JUSTINIAN

JUSTINIAN

H. N. Turteltaub

A TOM DOHERTY ASSOCIATES BOOK
NEW YORK

JUSTINIAN

Copyright © 1998 by Harry Turtledove

This book is printed on acid-free paper.

Edited by Patrick Nielsen Hayden

A Forge Book
Published by Tom Doherty Associates, Inc.
175 Fifth Avenue
New York, NY 10010

Forge® is a registered trademark of Tom Doherty Associates, Inc.

Design by Ellen Cipriano

Library of Congress Cataloging-in-Publication Data

Turteltaub, H. N.
Justinian / H.N. Turteltaub. — 1st ed.
p.   cm.
"A Tom Doherty Associates book."
ISBN 0-312-86699-2 (acid-free paper)
1. Justinian II Emperor of the East, 669?–711—Fiction.
2. Byzantine Empire—History—Justinian II, 685–695, 705–711—Fiction.
I. Title.
PS3570.U758J8   1998
813'.54—dc21   98-14338
CIP

First Edition: August 1998

Printed in the United States of America

0   9   8   7   6   5   4   3   2   1

JUSTINIAN

MYAKES

....

I s that you, Brother Elpidios?

No, wait, don't speak. I know it's you, for I recognize your step. I may have had my eyes burned out, but my ears see for me now. And, as the saying goes, a robe is revealed in advance by its border. So in the same way the stride reveals the man. You should fix the strap on your left sandal. It's loose, and flaps when you walk.

Have you got the book with you?

Ah, there it goes down on the table. Turn to the first leaf, I pray you. Justinian is gone from men these past twenty years—as long as I've been blind—but not all his deeds were wicked, and many of those that might be reckoned so were on such a scale that they deserve to live in the memories of men, too.

I knew he had been working on the tale of his life for years, writing every now and then as he found a few minutes' leisure. When the end came, there at Damatrys, he put it into my hands. I got caught soon enough afterwards, of course, and blinded. I remember how red the irons glowed when they brought them to my eyes. I remember the smell, like the baked white of an egg. They were merciful, in their way. Helias could have struck off my head. He thought about it, Lord knows. Instead, he had me brought here, and his men let me keep the book.

Read now, Brother Elpidios. Read. If, one day, you write the chronicle of days gone by of which you've talked so much, let what Justinian did and said have its place there. And if not, that's as God wills. The tale is worth the hearing either way; by God and the Virgin I swear it.

What's that? Yes, of course you may ask me questions. By your voice, you're young, and, even if you had my years, there's much here you didn't see, much here you couldn't know. So ask. And if, every now and then, you find me interrupting unasked, I pray you forgive me. For old men will talk, and blind men, too. When I speak back and forth with someone, for that time it's as if I see his face in my mind. I don't know how close the face I see matches the face that is, but for me it must do.

So read now, Brother Elpidios. Read.

BOOK A´

JUSTINIAN

I am Justinian, Emperor of the Romans. Oh, they stole the throne from me once. They mutilated me. They shipped me off into exile. They thought—fools!—they were done with me. But I came back, and they have paid. How they have paid! And they will go on paying, too, so long as one of them is left alive. The Empire is mine, and I shall keep it.

I was born to rule. I could not have been more than four years old when my father, the fourth Constantine and the fourth generation of the dynasty of Herakleios to rule the Roman Empire, sat me on his knee and said, "Do you know, son, why we named you Justinian?"

"No, Papa," I answered. Up till that moment, I had never imagined my name had been given for a reason. It was just what people called me.

"I will tell you, then," he said. You could hardly see his lips move when he talked, so luxuriant were his beard and mustachios. They say his father, Constans, was hairier yet. I do not know. God never granted that I see my grandfather. Rebels on the western island of Sicily murdered him the year before I was born.

My father resumed: "Do you know who the first Justinian was?"

I shook my head. I had never heard of anyone but me with the name. Now I was jealous, for I thought I had it all to myself.

"He was an Emperor, too," my father told me. "He was a great conqueror and a great lawgiver. If you can be like him when the time comes for you to take the throne, you will make the family proud. That is why we gave you the name: to give you a mark to aim at."

If I said I knew then what he meant, I would be lying. But I already knew there had been a great many Emperors of the Romans, so I asked, "When did this other Justinian live?"

My father muttered under his breath and counted on his fingers. At last, he said, "The first Justinian died forty-five years before your great-great-grandfather won the throne for our line from Phokas the monster, the usurper."

"Good. People will remember me instead," I said, "for he has been dead a very, very long time." I tell this without embarrassment; as I said, I had but four years.

Then my father's mouth opened so wide, I could see not just his lips but his teeth and tongue and the back of his throat as well. He laughed loud enough to make two servants come running in to find out what had happened. He waved them away. When they had gone, he said, "That is not such a long time, son, not as we Romans reckon it. The first Emperor, Augustus, was six hundred years dead when Herakleios beat Phokas: more than six hundred fifty years now."

The number was too big to mean anything to me. I had learned to count to twenty, using my fingers and the toes that peeked out of my sandals under the hem of my tunic to help me along. I did not know what it meant to be a Roman, to live with the memories of all those years cloaked around me.

The next spring, the Arabs came to Constantinople. When I was a boy, I knew old men who said that, when they were young, no one at the Queen of Cities paid the Arabs any mind or had even heard of them. How the Roman Empire wishes that were true today!

Herakleios, my great-great-grandfather, beat back the Persians after years of desperate war and restored to Jerusalem the piece of the True Cross the Magians and fire worshipers had carried away when they conquered the holy city.

God rested on the seventh day. Herakles, I suppose, rested after his twelve labors. Herakleios's labors were greater by far than those of the pagan Greek, but did God who had Himself rested allow my forefather any rest? He did not.

Forth from the desert, from the abomination of the desolation, the Arabs swarmed like locusts. They had always been there, I suppose: tent dwellers, nomads, lizard-eating savages. But in Herakleios's time the heresy preached by their false prophet Mouamet made them all brothers and sent them out a-conquering.

And Herakleios, who had celebrated the return of the holy and life-giving wood to Jerusalem, now had to take it up once more and bring it to Constantinople. For the Roman Empire was weak after decades of war with Persia, and had not the strength to withstand the onslaught of new invaders. Palestine and its holy city were lost, and Syria, and Egypt with Alexandria beside it.

(And if we Romans were weak, the Persians were weaker still, and had fallen into civil strife after their war against us failed. The Arabs conquered them one and all, and they have remained under the rule of the followers of the false prophet until the present. They would have done better to leave us alone.)

The great Herakleios's son, Herakleios Constantine—my great-grandfather—ruled but a few months. He suffered from a sickness of the lungs, poor soul. May God have judged him kindly.

When he died, he left behind a young son, my grandfather Constans. But the great Herakleios's second wife, Martina, sought to raise her son Heraklonas, the half-brother of Herakleios Constantine, to the throne in Constans's place. She and Heraklonas got what usurpers deserve: her tongue was cut out, his nose was cut off, and they were sent into exile on Rhodes.

They stole my throne. They cut off my nose. They exiled me. They treated me as if I, fifth in the line of the great Herakleios, had no proper claim to the throne. How I treated them I shall tell in due course.

To return to my grandfather: in his reign, we Romans fought back against the Arabs in every way we could. We sent out a fleet to reclaim Alexandria by Egypt from them, though it remained in Roman hands only a year before the deniers of Christ took it back, and it has stayed in their possession ever since.

From Egypt, the Arabs swept west toward Carthage and the lands surrounding it, lands the Romans had regained from the Vandals during the reign of the Justinian for whom I was named. That was one of the reasons Constans went to Sicily, where he met his death: he used the island as a base from which to assail the Arabs in their movement against Carthage. And while my grandfather lived, Carthage stayed in Roman hands. How it was lost, again, will be told in its own place.

Even before this time, the Arabs, curse them, had done a thing the Persians never did in all their centuries of war against us Romans. They took to the sea, endangering the Roman Empire in that new fashion. Like

all the line of Herakleios, Constans my grandfather was a man who believed in going straight at the foe. He assembled the Roman fleet, and
met that of the Arabs off the coast of Lykia, the southwestern region of
Anatolia.

Before the two fleets joined battle, my grandfather dreamt he was
in Thessalonike. He told this to a man who knew how to interpret
dreams, asking what it meant. And the man's face grew long, and he said,
"I wish you had not dreamt this dream."

As I have said, I never met Constans, but I can imagine the fearsome
glare he must have given the fellow. "Why?" he would have growled.

The man who could interpret dreams had courage, for he answered
with what he saw: "Your being in Thessalonike signifies, 'Give victory to
someone else,' for that is the meaning of the words *thes allô nikê*. You
would do far better, Emperor, not to engage the enemy tomorrow."

My grandfather went out and fought the sea battle anyhow. He—

MYAKES

Christ and all the saints, Brother Elpidios, that's Herakleios and those
who sprang from him, right there in a sentence. They weren't always
right, but they were always sure. So Justinian could see that in his grandfather, could he? Too bad he never could see it in himself.

Go on, go on, I pray you. I did say I'd break in from time to time.
Go on.

JUSTINIAN

—fought the sea battle, and was defeated. Indeed, he was almost killed.
The Arabs boarded the imperial flagship. One brave soul there
stripped the robe from his back and pretended to be him, while another
helped him get across a narrow stretch of sea stained red with Roman
blood to a dromon not under such fierce attack. Both those heroes died,
but Constans came back safe to Constantinople.

The Arabs might have moved against the Queen of Cities then, but
they fell into civil strife. In the fourth year of my father's reign, though,
the deniers of Christ readied a great expedition, and in the spring of his
fifth year they came.

We Romans had not been idle. My father, learning of the Arabs'
preparations, ordered our shipwrights to work straight through the winter,

building and refurbishing the vessels upon which, along with the great walls of Constantinople, our safety depended. On learning the foe's fleet had set out from Kilikia, where it had wintered, and was bound for the imperial city, he and his brothers—the two junior Emperors, Herakleios and Tiberius (my uncles, in other words)—decided to hearten the workmen and sailors at the Proklianesian harbor, and they took me with them.

When I think back on it, I am astonished by how much I remember of the day: the sights, the sounds, most of all the smells of fresh-cut wood and rope and pitch. Perhaps I should not be surprised. Till then, I had spent most of my time with my mother, the Empress Anastasia, and with the women of the palace. Now I was decked out in miniature robes of deep crimson—for I was a prince myself—and borne along in a sedan chair right behind those my father and my uncles rode. I kept peeking out through the curtains to see as much of the city as I could.

The Proklianesian harbor lies on the southern side of Constantinople, just east of the harbor of Theodosios, the largest of the city's anchorages. It is not a harbor for merchantmen or fishing boats: war galleys lie there.

I had never seen dromons before. They were long and lean, some with one bank of oars, some with two. The bronze rams they carried at the bow were green and pitted from the sea; some had gray or purple-red patches of barnacles growing on them. The dromons carried wooden towers amidships, from which archers could shoot down at the decks of enemy vessels. Each had sockets for masts before and behind the tower, but the masts were not in place now.

I had never seen or heard such men as those who worked on the dromons and would presently sail them either. The sun had burnt them near as black as Ethiopians are said to be, and sun and wind and spray carved harsh lines in their faces. Some of them wore wool or linen tunics that did not reach their knees, others just a cloth wrapped around their loins, commonly with a sheathed knife on the right side.

When they saw me, they smiled and pointed and called to me. I remember how white their teeth were against beards and dark faces. I also remember how much trouble I had understanding their Greek. Compared to what I heard in the palaces, it was clipped and quick, hardly seeming the same language at all.

My father and uncles had no trouble with it. In fact, when they talked with the sailors, they dropped into it themselves. I had never heard them speak like that before. Now, of course, I too talk like an educated man among clerics and accountants, and like a sailor among sailors.

A party of workmen came up the docks, past me, my father, and my uncles. Some of them were carrying bronze tubes, not sea-green like the dromons' rams but bright and shiny, the color of a freshly minted forty-follis coin. Others bore contraptions of hide and wood. After a moment, I recognized them as bellows, oversized cousins to the ones the cooks in the kitchens used to make their fires burn hotter. I pointed to them. "What are those for? Will the sailors blow on the sails with them to make the ships go faster?"

My father, my uncles, and everyone else who heard me laughed. I knew then I was wrong. That made me angry. I stamped my foot and screamed as if I were being made a eunuch.

My uncle Tiberius turned to Herakleios and murmured, "Constantine should clout him when he acts like that." Herakleios nodded. My father did not notice the byplay. Even though I was screaming, I did. I screamed even louder, just to annoy my uncles the more.

My uncle called to a swarthy, hawk-faced man who walked along behind the workers with the tubes and the bellows: "Attend us, Kallinikos!"

The swarthy man approached and bowed very low, first to my father, then to each of my uncles in turn, and last of all to me. I was surprised enough to quiet down. "How may I serve you, Emperor?" Kallinikos asked. He was an educated man; I could tell that at once. Yet his Greek had a guttural undertone I had not heard before. Since the Arabs burst out of the desert, Syrian accents have grown scarce in Constantinople.

"Tell the prince Justinian," my father said, pointing to me, "why these men are fitting our ships with the devices you have invented."

"Of course, Emperor." Kallinikos bowed first to my father and then to me. He did not bow again to my uncles. I liked that. To me, he said, "Prince, these tubes will project out across the water and onto any ship that comes close to one of ours a liquid fire that will cling and burn it up."

"How is it made?" I asked.

Kallinikos started to answer, then hesitated, looking to my father, who said, "We should not speak of that here on the docks, where so many men can listen. The making of this liquid fire is a secret, and we do not want the Arabs to learn how it is done. Do you understand?"

He spoke gravely. I nodded. As he had intended, he had taught me a lesson: that secrecy could matter not only to a boy but to an Emperor. I have remembered.

My father went on, "Kallinikos here, being a good Christian man"— he made the sign of the cross, as did my uncles, as did I, as did Kallinikos himself—"came here to the Queen of Cities from Heliopolis with his invention, not wanting it to fall into the hands of the followers of the false prophet." All at once he looked quite grim. "And soon we shall see just how much use it is to us, too."

Two years before, the Arabs had captured Smyrna, on the western coast of Anatolia, and Kyzikos, which lies under Mount Dindymos across the Propontis from Constantinople, to serve as bases for their assault on the Queen of Cities. When full spring brought good weather and reduced the chance of storms on the narrow sea between Kyzikos and Constantinople, the deniers of Christ sailed up and laid siege to our God-guarded imperial capital.

With my father and my uncles, I watched from the seawall as their fleet drew near. I had never seen so many ships in all my short life; they seemed to cover all the water of the Propontis. I pointed out to them. "See how the oars move back and forth like a centipede's legs," I said. I had smashed a couple of centipedes in the past few days; good weather brought them out, as it did the Arabs.

"They're like centipedes in another way, too," my father answered: "If they bite us, we will die."

Out ahead of their fleet rowed dromons much like ours, save only that they lacked wooden towers amidships. Faint over the water, I heard for the first time the chant their oarsmen and soldiers repeated endlessly: *"Allahu akbar! Allahu akbar!"*

"What does that mean?" I asked my father.

" 'God is great,' " he answered absently. He was paying more heed to those oncoming warships than to me.

Our own dromons put out from the Proklianesian harbor and the harbor of Theodosios to meet them. A great cry rose from the men and women watching on the seawall: "God with us! Christ with us! The Virgin with us!" They drowned out the chant of the Arabs. The patriarch John held up a holy icon of the Mother of God, one made by divine hands, not those of men.

M Y A K E S

And now this Leo, the one who's been ruling us these past fourteen years, he calls icons graven images, and says we should smash all of them? You ask me, only a man with the mind of a Jew or a Saracen would say such stupid things. No doubt you reckon me a foolish old man, Brother Elpidios, but I doubt you'll argue with me there.

Come to that, Justinian and I met this Leo before he was so much of a much. I wonder what my master will have to say of him. I know, Brother: each thing in its own place. Read on.

JUSTINIAN

The sea breeze played with the patriarch's robes—gorgeous with cloth of gold and pearls and jewels—and fluffed out his great white beard.

After my encounter with Kallinikos, I looked for our dromons to breathe out fire like dragons and send all the ships of the misbelieving Arabs to the bottom at once. That did not happen, of course. Life is more difficult than it looks to little boys.

The Arabs' dromons sprinted toward ours, their oars churning the water to a frothy wake. Behind them, the other ships of the deniers of Christ made for the Thracian coast south and west of Constantinople.

Some Roman war galleys broke through the screen the followers of the false prophet tried to set between them and the transports carrying Arab soldiers. My father, my uncles, I, John the patriarch—everyone on the seawall—screamed in delight when a dromon rammed a fat merchantman right amidships. The dromon backed oars after striking. The hole it punched in the other ship's side must have been huge; you could watch the merchantman wallow and start to sink. Heads bobbed in the water: sailors and soldiers, trying to swim for their lives. The archers aboard our dromons must have had fine sport with them, and sent many souls on to eternal torment.

But my father's exultation did not last. "It is not enough," he said. "They will gain the shore, in spite of all we can do."

He was right. From the suburb of Kyklobion less than a mile from the Golden Gate at the southern end of Constantinople's double land wall to the town of Hebdomon four or five miles farther west, the Arabs beached their ships and swarmed ashore, onto the soil of Thrace. Peering west and a little south, I could make out some of the nearer landings. At that distance, the deniers of Christ in their white robes reminded me of nothing so much as termites scattering when the piece of rotten wood they infest is disturbed.

Out on the sea, the fight between the Arabs' dromons and our own went on. From their towers amidships, our bowmen could shoot down onto the decks of the enemy war galleys, and the Arabs could not reply in kind. Little by little, we seemed to gain the advantage.

But that was not what I wanted to see. "Where is the liquid fire?" I demanded, and then, louder: *"Where is the liquid fire?"*

Tiberius and Herakleios looked at each other. I suppose they were hoping my father would slap me across the face and make me be quiet. If he tried, I vowed to myself I would grab his hand and bite it. I had done that before, and drawn blood. Mostly, though, he indulged me, which never stopped irking my uncles. And why should he not have indulged me? I was then his only son. I indulge my little son Tiberius the same way.

M Y A K E S

Someone told me what happened to Tiberius, there at the end. He was just like his father at the same age, only more so. Do you know that story, Brother Elpidios? You do? All right. Take no notice of an old man's maunderings, then.

J U S T I N I A N

Where is the—" I was screeching now, like a cat when somebody steps on its tail. But a rising cry of wonder and delight from all along the seawall made my voice sound small and lost.

My father pointed out onto the Sea of Marmara. My eyes followed his outthrust finger. There in the water, not far out of catapult range from the wall, a dromon full of the deniers of Christ was burning, flames licking along the deck and smoke billowing up from them. Oh, Mother of Christ, it was beautiful!

The Arabs on the dromon ran about like men possessed, trying to put out the fire. They were not chanting their accursed *"Allahu akbar!"* anymore; they were screaming in terrified earnest. And as I watched them do their best to douse the flames, I understood why, for water helped them not at all.

One of those who followed the false prophet, lent strength, no doubt, by fear, picked up a great hogshead and poured it down onto the fire. It did not quench the flames. Instead, still burning merrily, they floated atop the barrelful of water and, where it stopped, they stopped, too, starting new blazes in those places. When the Arabs perceived that, their screams redoubled.

They might have learned as much merely by looking down to the slightly choppy surface of the sea, where more fire floated. Indeed, our dromon, the one that had projected the liquid fire onto the Arab warship, had to back oars quickly, lest the flames on the seawater cling to it and make of it a pyre to match its foe.

My father cried out in a great voice, "Fifty pounds of gold to Kallinikos, to whom God granted the vision of this wonderful fire!" All the people on the seawall cheered like men possessed. Danger was not banished from the Queen of Cities; far from it. But we took new heart from having a weapon our enemies could not match.

A few minutes later, my uncle Tiberius shouted in a voice that cracked with excitement: "Look! Another galley burns!" And, sure enough, the liquid fire was consuming a second Arab dromon. That victory was not complete, however, for our galley did not escape the liquid fire on the water and also burned. Some of its sailors swam to the base of the seawall, where the soldiers and people of the city let down ropes to rescue them. Others, poor souls, drowned.

Perhaps the deniers of Christ had intended landing marines at the base of the seawall. Along with the darts the catapults on their dromons could have hurled, such an assault would have stretched our defenses thin. They might have been able to make and then to take advantage of a breach in the land walls.

But if that idea had been in their minds, the liquid fire put paid to it. Their war galleys drew back from our fleet, and from the walls of the imperial city, protected by God. They made for the Thracian coast, there to guard the Arabs' great flotilla of transports from our dromons.

Seeing the Arabs' galleys withdraw, the men on the walls burst into cheers. "We've beaten them!" some cried. Others shouted out a Latin acclamation still used in the city: "*Tu vincas*, Constantine!"

I looked to my father, proud like any son to hear him praised. I expected him to show he was proud, too, and to show delight in the victory the Romans had won over the barbarians. But his long, thin face remained somber. "We've not won the war," he said, perhaps more to himself than to anyone else. "We've survived the first blow, nothing more."

I pointed out to sea, where those burning dromons still sent up thick pillars of smoke, and where the wreckage of other vessels, most of them belonging to the followers of the false prophet, bobbed in the waves. Our own warships protected the seawalls like a pack of friendly dogs guarding a farmhouse. "Look, Father," I said, maybe thinking he did not know what we had done.

He looked. Then he looked westward, where the Arabs were still swarming off the vessels that had reached the Thracian shore. "Now the battle begins," he said.

My father was right. The followers of the false prophet had not labored so hard nor come so far to flee when their first assault miscarried. It was to be four years before Constantinople saw the last of them. From April till September, the Arabs would attack the land wall or Roman troops would sally forth from it to raid their encampments at Kyklobion.

Sometimes they would catch the raiders before our men could regain safety. Then, often, they would kill them before our eyes to put us in fear. Sometimes our men would return in triumph, with prisoners and booty. I remember them singing as they led dejected Arabs up the Mese from the wall to the Forum of Constantine. Our headsmen put some of the prisoners to the sword, to avenge our own butchered men. Others were sold for slaves. Even besieged, our merchants would not turn aside from profit. The deniers of Christ should all have been killed.

They kept their war galleys busy on the Sea of Marmara. Thanks to the liquid fire, and thanks to the towers on our dromons that gave our archers the advantage over theirs, they quickly grew reluctant to fight great sea battles, as they had done when they came forth from Kyzikos. But they were always out hunting for merchantmen, and, because they were known to be hunting, few merchantmen put to sea. Deprived of much of the harvest of Anatolia that normally fed it, the city became a hungry place.

I did not know hunger. How could I? I was the Emperor's son. Having made its acquaintance since, I must say I do not regret missing the earlier introduction. But if those years when the Arabs besieged the imperial city were empty of bodily hunger for me, they were full of the spiritual hunger of loneliness.

When the weather began to grow chilly toward the end of the first September of the siege, the Arabs withdrew from their camps on Thracian soil, sailing back to Kyzikos to winter there. We rejoiced, though even then we expected they would return with the spring like migrating birds. And, near the time of Christ's birth, my mother presented my father with a second baby boy.

He named the boy Herakleios, partly because that name had been in the family for generations and partly, I think, because he had just made up his latest quarrel with my uncle of that name and wanted to put a tangible seal on their reconciliation. Herakleios proved a weak and sickly baby, which was an omen for the reconciliation as well.

Bearing my little brother left my mother weak and sickly, too. And, even for an Empress of the Romans with eunuchs and wet nurses and other serving women to attend her should she lift a finger, a new baby sucks time as greedily as it sucks milk. In looking after little Herakleios, my mother all but forgot about me. My father, with the weight of the Roman Empire on his shoulders, already seemed to have forgotten.

And so, by the time I had six years, I did whatever I chose, for who besides my father and mother would tell me no? Often I would gather up a couple of excubitores and, with them as escort, go atop the seawall to watch our dromons and those of the Arabs clash on the Sea of Marmara. The excubitores never protested when I put them to such work. Why should they? They were imperial bodyguards and I was the Emperor's son; therefore, their duty included guarding me. Aristotle could not have made a clearer syllogism.

When the warships did not put to sea, I sometimes had my bearers carry me to the land wall so I could peer down at the Arabs vainly trying to break into the God-guarded imperial city. I even went out to the lower, outer wall—once. When word of that got back to my father, he remembered me long enough to forbid it. That only made me want it more.

The bearers, as was natural, stood in too much fear of my father to give in to my wishes, and withstood even my fiercest tantrums. So did the excubitores. That wounded me to the quick. They were fighting men. Could they not see I wanted to put myself at the forefront of the battle?

When tantrums failed, another boy might have tried wheedling. Not I. I had a different plan. One morning on the inner wall, I turned to the excubitor standing alongside me and complained, "I'm too short to see anything from the walkway. Lift me up to the top of the forewall, Myakes."

The forewall running between crenellations is perhaps a foot thick and a little taller than a man's waist. It is so high it need not withstand stones from a catapult or the pounding of a ram, but only give cover to archers behind it.

Myakes frowned. He must have been thinking about something else, and only half heard what I said. "What was that, little Goldentop?" he asked, using a nickname the excubitores often gave me.

MYAKES

L ittle Goldentop, Brother Elpidios? Yes, Justinian was blond. So was his father, come to that. The house of Herakleios sprang from Armenia, that's true, but as soon as they got out of Armenia and found there were yellow-haired women in the world, they started swiving them. Why, Constantine once told me old Herakleios himself had a bastard boy by a Visigoth from Spain, and let her name him Athalaric after her own father. She must have been a beauty, or good between the sheets, to get away with that.

Oh, quit spluttering, Brother. If you don't hear worse from Justinian later on than you just have from me, I'll be much surprised, that I will.

Justinian? If you want to know the truth, he reminded me of nothing so much as a cat. His face was long—that was true of everyone in his family I saw, and of the others, too, if their coins don't lie—but it narrowed sharply from the cheekbones down, so that he had almost a woman's rosebud mouth and a pointed little chin. And he was graceful, too. Even that young, he always held his body just so: tight-strung, you might say.

JUSTINIAN

L ift me up!" I repeated. "I want to see what's going on out there."
Myakes frowned but did nothing else. To me, then, he was a man grown: he was man-tall, with a peasant's broad shoulders and broad face. He carried a spear taller than he was and a shield with Christ's holy labarum painted on it: χ ρ. I could make up my mind in an instant. Why could he not?

I did not realize two things, being but a boy myself. For one, though my father and uncles, like me, decided and acted all at once, not all men matched my kin in that; and, for another, Myakes was scarcely more than a boy himself, despite height, despite shoulders. When the sun shone on his face, you could see his cheeks and the outline of his jaw through the beard that sprouted there, a sure proof he had not long been able to raise it. Thus inexperience and uncertainty also made him hesitate.

At last, after what seemed a very long time but probably was not, he laughed and said, "Well, why not? Not much to see, but what there is, you can."

He leaned the spear and shield against the forewall and picked me up. I could tell at once how he had got to be an excubitor, for he was strong as a bull. He might have been lifting a mouse, not a boy. I felt I was flying as he set my feet on the forewall. He kept a grip on my waist, but only to steady me, not to hold me tight.

I had counted on that. I twirled away from him and ran along the forewall, saying as I went, "Promise you'll take me to the outer wall, Myakes, or I'll cast myself down between them right now!" I looked down at the outer wall, there perhaps a hundred feet in front of me. It was quite handsome, bands of stone alternating with brick, the same scheme the inner wall used. I have always had a good head for heights; I was not frightened or giddy. But I remember thinking, *How far down the ground looks!*

Myakes stared at me. "Come back here, little Goldentop," he said. "Don't make foolish jokes." He spoke the same kind of clipped, elided Greek the sailors in the Proklianesian harbor had used. I understood it better now, from more exposure.

"I am not joking," I told him, and I was not. Had he said no, I would have jumped. I suppose they would have taken whatever was left of my body and buried it in the cemetery of Pelagios with the other suicides.

Myakes did not say anything. He took a step toward me. I could not back away from him, for I was up against a crenellation. I bent my knees, readying myself to leap out as far as I could from the wall. But I had forgotten how much faster than a child an adult can move. Myakes sprang forward, grabbed me, and pulled me back onto the walkway of the inner wall even as I was trying to leap to my death.

"Now," he said, breathing hard (and, looking back, I cannot blame him, for what would he have told my father—and what would have happened to him?—had I jumped?), "I am going to give you a choice. I will take you back to your father the Emperor and we will both tell him our stories, or I will give you a beating here and now for what you just did. You decide."

I tried to kick him in the shins. He jerked his leg out of the way. I tried to bite him. He would not let me. I cursed him, using all the words I had learned from the excubitores. He let them roll off him like water from oil-soaked cloth. "You do it," I said then. "Whatever you do to me, my father would do worse." My father was not so mild with me as he had been before the Arabs came; he had worse worries now. He still would not often strike me, but when he did, it was as if a demon seized his arm, for he would not stop.

"Come, then," Myakes said. Recovering his spear and shield, he slung the shield over his back, took the spear in his left hand, and seized firm hold of my arm with his right. We walked along to the nearest fortified tower, for all the world as if he were taking me to piddle at a latrine there, nothing more.

The latrine was empty when we walked into it. It stank of endless years of stale piss, which offended me: in the palace, sewer pipes swept waste away before it grew so ripely odorous. Myakes did not turn loose of me for a moment. No doubt he thought I would try to run off if he did. No doubt he was right.

"Remember our bargain," he said, and set down the shield and spear. He must have had a kindly father for, while the chastisement he gave me left my buttocks hot and tingling, it was all with the open hand, never once with fist or foot or the metal-studded belt he wore. At last he said, "Maybe you will think twice before you play such games with me again."

"I will think twice," I said, but I knew I had made the right choice. Almost I told him how mild he had been, but I refrained. He might, after all, have decided to make amends. Instead, I went on, "Now that the bargain is sealed, take me back out to watch some more of the fighting."

"From the inner wall here," he said. "Not from the outer one."

"Not from the outer one," I agreed.

"Come, then," he repeated, and we went out together.

MYAKES

By She who bore God, I've never been so frightened as I was in those few minutes! I was sorry I'd offered the bargain as soon as it was done. Hit the Emperor's son? Me? Afterwards, he might have said anything at all: that I'd beaten him worse than I had, even that I'd taken him into the latrine to try and sodomize him. Who would Constantine have believed, his firstborn or a guardsman whose name he might not know?

But what would the Emperor have done to me had his firstborn splattered himself on the cobblestones? That bore even less thinking about. And if once I let Justinian get his way with such a ploy, he would try, or threaten to try, again till he owned me. My idea, such as it was, was to make sure that didn't happen.

God was kind to me. It worked. It did more than work: it made Justinian my friend. I'd never imagined that. Poor puppy, he must have been so ignored at the palaces that even the flat of my hand on his backside felt good because it showed I knew he was alive.

And here I sit, past my threescore and ten, blind and shrunken—

and how strange to hear myself spoken of as young and brawny and crammed to bursting with the juices of life. So many memories, most of them, I fear, so full of base carnality as to be sinful even to remember, and so I won't trouble your ears with them.

Eh? Oh, very well, just a few. But then you read again.

JUSTINIAN

For five springs in a row, the deniers of Christ sailed forth from Kyzikos against this God-guarded and imperial city. I grew to take their yearly arrival utterly for granted: anything that happens through half a boy's life becomes fixed in his mind as an ineluctable law of nature.

What a host of warlike men they threw away in their futile assaults! They could not breach the land walls, nor, as they found in the last year of the siege, could they undermine them. And, on the sea, the fighting towers on our dromons and the liquid fire they hurled gave us Romans the victory again and again. As if I were a pagan watching Christians martyred by fire in the arena, I stared avidly out from the seawall as the followers of the false prophet burned alive, the unquenchable fires on their galleys foreshadowing the flames of hell. Myakes usually stood at my side, as he had been since the second spring of the siege.

Toward the end of that fifth summer, the Arabs sailed away from their Thracian camps earlier than was their wont. Their warships withdrew from our waters. Cautiously, my father ordered our dromons across the Propontis to spy out the enemy. And when those dromons returned, they did so with hosannas and cries of thanksgiving, for the followers of the false prophet were abandoning their enterprise and their base there, and were returning in disgrace to the lands ruled by their miscalled commander of the faithful.

How we praised God for delivering us from the foe despite the multitude of our sins! And how many more sins, I have no doubt when looking back on the time with a man's years, were committed to celebrate that deliverance. Having then but nine years, I was limited as to the sins of the flesh, but poured two cups of neat wine into my little brother Herakleios, laughing like a madman to hear him babble and watch him stagger.

When my uncles saw little Herakleios, who would have been three then, they laughed themselves hoarse. When my mother saw him, she was horror-stricken—but she laughed, too. And when my father saw him, he laughed so hard, he had to lean against the wall to hold himself upright—and when he was done laughing, he gave me a beating that, like so many of his, made the one I had had from Myakes seem a pat on the back by comparison.

I went looking for my only friend, but did not find him, not then. I had a hard time finding any excubitores. Had an assassin wanted to sneak into the palaces and slay my father, that would have been the time to do it, with so many guardsmen off roistering. But, on that day of days, surely the assassins were off roistering, too.

"Nothing I can do, Goldentop," he said the next day, when I did tell him my troubles. "The Emperor is your father, and he has the right to beat you when you do wrong—and you did wrong." He spoke slowly, carefully, and quietly, not, most likely, for my sake, but for his own, for he must have been nursing a thick head.

With anyone else, I would have been angry, but Myakes could say such things to me, not least because with him, unlike my father and my other kinsfolk, I was the one who chose how much heed I paid. "Where everyone else is glad, I am almost sorry the Arabs have gone away," I said.

"What?" He stared at me. "Are you daft? Why?"

"Because now I won't be able to go out with you and watch the fights by land and sea," I answered.

Myakes laughed at that, but quickly sobered. "They didn't come here for your amusement," he said, his voice as serious as if he were talking to a grown man. Even when I was a boy, he always took me seriously; I had taught him, up on the land wall, I was not to be trifled with. He went on, "They came to sack the city and kill your father the Emperor and kill you, too, or make you a slave or a eunuch or both. War is not a game. If you go into it, you go into it with everything you have. Your father would tell you the same."

He was right, of course. I did not need to ask my father; I could hear the truth in his words. I have remembered them from that day to this, and when I war against the enemies of the Roman Empire, or against the vicious, treacherous dogs who overthrew me once and conspire against me even now, I fight with everything I have.

Even beyond the frontier between this Roman land, this Romania, and the dominions of the miscalled commander of the faithful, the Emperor's reach remained long. My father urged the brigands known as Mardaites to sweep down from their fastnesses onto the plains of Lebanon, which they did, overrunning nearly the whole of the country and discomfiting the Arabs no end.

And God also revealed His love for the Roman Empire and for the Queen of Cities in other ways. Although the followers of the false prophet had abandoned Thrace earlier in the season than was their habit, and although they sailed away from Kyzikos well before the coming of the autumnal equinox in the hope of avoiding the storms that wrack the Mediterranean with the arrival of fall, they could not escape the heavy hand of divine punishment.

A great tempest overwhelmed their expedition off the southern coast of Anatolia. The fleet was smashed to bits by Pamphylian Syllaion, with only a handful of men coming home to Phoenicia and Palestine and Egypt and Alexandria to tell the tale of what had befallen them.

Hardly had this news reached our God-guarded and imperial city when word came that three of my father's generals, Florus, Petronas, and Kyprianos, had crushed an Arab army, slaying, it was said, thirty thousand of the followers of the false prophet. Truly God was merciful to the Romans in that year and at that season.

Again and again, folk reveled in the streets of Constantinople. Again and again, the great church—the church of the Holy Wisdom— the church of the Holy Apostles, and all the other innumerable churches in the city filled as worshipers offered up thanksgiving to God and His wholly immaculate Virgin Mother for delivering the Roman Empire from the jaws of the Arabs. The sweet savor of incense rose from the churches in clouds so thick that for hours at a time you could scarcely discern the usual city odors of horse dung and slops.

Mauias, the Arabs' leader, concluded further warfare against Romania was useless because of our divine protection. He sent two men to Constantinople to seek peace.

All the imperial family received them sitting in a row: my father, I, my uncle Herakleios, my uncle Tiberius, and my brother Herakleios. This display of might, or at least of fecundity, was intended to overawe. The Arabs' envoys prostrated themselves before us. When they rose, one of them addressed my father, in whom, of course, all true power rested: "Very well, Emperor, you have won this round. The commander of the faithful will pay you a tidy sum to put the Mardaites back on the leash."

"He speaks Greek," I whispered to my uncle Herakleios. "He speaks good Greek."

He was glad to whisper back: like me, he was there only for show. "Why shouldn't he speak Greek? The Arabs still use it in their chancery, and Damascus was still a Roman city when he was a boy."

I started to say something more, but my father chose that moment to reply to the ambassador. I looked for him to hurl anathemas and the fear of hell like a churchman; how often, in years gone by, he had scorned the Arabs as infidels and heretics and urged our Roman people to defend not only the Queen of Cities but also the true and holy faith.

But what he said was, "He'd better. It'll cost him plenty, too, after everything he put us through the past few years. I'm going to squeeze him by the money bags till his eyes pop."

Of all the sovereigns in the world, only the Arabs' ruler stands in rank with the Emperor of the Romans. My father, then, addressed him as an equal through his emissaries, and not only as an equal but almost as a near neighbor. I thought—and think still—this beneath the dignity of the Emperor, but it was my father's way. Who would have presumed to differ with him?

In my years of lonely exile at Kherson, I watched men in the marketplace dicker for hours over the price of the smoked flesh and salted roe of the mourzoulin and other fish like it. So, like a man buying salt fish in the market, my father dickered with the Arabs. The haggling went on not just for hours but for days. In the end, coming to no agreement with Mauias's envoys, my father sent them back to Syria, and sent with them an ambassador of his own, John Pitzigaudis.

He chortled after sending them off by land, and told me and whoever else in the palaces who would listen to him: "John will do better with Mauias than I could with his emissaries. He's sure of heaven, for if by some mischance or great sin he winds up in hell, he'll dicker his way free out of the devil."

He knew whereof he spoke. He never lived to grow old—I am one-and-forty as I go over these words, and have not far from a decade more than he ever attained, while at the time of which I speak he was but twenty-seven—but even without great experience he was a keen judge of men. After long discussion, John Pitzigaudis came back from Damascus with an agreement that the followers of the false prophet were to send us three thousand nomismata, fifty high-bred horses, and fifty bondsmen a year for the next thirty years.

One of the eunuch parakoimomenoi, Stephen the Persian, rubbed his hands together in delight and crooned, over and over again, "Three thousand pieces of gold a year," as if every one of them were to be delivered straight to his chamber.

He carried on for so long and acted so foolish that at last my mother, who hardly ever spoke up to rebuke anyone, reminded him, "The money goes to the fisc, not to you." Stephen turned red, then white. He bowed to my mother and took his leave, but he was still mumbling of nomismata. I never saw a man with a passion for gold to match his, but then, he had no other passions he could satisfy.

MYAKES

J ustinian was wrong there, and he must have known it when he was writing, but you can't think of everything all the time. Only God can do that, eh, Brother Elpidios? There's another passion a lot of eunuchs have, and Stephen the Persian had it more than most: he was as nasty an item as I ever had the misfortune to meet.

What do I mean? What eunuchs hanker after, Brother, is *revenge*, revenge on the whole world. When you think about it, you can't hardly blame them, now can you? If somebody cut me like that, I would have—

Vengeance is mine; I will repay, saith the Lord? Oh yes, of course, Brother Elpidios. That is what the Holy Scriptures say. But not every man can follow them as well as we might like. If we could follow them better, we'd not need them so much, eh? Am I right or am I wrong?

No. Wait. Never mind. We can argue theology or you can read. We can't do both at once. I'd sooner you read, if you don't mind. Ah. I thank you, and may God bless you and keep you.

JUSTINIAN

N ews that the followers of the false prophet had agreed to make peace and pay tribute spread all through the world with amazing speed, proving to the lesser rulers that the Roman Empire, while diminished in extent from what it had been in the reign of Justinian my namesake, yet remained, as of course it shall forever, the grandest and mightiest empire of them all.

Realizing this once more, the lesser rulers hastened to send envoys to Constantinople to congratulate my father for what he had achieved and to confirm that he was also at peace with them. First, for their lands were nearest, came men from the Sklavinias, the little territories the petty kings and princes of the Sklavenoi have carved out of the land between the Danube and the sea. They brought bricks of beeswax and pots of honey to lay at my father's feet.

One of those feet was bandaged when he received the Sklavenoi, with myself, my uncles, and my little brother once more ranked beside him to lend ceremony to the occasion: he suffered from gout, and, when it flared, the slightest touch was to him like the fiery furnace into which the king of Babylon cast Daniel long ago. The whole of the Empire presently suffered from this, as I shall relate in its own place.

The Sklavenoi, fair-haired, round-faced men in linen tunics elaborately embroidered with colorful yarns, stared in awe at our crowns and the shimmering silk robes we wore and at the jewels and pearls decorating our raiment. Their pale eyes also went wide at the marble and gold and silver in the throne room, at our thrones of gold and ivory, at the precious and holy icons of Christ and the Virgin and the saints on the wall (although, being pagan, they appreciated the beauty and ornament that went into their creation, not the piety), and at the floor mosaics, which I believe they took for a moment to be real things rather than images.

While they spoke to my father in bad, mushy Greek, I turned to my uncle Herakleios and said, "It's as if they've never been inside a building before."

"They haven't, not a building like this," he answered. "They live in little huts with straw roofs, mostly by riverbanks. Christ crucified, if poverty is a virtue, they're the most virtuous people in the world. But they can fight."

I did not fully understand him, not then. How could I? I had spent all my life in the palaces. What did I know of huts made of sticks and straw? But I have learned. And when you are cold and wet and hungry, a hut is more a palace than a palace is when you have all you want.

Afterwards came emissaries from the khagan of the Avars—swarthy men with narrow eyes set on a slant, flat noses, and even flatter faces, all of them bowlegged from spending most of their time in the saddle. Their gifts to my father included a double handful of fair-haired young women: slaves taken from among the Sklavenoi, several of whose tribes were under the dominion of the khagan.

I reckoned them a paltry present—some of them looked to be only a couple of years older than I was myself. But my father and my uncles inspected them with scrupulous attention to detail. At last my father said, "I shall put them to work here in the palaces. I expect we'll get good use from them."

He laughed, something I had never heard him do at an audience, which is in most instances almost as formal and solemn as the celebration of the divine liturgy. My uncles laughed, too, and so did the Avar envoys.

Again, I did not understand. I had but nine years at the time.

We also received ambassadors from the Lombards, whose possessions in Italy were and are mixed promiscuously with our own. After all these years, I do not recall which of their dukes and princes sent us men along with those who came from their king. There were several; I remember that much. The Lombards fight among themselves and seek our support in their quarrels, just as we try to use them to our own advantage. As he had with the various Sklavenoi and the envoys of the Avar khagan, though, my father made peace with them and sent them away happy.

There also came to this God-guarded and imperial city an emissary from the king of the Franks, the blond tribe now ruling in Gaul. I was excited when I heard of his arrival, for, as I told my brother, "The kings of the Franks are called the long-haired kings, which means they have hair growing all down along their backs like hogs. Maybe their ambassador will, too."

Herakleios, who by then was four years old, received my news with the usual amount of fraternal trust: "You're making that up," he said.

"What? About the Frankish kings? I am not," I said, and hit him, whereupon the little wretch ran and tattled to my father, who hit me a good deal harder.

I still believe, though I have never seen one, the Frankish kings have hair growing down their backs like swine. Their ambassador did not. He had no hair on his cheeks and chin, either, though he let his mustache grow long and droop down over his mouth to show he was no eunuch. He could not even speak Greek, but had to mumble away in Latin while his interpreter—an Italian, I suppose—turned his words into ones we could understand. Once translated, those words seemed friendly enough. After an exchange of presents and of good wishes, he departed from Constantinople on the long road back to his cold, gloomy homeland.

When the Frank had left the throne room, my father, though still in full regalia, abandoned imperial solemnity for a moment. "We've got it!" he cried. "Full peace, complete peace, freedom from all care, north and south, east and west—we've got it!" He turned to me, to drive home the lesson. "Not since your great-great-grandfather's day, since Herakleios beat the Persians and the deniers of Christ had not yet burst out of Arabia to torment us, has the Roman Empire been at peace against all its many foes at once."

"Then it will probably be just as long," I said, "before we know such peace again."

He boxed my ears, right there in front of everyone. But I was right.

Having made peace with all our neighbors, my father decided to see if he could also create peace within the holy orthodox church. This was no easy task, for the clerics had been at strife with one another for as long as we had been at war with the Arabs and our other enemies.

Indeed, the two struggles bore no small relationship to each other. The Christian folk of what were in Herakleios's day the provinces of the Roman East, Syria and Palestine and Egypt, have for centuries wrongly emphasized Christ's divine nature at the expense of His humanity, even claiming that after the Incarnation He had but one nature, the divine. The fourth holy ecumenical synod, that which was held at Chalcedon, condemned the impious heresy, but the foolish obstinacy of the Syrians and Egyptians made them cling to it nonetheless.

By my great-great-grandfather's time, the Roman government had been trying to root out the monophysite heresy for almost two hundred years. This, of course, was as it should have been, for the one true and God-guarded Empire must have only one true faith; how else is unity to be maintained? But, as I said, the heretics were stubborn, and would not abandon error.

My great-great-grandfather Herakleios sought a theological formula both the orthodox and the monophysites could accept, seeking to plaster over the differences between them rather than destroying the heresy. The patriarch of Constantinople in his day was himself of Syrian blood, and had monophysite ancestors. This fool of a Sergios suggested the Emperor declare that, while Christ did indeed have two natures, a single—divine—energy animated them.

Herakleios, being a better soldier than theologian, duly did this. The patriarch of Rome—the pope, as he is often known—at the time, a man named Honorius, assented in the doctrine of one will, if not energy, in Christ. The monophysites rejoiced, recognizing this doctrine as their own heresy in sheep's clothing. But the patriarch of Jerusalem anathematized Herakleios's formula.

So did many other leading theologians, so many that my great-great-grandfather recognized he had gone too far. But he also wanted to maintain such goodwill as he could from the monophysites of Syria and Egypt, for the ungrateful wretches, far from aiding him in the fight against the followers of the false prophet then erupting from Arabia, were welcoming the Arabs as liberators from Roman rule: to those who denied Christ, one group of Christians was no more offensive than any other.

And so, thinking he was doing something great, Herakleios put forth his statement of faith, forbidding discussion of whether Christ had one energy or two and declaring that, as Pope Honorius had said, He had but a single will. The monophysites, once more, were pleased, the orthodox dismayed. This new doctrine prevailed in Constantinople, but was condemned in Jerusalem, in Carthage, in Numidia, in Mauretania . . . and in Italy, where all the popes after Honorius rejected his formulation.

My grandfather Constans attacked his theological opponents with as much energy as he used to fight back against the followers of the false prophet. He sent troops from Ravenna in Italy down to Rome and seized Pope Martin and Maximus, who had crossed from Africa to strengthen Martin's zeal against the monothelite doctrine. The two holy men were fetched back to the imperial city, tortured when they refused to renounce their faith, and, that also failing to make them recant, exiled to Kherson.

Having known exile in Kherson, I declare that my grandfather was truly a hard man.

So matters stood when my father became Emperor of the Romans. In the early years of his reign, he had little time or energy of his own to devote to affairs of the church, though I know God was always in his mind and in his heart: all his strength went first toward avenging the murder of his father in Sicily and then to defending Romania against the great Arab onslaught.

Those things accomplished, though, he turned his mind toward matters spiritual—and also, I do not deny, toward matters purely pragmatic. When he announced he was going to convene an ecumenical synod and formally overturn monotheletism, my uncle Herakleios demanded, "How can you go against the will of the founder of our dynasty and that of your father—and mine?"

"Nothing simpler—I have a will of my own," my father answered. I was studying irregular verbs with a pedagogue certainly old enough to have known Herakleios the founder—and maybe Phokas before him. My attention wandered away from the aorist passive participle of *syndiaphero*. Theology is far more important than grammar; misspeaking will get you laughed at, true, but misbelieving endangers your immortal soul.

And watching my father and uncle quarrel was fascinating, too. My father, Uncle Herakleios, and Uncle Tiberius were all Emperors in name, but every bit of power lay in my father's hands. The only things his brothers got to do was wear fancy robes and appear beside him on ceremonial occasions. How they resented that!

Now Herakleios shouted, "We'll be the laughingstock of all Christendom, east and west, if we turn our backs on beliefs we've supported these past fifty years."

"And what have we got for all that support?" my father shot back. "Will the monophysites in Syria and Egypt rise up for us against the Arabs because we confess Christ's two natures have but one will? It doesn't look that way to me. By the Virgin, they're even starting to go over to the creed of the false prophet. And the popes have been throwing anathemas at us ever since Honorius dropped dead."

"If it weren't for our great-grandfather, we'd be nothing," my uncle insisted. "If it weren't for him, the Roman Empire would be nothing. Just on account of that, his views deserve respect."

My father glared. "Even with the great Herakleios at the root of the family tree, you *are* nothing," he said. "And *my* views prevail now, not his. And most especially not yours, my brother."

A short, deadly silence followed. At last, Uncle Herakleios bowed very low. "Emperor," he said. I have never heard a word freighted with so much poison. He stormed out of the chamber, his robes flapping as he went.

My pedagogue had been blind to all this. In truth, he was almost blind, being so shortsighted that anything out past the end of his beard was but a blur. I was told he had grandchildren, but I wondered how, for if ever a man was wedded to ink and papyrus, it was he. I am not surprised I have forgotten his name. Now, with my uncle's furious footsteps still echoing in the hall, he said, "And the genitive singular of the participle is—?"

"*Syndienekhthentos*," I answered absently. I did not love my lessons, but I learned them. Fear of my father made sure of that.

"Very good!" The old man beamed. He had not expected me to know that one. He raised his creaking voice: "Your Majesty, you have here a scholar among men."

He meant it as nothing but one more piece of the idle flattery the Emperor hears every waking moment of every day. It was more idle than most, too, by God; Romania needs soldiers these days, not scholars, if she is to survive.

"Let him be wise," my father said, "so long as it does not harm his piety." My pedagogue looked dismayed but, lacking the spirit to disagree with the Emperor of the Romans, bowed his old gray head in acquiescence.

The very next day—my father being a man who wasted time neither in making up his mind nor in acting once it was made up—the patriarch Theodore was summoned to the palaces. Like his predecessors since the days of Herakleios, Theodore held to the monothelite doctrine. When my father announced he intended to convene an ecumenical synod to overthrow monotheletism, the patriarch protested, "But, your majesty, consider the holy words of Dionysios the Areopagite, who spoke of a single human-divine energy in Christ. Surely this also applies to His will, which unites the natures in His person."

"I do not believe that," my father said, folding his arms across his chest and glaring at Theodore. "How can Christ be perfect man if he lacks a human will?" Theodore tried to go on justifying his belief. My father cut him off: "You will not confess that Christ has two energies and two wills, without division, without change, without separation, without partition, and without confusion?"

Theodore had courage. "No, Emperor, I will not. I cannot."

The following day, my father removed Theodore from the patriarchal throne. He replaced him with a certain George, who was reputed to be more pliable and who lived up to his reputation. The imperial summons to an ecumenical synod went out in short order.

MYAKES

You weren't yet born when that synod was held, were you, Brother Elpidios? No, of course you weren't—that was fifty years ago now. And yet, when I reach back into my memory, it seems like I can touch it. That's what happens when you get old: time squeezes together, till everything that ever happened to you feels like it happened year before last, no more.

I can't see, but I don't need to see to know my beard is white, and my hair, too, what I have of it. I can hear how mushy my voice is, and no wonder, for I haven't many teeth left these days, either.

But in my memory, I'm just a stone's throw from the young, strong, swaggering excubitor who guarded the Emperor—and his son—at the ecumenical synod, and who kept order there, too. And order needed to be kept, let me tell you.

What do I mean? You're a learned man, Brother, so surely you'll know: how many bishops came to Constantinople for the synod? Two hundred eighty-nine, you say? How fast you rattle out the number! I said you were a learned man. If it's in a book—*the* Book or any other—you know where to find it and what to do with it once you have it. Think for a moment, though. Here were two hundred eighty-nine bishops, from all the ends of the earth, brought together in one place. Some of them, now, wanted monotheletism done away with. Some of them, though, some of them didn't. Like Theodore the patriarch that was, they believed what they believed.

Much good it did them.

JUSTINIAN

The ecumenical synod was convened at the great church of the Holy Wisdom in November of the twelfth year of my father's reign, which was also the eleventh year of my age. By then my father had concluded no more bishops than the two hundred eighty-nine already present in the imperial city would arrive, bad weather having made the Mediterranean unsafe for further travel in that season—as the followers of the false prophet had discovered, to their sorrow and our great joy, two years before.

How gorgeous the bishops were as they stood to hear my father speak from the ambo of the great church to open the synod, how gorgeous and how varied. For though they were all Christians, all part of God's holy and universal church, yet they were also from many lands, with robes of different cut and many colors so that, assembled there, they put me in mind of Joseph's coat.

As my father spoke, setting forth the reasons for abandoning the false doctrine of the one energy and one will in Christ, his words came echoing back from the high dome of the church. When the Justinian for whom I am named first saw that dome, which his architects created in accordance with his vision, he cried out, "Solomon, I have beaten you!"

Thanks to the wicked Babylonians, we have not the chance to compare Solomon's temple to the church of the Holy Wisdom. By the awed looks on the faces of the bishops—especially those from beyond the borders of the Roman Empire—who gaped at the wonder Justinian had wrought, most would have agreed with him.

I was particularly struck by the amazement on the face of one man, a plump, fair-haired latecomer from somewhere in the west who, as luck had it, had been on pilgrimage to Jerusalem when my father sent out the summons for the synod, and who came up to Constantinople to take part. You would have thought he found himself unexpectedly transported to heaven, not in a human church, no matter how magnificent. I wondered in what sort of drafty cow barn he did his own preaching.

His robe was among the plainest there, being merely dark blue wool, but, as he had been a pilgrim before coming to the Queen of Cities, that said nothing as to the wealth of his see. He joined with the other bishops in applauding my father. After my father stepped down from the ambo, George the ecumenical patriarch replaced him there. He proceeded to make the same points my father had, but took four times as long doing it, as he cited every relevant Scriptural text and passage from the holy fathers to bolster his position.

Most of the bishops listened attentively. Some were scowling: they, I guessed, were those who still favored monotheletism, and who were mentally preparing texts and passages of their own with which to defend the doctrine in the sessions that lay ahead. Even as a boy of eleven, I could have told them they were wasting their efforts. When the Emperor convenes an ecumenical synod of the church, it ratifies the doctrine he has established. So it has been since the days of the first Constantine; so it shall always be. The Emperor, after all, being God's vicegerent on earth, is specially concerned with maintaining the faith.

Learned though it was, I found George's oration tedious. Watching the bishops, trying to guess who would cling to the doctrine of the one will and energy and who would gladly abandon it, was a more interesting game. And then my eye fell once more upon the pilgrim bishop from the distant west. His jaws were working furiously as George spoke. I thought he was about to burst out in a tirade against the holy ecumenical patri-arch, thereby disrupting the synod.

Then he tilted his head to one side and spat something onto the floor of the great church. That done, he popped something else into his mouth, whereupon his jaws began working once more. Chew, spit, pop . . . chew, spit, pop . . . After several of these cycles, I realized he was eating salted olives.

I had all I could do to hold my face still. Here we were in the grandest shrine ever built by man, on the solemn occasion of an ecu-menical synod—only the sixth such in nearly seven centuries of Chris-tendom—and this backwoods bishop reckoned nothing more important than the snack he had brought with him. Had my father stayed and seen him, he would have been less amused than I was.

At last, George droned to a halt, having run out of citations to hurl at the clerics assembled before him. He had not noticed the hungry bishop; like my pedagogue, he believed the most perfect reality lay in ink on paper.

The pious bishops broke up into knots. The murmur of theological disputation rose up into the dome of the church of the Holy Wisdom. I turned and caught Myakes' eye. "Do you speak Latin?" I asked him.

"A little, Prince," he answered; I had outgrown "Goldentop." "Sol-diers, we use it some."

"Good," I said, and pointed to the peckish bishop. "I want to meet that man, and he may well speak no Greek. You will accompany me." I was learning to command, even so young.

Accompany me he did. We steered our way through the assembled prelates, some of whom moved toward me to give me their views on the one or two wills and energies, presumably in the hope these would reach my father (a wasted hope even if realized, his mind being unalterably made up), while others drew back from Myakes' shield and spear. The western bishop looked up in surprise at finding himself my target.

He had manners. He bowed and said, "Good day, Prince Justinian," in Greek not too vile. He must have learned it on his long journey from the barbarous west.

"Good day," I answered. "Tell me your name, and where you are from."

He bowed again. "I am Arculf, bishop of Rhemoulakion, a small city in Gaul," he answered, and paused to eat another couple of olives.

I saw more pits than I had expected on the ground by his feet. "Do you do nothing but eat?" I asked him, pointing down to them.

The Gallic bishop flushed; as he was so fair, you could watch the color mount from his throat to the very top of his head, exposed by his tonsure. He was so flustered, he forgot his Greek, and spluttered out something in Latin. I glanced over to faithful Myakes, who translated for me: "He is embarrassed, for you have seen what a glutton he is. He fights the sin as best he can, but that best is not yet good enough."

"Thank you," Bishop Arculf told him. He went on for himself, in Greek once more, "I pray in Jerusalem at the church of the Holy Sepulcher for God to take this sin from me. It does not happen yet." He rolled his eyes mournfully. "Now I pray here, too, at the church of the Holy Wisdom. Sooner or later, God *will* hear me." His round face filled with serene faith.

"How do you stand on the question of Christ's wills and energies?" I asked. I was jealous he had been to Jerusalem, which the followers of the false prophet stole from us in the days of my great-great-grandfather.

"I believe with your father the Emperor of the World," Arculf said. "Christ has and must have two wills, two energies. All Christians in the west believe this."

"What of Pope Honorius?" I asked. "He agreed with Sergios of Constantinople that Christ has only one will."

Arculf looked at me in a new way before he answered. "You know these things," he said, almost accusingly. Before, he had been polite to a boy who was a prince; now he saw he had to weigh his words, as if to a man. I looked smug. At my side, Myakes looked proud. He had no learning to speak of, but admired mine. Arculf went on, "If Pope Honorius says this, if the holy ecumenical synod decides he says this, let him be anathema with others who say this."

"I agree," I told him. "Let all who confess one energy and one will be anathema. Let their bones be dug up." He did not understand that, not even after Myakes did his best to turn it into Latin. I realized it was Constantinopolitan slang, not ordinary Greek, and explained: "It means, 'Down with them. No mercy to them.'"

Little did I dream then that one day the worthless, fickle city mob would be screaming for my bones to be exhumed. Well, the wretches who led and misled them are mostly dead now, and those who still live shall not live much longer.

"'Let their bones be dug up.'" Arculf fixed the phrase in his memory. He said, "You are very sure of the right dogma, Prince."

"Of course I am," I told him, surprised he was surprised. "My father has decreed it, the ecumenical patriarch has agreed to it, now the holy ecumenical synod will ratify it. It must be true."

Had he argued with me, I would have screamed for all the assembled bishops to hear that he was an infamous heretic, and likely would have ordered Myakes to clout him in the side of the head with his spear shaft, too. But he had already said he supported the doctrine of two wills and two energies, and all he added now was, "Yes, and the popes of Rome also confess as you and your father do."

"Yes, and the popes of Rome," I agreed politely. The popes do deserve honor, for their line goes back to Peter, the rock upon whom Christ founded the church, but Rome itself, from all I have heard, is a village if set alongside Constantinople, which is also the true and only capital of the Roman Empire these days. To remind Arculf of the difference, I waved my hand all around, saying, "Is this not the grandest church you have ever seen?"

Words failed him—literally. He was eating yet another olive, and choked on the pit. I thought for a moment God was about to punish him most severely for profaning the church of the Holy Wisdom, but he spat out the stone when Myakes thumped him hard on the back. Even afterwards, he was reduced to spluttering in Latin, which I could not understand.

Myakes followed enough to make sense of it for me: "He says this is the grandest church he has ever seen. He has seen many in the west and in Jerusalem and in Alexandria, but this is the finest. He says he thinks God must be holding up the dome, because otherwise it would fall."

I smiled at that, which was a thought I have often had myself. Arculf recovered his Greek then, and went on, "Constantinople and the Roman Empire are full of holy things."

"I should hope so," I exclaimed, and pointed to a large, ornate silver chest heavily encrusted with precious stones that stood not far from the ambo where first my father and then the patriarch George had spoken. "In that chest, for instance, lies the holy and life-giving wood of the cross upon which our Lord and Savior Jesus Christ suffered. We venerate it each year at Easter, as you shall see if you stay with us."

Arculf made the sign of the cross himself. I and then Myakes imitated him. He said, "This is a great and holy thing, truly. But I also see and hear of many small and holy things. The icon of Saint George, the one on the stone column."

Now I felt embarrassed, for I did not know of this icon. "Tell me what you saw and heard of it," I urged him, not wishing to show my ignorance.

"I only hear this," he said. "They say a man, a witless fellow, strikes at the image with his spear." The last word came out in Latin, but it was one Myakes knew. "The spear goes into the column of stone. The man's hands go into the column, too, and all his ten fingers; they are stuck there." Arculf held out his own hands, the fingers extended, to show what he meant. He made as if to pull back and be unable; he had no small skill as a mime, though olive oil greased the skin of his right index finger and thumb.

He went on, "He is stuck, as I say. He prays—with tears, he repents. And God, 'who desireth not the death of a sinner, but rather that he may turn and live' "—he quoted from Ezekiel—"lets him go. But the marks where his fingers go into the stone, these are there to this day. It is a great icon, true?"

"True indeed," I said, and crossed myself again.

Then Arculf told me of an image of the altogether immaculate Virgin Mother of God. Inspired by the devil, a Jew took it down from the wall on which it had been set, threw it into a privy nearby, and then shat on it to dishonor Christ. A pious Christian, learning what had happened, rescued the icon, cleaned it, and washed it in pure water.

"Ever since that day," the Gallic bishop said, "it gives out from itself a pure oil, a good-smelling oil, that cures sickness better than any man of medicine. I see this image, I see this oil, with these eyes." He touched each eyelid with his index finger so I could not misunderstand. "These icons have much strength, true?"

"True," I repeated, making the sign of the cross once more. Now I had always known of the power of holy icons; had not the one human hands did not create helped defend this God-guarded and imperial city against the attacks of the followers of the false prophet? But Arculf seemed to be seeing these things with fresh eyes, and he made me see them so, too. Since that day, I have advanced the holy images in every way I have thought of, including some never used before in all the days of the Roman Empire.

M Y A K E S

Is that where he came up with his idea? Brother Elpidios, you could knock me over with a feather, and that is the God's truth. If I've thought of Bishop Arculf of Rhemoulakion or whatever the name of his town was three times in these past fifty years, it's a miracle, nothing else but. But it seems he never escaped Justinian's mind, which only goes to show you never can tell.

Old fool that I am, I'd forgotten about that icon of the Mother of God, too. I wonder how the Emperor Leo would explain its power, I do, I do. But he might have a way. He was always tricky, Leo was. Well, enough of that. Go on.

J U S T I N I A N

As have all such, the sixth holy and ecumenical synod, the third held in Constantinople, proceeded on the course the Emperor had set for it from the beginning. I headed an ever-increasing number of the sessions myself, for my father began to be concerned with reports that the Bulgars, a loathsome tribe then newly arrived at the Danube, were raiding Roman cities and farms south of the river. He dared not let my uncles preside; both Herakleios and Tiberius, as I have noted, were vehemently of the monothelite party (although I feel certain they would have espoused orthodoxy with equal vehemence had my father favored monotheletism).

Thus I presided over the debates of the learned—and the not so learned—theologians as they worked their way toward consensus. Only one voice was consistently raised in opposition to the doctrine of Christ's two wills and two energies: that of Makarios, patriarch of Antioch. His patriarchal see being under the rule of the followers of the false prophet, he could uphold his own misguided beliefs without fear of retribution from the Emperor.

Like Theodore, former patriarch of Constantinople, Makarios justified his vile and erroneous dogma by means of Dionysios the Areopagite's phrase referring to the divine-human energy of Christ. The rest of the bishops hurled against him a great barrage of quotations from the Scriptures and from the writings of the holy fathers of ancient days. He refused to own himself beaten, but his views, plainly, were those of but a tiny minority of the assembled clerics.

Winter wheeled round toward spring. Lent began, ushering in the approach to the day of our Lord's holy resurrection from the dead. And then, at the fifteenth session of the ecumenical synod, one of Makarios's few backers, a scrawny cleric named Polykhronios, who had made himself notable both for ostentatious piety and for what was obviously a lifetime's abhorrence of cleanliness, presented me with a memorial addressed to my father.

"Thank you, your reverence," I said, thankful mostly that he withdrew once more into the ranks of his fellow bishops.

"Read it, Prince!" he called in harsh, Syrian-accented Greek. "The salvation of your soul depends on it!"

A man who is ostentatiously pious can sometimes also get by with being ostentatiously rude. And, since the synod had been summoned for the salvation of souls, I could hardly disregard him. The memorial was legibly written; I could not dispute that. My lips moved as I rapidly took it in. "Your reverence," I said, "I see little here different from the views the assembled bishops have decided to be heresy and error, and so I—"

"They are not heresy and error!" Polykhronios shouted in a great voice, so that his words came echoing back from the dome of the great church. "They are the truth!"

When he interrupts the son of the Emperor of the Romans, even a man of ostentatious piety has gone too far. The ecumenical patriarch George said, "Reverend Polykhronios, surely you forget yourself. We who have gathered here at the Emperor Constantine's urging—"

"The truth!" Polykhronios all but screamed. He pointed to the memorial, which I still held. "Set those holy words on a dead man's chest and he will live again, just as Lazarus did when Christ called, 'Come forth!' "

He could not have cause greater commotion among the assembled bishops had he set fire to the great church. Some shouted that he was a fool, others that he was a madman. But still others, including a surprising number who till that time had seemed warm in their support for the doctrine of the two wills and two energies, shouted just as loudly in support of Polykhronios. One of them pulled the beard of a man who had remained loyal to that doctrine. His victim hit him in the pit of the stomach. They fell to the floor together, kicking and clawing at each other in what looked like a death struggle.

"Order!" I cried. "Let us have order!" That seemed to be only the first fight to break out of many that were simmering. What would my father do to me if, at a session over which I presided, the holy ecumenical synod degenerated into brawling and riot, making him a laughingstock not only throughout Christendom but also to the Arabs? Some lessons I did not want to learn. "Order!" I cried again, but my voice was still a boy's, high and shrill. They did not heed me.

I glanced back to the excubitores in mute appeal. Thank God, there behind my left shoulder stood faithful Myakes. His eyes asked a silent question. I nodded—desperately, I suspect.

"Order!" he and his comrades yelled together, a deep roar that cut through the bishops' bickering like a knife slicing cheese. The guardsmen slammed the butts of their spears down on the stone floor, so hard I hoped they did not crack it.

For a moment, I had silence. Into it, I said, "I do not think Poly-khronios can do what he says he can." That threatened to start the hub-bub anew. I looked back at Myakes again, and again he and his fellow excubitores struck their spears against the floor, which bought me another brief, tenuous stretch of quiet. I went on, "Let him prove it, if God grants him the ability." I pointed to him. "If the dead man does not rise, will you admit the doctrine of the one will and energy is wrong?"

"He will rise," Polykhronios declared, so confidently that I wondered if he knew exactly whereof he spoke.

George the ecumenical patriarch of Constantinople, whose church that of the Holy Wisdom was, said, "No corpse shall defile and pollute this shrine."

One of the excubitores shouted out, "Take the stiff to the Baths of Zeuxippos! He'll come clean there, by Jesus!"

Whoever he was—I could not tell—he brayed laughter like a don-key. The rest of the guardsmen laughed, too. But Polykhronios cried, "Yes, to the Baths of Zeuxippos!" and in a moment all the assembled bishops had taken up the cry. And to the Baths of Zeuxippos we went.

MYAKES

I didn't mean it for anything but a joke, Brother Elpidios. How was I supposed to know they'd take me up on it? So Justinian never knew I was the one who yelled, eh? I didn't think he did. When you get right down to it, I'm glad he didn't.

Did I think Polykhronios could raise the dead? I tell you this, Brother: *he* surely thought he could. I'd never heard anybody claim that before. Matter of fact, I've never heard anybody claim that since. If he could do it, I wanted to be there to see it happen, you had best believe that.

JUSTINIAN

Though rebuilt after a fire in the reign of my namesake, a century and a half before the time of which I write, the Baths of Zeuxippos, between the palaces and the hippodrome, are far older than that; they were built by the Emperor Septimius Severus, more than a hundred years before Constantine the Great accepted Christianity and transformed Byzantium into Constantinople. I mention this because the baths were ornamented in pagan style, with eighty statues of philosophers and poets and even figures from their false mythology. Many of the bishops drew back in dismay on seeing them, some making the sign of the cross.

George the patriarch of Constantinople also crossed himself, but more as a gesture of peace than as one intended to turn aside evil. "They are but memories," he said.

And, to my surprise, Polykhronios agreed. "As Christ cast out demons, so shall the words of His pure and holy faith protect us against any lingering wickedness here," he said, holding the memorial before him like a shield.

We then had some little wait while the excubitores went into the city to find the body of someone newly dead. Polykhronios, I regret to say, showed no interest in using the baths for any but his own purposes. In the warm, steamy air within the bathhouse, his sharp stink seemed stronger than ever. Arculf bought a handful of chickpeas fried in olive oil from a vender for a copper or two and popped them all into his mouth at once, so that his cheeks puffed out like a squirrel's.

Presently the guardsmen returned, carrying the linen-wrapped body of a gray-bearded man who looked to have died of some wasting sickness, for he was skeletally lean. The aromatic odors of the wine and spices with which he had been washed fought against Polykhronios's reek.

Behind the excubitores came the fellow's kinsfolk, now wailing and beating their chests and pulling their hair, now looking hopefully to Polykhronios. "Make him live!" they cried. "Make Andreas live again!"

"Live he shall," Polykhronios said. A woman whose lined face bore the stunned expression of one who has lost someone dear—Andreas's widow, she proved to be—fell on her knees before him and kissed his dirty feet.

The excubitores laid the corpse on a silver table that at other times might have held casseroles of fish, cheese, and vegetables, or perhaps salt pork and cabbage cooked in fat, along with fruit and honey cakes for the pleasure of the bathers.

Polykhronios was about to set his monothelite memorial on dead Andreas's chest when another delay ensued: a runner came hotfoot from the palace ordering that he do no such thing until the Emperors Constantine, Herakleios, and Tiberius got there to witness the promised miracle.

By the time their sedan chairs arrived, the excubitores had to use spear shafts to clear a path by which they could approach the makeshift bier. Word of what Polykhronios intended had spread quickly through Constantinople, as rumors have a way of doing, and throngs of people, many of them arguing the theology of monotheletism with as much sophistication as the bishops of the ecumenical synod, gathered in the Baths of Zeuxippos to learn whether Polykhronios could do as he said.

My father limped in leaning on a stick, with his foot bandaged; his gout had been plaguing him again. In spite of that, he was making ready to attack the Bulgars when the weather grew more certain. He took his place by the patriarch of Constantinople. My uncles, by contrast, ranged themselves with Makarios of Antioch and his followers. Nothing would have made them gladder than having Polykhronios vindicate the first Herakleios's dogma.

"Go ahead," my father told the man who claimed he could raise the dead.

Polykhronios bowed and, stepping up to Andreas's corpse with portentous stride, set his memorial on its chest. Everything in the bathhouse was silent as the tomb, save only a long indrawn breath from the dead man's widow.

Andreas did not move. He remained as he had lain since the excubitores set him on the silver table. "Live!" Polykhronios told him. But his eyes did not open, his chest did not begin to rise and fall, his pale, still, waxy features did not grow ruddy with vitality. In a word, he remained dead.

Several bishops sighed then: the monothelites who had hoped to see their doctrine proved in one fell swoop. A moment later, other bishops also sighed, these, I thought, with relief: the men who, like my father, supported the doctrine of two wills and two energies.

Thinking of my father, I glanced toward him. He had just finished signing himself with the holy cross, and now stared balefully at Polykhronios. "False priest, you are a fraud, and your dogma an error," he said, as if passing sentence. And so he was—sentence on monotheletism.

Andreas's widow let out a great wail of cheated hope, and would have attacked Polykhronios with clawed fingers had Myakes not seized her shoulders and held her back. As for Polykhronios himself, he answered only, "I am not beaten yet." He tugged at the dead man's shroud so his memorial could rest directly on flesh. Even after that, though, Andreas lay unmoving.

"Live!" Polykhronios said, this time in some annoyance, as if the corpse were a willful child disobeying its father. He muttered into dead Andreas's ears. I could not hear everything he said, but I think it was incantation, not prayer. Whatever it was, it had no effect.

After an hour passed with no resurrection, the assembled bishops grew restive. Arculf began popping handfuls of chickpeas into his mouth once more (in truth, he had not stopped doing that all through Polykhronios's performance, but he had slowed down).

And George the ecumenical patriarch of Constantinople, with wickedly sardonic glee, quoted from First Kings, the passage wherein Elijah mocked the priests of Baal when they proved unable to summon him: " 'Cry aloud, for he is a god; either he is musing, or he is gone aside, or he is in a journey, or peradventure he sleepeth, and must be awaked.' "

Some of the bishops, recognizing the allusion, laughed out loud. Arculf was swallowing as George spoke, and almost choked to death. Hatred flashed in Polykhronios's dark eyes, but it surely was, as the corpse on the silver table attested, hatred of an impotent sort.

Polykhronios kept trying to persuade dead Andreas to live until my father at last lost patience with him. This took longer than I would have expected, but when it happened, it happened all at once. Pointing first to the memorial on Andreas's unmoving chest and then to Polykhronios, he demanded, "Having seen your own failure, do you now admit the error of your dogma?"

To my amazement—to everyone's amazement—Polykhronios shook his head. "No, Emperor, I do not," he declared. "Since the doctrine is perfect and true, the error must lie in me, and I—"

As I said, once my father lost patience, he lost all patience. He allowed the bishop not another word, but shouted, "Let Polykhronios be anathema!"

"Let Polykhronios be anathema!" Baying like wolves, the bishops took up the cry, loudest among them George. Polykhronios's protests were overwhelmed in an avalanche of scorn, and the anathema duly recorded for all time in the acts of the holy ecumenical synod.

On Holy Thursday, as was the custom each year, the three pieces of the holy and life-giving wood of the True Cross were removed from their case and set on a golden altar in the center of the great church. As always when the case is opened, a scent like that of all the flowers in the world came forth, and everyone in the church of the Holy Wisdom sighed with pleasure.

My father advanced to the holy and life-giving wood, bowed his head, and kissed it. After him came my uncles Herakleios and Tiberius, the junior Emperors. Then it was my turn. Though I had performed the ritual every year of my life since I could toddle to the altar, it took on a special meaning with the bishops assembled for the ecumenical synod watching as I brushed the True Cross with my lips. The wood was smooth from countless kisses. At each knot, oil with that special fragrance welled forth. After Easter, that oil would be gathered and used to treat the sick, for whom it was a surer cure than any physician could give.

My brother Herakleios followed me to the True Cross. After him came Christopher the count of the excubitores—the commander of the imperial bodyguard—his mandator or chief deputy Theodore of Koloneia, and the other leading soldiers of the realm. I remember Florus, Petronas, and Kyprianos, still basking in the glory of their victory over the Arabs three years before, and the first appearance in the great church of a new general, a round-faced man named Leontios, who had won distinction in the endless skirmishes in Armenia. The procession of warriors continued until all the excubitores had kissed the life-giving wood.

On Good Friday my mother, the Empress Anastasia, led a similar procession of the women of the court. And on the Saturday of the Passover Sabbath, the bishops who had come to the imperial city for the sixth holy and ecumenical synod joined patriarch George of Constantinople and the other clerics who served the great church in adoring the life-giving wood. When the lips of Arculf of Rhemoulakion touched it, I wondered if he would leave on it oil different from that which it secreted of its own accord, as he had been eating olives again while the procession of bishops formed. But the man behind him made no complaint, so perhaps he had managed to wipe his mouth on his sleeve.

By Easter, which fell in that year on the fourteenth day of April, the ecumenical synod had nearly finished its work. Had that not been so, the assembled bishops would have faced my father's displeasure, for he, who had waited in Constantinople while the holy season—and three precious weeks of spring—passed, was eager to depart and assail the Bulgars. This he did, less than a week after the day of our Lord's resurrection from the dead, satisfied the synod had defined the faith as he desired.

He left me to preside while the bishops discussed other matters of canon law unrelated to the doctrine of Christ's two wills and two energies. On some of these, they in the end reached no firm conclusion, a failure like that of the holy fathers who took part in the fifth holy ecumenical synod, the one convened by the Emperor for whom I am named, the first Justinian, almost a century and a half earlier. Before my treacherous overthrow, I made good the deficiencies of those two synods, summoning my own to deal with matters they had neglected.

The other remaining subject of debate was that of anathemas. Polykhronios had richly earned his: there everyone agreed. Past that, consensus faltered. Four patriarchs of Constantinople ended up condemned: Sergios, who first proposed monenergism to the Emperor Herakleios, and his successors, Pyrrhos, Paul, and Peter, who upheld monenergism and monotheletism.

Some of the bishops more aggressive in their piety, and some of those from the western lands, also suggested anathematizing Herakleios and Constans. When one of their number proposed casting my great-great-grandfather and my grandfather into the outer darkness of anathema, applause rang out in the great church.

"No!" I shouted. "I forbid it!"

They stared at me. I had not quite twelve years then, and my voice had not broken. But I was older than Constans had been when he became Emperor of the Romans, and only a bit more than five years younger than my father when he gained the rule—and he had also been administering affairs in Constantinople for some time before that. I had no excubitores at my back; they had accompanied the Emperor in his campaign against the Bulgars. I knew what he would say, I knew what he was liable to do, if he returned to the imperial city to find his ancestors condemned to anathema.

The bishop who had made the proposal said, "Prince, they deserve the sentence no less than their misguided patriarchs. After all, it was your grandfather who made the holy Pope Martin and Maximus the Confessor suffer on behalf of the doctrine we ourselves have declared true and correct, and so—"

"No!" I said again. "It shall not be." I did not need to think of my father's certain rage; I was filled with rage myself, rage at the idea that these little, sniveling men—for so they seemed to me at that moment—could think of declaring my kinsmen heretics. "Without Herakleios and Constans, we should have no universal Empire to accompany the true and universal faith. The Queen of Cities would belong to the Persians or the Avars or the Arabs. Let the Emperors enjoy credit for what they did, and do not judge what you cannot match."

After a moment, bishops who lived within the boundaries of the Roman Empire spoke up in support of what I had said. All of them, of course, remembered how my father had turned back the followers of the false prophet; most recalled the ceaseless exertions of my grandfather against the Arabs; and a few, the old men among them, had seen my great-great-grandfather repel the Persians and the Avars both. If they accepted my father as Romania's savior, how could they deny the similar achievements of his ancestors? They could not.

Once that move was defeated, the ecumenical patriarch George had his revenge on the westerners who had thought to condemn Emperors of the Romans. His voice smooth and sweet as scented olive oil, he said, "Honorius the bishop of Rome confessed one energy in Christ. If we anathematize the patriarchs of Constantinople for this false doctrine, how can we look approvingly upon it in other prelates? Let Pope Honorius be anathema!"

Oh, how the bishops from Italy and Gaul and Africa screamed and bellowed at that! They might have been so many just-castrated swine. Fat Bishop Arculf of Rhemoulakion turned not red but so dusky a shade of purple that I feared he would suffer an apoplexy on the spot.

But the western bishops, though raucous, were few. And those from within the Roman Empire not only outnumbered them but had grown weary of their constant prating of perfect orthodoxy in doctrine. Here was not merely one of them but their patriarch shown by the words written in his own hand to be a misbeliever. Like Polykhronios, like Sergios, like the rest, Pope Honorius was condemned in the acts of the sixth holy and ecumenical synod. No doubt he shall suffer in hell for all eternity on account of his errors.

Having anathematized Honorius, the synod had in essence completed its labors. All that remained was for the Emperor of the Romans to ratify what it had done and dismiss the assembled bishops. But my father, as I have said, had left the Queen of Cities to campaign against the Bulgars, the barbarous horsemen who had begun to harass the Romans living nearest the Danube. And, on returning to Constantinople, he found trouble more urgent than any the bishops of the ecumenical synod had caused. Thus those bishops remained assembled, though no longer meeting, until almost the autumnal equinox.

M Y A K E S

People nowadays say Constantine didn't take the Bulgars seriously enough. What? How do I know what people say nowadays, Brother Elpidios? Well, there you have me. Am I blushing? I ought to be. Twenty years ago, when I was still out in the world, people said Constantine didn't take the Bulgars seriously enough. There. Are you happier, Brother? You'd make a fine canon lawyer, I have no doubt of that.

Whenever people say—said—that about Constantine, it makes—*made*, excuse me—me angry, for it isn't so. He had detachments from all the military districts of Anatolia cross into Thrace for the campaign. Why not? We were, for once, at peace with the Arabs, and they were paying us tribute. He didn't figure they'd jump us from behind, and he was right.

Most of the troops from the military districts slogged north toward the Danube on horseback. The rest, along with us excubitores and the Emperor, sailed up the coast and inland by way of the Danube. The Bulgars, in those days, didn't live south of the river. They stayed up beyond it, in the swampy country in the angle between the Pruth and the Seret. They had a sort of a camp there: not really a town, but a bunch of tents all in the same place, and ringed round with palisades of brush and sticks and whatnot, as much for keeping their cattle in as for keeping enemies out.

They must have been pissing themselves when we came up toward that camp, let me tell you. We made a proud spectacle: thousands of men on horseback, all of us in chainmail that glittered in the sun, the imperial guards with silk surcoats dyed in all sorts of bright colors, banners and crosses and icons going before the companies and regiments and divisions of the army. The Bulgars took one look at us, fled back inside the camp, and didn't come out for three days straight. We could have gone right in after them, too, easy as you please.

But what's that the Book of Proverbs says? "Pride goeth before de-struction, and an haughty spirit before a fall"? Yes, that's the passage I meant, Brother Elpidios. Thank you. You give me those so quick, I don't have to grope for them with my own poor wits. We thought the Bulgars would flee back to the eastern lands they'd come from, but they didn't.

Oh, other things went wrong, too. The soldiers from the Anatolian military districts didn't care for the country they were in: it was damp, it was boggy, it was misty, it was everything the land they were used to wasn't. And everybody remembered that the last Roman army that had gone north of the Danube was the one that had mutinied and murdered Maurice, back an old man's lifetime before. No one said anything about that, but you could tell it was in people's minds.

Even with that, though, everything might have been all right if only Constantine's gout hadn't flared up. But flare it did, not only in his big toe—which was where it usually bit him—but also in his heel and up the calf of his leg.

I happened to draw guard duty outside the imperial pavilion the night everything went sour. He should have been asleep in there. He'd brought up a featherbed covered in silk and stuffed a cubit thick with goose down, so soft it'd be sinful for a proper monk to think about it, let alone lie down on it. You'd take oath a man could set that featherbed on knives and still sleep sound.

Except Constantine couldn't. He'd moan and he'd curse and he'd moan a little more and he'd curse a lot more. What he wanted to do, I think, was scream, but he wouldn't give in to the pain enough for that. Finally, when the stars said it was getting close to midnight—time for me to roll up in a blanket a lot scratchier than what Constantine had—he came hobbling out on two sticks, his leg all swaddled like a baby and bent so his foot wouldn't accidentally bump the ground and make him hurt even worse than he did already.

He looked bad. He looked old. He couldn't have been thirty yet, but shadows from the torchlight filled and deepened all the lines in his face. You could see white streaks in his beard. Even in the torchlight, he was pale. "Mother of God, help me," he groaned. "I have to get some rest."

I glanced over at my partner, a thick-shouldered Armenian named . . . named . . . well, whatever his name was, all those years ago, he looked as worried as I felt. "Wine with poppy juice in it, Emperor?" I suggested.

Constantine shook his head. His face was shiny with sweat, not on account of the heat but because he was maybe a step and a half away from keeling over dead. "I can't," he said. "I need my wits about me. I've beaten all my other enemies, all around the borders of the Empire. Once I smash these louse-eating Bulgars, too, I'll have made a clean sweep."

My partner and I looked at each other. What were we supposed to say, Brother Elpidios? *You have to stop or you'll die?* For one thing, we didn't know that was so. Only God knows such things. And for another thing, do you think Constantine would have listened to us? If you had any sense, you wouldn't have bet a forty-follis copper piece against a stack of gold nomismata that any Emperor from the line of Herakleios would listen to anybody. By the way he sounded, Constantine didn't care whether he went on living or not, so long as he got rid of the Bulgars.

He said, "I'm going back inside, boys. I *will* get some rest." He was giving orders not to us but to his own body, which didn't much feel like obeying. But he was clumsy with his sticks, because he didn't need them all that often, and as he turned himself around to go back, he whacked himself right in the sore foot with one of them.

Poor devil. He started to fall down. I grabbed him, so that didn't happen, but he threw back his head and howled like a wolf. Everybody awake in our camp must have heard him, and he probably woke half the troopers who were sleeping. Except for the sizzle of my own eyeballs cooking, it was the most dreadful sound I ever heard. Christ, wouldn't surprise me if it woke up Asparukh, the Bulgar chief.

He clamped down on it fast as he could—made his mouth close and bit the inside of his lower lip, hard, maybe to make one pain fight another. "I *will* rest," he said again, in a ghastly voice, and a little blood trickled down off his lower lip.

He made it back inside. My partner and I, we closed the tent flaps after him. He wouldn't rest, not after that. He hadn't a prayer, and we couldn't do a thing to help him. After a while, our reliefs came. I didn't think I'd sleep, either, but I did.

The sun woke me. I sat up, praying God had worked a miracle and healed Constantine overnight. Then I heard a groan from inside the imperial pavilion and knew it wasn't so. God works miracles when He feels like it, not when you feel like it. I snagged myself a mug of wine and went over there to find out what Constantine was going to do. The only thing I was sure of was that, if we attacked, he couldn't lead.

I got to the pavilion about the same time Florus and Kyprianos did. Florus was the ugliest man I've ever seen, with a big nose, no chin to speak of, and big ears that stuck out like open shutters on two sides of a house. Kyprianos, now, Kyprianos looked like a pretty catamite grown up to middle age. You ask me, though, Florus made the better general.

Constantine came out to meet the two of them. He looked worse by daylight than he had in the middle of the night. The purple circles under his eyes said he hadn't slept at all, not even a little bit. When he said, "If I don't get relief, I'm going to die," Florus and Kyprianos both nodded. He meant it, and they could tell as much.

Florus pointed north, toward the Bulgars' camp. "What about the barbarians? What do we do with them if you're not here?"

The Emperor made a rude gesture. "Drag them out of hiding with your lances. You won't need me here for that. They're frightened spit-less of Roman power. Make them come out and fight and you'll smash them."

"We shall do as our glorious sovereign commands!" Kyprianos cried. He wore chainmail, but he talked like a courtier.

Florus said, "The men won't like that you're going, Emperor. They'll think you're leaving them in the lurch."

"I have to go," Constantine answered. He wasn't lying about that; just standing up on one foot and two sticks took an effort that left him white and trembling. "I'm sailing down to the baths at Mesembria; after I soak there, I always feel better. I expect I'll see you soon, with captives and booty to show me."

"We shall drag the barbarians forth from their lairs and crush them in your name," Kyprianos said. Constantine nodded. An Emperor always hears yes. Who'd dare tell him no? And Kyprianos wasn't the worst soldier around. He'd helped beat the Arabs a few years earlier, when they'd lost thirty thousand men. I guess he really thought he could do what he prom-ised. But Florus, I noticed, didn't say anything.

Along with five shiploads of excubitores—me among 'em—Con-stantine sailed down the Danube and then south along the Black Sea coast to Mesembria. It sits out on a rocky peninsula, and makes a good harbor. The Emperor took the waters there. Before too long, he was feel-ing . . . not good, but better.

"We should be getting news," he'd say, and try to put his sore foot on the ground. "We should be getting news." He must have felt like a bear in a cage. He talked about going back up to the frontier and taking over again, but he wasn't up to that. He waited. we all waited. If you weren't soaking your foot, Mesembria was a boring place to get stuck. Even the whores were clumsy . . . Sorry, Brother. That just slipped out.

By luck of the draw, I was attending Constantine when the first messenger arrived from the north. We'd just come out of the basilica called the Old Metropolis, where the Emperor had been praying for vic-tory. A fellow who looked like he'd just about killed his horse getting there galloped up, jumped off the poor, worn beast, and threw himself facedown in the street. "Emperor!" he cried.

"Get up, man," Constantine said. "What news?" He quivered like a bowstring when you've strung it too tight.

The messenger didn't get up. I suppose he didn't want Constantine to see his expression. Still grinding his face into the dirt of the street, he cried, "Disaster!"

Constantine took a step toward him. By the look on his face, he aimed to murder the poor luckless messenger right then and there. Not quite by accident, looking clumsier than I was, I bumbled out between the Emperor and the fellow who'd brought bad news. Constantine had to stop, just long enough to let him start thinking. He was headstrong, but God help you if you thought he was stupid. "What happened?" he ground out.

The messenger spewed out this great long tale of woe. The meat was what Florus had said it would be: without Constantine there, the men wouldn't go forward against the Bulgars. Some of them started saying the Emperor ran away. Then they panicked and ran away themselves, even though the Bulgars weren't after 'em.

"The wicked flee where no man pursueth"? No, not quite, Brother. The stupid fled where no one pursued, more like.

Of course, after a little while the Bulgars figured out the Romans weren't trying to lure them into some kind of trap and really were running away. They came to the Danube and crossed it, sweeping up our soldiers as they went. By the time the messenger got to Mesembria, the barbarians were already down to the Haimos Mountains and threatening Varna, not fifty miles north of where we were.

Constantine listened to it all without twitching a muscle. "Ruined," he said at last, and nothing more. I didn't know what to say. There wasn't much I could say. He wouldn't be able to put together another army like the one he'd thrown away, not for years—too many men gone. *Ruined* was about right.

He kicked at the dirt, hard, with his bandaged foot. I don't want to imagine the pain that must have cost him. His face didn't so much as twitch. We sailed for Constantinople the next day.

JUSTINIAN

My father's return to the imperial city took everyone by surprise. Stephen the Persian was particularly vexed, for he had no chance to prepare a triumphal procession to celebrate the extermination of the Bulgars. But when my father reached the palace—bare moments after

word he was in the city came to us—one look at his face said no procession would be needed.

"Father," I said proudly, stepping forward when everyone else hung
back, "the acts of the holy ecumenical synod await your review and approval."

"That is good," he said, and seemed to mean it; he was a good and
pious Christian, as concerned with the world to come as with our own.
But he had other things on his mind. "I shall review those acts . . . eventually."

Still full of myself and what I had done while he was gone, I demanded, "Why not now?"

"Because we were beaten, and beaten badly," he answered, getting
all the poison out in one sentence.

I gaped, speechless. Despite the grim, pain-filled expression he bore,
the last thing in all the world I had imagined was that my father, who
had turned back the followers of the false prophet and had received envoys not only from them but from all the lesser kinds of the inhabited
world, could have gone down to defeat at the hands of a band of ragged
barbarians.

My mother, normally of sunny disposition, made the sign of the cross
and burst into tears. One of the golden-haired Sklavinian maidservants
the khagan of the Avars had presented to my father, a pretty little thing
who had been baptized under the name of Irene, dropped the goblet of
wine she had been carrying to him.

Some of the wine splashed the robe of Stephen the Persian, who
was standing near my father. The eunuch stared down at the red stain
for a moment, then, quite coldly, slapped her across the face. "Clean up
the mess, you clumsy whore," he hissed in a voice that might have been
chipped from ice.

I gaped again; the imperial court was never subjected to such unseemly displays. But my father, lost in his rage and misery, said nothing.
Irene stood stock-still long enough for the print of Stephen's hand to
form itself in red on her cheek. Then, bowing, she said, "I sorry. I fix,"
in the broken Greek she had learned, and hurried away. Coming back
with rags, she began mopping up the wine on the floor.

No one save Stephen and I looked at her, he in satisfaction, I in
stupefaction. Everyone else formed a tableau as frozen as the mosaic scene
Irene labored on hands and knees to clean. When my eyes moved away
from her, I found myself, as it were, turned to stone as well, for my father
was staring at—trying to stare down—his two younger brothers.

Herakleios and Tiberius had not burst into tears when my father

admitted his defeat. Far from it. By their gloating expressions, they had
everything they could do to keep from cheering out loud, or perhaps even
from turning handsprings like acrobats earning coppers in the Forum of
Theodosios. All three of them had been crowned Emperor, but all power
had been in my father's hands since my grandfather was murdered in
Sicily: thirteen empty years for my uncles. Now my father, instead of
moving from triumph to triumph, had blundered. His brothers had to be
wondering, could they strip that power from him?

He knew what they were thinking. How could he not have known
what they were thinking? Had he been born second or third rather than
first, he would have been thinking the same thing himself.

My brother Herakleios let out a loud, wet cough. Even he had been
watching my father and my uncles trying to stare one another down. His
name, as I have said, was a bone my father had tossed to my uncle after
one of their earlier fights. Most of the time, though, my father did not
deign to toss bones. He was *the* Emperor, after all, and commonly was to
be appeased, not the appeaser.

But today, sensing his weakness, his younger brothers gave as good
as they got. Instead of breaking under his gaze and slinking off with shoulders slumped and eyes downcast, they stood straight against him. Nor did
they glance suspiciously at each other, as sometimes happened: they knew
that, if they cast down my father, only one of them could take up the
reins of power they both wanted. Without casting him down, though,
neither of them could seize those reins, and for once they remembered as
much.

My little brother coughed again, and again, and again, and began
to turn blue. That drew my father's notice. He went over to young Herakleios and took him in his arms, which made me angry and jealous. My
uncles Herakleios and Tiberius strode away, as if they had won a victory,
and so, perhaps, they had.

Herakleios—my brother, not my uncle—slowly came out of his par-
oxysm and, rather to my disappointment, regained his natural color. My
father ruffled his hair, which was darker than mine, and sent him on his
way, then turned to me. "Speak of the synod," he said.

I did, retailing to him the arguments over the anathemas and how
I had kept the names of our ancestors from being maligned for all eternity.
He nodded to me: for the first time in my life, as one man to another.
"You did well," he said, "in that and in the matter of Pope Honorius.
Misbelief must be uprooted no matter where it hides. Even if the affairs
of men suffered, those of God went well, and for that I thank you. It's
more than my brothers would have done, Lord knows."

"Thank you, Father," I said, probably sounding surprised, for I was unused to praise from him.

"You're growing up," he said. His tone too was less certain that it might have been; I daresay he found the idea startling. But he faced it head-on, as was always his way. "High time you wore an Emperor's crown on your head, not just a prince's circlet. If you can do the work, you deserve the rank."

Now I know I stared. If he crowned me Emperor, that pushed Herakleios and Tiberius even further into the background, for my rank would vault over theirs, and I would be my father's formally designated heir. In a small voice, I asked, "What will my uncles say to that?"

"I will tend to your uncles, never fear," my father promised.

Herakleios and Tiberius tried to tend to my father first. I think they might have done it anyhow, but hearing that he intended to acclaim me Emperor—for he made no secret of that: to the contrary—forced their hand.

Soldiers from the Anatolian military districts—the men who had run away from the Bulgars rather then routing them while they had the chance—began trickling into the imperial city, seeking passage back to the farms they worked when not summoned to war. They blamed their ignominious defeat not on their own vile cowardice, but on my father's having abandoned them: fools, wretches, liars, knaves! My uncles went out among them, not to calm their discontent but to fan it.

MYAKES

They tried to get us excubitores to go against Constantine, too. That didn't go far; we knew why the Emperor had had to sail away to Mesembria. Then they tried saying things like, "Do you want that spoiled brat telling you what to do when Constantine is gone?"

Now, not everybody got on with Justinian as well as I did. He wasn't shy about saying just what was on his mind, and who would talk back to the Emperor's son? Nobody, or nobody with any brains, anyhow.

But the thing of it was, what had Herakleios and Tiberius done to show they were anything much, either? They hadn't done a thing. Of course, one reason they hadn't was that Constantine never gave them the chance to do anything. Still, when you got down to it, they hadn't proved themselves. And, by the way they whined about Constantine and

Justinian, they were on the bratty side themselves. So we excubitores, we listened but we made no promises.

The troops from the military districts, now, they were another matter.

J U S T I N I A N

Herakleios and Tiberius flattered the soldiers who stamped through the streets of Constantinople and crowded the barracks at Sykai, across the Golden Horn from the imperial city. To hear them talk, the men had had victory in their grasp until my father snatched it away. The troops from the Anatolian military districts lapped that up like porridge sweetened with honey. Far easier for them to believe their failure someone else's fault than their own.

Rumors of what my uncles were about did not take long to reach my father. "I'll settle them," he told me. "If they think I'm a poor excuse for an Emperor, let's see how they like life without the title."

He summoned the nobility of Constantinople to the palace. As if nothing were amiss, he also summoned my brothers, who sat in their accustomed places at his left hand. More excubitores than usual stood close by my father, and they wore mailshirts, which was not common practice, but neither was it unknown.

Rising, my father said, "We all look with pride on what Prince Justinian has accomplished these past months for our holy and orthodox church." He walked over, stood beside me, and set a hand on my shoulder. "For his work, and to make clear my will as to the succession, I intend to proclaim him Emperor."

"*Tu vincas*, Justinian!" I think the first to make the ancient Latin acclamation was faithful Myakes, although, as he stood behind me, I cannot be certain. I am certain the excubitores raised the shout before the assembled nobles did. I saw that some of the imperial guards, off to either side of the throne, raised their weapons as well. In a moment, the palace rang with my name and the wish that I conquer.

Ceremony's iron law kept me from turning my head, but I let my eyes slide over to my uncles. They too joined in the acclamations—what choice had they, being where they were?—but their faces declared the words they mouthed lies.

And worse lay ahead for them, for my father went on, "And, since my God-guarded brothers during this same time did nothing save sluggishly eat and drink, and since they aligned themselves with heterodox frauds anathematized by the sixth ecumenical synod, they have brought the imperial house into as much disrepute as my son will bring luster to it. Is it your will, then, powerful men of Constantinople, that I revoke the imperial rank my father conferred upon Herakleios and Tiberius?"

Again, the excubitores cried out first: "Let it be revoked!" Again, the nobles my father had gathered could follow or risk their riches and perhaps their lives. Cowed, they followed . . . all save one.

There was a stir in the brightly clad rows of prominent men as a certain Leo, a functionary in the imperial mints, came forward to stand before my father. True to his calling, he reached into the leather pouch he wore on his belt and drew from it a gold coin, which he held up so the torchlight flashed from it.

"Emperor, this is a nomisma of Carthage," he said in a loud, harsh voice; Carthage then remained under the sway of the Roman Empire, not yet having been fecklessly thrown away by the bungling brigand who stole my throne from me. "Do you see the stamp on it? You and your brothers, Emperors all three. Do not cast them down now. That would be treason against them, for they were raised up at the same time you were."

From that day to this, I have wondered what Leo thought he would accomplish with such foolish freedom of speech. Was he in the pay of my uncles? I had never seen him around them before. Or did he think his simple words would make my father change his mind? Could he have been so naive?

Whatever he was, he paid for it. My father turned to a couple of the excubitores nearest him and said, "This dog's tongue is too forward. Seize him and take him to the executioner, so he can cut it out."

Leo did not even try to flee. He stood staring till the guardsmen laid hold of him and, amid awful silence, began to drag him away. Then, seeming to regain some of his senses, he cried out, "We confess a Trinity in heaven. Let there be a trinity on earth as well!"

Up to that moment, my father had dealt with the unseemly inter- ruption as smoothly as might be expected. Hearing his brothers compared to Persons of the holy Trinity, though, enraged him, and he shouted to the excubitores, "That will cost him his hands and feet along with his tongue! Tell the executioner."

After Leo got what he so richly deserved for his insane insolence, my father looked around the throne room again, as if seeing whether anyone else had the temerity to challenge him. The nobles all tried to pretend they were elsewhere, none of them anxious to meet Leo's fate. Then my father turned his terrible gaze on his brothers.

Tiberius quickly bowed his head. My uncle Herakleios was made of sterner stuff, which was, I suppose, why my father occasionally had to placate him but always rode roughshod over Tiberius. Today, though, my father would placate no one. At last, Herakleios too lowered his eyes in submission.

And then my father looked at me. I met his gaze unflinching. Partly this was pride—was I to humble myself when he had just cleared the way to exalting me above everyone else in the Roman Empire save him alone? And partly, I admit on this page where I must be truthful before the Lord, it was calculation. Having just degraded my two uncles, my father could hardly take vengeance against me. Upon whom would he then rely? My brother? Little Herakleios was not even in the throne room, being confined to his bed by yet another sickness. He had already come close to dying several times in his short, unhappy life. He would have to succeed only once to ruin all my father's plans if he set me aside along with my uncles.

Whatever my reasons, I had gauged my father aright. When he saw I would not bend my neck before him, he nodded and said, "This is the spirit an Emperor must have to rule, yielding to nothing and no one until he is dead."

I have remembered those words all my life, and lived by them.

My uncles, also being of the line of the great Herakleios, had their share of his indomitable spirit. Had they accepted their demotion and lived quietly afterwards, I think my father would have left them at peace: had he wished to inflict harsh punishment on them, he could have done so at the outset, rather than merely depriving them of the imperial dignity.

But Herakleios and Tiberius, having had the title of Emperor since they were children, had never lost the appetite for the power accruing to the title, power they had never tasted but always seen, just as in the pagan myth Tantalos never ate the grapes that hung always barely out of reach.

And so, rather than choosing retirement, they slipped out of the palace before dawn broke the next morning and rowed in a small boat across the narrow water of the Golden Horn to Sykai. Forgetting what had happened to Leo in the throne room, they used his argument with the soldiers from the Anatolian military districts, and succeeded with it better than they deserved.

My father and I had our first inkling of this at breakfast, when a servant, looking apprehensive (and rightly so!), reported to us that Herakleios and Tiberius were neither in their bedchambers nor, so far as anyone could tell, anywhere within the great palace. The eunuch said,

"Perhaps they have withdrawn to a monastery, there to pursue a contemplative life."

"I don't believe it," I said loudly. "They're plotting against me."

"I don't believe it, either," my father said; he knew what spirit his brothers had in them: one all too much like his own. He dipped the bread he was eating in fine olive oil, then took a sip of wine. "I don't think we'll have to wait long to find out, one way or the other."

He soon proved right. A great many ferries pass back and forth between Sykai and the Queen of Cities, and this day those entering Constantinople were filled with soldiers from the Anatolian military districts. Some of them brandished swords, not knowing or not caring that the penalty for rioting with swords was the amputation of their thumbs. Their cry was the same as that Leo's had been: "We believe in a Trinity: let us crown the three"—by which they meant my father and both my uncles.

Had they been a true army, they could have launched civil war within the walls of the God-guarded and imperial city that had repelled all foreign foes. But they were not an army, and Herakleios and Tiberius, who had never commanded soldiers (their function in the Empire having been purely ceremonial), could not make them one. They were only a mob. When my father heard reports that they were robbing shops and sacking taverns, he smiled from ear to ear.

I did not understand. "This makes them worse, not better!" I cried. "Not only are they traitors, they are criminals, too."

"Criminals are easier to deal with," he answered, then turned to Stephen the Persian. "Bring Theodore of Koloneia to me."

The eunuch bowed and soon returned with the patrician. Theodore was a blocky, muscular man with features that looked chiseled from granite—if you allow that the sculptor, after thinking he was done, went back and started several new cuts he then decided not to finish: half a dozen scars seamed Theodore's cheeks and nose and forehead. Although he was only the mandator—the chief deputy—to Christopher the count of the excubitores, he had far more to do with commanding them from day to day than the count did.

MYAKES

Ah, Theodore. Been a good many years since I thought of him, and that's a fact. What? Justinian mentioned him before? I missed it. I am sorry. I am old. He was one harsh man, every bit as rough as Justinian makes him out to be here. A few years after this, still far from an old man, he retired to a monastery. I wonder how he fared as a monk: he was used to having people obey him, not to obeying other folk himself.

But if he was harsh, he was also able. He had to be, to rise so high with a nature like that. Give him time in a monastery and he'd probably wind up the abbot there. And then *Kyrie eleison* on all the monks under him! He'd enforce every last rule St. Basil ever thought of, and likely a good many Basil never imagined.

Unseemly levity, Brother Elpidios? What? You think I was joking? Read on about Theodore, then. Did I tell you he was sneaky, too? You don't have to believe me. Justinian will tell you. He was there, along with me.

JUSTINIAN

My father and Theodore put their heads together. My father was all for mustering the excubitores and turning them loose on the Anatolian rabble. "If they ran away from the Bulgars, they'll shatter like glass facing real soldiers," he growled.

But the patrician said, "Emperor, I'll do that if you command it, but it's a waste of lives on both sides. I can do it for you cheaper, if you'll let me." He spent the next little while explaining how.

My father was not a man greatly given to laughter, but he laughed then, loud and long. "By the Virgin, Theodore, I should have left you in command against the Bulgars, not those blockheads who called themselves generals. How many men will you need, do you suppose?"

"A troop's worth, to make sure the soldiers don't mob me before I can harangue 'em," Theodore answered. Then he turned to me. "If the prince comes with me, too, it will make the offer look better."

I very much wanted to go; if I could do anything to keep my uncles from stealing my rightful place in the succession, I would. But I looked for my father to hesitate: if Theodore betrayed him and handed me over to Herakleios, Tiberius, and the soldiers they led, that would greatly aid their cause and hurt his.

He, however, nodded and replied at once: "Yes, take him." Not until years later, when the throne was mine, did I realize he dared not let any doubt he might have had show. That could have put doubt in Theodore's mind as well, which was the last thing my father wanted. The best way to keep your subjects from doubting you is to look sure, regardless of whether you are.

Theodore of Koloneia was like my family and unlike most other

men I have known in that he made up his mind quickly and wasted no
time in acting upon whatever he decided. By the time the sun reached
its high point in the sky, he, I, and the troop of excubitores he had asked
for had left the palace and were on the way to the Forum of Constantine,
the plaza commemorating the founder of the imperial city, the Emperor
who, like a thirteenth Apostle, made the Roman Empire Christian.

Even before then, Theodore had sent runners to every quarter of
Constantinople, calling on the soldiers of the Anatolian military districts
to assemble at the Forum to hear him and me. "That could get sticky,
Prince, if your uncles the junior Emperors—the *former* junior Emperors,
I should say—show up there, too," he told me. "But I don't think they
will. I think they'll suspect a trap, and so stay away."

"I think you're likely right," I answered. "They have to suspect
everything and everyone now. If we can keep them afraid instead of bold,
we shall win. If you are afraid, you do not deserve to rule."

Yes, I was parroting my father, but his words had struck deep into
my soul. Theodore's hard features showed little expression, but I thought
he looked on me with approval. And Myakes, who marched along with
the rest of the excubitores, beamed and winked at me. He knew my
nature: no one better.

When we got to the Forum of Constantine, we found it full of rowdy
Anatolian soldiers, many of them so full of wine you could get drunk
from their breath. The excubitores, a disciplined band in the midst of
these wild men, cleared a path for Theodore and me up to the base of
the porphyry column on which stood a great statue of the first Constantine decked in a gilded crown with sun rays spiking out from it as if he
were the false god Apollo himself.

"Soldiers of the Empire, hear me!" Theodore shouted, and then,
"Soldiers of Constantine, hear me!" That was clever, for it reminded the
mob that the present Emperor bore the same name as the one in whose
Forum they had gathered. Faster than I had expected, he got something
close to quiet.

Into it, he said, "Soldiers of Constantine, I won't take up much of
your time. I just want you to remember a few things. Who beat the Arabs?
Was it Herakleios? No. Was it Tiberius? No. It was Constantine—*the*
Emperor. Who got the followers of the false prophet to pay us tribute?
Who got the Sklavenoi and the Avars and the Lombards and the Franks
to pay us tribute? Was it Herakleios? No. Was it Tiberius? No. It was
Constantine—*the* Emperor.

"In fact"—he warmed to his theme—"just what the devil *have* Herakleios and Tiberius done? When you look at it, boys, they haven't done a damn thing. For years now, they've sat around the palaces drinking fancy wine and pinching pretty girls on the bottom. It's nice work if you can get it, aye, but does it set you up to be *the* Emperor? Not on your life.

"Christ crucified, lads," Theodore went on, "Constantine's son has already done more than either one of those worthless brothers, and he's only twelve years old. Here, Prince, you tell them about it. You don't need me."

I did not yet have a man's height. Myakes set his shield on the ground and motioned for me to stand on it. When I had done so, he and a couple of other stalwart excubitores lifted the shield, with me on it, so the soldiers from the Anatolian military districts could see me. And when they did see me so upraised, the silence they gave me was deeper than any Theodore of Koloneia had got. This, of course, was not merely for who I was but for who I might become: being raised on a shield is, or can be, the first step in the coronation of an Emperor.

I glanced down at Myakes, thanking him with my eyes for his quick wits. He winked at me again. In that moment, whatever nervousness I might have felt addressing a plaza full of unruly warriors, all of them angry at my father and therefore at me, vanished. I said, "Soldiers of Romania, who guided the two hundred eighty-nine bishops to the true doctrine of Christ's two energies and two wills? Was it my uncles? No—it was my father and I. Thanks to us, there is once more peace in the church all through the inhabited world."

Most of the soldiers cheered at this, but a few let out hisses and catcalls. By their looks and accents, most of them were Armenians, whose church, being both heretical and in the iron grip of the followers of the false prophet, has to this day, almost thirty years after the time of which I write, failed to ratify the sixth holy and ecumenical synod.

M Y A K E S

You'll remember, Brother Elpidios, that the true name of Philippikos who overthrew Justinian that second time was Bardanes, so he was an Armenian himself. That accounts for the synod he called, the one that condemned the sixth ecumenical synod. Whatever you call him, though, he lasted only a couple of years on the throne himself, and then he went onto the dung heap, and his miserable synod with him.

What? You didn't remember that? I forget—twenty years ago, when Justinian met his end, you were a boy, or at most a youth. What did you care then about Philippikos's real name? How time goes, Brother. How time goes.

JUSTINIAN

I went on, "When that fraud of a Polykhronios said he could use the lying doctrines of the monothelites to raise the dead, who hoped he would? My uncles—my father's brothers. With my own eyes I saw them. And did he raise the dead? No! God let that poor man stay dead, to show us that dogma was false. My father didn't believe. I didn't believe. But my uncles did! After that, soldiers, do they deserve to wear the crown?"

Many men shouted, "No!" But others kept up their vain and foolish chant: "We believe in a Trinity—let us crown all three brothers!"

"Hear me, then, soldiers!" I cried to them. This was to have been Theodore of Koloneia's part, but I had been with him and my father when they devised their scheme, and I was up on the shield now. So I was the one who set it forth: "Let ten of your leaders come forward to me. They will meet with my father and the nobles of the Empire to discuss this matter. The rest of you, go back to Sykai. By God I swear you will learn from your leaders tomorrow what my father has decided."

I waited, looking out at them, watching them chew that over to see what it tasted like. They must have liked the flavor well enough; the only trouble we had was keeping the number of self-proclaimed leaders down to ten, for ten times that many tried to come forward. But ten would do nicely, and the excubitores, under Theodore's direction, chose a mix of officers and private soldiers who did indeed seem to have some gift of leadership.

The rest of the men from the Anatolian military districts dispersed more readily than I had dared hope. We had heard them; we had spoken to them; they were satisfied. And, being satisfied, they streamed out of the Forum of Constantine toward the wharfs on the Golden Horn for the trip back across it to Sykai.

"Tomorrow," I told Theodore, "we must give orders that no ferries are to cross from Sykai to the imperial city."

"Prince, I have already made those arrangements." Theodore paused, studied me, and slowly nodded. I walked straighter. I felt I had passed a test.

We took the self-styled leaders of those who favored restoring imperial rank to Herakleios and Tiberius back toward the great palace. As we marched east along the Mese, the excubitores surrounded these men more and more closely. Taking alarm at last, one of them cried, "Are we ambassadors or prisoners?"

"I promised you would see my father," I answered, "and so you shall." That kept the leaders quiet as we hustled them along toward the palace.

See my father they did. As soon as they were inside the palace, the excubitores laid hold of them and stripped them of their weapons. Then, with Theodore of Koloneia and me leading the way, they frog-marched the wretches into the throne room.

"So," my father said, fixing them with a glare that had chilled my blood often enough, "you are the traitors who want to give my worthless brothers their crowns back, are you?"

The fellow who had asked if they were prisoners—an officer named Theophylaktos—repeated the senseless jingle they had been bawling all along: "We believe in a Trinity—let us crown all three brothers."

"No, let us not," my father said, his voice deadly cold. "What I believe in, now, is rooting out treason wherever I find it." He turned to Theodore. "Illustrious patrician, take them to the Kynegion and dispose of them, then take the bodies across to Sykai and hang them on gibbets so the troops from the Anatolian military districts have something instructive to contemplate."

Theodore bowed. "Emperor, workmen are already building the gibbets." He nodded to the excubitores, and they took the wretches off to the Kynegion—an amphitheater near the sea, where miscreants were frequently dispatched—for execution. Theophylaktos and the rest bawled like castrated bullocks, screeching they had been betrayed—as if they, having betrayed their sovereign, had any cause for complaint.

All went just as my father and the patrician Theodore devised. Indeed, they even added a refinement: they had scribes write the word TRAITOR on ten large placards, and hung one around the neck of each executed man. Thus, when the executioners tied the wrists of the dead leaders to the upthrusting arms of the gibbets, the corpses displayed the reason for which they had been put to death.

By the altogether immaculate Virgin Mother of God, I wish I could have been in Sykai when the soldiers from the Anatolian military districts woke up and found out what had become of the fools who, they thought, were getting what they wanted from the Emperor. Instead, those fools got what they deserved.

The soldiers could not even take their worthless outrage to

Constantinople, for no ferries were crossing the Golden Horn and, should they have tried to march around it, the gates of the city wall were closed against them. Later that day, ferries did go to Sykai, but the only place their captains would take the soldiers was across the Bosporos to Anatolia.

When the soldiers made as if to balk at this, the captains delivered to them my father's warning: "Go home to your farms now, while you still have the chance. Otherwise, you will envy the fate of your leaders."

I am told the men looked long on the ten bodies hanging from the gibbets, then began filing onto the ferries. By the time the sun set, the whole disgruntled lot of them were back in Anatolia, and no one in Constantinople said one word more about crowning Herakleios and Tiberius again.

Somehow, my uncles got back into the city and returned to the palace without my father's knowing of it until they appeared at breakfast the next morning as if nothing had happened. "Go ahead," he told them. "Sit there smug as you like. The crowns will never go on your heads again."

"That's for God to decide, not you," Tiberius said, meaning, I suppose, that my father could not know whether he would die tomorrow, and perhaps also that he and Herakleios might have a hand in my father's demise.

Then Herakleios pointed at me and said, "Better we wear the crowns than this arrogant little bugger."

With ten casually spoken words, my uncle snuffed out the last of my boyhood. I thought we had always got on well, Herakleios and I; we used to mutter to each other as we sat through endless ceremonies where our role was purely ornamental. But my uncle, having seen himself demoted, could not bear the thought that I might gain one day that to which he could no longer aspire: not only rank, but power. I was not his nephew any more, only someone who stood between him and what he wanted above all else.

My father said, "He's done well, by the Virgin, and he's done things for me—the ecumenical synod, to name just one. You, Herakleios, you just want to do things *to* me."

"Give Tiberius and me our rights," Herakleios said. "That's all we ask."

Tiberius added, "Our father crowned all three of us. Who are you to take away what he gave?"

"Yes, our father crowned all three of us," my father answered, "but he set *me* to rule from the day he sailed off to Italy and Sicily. Somehow you always manage to forget that. Who am I, you say? I am the Emperor, *the* Emperor. Give you your rights? I'll give you more than that—I'll give you your deserts!"

Having made up his mind, my father, as was his way, acted at once. He summoned once more the nobles of Constantinople, before whom a few days earlier he had demoted Herakleios and Tiberius from the imperial dignity. Now, though, instead of sitting beside him, they stood in front of the throne like any other men who were to be judged. *I* sat at his left hand, and my little brother to my left.

My father gave my uncles one last chance even then, asking them, "Well, Herakleios; well, Tiberius—what am I now? Am I your brother or your Emperor? If you tell me I am your Emperor, all will be well for you. But if you say I am only your brother—" He let them draw their own conclusions.

Tiberius stood silent, perhaps hoping silence would be taken for acquiescence. But Herakleios turned, as if appealing to the courtiers and bureaucrats who had been brought together to hear his fate. He answered, "You are our brother, and the eldest, and we honor you for that. But we cannot call you our Emperor, for our father, the Emperor Constans, crowned us all together at the same time."

"Tiberius, is this your word also?" my father demanded.

Miserably, Tiberius nodded. He and Herakleios looked to the nobles of the city for support. They found . . . none. My father had saved the city from the Arabs, my father and I had restored peace to the church— and my father had mutilated Leo for daring to speak on my uncles' behalf.

"So be it—you have condemned yourselves," my father said to Herakleios and Tiberius. Sighs ran through the throne room: the moment, though expected, was hard when it came. My father passed sentence: "You shall have your noses slit so that, being physically imperfect, you shall no longer be able to aspire to the throne, and you shall be sent into exile."

Tiberius simply stood and stared, perhaps accepting his lot, perhaps unable to believe he was about to suffer the deserved fate of all failed plotters and rebels. But Herakleios stabbed out a finger at my father and cried, "May what you give me fall on you one day, *brother*!" Then that finger, which at the moment seemed long and thin and sharp as a claw, pointed first to me and then to my little brother. "And may it fall on your heirs as well!" To emphasize what he said, Herakleios spat on the mosaic-work floor.

My father made the holy sign of the cross to turn aside the words of evil omen. So did I. So did my brother, clumsily and a beat late. So did the assembled nobles and the excubitores who crowded the throne room. Neither my brother nor my father lived long after that, but on neither of them did Herakleios's curse fall. On me, by the incontestable judgment of God, it did.

But my uncles, whom the excubitores now led away, never were seen in this God-guarded and imperial city again. Herakleios's curse fell on me, aye, but I have overcome it like every other obstacle in my path. And with him and Tiberius gone, no more obstacles stood between me and eventual imperial rank.

I wondered whether my father would immediately have me crowned as a junior Emperor, now that my uncles were vanished from the scene. In fact, I expected him to crown me: had I not earned a coronation of my own for helping to persuade the soldiers from the Anatolian military districts to stay loyal to him and not go over to Herakleios and Tiberius?

But no ceremony seemed forthcoming. Emboldened by my new status as heir apparent (even uncrowned), I asked him why not. To my relief, he took the question seriously instead of growing angry, and replied, "I think my father made a mistake by crowning all three of his sons. I don't want to imitate him. If I crown you, how can I keep from crowning your brother with you? And if I crown you both, I sow the seeds of strife for a new generation."

"I don't think little Herakleios could ever be a danger to me," I said. I did not think my younger brother was likely to live out the year, but I did not say that to my father.

He set a hand on my shoulder. "You never can tell, son," he said. "When I was a boy, my brothers were so much smaller and younger than I was that I didn't think they could be dangerous, either. But as you both grow older, differences in age become less important than they are when you're children. And so I was wrong, and you might be, too. You never can tell."

When I look back on all the twists of fortune that have gone into the skein of my life, I have to say he was right about that.

And then any notion of crowning me was forgotten, for the Bulgars sent three envoys to Constantinople seeking tribute in exchange for refraining from penetrating deeper into Romania than they already had. Having seen so great a part of his force heedlessly thrown away, my father felt he had little choice but to pay the barbarians what they demanded.

He summoned them to the throne room to impress them with the splendor still remaining in the Roman Empire. My brother and I, as part of that splendor, sat at his left hand. Our three seats were the only ones there; the two additional thrones formerly occupied by my uncles had vanished, I never learned whither.

The Bulgars—their names, as best I can set them down in Greek letters, were Krobat, Batbaian, and Kotrag—were quite the ugliest men I had ever seen. They were short and squat and swarthy, with wide, flat faces, noses almost bridgeless, and narrow eyes set in their heads at a slant. They could raise hardly more beard than a eunuch; a few hairs sprouted on their cheeks and chins, and a few more, enough to make up scraggly mustaches, on their upper lips. They smelled of horses.

Instead of silk and linen, they wore fur and leather, and also, as if to make up for their physical hideousness, great quantities of gold: rings and armlets and necklaces and clasps and even, in the case of Krobat, who was their leader, hoops in his ears. I stared, never having seen a man decked out in that effeminate style.

They all spoke Greek, after a fashion. My father ignored their twit-tering accent and their endless solecisms, treating them with as much dignity as if they had come from the misnamed commander of the faithful in Damascus. The question was never whether to pay them, only how much, for my father reckoned himself unable to drive them back north of the Danube.

He did not let them know that, however. Instead, he made sure that, wherever they went in Constantinople, they were sure to see large numbers of soldiers, as if he were contemplating renewed war should their demands prove exorbitant. The ploy worked. They cut their demands in half, and then in half again.

"Your people has no great need for gold," my father told Krobat, pointing to the numerous ornaments of precious metal adorning the bar-barian. "It is only a symbol of the relationship between us." He then had to spend some time making sure Krobat knew what a symbol was. That done, he went on, "If the symbol is more expensive than the war it replaces, we would sooner fight."

In his bad Greek, Krobat said, "You talk like—what is name?—fish merchant. Like fish merchant, yes." He sneered. He had big yellow teeth, made for sneering.

My father simply stared at him. So did I, adding my indignation to his. My brother may well have done the same thing, but I did not shift my eyes to look at him. I kept staring at Krobat, letting him know without words he could not address an Emperor of the Romans thus.

Silence stretched. At last, Batbaian muttered to his leader in their ugly tongue. Krobat muttered back, angrily. But when Kotrag also spoke to him, he returned to Greek and growled out something that would do for an apology. My father dipped his head to accept it, and the dickering went on as if the insult had never occurred.

MYAKES

Constantine had that knack for looking at you—looking through you—so you knew he thought he had every right to command you, and you believed it, too. Yes, Brother Elpidios, Justinian had it, too. I was about to say so. Patience is a virtue, or so I hear tell. The veterans among the excubitores said Constans had it, so it must have run in the blood. Herakleios, now, Herakleios was forty years dead by then, but he couldn't very well have been without it, not with everything he did.

What's that, Brother? What do I think of Leo, the Emperor we have now? Aside from the icons, I expect you mean? Well, you could compare him to Constantine, I suppose, on account of they both held the Arabs away from the imperial city. But you have to remember, Brother, I knew Leo when, as they say. He may be a strong Emperor now, but he wasn't born to it, and I'd bet that shows.

And who knows what his son, his Constantine, will turn out to be like when his time comes to wear the crown? Is the story they tell true, that when he was a baby he shit himself in the baptismal font? Not the best omen you could have, no indeed it isn't.

You ask me, they don't make 'em the way they used to, and that's a fact. The world isn't the place it was when I was young, and I don't need eyes to see as much. But then, what old man doesn't say the same?

JUSTINIAN

The sum the Bulgars finally agreed to accept was twenty pounds of gold a year: fourteen hundred forty nomismata. They went back to Asparukh with the first year's installment in their saddlebags, and seemed happy enough to get it.

After they were gone from the capital—not before—I said, "That's not what I would have done, Father. I'd fight the barbarians and beat them once for all."

"When the Roman Empire is yours, you'll do as you judge best," he answered. "Now it is mine, and I reckon this course best. We have peace on all our borders, to give us time to recover from our wars, and we take in more than twice as much gold from the followers of the false prophet as we pay out to the Bulgars."

To my surprise, I found myself agreeing with Krobat, at whom I had scowled a few days before: I thought my father *was* running the Empire as if it were a fishmonger's shop, calculating every follis of profit and loss. But, as he had spoken, I dared not continue the argument, and while he lived we paid the Bulgars their tribute.

The sixth holy and ecumenical synod held its final session a few days before the fall equinox. By then the two hundred eighty-nine bishops, who had labored for ten months, were anxious to depart for their homes, especially those of them who had to travel by sea. My father and I presided together over that last session, which was held in the great church.

"By your acts," my father told the assembled bishops, holding up the copy of those acts to which they had affixed their names, some in the uncial script in which books are usually copied, some in the newer cursive, "by your acts, I say, you have restored peace to all us Christians. May that peace be deep and lasting."

He made the sign of the cross, as did many of the bishops who listened to him. During those last few years of his life, peace was very much on his mind, as if, having seen so much of war and strife in the earlier years of his reign, he wanted to avoid them at all costs thereafter. Understandable enough, I suppose, but not my way.

He went on, "By your acts, you have also rightly defined our holy Christian dogma for the rest of time. A thousand years from now, men may not remember your names—though some of you, surely, shall be among the saints—but, whenever they confess Christ's two natural wills and energies, they will remember what you have done here."

I had not thought of the synod's work in those terms, but no doubt he was right, just as today, no doubt, many confess that Christ and God the Father are of the same substance without ever thinking of St. Athanasios, who saved our holy church from the vile and infamous heresy of Areios.

It seemed also to have been a new thought to many of the bishops, but one of which they approved, not least because it magnified their importance in the scheme of things. Bishop Arculf of Rhemoulakion, for instance, paused long enough in eating whatever he was eating on that particular day to clap both hands together. Arculf did not return to the synod I summoned ten years later to decide questions of canon law left behind by the fifth and sixth ecumenical synods. I sometimes wondered if he safely reached his home in distant Gaul. Later, to my surpise, I learned.

George the ecumenical patriarch blessed the assembled bishops and thanked them for giving of their piety and wisdom for the benefit of all Christians throughout the inhabited world. The bishops bowed to him and then filed out of the church of the Holy Wisdom for the last time. The world will not soon see such a gathering of great theologians again.

M Y A K E S

Aye, Brother Elpidios, Justinian was pious. No one, not even his enemies—of whom he had a great whacking host—would have denied that. But I don't think it's from piety alone that he has such fond memories of the ecumenical synod. That was the time, that was the place, when he first started doing things on his own. He found out he could, and he liked the feeling.

Me? Yes, I think the bishops were a good and pious bunch. They started only a couple of tavern brawls I know of, and over the space of most of a year that's pretty fine, don't you think? And only one woman I heard about claimed a bishop got her with child, and not everyone believed her.

You say your standards are higher, Brother? Well, you have to remember, you're a holy monk, and I was just an excubitor. In those days, I started tavern brawls aplenty, and if no pretty girl said I put a loaf in her oven, it wasn't for lack of trying. Yes, I was a sinner. And Constantinople was a good town for a young man—oh, all right, for a sinner—to be alive in, too, that it was.

What's that? You never saw the place? You never saw Constantinople? Well, yes, now that I recall, you have said you were born in the provinces, and of course you've been here since you were young. But you've missed something mighty fine, that you have. There's not another place like the Queen of Cities in the whole wide world, not half there isn't. Damascus? Damascus can't hold a candle to it. Thessalonike? Thessalonike's not a bad town; I was there with Justinian. He'll talk about that later on, I expect. But Thessalonike *is* a town. Constantinople's a city—it's *the* city. They don't call it that for nothing, you know.

How is it different? Well, just for starters, it's got more people in it than you can shake a stick at. You'll never in all your days see so many people all in one place. You'll never in all your days smell so many people all in one place, either. It's a strong odor, but it's not always a nasty one. And in Constantinople, there always seemed to be a hint of spices and perfume to it—it's not just ordure and folks who've gone too long between baths. Ah, maybe that's an old man's memory playing tricks on him, but maybe it's not, too.

But where else could you walk down the street and see good old ordinary Romans and blond Slavs and Arabs in robes and Persians in hats that look like chamber pots and Lombard merchants with greasy hair and folk from who knows where bumping elbows with one another and not even hardly noticing they were doing it? You ever notice how, when a stranger comes into a village or a little town, everybody gives him the once-over, even if he's a Roman like everybody else? It's not like that there. There's too many people for them to keep track of who belongs and who doesn't, so they treat everybody like he belongs. Takes some getting used to, I know, but it's true. And they'll swindle their fellow townsmen just as happily as they will a stranger, too. Oh, aye, indeed they will. They'll steal the tunic off your back and sell it to you before you notice how you got to be naked.

But you can get anything you want there. Anything at all, I think. If you can find it anywhere in the world, you can find it in Constantinople. That means churches, too, mind you, Brother Elpidios. When you think of Constantinople, you think of the church of the Holy Wisdom, of course, and maybe the church of the Holy Apostles, too, where they bury the Emperors and their kin—you'll hear about that in due course. But those are only the big ones. They've got other fancy ones dedicated to the Virgin and John the Baptist and Saints Sergios and Bacchus and . . . I could go on for a while, but you get the idea. And they've got little tiny churches that maybe only a dozen people can crowd into at a time, some of them dedicated to saints nobody three blocks away ever heard of. Something for everybody, like I say.

Even leaving the palaces out of the bargain, you've never seen the like of some of the houses there. They don't build 'em like that out in the country, let me tell you. I grew up in a shack made of mud bricks; my old man had to shore it up after every big rainstorm. Not like that in the city, no sir. The fancy brickwork the rich folks have on their houses—Lord! Baked bricks, one and all, and not just baked bricks, but bricks baked in different colors to make pictures or designs. Makes me shudder to think what work like that must cost, so it does.

No, poor folk don't have anything that fancy, of course, but they do live in stone houses or ones made of baked brick. Some of 'em just have rooms in big buildings, four or five stories high, they put up so they can crowd more people into the same space. You won't see anything like that anywhere else, either.

The main streets are all cobblestoned, so you can use 'em in any weather. That's not so in the alleys, I grant you, but still. How many times have you gone outside in the rain and sunk up to your backside in mud? A good plenty, I don't doubt, same as me—same as anybody. But you don't have to, not in Constantinople. Not all the time, anyhow.

And the things you can buy! Let me tell you, Brother Elpidios, along the Mese there's everything your heart could desire. There are shops that sell frankincense and myrrh from down in Arabia, and others that sell amber from way up north somewhere—God must know where the stuff comes from, but I don't, not exactly. There are coppersmiths and jewelers and potters and leatherworkers and candlemakers and oil sellers and boatbuilders and fishermen and weavers and tailors and cattle drovers and wool dealers and butchers and bakers and glassblowers and scribes and . . . and I don't know what all. Everything!

What's that? You can find people who do those things in every town? You can find one or two, maybe, most places. In Constantinople, there are dozens, sometimes hundreds, of people who have the same trade, so you can pick exactly the one you want, the one who does your kind of work at your kind of price (or who's sly enough to make you think it's your kind of price, anyhow).

And you will find trades at Constantinople you won't see anywhere else. Silk weavers, for instance, and the dyers who make the purple for the Emperor's robes. There's always the stink of rotting sea creatures round their shops, but you can buy the meat from the murexes for cheap, because they don't use most of it. Take 'em to a tavern for the cook to fry up in bread crumbs and olive oil, and they're as tasty a little supper as your heart could desire.

Oh, the taverns! If you had gold in your pocket, you could drink with the lords of the city, so you could, and the places they'd go were near as fancy as their houses, don't you doubt it for a minute. Some of them liked buying excubitores drinks; they hoped we'd tell them things about the Emperor. Gossip in Constantinople's like nowhere else, too. Anybody who let his mouth get ahead of his wits didn't last long, though. Things went down from there, too, down to dives nastier than I've ever seen anyplace else, dives where the wine was vinegar and the beer was mule piss—and piss from a sick mule, at that. Some folks, though, don't go to a tavern to talk. They go there to drink. Vinegar and mule piss will get you where you want to go, if that's all you've got in mind. Like I keep saying, something for everybody.

Girls for every price, too. No, I don't remember how fancy a wench it was who said a bishop put a loaf in her oven. A bishop, though, you'd think he'd want something choice along those lines, wouldn't you? Yes, of course I mean if he was sinner enough to want anything along those lines at all. You could find 'em—if you were looking—in taverns, or strolling along the Mese (after all, they were for sale, too), or in brothels, too, of course. Some of 'em ended up marrying well; some saw the light and went into convents (Eh? God bless them? Of course, God bless them—did I say anything different?); some just got old and ugly. Some weren't that young and weren't that pretty to start with. They couldn't charge as much, unless they did things none of the others felt like doing. Oh, sure enough, a young man with a little gold—or even a little silver— in his belt pouch could have himself quite a time, that he could. . . .

Aye, if I hadn't had my eyes burned out, I'd likely be a sinner still. I make no bones about it. All things work for good in the end, is that what you said there? I won't argue, Brother Elpidios. How could I argue with the likes of you?

J U S T I N I A N

A couple of months after the end of the sixth holy ecumenical synod, my father suffered his first attack of stone. I learned of it when my mother, at most times a quiet woman, let out a shriek at dawn one morning that had everyone in the palace rushing toward the bedchamber she and my father shared.

Because the rooms holding my bed and Herakleios's were close by that of my parents, I was among the first into the imperial bedchamber, and what I saw there made me slam the door in the faces of those who came more slowly, including my own brother. My father lay senseless on the floor; a shattered chamber pot close by had spilled a night's worth of piss over it and over his tunic.

Even as I turned back from the door, he groaned and sat up, one hand going to the small of his back. His face was pale as parchment. "Mother of God, help me," he said in a voice not his own, and then, wonderingly, "She *has* helped me—the pain is gone." He got to his feet and, though he swayed a little, did not seem on the point of falling.

"What happened?" my mother demanded. Her nightgown was wrinkled from sleep, her fair hair wild around her head. I could not remember the last time I had seen her anything but perfectly robed and coiffed.

"I woke up, perhaps half an hour ago," my father answered, plainly explaining as much to himself as to her and me. "At first I thought it was the gout again, but the pain lay here"—he touched his back again— "not in my foot. It moved—slowly." He ran a hand down his back, toward the bottom of the cleft of his buttocks. Even the memory of the pain made sweat bead on his face, though the bedchamber was cool. "It felt—it felt as if there were a torch soaked in liquid fire burning inside me, all the way down. I got up to make water, hoping to squeeze the pain down further, and—I woke up on the floor." Suddenly noticing his tunic was soaked and dripping, he let out a hoarse cry of disgust.

At that moment, someone rapped on the door, a loud, peremptory knock that cut through the Babel out in the hallway. "Let me in, curse it!" a man—presumably the fellow who had knocked—called in a loud, deep voice. "How the devil am I to attend my patient with him on one side of the door and me on the other?"

I looked a question to my father. He nodded, saying, "Let Peter come in—but no one else, mind you. A physician will do me no harm, though he probably won't do me much good, either."

I opened the door a palm's breadth, repeating my father's command as I did. In spite of it, the forward rush almost overcame me: it was as if a besieging army had broken in the gate of a city. But a big, burly man with a thick black beard threw a couple of judicious elbows that doubled over the men just behind him. Peter got in, then helped me shut and bar the door once more before anyone else could follow.

That done, he turned to my father and, as ceremony required even under those circumstances, began to prostrate himself before him. When my father waved for him not to bother, he said, "Tell me your symptoms." My father did, in words almost identical to those he had used with my mother and me. Peter listened attentively, then said, "You passed a kidney stone, Emperor. What you felt was it moving from your kidney down to your bladder. It may stay there, or you may pass it out of your body sometime in the next few days when you make water."

"Will I get more of them?" my father asked. "One, let me tell you, was enough for a lifetime."

"Everyone who suffers from stone says the same thing. Thank God, if you care to, that yours passed quickly instead of lingering for hours or even days," Peter said. My father shuddered. The physician went on, "Will you get more?" He spread his hands. "God alone knows. I pray you don't." He hesitated, then said, "Suffering from stone, Emperor, along with your gout, is not the best of signs."

My father shrugged. Could the soldiers from the Anatolian military districts who said he ran away from the Bulgars have seen him them, they would have quivered in shame. "Akhilleus chose glory over length of days, or so the pagans say," he told Peter. "My family has a way of dying young—my father to a murderer, his father to consumption. My life may not be long, but already it has been full. Having saved the Empire from the followers of the false prophet and our holy Christian church, I leave the rest in God's hands."

Peter crossed himself, then bowed very low. So did I; I had never seen my father more worthy of respect. Holding faith in the face of pain is the hardest thing a man can do, and he did not merely hold it: it shone forth from him, as light does from a lamp.

The clamor in the hall got louder. "What shall I tell them?" Peter asked.

"Tell them I had an attack of stone. Tell them it has passed, and I am well again." My father smiled a thin smile. "All that has the advantage of being true. Tell them also that in most cases the stone does not recur."

From what Peter had said, that was not true. A physician, however, being able to do so little against illness, carries hope as a standard medicament. And Peter, with his big voice and bluff, blustering manner, was the perfect man to put forward what my father wanted everyone to believe. By the time he was done haranguing the servants and guardsmen out in the hall, they all sent up cheers and cries of thanksgiving to God that my father's trial had been so light and so fortunately ended.

Also in the hall, close to the door, stood my brother. Despite Peter's glib, fluent speech, Herakleios's face, always pale and thin, remained tight with worry. He knew illness too well to believe it could be so casually dismissed.

He looked a question at me. I nodded, as reassuringly as I could. After a moment, he nodded, too. I have always wondered whether he believed me.

My father's next attack of stone came halfway through the spring.

M Y A K E S

Those last four years of his life, Constantine wasn't the same man he'd been before. Better? Worse? I don't know, but different. Maybe some of it had to do with losing to the Bulgars. Up till then, he must have thought he was invincible. And why not? He'd beaten every foe he faced, and the Arabs seemed more dangerous than anyone imagined the Bulgars could be. So what happened with the barbarians likely had something to do with clipping his feathers.

But it wasn't only that Constantine didn't go to war with his neighbors any more. He softened, you might say: the bursts of temper he'd loose against anyone who got in his way—the same sort Justinian had and, from what I heard, the same sort Constans had had, too—they stopped coming.

Again, part of the reason for that may be that he didn't have to worry about his brothers any more. But more of it, I do believe, sprang from his being sick so much of the time. He suffered a lot from stone. From all I've heard, there's no worse pain a man can know. A woman in childbed, maybe, but not a man.

I must say I don't see the justice of it. Never have. He knew what he'd done. Justinian puts the words in his mouth: he'd saved the Roman Empire and reunited the church. And what did he get? Hell on earth and an early grave. No, I don't see any justice there.

What's that, Brother Elpidios? Who am I, to question God's judgment? Nobody at all—just an old blind man. And I don't question, not really. But I don't understand, either.

JUSTINIAN

Between my father's first attack of stone and his second, I grew taller by the breadth of a couple of fingers, nor did my growth slow after that: I was entering my thirteenth year, and making the passage from boy to man. My shoulders thickened (though I have always been slim), my muscles hardened, I began to have more than down on my cheeks and around my private parts, and my voice, absurdly, was a boyish treble one moment and the next the deep note I have struck every since.

In the course of those few months, the world became a different place. My brother Herakleios was suddenly not just smaller than I but on the the far side of what seemed an unbridgeable chasm. My father and I, by contrast, constantly butted heads, as if we were an old ram and a young charging at each other in springtime. If he said it, I was certain it was wrong, for it came from his lips. And what I was certain of, I said—in no uncertain terms. He did not take kindly to that, something I understand better now than I did at the time.

And, like a young ram, I began to take notice of the ewes. I had known for some time what passes between man and woman, but when I was a boy it struck me as so absurd and unlikely that I could not take the notion seriously, though both my father and Myakes assured me it was true. Why on earth would any man want to do *that*, and why would any woman let him if he did?

Then one day, in a hallway in the palace, I walked past a serving girl who was carrying some freshly washed bed linen out to dry in the sun. Being still wet, the bedclothes had also wet her tunic, which clung to and revealed the shape of her breasts and nipples. I gaped at them, and my body stirred in a way I had not known before.

I stopped and stared after her. I had, of course, seen how women walk before that day, but I had never *seen* it till then. Perhaps noticing that my footsteps no longer sounded in the passage, the serving girl looked back over her shoulder. When she saw how I was looking at her, she smiled saucily, then turned a corner and disappeared.

That night (or was it the night after?—so many years have gone by, I confess I am not certain) I had a dream unlike any I had ever dreamt. Not surprisingly, the serving girl was in it. Somehow she was dry and wet, in her tunic and bare, all at the same time. I moved toward her . . . and then I was awake, alone, in my bed in the darkness.

My nightshirt and the bedding were wet. I thought for a moment I had pissed myself in the night like a baby, but quickly realized it was not urine that had spurted from me. My body still glowed with the remembered sweetness. Wishing I could remember the dream of the serving girl in more detail, I rolled over and went back to sleep.

M Y A K E S

Oh, don't cough and splutter so, Brother Elpidios. Yes, of course I know it's Satan who sends such dreams, seeking to lead men away from virtue and toward sin and lasciviousness. But they are sweet while they last, as Justinian says, aren't they?—and this was his first one.

You say you don't think they are? Well, you can say what you like, Brother. God gave us free will, after all, didn't He? Aye, you can say what you like, but that doesn't mean you can make me believe it.

Is there going to be more of such filth? How should I know? When Justinian gave it to me, I never saw anything but the outside, and I'm not likely to set eyes on anything more than that now, am I? Do you want to stop reading? Your purity and chastity wouldn't be challenged then.

Ah, you think you can overcome any challenge you find? I'm glad to hear it, that I am. Read some more, then.

Am I laughing at you? Brother Elpidios, like I said, I'm an old blind man. Would I do such a thing? I'll keep all my snorts to myself from now on, I promise.

JUSTINIAN

I had looked at the serving girl, and she had smiled at me. I wondered how to proceed from that point to the operation that, although it still struck me as preposterous, might in fact perhaps have had something to recommend it.

Before this time, as I have written, the only times I had anything to do with the serving women in the palace was when I wanted them to fetch me something or to take something away. Except for those times, I had, like any foolish boy, done my best to pretend they did not exist.

Now, awkwardly, I began to change my ways. Having gained one smile with a smile, I started smiling more, especially at those among the serving women whose smiles I most wanted in return. And, indeed, I did win some of those smiles. Looking back, I marvel that I should have been so anxious. Not only was I young and reasonably well favored, I was also the Emperor's son and likely heir. The combination should have made me irresistible. In fact, it did, but I took a while to realize that.

About a week later, I had another of those disturbing, delightful, and messy dreams. I do not remember what happened in that one so vividly as I do the first, but when I awoke from it I understood what had happened more quickly and with less confusion than before. I vowed to myself that the next time I found such pleasure, it would not be in a dream.

One of the serving girls at whom I had formed the new habit of smiling was the yellow-haired Sklavinian who had been baptized as Irene. She was, I think, closest to my age of all the servants the khagan of the Avars had given to my father three years before. She, to my disappointment, did not smile back, but would nod and say "Good day" in her halting Greek.

Then one day a couple of days after that second dream, I happened to be coming back from the kitchen, where I had just absconded with a bun stuffed with raisins and honey and chopped nuts, when she came out of a storeroom and almost ran into me.

"I sorry," she said nervously. Even the higher-ranking servants could beat her if she did something wrong; Stephen the Persian, no doubt among others, had taught her as much. If she displeased me, she must have thought I would have her tied in a sack and chucked into the Bosporos, as I suppose I could have.

But I said, "It's all right. No harm done." And, indeed, none had been. To prove I meant it, I smiled at her. As usual, she did not smile back. Then I had a better idea. I tore the sweet bun in half, giving her the larger piece.

She did smile at that; her whole face lit up. Our fingers brushed when I handed her the bun; mine, afterwards, felt as if they were on fire. "I thank you very," she said, and ate the bun in a couple of bites. "This good," she added with her mouth full, and then went on to chatter about food for a while, mostly in Greek but every now and then slipping back into her barbarous dialect. I gathered she did not much care for the pungent sauces and spices with which we Romans are in the habit of making our fish and vegetables and meat piquant.

She could have been talking about the antipodes or stirrups or tadpoles. It would not have mattered to me. I was not listening to her, not with the tenth part of my mind. I was watching, entranced, the way her eyes shone; the way her pink lips moved, showing me every now and then her white teeth and the tip of her tongue; the curve of her jaw, the curve of her neck, and other curves covered but not hidden by the linen tunic she wore.

Irene did not take long to notice how I was staring. She smiled again then, a different smile, one that made me think our ages had a large gap between them after all. It was, I realize now, a woman's smile, not a girl's. At the time, it alarmed me as much—almost as much—as it aroused me.

"You give me, Prince," she said. "I give you, too. Come." She stepped back into the storeroom from which she had just emerged, and beckoned for me to follow. I do not know what I thought she had in there: some little trinket hidden away, perhaps.

I went in there with her. It certainly was the ideal place in which to hide a trinket: shelves on all four walls reached from the floor almost to the ceiling and were crowded with pots and dishes on one side of the room, lamps and braziers on the other. Some were of brass, others of clay; the likes of Irene would not have been allowed to have anything to do with vessels of silver or gold.

She walked around me and looked out into the hallway. I did not understand why, as no one had been out there, nor, as best my ears could tell, was anyone there now. Suddenly, she shut the door. The storeroom plunged into gloom, for only a small window above the shelves on the far wall let in any light.

Alarm rose in me again. Had someone—my exiled uncles, perhaps—bribed her to try to stick a knife in me? I had a knife of my own on my belt. My hand went to it. I was lucky: she did not see me, for she was pulling her tunic off over her head.

"I give you," she said again, tugging down her thin linen drawers and letting them fall to the floor. "Prince, I give you. You like?" She stood where she was for a moment, so I could see her. There was plenty of light for that.

She was very fair, her skin where the light did not touch it white as milk, the nipples on her small, firm breasts a pale pink, the hair in her armpits and between her legs as light as that on her head, whereas mine in those places was several shades darker. I remember all this as vividly as if it were yesterday, yet how much of it I truly noticed in those first few stunned heartbeats I cannot say. She was a woman and she was naked in front of me, and that was—enough? Dear God, how much more than the imagination truth is!

Seeing me gaping, she smiled that ancient, secret smile once more. "You no do before?" she asked. Numbly, I shook my head. It was a foolish question; had I had practice in such things, she would already have been down on the ground with her legs spread wide. But she said, "Never mind. No worry. I show you all things," and stepped forward into my arms.

Between the two of us, we managed to get my robe and drawers off me in not much more than twice the time I would have needed were I undressing for bed alone. I almost brought my hands up to cover my privates; though Irene seemed to feel no shame at letting me see her, I was shy when she looked me up and down.

She spread my robe and her tunic on the floor, then got down on them. I got down beside her, my heart pounding as if it would burst from my chest. Even with the clothes as makeshift mattress, the floor was hard. I did not care.

As she had promised, she showed me all things: where my hands and mouth should go on her, and what they should do when they got there. In this, unlike the instruction I still endured from my pedagogue, I proved a quick study. Some of her sighs and little moans, no doubt, were to build my pride, but some of them, I think—I hope—were real.

Nor were her hands and lips idle, though she did not grasp my manhood as I touched her secret place, fearing, no doubt, I would spurt too soon if she did. But then, as it became obvious our joining would not be much delayed, I wilted like a candle in a hot room. A boy's nerves: I did not know how to be a man, in this most virile way of all.

"I fix," Irene murmured in a tiny voice, mindful of any passersby in the hall. She had me lie on my back, then crouched beside me and bent her head to the flagging part. In a moment, it flagged no more, but stood tall and stiff as the column in the Forum of Constantine, head poking proudly from the foreskin. Of such sensation I had never dreamt.

But yet another lesson awaited me. Seeing me proud once more, Irene straddled me, took me in hand, and guided me into her. She sank down upon me with a soft sigh, and I was engulfed to the hilt.

She raised herself, then lowered again. From my dreams, I had memories only of the explosion. Now I discovered how delicious reaching it was. When Irene found I would not spend myself on the instant, she moved more vigorously. I began to move, too; no doubt I was clumsy, but who is not, the first time?

Presently her breath came in gasps, as mine had been doing for some little while. She took my hands in hers and brought them up to her breasts. I squeezed, and was afraid I had hurt her, for she whimpered deep in her throat. But she squeezed me at the same instant, down there where we were joined, several times, one right after another. And I, I spurted my seed deep into her.

A moment later, as Irene scrambled off me, something hot and wet splashed down onto my leg. "Good," she said. "It fall out. Less chance baby." Now that our passage was done, she became all brisk practicality, getting into her drawers, tugging her tunic out from under me, and dressing with smooth haste. I did my best to imitate her.

When we were both clothed, she opened the storeroom door, saw no one in the hallway, and tugged at my sleeve so I would go out first. That made sense: she might have had—indeed, had had—some legitimate business in there, which was not true of me. The precautions, though sensible, were needless; the hall was so quiet, it might have been deserted since the palace was built.

She came out, closing the door behind her, and I—greatly daring, I thought—set a hand on her shoulder. "Can we do—this—again?" I asked.

She looked astonished. "You a prince, I a servant, a slave," she said, pointing out the obvious, as if she were telling me, *This is the sun; that is the moon.* "How I say no?" Then she looked worried, no doubt fearing I would be offended to think she gave herself to me only because of the difference in our ranks. "I do anyhow," she added. "Sweet, good, make me feel good."

Looking back, I still think some of that was true. At the time, I drank it down as if it were unwatered wine from Thasos. I felt nine cubits tall and five cubits wide, ready for anything, especially anything female. "Another time, then," I said grandly, and left her to get back to her work.

M Y A K E S

....

You did that very well, Brother Elpidios: only two or three coughing fits the whole time. What? Is that what my first time was like? Oh, not that different. I was a year or two older, and Maria was a maiden, too, so neither one of us was sure what we were doing, but we managed, so we did. I was on top, not the other way round.

How about you, Brother? . . . What? You *never*? Vowed chastity before you could even think about breaking your oath, you say? That's—very holy, Brother Elpidios. No wonder you're so curious about what the real thing is like.

How does it compare to *what*, Brother Elpidios? I tell you frankly, I don't know. Sorry I can't tell you, but I've never found out, nor been curious, if you really want to know. Eh? What's that? No, of course the abbot doesn't have to know you asked the question. Nothing wrong with curiosity, I say. If you weren't curious, you wouldn't be reading Justinian's book, isn't that right, Brother?

Yes, you can read some more now, if you've a mind to. When you read, I hear his voice inside my head. Isn't that strange? I remember it changing, just as he says.

J U S T I N I A N

....

Not only did I seek out Irene whenever I found the chance, I also got in the habit of going around with a sweet bun or two from the kitchens. Having caught one fish with that bait, I went angling for others—and my luck, while not perfect, was good enough to make me a happy, or at least a sated, young man. Though the first lesson teaches most of all, I learned a good deal afterwards, too.

That was a happy time for me, that little stretch of years beginning my manhood: the happiest time I have ever known, save these past few years when I have found revenge a pleasure surpassing the love of woman, as the Psalmist said with somewhat different meaning to the words.

My father had the peace he desired, the peace he had bought and paid for. He took great delight in it, in spite of, or more likely because of, his growing bodily infirmity. Gout and stone continued to wrack him, though he was, or should have been, still in the prime of life, and he pissed blood after some of his attacks.

His physician, Peter, muttered darkly at that symptom, but Peter, I was discovering, was given to dark mutters at any excuse or none. A man's body can go wrong in so many ways, and God has given us knowledge to fix so few of them, that anyone choosing the physician's trade, if not a bit mad merely for entertaining the desire, will be driven so by the frustrations of his craft.

And yet . . . I touch my nose and I remember that not all the doctor's art is useless, or not entirely so.

In sickness and in health, as I said, my father maintained peace, both with the Empire's neighbors and within the church. This latter required some effort, for, as we learned a couple of years after the fact, when the bishops of Rome translated the acts of the sixth holy ecumenical synod into Latin for the benefit of the westerners too ignorant to have learned Greek, in the anathemas they mentioned Pope Honorius but deleted his title, so as not to have to acknowledge his heresy to that part of the world administered by the see of Rome.

On hearing that, I grew furious. "You ought to order the exarch of Ravenna to send troops down to Rome and force the pope to tell the whole truth," I said to my father.

But he shook his head. "For the sake of preserving the work of the synod, I shall practice economy here," he said.

Economy is the term theologians use for overlooking differences without doctrinal import. Without it, I suppose, there would be endless friction in the church, as if sand were poured into the gearing of a waterwheel. But too great an exercise of it countenances heresy.

I said as much to my father; I was at the age where I challenged him more freely than I had. He shook his head again. "The anathema against Honorius remains. He is who he is, and burns in hell for what he did, regardless of whether they give him his proper title."

I could not sway him, though I said, "Surely the pope who gave the order for this lie after sending bishops to the ecumenical synod will also burn in hell."

"Agathon, the pope who sent bishops to the synod, is dead, and facing the decrees of a judge greater than I," my father answered.

"His successor, then," I persisted. I had not heard that Agathon was no longer among men, but then Rome, being at the very edge of the Empire, seldom drew my notice.

And my father said, "His immediate successor, Leo, has also suffered the common fate of mankind. The new bishop of Rome, a certain Benedict, has in his brief time been a good enough man on the whole—one more reason to stay quiet about the way the anathemas were translated."

And, indeed, Benedict and my father exchanged a couple of cordial letters, my father writing in Greek, which the papal secretaries could render into Latin for the bishop of Rome (I hoped more accurately than they had the anathemas), and the pope in Latin, which, despite its being little used in these parts save in the army and, to a lesser degree, among lawyers, we managed to puzzle out.

One day my father summoned me and my brother Herakleios to the metropolitan's church near the palace, a crumbling wreck of a building seldom used for anything. I went unwillingly, for the summons meant I could not keep an assignation I had made with some girl or another: at fifteen, which I was then, you feel your life will be blighted forever if you do not dip your wick on the instant. But, had I disobeyed my father, I knew perfectly well what sort of unpleasant things would have happened to me, and so, though unwilling, I went.

I was surprised to find not only my father but also George, the ecumenical patriarch, awaiting Herakleios and me. I was even more surprised to find Theoktistes the barber waiting with them.

"What's this, Father?" I asked. "You're not making us into monks, are you?" Herakleios laughed at that—one of the few times I remember making him laugh—but I wondered if I was joking. Had my father decided for some secret reason of his own to be rid of us, what easier way than shaving our heads and clapping us into a monastery? Monastic houses are easy to enter, but hard to leave.

But my father shook his head. "No, hardly," he said, and I relaxed. He went on, "The bishop of Rome, this Benedict, has asked if he might become your spiritual father, and I have agreed." He made the sign of the holy cross. "A man can never have too many prayers in this world, and those from a good and pious man will surely be effective. As a token that I do agree to this spiritual adoption, Justinian, I will send him a lock of your hair, and one of yours, too, Herakleios."

That explained why Theoktistes was there, then. George the patriarch, who was present in lieu of the pope, prayed while Theoktistes snipped a lock from where my hair grew long behind my ears and then did the same with my brother, whose hair was several shades darker than mine. The barber wrapped my hair in a square of red silk, Herakleios's in a square of green, and handed them both to my father.

"Well done," my father said, as if Theoktistes did not make his living trimming hair. "I shall have the artisans fashion a container suit-ably fine for such a rich gift, and send it on to the pope in Rome. May his prayers sustain both of you as the blessing of the bishops of Rome have helped me since I decided to convene the ecumenical synod and restore and renew the orthodox faith."

"May it be so," Herakleios and I said together, both of us crossing ourselves. Alas! God, Whose judgment in all things is beyond the ken of mere men, chose for His ineffable reasons not to grant my father's wish.

My brother Herakleios died three months to the day after Theoktistes cut the locks from our hair. When he fell ill, no one, not ever Peter the physician, was much concerned; over the years, he had shown he fell ill at any excuse or none, and always managed to recover.

But not this time. I hardly remember the earliest course of his illness; at most, I would have thought something like, *Mother of God, has the little wart caught* another *cold?* He milked his diseases for all they were worth, and I often wondered whether he was as sick as he made himself out to be, or if he was faking to get sympathy he did not deserve.

After a couple of days, neither I nor anyone else thought he was faking. His fever rose till his face looked and felt like red-hot iron. He coughed and coughed and coughed and would not—could not—stop. Weak lungs had been the death of our great-grandfather, and they were the death of Herakleios, too. Peter did everything he could, with poultices and plasters and fomentations smelling tinglingly of mint, but to no avail. After raving in delirium, Herakleios slipped into a sleep from which he never wakened. He had just reached his tenth year.

Anyone's death brings mourning and lamentation from those who knew and loved him. A child's death comes doubly hard, for in it the natural order of things is reversed and the old must lay the young in his grave. And when the child who died was son to the Emperor of the Romans, that cast all of Constantinople into gloom.

Because Herakleios, like me, had never been crowned junior Em-peror, my father chose not to bury him in the church of the Holy Apos-tles, which has served as the final resting place of Emperors and their consorts since the days of Constantine the Great. Instead, he was laid to rest in one of the *hypagogai*, the underground vaults, used for the inter-ment of the nobles of the imperial city.

My father, my mother, and I, all wearing black robes, all beating our breasts and wailing, followed the servants who bore my brother's pit-ifully small corpse, shrouded in white linen, to its tomb. Beneath the rituals of grief, my feelings were curiously mixed. He was my brother, true, and I had grown used—resigned might be a better word—to having him around. But then again, in the imperial family, having brothers was dangerous. I needed to look no further than the case of my father and my uncles to prove that to me. Suppose I became Emperor of the Romans. Would Herakleios have tried to steal the throne from me, as his uncle Herakleios tried to steal it from my father? Maybe I was better off without him.

"Surely God will take his soul into heaven!" my mother wailed. "Poor chick, he was too young to have stained himself with sin."

I made the sign of the cross. Now that Herakleios was gone from the earth, I did wholeheartedly wish him to join God rather than having demons drag him down to eternal torment. But I also crossed myself for the sake of my own soul. Every fornication with a maidservant, back to that first one with Irene, smote me like a slap in the face. How would I defend myself before the Judge of All when my time came to stand in His presence?

Fear of death fires every man's faith. Could we live our lives thinking each moment likely to be our last, how much better and more pious the world would be!

We went down into the *hypagoge* and laid Herakleios's body in the niche that had been readied for it. Lamps made the underground chamber bright; incense spiced the still, quiet air. George the ecumenical patriarch prayed for my brother's soul, though what he might have said that would have moved God if my mother's plea failed was beyond me.

Then the mourners who had accompanied us departed one by one, taking their lamps with them, until at last only we and the patriarch and a single lamp burning before Herakleios's last resting place were left. We went upstairs. He stayed behind, all alone. Soon, so soon, the lamp would gutter out, as had his poor life.

It had begun to rain while we were in the *hypagoge*. "The very heavens mourn your loss," George said.

"If the heavens mourn, why did they allow it?" my mother said harshly. George did not answer. That question has no answer, nor ever had, nor ever shall have, save only the will of God, which may not be questioned.

Sorrows hunt in packs, or so it seems. Just when you are over the first—or sometimes before you are over the first—along comes another to tear at you, till you wonder how you can bear griefs piled one upon another like Pelion upon Ossa. The only way to make them more terrible would be to have them known in advance, as they are to God, and even that might let you prepare for them, so far as it is granted to mankind to prepare for anything.

Autumn passed into winter, winter into spring, spring into summer. I wish I could say the sense of sin that filled me at my brother's funeral persisted and enabled me to maintain bodily continence, but I know too well it is not so. Within weeks—no, the truth here: within days—I found a new washerwoman (a girl, actually; she was younger than I) who stirred me, and nothing would do but that I storm the fortress of her virginity, which, I discovered in due course, someone had conquered before me. My life, as life has a way of doing, went back to its usual rut, in all senses of the word.

The same was true for my parents, though for them, and especially for my mother, sorrow lingered longer. My father seemed in better health than he had in some time, being less afflicted by both his gout and his kidney stones than had been so of late. Perhaps to celebrate his reborn feeling of well-being, one hot, muggy evening not long after the summer solstice he doused his plate of roast kid with half a pitcher's worth of fermented fish sauce.

I remember my mother wagging a finger at him. "I wish you wouldn't do that in this weather," she said in mild reproof. "Fish doesn't stay good."

"Oh, rubbish, Anastasia," he said, and, to show he would not be thwarted, poured on the rest of what was in the pitcher, till his meat was fairly swimming in sauce, far more than he would have normally used. He ate it with every sign of enjoyment. Being the man he was, he would have done that, I am certain, even had he despised it, but he always was fond of kid in fish sauce.

Dessert was as splendid a honey cake as the cooks ever made, with fine, fine flour mixed with boiled must to give the sweetness a winy tinge, and covered over with candied figs and apricots. Had it been given to me alone, I would have gone through it like an army sacking a town without a wall; as things were, I begrudged my parents the slices a servant set on their plates.

My father did not finish his, at least not right away. He left the table suddenly, with a startled look on his face. "I'll be back," he told my mother and me. "Keep eating." Had he not spoken up, we should have had to stop, too, the custom being that everyone is done when the Emperor rises.

He returned some little while later, by which time I had done formidable damage to that part of the cake which had not been served out at once. In the lamplight, his face was shiny with sweat and a little pale as he sat down once more. "Are you all right?" my mother asked, for he had been fine when he left.

His chuckle sounded both forced and self-conscious, which last was most unlike him. "Perhaps I should have listened to you about the fish sauce, dear," he said—again, the sort of admission he seldom made. "That was—unpleasant."

He picked up his slice of honey cake and began to eat, but had taken only a couple of more bites when he had to rush away again. "There, do you see?" my mother said severely when he came back once more. "You've gone and given yourself a flux of the bowels."

"So I have," he said through clenched teeth. He made no move to finish the cake now, but gulped wine, no doubt hoping it would restore him. A little color came back to his face, a hectic splotch of red over each cheekbone. He breathed slowly and carefully, as if each inhalation hurt.

"Maybe you should go to bed, Father," I said, for he had not looked much worse during his most savage attacks of stone.

"Yes, maybe I should," he answered, and I knew then he was seriously ill. He rose and started for the door. Halfway there, his departure turned into an undignified dash. With that gait, he was running for the latrine, not the bedchamber.

"I'm going to send for the physician," I declared, as if I expected my mother to argue with me. Had she argued, I would have overridden her. But she said not a word. She nodded to me, her eyes wide and worried. I pointed to a servant and told him to fetch Peter at once.

Instead of leading Peter to my father, the idiot brought him back to the dining room. The physician looked first at my mother, then at me. "Dyspepsia?" he asked. He could be more cutting with fewer words than any other man I have known, the others approaching him also mostly being physicians. Seeing so many sick and dying people they have but small chance of helping does something to their spirits, just as experience in war inures a man to gore.

"We are well, thank God," I said, resolving to have the servant whipped for his stupidity, which I did the next day despite the chaos engulfing the palace. "You need to attend my father." I explained the symptoms, and how they had suddenly come upon him.

Peter looked grave. "You did well to call me. Anything with bad fish in it is not to be taken lightly." He bowed to me, then to my mother, and hurried off toward the imperial bedchamber.

Now I drank unwatered wine, a large goblet, though in hopes of restoring my spirit rather than my body. My mother spent the time until the physician returned praying quietly to God and to the altogether immaculate Virgin. I prayed, too, wishing all the while I could do something more. For as long as I can remember, I have been one who prefers acting to waiting for the actions of others. Here, unable to act, I felt it acutely.

When Peter returned, I did not like the flat, blank expression he wore like a mask. "Well?" I demanded, my voice cracking; I was, after all, but newly turned sixteen.

"He is not well, Prince, not well at all," the physician answered. "He suffers from a violent derangement of the entrails, with the bloody flux typically accompanying such derangements."

"I told him not to drench his kid in fish sauce," my mother said.

Peter bowed. "Would that he had listened to you."

"What can you do for him?" I asked, always the critical question when dealing with a physician. Identifying an illness is oftentimes easier than treating it.

"I have given him a large dose of poppy juice," Peter answered. "Not only will this relieve some of the discomfort from which he suffers, but its constipating action should to some degree oppose his diarrhea."

"To some degree?" I said, surprised. Like anyone who could afford it, I used poppy juice to fight disturbances of the bowels. It always plugged me tighter than the bung driven into a barrel for days at a time.

But the physician replied, "Yes, to some degree, Prince. As I said, this is a violent derangement, and I would hesitate to offer a prognosis before seeing how nearly the poppy brings the flux under control."

With a small shock, I realized he was telling me my father's life was endangered. My mother grasped that a moment after I did, and let out a keening cry of despair, as if my father had already passed from the world of men. My father had been strong for her when Herakleios died. Who now would be strong if my father died? No one but I could do that. Becoming a man, I discovered, had aspects less enjoyable than hiking up a maidservant's tunic and yanking down her drawers.

"It will be all right," I told my mother, though I knew nothing of the sort. She nodded, trying to reassure me as I was trying to reassure her. I got up from my seat. "I'll go see him now."

"And I," my mother said, her voice small but determined.

Peter hurried ahead of us. I started to order him back, then held my tongue. My father might tolerate a physician catching him squatting over the pot, but would not want me or my mother to see him in the throes of such fleshly weakness.

After going into the bedchamber, Peter emerged and nodded. "The drug has begun to take effect, at least on his spirit," he said. "He does want to see both of you, though." As if he were a common servant himself, he held the door open for my mother and me.

Even before I went inside, the sickroom stench hit me. I knew it all too well from my brother's room: a combination of the chamber pot, sour sweat, and medicaments of one sort or another. Here, though, the odor was sharper, harsher than I had smelled it before; it had a metallic stink I could not place till I remembered the doctor had spoken of a bloody flux.

My father lay on the bed as if he had been poured there, as if not even an earthquake that threw the palace down around him could make him get up and move. His eyes traveled slowly from me to my mother and back again. The lamps were not bright, but his pupils were so small, he might have stood in noontime sun: an effect of the poppy juice, I learned later.

"Bless you," he said to both of us. His voice was thick and slow and slurred, as if he were drunk. "Pray for me. I have—things—left to do." He seemed to want to say something more, but his eyelids slid down over his eyes. A moment later, he began to snore.

"How large a draught of the poppy did you give him?" my mother asked.

Peter had spirit, answering, "As large as I judged he could stand. If his dysentery is not abated . . ." He spread his hands. "If God grants my prayer, he will sleep the day around and be better when he wakes."

"And if not?" I said roughly.

Before the physician could reply, my father grunted softly in his drugged sleep. The latrine stink grew gaggingly thick; so did the iron odor of blood. "He's fouled himself!" my mother cried. She rushed to tend him with her own hands.

As she gently stripped my father of his robe and wiped the blood-streaked dung from his buttocks and legs with cloths she wet from a pitcher, I looked to Peter and saw him make the sign of the cross. He caught my eye and murmured, "Pray indeed, Prince. It's out of my hands now." He pitched his voice low so my mother would not hear, but how could she help but understand that for herself?

For the next three days, she cared for my father herself, driving away the servants who tried to help. Me she tolerated, and Peter the physician, though him just barely—and less and less as it became clear his nostrums would not make my father well. She must have slept some during that time, but if she did, I did not see it.

My father's life flowed out of him in a foul-smelling tide. If the poppy juice could not stem the dysentery, it did keep him from feeling any great pain. When he was awake, which happened at irregular intervals by both day and night, he knew who my mother and I were.

I do not think he knew he was dying. Because of the drug, he had no clear notion of time. Once he exclaimed in surprise that suddenly it was night, when a moment before the sun had been shining into the bedchamber. The hours between simply did not exist for him.

Not long before the end, he looked at me and said, "High time we found a girl for you, Justinian. By your age, I'd already married your mother."

"Yes, Father," I said. He surely knew I was no virgin: he wanted me to have a wife. Though I seemed obedient, the idea of being limited to one woman did not appeal to me. Still, he was right: for the sake of the dynasty, I needed an heir, and a legitimate one. And even had he been wrong, who would contradict a man on what was plainly his deathbed?

Someone—I do not know who—perhaps my mother, perhaps Peter, perhaps Stephen the Persian or some other palace functionary—summoned George the ecumenical patriarch to administer the sacrament of unction to my father. George looked in need of unction himself; his own health was visibly failing. My father did not wake while the patriarch anointed him and prayed for the forgiveness of his sins.

He roused a little while afterwards. His eyes found mine. He inhaled once, deeply. I thought he was going to tell me something. Ever so slowly, his breath sighed out. His eyes stayed open. When I moved, they did not follow me. I gestured to Peter. He felt for a pulse, then let the wrist drop, limp. First the right, then the left, he closed my father's eyes.

MYAKES

After Herakleios, none of that dynasty lived to grow old. They didn't last long, but God and all the saints, they burned hot while they were here.

Strange to think about it, Brother Elpidios, but, do you know, Constantine could be alive today. He'd be eighty, more or less: a great age, aye, but not an impossible one. He was a fine man while he lived, maybe even a great one when you remember all he did while he ruled.

And he's been gone these past forty-five years and more, and who thinks about him today? You and me inside this monastery, and nobody else in the whole wide world. That's what fame in the world is worth. Peace with the Lord is better. Or maybe having some fun in the world and *then* peace with the Lord.

Oh, don't click your tongue between your teeth at me, Brother. Weren't you the one who was asking questions about women and—? All right, I'll not go on, not if you say it upsets you. It didn't upset you then. It—

Yes, Brother. Constantine. A fine man, as I say, and a pious man, a good Christian. Yes, if he'd lived longer, he might have tried holding the Empire on a more peaceful course. But he didn't live longer. That left it up to Justinian. He had his own ideas about things and, now, no one to tell him no.

JUSTINIAN

M y father's washed and anointed body lay in state in the throne room for two days. He faced east, as is the custom, his arms formed in the sign of the cross on his chest, a holy icon in his right hand. Candles and incense burned to either side of him. My mother and I spent most of our time there, lamenting, while nobles and clergy and soldiers and common people filed past to look on him one last time and to mourn with us.

We laid him to rest in the church of the Holy Apostles; he being the Emperor, no other choice was conceivable. For the second time in little more than half a year, my mother and I, dressed in black, paraded through the streets of the God-guarded and imperial city to lay our nearest kin to rest.

My father's body, still dressed in imperial robes as it had been while it lay in state, rested in a wooden coffin on a black-painted cart drawn by a pair of lowing oxen. Excubitores in black surcoats, their spears fixed with black streamers, marched to either side of the cart. Behind my mother and me came a great crowd of nobles and palace servants, all of them crying out their grief that the lord of the inhabited world, the vicegerent of God on earth, was dead.

The people of Constantinople lined the Mese and packed the squares of the city to bid my father a last farewell. "What will we do without Constantine?" my mother shrieked, over and over again.

I set my hand on her shoulder. "I will care for the Empire now," I said, "and care for you as well."

She shook me off. "I pray to God you make a good Emperor, as you

are a good son," she said, "but you are not my husband, nor can you be."
She was far from an old woman, and I, at thoughtless sixteen, did not
understand how much of her life had come to an end along with my
father's.

Past the church of St. Euphemia, through the Forum of Constantine,
and through the Forum of Theodosios the funeral procession made its
slow, sorrowful way. Then we proceeded northwest up the Mese toward
the Kharisian Gate, past the church of St. Polyeuktos—after the church
of the Holy Wisdom, perhaps the grandest in the city—past the column
of the Emperor Markianos on the opposite side of the thoroughfare, and
on to the church of the Holy Apostles, less than a bowshot from the
remnants of the first inadequate wall Constantine the Great had built for
the new Rome that came to bear his name.

The church of the Holy Apostles resembles that of St. John in Ephe-
sos, being of cruciform plan with five domes. The excubitores lifted my
father's coffin down from the cart and carried it into the church. The
mosaic on the floor of the narthex showed Constantine the Great offering
the basilica to Christ. My mother and I both crossed ourselves as we
walked over the mosaic and into the church itself.

After setting the coffin on a stand next to the altar, the excubitores
withdrew. My mother went up into the women's gallery, whence she
could gaze down on my father, or the mortal part of him, for the last
time. George the patriarch prayed for my father's soul, as he had for that
of my brother, and also prayed for the Roman Empire, as is usual when
an Emperor passes from men.

"We are fortunate," he said in a slow voice that put me in mind of
nothing so much as a tired man scuffing through dry leaves (plainly his
patriarchate would not long outlast my father's reign), "we are fortunate,
I say, that Constantine, who must now sit at the right hand of God, left
behind for us a successor who, being just now arrived at the first flush of
manhood, will surely rule for many long and prosperous years."

I stood straighter. Till then, I had been so consumed with my father's
passing and with readying his funeral, I had not thought ahead to what
would be my reign. Now I did, just for a moment. My father had not run
the Roman Empire as I would have, nor had he heeded me when I told
him as much. The power had been his. Now it was mine. I could make
changes. I *would* make changes—soon.

George having finished celebrating the liturgy, my mother came
back down to the main level of the church. The excubitores returned
and, lifting the coffin, carried it down the marble stairs to the mausoleum
below. I followed, as did my mother and George. The ecumenical

patriarch had trouble going downstairs; after a moment, a priest hurried up to lend him support.

Despite torches and candles and lamps, the air in the mausoleum was cool and rather damp. I went from one sarcophagus to another, reading the great names: the first Constantine; the first Theodosios, who beat the last pagan army in the west and ended the Olympic games; the second Theodosios, who erected the walls fortifying Constantinople to this day; the Justinian for whom I was named; and my great-great-grandfather, Herakleios. My father would rest in worthy company.

The excubitores set down the coffin that had borne my father from the great palace to the church of the Holy Apostles. They lifted his remains from the coffin and placed him in the stone sarcophagus that awaited him. When they set the lid on the sarcophagus, my mother wailed anew.

"Console yourself, Empress, with the knowledge that your husband has gone from this world into one far better, one where he will know God face to face," the ecumenical patriarch told her, pausing for a moment in his prayers.

"What you say is true," my mother answered through her tears, "but life is hard for those left behind." That also being true, George bowed his head in silent agreement. His lips had a bluish tinge to them; before long, he too would know God face to face.

When the last prayers were over and we went out of the mausoleum, the young, strong priest had George put an arm around his neck and bore most of his weight and the climb upstairs. While performing his ecclesiastical duties, the patriarch was strong and vigorous. When he had to be a mere man, he faded. Either his spirit or the spirit of God working within him imbued him with holy zeal, in the same way that soldiers in the heat of battle perform prodigies of valor they cannot even contemplate when times are quiet.

Once on the main level of the church, George sank panting into a chair with a back of carved ivory that had been placed by the altar, perhaps, for just such a need. I strode up to him and said, "I hope you will be well soon." That was true; I did not expect it, but I hoped.

He caught all the meanings underlying my words. "I will be well enough," he said, "for your coronation."

I assumed the imperial crown four days later, a week to the day after my father's passing. Instead of the black robes of mourning, I donned for the first time the full imperial regalia: the long red tunic, the *skaramangion*; over it the cloak known as the *sagion* or, in the ancient usage, the *chlamys*, in purple with gold-embroidered border and ornamented with shimmering pearls; the long bejeweled scarf of the *loros* draped over my chest in the shape of the letter chi—X—symbolizing Christ's holy and victorious cross; and on my feet the *tzagia*, the purple boots, permitted to the Emperor alone.

The procession from the great palace to the church of the Holy Wisdom was not what I had imagined it would be when I was small. I had thought of being crowned a junior Emperor like my uncles, and had expected them to be there along with my father and my brother. But they were mutilated and exiled, and my brother and father dead. I was the center of every eye, and would be for as long as I ruled—*for the rest of my life*, I thought, not knowing all that lay before me.

My mother, still in black, walked behind me to the great church. Excubitores, now resplendent once more rather than somber, kept back the people who crowded close. Some of the people's exuberance, surely, was due to the pleasure Constantinopolitans take at spectacle of any sort, but more sprang from the silver miliaresia and gold nomismata palace servitors flung into the crowd as largesse to celebrate my coronation.

Late in my father's reign, the imperial mint was lucky enough to find a certain Cyril, an engraver of such genius that he could show a man's perfect portrait in the compass of a coin no broader than a thumbnail. Having made the last nomismata of my father's reign marvels to behold, he now worked his magic with me. Some of the gold pieces the servitors gave out had my picture on them, as I looked then: under the imperial diadem I would don that day, a long, thin face with rather pinched cheeks and a narrow, pointed chin. As my beard was still thin and spotty, I shaved my cheeks and jaw, a practice I would soon give up. I do not know what prodigies of labor Cyril required to ready these new nomismata for the day, but ready they were.

And ready—and more than ready—the crowds were to receive them. Fights broke out among the people struggling for them, as always happens at such affairs. So long as men battled only with fists and elbows and knees, the excubitores took no notice of their sport. But when, just as we arrived at the church of the Holy Wisdom, one ruffian stuck a knife into another not twenty feet from where I stood, the guardsmen waded into the crowd and seized him. The victim, I believe, recovered.

Stephen the Persian turned to me. "Emperor, must we give out this largesse?" he asked in his sweet eunuch's voice. "It brings with it nothing but strife."

"We'd have worse strife if we didn't," I answered. "The people expect it, and if they don't get what they expect . . ."

He sniffed. "Mob rule," he said disdainfully. And, though I think more than half his objection sprang from spending the money, I have seen enough of *demokratia* since that day to admit he had a point. And since, in his blind avidity for gold, he incited the mob against him (among other outrages) . . .

But my pen races years ahead of events. To divert the city mob from its squabbles over coins, I signaled for the excubitores to raise me on a shield, thereby showing the army accepted me as legitimate heir to my father. The four men chosen for the ceremony were Christopher the count of the excubitores; his mandator, Theodore of Koloneia, of whom I have already had a good deal to say; a captain who must then have been prominent but of whom I remember nothing save a huge black mole right between his eyes; and faithful Myakes.

I promoted him to officer's rank so he would not seem out of place alongside his colleagues in the ceremony. To my surprise, he tried to refuse the promotion, surely one of the rare instances in the history of the Roman Empire where a man sought to avoid aggrandizing himself rather than the reverse. But when I ordered him to accept, he obeyed, for how can any man refuse the command of the Emperor?

M Y A K E S

Christian humility, Brother Elpidios? I wish I could take credit for it, but that's not what made me want to stay a simple soldier. Why did I? Nothing simpler: I was happy right where I was. The duty was easy, the pay was fine, I had plenty of good food to eat and good wine to drink, and the girls were just as impressed by a plain excubitor as they would have been by a fancy one, if you take my meaning.

Officers yelled, officers worried, officers had to keep track of a pack of wild men like me. From where I stood, it looked like too much work to be worth the bother. And when Justinian promoted me in spite of my squawks, I found out I was right: it *was* too much work to be worth the bother.

But he's right. Once he'd said yes, I couldn't say no.

These four men, then, hoisted me up on that shield for the crowd to see. Though no Emperor had been crowned for almost a generation, the people knew (and some, at least, had been rehearsed in) their role. "*Tu vincas*, Justinian!" they shouted, and then other acclamations, some of them quite antiquated, suitable for the occasion: "Many years, Justinian!" "Justinian, ruler of the world!" "Flourish, Justinian, bestower of honors!" Then came a new acclamation, one devised by Stephen the Persian: "Hail, Justinian, restorer of a rich name!"

I stood on the shield, supported by the stalwart shoulders of Myakes and of the three other officers of the excubitores, waving out to the people, letting them see me, and letting them get used to the idea that I rather than my father would be appearing on ceremonial occasions from now on. They waved back at me and kept on cheering, more, I daresay, for the diversion I represented than for any virtues inherent in myself. An elephant might have done even better, but we had no elephants, so they had to content themselves with me.

After the city mob had gawped at me long enough, I looked down at Christopher and hissed, "Get on with it!" The count of the excubitores, Myakes, Theodore of Koloneia, and that captain, whoever he was, slowly carried me into the church of the Holy Wisdom. The folk outside bore up philosophically at being deprived of my presence, for the palace servitors threw fresh handfuls of coins into the crowd.

The people inside the great church were of more consequence to me, for I would rule through the high-ranking bureaucrats and soldiers and clerics who packed it tight. Their robes made a bright rainbow of color within the church. These men—and their wives and daughters and, no doubt, concubines in the women's gallery above—shouted acclamations as the common people had outside.

I stared down from my high perch. Along with the army, these men had to acknowledge me their sovereign, as they were doing. Then one of my bearers missed a step. That, added to my own inattention, nearly made me fall off the shield—whose bronze surface was smooth, almost slick—and smash my head on the floor of the great church. A worse omen at a coronation I can hardly imagine. But Myakes, bless him, reached up with his free hand and caught me by the ankle till I steadied, just as he had stopped me from leaping off the city wall when the deniers of Christ besieged Constantinople.

We reached the ambo without further mishap. George the patriarch stood there waiting, leaning on a stick to take some of the weight from his legs. His vestments of silk and wool, worked with gems and pearls and gold threads in the shape of many crosses, rivaled the imperial regalia in splendor.

On the ambo rested a cushion of purple silk embroidered with eagles in gold thread. And on that cushion sat the crown that had for so many years been my father's. Its golden circle of bejeweled and enameled panels, the glittering *prependoulia* that dangled from it, and its surmounting cross were of surpassing magnificence.

Theodore of Koloneia caught the eyes of the rest of my bearers. At his nod—not that of Christopher, his nominal superior—all four men went to one knee, lowering the shield so I could descend. They rose once more. Having gained my full height by then, I was taller than any of them, though they were all thicker through the shoulders.

George the ecumenical patriarch beckoned. I went to him. Setting his hand on my head, he called out, "Holy!" in a voice so loud and deep, no one would have guessed him ill. At the coronations of Frankish kings, I have heard, they are smeared with scented oil, in imitation of Biblical practice. No such ritual existing among us, the patriarch offered the customary prayers for the occasion, altering them slightly to stress Christ's two energies and two wills, as defined by the recently past ecumenical synod, and finishing, "May God bless His servant and our master, the Emperor Justinian!"

Had my father been crowning me junior Emperor, the patriarch would have stepped aside then and let him set the crown on my head; junior Emperors are made—and unmade—by the will of *the* Emperor. But my father was gone. George crowned me, a sign I was receiving the symbol of my new station by the will of God.

The crown was heavy, almost oppressively so. It surprised me; gold combines small bulk with great weight. I wondered how my father had put up with wearing it hour after hour, day after day, year after year. And now, having worn it so long myself, I take its weight altogether for granted. When the mad-dog usurpers mutilated me and exiled me to lonely Kherson, on the peninsula jutting down into the Black Sea from the north, my neck felt curiously limber for some weeks, so accustomed had it grown to supporting the crown along with my head. I had to get used to it all over again when I took back what was rightfully mine, a burden I assumed with pleasure.

No matter how heavy the crown felt there in the great church, I knew I had to bear it without complaint or flinching. And so I stood very straight and very still, looking a challenge out to the dignitaries who were looking in at me and trying to take my measure.

I do not know what they thought of me as they shouted for the acclamations—"*Tu vincas*, Justinian! Many years to the Emperor Justinian!"—that, with those of the people, with my being raised on a shield by the soldiers, and with the patriarch's coronation, formalized my accession to the throne. What I thought was, *Now I rule you all—and you had better obey.*

BOOK B´

JUSTINIAN

R omans!" I said loudly, pitching my voice to carry and doing my best to make sure it stayed deep, "Romans, I stand before you full of grief, grief that my father, who fought so fiercely to force back the followers of the false prophet, now no longer dwells among men and rules Romania, but has so soon gone to earn God's reward for his greatness here on earth."

I made the sign of the cross. So did the ecumenical patriarch. So did many of the dignitaries in the great church. Many of them were up on their toes, leaning forward slightly so as to be able to capture every word and from those words to try to divine the future course of the Roman Empire.

That suited me. I had no intention of hiding my aims—on the contrary. I said, "As much as my father wished to be most beloved by the barbarians, so he who is now Emperor of the Romans wishes to be most feared by them all. So that no barbarians might invade our provinces and do them harm, we shall, as soon as may be, trouble them with continuous attacks."

A sigh went through the church of the Holy Wisdom. The wars would not begin at once—it was too late in the season to start a campaign—but begin they would. My father had told me I could set my own course when the Empire rested in my hands, and I aimed to do just that.

"Romans, 'Tu vincas!' should not be only an idle acclamation, spoken and then forgotten," I said earnestly, "nor is passivity preferable to fighting. The peace we have with the Bulgars—a peace existing for no other reason than that it is bought and sold—is shameful and slavish. Better by far to bear wounds in our bodies than in our souls. Before long, the barbarians shall learn a lasting lesson."

I paused. The notables cheered. Nothing else was possible. I was the Emperor. I had defined, as I had the right to define, the direction the Roman Empire would take. Their task was to make it go in that direction, nothing more.

They sensed as much, giving me the cry of "Tu vincas!" again, over and over, till the ancient Latin words came echoing back from the great dome that, as some writer from the age of my namesake says, seems more as if it is suspended from the sky by a golden chain than a part of any merely earthly building. I paraphrase without the book before me, I fear.

Up to this time, all acclamations had gone to my father, save for rare moments like that in the Forum of Constantine. Hearing hundreds of prominent people shouting my praises was heady as strong wine. I had not yet learned those nobles and clerics and soldiers would acclaim a usurper, a rebel, a tyrant, as fulsomely as their legitimate lord.

With the crown on my head, I strode out of the great church to receive fresh plaudits from the people. I already knew the city mob was fickle; anyone attending two days' racing at the hippodrome could have said as much. But for now they were all with me, and I basked in their acclaim like a fence lizard basking in the sun.

On the procession returning to the palace, the servitors helped keep the people happy by throwing more coins out to them. As at the church of the Holy Wisdom, struggling over the nomismata and miliaresia seemed as enjoyable as having them. A tagline from some pagan play ran through my mind: "Man seeks God and, seeking, finds Him." And is not gold a god for far too many?

When I was back at the palace—my palace now—I thought of summoning a serving girl to my chamber and celebrating my accession in the most enjoyable fashion I could imagine. Then, all at once, I recalled my father's deathbed words to me. He had been more than half out of his wits with sickness and poppy juice, but that did not mean he had made no sense.

Instead of some lively wench, I called for Stephen the Persian. When he came before me, he prostrated himself. That took me aback:

another reminder *I* was the Emperor. I told him to rise and then said, "Fetch my mother and, having brought her, you stay as well. I would take counsel with the two of you."

He bowed in obedience and hurried away. Like every palace servitor, he had always been attentive to my wants. What he was now was as far beyond attentiveness as that was beyond indifference. I had not realized the power the Emperor enjoys until it fell into my hands and I could feel of it.

Stephen returned with my mother a few minutes later. The eunuch parakoimomenos wore a fine robe of sea-green samite shot through with silver threads, a fitting bit of splendor for my coronation ceremony but an odd contrast to my mother's black wool of mourning. Her face bore a curious mix of expressions: partly the stunned sorrow that had held her since her husband died, partly pride that her son should have succeeded to the lordship of the world.

Both of them stood silent. After a moment, I saw they were waiting for me to speak, another imperial perquisite I had not before encountered. I came straight to the point: "I think I should wed, and as quickly as possible, too."

My mother nodded at once; she too remembered my father's words. "I think you are wise. You are the last man of your line, and God's will is unknowable to us. We have seen that." Her voice went ragged with pain as she crossed herself. "If the family is to go on . . ." She nodded again.

"While I would not presume to disagree with the Emperor's wise words . . ." Stephen's strange voice was, as always, dulcet, beautifully modulated. He was a courtier through and through, to disagree by denying he was disagreeing. His decorous pause allowed me to order him to silence if I so chose. When I waved for him to go on, he did, saying, "The treasury, having been strained by today's festivities, will for some little while be in poor condition to absorb the further expenses inherent in a wedding celebration, and so it might be more prudent to wait and—"

Now I did cut him off, with a harsh, chopping motion of my right hand. "The nomismata in the treasury are not yours, Stephen," I said sharply. "They belong to the Empire, and to the Emperor—to me. If I say they shall be spent on my wedding, they shall. Do you understand?"

Stephen bowed. "I do indeed, Emperor. My only thought was to serve both you and the treasury as well as I could."

Looking back on it, I suppose he hated me. At the time, I neither noticed nor cared. He would obey: that was what mattered. I turned to my mother. "But whom shall I marry?" I knew, by then, a good deal about bedding serving maids . . . and just enough to realize that was not the same as picking a wife. I did not even know which of the notable men of Constantinople had daughters of marriageable age; the women of the wealthy and prominent live sheltered lives, and are not casually seen by men outside their families. I certainly did not know which of those daughters of marriageable age might suit me.

"We must think carefully," my mother said, her voice more lively than it had been since my father first took ill. "We must look at the character of the girl, at who her relatives are, at—"

"Her dowry," Stephen the Persian put in.

My mother nodded, albeit reluctantly. "That does matter, but less here than it would in another marriage. If the Emperor must depend on his wife's bride-portion for what he needs, the Roman Empire has fallen on hard times indeed."

"True," Stephen admitted, "but, everything else being the same, more is better than less. Gold never goes to waste." Yes, he was one of those who spoke the word "gold" as another might say "God." I noted that then, and put it to use later.

"I shall inquire," my mother said. She had something to do now, some direction in which to go. The smile she gave me was wan, but it was a smile. "Is there anything more, Emperor?" It was the first time she called me what I now was.

I shook my head, dismissing her and Stephen. Having given them a purpose, I soon found one of my own, the one I had rejected before. Soon, I was frolicking with one of the blond Sklavinians, not Irene, but another one. If I was to be restricted to a wife thereafter, I would enjoy myself while I could.

One thing I quickly discovered: when the bridegroom is to be the Emperor of the Romans, every family in the city has an eligible—indeed, an ideal—daughter, or imagines it has. Some of these my mother quickly eliminated from consideration. No, I did not want to marry the headsman's daughter; or a screaming harridan of thirty-five who remained unwed and undoubtedly virgin because every man who got near her had fled in terror; or a girl who, although of the requisite age and social standing, had the misfortune—or the greed—to be wider than she was tall.

"She would not suit you," my mother said seriously, speaking of this last candidate. "There are appetites, and then there are appetites."

I stared at her. It was the first time I had ever seen, ever thought of, her as a woman rather than merely as my mother, the first time I truly realized what losing my father meant to her. Not knowing what to say, I kept silent.

Over the next few weeks, she and Stephen the Persian winnowed the list down to three. "Among these, I cannot choose," she said. "Best you should meet them all, and pick which one suits you."

And so I did. Zoe, the daughter of Florus the patrician, was like the general in being clever and plainspoken. Unfortunately, she also looked like him, and Florus, while fearsome to his foes, was also fearsome to behold. I was sure Florus's status and her own good sense would get Zoe a match one day, but it would not be with me.

Anna was the daughter of John, the eparch of the city. But, although John had the brains to administer Constantinople, a quarter hour's conversation convinced me Anna had none in her head or concealed anywhere else about her person. She was pretty and well made, which tempted me, but, before making up my mind, I decided to see the third of the girls my mother and the parakoimomenos thought a possible match for me.

Before I did meet Eudokia, I teased my mother, saying, "This whole business reminds me of the way I'll choose a new patriarch when old George dies. The synod of bishops will send me three names, and I'll pick one from among them."

"Choose wisely then," my mother answered. "Choose wisely now, too."

And so I met Eudokia, the daughter of Philaretos. Her father was count of the walls, the officer in charge of maintaining the Long Wall, the fortification protecting the part of Thrace nearest Constantinople from barbarian attack. Philaretos was a less prominent man than either Florus or John, which had advantages and disadvantages both. While he brought less influence than either of the other two men, he was also less likely to get above his station and think that being father-in-law to the Emperor entitled him to conduct himself as if he, not I, ruled the Romans.

I dined with Philaretos and his family in the tribunal of the nineteen akkubita, a ceremonial hall that, Stephen the Persian assured me, had been built in the reign of Constantine the Great. The count of the walls was bluff and affable, his wife Marina plump and pleasant. Her father having lately died, she and my mother, who were about of an age, commiserated together.

Philaretos also had a couple of sons, one older than I, one younger. Neither of them said much; no doubt they had been told to keep their mouths shut unless I spoke to them. Beyond bare politeness, I did not. I was more interested in their sister.

Eudokia was close to my age: half a year younger, it turned out, when we compared birthdates. She was less lushly put together than Anna, but far from displeasing, unlike poor homely Zoe. Her hair was dark, like her father's, but showed little reddish glints when the lamplight shone on it. Her eyes were an interesting color, somewhere between brown and green; I wondered whether Philaretos or Marina had a Sklavinian or a German down near the roots of the family tree.

She said, "Thank you for inviting us into the city, Emperor. Because of my father's post, I come here less often than I would if I could." When she smiled—not brazenly, but not as if in apology, either—she showed good teeth. I liked her voice, too: not squeaky, not raspy, but smooth like well-aged wine.

"But do you come less often than your father would like?" I asked. "Out in Thrace, you have less chance to spend his money."

"If you marry her, Emperor, that'll be your worry, not mine," Philaretos said with a laugh: more than most men would have dared, sitting where he was.

"He'll be able to afford it better than you can, Father," Eudokia said, which was also daring—though certainly true.

The feast, and the talk afterwards, went on longer than they had when I was meeting Zoe or Anna. The servants kept bringing in wine, and we kept drinking it. Philaretos did a hilarious impression of a Bulgar with a hangover. Even my mother and his wife, in mourning though they were, laughed till they had to hold on to each other to stop.

When, sometime close to midnight or perhaps after it, we rose from the table, Eudokia said, "Thank you again for inviting my family and me here, Emperor. I enjoyed myself."

I realized I had enjoyed myself, too. I had not particularly expected to; I had looked on the dinner as something I needed to do, not something I wanted to do. A woman with whom I could enjoy myself—if that was not a recipe for a wife, what was?

My mother was in a sour mood the next morning, probably from too much wine and not enough sleep. "Are you trying to imitate Philaretos's Bulgar?" I asked, and won from her half a smile. Then I said, "Of the three of them, I choose Eudokia."

That did lighten her mood. "Oh, good," she said. "I hoped you would, but I wondered if you would rather have Anna because of her looks. Not that Eudokia isn't a nice-looking young girl," she added hastily, as if afraid she might make me change my mind.

"I like the way she smiles," I said.

"The night I met your father, I was too nervous to smile," my mother said; by the look in her eye, that night was very close to the present in her mind. "He forgave me." She seemed to come back to thinking about me. "May God grant you and Eudokia many years, many children, and much happiness." She crossed herself. So did I.

God has His own purposes. He must weigh the happiness of my family against other matters in His scales, and find it comes to not so much. Of course, He has all of His plan before His eyes at all times, where for us humans it unfolds bit by bit.

MYAKES

Justinian hit too close to the mark there, Brother Elpidios. And he didn't see all of it, though he heard the last. Anastasia had to witness every bit of that house's misfortune, right down to the end. I wonder how she bore so much sorrow, and what happened to her at last. So many things we never get to know.

JUSTINIAN

Stephen the Persian conducting the negotiations over Eudokia's dowry, those went quickly and were settled to my entire satisfaction. "Maybe I ought to put you in charge of the treasury," I told him. I was joking at the time, but remembered the words later, he having proved himself both skilled and diligent.

We announced the betrothal just after the end of summer, with the wedding to be held in November. At my mother's invitation, Eudokia and her family were installed in the great palace, Philaretos delegating his duties to a subordinate until the wedding. Before my father died, he had paid the Bulgars their yearly tribute, so we had no reason to expect trouble either from them or from the seven Sklavinian tribes they had brought under their control—and, indeed, all remained peaceful in the north, as it did with the Arabs. Their misnamed commander of the faithful sent an ambassador congratulating me on my accession, I suppose in the hope I would continue my father's policy on that frontier as well. I did not say no. I did not say yes.

Having Eudokia in the palace was awkward in a way my mother might not have considered on inviting her. On the wedding night, Eudokia needed to show herself a virgin, which meant I could not indulge myself with her beforehand. But with her there, I hesitated to

take the serving girls to bed, lest they bring back tales to her or, fool-
ishly, put on airs before her. And so, till the wedding day, I lived a
nearly monkish existence, and was often short-tempered—no, angry—
on account of it.

Everything concerning the Emperor must be magnificent, with his
wedding no exception to the rule. Servants set up tables in every forum
in the imperial city, to feast the people. I ordered chariot races for the
amusement of the city mob. Though such amusements are no longer the
all-consuming passion of the city as they were in the days of my namesake
a century and a half ago, the people would have thought me mean and
niggardly had I omitted them.

As Stephen had said, all this took large sums of gold. I wished my
father had not paid the Bulgars, and I wished we collected more in tribute
from the followers of the false prophet, for most of what the Empire raised
in taxes on land and crops and commerce was promptly spent again on
soldiers and dromons and buildings. But, despite dark mutterings from my
ministers, we had enough.

The day we had set dawned crisp and cool and clear. "A good
omen," I said to my mother as we got ready to parade to the church of
the Holy Wisdom so the ecumenical patriarch could perform the marriage
ceremony. "The way it's rained the past week, I was afraid we'd have to
splash through puddles all the way there."

"Your bride will be lovely," she answered, and then went on, "You
chose well, son. Eudokia is a fine girl; the more I see of her, the more I
see to like."

"Yes," I said enthusiastically, responding more to the first part of
that than to the second, though I was looking forward to seeing far more
of Eudokia than I had yet. I was also curious, as the only virginity I had
been involved in losing up till then was my own.

Stephen the Persian came in and fussily adjusted the way the ends
of my *loros* crossed each other. I wore the same regalia as I had to my
coronation, and, as I had then, I went bareheaded. Today I would don,
not the Emperor's crown, but that of the bridegroom.

I could not see how Eudokia looked as we left the palace (which
served for her in place of her parents' home), for, as was customary, she
was veiled against all intrusive eyes, mine included. Her white silk gown,
though, fit tight enough to give me a new idea of her figure, and I liked
what I saw there.

When we got to the church of the Holy Wisdom and walked up
to the altar, George struggled to his feet to perform the marriage service. He was, by then, almost literally on his last legs, but still managed

to make his voice carry as he asked us if we both consented to the marriage.

"Yes," I said, and then had to repeat myself so anyone but he and Eudokia could hear me.

Her voice was not loud, but very clear: "Yes."

One of the priests attending the patriarch handed him a sheathed sword on a belt. Swollen fingers fumbling, he girded it round my waist, a symbol of imperial power. Then, slowly, he turned to the altar and lifted the crowns of marriage from it. Where most folk make do with tinned copper, ours were of gold. He set one on my head, the other on Eudokia's. Between where the crowns had lain stood a golden goblet. The patriarch offered it first to me, then to my bride. We shared the wine the goblet held, Eudokia lifting her veil just enough to drink.

George read from the letter to the Ephesians, and from the book of John. He prayed for long years together for us, for happiness, for children, for prosperity—"for you and for the Empire," he said, as he would not have at a wedding for bride and groom of lower rank.

Eudokia set a golden ring on my finger, its bezel showing Christ joining a couple together in marriage. I gave her an iron ring in return; a golden wedding belt waited at the nuptial chamber. George took the crowns of marriage off us and handed them to Myakes, who, despite my mother's grumbles and Stephen's sniffs, served as my groomsman. He hurried off to set them on the posts of the marriage bed for luck.

Once the crowns were off, George blessed us one last time, bent his head in silent prayer, and then, with an effort, straightened. "Justinian and Eudokia are wed," he said. "What therefore God hath joined together, let not man put asunder."

After that, we paraded back to the great palace, to the cheers of the nobles and officials and officers who had filled the church of the Holy Wisdom, and to those of the common folk of Constantinople as well. No sooner were we out of the church than the epithalamia began. The farther we went, the louder and bawdier the wedding songs got. If Eudokia had not known what we would soon be doing—and, since she was a well-brought-up maiden, she might not have—she would have been left in little doubt by the time we got to the palace.

The wine was already flowing freely there; mimes and dancing girls entertained the guests. My mother being the only family I had left in the world, she and I and Eudokia went into an antechamber for the ceremony of removing the bride's veil. I had, of course, seen Eudokia's face before, but in theory I might not have.

Seeing my mother nod encouragement, Eudokia took off the veil.

Under it, her cheeks were flushed, perhaps from the crisp breeze outside, perhaps from excitement, too. "My husband," she said, sounding proud of herself, as well she might have.

"My wife," I answered, and then added, "My beautiful wife." She looked down at the floor for modesty's sake—she had indeed been properly brought up. But she was smiling.

"God and the Virgin bless both of you, my children," my mother said.

I was not thinking of God at that moment, and of no virginity save my bride's. "Fix your veil again," I told Eudokia, "so I can lead you to the nuptial chamber." *So I can make you truly my wife*, was what I meant. As the white veil concealed her features once more, I thought she looked nervous, and wondered what, if anything, her mother had told her of what happens on a wedding night.

Everyone cheered when my mother and Eudokia and I came out, because everyone knew where Eudokia and I were going and what we would be doing once we got there. A good many people followed us down the hall, bawling out epithalamia on that very theme. Some were far more specific than any sung on our way back to the palace. I wondered what Eudokia made of such gleeful obscenity. Just before we reached the door to the bedchamber, she giggled. That seemed a good sign.

Even after we went inside and closed the door behind us, the loud, lewd racket went on. The bed had on it only a plain white linen sheet. On the posts, faithful Myakes had hung the marriage crowns. "Take off your veil," I said to Eudokia. "We're alone now." Soon she would take off more than the veil, but maybe she did not want to think about that yet.

And I still had to give her the marriage belt, which lay, wrapped in white silk, on a table by the bed. I unwrapped it. How the bright gold glittered!—twenty-one small medallions and two large ones on either side of the clasp showing Christ joining the right hands of bride and groom together. I carried the belt over to Eudokia and put it round her waist. It fit perfectly: a maidservant must have measured her for the jeweler. She looked down at herself and at the splendid ornament. "How beautiful," she whispered.

This was the first time I had touched any part of her but her hands. I let my own hands linger on her hips. "How beautiful," I said in an altogether different tone of voice.

She cast down her eyes once more—a modest bride indeed. But there is also a time when modesty should end, and that time had come. Leaving one hand where it was, I raised the other to her chin and tilted her face up to mine. She looked nervous but determined, which, under the circumstances, was as much as I could expect.

I quickly discovered she knew nothing about kissing of the sort in which a new groom and his bride are apt to engage. She learned fast, though. My own first instructions in these mysteries were close enough in time that I remembered them and used them as a guide in teaching her.

While we kissed, we clung to each other ever more tightly. My manhood rose. As it was pressed between us, she must have noticed, but she gave no sign that she did, perhaps again from modesty, perhaps because she simply did not know what to do. I took one of her hands in mine and guided it down there. She started to pull away when she felt the bulge, but I held her hand there.

"That is—" she said, and then stopped: half a statement, half a question in two words.

"Yes, it is," I answered, my voice full of what I would rather call enthusiasm than raw lust. I took my hand away; after a tiny hesitation, she left hers where I had put it. I nodded: another lesson learned. I needed both hands to undo the catch of the marriage belt. My fingers trembled as I worked it. "A pity to take this off so soon after putting it on you, but . . ."

Then I had to step away from her for a moment, to set the belt on the table once more. When I came back to her, I began to undo the catches that held her wedding gown closed. She stood very still under my hands. I slid the gown down off her. It puddled at her feet. The small nipples on her breasts were tight and hard, more, no doubt, from nervousness than passion. I bent my mouth to them, first one, then the other. Her breath caught. "That feels—" Again, she did not finish, but she put on hand on the back of my head to keep me at what I was doing.

Presently, I pulled her drawers off her, so that she stood naked before me. "I am a lucky man today," I said, and smiled the smile I had been practicing since before the little Sklavinian girl took me into the storeroom.

Then it was my turn to divest myself of my robes. When I was through, Eudokia stared at me. I knew how women were made, and had learned from her nudity only the particulars of her body. In my nakedness she saw for the first time the generality of maleness. My erection stood out as straight as if I were about to fence with it.

"I'll try not to hurt you," I said, taking her hand and walking with her to the bed, "though it may, the first time." I spoke as if I knew in detail, wanting to make her feel easy, although, as I have said, the only virginity I knew was my own. Losing that had not hurt—by no means!

We lay down together. I did not go into her at once, but kissed her and caressed her with my hands. When I stroked her secret place, she sighed and her legs, which she had held tightly closed till then, opened of themselves. After a while, my mouth followed my hand. A maidservant had taught me that a year or so before—sucking the fig, she called it. She and several others had seemed to like it more than a hand stroking the same place, and so, by her little gasps, did Eudokia.

Without my asking, she took me in her hand, and laughed to feel me throb against her palm. Then, on hands and knees, I got up over her and guided myself inside her. She being wet, I went in easily—until, all at once, I was halted. Eudokia's face, which had been full of surprised delight, twisted in pain. She was indeed a maiden. I had not had any serious doubts on that score, but proving it was a relief.

"We must finish what we've begun," I said, and she nodded. I thrust with all my strength, and broke through the barrier. Eudokia did not cry out, but her breath hissed through her nostrils. I have heard soldiers make that sound when they take a wound. "Is it all right?" I asked after a moment. She nodded again. Slowly, I began to move inside her.

But as my own heat built, I forgot about restraint, and soon gasped out my spasm of delight. When I came back to myself, I saw her eyes were tightly closed. A tear had run down the side of her face from each of them. She hissed again when I slid out of her. I looked at myself, at her, at the stained sheet, and nodded, happy with the world. No one would have cause to doubt I had taken her maidenhead.

She too sat up and looked at the blood that had come from between her legs. "You are truly my wife," I said.

"Yes." Eudokia got off the bed and, walking as if she had been on horseback for a long time, poured some water from a pitcher into a basin, soaked a rag in it, and washed her private parts. After a moment, I did the same. A wedding night of one round only is a poor wedding night indeed, and I had in mind teaching her some things I had not shown her before our first joining. Being clean would help.

If I had the stamina now that I did then, or if I had known then what I know now, the night might have been even more memorable, but it was quite fine enough as things were. Some time along toward midnight, I stripped the sheet from the bed, put on my robe, and displayed the trophy to all the wedding guests who had not yet drunk themselves to sleep or gone off with a dancing girl. Loud, raucous cheers greeted me. "What are you going to do now?" someone shouted.

"Go back in there and put some more stains on it," I answered, and the shouts that came echoing back were even more raucous than before. To whoops of laughter, I shut the door and proceeded to do as I had said.

I woke the next morning to sunlight streaming into the bedchamber. Eudokia lay naked beside me. I thought about waking her with the same music to which we had fallen asleep: when you are but sixteen, you can contemplate such things after a night like the one we had had. But even at sixteen, that next round was far from urgent. I rolled over and yawned and stretched, feeling lazy and contented.

Eudokia's eyes came open. She let out a startled squeak at finding herself in bed with a man, but quickly remembered how and why that had happened, proof of which being that, although she started to cover herself with her hands, she stopped with the motion half begun and let me look all I pleased.

"My husband," she said. Her eyes traveled from my face downwards. Sure enough, I had begun to rise again. I do not know whether she was impressed; being ignorant of the ways of men, she had no standard for comparison. Looking back across a quarter of a century, I am certainly impressed. And so we did play that same sweet tune over again.

M Y A K E S

There, you see, Brother Elpidios, you read that all through with only a handful of wheezes and hardly a splutter. First times are strange, but after you've done something once, the second time is always a lot easier.

What do you mean, that wasn't the reason you had an easier time here? Oh. The other was just fornication and this was talking about real marriage, and so not a sin in the eyes of God? I see. If the difference makes you happy, Brother, far be it from me to argue with you, even though Justinian was doing the same things as before.

Not all the same things? Oh, sucking the fig. Yes, they like that, same as we like it when they play the flute for us. No, when you get right down to it, I don't think there's anything in the Holy Scriptures against it. It's not the sin of Onan, for how can a woman spill her seed out on the ground? She has no seed to spill, now does she? She's just fertile soil where a man's seed can grow. You might even say he's watering that ground, eh?

If you're really so curious, Brother Elpidios, why don't you ask the abbot what he thinks? You're not *that* curious? Mm, might be just as well. Read some more, why don't you?

JUSTINIAN

Marriage agreed with me. Being able to slake my lust whenever I felt like it agreed with me. And Eudokia and I got on when even when not joined together panting on the marriage bed. She had an odd, sideways way of looking at things that went on in the palace—I suppose because she was not accustomed to the life from birth, as I was—that made me take the ancient customs less for granted, too.

George the ecumenical patriarch died in the spring of my first year as Emperor. After rather less bickering than usual, the local synod of bishops chose the three men from among whom I was to choose his successor: Paul, Kallinikos, and Theodore. Now, Theodore is far from the least common of names, but having it presented here gave me pause. I asked Niketas, who as synkellos to George administered churchly affairs until a new patriarch was installed, "Is this the same Theodore my father deposed because he was a monothelite?"

"Emperor, it is," he said, "but since the sixth holy and ecumenical synod anathematized the doctrine to which he formerly adhered, he has truly repented of his earlier error. His orthodoxy is now complete and unquestionable."

"Complete, maybe, but far from unquestionable," I answered, and ordered Theodore brought before me.

It proved to be as Niketas said: he was indeed of perfect orthodoxy. "The Holy Spirit speaks through each ecumenical synod, and makes God's will clear," he declared. "I was in error, but am no longer. Restore me to the patriarchal throne, and I shall prove to you the truth of what I say."

The other two prelates the local synod had named were also worthy men, each of them later serving as patriarch of Constantinople. Now, though, reinstalling the man my father had ousted struck my fancy. I ordered it, and it was done.

"Your father would never have done that," my mother said after I announced my decision. "He never abandoned a friend, and, more important, he never forgot a foe."

I tossed my head. "I am not my father," I said. "Just because he did things a certain way doesn't mean I have to do them that way, too." I was still arguing with my father, as boys do on the way to manhood. Now, though, he could no longer answer back, so I, unlike most boys, won all the arguments.

That would have been better had I been right all the time. Well, I have learned—painfully, as such lessons are often taught. By God, by the Virgin, by the saints, I forgive no foes today.

Everyone who advised me—not my mother alone—seemed passionately convinced all matters should remain as they had been in the time of my father. This applied even to Theodore, the restored patriarch. "If you but continue on his course, Emperor," he said, "the Roman Empire will do well."

"Is that so?" I said. "Shall I depose you, then, because he did?"

Theodore suffered such a coughing fit, he had to retire from the throne room. I laughed till my sides ached at getting the better of the prelate. But, while he no longer importuned me after that, the bureaucrats and soldiers who came before me kept trying to hold back even the idea of change.

This, of course, accomplished the opposite of what they wanted, making me even more eager than I had been to overturn my father's arrangements regardless of whether they had been foolish. What lad has ever reached sixteen years without being certain everything around him is the creation of a pack of doddering idiots and deserves nothing better than being tossed upon the rubbish heap? I had no patience for what had been done; my mind turned instead to what I might do.

As I say, every lad of like age is full of the same ideas, being convinced to the uttermost depths of his soul that all the people older than he, and especially all kinsfolk and men of authority older than he, have not a counterfeit follis's worth of sense among them. Most lads, though, have to accept the authority of their elders, possessing no power, no wealth, of their own.

I was not most lads. I was Emperor of the Romans. I had all the power of the Empire behind me, and all the wealth, too. I could do as I chose, not as anyone chose for me. It had not been done that way before? Precedent and conventional usage argued against it? So what?

Furthermore, I saw—I was certain I saw—an opportunity to which my so-called counselors were deliberately blinding themselves.

After the failure of their impious and infamous assault upon this God-guarded and imperial city, the Arabs had fallen into disarray. Mauias, their longtime ruler, passed from this earth into hellfire two years after they gave up the siege. Upon his death, several misnamed commanders of the faithful held their throne in Damascus in quick succession, none securely. Abimelekh, the latest, had gained it in the same year I did, though already older than my father at his death.

Through all the turmoil among the deniers of Christ, my father had sat quiet, content to receive the tribute Mauias had agreed to pay after his fleet was destroyed and his army beaten. He preferred that to battle.

I thought otherwise. Summoning my advisers, I said, "With the followers of the false prophet quarreling among themselves, should we not seize the moment to take back some of the lands they stole from the Romans during the reigns of my grandfather and my great-great-grandfather?"

The sakellarios, a dour man named Romanos, said, "The treasury has not the gold for a long campaign, Emperor."

"Since we are at peace, should we not remain at peace?" John the city eparch said, though nothing outside Constantinople was properly his area of concern.

And Christopher, the *comes excubitorum*, said, "Having been little used of late, the army will not be at its peak fighting condition."

I clapped a hand to my forehead. "We have not fought and so we cannot fight? The longer we do not fight, the worse we will fare when the time for fighting comes! If we stay at peace for a generation, will we be altogether destroyed when war breaks out?"

"That is not what I meant, Emperor. I—" Christopher began.

I cut him off, declaring, "I do not care what you meant. I heard what you said, and I did not care for that, either. We shall take advantage of Abimelekh's weakness, and the war, undoubtedly a short and successful one, will more than pay for itself."

"Such promises are more often made than fulfilled," Romanos said sourly.

"You have heard my will expressed. You shall carry it out," I said. They all bowed in submission. I glowered at Romanos. I did not need a treasurer who told me why I could not do things. I needed one who would find ways for me to do as I wanted. If this copper counter obstructed me, I would replace him—and I knew with whom.

But that could wait. More urgent was picking the proper general to lead the campaign against the followers of the false prophet. Christopher the *comes excubitorum* I dismissed out of hand. The only military virtue I had seen him display was looking splendid in his gilded shirt of mail. That sufficed in Constantinople. In the field, it did not.

If I appointed Theodore of Koloneia commander of the army, that left the imperial bodyguards with no one to keep a tight rein on Christopher. I decided I dared not take the chance. Theodore also stayed in the imperial city.

Of the three generals who had beaten back the Arabs in my father's day, Kyprianos had by this time met the common fate of mankind. When I asked Myakes what he thought of Petronas, he rolled his eyes. "He promises more than he can give," he said.

"What do you mean?" I asked.

Myakes explained how, in my father's expedition against the Bulgars, Petronas had promised victory after my father went off to Mesembria on account of his gout. I knew too well he had no victory there, only defeat and humiliation. And so I resolved not to name Petronas to high command.

Florus, now, was another matter. No one faulted either his cleverness or his generalship. And yet . . . having had the chance to marry Florus's daughter but instead having chosen another, I hesitated. Did he harbor, did he hide, did he nurture resentment under that clever mask? If he did, his strategic ability might prove more dangerous to me than to the deniers of Christ. When my house rose to power through civil war, when my grandfather was murdered as the overture to uprising, I had to make these calculations. Florus might have done well, but I did not send him east.

Having eliminated all these candidates, I summoned a man I knew much less well, a man of my father's generation: Leontios, whom I last remembered seeing at the time of the ecumenical synod. He was as I remembered him: round-faced, broad-shouldered, with open, smiling features and a hearty manner.

"Turn me loose on them, Emperor," he boomed. "That's all I ask—turn me loose on them. I'll beat 'em for you. You just see if I don't."

This was what I wanted to hear. One of the things I had already found out, though, was that the Emperor always heard what he wanted to hear, or what the man speaking to him thought he wanted to hear, regardless of its truth. And so I asked Leontios, "Why are you so confident?"

"Why? I'll tell you why, Emperor." He had the habit of repeating himself. As he spoke, he ticked points off on his fingers, something else he did all the time. "The Arabs, they've been through civil war. And they've been through famine. And they've been through plague. And the Armenians hate them, because the Armenians, they're Christians even if they're heretics, and they don't have any use for the false prophet. If I march an army into Armenia, the princes there, they'll rise up and help my boys throw the Arabs out. That's why I'll beat 'em."

"Good," I said—and the reasons he had named *were* good. Coupled with his confidence, they gave me reason to hope he could do as he claimed. I said, "I shall send you forth, Leontios, and may God grant you the victory you deserve. And, to help ensure it, I will write to the Mardaite chieftains and turn them loose against the deniers of Christ, too."

Leontios's eyes glowed. "That's fine, Emperor. That's mighty fine. With them and me hitting the Arabs at the same time, their caliph"— having fought a good deal in the east, he used the Arabs' own name for their miscalled commander of the faithful—"he'll be itching so many places at once, he won't know which one to scratch."

He was not an educated man. He was not a particularly clever man. But he had a bluff vitality to him that made those deficiencies matter less than they would have in many another. Soldiers followed him, not just willingly but eagerly. I also heard that women fell all over him, but that, true or not, had nothing to do with matters military.

He having satisfied me, I sent him forth. And, thanks to him and to the Mardaites, I showed my quivering, cowardly advisers what fools they were. Leontios ravaged that part of Armenia under Arab control, and succeeded so well there that he went on to plunder not only Iberia but also Media, the northwesternmost province of what had been the Persian Empire before the followers of the false prophet burst from the desert and subjected Romania's ancient foes.

From all these lands he sent back to Constantinople a large sum of money, which was most welcome. I knew the fisc would make good use of every follis Leontios sent, too, having replaced Romanos as sakellarios with Stephen the Persian. Many eunuchs could care for my comfort as well as Stephen had; few men, entire or not, had the gift of caring for the revenue accruing to the imperial treasury.

And while Leontios was campaigning in and beyond Arab-held Armenia, the Mardaites ravaged the borderlands from Mopsuestia in Kilikia—not far from Antioch—north and east up to the Roman province of Armenia, from which my general had set out. For a long time, their depredations kept Abimelekh from responding in any way to Leontios's invasion.

God granted us Romans another boon at this time, in that one more spasm of civil war convulsed the deniers of Christ not long after Leontios attacked them. Distracted as Abimelekh was—one of the rebels against him even succeeded in briefly seizing Damascus, his capital—he could not hope to withstand our armies. And so, for almost three years, we swept everything before us.

As Mauias had after his force shattered itself against the walls of this God-guarded and imperial city, the miscalled commander of the faithful sent an embassy to Constantinople, asking our terms for breaking off the conflict. Abimelekh's ambassador, a Greek-speaking Christian named Mansour, had the gall to protest that I had broken the thirty years' truce to which my father had agreed.

In his presumption, he might as well have been one of my own advisers, not Abimelekh's. "I am not my father!" I shouted to him, as I had to my own bureaucrats. "Unless I so choose, his acts do not bind me. Here, I do not so choose."

Mansour bowed his head. What I had said was simple truth, as any fool could see. Was Abimelekh likely to do exactly as his predecessors had in all things? Of course not! It was a diplomat's trick, an effort to make me feel I was in the wrong. But I did not fall for it.

Having put old Mansour in his place, I turned him over to the diplomats whose job it was to negotiate the fine details of treaties and let him haggle with them. Unlike my father, I reckoned it beneath my dignity to dicker like a tradesman with foreign envoys.

And I had other things on my mind. I had never sired a bastard on any of the serving girls with whom I had dallied, but Eudokia's courses failed and, presently, her belly began to bulge. I puffed up with pride like a pig's bladder. To tell the truth, I had feared my seed was cold within me, and was relieved and delighted to find this not so.

"What shall we name the baby?" Eudokia asked when she was certain she was with child.

I had been thinking about that since we both began to wonder. I would have liked to name a boy Herakleios, after the founder of my dynasty, but that also meant naming him after my uncle, the traitor. "We'll call him Constantine," I said instead. I had not been overfond of my father, but he had been a strong Emperor—and the name would make my mother happy.

Timidly—more timidly than she usually spoke—Eudokia asked, "And if it should be a girl?"

My mind and my hopes being set on getting an heir, I had not worried about what name to give a girl. By chance, Eudokia herself bore the same name as the first Herakleios's first wife, from whom I am descended. "There's always Maria," I said, a careless, indifferent answer that left Eudokia visibly discontented. As I was assotted of her, I did not want that, and so put some thought into my next essay: "What about Epiphaneia? That's the name of the first Herakleios's mother."

"Epiphaneia." Eudokia tasted the name on her tongue. Her brow smoothed. "Yes, it will do."

That problem was easily solved. For my part, whenever I spoke of the child to come, I called it Constantine. Everyone around me took up the habit, as was only natural: an Emperor needs a successor. Sooner than leaving the throne empty, an Emperor might marry three or even four times, I would say.

MYAKES

Brother Elpidios, if you set fire to the book, you won't be able to read the rest of it. What do you mean, you don't care? You've come all this way, you've read lewd things and turned—well, hardly a hair, and now you want to feed the codex to the brazier a leaf at a time? I don't understand, and I'll own as much. Justinian was just talking about what he might have done if—

Heresy? Blasphemy? Brother, if you don't calm down, you'll feed yourself to the brazier a leaf at a time, sounds like. Tell me what's on your— Oh, marrying three or four times. He wasn't talking about it for the sake of fornication, Brother Elpidios, but for the sake of getting an heir. "It is better to marry than to burn," eh?

Not three times? Especially not four times? Not even to keep the Empire from the threat of civil war? You don't think an Emperor would be able to find a priest who would give him a dispensation for something like that? What? You'd break from communion with a priest who did something like that, you'd go into schism? You're a . . . pious man, Brother Elpidios.

In any case, you don't need to burn the book. Justinian married only twice, and canon law says nothing about that, now does it? He was only saying what he thought about a might-have-been that never was. Maybe he was wrong. It wouldn't have been the only time, God knows.

What about *me*, Brother? No, I never married, and yes, maybe I'll burn for it. I was like Justinian before he wed Eudokia, and I didn't have his excuse of being a young pup. I liked women so well, I never settled on any one woman. Life is like that sometimes. It'll get right past you if you don't watch out, and then you look back and you say, "Oh, Lord, what have I done?" Or you say, "What have I missed?"

Do I repent of my sinful ways? I've been a blind monk these past twenty years. If I haven't repented by now, when do you suppose I'd get round to it?

J U S T I N I A N

I had hoped to get even more from the Arabs than we ended up acquiring, but they scored a victory or two of their own to begin balancing ours: they captured Kirkesion, our outpost on the eastern Euphrates, and raided west from Antioch. The arrival of that news made Mansour more stubborn than he had been.

Even so, thanks to the invasion of Armenia I won far better terms from Abimelekh than my father had from Mauias. Mansour agreed to pay us a slave and a high-bred horse for every week of the year, an arrangement much like the former one, but Paul the magistrianos, at the urging of Stephen the Persian, held out for a large increase in the amount of gold we were to receive each year.

When he came to me to report what Mansour had conceded, his eyes were round and staring. "A thousand nomismata a *week*, Emperor!" he exclaimed. "We were getting only three thousand a year before."

"You see?" I said triumphantly. "I knew we'd hurt the deniers of Christ. You may agree to that, Paul, but make certain you don't sound too eager doing it."

"I understand," he said. Then he coughed. "While the payment lies at the heart of the treaty, Emperor, it is not the only provision involved. In Abimelekh's name, Mansour has proposed an arrangement the likes of which I have never heard before; you must weigh its advantages and disadvantages for yourself."

"Tell me, then."

"He says that, while his master Abimelekh commonly controls Armenia and Iberia, our continued raids on those lands and the uprisings they spark create such disruption that he cannot collect the taxes owed him—"

"Good!" I said.

But Paul continued, "Mansour also says we do not bring in enough money from the raids to make them worth our while, either. Through him, Abimelekh proposes that both sides give over warfare in those provinces, that we let the Armenians and Iberians carry on their lives in peace, and that we then tax them and divide evenly the money we receive."

"That *is* a novel suggestion," I admitted, rubbing my chin. Whiskers rasped under my fingers; my beard had thickened to the point that I was letting it grow. "But is Abimelekh sincere in this, or only trying to keep us from raiding Armenia and Iberia?"

"I cannot judge, Emperor," Paul said. "Mansour seems sincere, but he is an ambassador. Did he not seem sincere, he would fail of his purpose."

"Let me think on it," I said, and sent him away. I summoned him again two days later. He having prostrated himself before me, I said, "So Abimelekh says we should stop these attacks because they cost both sides money, eh?"

"That is how Mansour represents the matter, yes," the magistrianos answered, diplomatically cautious.

I pounced: "Will Abimelekh then agree likewise to share the tax revenues from the island of Cyprus, and to order his fleets to leave off ravaging its coastal towns? If he is sincere, he will agree to stop raiding as well as to keep from being raided."

Paul's bow showed respect for my person now, not merely for the imperial office I happened to hold. "I shall put the question to Mansour, exactly as you have put it to me, and shall immediately report to you his response."

That response was in essence no response: on the grounds that the matter of Cyprus was beyond the scope of his instructions and that he dared not decide without having consulted his principal, Mansour felt compelled to write to the misnamed commander of the faithful in Damascus before replying. The letter went east, negotiations pausing while we awaited Abimelekh's reply.

With the impatience of youth, I chafed at the delay. Paul tried to calm me, saying, "Emperor, we remain at peace with the Arabs while the letter and its reply go thither and return hither. A bit of time—"

"A bit of time?" I burst out. "Weeks, a bit?" Waiting seemed unconscionable. Even now, when I have had to wait years to return to my throne, I hurl myself headlong into every enterprise. Then, I daresay, I had no patience whatever.

After what seemed a very long time, a messenger brought Abimelekh's answer to the imperial city. His arrival made the delay seem, if not worthwhile, at least tolerable, for the Arabs' ruler agreed to codominium over Cyprus as well as over Armenia and Iberia. That agreement, I had hoped, would let us complete the treaty, but Mansour, at Abimelekh's urging, raised yet another issue.

Paul the magistrianos brought the matter to me: "Emperor, the commander of the faithful"—almost like Leontios, he was so used to dealing with the Arabs, he did not append *misnamed* to Abimelekh's title—"urges you to take an unusual step in securing the border between his land and making sure no trouble that endangers the peace being arranged between us, which peace, he adds, he will at once assent to upon your agreement to his proposal."

"And that proposal is . . . ?" I asked.

"Emperor, he asks you to remove and resettle the Mardaites, whom he terms brigands and bandits and robbers and thieves, taking them into Roman territory and away from his own."

"You don't like the idea," I said. Though he had continued to speak dispassionately, diplomatically, Paul had made that very clear. By the way his nostrils flared, by the way he quivered ever so slightly, Abimelekh, as far as he was concerned, might have been demanding we serve him up a stew of Christian children as prerequisite for ratifying the treaty.

Having been given permission to speak his mind, he exclaimed, "Emperor, I do not! The Arab's offer is a snare, a delusion, a deception. For a generation and more, the Mardaites have stood like a wall of bronze on the Roman Empire's eastern frontier. Removing them, resettling them, would accomplish nothing but a mutilation of the Empire. Your father used them to keep the Arabs busy close to home so they could not attack us, and you yourself augmented Leontios's campaign by loosing them against Abimelekh at the same time as he invaded Armenia. What we have done before, we shall surely need to do again."

"And yet," I said musingly, "when the Arabs make a treaty, they generally honor it, don't they?—they being our most civilized neighbors." Though plainly reluctant, Paul had to nod. He could scarcely do anything else, since our other neighbors included, then as now, barbarians like the Lombards and the Bulgars, as well as Sklavinian tribes like the Croats and the Serbs, who hardly deserved to be called even barbarous. I went on, "If the deniers of Christ may be relied upon to keep agreements once made, would it not be wise to shift proven fighting men and their families to frontiers where fighting is likelier to break out unexpectedly?"

"It goes against all traditional usage," Paul said, his voice stiff with disapproval.

He spoke as if he were a bishop arguing a theological position by citing the view of the church fathers of old and the text of the Holy

Scriptures. But the Scriptures are divinely inspired, while the Roman Empire's dealings with its neighbors (save insofar as God guards us) are but human, and therefore mutable.

Besides, arguing tradition to a man who has not yet seen twenty years is like arguing chastity to a billy goat: no matter how eloquent you are, he will not listen to you. I said, "Perhaps we can resettle some of the Mardaites elsewhere and leave some of them in place. We truly could use such warlike men in other parts of the Empire. Abimelekh has compromised in these negotiations before; maybe he will again. Put the matter to Mansour as I have stated it."

"But, Emperor—" Paul began to protest anew.

I cut him off. "I *am* the Emperor of the Romans, and as Emperor of the Romans I command you. Obey or abandon your office."

"Yes, Emperor," Paul said, in tones suggesting I had given him over to martyrdom. But obey he did, as all subjects of the Emperor of the Romans must.

MYAKES

Do you know, Brother Elpidios, the things you do sometimes end up causing other things you never would have—never could have—expected. When Justinian ended up shipping those Mardaites to Europe— I daresay he'll have more to tell about that soon enough—one of them was a little brat who then would have been . . . oh, I don't know how old exactly, but not long past the age of making messes in his clothes.

What? Oh, aye, Brother, there would have been a lot of brats like that. The one I'm thinking of in particular, though, came out of Germanikeia in northern Syria. Does that give you enough of a clue? Why, so it must—I hear how you suck in air in surprise. Yes, the Emperor Leo who rules us now was one of those resettled Mardaites.

Who can guess how things would have turned out if Leo and his family had stayed behind in Germanikeia? Who would be Emperor of the Romans now? Would there be an Emperor of the Romans, or would the Arabs have taken Constantinople in that second siege? It would be a different world, one way or another, that's certain. Would God allow such a thing?

No, don't consult the Scriptures *now*, Brother Elpidios. It will wait. You have Justinian's book in front of you. Read that instead.

While we were awaiting Abimelekh's reply to Mansour's letter asking if he would accept partial rather than complete resettlement of the Mardaites, Eudokia went into labor. Looking back on these leaves, I realize I have scanted my wife, saying little about her since the time we were wed. I can offer no better defense than saying quiet contentment leaves little to record.

My mother brought me the news. "I have attended to everything," she said. "I have summoned the midwife, I have summoned Peter the physician, though God forbid he be necessary, I have summoned the patriarch to bless the baby and to exorcise the evil spirits that attend a birth, and I have ordered a girdle brought from the monastery of the Virgin to make the labor easier."

I bowed to her, as if I were a servant. "And what is left for me to do?"

"Wait," she snapped. "Pray. When the time comes, receive your son or daughter in your arms and say what a beautiful child it is. It won't be—newborns are of an odd color, and their heads are apt to be misshapen. Say it anyhow. Eudokia will expect it of you." Having outlined her plan of campaign and given me her orders, she went off to help Eudokia through her trial.

I waited. I prayed. Those palling, I called for wine. Eventually, I fell asleep. I woke in darkness. My head ached. It was the eighth hour of the night, two thirds of the way from sunset back to sunrise. I called for more wine, and some bread to go with it. Sopping the bread in the wine, I made a nighttime breakfast of it. I prayed some more. I waited some more.

Presently, I summoned a serving woman and told her to bring me back word from the birthing chamber. When she returned, she said, "The physician—Peter is his name, yes?—is busy in there, and shouted at me to go away. I told him you had sent me, and he told me to go away anyhow." Her eyes were wide and astonished: Peter had defied me. "He was most rude."

I hurled across the room the heel of bread on which I had been nibbling. That Peter had shouted was of small moment to me. That he was busy in there, though, made me tremble with fear.

On the one hand, it is against all custom for a husband to enter the chamber where his wife is giving birth. On the other hand, that which is pleasing to the Emperor has the force of law, as the jurists who served my namesake put it. And if I scandalized the midwife, I expected a few nomismata would put things right.

Serving women fled gabbling before me when they saw where I was going. I sighed. I would have to put things right with them, too. I was about to round the last corner when I heard the high, thin, indignant cry of a newborn babe.

The midwife was holding the baby. It had already been washed and swaddled in woolen wrappings. She nodded to me; thanks to the servants, she had known I was coming. "Emperor, you have a daughter," she said, and held the baby out to me. "What will you name her?"

"Epiphaneia," I said shortly. I did not take her from the midwife. Instead, I started for the chamber in which she had been born. The midwife moved to put herself between me and the door. We stared at each other. "My wife," I said. "Eudokia."

"Pray for her," the midwife said, and made the sign of the cross. "It was a hard birth, and she began to bleed. I could not make it stop. I wasted no time calling in the physician, Emperor. Your mother was there—she's in there yet—and she will tell you the same. I know Peter; he is better than most of the butchers who go by the name of doctor. But there is only so much to be done—" She held out the baby again. "You have a fine daughter here, strong and healthy."

"Stand aside," I snarled, and in my fright and fury I would have struck her had she dared disobey. That she did not; she scuttled aside like a frightened mouse. But, at the same time as I set my hand on the latch, a great burst of lamentation came from inside the chamber. I knew my mother's cries of anguish: how could I not, having heard her mourn my brother and my father? Mixed with them were Peter's vile but helpless curses. Death had beaten him again.

Numbly, my hand fell away from the door. As if from very far away, I heard myself say, "*Kyrie eleison. Christe eleison.*" I felt as if I had been rolled in ice: cold and stinging at the same time. A woman who lies down in childbed risks her life, no less than a man going off to war. We men do not think on this, not until—or unless—we are are forcibly reminded.

The door to the birthing chamber opened. Out came my mother, her face haggard and drawn. When she saw me, she cast herself into my arms, tears flooding down her cheeks. "Too much, God!" she screamed. "Too much. How can You let one person, one family, suffer so much?"

I had no tears, not yet. Those would come later, when I started to believe. Now . . . now Peter the physician came out. He had washed his hands and arms, but Eudokia's blood, still fresh and red, splotched his tunic; on looking more closely, I saw it under his fingernails as well. Behind him lay a still form covered by a sheet. The sheet was stained with blood, too.

Noting the direction in which my eyes had moved, he made haste to close the door after himself. Then he stood very straight, as if he were a sentry acknowledging a general's presence. "I failed you, Emperor," he said baldly. "She hemorrhaged. I did everything I could to stop it. Nothing worked." He spread his hands—*his bloodstained hands*, I thought, although, as I have said, the only blood physically on them lay under his nails. "Do what you will with me."

It occurred to me then that I could order him slain, as Alexander had the physician who could not save his beloved companion Hephaistion. The temptation, the desire, were very strong. That must have shown, for Peter's face, already pale, went paler. "Get out of my sight," I said, my voice thick with the fury I strove to hold in.

Peter, if not wise enough to save either my father or my wife, had the sense to obey me. His withdrawal was the next thing to headlong flight. He did not show himself before me for some weeks thereafter. By then, my grief having lost its edge, I was willing to suffer him to live.

My mother took Epiphaneia from the midwife. The baby made noises that put me in mind of an unhappy kitten. As the midwife had, my mother held her out to me. "Take your daughter," she said.

But I backed away as if she had offered me a viper. "No," I said. "If it weren't for her, Eudokia would be, would be . . ." Then I felt myself start to cry, although I had not willed it. I tried to stop. I could not. I stood there in the hallway, tears streaming down my face, my hands balled in useless fists at my sides.

My mother gave the midwife back the baby. She took me in her arms. We clung to each other and wailed to a Heaven that had proved itself deaf to us. My brother, my father, my wife, all young, all stolen from me in the span of four years. To this day I pray God forgives me for the blasphemies I loosed against Him in the madness of my grief.

The door to the chamber where Eudokia had died opened once more. Out came the ecumenical patriarch, looking as grim and mournful as Peter the physician had. Thinking back on it, seeing the man's face once more in my mind, I recall that the patriarch was Paul, not Theodore, who had suffered a fit of apoplexy and expired while conducting the divine liturgy a little more than a year after I restored him to his throne: not the worst way for a bishop to be called to God.

Paul must have heard my vain, useless, senseless railing against the Lord of all. Being a kindly man, he forbore to mention it, saying only, "Because of her great virtue, your wife is surely in heaven even as we speak." He made the sign of the cross.

I remembered myself enough to do the same. "I am glad you were here to give her unction," I said.

"As I am," he said gravely, "even if I was summoned for another purpose." He turned to the midwife and pointed to tiny Epiphaneia. "But you are blessed with a fine and, God willing, healthy daughter to remind you of her."

"Get out!" I shouted. Had my mother not restrained me, I would have set on him. But she held me back, and Paul, shock and fear both on his face, half staggered away from me. "Get out of here!" I cried again. "I never want to have anything to do with her—never, do you hear me? She killed my wife. She killed Eudokia. If it weren't for her . . ." I dissolved in tears once more.

Paul crossed himself again. "You are distraught, Emperor," he said, which was certainly true. "When you are more fully yourself, I trust you will change your mind. You cannot blame the child for what is surely God's will."

But I did blame Epiphaneia, and I never changed my mind. I could not stand to be near her; she reminded me too much of what I had lost. And even the marriage I eventually tried to arrange for her was as much a punishment, a revenge, as anything else.

Having already written overmuch in these pages of funerals, I shall say little here of Eudokia's. She was laid to rest in the church of the Holy Apostles, in a sarcophagus of rose-pink marble. May God have had mercy upon her. If I am lucky enough to be forgiven the many sins staining my soul, I shall see her again in heaven.

With Eudokia I buried, I think, a great part of my own youth. It is, I daresay, no coincidence that shortly after this time I summoned to the palace Cyrus the engraver and ordered him to mint nomismata of a new type, showing me as the man I was rather than the beardless youth I had been. The portrait he produced for these new nomismata had all his usual skill. I approved it, and the goldpieces were duly struck. Yet it left me dissatisfied in a way I could not define even to myself. I was searching for something else, but would not find it for another couple of years.

MYAKES

Well, Brother Elpidios, I have to say Justinian is right when he talks about himself so. Up till Eudokia died, he could be playful every now and again, but not afterwards, not for years and not until a lot of water had flowed under the bridge. When he lost her, he lost something special, something he couldn't find anywhere else.

Me, Brother? Yes, I liked Eudokia pretty well. Can't say I was what you'd call close to her. That wouldn't have been fitting, not with another man's wife. But she treated me—she treated all the excubitores—like flesh and blood, not like part of the furniture. She was a soldier's daughter herself, you'll remember. That probably helped.

What? Did I upbraid and exhort Justinian to pay poor Epiphaneia more heed? You don't upbraid and exhort the Emperor of the Romans. I mentioned her once or twice. Every time I did, he gave me a look fit to freeze my marrow. I'm not stupid. I got the idea, and shut up.

J U S T I N I A N

Emperor of the Romans though I was, the world did not stop turning because of my sorrow. Abimelekh eventually responded to Mansour's question. Paul the magistrianos brought me that response, along with Mansour's graceful expression of consolation and condolence, which I listened to although I did not much want to hear it.

"Mansour says Abimelekh says he will accept a partial resettlement of the Mardaites . . . provided it includes at least twenty thousand men of fighting age," Paul reported, his tone going from sympathetic to cold and sardonic in the space of a sentence.

"Good heavens," I said, "he wants us to take away the substance and leave behind only the shadow. I doubt the Mardaites have more than twenty-five thousand men under arms all along our border with the Arabs."

"Exactly so, Emperor," the magistrianos replied. Had I not been Emperor of the Romans and he, like everyone else within the Empire, my servant, I have no doubt that, instead of agreeing, he would have said *I told you so.*

"He asks too much," I said. "He is the one who wants this treaty, not I. Tell Mansour the war goes on if that number does not come down." Paul bowed and departed. I had no doubt he would convey my words exactly as I intended, for I meant every one of them. I was ready—I was more than ready—to hurl Leontios into Armenia once more. If Abimelekh wanted to avoid more war, he could meet my terms.

And the numbers did come down. Paul and Mansour haggled like a couple of old women trying to get the better of each other over the price of a sack of beans. At last, Paul came to me, reporting, "He is down to fourteen thousand, Emperor. I had hoped for twelve, but—"

"Tell him twelve thousand or war," I said. "If you hoped for that, we shall have it."

And we did have it. Faced with that bald choice, Mansour capitulated. Paul and Mansour having drawn up the terms of the treaty, I signed two parchments in scarlet ink and affixed my seal to each of them. Paul then accompanied Mansour to Damascus, where Abimelekh, observing virtually the same ceremonies I had, also signed and sealed both copies of the treaty. He kept one and sent the other back to this imperial city with the magistrianos, to whom he had shown every honor while Paul was in Damascus.

Also accompanying Paul on the road back from Damascus was the first year's payment of the new tribute: fifty-two thousand gold nomismata, more than seven hundred pounds of gold. Some of the coins were old Roman mintings, dating from before the days when the Arabs stole Syria and Palestine and Egypt from us. Some were newer, obtained from us in trade. And some were their own issues, imitating ours. But all were of the same weight and purity, as the treaty had specified. Seeing them, I felt like Midas in the pagan myth.

The treaty having been completed, both Abimelckh and I sent messengers to the chieftains of the Mardaites, ordering them to assemble at Sebasteia, in the eastern part of the military district of the Armeniacs, for resettlement. Several of the messengers did not return. Some of them were returned to officials of the misnamed commander of the faithful and to my own officers—in pieces. The Mardaites were convinced the orders they had received were a trick on Abimelekh's part to lure them from their mountain fastnesses and destroy them. And, I daresay, had the Arab thought of such a ploy, he would have used it.

Paul the magistrianos and several of my other advisers were almost jubilant on account of the Mardaites' intransigence: if my plans failed, they would regain lost influence. But I did not intend to fail. Summoning Paul and the others, I said, "I will travel to Sebasteia myself. If the Mardaites know I am there, they will not be afraid to go there themselves. Let word of my journey go forth."

Word went forth, and, in due course, so did I. Up till then, I had never traveled far from Constantinople. Oh, I had been out of the imperial city now and again, once or twice visiting Philaretos by the Long Wall and often crossing the Bosporos to hunt in Asia, but my life had revolved around the palace, the court, and the city.

I was anxious to leave for more reasons than one. Not only did I want to see more of the Empire I ruled, but I was also eager to leave Constantinople behind for a while, to escape the memory of Eudokia.

And so, riding my own horse rather than traveling in a cart or horse-drawn litter, I set off across Anatolia for Sebasteia.

Until you have seen more than your own home, you do not understand even that home, for you have nothing with which to compare it. So I discovered in this journey. I knew Constantinople was the greatest city in the Roman Empire. Knowing that, I expected other cities to be very much like *the* city, but smaller. It was not so, I saw. Most of the towns along the way to Sebasteia were hardly more than fortresses, strongpoints from which to defend the local countryside. Ruins around the walls said many had once been more than that, but how can a town survive, how can its hinterland feed it, when it is continually oppressed by war, as the towns of Anatolia had been since the Persian invasions in the reign of Phokas a long lifetime before?

So much of the countryside, both in the coastal lowlands and in the plateau that makes up the heart of Anatolia, was also all but empty. Save for the soldiers settled on the land in the military districts in exchange for their service in time of need, broad tracts of what should have been good crop- and pastureland had no farmers or herders on them. Who would want to, who would be mad enough to, work land that would surely be despoiled by an invader in a few years' time?

But the land needed to be worked, for the sake of the towns and for the sake of the fisc. The Mardaites whom I would meet in Sebasteia would not be nearly enough to fill these broad territories, and, in any case, I had more urgent need for them in Europe. Still, I resolved that, if ever I had more folk to resettle, I would put them in Anatolia.

Sebasteia lies just north of the Halys River, a dusty fortress of a place much like the other dusty fortresses I had seen. But when I was riding down the road from Sebastopolis and Siara and first drew near Sebasteia, I cried out in wonder, saying, "Have they given their fields over to flowers?" For the precincts surrounding the town were awash with bright colors, reds, and blues and golds and greens, as splendid a sight, and as unexpected a splendor, as I have ever found.

They were not flowers. They were, as I discovered on coming closer, the tents of the Mardaites. Twelve thousand warriors and their families are not just an army; they are a city. And all that city did me honor as I rode through it, men in white robes and others in rusty mailshirts prostrating themselves in the dirt and shouting my praises in Greek, in Arabic, in Armenian, and Persian, and, for all I know, in other tongues as well.

Sebasteia's garrison had been beefed up by summoning some of the soldiers off their fields in the Armeniac military district. Even so, the local commander, a certain Basil, was nervous. "They outnumber me, Emperor," he said. "They outnumber me by a lot. If they want this place, they can take it."

"Why on earth would they want it?" I said, very much as if I meant it. "The only reason they have come here is to meet me before they resettle them. We'll invite the chiefs into the city and feed them full of wine and mutton. We'll feed the warriors full of wine and mutton outside the walls, and give their brats candied figs. Everyone will stay happy, and then, a few at a time, everyone will start on the long road west. No one will even think of doing anything else."

He gave me an odd look, one I did not fully understand until later. I did not realize then how, while I took intrigue utterly for granted, having grown to manhood at its very heart, the court, others, especially others far from Constantinople, had to have things spelled out for them. Very well: the Mardaites could, if they so desired, take Sebasteia. We could do nothing about that, not in a military sense, for the time being. The key, then, was making sure they did not so desire—that, in fact, the idea of taking Sebasteia never so much as entered their minds.

How to do that? But putting extra men on the walls, by having the garrison prepare to sell its lives dear if attacked? What better way to show the Mardaites our secret fear, to plant the idea of attacking in their minds when it might not even have been there before? They were warriors; they could smell weakness.

We gave them nothing to smell. By proceeding as if everything was perfectly normal, we made certain everything stayed perfectly normal. I got drunk with their chiefs, and listened to stories of throat-cuttings and town-burnings all along the border, mostly told in a vile Greek I had trouble following. Even when I could not follow, I kept smiling, and promised them many throats to cut and many towns to burn in the places they were going. I promised no one would collect taxes from them for five years. I promised myself I would make sure the wine was better at the next such carouse, but the Mardaites did not need to know about that.

Band by band, a few hundred at a time, they set out west along the highway back to Constantinople. By the time four or five bands had departed, the ones who were left were a far smaller threat to the town or the garrison. Basil looked at me as he might have at a wizard. I looked at him with something like pity, doubting any chronicler would ever remember his name.

I soon headed west across the same highway myself. When in the course of my journey I came to Ankyra, about halfway between Sebasteia and the imperial city, I passed the night in the fortress there. Indeed, the capital of the military district of the Opsikion is little more than its fortress these days: the citadel, a strong rampart with pentagonal towers, sat on its hill overlooking a bathhouse, grand public buildings, several churches, and many, many houses—all dusty ruins, destroyed first in the Persian invasions and then in the onslaughts of the followers of the false prophet. As at so many stops on my journey, the contrast between what had been and what was now saddened me.

At the feast that night, a black-haired serving girl made certain my wine cup was never empty. When, wobbling as I walked, I went back to the chamber in which I was to sleep, I found her waiting under the covers for me. I started to order her out of the room, having had no congress with women since Eudokia died.

Before I could speak, though, she flipped back the blanket, the flickering lamplight showing she was naked. "Come," she said. "It is only a night." Her accent, absurdly, reminded me of Myakes'.

Had I had less to drink I think I should have sent her away, her abundantly displayed charms notwithstanding. But "wine is a mocker, strong drink is raging." My lust raged in me, and I had not the will to withstand it. Throwing off my robes, I got into the bed as naked as the girl and took her with the light still burning.

She was gone when I woke the next morning. My head pained me, as did my conscience, fornication being a sin in the eyes of God. But, oddly, along with the guilt I also knew a curious sense of release, as if I had taken a long step toward accepting that Eudokia's death was in the past, and irrevocable.

Those two feelings warred in me until I returned to the imperial palace. No sooner had I arrived than my mother thrust Epiphaneia in my face, exclaiming, "See how much she has grown while you were gone? See how she can smile now? Smile for your father, little pretty one."

Ephiphaneia smiled a toothless smile. I recoiled from it as from a demon; seeing the baby still reminded me unbearably of her mother's fate. My own mother began to cry. I pushed past her, and past my daughter, calling loudly for wine as I went. I stayed drunk for two days and bedded three maidservants. Yes, a sin—two sins—but sins that pushed aside pain.

MYAKES

H e was a man, Brother Elpidios, and not a perfect one. You'll notice he admits he was a sinner. I've known a whole great swarm of men, out in the world and here in the monastery, too, who, if you listen to them talk, never did one wrong thing in all their born days. Well, maybe so, but maybe not, too. I haven't heard of a whole lot of people walking on water lately. Have you?

No, I wasn't along on this trip to Sebasteia. I'd come down with a flux of the bowels, and for a while there I wondered if I was going to go the same way Constantine had. I ended up getting better instead, but I was flat on my back for more than a month.

I'll tell you something, though. If I had been along, I'd have arranged to put a girl in Justinian's bed. That was the medicine he needed, sure as sure.

Yes, I'm a wretched reprobate. God will punish me. No doubt you're right about that, Brother. God has already punished me in this world, and He has all eternity to do as He likes with me in the world to come.

But I don't have all eternity here. I don't know how much time I do have, but I'd doubt it's a whole lot. I'd like to hear some more of the words Justinian left behind, if you don't mind too much.

JUSTINIAN

I had peace with the followers of the false prophet, and had it on better terms than my father had managed to wring from them. Not only that, but Abimelekh faced yet another uprising against his rule. My judgment was that my eastern frontier was as safe as it would ever be. I called up the cavalry from the military districts of Anatolia and ordered the horsemen to cross into Europe, as my father had in his ill-fated campaign against the Bulgars.

I intended to campaign against the Bulgars, too, and sent their emissaries away empty-handed when they came to collect the tribute to which my father had agreed. But the campaign I had in mind would not merely put the Bulgars in their place; it would also deal with the Sklavenoi, some of whom were under the control of the Bulgars and some of whom, in their revolting freedom, plundered Roman settlements all on their own. The suffering the land south of the Danube had endured made that of Anatolia seem as nothing beside it.

As had my father and grandfather and great-great-grandfather before me, I took the field in person. If the soldiers would not perform well under my eye, they would never perform well. And the Sklavenoi were so barbarous, I was certain they could produce no leaders with the wit to stand against us.

They were also divided among themselves, each little Sklavinia existing in a state of squalid independence, as often at war with its neighbors as with the Roman Empire. Like a foolish man in a fight who covers up where he has been hit rather than trying to anticipate where he will be hit next, they (or at least those not dominated by the Bulgars, who had better sense) were not likely to come to the aid of one another.

I had been out to the Long Wall before, but no farther. Philaretos, the count of the Long Wall, greeted me at Selymbria, the town anchoring the wall to the Sea of Marmara. I had not seen him since Eudokia's funeral. "God grant that my granddaughter thrive," he said, "for she is all I have left by which to remember the girl."

"God grant it," I echoed, and said no more. He made the sign of the cross, thinking me pious. But what I meant was more on the order of, *God had better grant it, for I intend to have nothing to do with it.*

The Long Wall is different from that of the imperial city. Rather than alternating courses of brick and stone, it is built of hard, pinkish cement with chunks of brick embedded in the cement. It also, I must sadly say, differs from Constantinople's wall in its effectiveness, or lack thereof. Where, along with the protection of God, Constantinople's wall has kept the city inviolate since it was built, barbarians have repeatedly penetrated the Long Wall and plundered the suburbs it was meant to protect. Stretching more than thirty miles from the Sea of Marmara to the Black Sea, the Long Wall was too long to garrison adequately.

Still, though, it did offer the regions nearest the imperial city some protection. Passing beyond it, I felt I was leaving safety and entering land that, while nominally under the rule of the Roman Empire, was in fact detached from Romania. I aimed to make Roman rule real there once again, and nominal no more.

Had I wanted to push the army straight down the Via Egnatia, the military highway of the Romans for the past eight hundred years and more, I could have been in Thessalonike very soon. But I had planned a campaign, not a military parade, and so in search of Sklavenoi the army plunged off the highway and into the forested, sometimes marshy valleys that lay to the north.

I prayed at the church of St. Glykeria in Herakleia (or, as the antiquarians call it, Perinthos), and had my prayer answered the very next day, the army flushing out several little Sklavinian farming villages north of the town. The barbarians seemed utterly astonished at the presence of Roman soldiers in land they obviously believed to be theirs.

None of them spoke Greek. I had their headmen haled before me and asked them, "Would you sooner die or obey me?" I thought at first that my interpreter had suffered a coughing fit, but he was merely translating the question into their hideous, guttural dialect. Their answers were as full of choking, wheezing noises.

"They say they will obey, Emperor," the interpreter said.

"Good. I thought that would be a choice even a Sklavinian could understand," I said. "Since they say they will obey, tell them I am going to resettle their whole clan or tribe or whatever they call themselves in Anatolia. Tell them they can farm there and pay taxes to the fisc and furnish us with soldiers when we need them."

"Emperor, I can tell them they will farm," the interpreter said. "I can tell them they will give us soldiers. But I cannot tell them they will pay us taxes. Their language has no words for such things."

"What? They don't know about taxes?" I threw back my head and laughed. "Very well. Tell the poor barbarians what you can. They'll learn about the other soon enough. The officials of the fisc will give them detailed lessons, I have no doubt."

A small escort of Romans led the Sklavenoi down the Via Egnatia and then east toward Constantinople, whence they would cross into the empty lands of Anatolia. I allowed them no more than they could carry in their hands. Considering how little they had, I did not greatly deprive them.

The season being summer, the millet and barley in their fields were too far from ripe to feed my army. They did, however, have a good store of grain hidden in underground pits, as those familiar with their habits had foretold. We added that to our own supply, and our horses had good grazing in the fields.

It soon became clear that, although we had captured their villages, we had not sent all of the Sklavenoi off to the imperial city for resettlement. Some of them must have escaped into the woods and run off to warn their fellow tribesmen, for the next Sklavinian settlements we came upon were deserted, not only the people but also the livestock being gone.

I required no training in logic to realize the Sklavenoi from the abandoned villages were in turn surely letting more barbarians know we were on the march. A young officer familiar with the Sklavenoi, Bardanes the son of the patrician Nikephoros, confirmed my impression—not, I say, that it needed much confirmation. "Emperor, the next ones we meet will resist us," he said.

"No doubt you're right, Philippikos," I replied, and he beamed at me: he preferred that thoroughly Greek name to the Armenian one his father had given him as a sign of his ancestry. I went on, "I trust the army will be ready to meet their onslaught man to man, shield to shield."

"In an open fight, we'd smash them to bits," he said. "They aren't likely to give us an open fight, though. They'd rather spring ambushes, and"—he looked around—"this country is made for that sort of thing."

He was right, the land being rough and broken and woody, the roads leading north off the Via Egnatia no better than cattle tracks and, now that we had moved a couple of days' journey inland, sometimes disappearing altogether. He was also right about the Sklavenoi. As our horsemen, having no other choice, went up a game path in single file, javelins flew out of the woods and wounded one of them and two horses. After that, I dismounted some of the soldiers and sent them through the undergrowth to either side of the road. The Sklavenoi shot arrows, some poisoned, at them, but they caught and killed a good number of barbarians, too. Our advance through the Sklavinias continued.

Not all the Sklavinian chiefs and petty kings fled on hearing of our approach. Some yielded themselves and all their people up to us. I resettled them just as I had the Sklavenoi we had captured and overcome in war, although I allowed them to take along their livestock and carts and wagons filled with their belongings, the better to start their new lives in Anatolia.

You could never tell what would happen in any particular little Sklavinia. All depended on the will of the chieftain who ruled that patch of ground. Rather more of them, I think, chose to fight than to surrender. Their poisoned arrows were weapons not to be despised. Several of our men died from them, while others were mutilated: the sole cure the physicians knew was to cut away the flesh around the arrowhead to keep the venom from spreading throughout the victim's system. The physicians gave these poor fellows great draughts of wine infused with poppy juice before plying their scalpels, but screams still echoed through the gloomy forests of Thrace.

A certain Neboulos was kinglet of the largest and strongest Sklavinia not under the control of the Bulgars; it lay north and east of Thessalonike. This Sklavinian had the arrogance to send envoys to me warning me not to enter the territory he reckoned his. "You do that, he kill all your men, all your horses," one of these men said in bad Greek.

"He will have his chance," I said.

"He kill you, Emperor, in particular especial," the envoy warned redundantly.

"He will have his chance," I repeated, and sent the Sklavenoi away with the message that Neboulos could either yield or face the weight of Roman wrath.

That evening, our army camped by a stream with a marsh and reeds on the far bank. More reeds grew on the western bank, where we were encamped. I took my horse down to the edge of the stream to water it and to get a drink for myself, having been in the saddle all day. Nikephoros's son Bardanes (or, again to use his own coining, Philippikos) went down to the stream alongside me, intent on the same errands. Stooping to fill a cup of water for himself, he suddenly froze in place. Then he pointed to one of the reeds that seemed to me no different from any of the others. "Do you see that, Emperor?" he asked quietly.

"Yes, I see it," I said. "But what—?"

Bardanes did not answer, not in words. Instead, he reached out and yanked the reed out of the water. It had, I saw to my surprise, neither roots nor leaves, being merely a length of stem. A moment later, I got another, larger, surprise. A Sklavinian popped to the surface where the reed had been. Bardanes had dropped it and snatched up his bow. I quickly drew my sword.

At Bardanes' peremptory command in the Sklavinian language, the man came up onto the bank of the stream. Water dripped from his long yellow hair and from his beard. He was naked but for a sword belt. Bardanes spoke again. The Sklavinian loosed the belt and let it fall. A couple of the excubitores came hurrying up to take him away. He went off between them, careless of his unclothed state.

"How did you know he was lurking there?" I asked Bardanes.

"Emperor, hiding in the water is a favorite Sklavinian trick," he answered. Picking up the reed, he showed me its entire length had been hollowed out. "They'll stay down there for hours, even a day, at a time, breathing through one of these, waiting till their enemies go away. But you can usually spot them, because they cut the ends of the reeds straight across, where a naturally broken reed"—he pointed to a couple—"has a jagged end."

"Cunning," I said. "Barbarously cunning. With tricks like that, no wonder they've given us Romans so much trouble down through the years."

"I'm glad I spied this one," Bardanes said. "Who knows what mischief he might have done had you come here alone?"

"Who indeed?" I said. "Thank you, Philippikos."

MYAKES

So that was how Bardanes Philippikos caught Justinian's eye, was it? I didn't happen to be one of the excubitores who came and got the Sklavinian, so I couldn't have told you the tale for certain. He saved Justinian's life, eh? Or he made Justinian think he had, which amounts to the same thing.

Philippikos turned out to be more dangerous than any dripping Sklavinian, to Justinian and to me, but that tale is a long way down the road as yet. We haven't even got to Thessalonike, have we? No, I didn't think so. Still a good ways to go yet.

JUSTINIAN

On our entering the country Neboulos claimed as his own, opposition from the Sklavenoi did become fiercer, as the men he had sent to me warned it would. Bands of barbarians, some armed with shields and javelins, would burst from the woods and undergrowth and rush the lines of Roman horsemen, shouting horribly. When we stood fast, they would melt away as quickly as they had advanced. I do not care to think what might have happened had we shown flight during any of these attacks: that would have fanned the fire of Sklavinian impetuosity, where in fact our steady demeanor damped that fire.

Skirmishes though these were, in them we both gave and received wounds. In them, too, I learned hard lessons about the aftermath of battle, where the cries most commonly are not, as the poets would make you think, the exultant shouts of the victors but the groans and screams of hurt men from both sides.

I went with the physicians as they did what they could to repair the damage edged metal had wrought. But, though churchly law forbids it as murder, the kindest thing a physician can do for a Sklavinian with his guts spilled out on the ground is to cut his throat and let him die at once, and, while cauterizing the stump for a Roman who has lost a hand may perhaps, if God so wills, save his life, the fresh torment the hot irons inflict will make him wish for a time it had not.

After the first small battlefield, I was simply numb with disbelief. After the second, I drank myself into a stupor to keep from thinking about what I had seen. After the third, I summoned Myakes to my pavilion.

When he came in, he had a blood-soaked bandage on his left arm.

"You're hurt," I exclaimed. That he could be hurt made the horrors of battle even more immediate than they had been: if such a thing could happen to him, it might even happen to me.

But he shrugged off the wound, saying, "You should see the damned Sklavinian." His voice was thick and rather slurred; he had had some of the physicians' poppy-laced wine to ease his pain while his injuries were sewn up.

"How can you go into a fight, knowing something like this or worse is liable to happen to you?" I asked, meaning not that alone but also, *How can you obey the orders of superiors who send you into fights?*

He shrugged again. "You can die of the plague, you can cough yourself to death, you can get a flux and die of that the way your father did, the way I almost did last year, you can be smashed in an earthquake or burn up in a fire, you can get a scratch and have it fester and rot. You go into a battle, either you win or you have a fair chance of dying quicker and easier than a lot of other ways."

I had not looked on the matter from that point of view. Having lost my brother, my father, and my wife in quick succession, I thought of death as something to be avoided, averted, shunned. Myakes' way made more sense. Sooner or later, I *would* die, try as I would to flee my fate. Furthermore, as a Christian, I knew in my heart the world to come was far preferable to the one in which I passed my bodily existence.

Making the sign of the cross, I said, "You are wiser than I." I doubt I ever sounded humbler than at that moment.

"Me?" Myakes first stared, then started to laugh—yes, he was drunk. "There's a joke for you, Emperor. All I am is a half-bright soldier who wasn't smart enough to keep a howling barbarian from taking a slice out of him. If that's wise, Christ have mercy on the foolish." He crossed himself too.

Superficially, he was right. But that did not make me wrong. He accepted the world as it was and did his best within those confines. I have often wished my nature were more easygoing. But it is not, and I have come to accept that.

We pressed deeper into the shadowy realm Neboulos had built up within the confines of the Roman Empire. I say shadowy not only because his rule had no right to exist, but sprang like a toadstool from the shadow of Roman weakness, and also because, in the forests the Sklavenoi infested, we were literally in shadow so much of the time that we once got east and west confused and cried out in fright to discover the sun, as we thought, rising in the west one morning. But it was no prodigy, only our own error.

Captured Sklavenoi told us where Neboulos made his headquarters. When—after some fumbling and mistakes, as I have said—we came to that valley, we found what was not quite a town and not quite a nomad encampment like that of the Bulgars which my father had assailed. The Sklavinian kinglet had circled the huts of his people with a number of wagons, making a fortified position of no small strength.

From inside those wagons, and from behind them, and from below them, the Sklavenoi howled defiance at the Roman host. Brandishing their javelins, they screamed what had to be bloodcurdling threats in their revolting dialect. And, indeed, had we had to storm our way past those wagons, it might well have cost us dear.

But the Sklavenoi, in their barbaric ignorance, did not yet fully understand all that facing Romans entailed. We won our wars not merely thanks to the courage of our soldiers (though when that was lacking we failed, as my father had against the Bulgars) but also by using the wits God gave us. And so, seeing the wagons full of fair-haired savages, I said, "Let the liquid fire be brought forth."

Acting on my command, my officers determined the best way to employ the fearsome fire that had routed the followers of the false prophet when they sought to capture Constantinople. The wind was blowing out of the west, so they chose to use the fire-projecting tubes and bellows on the western side of the Sklavinian position, to let the breeze spread the flames it created. The one drawback to the liquid fire was that it had to be projected onto the target to be burnt from a range far shorter than bowshot. The corresponding advantage, this first time, was that the Sklavenoi would not know what we were doing with the fire until we had done it, by which time it would be too late.

To distract them further, a large contingent of cavalry from the Anatolian military districts delivered a spirited attack against the eastern side of their wagon wall. If our men broke in there, well and good. If not, they would at least help distract the barbarians from the truly important point.

Distract them they did; through the gaps between wagons, we saw hide-clad barbarians carrying throwing spears and bows and arrows rushing toward what looked to be the most threatened area. At my signal, the excubitores advanced on foot against the barrier the Sklavenoi had thrown up, their shields protecting the relative handful of artisans who trundled along the carts that carried the liquid fire and the bellows and bronze tubes through which it was projected.

My greatest fear had been that the Sklavenoi would swarm out from their wagons and try to overwhelm the excubitores by weight of numbers. But we had cavalry on either wing to protect the imperial guards, and they, with their mailshirts, helms, and shields, and with their spears and swords, had to be foes to make unarmored barbarians think twice about engaging in close combat with them.

M Y A K E S

If Justinian was nervous, Brother Elpidios, I have to tell you I was about ten times worse than that. The Sklavenoi were screeching and shrieking louder than anything you can imagine. Boys—maybe girls, too, for all I know—kept running up and bringing them bundles of javelins and whole great sheaves of arrows.

I was in the front rank as we marched up to the wagons. *That's* what I got for being an officer, that and a fancier shield and a helmet with a tuft of red-dyed horsehair sticking up out of the top. So the Sklavenoi didn't want to kill me just on account of I was there, the way they did your ordinary excubitores. They especially wanted to kill me because I was close to 'em and I looked important. Lucky me.

By the time we got near enough their wagons for the clever lads with the liquid fire to do their work, my fancy shield had so many javelins and arrows stuck in it, it looked like it was practicing to be a hedgehog. One javelin hit me square in the chest, but my mailshirt—Mother of God, thank you—didn't let it through. And a couple of arrows clattered off my helmet, too.

Some good men weren't so lucky. My chum Anastasios, who'd eaten beans with me ever since I joined the imperial guards, took an arrow right in the eye. Like I told Justinian, not the worst way to go. He never knew what hit him, anyhow—that one would have killed him whether it was poisoned or not. And he was far from the only one who fell, too.

The biggest thing we had going for us was that the Sklavenoi didn't know—

What? Justinian says the same thing? All right, then, tell me what he says. He'll probably put it better than I could, anyway.

Our greatest advantage, as I have said, was that the barbarians, being ignorant of the liquid fire, did not fully grasp why this body of foot soldiers was approaching the wooden rampart from which they were conducting their defense. Like the Achaeans when the warriors of Troy reached their beached ships, they aimed to keep fighting against us as fiercely as they could.

But we Romans had rather better incendiary tools at our disposal than our Trojan ancestors had known in that earlier age. A trumpet blared a command. The excubitores in the front rank stepped hastily to one side or the other, exposing the tubes and bellows and the men who worked them.

Eager as a small boy, I watched events unfold. Truly, I felt swept back to my own boyhood, having last seen liquid fire employed against a foe in the final year of the Arabs' siege of the imperial city. "Now!" I shouted to the military engineers. "Burn them now!"

They could not have heard me, not from so far away through the din of battle. And the Sklavenoi were showering them with missiles of every sort. Without the protection of the excubitores' shields along with their own, several of them were struck down in quick succession. But, having prepared for that case as well as every other, they brought up replacements and went on with their work.

Torchbearers sprang out in front of the mouth of each of the half-dozen bronze tubes aimed at the enemy. A javelin knocked one of them down, but a brave military engineer snatched up his torch in the nick of time and held it to the tube's mouth. Thus all six streams of flame were projected together against the wagons of the Sklavenoi.

Great, thick clouds of stinking black smoke rose from the streams of flame. The barbarians' shrieks of horror were as sweet as honey, sweet as wine, in my ears. I shouted with glee to watch some of the heathen Sklavenoi, caught in the fire, twist and writhe and burn, gaining for themselves in this world a tiny foretaste of the eternal flames of hell they would assuredly know in the next.

They were brave. Some of them, careless of our soldiers, rushed out between burning wagons to pour buckets of water on the liquid fire to try to douse it. But their efforts led only to fresh cries of dismay, for the Sklavenoi discovered, as had the followers of the false prophet before them, that the liquid fire continued merrily burning even though soaked with water.

We had at first set four wagons ablaze. God, in His kindness to us

Christians, then granted that the breeze from the west, which had been fitful, began to blow more strongly. It carried flames and burning embers not only to the wagons close by those we had ignited, but also to the thatched roofs of the huts in the village the wagon circle had been made to protect. Along with the guttural shouts of Sklavinian men, the high, shrill cries of women and children came to my ears.

The fire reaching the huts, the battle was as good as won. While some of the Sklavenoi did continue trying to withstand us, others turned instead to fighting the fires, and still others, abandoning fight and fire both, ran for the shelter of the woods. Our soldiers were hunting them like partridges, having great sport. I let that go on for a short time, but then sent forth a new order: "If the barbarians wish to surrender, let them. The more captives we take, the more we can resettle in the empty lands of Anatolia." After a moment, I had another thought: "A pound of gold to the man who brings me Neboulos, the so-called kinglet here."

Because the village was burning, the Roman soldiers herded the prisoners into the fields nearby. They had to keep some of the Sklavinian women from slaying themselves because their husbands had been killed; officers familiar with the character of the Sklavenoi told me their women were more tender in this regard than those of any other people we know. Our men threw the corpses of those husbands—and of the women and children who died in the village—into a large pit they made some captives dig.

No one brought me Neboulos. I hoped he had fallen in the fighting and been burned beyond recognition but, on questioning Sklavenoi through men who knew their tongue, discovered no one who admitted having seen him go down. Disappointed, I concluded he might well have escaped as Sklavinian resistance crumbled.

Commanders were busy rewarding Roman soldiers who had fought well: some with promotions, some with money, and some with their pick of the Sklavinian women among the prisoners. One of the barbarians tried to keep his attractive wife from going off with the soldier who had chosen her for his enjoyment, and was promptly speared to death. The woman shrieked and wailed; the soldier led her away anyhow. As someone—as I write these words, I cannot remember who—said in the early days of Rome, "Woe to the conquered."

One of the prisoners, a yellow-haired woman of outstanding beauty despite a large smudge of soot on her cheek, struck my fancy. Approaching an officer who was making sure the Romans did not quarrel over their rewards, I asked, "May I be considered to have fought well?"

He looked startled for a moment, then bowed and replied with a smile: "Emperor, without your orders, we would not have fought at all. Since we won, you must have given good orders, which is surely the same thing as fighting well."

He could hardly have said no, but I liked the way he said yes. Pointing to the woman I wanted, I said, "Have her brought to my pavilion."

When the Emperor of the Romans travels, even to war, he travels with as close a reproduction of the comforts of the grand palace as his servants can give him. At the time, never yet having traveled as a mutilated exile on the deck of a miserable little ship with only bandages and a loincloth to call my own, I took for granted such luxuries as a wide, soft bed, hanging lamps, and a tall, heavy wooden chest that held not only my robes but also a gilded suit of mail in case I wanted to join in the fighting myself.

I also traveled with a large retinue of palace servants, some eunuchs, some whole men. I ordered them to bring me a jar of good wine and two cups, and then to go away and stay away till morning: "I shall be entertaining tonight," I said grandly.

My servants retired, sniggering. "Entertaining, eh?" I heard one of them say to another. "He'll be entertained, is what he'll be." His friend laughed. I paced impatiently about the pavilion, waiting for the Sklavinian woman.

The soldiers did not take long to fetch her. They had scrubbed the soot from her face, but she still wore the same smoke-stained wool tunic, decorated at the bodice with flowers and fantastic birds embroidered in red and blue thread, she had had on when I first saw her.

She stared around the pavilion in dull wonder. Lamps of glass and silver, a bed that stood off the ground on legs, my own gorgeous raiment, perhaps even the tall chest—all these must have been strange and splendid to her. I had by then seen the inside of Sklavinian huts. Only the richest of the Sklavenoi were well enough off to be reckoned poor. The rest had less, much less, than that.

"Do you speak Greek?" I asked her. She shook her head. I shrugged. What we would be doing did not require much in the way of words.

I poured her wine with my own hands. Not even my generals enjoyed such an honor. She stared down into the cup. Except when they got it by trade or theft from the Romans, the Sklavenoi did not drink wine, having instead a barley brew of their own, so she may not have known what it was. After a taste, though, she gulped the cup dry. I drank a little more slowly. When I held out the jar to her, she nodded. I filled her cup again. She drained it as quickly as she had before.

I pointed to the bed. She looked at it, at me, at it again. She must have known why I had summoned her to my pavilion. She must have known, too, I was no man of ordinary or even of merely high rank; whether, in her barbarian ignorance, she realized I was the Emperor of the Romans, I cannot say.

She held out the wine cup to me. I poured for her once more, willingly enough; if that would make her tractable, all the better. I had been wondering if I would have to fight her or beat her into submission, and wondering also whether that would kill my enjoyment or spike it.

She drank down the cup, then said something in her own language. I knew none of that, but from the flat, resigned tone could guess what she meant: something on the order of *Might as well get it over with*. She pulled the long tunic off over her head, let it fall to the ground, walked over to the bed, and lay down.

I stared at her a moment before undressing myself; she was as well made as she was beautiful, which says a great deal. When I lay down next to her, she did not turn her head toward me, but kept looking straight up at the poles and ropes supporting the pavilion and the silk cloth stretched over them.

I bent my mouth to hers. She let me kiss her, but her lips did not respond in any way. She lay there, still, unmoving, expressionless, as I kissed and fondled that splendid body. Even when I brought my tongue down to her hidden parts, she did not stir. I thought she thought she might escape by not responding. That angered me.

Roughly, I pulled her legs apart and poised myself between them. Roughly, I thrust myself into her. She was wet enough, from my spittle if nothing else. I forced myself hilt-deep, drew back, rammed again. All the while, I watched her face. She might not have been there with me at all, but somewhere far, far away.

I took my pleasure, and did not withdraw afterwards. Being a young man, I knew I would soon rise again. And so I did, and began the act once more. Save that she was warm and breathing, it was like carnal congress with a corpse. Only after I spent myself a second time and pulled out of her did she move: she rolled onto one side and drew up her legs. I thought about taking her again, this time from behind, but before I could, I stretched out to rest a bit and let my spear regain its strength . . . and I fell asleep.

It was, no doubt, one of the stupider things I ever did, but war and wine and venery had their way with me. Had she so chosen, the Sklav-inian woman could have found a knife, could have smashed in my skull with the wine jar, could have done any of a multitude of deadly things. Murder is easy. I should know.

On waking, some time in the middle of the night, I realized how lucky I was *to* wake. I had twisted so that I lay on my side, facing away from the Sklavinian woman: a posture not far from the one she had assumed. Since she had not slain me, I decided I would enjoy her again. Before I rolled over to do just that, though, I took a deep breath.

My nose wrinkled. "Ignorant barbarian," I muttered to myself. By the odor, either she had not know enough to put the lid back onto the chamber pot after she used it or she had not known enough to use it at all, but had done her business on the ground like an animal.

I did roll over then—and discovered she was not in the bed. Confused, I wondered where she had gone: she could not have escaped the tent, not with guards and servants all around, and what point to hiding anywhere inside? I sat up, and I saw her.

While I slept, she had taken her linen tunic, twisted it into a rope, tied one end to the bronze handle of my clothes chest, and tied the other in a noose around her neck. The handles were about at chest height; she had had to lie out at full length to strangle herself, which was exactly what, in grim silence, she had done. She must have been determined to perish, for she could have saved herself by getting up on her knees before consciousness left her. Her eyes stared sightlessly in a face almost black. What I had smelled was the result of her bowels letting go as she died.

"Mother of God, help me," I whispered, and made the sign of the cross. I started to shout for my servants, but then checked myself. What could be a greater rebuke, a greater humiliation, than a woman who killed herself after I brought her to my bed? The servants might never have the nerve to bring it up in my presence, but that would not keep them from spreading the tale when we returned to Constantinople. A servant who does not gossip is a servant who has had his tongue cut out.

Abruptly realizing I was naked, I quickly put on the robes I had doffed to have the Sklavinian woman. Then I undid the knot attaching her makeshift rope to the wooden chest, and after that the knot around her neck. Touching the dead flesh I had caressed not long before made my own flesh creep but, mastering my revulsion, I dragged her body behind the chest, where it would not be seen if I opened the tent flap.

And I did open the tent flap. A couple of excubitores stood guard in front of the pavilion—not too close, for they knew better than to eavesdrop on the Emperor, or rather, to risk getting caught eavesdropping on the Emperor. The moon, shining through scattered clouds, showed the night to be more than half spent. The camp was quiet, almost everyone asleep, for which I thanked God. "Is anything wrong, Emperor?" one of the guards asked as they hurried up to me.

"What could be wrong?" I answered, doing my best to sound bluff and cheerful. "One of you go fetch me Myakes. Something I need to ask him."

The excubitores looked at each other. I could read their thought: *won't it wait till morning?* But I was the Emperor. One of them trotted away, shrugging as he went.

He came back with my faithful friend almost as soon as I had hoped. As Myakes drew near me, I smelled stale wine on his breath. Even torch-light made him blink and squint: he had been celebrating our triumph himself. "Go off to bed," I told the excubitores who had been guarding the pavilion. "I'm safe enough with Myakes here."

They looked at each other again. Obeying might get them in trouble with their superior. Disobeying *would* get them in trouble with me, the Emperor of the Romans. Sensibly, they obeyed. "Thank you, Emperor," one of them called over his shoulder as they left.

I went into the tent, holding the flap open for Myakes to follow. As soon as we were both inside, he asked, "What's gone wrong, Emperor?" Though never what a pedant would call a clever man, Myakes was no one's fool.

Wordlessly, I pointed around behind the clothes chest. He walked over to see what I meant, and suddenly stopped dead. As I had, he made the sign of the cross. "She did it herself," I said quickly, not wanting him to think I had killed her for the mere sport of it. I have done a deal of killing since, but never for the mere sport of it—which is not to say I have taken no pleasure in the destruction of my foes. In a few words, I explained how I had discovered her body.

He nodded, clicking his tongue between his teeth a couple of times. "She probably watched her man get killed earlier today," he said. "These Sklavinian women, they're not like Romans—they don't want to live without their husbands."

Having heard that more than once before, I accepted it all the more eagerly now. "Even if the blame does rest with her, though," I said, "the embarrassment will be mine. Unless— Has the grave in which we flung the bodies of the barbarians been filled in?"

"No, Emperor," he answered, and then, without so much as a hes-itation, "You want me to toss her into the pit?" No, Myakes was no one's fool.

"That's just what I want," I said. "She's a pagan, and damned, and a suicide and so doubly damned; it's not as if I'm depriving her of Chris-tian burial."

Myakes only grunted. That aspect of things worried him not at all.

He picked up the linen tunic, untwisted it and shook it out as a washerwoman might a towel, and then put it back on the corpse, which turned out to be a harder job than I had thought it would. But when I said as much, he replied, "Be thankful she hasn't been dead long, and started getting stiff. That would really make things tough." He paused, then added, "It would be the devil's own time carrying her that way, too."

Having dressed her, he stooped, slung her over his shoulder, and, grunting again, rose. I nodded in approval. Her face lay against his chest, and her fair fell down over it, obscuring it further. And it would be dark outside. "If anyone stops you—" I began.

He followed my thought perfectly, interrupting, "I'll say she's drunk herself blind. Everything should be all right, Emperor. Will you open the flap for me? I ought to be back pretty soon."

Open it I did, and out into the night he went.

M Y A K E S

Well, Brother Elpidios, what the devil was I supposed to do? She *was* dead. I hadn't killed her, and Justinian hadn't killed her, either. She was a pagan who'd killed herself. What? She wouldn't have done it if he hadn't abused her? Maybe, but maybe not, too. It's not a lie, what I told him about Sklavinian women. If their husbands die, sometimes they *will* kill themselves. It's something they do, the way we Christians cross ourselves. Of course, they can only do it once.

No one did stop me till I got to the camp gate nearest the burial pit and the prisoner pen. I saw a couple of other soldiers carrying women through the camp, as a matter of fact; it was that kind of night. The ones in their arms probably were just drunk, though.

The gate guards laughed as I came near them. "Used her up, did you?" one of them said.

"You might say so," I answered. "What with the wine and everything else"—I grinned and rocked my hips forward and back—"she's gone." And Lord, wasn't that the truth?

All of a sudden, he made a nasty face. "Aii, get her out of here!" he exclaimed. "She stinks—she's gone and shit herself." His comrades all got out of the way then. They didn't want anything to do with me, not after that.

It was easy as could be. The moon ducked behind a cloud right after I walked out of the gate. The night turned black as the soot above a lamp that's been hanging in the same place for twenty years. Instead of going all the way out to the prisoner pen, I stopped by the burial pit. It was closer. Nobody saw me heave her in. Nobody heard the soft thud her body made, landing on the others. I waited long enough so it would seem I'd gone to the pen. Then I walked back to the gate. The guards jeered at me. I swore at them, enough to sound convincing. They laughed and waved me by.

I went back to Justinian's pavilion.

How do I feel about it, Brother Elpidios? I'd sooner not have done it, I'll tell you that. But the Emperor told me to, so I did. I haven't thought about it much since then; some things you'd rather not remember. You ask all the questions, Brother. Let me ask you one for a change. Suppose Justinian had told *you* to dispose of her. What would you have done then?

JUSTINIAN

When the tent flap fluttered open, I reached for a sword—you never lose by being too careful or worrying too much. But it was faithful Myakes. "You took care of it?" I asked him.

"I did, Emperor," he said. "No one's the wiser." His eyes went to the jar of wine I had ordered brought for the Sklavinian woman and me. After what he had done, he needed fortifying. I waved for him to help himself. The cup he picked up and filled was the one from which she had drunk, but I—

MYAKES

Mother of God, Brother Elpidios!

JUSTINIAN

—did not tell him that, he having done me a great service. He drained the cup, then set it down with a sigh. "Ah! Better."

"If you want gold for this, you have it," I told him. "If you want rank, you have it. If you want—"

"Emperor, what I want is to go back to bed," he said. That also being in my power to give him, I waved him out of the pavilion. I lay down myself, though I did not sleep the rest of the night.

And the Sklavinian woman? No one ever asked me about her, the early shifts of guards assuming I had sent her away after I went off duty, the late shifts believing her already gone before they arrived. When you are of no consequence, how easy you are to forget! I found that out for myself, a few years later.

I greeted the replacements for the two guards I had sent away after summoning Myakes, and sent them away, too, clouding matters further. Not that I needed to worry, as things turned out: what did one prisoner, one woman, matter?

The next morning, we began the hunt for Neboulos.

Word of what we had done to the Sklavinian kinglet's stronghold spread rapidly among the barbarians. Some of them did go on hiding in trees and flinging javelins at us when we passed below; some kept shooting arrows at us out of the bushes alongside the tracks we traveled. Here and there, villagers would offer battle when the Roman army came into sight.

But, ever more often as my advance through the Sklavinias continued, the Sklavenoi yielded rather than fighting. Columns of wide-faced, fair-haired men and women went tramping down the forest paths toward the Via Egnatia and, ultimately, toward Anatolia. A few of them, when they found the chance, bolted into the woods, preferring their native wild lawlessness to life within the boundaries of the civilized world. By far the greater number, though, let themselves be resettled without the least difficulty, as reports reaching me in the field made plain.

One great reason so many of the Sklavenoi surrendered was the impression the liquid fire made on those who escaped from Neboulos's village. The tales they spread among their tribesmen grew in the telling, too, as such tales have a way of doing.

Bardanes Philippikos came up to me of an afternoon, bringing with him a Sklavinian whose long yellow beard had ugly streaks of gray. Bardanes' swarthy face bore an amused expression. "Emperor, this fellow wants to see the dragon we used to burn up Neboulos's wagons," he said.

"Does he?" I did not smile. I made a point of not smiling. "Tell him he may not see it. Tell him God gave that dragon to the Emperor of the Romans, who looses it against his enemies. It is not to be seen by the common run of barbarian, unless he be a foe facing the fire."

Bardanes started to laugh. I looked very fierce. If the Sklavenoi believed what I was saying, they would be more inclined to give up. His expression changed. He translated my words into the nasty grunts the yellow-bearded man used for speech. The Sklavinian gave back a guttural torrent of sound. When he was through, Bardanes said, "He thinks you are some kind of wizard."

"Good," I said. "Tell him that if the Sklavenoi anger me enough, I will turn them all into mice. Tell him to tell some of his friends, and then let them go into the forests to spread what I say to their kinsfolk who still skulk out there." If the foe was superstitious, I would take advantage of it.

Bardanes translated again. The Sklavinian stared at me. His eyes were big and wide and blue and stupid. His hand twisted in some sort of apotropaic pagan gesture, he being too ignorant to make the sign of the holy and life-giving cross. I scowled at him, stuck out my front teeth ahead of my lower lip, and said, "Squeak!"

The barbarian almost wet his trousers. Bardanes looked as if he would burst, but did not let out the laughter he held inside. In Greek, he said to me, "Now I see what you are doing, Emperor: you are playing on his fears."

"Of course I am," I answered, surprised as I had been with Basil that anyone would need such a lesson. Well, at least Bardanes understood it when it came in front of his face. My time at the imperial court, and particularly my time on the throne, had shown me how seldom men grasp the lessons they are offered.

On through the hills and valleys of Thrace and Macedonia we went, cleansing them of Sklavenoi either through their voluntary surrender or by fire and sword. I wondered if I had Mardaites to spare for Thrace, to set up a military district there like those in Anatolia. If I could find the men for a military district, their presence on the land would protect Constantinople against barbarous assault.

No matter where we went, we did not catch up with Neboulos. That grated on me; I was never one to like the ends of a knot left loose. I doubled the reward for his capture, then doubled it again, but he still eluded us. Like water through a clepsydra, time was running out in the campaigning season. And then, as I began to despair of laying hands on the Sklavinian kinglet, he once more sent me envoys.

These men were not so arrogant as his previous ambassadors had been. They wriggled on the ground before me like worms. When at last they rose, their tunics were filthy and covered with leaves and twigs. Their spokesman came straight to the point: "Neboulos yield to you, you let him live?"

I thought it over. I would sooner have taken his head, but leaving him alive and in my hands was better than letting him run loose through the winter, rebuilding strength with no Roman troops around and probably compelling me to fight this campaign all over again. "I shall let him live," I said, not without an inner pang.

"You swear this?" the Sklavinian asked. "Swear by your god, your funny god, god no one can see?"

I crossed myself. "By God, by the holy Mother of God, and by all the saints in heaven, I swear no harm will come to Neboulos if he comes to me of his own free will."

"He come," the Sklavinian said. "He come three days' time. You stay here, no fight, no burn, three days' time?"

I hesitated before answering. The Sklavenoi might have been trying to buy time for some mischief, or even for a full-scale assault on us Romans. If they did try that, though, I was confident they would regret it. And so I said, "Very well. We shall stay here for three days without making any attacks. But if by the end of the third day Neboulos has not yielded himself up to me, there will be such a great burning that any crow flying across the Sklavinias will have to carry its own provisions, for it will find none here."

The Sklavinian wheezed. At first I thought him consumptive, then realized he was stifling laughter. He translated my remark for his comrades, who evidently had no Greek. They laughed out loud. What I had intended as grim threat, they took for a joke. Truly there is no reasoning with barbarians!

I cast a wide net of scouts around the open meadows where we encamped. If the Sklavenoi contemplated assailing us, they would not catch us napping. The wait in one place, I must say, did the army good, and was in particular a boon to our wounded, who no longer had to endure jouncing along over roads more imaginary than real in our supply wagons. Several men the doctors had given up for lost recovered, thanks in great part to the quiet rest they were able to enjoy.

And, on the third day, true to his promise, Neboulos came to our camp. He rode in alone, on a better horse than any other I had seen in the Sklavinias. I received him on a portable throne, surrounded by servants and excubitores, reproducing as best I could in the field the splendor of the great palace of Constantinople.

When he dismounted, one of my grooms took charge of the horse. Chainmail rattled on his shoulders as he walked toward my high seat. He also wore an iron helmet, which, like the mailshirt, looked to have been taken from a Roman soldier. He had a sword on his belt—and almost died under the spears of the excubitores when he drew it. But, instead of attacking me, he stabbed the sword deep into the ground. He took off the helmet and hung it on the sword hilt. Then he undid the mailshirt; his armor clattered about him, to use the Homeric phrase, as he let it fall to the ground.

"Emperor, you are too strong for me," he said in Greek that, like his horse, was better than I had looked to find among the Sklavenoi. "I surrender myself to you."

Standing there before me in plain linen tunic and baggy wool trousers, he cut a surprisingly impressive figure. He was not tall—I overtopped him by half a head—but very wide through the shoulders and narrow in the waist, with arms as thick as a thin man's legs: a warrior to reckon with. For a Sklavinian, he was handsome. True, his face was broad, but his features, though blunt, were regular. His eyes were wide and candid and a very bright blue; on a woman, they would have been devastating. He trimmed his buttery hair and beard more closely than most of his countrymen. Looking at him, one might have imagined he was a quarter of the way along the line toward becoming a Roman. He was older than I, but not old: thirty, thirty-five at the most.

"You would have done better—for yourself and for your people—if you had surrendered before," I said.

Those massive shoulders rolled in a shrug. "I thought I could beat you. Till now, I never met any man I could not beat. But you have too many horsemen in iron shirts, and that fire you throw"—it was not a grimace of fear, but one of anger, frustration—"I cannot match it, and my men will not stand against it. And so—you have me."

"And what shall I do with you?" I mused. I had promised not to kill him, and I keep my promises, as both my friends and my enemies have reason to know. I had not promised, however, not to lock him in a tiny chamber somewhere, feeding him bread and water till he eventually had the good grace to expire.

I had not been talking to him, either, but to myself. Nevertheless, he answered me: "Emperor, you send my people off beyond the edge of the world, is it not so? Send me with them. Let me lead army of them for you. You are too strong for me, but I know I can beat every other man who was ever born of woman."

If he could be trusted, it was not the worst idea in the world. The Sklavenoi I was resettling in Anatolia could fight; many of them had been captured in battle at the point of a spear. I intended making military peasants of them, paying them some small wage each year, with which they could maintain their equipment and mounts, and summoning them at need to war. My plan had been to put them under the command of Roman officers, but they might fight better for one of their own. "Neboulos," I said, "if you think you will be a kinglet in Anatolia, as you have been here, think again. The Roman Empire has only one Emperor, and I am he."

Those wide blue eyes went even wider. "You are Emperor. I am your man. I will help you against your enemies." Then he smiled—a provocative smile, almost the smile a man would use to try to bring a woman to his bed. "And, Emperor, you owe me four pounds of gold."

"I what?" I said, partly in amazement, partly because his Greek, while good, was not perfect, and I wondered if I misunderstood him.

But he repeated it: "You owe me four pounds of gold," he said, very clearly. Seeing me still gaping, he condescended to explain: "You say you will give one pound of gold to man who brings me to you. No one does it. You say you will give two pounds. No one does it. You say you will give four pounds. I bring me to you. Here I am." He thumped his chest. "You owe me four pounds of gold."

I could have killed him on the spot for such effrontery. But I had sworn an oath to let him live—and, in any case, I was laughing too hard to think of the headsman's sword. And so, with a smile, he began to betray me.

M Y A K E S

Ah, Neboulos. I haven't thought about Neboulos in going on forty years not more than once or twice, anyhow. He was a piece of work, Neboulos was, no two ways about it.

You've never *heard* of him, Brother Elpidios? Not till you read of him in Justinian's manuscript, you say? God and all the saints, you've made me feel ancient often enough before. Why should one more time bother me? And, thinking about it, his heyday was here and gone years before you were born, so there's no real reason you *should* have heard of him, but still . . .

I wondered if Justinian *would* kill him when he came out with that, "You owe me four pounds of gold." Every excubitor who heard him was either snickering or rupturing himself trying not to snicker. Justinian's temper was always chancy, though. If he'd taken it the wrong way, Neboulos was one dead Sklavinian, oath or no oath. But then Justinian laughed, and when the Emperor laughs, everybody laughs.

Neboulos? Yes, he laughed, too.

After Neboulos came into our camp, warfare against the Sklavenoi ended. We rounded up some thousands more of the barbarians and sent them on toward Constantinople for resettlement. In this, Neboulos made himself useful, persuading several petty chiefs they would do better to yield than to waste their lives in useless battle.

With the Sklavinias under Roman sway, I brought the army down to Thessalonike, which, although the greatest European city in the Empire after Constantinople, had been twice besieged by the Sklavenoi over the years, and might have fallen to them if not for the miracles wrought by St. Demetrios, its patron.

I rode into Thessalonike on a white horse, at the head of the soldiers. The people of the town went wild to see me. For so long, Thessalonike had been a Roman island in a Sklavinian sea; now it was linked again to the larger part of the civilized world. Seeing Neboulos walking behind my horse, the inhabitants jeered and cursed him, for they had feared his growing power.

He took no notice of the jeers. Even when they began to pelt him, first with rotten vegetables and then with stones, he dodged only those missiles aimed directly at him, and did so with a quick economy of motion that kept all but a couple from striking him.

"Let him be!" I shouted to the crowd. "He is mine!" The Thessalonikans bayed wolfish approval at that, no doubt construing it to mean I had in mind for him a fate more bitter and lingering than any a mere mob could inflict. Would they had been right. In fact, though, it was only that I admired the courage and self-possession with which he faced them, and did not wish to watch him slaughtered as part of the celebration of my arrival.

Seeing Thessalonike and its walls, I understood how (with the help of St. Demetrios) it, like Constantinople, held out in the face of everything its foes could do. It rises steeply from the Thermaic Gulf, the Via Egnatia entering it less than half a mile from the sea. The citadel stands on the high ground in the northeastern part of the city. The circuit of the walls (counting the seawall, which is in a poorer state of repair than the rest) is about three miles. More than a hundred towers, some rectangular, others triangular, gave Roman soldiers fine vantage points from which to fight.

Kyriakos, the bishop of Thessalonike and also, in effect, its governor, greeted me just inside the Kassandreia Gate. "God bless the Emperor

Justinian!" he cried, "the God-crowned maker of peace, benefactor to this city, pious and faithful to Jesus Christ our Lord!"

"God bless Thessalonike," I replied, to which the people cheered. "Through His help and that of the great martyr, Saint Demetrios, we have triumphed against our foes, who are also the foes of the saint." The Thessalonikans shouted louder for their beloved saint than they had for their city.

Kyriakos leading the way, we paraded through Thessalonike. When we passed under a great triumphal arch perhaps a bowshot inside the wall, he crossed himself, saying, "This was built by the arch-persecutors, Galerius and Diocletian."

Reliefs on the arch showed prisoners—easterners: Persians, perhaps— pleading for mercy before a Roman Emperor in antique costume like that which Constantine the Great is often seen wearing on his monuments. As the bishop had said, Galerius and Diocletian savagely persecuted Christians, and no doubt suffer the pangs of hell because of it. But without their victories, the Roman Empire would have suffered untold grief at the hands of its enemies. How was I to feel about them, then? How I felt, at the time, was puzzled.

Just north of the triumphal arch was an impressive church dedicated to St. George: Thessalonike seemed to have, and to need, several churches favoring the military saints. It also had, along the Via Egnatia, a church dedicated to the Mother of God. "In here," Kyriakos said proudly, "rests an icon of our Lord which human hands did not paint." His pride was justified, for by possessing such a holy image Thessalonike showed itself to be no provincial backwater, but a city to be reckoned with.

Shortly after passing the church dedicated to the Virgin, we turned north up a meaner, narrower street leading to the church of St. Demetrios, a church worthy of standing comparison to any I have ever seen, save only the great church in the imperial city. It is an old-fashioned basilica, rectangular in plan, with a wooden roof and with a transept giving it something of a cruciform appearance.

"Here we shall celebrate the divine liturgy," Kyriakos said, "celebrating also your glorious victory against the godless Sklavenoi who have for so long oppressed and harassed Thessalonike."

Notables, both priests and laymen, filled not only the wide nave of the church but also the aisles to either side, aisles separated from that nave by columns of red, green, and white marble, a stone with which Thessalonike is abundantly supplied. I admired the mosaics of St.

Demetrios and others, who I learned were a prefect Leontios (the coincidence of names amused me), who had built the first church on the site more than two and a half centuries before, and Kyriakos's predecessor, John, who had led the defense of the city against the Sklavenoi during my great-great-grandfather's reign.

At the close of the liturgy, I took communion from Kyriakos, eating of our Lord's flesh and drinking His blood. Afterwards, the bishop introduced me to a whole great swarm of prominent Thessalonikans, men whose names vanished from my head the moment I left the city they inhabited. And why not? Men who think themselves worth remembering come to Constantinople, to see if they can prove it.

A partial exception was Dorotheos, commander of the garrison of Thessalonike. Even he, though, was less than he might have been, allowing Kyriakos to take the leading role in administering Thessalonike; in that, though, he but acquiesced to a long-standing tradition of episcopal control in city affairs.

To me, Dorotheos said, "You have done a great thing, Emperor, in subduing the Sklavenoi hereabouts. They've made life miserable for us the past hundred years."

"Your hinterland is free of them now, for I've cleared them out by the tens of thousands," I answered, and then paused, struck by a happy thought. I had been contemplating making Thrace a military district on the order of those in Anatolia; doing the same around Thessalonike would give the city warriors on whom to draw should the barbarian menace revive. I said, "I will send military peasants here, to settle on some of the lands cleared of the Sklavenoi. And you, Dorotheos, you I shall name the first commander of the military district of Hellas." At the last moment, I chose that more sweeping title instead of naming the district after Thessalonike.

"Thank you, Emperor!" Dorotheos exclaimed. We both knew, of course, that great stretches of Hellas remained outside effective Roman control—indeed, outside any Roman control at all—being overrun by more bands of Sklavenoi. All the same, the name offered the promise of eventual redemption for the territory named.

Then Kyriakos said, "What a splendid promotion for you, Dorotheos," in tones suggesting he did not find it splendid at all. I realized the bishop was used to being the leading man in Thessalonike, and found anything tending to aggrandize a rival distasteful in the extreme. I also realized I would be wise to do something to placate Kyriakos, as he would probably remain more important here than Dorotheos even after the military district of Hellas was established.

At a supper later that evening, I found a way to grant Kyriakos a favor without diminishing the new authority I was conferring upon Dorotheos. The centerpiece at the feast was a roast kid basted with olive oil and crushed garlic. Watching Neboulos amused me; while relishing the fatty richness of the dish, he cut away the crisp outermost slices of meat and shoveled on salt with both hands to kill the taste of the garlic, the Sklavenoi, like many barbarians, being less fond of it than we Romans.

When he noticed my eye on him, he said, "Emperor, I am glad again I surrender to you. You Romans live by sea, make all salt you want. You do not sell salt to me. You do not sell it to my people. Now at last I can eat all I want." And he reached for the saltcellar again.

"Selling salt is against our law," I said, and let it go at that. Without salt, preserving food is much harder. That makes the stuff a weapon of war, hardly less than iron. Anyone selling his foes that which strengthens them deserves what happens to him.

Neboulos sprinkled still more salt over the fresh surfaces of kid his knife exposed. Turning to Kyriakos, I adapted the text of the Book of Matthew, saying, "In the Sklavinian you see a man for whom the salt has not lost his savor."

"True enough, Emperor," he said, and then, lowering his voice, "I would not mind if, like Lot's wife, he were turned into a pillar of salt. Not only would we be rid of him as a man—which, thanks to you, we are in a different way—but we could break him up and sell him for a good price."

I laughed, but quickly grew thoughtful. "You want to sell salt for a good price? I'll tell you what I'll do: I'll give the church of Saint Demetrios a salt pan all to itself, and all the revenues from it, to thank the saint for aiding us against the Sklavenoi. Let the salt pan be entirely free: you'll pay no taxes for it, and you will not be obliged to furnish salt from it to the soldiers without payment. Does that suit you, Kyriakos?"

"God bless you, Emperor!" the bishop exclaimed, which I took for an affirmative.

"My secretaries will draw up the edict tomorrow," I said, and Kyriakos looked more joyful still. Thessalonike lying by the sea, granting the church he headed the privilege of producing its own salt would bring it extra revenue without seriously inconveniencing the garrison, which had other salt pans upon which to draw. It also helped salve the bishop's bitterness at the greater authority Dorotheos was to acquire.

If I could not live in Constantinople, I would sooner make my home in Thessalonike than in any other city I have seen. But I could not stay there long. It was already September, the beginning of a new year, and I wanted to strike a blow at the Bulgars before returning to the imperial city for the winter.

To reach the Bulgars, the Roman army had to pass through the territory of the seven tribes of Sklavenoi they had subjected to themselves when they settled south of the Danube after my father failed to crush them north of the river. The roads leading up to that country were frightfully bad. Even when it was under Roman rule, it had been a raw frontier district, and it had been ravaged by Goths and Huns and Avars and Sklavenoi and Bulgars; whatever highways had existed were now dirt tracks at best, memories at worst.

The Sklavenoi of the Seven Tribes tried to withstand us from villages surrounded by a circle of wagons, as Neboulos had; the dreadful roads must have prevented word of what we could do to such works from reaching so far north. Liquid fire proved as effective against them as it had against him.

He stood at my side as the flames leaped forth and seized the wagons. "How do you Romans do that?" he asked me, watching the Sklavenoi try and fail to douse the flames, watching our soldiers take advantage of the chaos the fire caused and cut down the barbarians.

"It is a gift from God," I answered. Neboulos was free enough within the camp, but not so free as to be able to sniff around the wagons where the liquid fire and the tubes and bellows used to project it were stored. I had warned his guards their heads would answer for that. They believed me, which was as well, for I meant every word of it.

"Your god is a strong god," Neboulos said. He knew little of the true and holy Christian faith, worshiping instead the lying demons who, calling themselves gods, have deceived and damned the Sklavinian race.

These Sklavenoi did not resist so stoutly as had the barbarians Neboulos had led. On our breaking into their village, they threw down their bows and javelins and cried for mercy in their own tongue and in such fragments of Greek and even of Latin (this having been, before the barbarians' invasions, a Latin-speaking land, they must have learned it from a few surviving peasants) as they had. We took prisoners by the thousands, and sent them down toward the Via Egnatia for resettlement.

Among the prisoners were many comely women. As far as I was concerned, the soldiers who wanted them were welcome to them.

Having defeated the Sklavenoi of the Seven Tribes, we pushed north and east over the Haimos Mountains, invading the land the Bulgars held directly. They fled before us, driving their herds of cattle and sheep with them. Unlike the Sklavenoi, who lived in villages and farmed, the Bulgars were nomads without fixed abode, and the more difficult to bring to battle against their will on account of that.

We might yet have punished them as they deserved, they being unprepared to resist so many Romans roaming through the land they had stolen, had not the weather turned against us. It might as well be a different world north of the mountains; the olive does not grow there, nor does the grapevine: the winters in that benighted province are too fierce to let either survive. And the first snowstorms came early that year, covering the land in white.

The chief quartermaster, an officer named Makarios, approached me with a worried look on his face. "Emperor, we have campaigned all through the summer," he said. "We have not the supplies, especially for the horses, to go on in the face of snow."

"We'll take what we need from the peasant villages, and—" I broke off. I had already seen how peasant villages, there north of the Haimos range, were few and far between. I had not intended in any case to winter north of the mountains; ordering an army to winter in barbarian territory was what had brought Maurice down in ruin and set in train the events that raised my family to the throne. I did not aim to start some other family's rise to power at my expense. But having to withdraw with my attack barely begun also galled me. I said, "We will go on for another few days and see what happens." Makarios bowed and withdrew.

What I hoped would happen was that we might get a break in the weather, another week or two of mild days after that snowstorm, in which we could strike at the Bulgars, plundering their herds if nothing else. Instead, less than half a day after the first snowstorm ended, another blew in.

This time, it was Myakes who came to me. As perhaps no one else would have dared, he told me the truth, straight out: "Emperor, even the excubitores are starting to grumble at staying here so long. And if we're grumbling, the cavalry from the military districts has to be fit to be tied. They've already missed the harvest, and they didn't like that. They aren't fond of being stuck up here, not even a little they aren't."

Not only had unhappy soldiers overthrown Maurice, they had also murdered my grandfather and ruined my father's campaign against these same Bulgars, inspiring his brothers to try to cast him down from the throne. An Emperor whose soldiers were unhappy with him was an Emperor whose throne shook under him.

"Thank you, Myakes," I said. Not getting everything I wanted was always hard for me. Here, though, I saw I had no choice. "We'll go on for today, and see what we can do. Come tomorrow, it's back to the imperial city."

We did little that day, seeing neither Bulgars nor their herds. When we encamped for the evening, I announced our return to the whole army. They could scarcely have been more joyful had I told them Christ was coming back day after tomorrow. Their delight showed me Myakes had been right, and also showed me I would have had little service from them had I insisted on continuing the campaign.

They did not complain about going through Bulgar-held territory on the way to a pass through the mountains closer to Constantinople than the one by way of which we had entered the chilly northern land. Nor did they complain about acting like soldiers on the march, which is to say, about plundering and burning everything in their path. They would have burned for the sport of it, arson being deeply ingrained in the warrior's soul, but they did so all the more enthusiastically for being able to warm themselves at the fires they set.

As before, the Bulgars ran away from us. Their rule, when fighting Romans, seemed to be to advance when we retreated but to retreat when we advanced. Oh, a few of their scouts always hung close to the army, now and then exchanging arrows with our own outriders, but they always fled when we sent larger detachments after them. By the time we started traversing the pass that would take us back to Romania, I took them for granted, as a man takes for granted the taste of the pitch that makes his wine keep longer than it would otherwise.

That quickly proved a mistake, as did my earlier contemptuous estimate of the barbarians' strategy. They had placed an army in the pass, intending to block our way south. Their standards were horses' tails—one, two, three, or more—mounted on poles. Behind their line, drums thumped, echoing and reechoing as the khagan of the Bulgars shifted his men to meet our dispositions. As we drew near, the barbarians screeched what were surely insults at us in their unintelligible language.

My own speech to hearten the soldiers was simplicity itself. Pointing south, I said, "There lies the Roman Empire. There lies the God-guarded imperial city. There lie your homes. And there stand the Bulgars, between you and those homes. Will you let the barbarians keep you from them?"

"No!" the men shouted with all their might. Their outcry startled the Bulgars and silenced them, if only for a moment.

"Then forward!" I said, waving toward the foe. "We shall ride through them, we shall ride over them, and we shall return to our own land once more." At my command, the horns blew the order to advance.

Thud! Thud! went the Bulgars' drums. Shouting their war cries, they rode at us, too. Both sides loosed arrows, which began to fall like deadly rain. Hearing thousands of men shouting my name as a war cry made the hair on my arms and at the nape of my neck prickle up in awe.

The fight was very simple, the Bulgars wanting to trap us and crush us, our own men battling bravely to return to the Roman Empire after having traversed a large part of the enemy's territory. We were better horsed than the Bulgars, and wore iron while they were in leather. And so we broke through, scattering them before us and leaving large numbers of them dead on the ground. I drew from this combat an important lesson: never to let the foe place himself between my army and my own heartland.

M Y A K E S

Why am I coughing, Brother Elpidios? Being an old man isn't reason enough? Justinian's right: that was a good lesson to learn. He forgot it once, years later, and paid dear for forgetting.

But that's not all. You've been reading a good many days now, Brother. I haven't often heard Justinian shade the truth, but he does here. Aye, we broke through, but to hear him talk about it, it was as easy as smashing up the Sklavenoi. It wasn't like that, not even a little bit. I wish it had been.

The Bulgars' horses were little and scrubby, but they were fast. Their bows shot farther than ours—not a lot, but some. And the leather they wore had been boiled some kind of way, till it was almost as hard as iron. As for the damned Bulgars themselves, they were as tough as you could want. Still are, I guess, come to that.

Does Justinian say how many dead *Romans* lay on the ground? No, eh? Well, there were plenty. If we hadn't outnumbered the Bulgars, I think they would have beaten us. We made it into Thrace, aye, but we weren't a happy bunch afterwards. Just as well winter came down hard; we went home, the men from the military districts back to Anatolia and the excubitores to Constantinople, and the Bulgars, they stayed home, for which we were all duly grateful, especially, I think, Justinian.

All the while we were traveling through the country the Bulgars had stolen from my father, during the battle against them, and on the road through Thrace back to the imperial city, I studied Neboulos. He affected not to notice me, but his blue eyes were watchful, too. Yet he said nothing, knowing, I suppose, his fate was not in his own hands.

Like any barbarian seeing Constantinople for the first time, he gaped at the city's walls and then, all over again, at the wonders they contained. "So many people, all in one place," he marveled, and then, in his clumsy Greek, asked me, "With so many people here, why do you want us Sklavenoi, too?"

"The countryside is emptier," I told him. "Even Constantinople has fewer people and more open spaces than it did a hundred years ago."

"Hundred years?" He shook his head. "Who remembers so long ago?"

"Augustus, the first Emperor of the Romans, ruled in the time of our Lord, Jesus Christ, almost seven hundred years ago," I replied. "God has never allowed a break in the line of Emperors from that time to this."

Neboulos looked at me. By his expression, he thought I was lying to impress him. Then he looked from me to the marvels of Constantinople once more. They presented a better argument as to my truthfulness than any I could offer, for no barbarians, their thoughts rooted only in the present, could have conceived of them, let alone built them. When he turned back to me, his face was troubled. "How do you stand living in shadow your ancestors cast?" he asked.

"They are our guides," I said. "We follow them as best we can. And, because we know Christianity, where they were mired in pagan falsehoods, we have surpassed them."

"This god who gives you fire is strong," he admitted. "He drives away all other gods you used to have?"

"Yes, you might say that," I answered: how to put it any more clearly to a letterless barbarian ignorant of the true and holy faith except insofar as he might have delighted in plundering a church of its treasures should he have managed to take a Roman city.

"And I," he said, thumping his thick chest with a big square fist, "I will be strong for you. I drive away all enemies you have now."

He had not pestered me about that notion of his, not in Thessalonike, not in the Bulgars' country, not on the return from that country to the imperial city. Had he pestered me about it, I should naturally have come to suspect him. But now, when we were just across the Bosporos from the many Sklavenoi I had resettled in northwestern Anatolia, seemed an equally natural time for him to inquire about my plans for him. In my mind's eye, I saw him leading a force of fair-haired warriors combining Sklavinian cunning and Roman discipline. Further, I saw myself loosing him, like an arrow from a bow, straight at Abimelekh's heart.

Not yet having learned the full depths of Sklavinian cunning, I said, "So you will make me an army from among your fellow tribesmen, will you?"

"Yes, I will make you army," he said, and his eyes glowed bright as stars. "I will make you *special* army. You show me your enemies. You take me to them. I drive them all away."

That fit in so perfectly with my own thought of a moment before, I said, "Let it be so. I shall send you to Anatolia. Make me an army. Make me a *special* army, Neboulos, and I will show you all the foes you want."

"I am your slave," he said.

Stephen the Persian prostrated himself before me, as he had in the days when he served in the palace rather than the treasury. "Emperor," he said in his eunuch's voice on arising, "I have seen how much gold your campaign against the Sklavenoi and the Bulgars cost, and I am pleased to be able to tell you that, when the tribute from the Arabs and the taxes collected within the Roman Empire are both taken into account, we have gathered in more than you expended."

"That is good news," I replied. "Your predecessor always seemed to be finding reasons for me not to do the things the Roman Empire requires of me. You, now, you find the gold with which I can do those things. That is what I want in a sakellarios, Stephen."

"So I have interpreted my duties from the beginning," Stephen said. "I should also like to commend to your attention a certain Theodotos, a former monk from Thrace, who has ably served your cause, being most ingenious in sniffing out those who would keep from the fisc monies rightfully belonging to it."

"If he does that, he is truly given by God," I said, playing on the meaning of Theodotos's name. Stephen's beardless cheeks plumped as he smiled. I went on, "Bring his name to me again, that I may reward him for his diligence."

"I shall send you a written memorandum, Emperor, detailing his contributions in full," Stephen said.

"Better yet," I told him, and he bowed his way out of the throne room.

That evening, I took supper with my mother. I had, I confess, been avoiding her since my return to Constantinople, for she kept assailing me with the multifarious virtues of my daughter Epiphaneia, a subject on which I remained resolutely deaf. The more she praised the child, the less desire I had to learn whether any of the praise was true.

Indeed, the only reason I consented to dine with her was her promise not to raise the subject of Epiphaneia at the meal. That promise she kept . . . in a way. Instead of talking about Epiphaneia, she talked instead about prospects for my remarriage. "How happy you will be," she said, "when you hold a child in your arms and give it all the love that pours from your heart."

"You know, Mother," I said, "if you were looking for a way to put me off the idea of remarriage for good, you couldn't have found a better one, not in a year of trying." For I heard all too clearly the unspoken reproach that I did not hold Epiphaneia in my arms and give her my love.

I now realize my mother was right; I had an obligation to my family and to the Roman Empire to remarry and to produce an heir as soon as possible, thereby securing the succession and reducing the risk of civil war. But I still mourned Eudokia, and the thought of yoking myself to a new wife held no appeal. And if I lost a second wife as I had the first, grief, not love, would pour from my heart. The previous few years, I had had enough of grief and to spare.

And I was still very young. When you are twenty or so, an endless sweep of years seems to stretch out before you. Ignoring the past history of my family, I was certain I had all the time in the world to marry again and get an heir. Little did I know then the fate God, in His ineffable wisdom, had decreed for me.

And further, not to put too fine a point on it, I was and am a man of my house, meaning a man of strong will. The quickest way to set me against an idea forever was and is to urge it on me too strongly. No donkey or mule could dig in his heels more stubbornly than I under such circumstances. The course my mother advocated was one for which I did not care, the more vehemently and persistently she advocated it, the less I cared for it.

She was stubborn herself, no doubt having acquired the trait from my father if it was not inborn in her. All through the time before my throne was stolen from me, she kept urging no, she kept nagging—me to wed again. I can think of no more important reason for my failure to do so then.

Thinking to distract her so I could finish my supper in peace, I said,

"I hope you don't miss Stephen the Persian too much here in the palace. He is as good in the treasury as I hoped he would be, and the hopes I had for him were of the highest."

Distract her I did. "That eunuch is a shark in man's clothing," she said, her eyes flashing angrily. "Were it not for his robes, you would see the pointed fin on his back. He has not held office long, but already everyone in the city hates him."

"What better recommendation for a tax collector?" I said with a smile.

"Don't joke about it," my mother snapped. "He goes too far—he goes much too far. Anyone who dares protest either how much he collects or how he collects it suffers. He is fond of the switch and, if that fails, the whip."

I shrugged. "The fisc must be fed, or the Roman state starves."

"He is a bloodsucking wild beast, and he thinks the fisc is the soul of the Roman state, not its belly. I told him as much, to his smooth, fat, evil face. I told him he was making you hateful to your subjects, too."

"And what did he say to that?" I asked.

"He said that, if he didn't collect all he could, he would make himself hateful to you," my mother replied, "and that is not all—"

"And do you think he was wrong?" I broke in.

My mother held up her hand. "You are the Emperor now, and so you may speak when you like. But you are also my son, and so you will hear me out. I had not finished." She paused, waiting to see how I would respond. She was indeed my mother, no matter how annoying to me she made herself at times, so I waved for her to go on, which she did: "As I was saying before you interrupted me, that is not all your precious Stephen the Persian said, nor all he did. He said I should mind my own business and let him mind his—"

"An excellent idea," I said.

She kept on talking, right through me: "And he picked up one of the switches he uses to thrash those who will not pay what he demands, and he hit me once across the back with it, as if I were a schoolboy who had not learned his lessons."

She was my mother. Had she not also been nagging me, pushing me in directions in which I did not wish to go, no doubt I should have been outraged. As things were, the first thought crossing my mind was, *Good—you deserve it.* Saying that, though, would only have made our quarrel worse. What I did say was, "Now that I am back in the imperial city, I will tend to matters of the fisc myself. You need never have anything to do with Stephen the Persian again."

It was not enough. Looking back, I see that. At the time, I deemed it the height of generosity. My mother's mouth thinned to a pale, narrow line. "Thank you so much, Emperor," she said, and left the dining chamber quite abruptly—and quite against etiquette.

I do not think she spread the story through the city. In spite of our spats, she was always loyal to the family. I know I did not spread the story. Nevertheless, it did spread, which meant it must have spread from the lips of Stephen the Persian, boasting of the power he wielded. Perhaps he made himself feared with such tales; he surely made himself hated. And, as my mother had warned me, he made me hated, too. We both paid the price for it a few years later.

"Emperor, have mercy!" The fat little man—John, his name was—arose from his prostration with a wail like that of a distraught mourner in a funeral procession. "Have mercy on the pitiful island of Cyprus!"

He was the archbishop of Cyprus. Even so, having learned that anyone coming before the Emperor of the Romans on his throne will make a small problem seem large and a large one seem the end of the world, I discounted at least half that anguished wail. What remained after such discounting, though, was enough to concern me. "Have mercy on Cyprus?" I said, raising an eyebrow. "I thought I have had mercy on Cyprus, arranging for the taxes from the island to be shared between us and the followers of the false prophet. The island has had no share of fighting ever since."

"Not no fighting, Emperor—less fighting," John said. "Your armies and those of the Arabs' miscalled commander of the faithful do not clash there, but strife between their villages and ours remains. And we Christians there have to pay a tax for the privilege of practicing our true and holy faith."

"Do they make you pay that tax over and above their half of what they collect? Or is it part of that half?" I asked, knowing the deniers of Christ made their Christian subjects pay that tax through all the lands they ruled.

John's face twisted; he must have hoped I would not ask that question. "As part of their half of the total tax to be paid," he said unwillingly.

"Idiot!" I shouted, and he blanched. "Blockhead! Imbecile! Cretin! Dolt! For a tax which he is within his rights to levy, you want me to go to war with Abimelekh?"

"And for the harassment our villages endure, yes," John said.

"It is not enough, not close to enough," I told him. "Begone! Since you are in a Christian land here, go to the church of the Holy Wisdom and thank God for my mercy in not sending you home with stripes on your back. And while you are there, pray to God to grant you some of His wisdom, for plainly you have not got enough of your own."

He fled. Some of the oldest courtiers had served since the last days of my great-great-grandfather's reign, nearly half a century before. They united in telling me they had never seen anyone withdraw from the imperial presence so precipitously. "Anybody'd think he'd been struck with the urgent squats," one of them said, chuckling.

I froze him with a glance, whereupon he withdrew from my presence almost as fast as John the Cypriot had done. I remembered too well how my father had died. At the next imperial audience, the old fool did not attend me, pleading an indisposition. I sent word that the longer he remained indisposed, the happier I would be. He never returned to court, and died the following year. His funeral, for that of a man of such high rank, was remarkably ill-attended.

John soon went back to Cyprus, sadder and probably not wiser. His pleas, even if I could not honor them, left me thoughtful. If I resettled the Cypriots on territory definitively Roman, I could gather for myself all the taxes they yielded, sharing none with Abimelekh. Since the treaty between us said not a word about such resettlement, I would have been within my rights to do so.

But the time was not yet ripe. The war with the Bulgars might well have continued into the following campaigning season, and I did not wish to embroil myself with them and with the followers of the false prophet at the same time. So long as Abimelekh paid his tribute as he should, Cyprus would have to wait.

Not long after John had returned to Cyprus, the ecumenical patriarch Paul approached me, saying, "Emperor, your piety is renowned among Christians throughout the civilized world."

"For which I thank you," I said. His opening obviously being preface for a request of one sort or another, I said no more, waiting instead to see how he would proceed.

"The sixth holy and ecumenical synod was a splendid jewel in your father's crown of accomplishments, perhaps the most splendid in all his reign," he said.

"Perhaps, though he would have been in a poor position to call the synod had he not protected Constantinople from the deniers of Christ," I returned.

"Rooting out the misguided doctrines of monotheletism and

monenergism weighs more in the scales of God, Who surely aided him in preserving the imperial city so that he could restore correct dogma to the true and holy faith," the patriarch said.

"It may be so," I admitted after a little thought, for who can deny that the world to come, wherein we shall exist for all eternity, is of greater moment than our tiny eyeblink of life here on earth?

"It *is* so," Paul declared, luminous faith on his face. After a moment, he went on, "Magnificent as the ecumenical synod was, however, and marvelously as it established the doctrines of the holy Christian church, its work, regrettably, was incomplete. As had the fifth ecumenical synod before it, convened by the great Roman Emperor who bore the name with which your father endowed you, it dealt with doctrine at the expense of discipline."

I knew that, as my father had known it before me. Some questions of discipline, now, had awaited settlement for nearly a century and a half: not surprisingly, dogma had to be established first, whereupon, all too often, the zeal of the holy fathers flagged. I asked the question he no doubt expected me to ask: "What remedy do you propose?"

"A new synod, Emperor," he replied, "one that will deal solely with the matters of discipline the last two holy and ecumenical synods failed to cover. You must agree, these matters have gone neglected too long."

"I do agree," I said.

Paul took no notice. Once started on a chain of thought, he would pursue it link by link, even if the person to whom he was speaking had skipped several links and reached the end before him. Now he said, "Matters such as ordination, proper clerical dress, simony, and alienation of monastic property stand in urgent need of definition and legislation. So do less purely ecclesiastical matters like marriage and public morality, manumission of slaves, and the correct representation of our Lord Jesus Christ and the suppression of base and ignorant superstition."

He ticked off the points on his fingers, one by one, as if to make sure he omitted none. Plainly, he had forereadied them. I thought more of him for that, not less, having had many hours of my life wasted by lackwits unprepared for the audiences they had gained with me.

"All those matters, and others as well, do need regulation," I said. "I agree."

He gaped at me in glad surprise. "You do?"

"I said so. Twice, now." I put a hand on his shoulder. "Begin getting ready for the synod at once. Send out letters to bishops within the Roman Empire, to those under the control of the Arabs, and to those in the western lands the blond German barbarians rule. Set the date for the synod as, hmm, two years from now. That will give all the clerics wishing to attend time enough to come to Constantinople, and will give us plenty of time to prepare for their arrival."

He bowed. "Emperor, you are generous beyond what we deserve."

"Nonsense. Without the church, how shall we be saved?" After a moment, I went on, "And I want as many bishops from the western lands as possible to come. There were only a few"—I particularly remembered Arculf of Rhemoulakion—"at the holy ecumenical synod, which I suppose is why they would not admit their Pope Honorius was anathematized at the synod. I want no such, ah, misunderstanding after the synod to come."

"Quite right, Emperor," the ecumenical patriarch said. "The pretensions of the bishop of Rome grow tedious at times. Peter may have founded their church, but Andrew founded ours, and he too was an apostle. And Rome, these days, is a contemptible ruin of a town, as your grandfather discovered when he traveled to the west, while Constantinople is and shall always be the grandest city in Christendom. Let the ignorant western bishops see our magnificence and taste of our learning and return to their own lands better and wiser men."

"They will be as good as they will be," I replied. "Let them return with correct doctrine, and spread it through those barbarous regions."

"Yes, Emperor. That, too," he said.

M Y A K E S

Everyone who talked with Justinian around that time did his best to talk him out of resettling the Cypriots then and there. In all the hundreds of years of the Roman Empire, I don't think there's ever been such a man for resettling people as Justinian was. If you lived somewhere and your ancestors had lived there for the past five hundred years, to him that was plenty of reason all by itself to move you someplace else.

You know what it puts me in mind of, Brother Elpidios? It puts me in mind of the Assyrians in the Holy Scriptures, who resettled the ten tribes of Hebrews so well, they've never been heard from since. Ah, now I've gone and surprised you—I hear it in your voice. Yes, I've paid attention when they read the Holy Scriptures here. Why shouldn't I? I'm an old blind man; being read to is all I'm good for.

Anyway, this time we managed to keep him from shipping the

Cypriots to Anatolia. He would sometimes listen to reason, and with everyone telling him to wait, to be patient, where reason lay was pretty plain this time.

Sometimes, of course, he wouldn't listen to anyone or anything at all. Life got . . . interesting then, for him and for the whole Roman Empire.

J U S T I N I A N

The next spring, I crossed over into Anatolia to see how the Sklavenoi I had resettled were getting along, and how Neboulos was progressing with the creation of the so-called special army. Most of the Sklavenoi had been transferred to points along the Gulf of Nikomedeia, the easternmost projection of the Sea of Marmara. Had I given more detailed orders to the men bringing them into Romania, they would have been widely scattered across Anatolia. As things were, though, their keepers had taken them along the military road to the eastern frontier, from Chalcedon across from the imperial city to Libyssa and then to Nikomedeia, and there, perhaps forty miles from Constantinople, had turned back toward the capital, leaving the Sklavenoi to fend for themselves.

That the sturdy barbarians had done. As I traveled the military road myself, I saw a good many thatch-roofed huts like those the Sklavenoi had made in the villages I had captured the year before in Thrace and Macedonia. The men and women working in the fields were fair-haired Sklavenoi, the sun making their yellow locks shine like gold. Although not long in their new homes, they had wasted no time in buckling down: sensibly so, for, had they dawdled, they would soon have begun to starve.

From Nikomedeia, the military road runs east. Another, lesser, road goes south from the fortified town toward Nikaia, site of the very first holy ecumenical synod. It leaves the Gulf of Nikomedeia at the harbor of Eribolos, ten miles south of Nikomedeia. I did not follow the road all the way to Nikaia, but went west along the southern shore of the gulf about halfway to the seaside town of Prainetos, for more Sklavenoi, Neboulos among them, had been resettled thereabouts.

Only a track hardly deserving to be called a road ran from Eribolos to Prainetos; most travelers from one to the other would have gone by sea. Sometimes there were cliffs right at the water's edge, with more high ground lying farther inland. But here, as on the flatter terrain north of the gulf, Sklavinian farmers were out in the fields, tending their crops and minding their flocks and herds.

As he had before he surrendered to me, Neboulos made his home in a village larger and wealthier than the mean Sklavinian mean. When, accompanied by my excubitores, I rode up to that village, I saw fair-haired men wearing leather jerkins practicing with javelins in a field close by. Neboulos himself stood among them. I could not follow his barbarous dialect, but he seemed to be congratulating the warriors who threw well and upbraiding those who did not.

A broad, sincere smile was on his face as he left the Sklavenoi and approached me. "Have a care, Emperor," Myakes muttered. "Anybody in charge of soldiers who looks that cheerful, there's something wrong with him."

"Ah, Emperor!" Neboulos called. "You come to see my special army—*your* special army? I have them go through their paces for you."

"That is what I came to see," I told him, wondering if he was not too eager to show off the barbarians. How convenient that he should have had a unit of them exercising just when I arrived. Was it too convenient? Word of my coming might have got there ahead of me, giving him the chance to show me what he wanted me to see.

Nothing I could do about that, though. Being shown what others want him to see is a bane of the Emperor's existence. Everything is always prettied up, everyone on his best behavior. And so I watched perhaps a thousand Sklavenoi march and countermarch, throw javelins, and shoot arrows at bales of hay. They did well enough to look to be a useful addition to the Roman army.

"Are these the only men with whom you've been working?" I asked Neboulos. "How many men do you propose having in the special army?"

"These are not only men, no," Neboulos answered. "How many men do you want in special army? You resettled lot of Sklavenoi in this country. If you want twenty thousand men, I give you that many."

"If you can give me twenty thousand men . . ." I felt weak and dizzy with desire, as if, like David spying Bathsheba, I had suddenly and unexpectedly come upon a beautiful woman in her nakedness. But my lust was for martial conquest, not carnal. With twenty thousand fierce Sklavenoi joining the cavalry from the military districts, I might be able to seize Damascus, the Arabs' capital. I might even be able to take back from the followers of the false prophet the holy city of Jerusalem, as my great-great-grandfather Herakleios had regained it from the Persians.

"I put twenty thousand men in your army, Emperor," Neboulos promised. "Maybe thirty thousand, even. We march where you march, we fight where you fight."

That promise he ended up keeping, too. My own euphoria did not last long, for I was used to men exaggerating what they could do in hope of gaining advantage they did not deserve. I would have been satisfied had he ended up giving me half of what he claimed, but, as I say, he, unlike so many, did fulfill his promise. That, unfortunately, proved to make matters worse rather than better . . . but, as I do too often, with such comments I get ahead of myself.

At Neboulos's command, the Sklavenoi cut the throats of enough sheep to feed me and my escort along with themselves, then butchered the carcasses and roasted them over fires made in pits they dug in the ground. They served us the mutton along with both wine and the barley drink they brew: rough fare, rougher even that I had eaten when campaigning against them, but filling and in its own way satisfying even so.

I had mutton fat in my mustache, and could smell it every time I inhaled no matter how often I wiped my mouth. Neboulos leaned over to me and asked, "Do I hear right, Emperor: your wife is dead?"

"Yes," I said shortly. Who could expect a barbarian to have manners?

"You stay here with us tonight, yes?" he said, and went on without waiting for my answer: "Shall I bring you pretty woman, to keep you warm, to keep you happy?"

Most times, most places, I should have said yes to that in those days. But hearing Neboulos put me in mind of the night after we sacked his village, and of the Sklavinian woman I had chosen from among the captives. "No!" I exclaimed, perhaps more sharply than I had intended.

Neboulos, being an ignorant heathen who knew no better, then asked, "If you do not want pretty woman, shall I bring you pretty boy?"

"No!" I said again, even more sharply that before: so sharply, in fact, that Neboulos's eyes widened in surprise. I explained: "In the law of the Roman Empire, those who partake of this impious practice are put to the sword: it is criminal, as the Holy Scriptures clearly set forth. Even bishops who succumb to it face harsh punishment. I know of one who was tortured and sent into exile, and another who was castrated and paraded through the streets for the people of his city to mock."

"Seems silly to make such fuss over this thing," Neboulos said, never having had the privilege of learning the precepts of the true and holy Christian faith. Then, though, he shrugged. "If you do not want pretty girl or pretty boy, I do not bring you pretty girl or pretty boy. You sleep by yourself. You are Emperor, you can do as you like."

I was not altogether by myself in bed that night, being accompanied by an inordinate number of mosquitoes. But pederasty is not only against the law of God and man, it has never been to my taste. And, remembering the one untamed Sklavinian woman, I was not anxious to try another.

What Neboulos had shown me left me encouraged on my return to the imperial city. He did seem at least to be attempting to do as he had promised when he surrendered up north of Thessalonike. Perhaps the special army he had vowed to create would be worth hurling at the Arabs. Better by far, I thought, to spend Sklavinian lives than Roman.

"Emperor," Stephen the Persian said, "I want you to examine these coins we have received from the followers of the false prophet in their latest tribute payment." His voice quivered with indignation. Stephen could be relied upon to take seriously anything pertaining to gold.

The coins he handed me were not Roman nomismata, though their obverses, copied from goldpieces of my predecessors, closely resembled our mintings. When I turned the coins over, though, I saw at once what had upset him. It was not so much that the deniers of Christ truncated the cross on the reverse of their goldpieces; thanks to their false religion, they had been doing that for some time. But the inscriptions on these new coins were not in the Greek and Latin characters we Romans use on our nomismata; they appeared instead in the sinuous, ophidian letters the Arabs employ to write their own jargon.

"What do they say?" I asked.

"Something extolling their false prophet and senseless god, I have no doubt," Stephen replied. "That they copy our coins is bad enough. That they do such a thing as this is much worse."

"I wonder how they would like it if we minted coins with legends calling their Mouamet a liar," I said, and then, in an altogether different tone of voice, "I wonder how they *would* like it if we minted coins calling their Mouamet a liar." The idea appealed to me, not least because it would be the plain and simple truth.

"That is an interesting notion, Emperor," Stephen the Persian replied, "but not one that is germane here, the question at hand being, what is to be done about the presence of these anomalous coins in this year's tribute?"

As I had seen, in matters having to do with money he was single-mindedness itself. The notion of calling the false prophet a liar and a blasphemer on our nomismata remained most tempting, for those coins pass current far beyond the borders of the Roman Empire, and it was an opportunity for us to tell the Arabs what we thought of their misguided, diabolically inspired heresy. Reluctantly, I brought my mind back to the question the sakellarios had asked, and I asked a question of my own: "Are these goldpieces of the proper weight and purity?"

"They are," he said, sounding as if he hated to admit it.

"Then this year, at least, we shall accept them," I said. "We can melt them down and remint them so these offending messages do not spread through the Empire. It is a nuisance, I know, but I am not yet fully prepared to go to war with Abimelekh."

"As you wish," he said, again unhappily. Listening to him, I got the idea that, for the sake of any tiny alteration in the goldpieces we received as tribute, he would have sent every soldier we had marching against the miscalled commander of the faithful.

Never having been one to turn the other cheek to slights no matter how small, I might under other circumstances have felt the same. When I did not, I wondered why, and realized I wanted to wait until Neboulos's special army should be ready before warring against the Arabs. Only then did I fully understand how much hope I had for that army.

"The tribute will stop, at least for a while, when we do go to war against the deniers of Christ," I reminded him. "I want to be certain we have enough in the treasury to fight for a long time even without the tribute's coming in, and also to run the state afterwards without it."

"You may depend on me for that," Stephen the Persian said. "I should also note that my colleague Theodotos, whom I commended to you before, has proved most ingenious in gaining for the fisc all taxes due it."

"Good," I told him. "Congratulate him on his diligence. Gold will be scarce when the Arabs leave off paying tribute. However large a store of nomismata we can build in advance will help us pay for the war. We must get this money, by whatever means prove necessary."

"By whatever means prove necessary," Stephen repeated. "You may depend on me—and on Theodotos—for that."

He was as good as his word, and so was Theodotos, who proved so capable, I promoted him to general logothete, a position of equal rank to Stephen's. Over the next few months, petitions pertaining to the collection of taxes increased sharply. So did the anguished tone of those petitions. When handing me one sheaf of them, the logothete in charge of petitions, a white-bearded bureaucrat named Sisinniakes who might have served the Empire since the days of my great-great-grandfather, said, "Emperor, these people hate your tax collectors so much, they and others like them are liable to end up hating you, too."

If I had not heeded that advice from my mother, I would not heed it from Sisinniakes, either. I stared at him until he lowered his eyes and muttered in embarrassment at having spoken out of turn. "The fisc must be served," I said. "Those who seek to cheat it of its rightful due must be discovered and made to pay in full. Remember, your pay comes from the treasury, too." He bowed and withdrew, leaving the petitions behind.

More soon came in to the palace: fools kept grumbling because the state that protected them from the ravages of the barbarians and the followers of the false prophet could not do so free of cost. But Sisinniakes was right at least to the extent that even the grumbling of fools could prove dangerous. And so, summoning Stephen and Theodotos to the throne room in the grand palace, I allowed some of those alleging my officials had wronged them to come before me and try to convince me they were right.

Stephen, as was his wont, dressed richly: he had the love of ostentation so common among eunuchs. His undertunic was of gold silk, the robe he wore over it of green. Gold rings gleamed on his fingers; a heavy gold chain stretched around his fat neck. The buckles of his sandals were also of gold.

Theodotos, by contrast, wore a plain black wool robe, as if he were still back in the Thracian monastery from which he had come. He was tall and thin and pale, a pallor accentuated not only by the robe but also by his hair (one lock of which kept flopping down over his forehead) and his long, thick, beard, which were both the color of pitch. His cheeks were hollow, he continuing to practice an ascetic way of life here in Constantinople, while his eyes, though dark, glowed as if from an inner fire.

The first to protest against his exactions was a certain Artavasdos, a wine merchant. After prostrating himself before me, he pointed at Theodotos and said, his voice quivering with fury, "Emperor, inside that monkish robe dwells a wolf. Do you know what he did to me? Do you know?"

"I collected the monies due the fisc," Theodotos said calmly. He sounded, as he usually did, as if he knew precisely what he was doing and would proceed on that course without hesitation. No wonder, then, I favored him, my own mind running in similar channels.

Artavasdos leaped into the air, a remarkable turn for such a short, plump man. "He came to my shop, Emperor, with soldiers. They tied my hands together with ropes and hung me up over a beam. Then they piled sawdust and chaff and such under me and lighted them with a lamp. They smoked me, Emperor, like a ham they smoked me over the fire, till I thought I was going to die, to make me tell them where I hid my money."

I turned to Theodotos, who was sorting through sheets of papyrus. "What have you to say about this matter?"

"Emperor, Artavasdos son of Symbatios owed the fisc the sum of"— a long, pale finger slid down the list of names he was holding—"twenty-four and seven-twelfths nomismata, said arrears having accumulated over the period of four years. After my visit to him, his debt to the treasury was paid in full."

"Did you owe this sum?" I asked Artavasdos.

His already swarthy face grew darker yet, rage suffusing it. He pointed at Theodotos again. "What he did, Emperor, only a monster would do, not a human being. I was choking in the smoke, coughing, wheezing, my shoulders like to be torn out of their sockets, and he stood there laughing—laughing, I tell you."

"Do you deny owing the fisc these twenty-four nomismata?" I demanded.

Suddenly getting my drift, Artavasdos stopped blustering. "No," he said in a small voice.

"Did he and the fisc take any more money than was owed?" I asked.

"No, Emperor," Theodotos said, and, most reluctantly, the wine seller agreed.

"Get out of here!" I shouted. "Get out of here and give thanks to the merciful Mother of God that I don't tear out your cheating tongue. You dare to rob the treasury, and then complain when you're caught? Good Theodotos here should have smoked you into ham, for you're a swine wallowing in the trough of our generosity. Get out!"

Court ceremonial forgotten, Artavasdos left at a dead run. He might even have been faster than John of Cyprus. Several men who I thought might be petitioners also hastily departed without pleading their cases before me. But one group in tunics plainly their best and as plainly none too good did come before me. Having completed their prostrations, they rose. Their spokesman, a loutish fellow as shabbily dressed as the rest, said, "Emperor, I'm called Ioannakis." Whoever had styled him *little John* had done so on the principle of contrariness, for he was large and burly, with a wrestler's shoulders. He went on, "I'm one of the heads of the carpenters' guild, and these here are some of my boys." His companions nodded.

He spoke a rough Greek, of a kind seldom heard in the grand palace, but seemed to be doing his best to be polite with it. "Say on," I told him.

Ioannakis pointed to Stephen the Persian; a lot of men pointed fingers in the throne room that day. "Emperor, that fellow is a bad one," he said. "He cut our pay for some of the repair work we've been doing here at the palace, and when we complained about it, he set ruffians throwing stones on us. Look and see for yourself." He pulled up one sleeve of his tunic, displaying a jagged, poorly healed scar on the big muscle of his upper arm.

"Emperor, the pay for these workmen comes from your privy purse," Stephen said smoothly when I looked a question at him. "I discovered them working more slowly than they should have, and adjusted their wages accordingly."

"That's a lie!" Ioannakis shouted, and several of the men with him shook their fists at Stephen and bawled coarse curses. "We were doing fine till he stuck his pointy nose in where it didn't belong, looking for ways to make us hungrier. Don't see *him* looking any too hungry," he added, staring insolently at Stephen's plump prosperity.

Imperturbable, the eunuch said, "It is not a lie. The work to be completed would not be finished by the time assigned, necessitating the reduction in wages previously mentioned. Following the reduction, the workers threatened to damage such work as they had already done. I found a way to force them from the area without summoning soldiers and provoking worse bloodshed."

Ioannakis and the other carpenters kept shouting and cursing, even after I raised my hand for silence. As Stephen's comments had already shown, they knew neither discipline nor respect for their betters. I gestured to the excubitores flanking the throne. Only when they slammed the butts of their spears against the marble floor did the carpenters come to their senses and quiet down.

Now I pointed at them. "If you cannot do that which is required of you, you have no business coming here and complaining to me of it. Obey those set above you and you will do better. Now go." I pointed again, this time to the way out.

But instead of obeying, as all subjects are obliged to do when the Emperor of the Romans commands, Ioannakis, hubris filling his spirit, shouted out to everyone who would listen: "This is a cheat! Do you see how he cheats us?" His vain, insane followers bellowed like nonsense.

Rage ripped through me. I pointed first to the carpenters, then to the excubitores—yet more pointing fingers on that day. "Seize these men!" I told my guards. "Cast them into prison until we can properly decide their fate."

Then Ioannakis and his henchmen did make for the door, but more excubitores stood there and prevented their leaving. The guardsmen who had been stationed to either side of the throne advanced on them, trapping them between two groups of soldiers. After a little scuffling, the arrogant, insolent, mannerless wretches were seized and taken away. Calm having been restored to the throne room, the rest of the day's audiences proceeded smoothly.

MYAKES

Yes, I was there, Brother Elpidios. Why didn't Justinian listen to the downtrodden workmen? I'll tell you why. He'd told Stephen and Theodotos to squeeze as much gold out of people as they could—he says as much; you've read the words. They were doing what he'd said. They were enjoying themselves doing it, true, but he didn't care about that one way or the other. He cared about obedience and about money. Anyone who got in the way of that had to look out.

We took Ioannakis and the other carpenters down to the Praitorion, the city eparch's headquarters on the Mese, and threw them into cells there. What I figured would happen was that the eparch would let them stew for a couple of days, tell them what idiots they'd been for insulting the Emperor, and send them home. It looked like a neat, clean way to get free of the mess.

Trouble is, I'd guessed wrong about Justinian. I thought he'd angry up and calm down and forget about things. But he didn't. The very next day, he sent an order to throw away the key for Ioannakis and his friends. They were still in prison—the ones who were still alive, anyhow—when he was cast down from the throne. And they were a long way from the only ones, too.

You're right, Brother. So far as I know, nobody in the Roman Empire ever did anything like that before Justinian . . . except for having people tonsured and shutting them away in monasteries, that is. What? It's not the same? I suppose not, especially if they let you keep your eyes before they shut you away.

Bitter? Why on earth would I be bitter? I thank God every day that I'm alive. Well, almost every day. Some days, certainly.

But for a few small raids by the Bulgars, the empire remained at peace over the next couple of years. And those raids were met promptly and well by the Mardaites whom I had resettled along the frontier with the Bulgars. My advisers had claimed I would tear down the brazen wall between the Roman Empire and the followers of the false prophet the Mardaites represented, but they were mistaken. The Mardaites did, however, build up a soldierly wall between the Empire and the Bulgars, a wall sorely lacking up to that time.

Abimelekh, the Arabs' miscalled commander of the faithful, continued sending me the annual tribute the treaty to which I had made him agree required of him. Each year, though, more and more of the goldpieces contained within that tribute were neither proper Roman nomismata nor close Arab imitations of our coins, but rather their newfangled mintings with inscriptions in their own tongue. Furthermore, the papyrus the deniers of Christ sold to our chancery was now marked not with the holy and life-giving cross, as had always been the custom, but with passages from the lying works of their false prophet.

Remembering my earlier conversation with Stephen the Persian, I summoned the engraver Cyril, saying to him, "I want you to ready for me new designs for our nomismata, these having inscriptions mocking Mouamet. Choose whatever texts you like, so long as they are properly insulting. If you have trouble coming up with ideas, talk with a priest or even with the ecumenical patriarch."

Cyril being a fine and pious Christian, I had expected him to leap gladly on the orders I gave him. Instead, he looked troubled, saying, "Emperor, must I change the coins that way?"

He did not speak disrespectfully, as the arrogant manikins who called themselves carpenters had done. The respect he showed helped me keep my temper. Instead of growing angry, as I might otherwise easily have done, I replied, "Good heavens, why on earth would you not want to do this?"

His earnest face twisted. "I don't know if I can make you understand, Emperor." He thought for a little while, then said, "Let me put it like this: a nomisma isn't something just for the moment. It's something that lasts a long time. You look through a pile of goldpieces, you'll see coins struck in the reign of Herakleios, of the first Justinian, of Anastasios, of Theodosios, even of Constantine. Those are scarce, God knows, but they show up now and again. Five hundred years from now, people will find *your* nomismata the same way. Seems a shame to put slogans on 'em for the quarrels of a moment, if you know what I mean."

Greek as it is customarily written, having many memories of ancient days in it, does not well reflect Greek as it is spoken by men of little education, as Cyril certainly was. In trying to call back to memory his words, I am certain I have made him more eloquent than he was. Yet sincerity blazed from him.

And, when backed by such sincerity, his words, commonplace though they may have been, had their effect on me. For the point he was making was an important one. Unlike some barbarian kingdoms, the Roman Empire spans the centuries no less than it bestrides the civilized world, extending even in these sorry days from the southern Pillar of Hercules where the Mediterranean meets the great outer Ocean to the Caucasus Mountains. Seen from that longer viewpoint, concerns of the moment all at once seemed less pressing.

I said, "Very well, perhaps mocking the Arabs' false prophet with slogans is not the best way to show we disapprove of what they are doing with their coins. But I do not intend to let them think they can get away with their outrages, either."

"Oh, no, Emperor!" the engraver exclaimed. "I don't want that, either. Let me see if I can find a better way to do it, so that anybody who looks at your nomismata even a thousand years from now will see how splendid they are."

"A thousand years from now," I murmured. I wondered who would be Emperor of the Romans then, and what his nomismata would look like. Surely they would be pure. From the days of Constantine the Great to my own, a span of more than three and a half centuries, the Roman Empire has struck coins of pure gold, seventy-two to the pound. I saw— and to this day see—no reason for that not to continue forever.

"I'll come up with something good, Emperor," Cyril promised. "I'll think and I'll sketch and I'll pray till I do. God will put something in my mind so I can give Him the glory He deserves."

"Let it be as you say," I said, dismissing him. And it *was* as he said, although two years passed before God graced him with the vision he immortalized in gold. The wait, though longer than I would have liked, was, I must say, worth it.

MYAKES

Somewhere right around the time he was writing those words, Brother Elpidios, the Arabs took the southern Pillar of Hercules away from us, and ran up into western Iberia, the land I've also heard called Spain. And nobody—nobody Roman, anyhow—knows how far to the east they've spread word of the false prophet. These are hard times for us Christians; if Constantinople had fallen in that last siege, there might not be any Christians left in the whole world today.

What's that, Brother? On account of our sins, you say? Maybe, but aren't the Arabs sinners and followers of a false religion? Why do they flourish, when all we do is suffer? Eh, Brother Elpidios? Why is that?

JUSTINIAN

That same summer, churchmen began arriving for the synod that would make good the lack of regulations issuing from the fifth and sixth ecumenical synods. Indeed, because it was intended to be a supplement to those synods, the ecumenical patriarch styled it in his letter of announcement the *fifth-sixth* synod, *penthekte* in Greek, and, I learned from western arrivals who had had the letter translated into the Latin more commonly used there, *quinisextum* in that tongue.

The synod itself was not to begin for another year. At first, I was surprised to learn of so many bishops coming so soon. But a moment's reflection sufficed to explain that. What man of sense, offered the choice between spending time in whatever dreary town he called home and in the Queen of Cities, could fail to desire the latter?

In that same otherwise quiet summer came a letter from the brother of Theodore of Koloneia, who served as bishop of the city from which Theodore had sprung. In it, he complained of the iniquities of the Paulicians, a heretical sect originating among the Armenians, by whose country Koloneia lies. Their crimes included not only misbelief by also idolatry.

Not wanting my name for the orthodoxy tarnished at a time when bishops from throughout the known world were gathering in the imperial city, I ordered the bishop to suppress these heretics (against whom, in an earlier outbreak, my father had also moved) by whatever means proved necessary, up to and including summoning troops from the Armeniac military district to break up their robbers' nests. Any who refused to recant their error or who returned to it after such recantation were to be burned alive.

After their leader, who, to help him escape detection, went by two names, Sergios and Titus, met death in this fashion, these Paulician heretics ceased to trouble the borders of the Roman Empire. To this day, I remain proud of having succeeded in putting them down once for all and in restoring the area to perfect allegiance to the orthodox faith.

M Y A K E S

What's that you say, Brother Elpidios? There are still Paulicians around, and they're still heretics and still bandits? I should be sad—I *am* sad, for I don't love heresy, not even a little bit. But that's not what I meant. I'm sad for Justinian's sake: it's one more thing he thought he did that turned out to be built on sand. That's the way of the world, isn't it?

Faith lasts, you say? God lasts? I pray you're right.

J U S T I N I A N

In the following year, a sufficiency of bishops having gathered, the fifth-sixth synod was convened. I ordered the sessions held in a domed hall of the great palace, for which reason I have sometimes heard the synod called that held in the dome. The westerners, in whose tongue the word *dome* is signified by *trullo*, are most prone to this usage.

As the synod opened, all the assembled bishops prostrated themselves before me. They having risen, I addressed them, as my father had addressed the bishops who had come to the imperial city for the sixth ecumenical synod.

"Holy fathers," I said, and my words came echoing back from the dome that gave the hall we were using its name, "employing me as His instrument, God has given you the chance to complete and perfect the work of the previous two ecumenical synods, which concerned themselves more with dogma than with discipline."

"You are the protector of the church, Justinian," the bishops responded. "Though we live in an age of corruption and despair, you will restore the light we once knew."

I made the sign of the cross, the bishops imitating my gesture. Such formal praise as that which they had just given me is not always sincere, but I basked in it nonetheless, knowing that by summoning the fifth-sixth synod I had become part of a chain of Emperors dating back to Constantine the Great who would be remembered forever for their association with the holy ecumenical synods. How could a Christian want a memorial better than defining the faith and its rules, rooting out error, and making the truth shine forth?

"The problems before us are many," I said. "Even now, almost seven centuries after the Incarnation of our Lord Jesus Christ, pagan practices persist among the peasants. We Christians also stand in danger of corruption by the mischievous ideas of the Jews. Our morals are appallingly lax, this holding true for both layfolk and clergymen. And further, both in the west where barbarians rule and in Armenia, certain unacceptable practices have taken root and need to be eradicated."

In mentioning the Armenians, I did not refer to the Paulician heretics but rather to the customs that had gained acceptance within the regular Christian church of Armenia. That church has never fully reconciled itself to the condemnation of the misguided doctrine of the single nature of Christ, and, being more often than not under the power of the followers of the false prophet, is not so fully susceptible to ecclesiastical discipline as I should like.

"We shall make the world new and pure and holy," the bishops chorused. "We shall correct all errors, remove all ambiguities."

And that, over the next few months, is exactly what they set about to do. With my approval, they took severest aim at suppressing worship of the demons who had fooled the folk of the days before the divine Incarnation into thinking they were gods. Even in my time, people would—people do—swear oaths by these pagan gods. The synod made those swearing such oaths liable to excommunication, as they richly deserved to be for their thoughtlessness.

Men and women trampling out the vintage remained in the habit of calling on Bacchus, the false god of wine, as they did so. They too were made liable to excommunication, as were those who celebrated Bacchus's festival, the Broumalia; the great festival of Pan (who, as every educated man knows, died shortly after the time of our Lord, as the pagan writer Plutarch acknowledges), the Bota; and the old pagan New Year's festival near the vernal equinox.

Village dances celebrating the pagan gods were also condemned, laymen participating in them being made subject to excommunication and clergymen to removal from their order. The same penalty applied to

those wearing masks—whether tragic, comic, or satiric—which were connected to the false cult of Dionysos.

The assembled bishops also outlawed divination, horoscopes, ven-
triloquism, and fortune-telling of all sorts because of their un-Christian
nature. God's will may not be influenced thus, and may not be known
until He chooses to reveal it in the fullness of time. Perhaps because
offenses of this nature are so common, the synod decreed six years' penance for them rather than excommunication.

As it should have done, the fifth-sixth synod also protected us Christians against the pernicious Jews, who yet persist among us, steadfastly
denying with their stubborn ignorance the reality of the new dispensation
decreed by Jesus Christ. The bishops ordered laymen excommunicated
and clergymen deposed who ate of the Jews' unleavened bread, who accepted medicine from Jews (whose reputation for skill as physicians no
doubt springs from Satanic assistance), and who bathed with them or had
other similarly intimate dealings.

While condemning these errors, the synod also perfected the laws
governing us Christians. It forbade picturing Jesus Christ as the Lamb
of God, ordaining that He be shown only as the man He was, lest the
ignorant conceive from the misrepresentation that God had truly sent
His Son to earth in lamb's shape. And it prohibited using the cross in
a floor mosaic, to keep feet from trampling on and profaning the holy
symbol.

Sensibly, the synod affirmed and strengthened previous condemna-
tions of adultery, fornication, abortion, and maintaining a bawdy house.
It banned gambling with dice, and also outlawed appearing as an actor
in a theatrical show. From the time when these rules were promulgated,
I vigorously enforced them.

MYAKES

That he did, Brother Elpidios, that he did. You should have heard
people grumble, too. You tell your Constantinopolitan he can't have
his shows, you tell him he can't throw the dice, and he won't be very
happy. I'd be lying if I said I never got down on my knees in the dirt
myself, matter of fact. Yes, I was at the sessions. Yes, I heard gambling
with dice condemned. Why did I do it? It's fun, that's why. I'm a sinner?
Now give me news I haven't heard.

Eh? What do you want to know? Did Justinian leave off his drinking
and fornicating after he set his signature on all those canons? He was

twenty-two years old, give or take a year, and Emperor of the Romans. What do you think he did?

You're right. That's what he did. If you already know the answers, why ask the questions?

J U S T I N I A N

As I urged it to do, the synod condemned certain practices followed by the Armenians and by the barbarians in the west. The Armenian bishops raised no objection to the four canons that sought to regulate affairs in their church, nor, at the time, did the few clerics who had come from the west complain about the forbidding of fasting on Saturdays during the Lenten season, about prohibiting the eating of meat from strangled animals, or about other small-souled, exotic, and newfangled usages prevailing in that part of the world.

And so the synod moved on to consider canons pertaining to marriage. It affirmed that men previously married who were ordained as deacons or priests could, and indeed were required to, keep the wives with whom they had exchanged the holy and sacred vows of matrimony.

Here Basil, the bishop of Gortyna on the island of Crete, who, being under the jurisdiction of the pope of Rome, had also helped represent Rome at the sixth ecumenical synod, protested, saying, "The custom in the west is different, and requires complete celibacy of priests and deacons. Those there who have wives must put them aside to be ordained."

"This is but another barbarous error on the part of western clerics," the ecumenical patriarch said. "Have they forgotten the words of the book of Matthew: 'What therefore God hath joined together, let not man put asunder'? For your reference," he added slightingly, as if Basil could not be expected to know, "this is the sixth verse of the nineteenth chapter."

Paul spoke as if explaining proper doctrine to a child, not to a fellow churchman. The bishops under the jurisdiction of the see of Constantinople made only the slightest efforts to conceal their amusement, having long since wearied of the arrogant pretensions of the popes, who, dwelling in the ruins of what was once a great city, think to dictate doctrine to the entire civilized world.

Basil of Gortyna held his temper. He said, "Practice in the west differs, and the differences are of long enough establishment to be tolerated under the principle of economy."

George and Daniel, Pope Sergios's regular legates in Constantinople, nodded in agreement. But Paul shook his head, saying, "The principle of economy covers differences of ritual without doctrinal importance. That cannot be said of rules pertaining to the proper ordination of priests and deacons."

Basil looked mournful. "The holy pope will not care to set his signature on canons going dead against the custom in his patriarchate."

He and the papal legates wrangled on with the ecumenical patriarch and the bishops from within the Roman Empire for some time over this matter and others, such as the canon that—only reconfirming the acts of the second and fourth ecumenical synods—placed Constantinople with Rome in patriarchal privilege, ranking after it only in the listing of the patriarchates.

I heard much of this later, for I did not attend all these sessions of the fifth-sixth synod, having other matters to occupy my attention. Chief among these was the return of the Cypriots, who again petitioned me to let them leave their island and settle within territory under the sole rule of the Roman Empire.

Where I had refused them before, I now accepted their pleas, resettling a good many of them in Bithynia, not far from the imperial city. Thanks to Abimelekh's insolent provocations with his coins and papyrus sheets, I was more inclined toward war than I had been previously, and, thanks to the exertions of Neboulos, who to my amazement was building his army to the size he had promised, more confident of the outcome.

In my honor, the Cypriots renamed the town in which I resettled them New Justinianopolis. This touched me even more than it might have otherwise, for their luck during the resettlement was not good: a storm sank some of the ships carrying them to their new home, while a pestilence raged among them after the transfer. But they sent John, whose acquaintance I had already made, to the fifth-sixth synod. Despite his previous foolishness, I was glad to see him there, as a sign of their making themselves at home.

Not long after the Cypriots had been moved to New Justinianopolis, Cyril the engraver asked for an audience with me. "Emperor, I have it!" he cried upon rising after prostrating himself.

"Splendid," I said agreeably, pleased to see one of my subjects so diligent in his service to me. *I have it!* being imperfectly informative, though, I asked, "What do you have?"

"The way you were seeking, Emperor; to show the deniers of Christ the folly of the ways and the glory of the true and holy faith," he answered.

I leaned forward on the throne; he had indeed engaged my interest.

"Show me what you have," I said, and beckoned him to me, a rare privilege for an artisan, even one so skilled as Cyril.

As he approached, he reached down to a pouch he wore on his belt. A couple of the excubitores who stood nearest the throne stepped between him and me, pointing their spears at him with warning growls. But he had not come with assassination in mind; all he drew from the leather pouch was a sheet of papyrus on which he had been sketching in charcoal.

The papyrus, I saw, was one of the new sheets from Egypt, one on which the customary cross had been replaced by verses from the work of the Arabs' false prophet. That made Cyril's sketches all the more glorious, for they could have been taken to symbolize Christianity's triumph over the wicked doctrines Mouamet preached.

One sketch showed a Roman Emperor recognizably resembling me standing by and holding a step-mounted cross, a cross such as had been commonplace on the reverse of Roman nomismata for centuries. Cyril had lettered an inscription around the rim of the circular sketch: D. IUS-TINIANUS SERVUS CHRISTI. Most of the letters were Latin, only a few Greek. "Lord Justinian, servant of Christ," he said, translating it into the tongue that had replaced Latin for most purposes in the Empire.

I nodded, but absently, for I was looking at the other sketch, which was of our Lord. Cyril had portrayed Him as Christ Pantokrator; the Ruler of All, His right hand flexed in a gesture of benediction, His left holding a book. The cross on which He was crucified appeared behind His head. Here the inscription read, again in a mixture of Latin and Greek letters, IES. CRISTOS REX REGNANTIUM. "Jesus Christ, King of Rulers," Cyril translated. He looked up at me. "Emperor, a nomisma with this on it will tell the followers of the false prophet what we think of him and of them."

"It will," I breathed. Coins go everywhere within the Roman Empire, and, thanks to the unchanging fineness of our gold, far beyond as well. A story told by a certain Kosmas, who sailed to India during the reign of my namesake, a century and a half before my time, comes to mind. An Indian prince asked him and a Persian merchant who was also present at his court which of them had a mightier sovereign. The Persian, of course, at once claimed his king was the mightier.

But Kosmas told the Indian prince, "Both rulers are here. By their coins shall you judge them." The Persian's silver was not bad in its way, but could not stand comparison to the gleaming Roman nomismata. And so the prince rightly judged the Emperor of the Romans mightier than the Persian King of Kings.

"One thing concerns me," I told Cyril. "These drawings are large"—

each was broader than the palm of my hand—"but a nomisma is small, scarcely the width of my thumb. Will you be able to reproduce them accurately in that cramped space?"

He drew himself up, the picture of affronted pride. "Emperor, my work satisfied your father, and it has always satisfied you up to now. Do you think I would do anything less than my best when making an image of our Lord?"

"I'm sorry," I said, one of the few times—in fact, thinking back, the only one I can remember—I ever apologized while sitting on the imperial throne. "How soon can you strike examples to show me?"

Cyril got a faraway look in his eye. "I would say three days, Emperor, but, like I told you, I want this to be my very finest work. Will five days do?"

"That will be fine," I said, having expected some considerably longer time. Looking back, I should have known better, for some of the coins the palace servitors threw to the crowds of Constantinople at my coronation bore my image, not my father's. The engravers could, at need, work very fast indeed.

And Cyril proved as good as his word—in fact, one day better. When he handed me the first five nomismata he had struck, I brought them close to my face and squinted at them, hardly believing he had managed to include so much in so small a compass. I could make out the individual hairs, long and flowing, on Christ's head and in His beard and mustache; I imagined I could read (though in truth I could not) the words on the book He was holding. On the reverse, my own image was also impressively detailed, down to the three jeweled pendants dangling from the fibula that held my chlamys closed.

I passed one of the nomismata to Myakes, saying, "Tell me what you think of this."

"I always think well of gold, Emperor," he answered with a smile, which I knew to be true, though he was not madly greedy for it as some men are. I had given him the coin with the side upward that showed me standing and holding the cross. He looked at it, nodded in a businesslike way, and turned the nomisma over. He studied the image of our Lord in silence for some little while, so long that I began to wonder whether he had caught some flaw I missed. Then, softly, he said, "Ahh."

My gaze went to Cyril. His expression was the one he might have worn had some beautiful woman come up to him and begged him to take her to his bed that very instant. With the possible exception of something like that, no artisan could have got higher praise than Myakes' murmur of awe had just given him.

To Myakes, I said, "Keep that coin for yourself." I gave Cyril back the other four nomismata. "And you keep these. You did everything I wanted my coinage to do, and did it better than I imagined it could be done."

"I thank you, Emperor, for letting me turn my wits loose and not ordering me to do the other," he answered, "and I thank God for letting my wits come across this idea—for putting it in my mind, you might say. He knows how to watch over His faith better than any of us does, I expect."

"You might as well be a bishop," I told him.

He held up his scarred, callused hands. "I'm better at what I do," he said. "Maybe one day, when I'm too old to use the awl and the punch and the chisel and the hammer as I should, I'll seek the quiet of the monastery. But not yet."

"Good enough," I said. "You can make me more splendid coins, then." He nodded, almost—although not quite—as happy as he had been when Myakes' involuntary, startled praise turned him to a bowl of barley mush.

I looked out at the bishops, each in his finest vestments, who had come to this God-guarded and imperial city at my urging. "You are agreed, then, holy fathers, that these canons complete and perfect the work of the last two ecumenical synods?"

"Emperor, we are," they chorused as one.

"Then let my signature and yours on the canons of this synod be proof of that." And, so saying, I dipped a pen into a jar of the crimson ink reserved for Emperors alone and set my name on each of the six copies scribes had prepared of the canons: one copy for the imperial chancery, and one each for the patriarchs of Rome, Constantinople, Alexandria, Antioch, and Jerusalem.

Paul the ecumenical patriarch affixed his signature next after mine, leaving a blank space on each parchment wherein Sergios, the pope of Rome, might set his name. After him came the three patriarchs whose sees still unfortunately groan under the heel of the Arabs' miscalled commander of the faithful.

And after them I had the pleasure of summoning John, the bishop of New Justinianopolis, who had been translated with his flock from Cyprus to Bithynia. His signature went immediately below those of the patriarchs. "Thank you for the honor you show me and my new city, Emperor," he said, bowing.

"I take great pleasure in seeing you here," I answered, and we beamed at each other. He might have been foolish, but our thoughts now ran in the same channel.

After John, the rest of the bishops who had attended my fifth-sixth synod queued up to sign the canons to which they had agreed. As more than two hundred had come to the imperial city, and as each man had to write his name half a dozen times, the ceremony took some time.

Among those signing their names were George and Daniel, who regularly represented Pope Sergios in Constantinople, and Basil of Gortyna whose see, as I have said, fell under the ecclesiastical jurisdiction of the see of Rome. George and Daniel signed without hesitation, as I saw with my own eyes. Bishop Basil also set down his name, but, having done so, said, "Emperor, I fear the holy pope will find some of the canons here hard to bear."

"If he knows what is good for him," I said, pitching my voice so all the assembled bishops could hear, "he will give his assent, and waste no time doing it. I have great things in mind in the east, and have no intention of wasting my time enforcing discipline on a barbarous, backwoods province like Italy. If the bishop of Rome withholds his signature, he shall be punished quickly and severely."

The bishops from within the heartland of the Roman Empire nodded, knowing they had to accommodate themselves to their sovereign's wishes. Of the far smaller number of western bishops, some looked alarmed, others indignant. The latter, I suppose, failed to remember how my grandfather, as other Roman Emperors had done before him, had used the exarch of Ravenna to seize a pope who flouted his wishes and send him off to imprisonment, exile, and torture. Although not eager to do such a thing, I aimed to if Sergios decided to be troublesome. Having him inflame dissent and argument was the last thing I needed when I was about to go to war against Abimelekh.

Leontios's broad, earnest face puckered into a frown. "Emperor, your father would never have done a thing like this," he said. "I fought the Arabs a lot of times for him, but he would never have done anything like this."

He had not lost his habit of repeating himself, but that was not why I glared at him. I had, by then, been Emperor of the Romans for seven years. Being told what my father would have done rankled. "He is dead," I answered, my voice cold. "I choose war against the followers of the false prophet, not this odious treaty of peace, which they have violated and under which the Roman Empire suffers. I thought of you to command my army and chastise them as they deserve. You have succeeded against them before. Are you afraid you cannot again?"

"I'm not afraid of anything," he said, puffing out his massive chest. "Not of anything. But it won't be as easy as it was before. Abimelekh's finally put down all the rebellions that plagued him, so it won't be easy, no indeed."

"That only means he'll be able to put a few more men in the line against us," I said. "We'll have the troops from the military districts, we'll have Neboulos and his special army of Sklavenoi—"

"Useless barbarians," Leontios muttered, which made me glare again, Neboulos having, to my continuing astonishment, trained up as many Sklavenoi as he had promised me. "Barbarians," Leontios said again. "Emperor, if you beat them with a Roman army, what makes you think Abimelekh won't beat them with an Arab army?"

"They fought well against us," I answered, exaggerating only a little, "and since then they've had a taste of proper Roman discipline," which was true. "Put them in the line with Roman soldiers to help stiffen them, and they'll do well, I feel sure. And besides," I went on, flattering him a little because, thanks to his previous victories, I did want him to command the army, "with you leading the host, how can we possibly fail?"

In due course, Leontios would show me how we could possibly fail. At the moment, the glow that lighted his features did not spring from the reflection of lamplight off his rather greasy skin. Like a sponge, he sucked up compliments. "Ah, Emperor, you honor me more than I deserve," he boomed, which also turned out to be true.

"I don't think so," I said, showing how little I knew of the future. "Now, let's decide how best to strike the Arabs a hard blow. When we do strike them, it should be in a way they'll remember for years."

"We'll hit 'em a good lick, Emperor, that we will," Leontios said. "A good lick, yes indeed."

"You have no more objections?" I asked.

"I wouldn't do it, Emperor," he said. "I wouldn't. I already told you that. But if we are foolish enough to do it—uh, that is, if we are going to do it—you're right, and we should hit 'em as hard as we can. I'll do my best to strike a hard blow against 'em, that I will."

I weighed him in the balance and did not find him wanting. Continuing to speak against my point of view, I told myself, took a certain amount of courage, courage that could also be usefully employed against the Arabs. I said, "Send out orders for the armies from the military districts to gather at their assembly points. Send orders to Neboulos and the special army, also. I shall personally lead forth the imperial guards to join them."

He bowed. "Emperor, everything shall be as you say."

While I contemplated war against the followers of the false prophet, Abimelekh contemplated desecrating a famous and holy Christian shrine. I learned of this as the result of an unexpected embassy from the lands controlled by the miscalled commander of the faithful.

Both ambassadors, as often happens, were Christians: Sergios of Damascus, the son of the Mansour with whom my father had often dealt, who served Abimelekh as finance minister; and Patrikios Klausus, the leader of the Christians of Palestine. "Emperor, we are in sore need of your aid," Sergios said after he and Patrikios had prostrated themselves before me. "Abimelekh, my ruler, plans to restore the temple at Mecca, which suffered in the Arabs' late civil war."

"Why is this a concern to me?" I asked with genuine curiosity. Though the center from which the Arabs' false prophet sprang out like a wolf, Mecca had never been under the dominion of the Roman Empire.

Patrikios answered me: "Emperor, for the restoration he plans to take columns from the grotto of Christ's agony at holy Gethsemane."

"An outrage!" I shouted. Had I not already decided to go to war against the Arabs, learning of the wickedness Abimelekh planned on perpetrating would have impelled me in that direction.

But Mansour held up a soothing hand. "We asked him not to do this, Emperor, hoping you might supply us with other columns to use in their stead."

"That I can do," I said at once. "This I shall do." In my mind's eye, I saw the fortress of Ankyra in central Anatolia, and what had been the city and was now the field of ruins below. Abimelekh could have a hundred columns from those ruins alone without making anyone notice they were missing. And Ankyra was but one of the scores of cities that had shrunk or died in the incessant warfare of the past ninety years. The miscalled commander of the faithful was welcome to our rubbish, even if I was about to go to war with him.

Sergios and Patrikios were effusive in their thanks. "We knew your generosity would let us preserve the holy place undisturbed," Patrikios said.

"No matter what happens," I promised, "I will send these columns to Abimelekh for his false temple at Mecca, so that he need not trouble a shrine belonging to the true faith." This promise I kept, preventing the desecration of the church at Gethsemane.

Perhaps I should not have said *no matter what happens*: in so doing, I gave a sort of warning of what I intended in aid of my campaign in the east. Sergios, however, took it a different way, saying, "Emperor, on our journey hither, we saw your new nomismata, and very beautiful they are, too."

"They are indeed," I said, "and show, as they should, Christ protecting the Roman Empire and the Roman Emperor."

"There is only one difficulty with them," Sergios said, "and that is that I fear my master, the caliph Abimelekh, will not accept them in his realm, since they contradict the teachings of his religion. He will have to pay you the agreed-upon tribute in coins of his own minting."

"We agreed it should be paid in nomismata," I reminded him.

He looked worried. "The weight of gold would be the same, Emperor, so you would not suffer any loss as a result of this. Only the images and legends of the coins would change."

"That was not part of the agreement we made."

Sergios looked unhappier yet. "Is this the word I should convey to the caliph? He will not be pleased to hear it, not even when I have the joy of telling him you have made arrangements to spare Gethsemane."

His words showed me courtiers in Damascus played the same games as did those of Constantinople, using good news to offset the bad and to keep their sovereign in as sweet a temper as they could. It is probably the same among the blond barbarians of the west. It is surely the same among the Khazars, who roam the plains north of the Black Sea. I have seen that with my own eyes.

To Sergios, I said, "If this message so distresses you, you need not deliver it to Abimelekh." Hearing that, he brightened. But I had not finished: "I shall give it to him in person," I said.

Sergios's face fell. So did that of Patrikios Klausus. Myakes suffered a coughing fit. If I had it to do over again, I would have held my tongue. But I did not have it to do over again. Abimelekh would be warned.

M Y A K E S

A coughing fit? I hope I did, Brother Elpidios. I like to have swallowed my tongue, is what happened. Lord have mercy, Brother, the only quicker way Justinian could have given Abimelekh the news that he was going to war with him would have been to send his own messenger.

Why did he do it? No, not stupidity, I don't think. Justinian was a lot of things, but not stupid. What's the word I want? The one left over from the old pagan dramas the fifth-sixth synod condemned? It means overweening pride, something like that.

Hubris? Thank you, Brother. Aye, that's it. He'd beaten the Sklavenoi, Leontios had beaten the Arabs, he had Neboulos and the special army, he didn't think he could possibly lose. So why not let Abimelekh know he was coming? He figured Abimelekh would spend that time shivering in his shoes.

Sounds like Leontios tried to warn him about Abimelekh. I don't have a whole lot of good things to say about Leontios, but he did try. Justinian wouldn't listen to him. He wouldn't listen to people, Justinian wouldn't. He went ahead and did what he thought he ought to do. When that worked, it worked fine. When it didn't . . . well, see what happened when it didn't.

JUSTINIAN

I ordered Neboulos's special army and the armies of the military districts to assemble at Sebastopolis, in the military district of the Armeniacs. Those soldiers having begun to move before I could, the excubitores and I traveled by sea to Amisos and then went down to Sebastopolis rather than making the whole long, slow journey by road.

As I left the ship that had brought me to Amisos, the officer in charge of the fleet said, "Good fortune go with you, Emperor, and God bless you and your army."

"Thank you, Apsimaros," I said. "May you have safe winds back to the imperial city." He nodded. His face was long and thin and pale. I believe he had German blood of some sort in him, which accounted not only for his looks but also for his peculiar name, one without meaning in either Greek or Latin.

The excubitores and I rode toward Sebastopolis the next day. I looked back and saw Apsimaros's fleet sailing west toward Constantinople. I sighed a little. If we could travel by land as readily and cheaply as by sea, governing the Roman Empire, feeding the cities, and collecting taxes would be far easier than they are. But even a paved highway like the Via Egnatia, while allowing soldiers to move rapidly from one part of the Empire to another, does not let good travel cheaply. Take grain in carts more than a couple of days' journey and its price doubles or worse. And so, very often, inland districts are more isolated than islands.

Too much time wasted on a wish that is and must for all time be idle. When, with the excubitores around me, I rode into the camp, I glowed with pride at the size of the army I had caused to be assembled. The tents of the cavalry forces from the military districts stretched over a wide expanse of dusty plain. Off to one side were other tents and huts, these run up in a less orderly fashion. I pointed them out to Myakes: "See how large Neboulos's special army is? As many men there as in the contingents from the military districts, I'd say."

"Looks that way," he answered, peering toward the Sklavenoi. "But how many of 'em there are is only half the question. The other half is, how well will they fight?"

"They fought us well enough when they didn't have to face the liquid fire," I said, nettled. "The followers of the false prophet can no more make the fire than the Sklavenoi can. What would keep the special army from fighting well, then?"

"Nothing I can think of," he said, which pleased me, but then he added, "Of course, the Arabs might think of something I can't," which did not.

Leontios rode out from the camp to greet me. "Here we are, Emperor, gathered together at your order and as you commanded," he proclaimed, redundant as usual.

I waved toward the half-separate camp of the special army. "As you see, we have the men we need to hit the deniers of Christ harder than they expect."

His round face went mournful. "Oh, aye, so we do, provided we don't come to blows and start fighting among ourselves first."

"What do you mean?" I demanded.

"The Sklavenoi are cursed thieves, is what I mean," he said. "Every time one of them gets near my Romans, he steals something: a knife, a chain, some money, it doesn't matter what."

Neboulos came up then, riding on a pony that struggled under his bulk. "Emperor," he cried, "these cavalry, they hate your special army. They taunt us. They say they screw our wives, screw our sisters, screw our daughters, when they fight us before. They laugh. They make us hate them worse than your enemies."

Both Leontios and Neboulos started shouting at me, forgetting my station in their quest for advantage. Then I shouted, too: "Silence!" Leontios remembered himself first, and bowed his head. Neboulos, less used to having anyone over him, went on for another sentence or two before realizing he was doing his cause more harm than good by such rudeness. When he quieted, I pointed to him and said, "Are your men stealing from the cavalry of the military districts?"

"Soldiers always steal," he said.

That had a good deal of truth in it, which I declined to notice. "Soldiers loot from enemies," I said. "They do not steal from their comrades. The warriors from the military districts are the comrades of the special army. Do you understand that?"

"Yes," he said, giving Leontios a look anything but comradely.

"Good," I told him. "You had better. The next Sklavinian who steals from a comrade will have his hand cut off. Do you understand *that?*" He nodded sullenly. I said, "Good. See that your men understand it, too."

"That's fine, Emperor," Leontios said, beaming. "That's fine and dandy."

I turned my gaze on him. "Are your men taunting the Sklavenoi, as Neboulos says?"

He looked less happy. "Urr . . . ahh . . . Some of them, maybe, Emperor. Some. A few."

"That must also cease," I declared. "All of us here in this camp must join together against the common foe: the followers of the false prophet. Tell the men from the military districts that any of them caught obscenely mocking their comrades in the special army will be given a choice." I smiled unpleasantly.

"A choice, Emperor? What kind of choice?" Leontios was not so swift to follow my thought as I would have liked.

"A choice of the part he would sooner lose," I answered: "his tongue, with which he boasted of the lewdness he had committed, or his prick, the instrument of that lewdness."

"You Romans, you like to cut things," Neboulos observed.

I ignored him, watching Leontios. The general's round face (which he was not good at keeping closed) said he had not truly reckoned the men of the special army his comrades. "I will make certain the cavalry from the military districts knows of this choice," he said at last.

"See that you do." When assembling my army, I had not considered that its separate parts might find each other as inimical as the Arabs. If making them all fear me more than they hated each other yoked them in common cause, make them fear me I would.

For all his former bold attacks against the Arabs, Leontios proved a cautious, even an apprehensive, commander. Instead of setting out at once and storming into territory held by the deniers of Christ, he spent day after day drilling the cavalry from the military districts and Neboulos's special army.

I chafed at the delay, but did not follow my first impulse and order him to advance. The reason he adduced for waiting was plausible enough:

planning cooperation between the Sklavenoi, who were foot soldiers, and the mounted men from the military districts. He tried several different formations, at last settling on one that placed the special army in the center of the line with cavalry on either wing and a body of horsemen behind the Sklavenoi as a reserve.

"The cursed butterheads can't move very fast, anyhow," he said to me. "We'll let them hold the Arabs and use the cavalry to get round the foe's flanks."

"Don't call them butterheads," I said. Two Romans had lost their tongues for taunting the Sklavenoi; four men from the special army had had their hands cut off for theft. The rest of the Romans, understanding they had been warned, accepted their fellows' punishment as something they had earned. I was less confident of the effect of my order on Ne-boulos's men, who were unused to discipline from their chieftains or any-one else save possibly their wives. I went on, "I wish we were already in combat with the followers of the false prophet. That would help pull us together."

"Soon, Emperor, soon," Leontios said soothingly. "Won't be long. We have to be ready. We have to prepare." Again he repeated himself. Again he said the same thing twice in slightly different ways.

I do not know whether Sergios and Patrikios, on their return to Damascus, told Abimelekh enough to let him anticipate my intentions, or whether the spies the Arabs keep in Roman territory (just as we keep spies in the lands they rule) sent word that our men were on the march. However he learned of it, the misnamed commander of the faithful hastily gathered together his soldiers and treacherously invaded Romania before we began our stroke against him. Thus was my wish for a speedy meeting with the Arabs granted, though not in the way I had intended.

Frontier guards all but killed their horses galloping back to Sebas-topolis with word of the invasion. "It's a big army they have, Emperor," one of the men said on being brought before me. "I didn't reckon they could put so many men in the field so fast, but I was wrong."

"And the standard they're fighting under," another scout added.

"What standard is this?" I asked.

The scout hesitated, then answered, "Emperor, they've skewered a rolled-up parchment on a spear and carry it before them, saying it's the treaty you've broken."

"Liars!" I shouted. "Satanic hypocrites! They're the ones who broke the treaty, not I. They've put their own false, filthy words on their coins and on their papyrus, and I'm going to punish them for their presump-tion."

"Yes, Emperor," the scout said hastily, bowing his head. "All I'm doing is telling you what I've seen and what I've heard."

"Very well," I said, reminding myself the messenger was not responsible for the news he bore. A thought occurred to me: "Does Abimelekh lead them in person?" I saw myself parading the miscalled commander of the faithful through Constantinople in chains before sending him to the mines to work himself to death.

But all the frontier guards shook their heads. "No, Emperor," said the one who had told me of the Arabs' lying standard. "It is his brother Mouamet, the prince of northern Mesopotamia."

A prince of the Arabs' ruling line struck me as good enough prey. Having dismissed the scouts, I took counsel with Leontios, discussing how best to defeat the Arabs and drive after them into their territory. When the general heard who commanded the followers of the false prophet, he looked solemn. "This Mouamet is not a warrior to be despised, not a man to hold in contempt, Emperor. He sheds blood without pity. When the Arabs were fighting their civil war, he took Mesopotamia and Syria and Armenia from the rebels and restored them to Abimelekh's rule."

"You've beaten the Arabs before," I told him. "Surely, since God is on the side of us Christians, you can win another victory." Leontios's large head bobbed up and down. Relying on his ability to duplicate the successes he had enjoyed in the past, I sent him away and summoned Neboulos.

"We fight soon, Emperor?" the Sklavinian chieftain asked. "I hear these Arabs, they come into your land like you come into my Sklavinia."

Ignoring the comparison, I said, "Yes, we will fight them. The brother of their ruler commands this army of theirs. I want to capture him and treat him as he deserves for breaking the treaty."

"You treat him as bad as Sklavenoi whose hands you cut off?" Neboulos said.

"Worse," I promised, at which he looked suitably impressed. I should have paid more attention to the tenor of the questions he was asking. Looking back, I see that. Unfortunately for the Roman Empire, at the time I did not.

We moved east from Sebastopolis the next day. We did not go as far as I would have liked, the Sklavenoi, who marched on foot, compelling the cavalry from the military districts to slow down so that the two parts of the army would not separate from each other.

Leontios rode up to me, fuming. "Look at those disgraceful barbarians," he said, pointing to the men of the special army.

"You have known for some time they are foot soldiers, have you not?" I asked, annoyed at the tone he took with me.

"Yes, Emperor," he said, but still without the proper submissiveness. He pointed again and, as was his wont, repeated himself: "Look at them. Disgraceful."

Look I did. The Sklavenoi were not marching in neat, well-ordered ranks and files. They ambled along in groups that might have been made up of friends or relatives or men who came from the same wretched little village. As they walked, they sang and joked and passed skins of wine back and forth. Their weapons stuck up at all different angles. They certainly lacked the disciplined appearance of the regiment of excubitores accompanying me.

But, however unaesthetic their progress might have been to the eye of the military purist—such as Leontios was giving every indication of being—they were moving along every bit as fast as the imperial guards. I pointed this out to Leontios. "Well, so they are, Emperor," he said. "And if anything goes wrong, which God forbid, you'll see them run a lot faster than the excubitores, too."

"What do you know of the Sklavenoi?" I said angrily. "You never fought against them—your station has always been here, in the east. *I* was the one who beat them, Leontios. It wasn't lack of courage that caused their defeat. We had liquid fire, and they did not. And they were broken into clans and tribes that did not support each other."

"Why should they support each other now, then?" he replied, not knowing when to give up the argument. "They're still broken up into clans and tribes, not so?"

"All of which have come under the leadership of Neboulos." I put ice in my voice. "General, your objections have been noted. You shall now carry on with the campaign and defeat the Arabs."

"Yes, Emperor," Leontios said tonelessly, and rode away.

When we encamped for the night, the disorder among the men of the special army was enough to distress me, too. I sent for Neboulos. He waved my concerns aside, saying, "Who cares how we camp? We fight good." Since that was what I had told Leontios, I let myself be persuaded.

Leontios sent scouts out a good distance ahead on our breaking camp the next morning. Well before noon, some of their number came galloping back, having encountered the outriders of the army Abimelekh's brother commanded. Horns rang out and banners waved, ordering my force to deploy from marching column to line of battle.

With so many thousands of men and horses involved, that maneuver is more complex than any of the dances concerning which the fifth-sixth synod registered its disapproval. Being practiced at the drill, the cavalry from the military districts went through their evolutions smoothly enough. The men of the special army performed less well. Not only were Neboulos and their officers shouting at them to hurry, but every Roman captain who could spare a moment screamed for them to move faster, lest they give not only themselves but also the entire army over to destruction.

By the grace of God, we had taken our position—perhaps fifteen to eighteen miles east of Sebastopolis—when the followers of the false prophet came into sight. Their scouts and ours exchanged arrows, our men raising a cheer when one of theirs pitched from the saddle and groaning if one of our own men fell.

Before long, the whole of the army the prince Mouamet led grew visible from the cloud of dust it had raised. The Arabs raised a great shout: "*Allahu akbar! Allahu akbar! Allahu akbar!*" Chills ran up my spine. I had heard that war cry as a small boy, standing on the seawall of Constantinople beside my father when the deniers of Christ came to besiege the imperial city. We beat them then. I expected us to beat them again.

"Christ with us! The Virgin with us!" the men from the military districts shouted back at the Arabs. They also shouted my name, loud and long: "Justinian!" The Sklavenoi were shouting, too, a great bellowing like the howls of wolves and the roars of lions. I sent one of the excubitores running over to Neboulos to ask what their war cries meant.

When he came back, he was grinning, and reported, "Emperor, the barbarian says what they're shouting is, 'We'll make soup out of your bones.'"

"That," I said, "is an excellent shout."

As the scout had told me, the Arabs did carry, in place of their usual banners, a rolled-up sheet of parchment or papyrus impaled on a spear. Their standard-bearer rode out ahead of their army and called out in good Greek: "We have not broken what we and you Romans agreed to with oaths." He waved the spear. "God will judge the truth, and take vengeance on those who abandon it."

My army waited to hear what I would do. Pointing to the Arab, I did some shouting of my own: "A pound of gold to the man who brings me that lying standard!" My voice carried, as it has a way of doing when I am angry. Up and down the line, a score of horsemen from the military districts spurred their mounts toward the man holding the spear on high.

Followers of the false prophet galloped out to meet the Roman cavalry. A small battle developed then and there, ahead of the larger one to come. Neither the horsemen from the military districts nor the Arabs drew back by so much as the breadth of a finger. Men tumbled from their horses, struck by arrow and sword and spear. To my anger and disappointment, the Arabs' standard-bearer kept on upholding the spear alleged to bear on it the treaty they alleged I had broken.

Fighting soon became general all along the line. From my position not far behind the special army, I soon lost sight of the ends of the left and right wings, tens of thousands of horses kicking up so much dust from the dry ground across which they galloped as to screen those distant formations from my view as if fogbanks lay between me and them. In front of me, Neboulos was screeching orders like a man possessed. What he was saying I do not know for certain, as he used his own idiom rather than Greek. The Sklavenoi he led shot their envenomed arrows at the followers of the false prophet, and hurled great volleys of javelins when the foe drew close enough to give those some hope of hitting.

Had the Arabs pushed close enough to try handstrokes, the men of the special army would have been at a disadvantage, they having most of them only daggers, not swords, with which to defend their persons. But the torrents of missiles the Sklavenoi loosed against them prevented their making that discovery for themselves.

Cavalry from the reserve went hurrying off toward the right, no doubt at the request of some officer I could not see. If the crisis had been invisible, so was the solution. That a solution had been found, however, I inferred from the Arabs' failure to break through our line of battle.

If the Sklavenoi in front of me wavered, I intended to throw the excubitores into the breach. My own guards were looking now this way, now that, eager to find a place where they could battle the deniers of Christ. They shouted for me to send them into the fray.

M Y A K E S

Some of them did. The troopers were young men, Brother Elpidios, and the horsemen from the military districts had been teasing us— they couldn't lose their tongues or their prongs for that. "Toy soldiers," they called us, and "sweets in fancy wrappers" on account of our gaudy surcoats, and other things I won't soil your ears with. We'd had some fights with them, and broken some heads, too.

Me? Shouting to get into a battle? I'd been in a battle, against Neboulos's men, and I found out it was a lot more fun to think about than for real. And I was past thirty by then, too, getting to the age where your blood doesn't boil quite so fast.

I wanted us Romans to win. I didn't want Neboulos's Sklavenoi to—what was the word Justinian used?—to waver, that was it. For one thing, if the special army did a lot of wavering, there weren't enough excubitores to plug the gap they would have made. For another, if they didn't waver that much, my men and I would be fighting the Arabs with the Sklavenoi alongside us. And if they turned their backs and ran then, who'd be left in the lurch? That's right, Brother Elpidios—me and my chums, that's who.

But it didn't happen. That first day, the special army— Eh? What's that, Brother? Justinian has a good deal more to say? All right, read some more of the manuscript. We'll see how what he remembers stacks up against what I recall. Somewhere in there, we might even find some truth.

JUSTINIAN

Had there been need, I would not have hesitated for a moment over sending the excubitores into battle. I knew how well they could fight; I had seen as much when we took Neboulos's village, and also on other occasions. I also knew they could protect my person as effectively, or perhaps more effectively, while fighting at some distance from me than gathered in a tight-packed mass around me.

Leontios had wanted the battle to unfold like the great victory Hannibal had won over the Romans at Cannae more than two hundred years before our Lord's Incarnation: the center—here, the special army—holding firm while the cavalry on either wing swept out and enfolded the foe in a box from which there would be no escape.

That was what he wanted. What he got proved a good deal less, he being no Hannibal and the Arabs proving far cannier than the Romans whom the wily Carthaginian had lured to destruction. When the wings of the cavalry from the military districts tried to fold round the followers of the false prophet, the Arabs' flank guards held them in check after scant progress. The deniers of Christ thus remaining unsurrounded, strategy became secondary to the courage displayed by the soldiers on both sides.

Here a Roman smashed an Arab in the side of the face with his sword, making the wretch reel in the saddle and then dispatching him with a blow to the neck that sent his soul to eternal torment and half severed his head from his body. There another Roman, already bleeding from a dozen wounds, grappled with an Arab and dragged him from his horse so they both fell together.

I also saw then what I remembered seeing when the followers of the false prophet besieged Constantinople in my youth, and what the history of their wars against the Roman Empire had shown: that they, despite their misbelief, had courage aplenty. When they rode close to the Sklav-enoi to ply them with arrows, one of them had his horse take a javelin square in the throat. The animal crashed down as if it had run headlong into a wall, allowing its rider barely enough time to kick his leg free so it was not pinned beneath the horse.

That rider could have fled away, back toward his own line. Instead, scrambling to his feet, he drew his sword and ran straight for the Sklav-enoi. He killed or wounded several of them before they dragged him to the ground once more and slew him.

Neither side giving way, then, and neither side being able to gain any great advantage, the fight went on from the time when it was joined till sunset without a substantial advance or retreat. If anything, we Ro-mans had the better of the day, and when evening came it was the deniers of Christ who withdrew from combat. But they made no great retreat, only pulling back out of bowshot and leaving enough skirmishers out ahead to show that they intended to renew the fight when morning came again.

Leontios also proved willing to halt for the night, which, considering how evenly the battle had gone on the first day, I could hardly protest. Roman forces made three rough camps, those of the cavalry from the military districts to either side and that of the special army in the center, corresponding in that way to the disposition of the soldiers during the battle.

I summoned Leontios, Neboulos, and other, lower-ranking officers to my pavilion to see if we could think of a way to do better than we had done. I was hoping these men, trained in war, would be able to see what I did not. In that I found myself disappointed. "We'll keep ham-mering at them, Emperor, keep hammering away," Leontios said. "Hit 'em enough blows and I expect they'll crack. How can they keep from cracking if we keep hitting 'em?"

"This is how you won your name as a general?" I exclaimed. Leontios assumed an injured expression. I felt like injuring him, but wondered if he had the brains to notice. I turned to Neboulos, thinking he might have imagination mixed in with his barbarous cunning. "How would you make the fight turn our way tomorrow?"

But all he did was shrug. "You pay us, Emperor, and we do not let Arabs through. You tell us what to do, we do it."

"We'll fight it out, then." I looked at Leontios. Since he showed no sign of having any better idea than that, I said, "It seems we can't enfold them with both wings at once, so why not put more weight on one wing and see if we can use it to break through their line?"

"Aye, I could do that, Emperor," he said. "I could." Plainly, he had had no thought past fighting tomorrow's fight as he had fought today's. He plucked at his beard. "Now which wing should I choose, do you suppose?"

"The left," I said, for no better reason that that I might have been more likely to say *the right*.

"All right, Emperor, I'll do that." And off he went. Someone had told him what to do, and he was fit to do it. I suppose my father had done that during his reign, too. I wondered how Leontios had won victories on his own not long after my father died. Maybe he had run across Arab generals as hamhanded as himself. We had one. Why not they?

Neboulos saw the same thing I had. "That is Roman general?" he said. "If he fights me, I beat him. To you, Emperor, I lose. I always remember that." He rose, nodded, and also departed. The lesser officers quickly went out into the night, leaving me alone.

Not many battles last two days, which is as well, for all through the night men who knew they were to continue fighting on the morrow had to listen to the cries and groans and screams of the wounded, knowing such could as easily as not be their fate when the sun rose once more. Some of the injured men had been taken from the field for the physicians to treat, but some, Romans and Arabs both, still lay between the two armies.

Then their mournful voices were joined by cries of alarm from the Roman pickets. I heard Romans calling to one another in excitement and alarm as they dashed over to the right and, from that direction, the sound of fighting. After perhaps half an hour, the racket eased.

Leontios reported to me what had happened: "Emperor, the sneaky bastards tried a night attack to see if we were awake, but we turned 'em back, we drove 'em away."

"Good," I told him. "I hope they paid plenty for their folly."

"I expect they did." His head went up and down, up and down. "There weren't that many of them. Pickets coming over were almost enough on their own. Soon as soldiers from camp joined 'em, the Arabs knew they couldn't do anything to us."

But they had. I remember watching a conjurer at the palace, once years ago. The man was full of empty, distracting chatter; he would wave one hand about, to keep his audience from noticing what the other was doing. And then, with that other hand, the one we had not been watching, he would pluck silk scarves out of thin air, nomismata from our ears, once even a kitten from a Persian skullcap. He was so good, I had his fee doubled. But set alongside Abimelekh's brother Mouamet, he was as a child.

Both armies were astir before sunrise, each fearing the other would contrive to steal the battle by striking first. Men breakfasted as they had supped, on whatever bits of bread and cheese and onions and salt pork they had with them. Then, their officers shouting at them to hurry, they rolled up the blankets in which they had slept—if, indeed, they had slept anywhere but on the bare ground—the cavalrymen mounted their horses, and horse and foot alike formed line of battle.

Looking over toward the left wing, I could not see that Leontios had materially strengthened it. Perhaps he had done so in such a stealthy way, both I and the followers of the false prophet were deceived. If so, well and good. If not . . . I sent one of the excubitores trotting off to him to inquire.

The guardsman came back a few minutes later. "Emperor, he says he didn't, because of the night attack the Arabs made on our right. He says that if they had made a larger attack there later on, they might have broken through if he'd thinned things out too much." He looked nervous, as any man might who was bringing the Emperor of the Romans news he would not care to hear.

"I gave him an order," I growled. "He said he would obey it."

"Yes, Emperor." The excubitor's nods were quick, placating. "He says he knows that, and he's sorry, and he'll take the blame if things go wrong."

"He certainly will," I said. But Leontios was, or was supposed to be, a general. If he put his own judgment on the scales against mine, I had to believe—or so I told myself—he had a good reason. I waved for the excubitor to leave my presence. Leave he did, as if glad to escape.

"*Allahu akbar! Allahu akbar! Allahu akbar!*" The Arabs' war cry rang out: pounding, rhythmic waves of sound lifting their spirits and casting down those of the men who would oppose them. The Romans and Sklavenoi shouted back, as loudly as the followers of the false prophet but more as individuals than as drops of water in a wave. That second day, their lying cry of "God is great!" outdid our shouts, I fear.

As before, fighting spread all along the line. I had hoped that, by concentrating our forces on one wing, we could break them. Since Leontios, in what he judged his superior wisdom, had chosen not to do that, my hopes had to shift: either we might beat them in straight-on fighting or, demonstrating that we ourselves were steadfast and could not be made to retreat, we might force the Arabs, rather than facing further combat, to retreat from Roman territory.

Prince Mouamet, I assumed, had plans that might be described as the mirror image of my own, with his chief aim to break through the Roman line by hard fighting. That he thought like a serpent had never occurred to me.

For more than an hour, Roman horsemen and their Arab counterparts shot arrows at one another and sometimes came close enough to one another to hurl javelins or to slash with swords. The followers of the false prophet did not assail the Sklavenoi in Neboulos's special army so strongly as they had the day before. That pleased me beyond measure. Turning to Myakes, I said, "The Sklavenoi have taught them respect."

"It looks that way," he replied, and then scratched his head. "I wonder why, Emperor. The barbarians—your barbarians, I mean, not the Arabs—didn't fight all that well yesterday."

"They fought like lions," I said indignantly. Myakes shrugged. I allowed him more liberties than most men, but even he fought shy of coming out and contradicting me. I pointed ahead, to the fighting. "If the Arabs don't think so, why aren't they pressing them harder today?"

"That I can't tell you, Emperor."

"Then keep your ill-founded opinions to yourself," I snapped, and Myakes bowed his head in submission.

I sent a messenger up to Neboulos, ordering him to advance on the enemy if they hung back from attacking the special army. The messenger returned with Neboulos's promise of obedience, but the Sklavenoi did not advance. I sent another messenger. He returned with more promises, but the special army remained where it had lined up. I cursed. Here I had a perfectly good army, but none of its generals felt like doing anything with it.

Then, in the very center of the line, an Arab trumpeter rode out ahead of the army Mouamet commanded. Raising a horn to his lips, he blew three loud, discordant notes.

The Sklavenoi—not all of them, but far and away the greater number of them, at least two men out of every three—left off what they were doing and stood very still and very straight. Neboulos shouted something to the special army in their own barbarous dialect. Thanks to the sudden stillness on the part of the Sklavenoi, I recognized his voice without possibility of confusion.

Never having bothered to acquaint myself with the ugly tongue the Sklavenoi speak, I did not understand what Neboulos had shouted to his men. Yet I did not long remain in doubt as to its meaning. As if with one accord, those men who had stood straight and still abandoned the line of battle they had been holding and trotted across the dry, dusty plain toward the followers of the false prophet.

Hope dies hard. Deceiving myself as long as I could, or even a moment longer, I said to Myakes, "See! They are attacking the Arabs after all."

Mournfully, he shook his head. Even then, he did not offer direct contradiction. He pointed ahead of us, the action there disproving my words more effectively than any countering words of his could have done.

For the Sklavenoi, although trotting toward the Arabs, were not attacking them. Nor did the deniers of Christ offer any injury to Neboulos or the special army. Instead, they welcomed them as comrades, as brothers. And the Sklavenoi reached up and clasped in friendship the blood-stained hands of the mounted Arab warriors.

Later, I learned that, the night before, the prince Mouamet, alarmed at Roman steadfastness, sent a man to Neboulos with a purse loaded with goldpieces, promising him also land for himself and the Sklavenoi in Syria and women of their choosing. Not content with the honors I had given him—not gratefully remembering I had let him live when I could and should have given him a slow, painful death—Neboulos, accepting the gold, turned traitor to the Roman Empire. The flank attack that had paralyzed Leontios was, I suppose, intended to draw Roman attention to the right and away from the center, and achieved its purpose all too well.

At the time, I knew none of this, although, as I say, I could hardly avoid noticing the brute fact of the special army's defection. I could also hardly avoid noticing that, the Sklavenoi having switched sides, the center of our line was a line no longer, only a gaping hole. The Arabs could not avoid noticing as much, either.

I drew my sword and shouted to the excubitores: "Forward! We'll fill the gap!"

Forward we went, I on my horse and the excubitores, afoot, all around me. We linked up with the leftmost end of the right wing of the cavalry from the military districts, the Sklavenoi who had deserted to the deniers of Christ having come mostly from the rightward section of their battle line. But an Emperor of the Romans and a regiment of the imperial guard could not hope to cover the ground some twenty thousand men had formerly filled. The remnant of the treacherous tribe still remaining in Roman ranks stretched themselves out toward us, trying to sew shut the tear in the fabric of our military cloak.

Had we had time to make these movements, we might have

managed them and saved the battle. But the prince Mouamet, having suborned Neboulos and the Sklavenoi, anticipated the effect of their defection and struck hard into the gap that defection had created. His horsemen, still screaming *"Allahu akbar!"* as if possessed by demons, stormed at what had been the center of our line and broke through, splitting the Roman army in half.

I had practiced with the sword. Any Emperor with a grain of sense will do as much, in case an assassin should get past his guards or in case those guards should turn against him, as happened to my unfortunate grandfather in the bathhouse on the island of Sicily. But I never thought to have to engage in swordplay in such desperate circumstances.

The Arabs, recognizing my regalia, made for me in large numbers. Being mounted, they overbore many of the excubitores who tried to stand in their way, and, had I not fought, I would surely have been slain or, perhaps worse, captured, a humiliation that had not befallen a Roman Emperor since the days of the luckless Valerian, who ruled two generations before the time of Constantine the Great.

"Die!" one of the followers of the false prophet screamed at me— in Greek, so I could understand and fear. He cut at my head. When I turned his stroke, sparks flew from our blades. Then I cut at him. His swarthy, bearded face took on an expression of absurd surprise, as if it had never occurred to him that I might do such an untoward thing. Barely in time, he parried.

"Christ with me!" I shouted, and spurred toward him. My horse was bigger than his. The two of them colliding, his had the worse of it, throwing him off balance. I slashed again. My sword bit. Blood sprayed from his wound, at the joining of his shoulder. He yowled, as a cat will if its tail is stepped on, and clutched at the injury. I smote him again, this time across the face. Features a gory mask, he pitched headlong from the saddle.

"Justinian!" cried the excubitores who were near me—though not near enough to have kept that wretch from assailing me. He was the first man I ever killed with my own hands. Seeing him fall, knowing I had overcome him, hearing the guardsmen acclaim me, made warm satisfaction surge through me, almost as if I had just had a woman.

Another Arab came trotting toward me. This time, not waiting for his onslaught, I set spurs to my own horse and myself attacked. That startled him; he must have reckoned me as oly and cowardly as his own leaders. He soon learned his error. After a sharp, hard fight, I beat down his guard and wounded him first in the arm, then in the side, and then in the neck. Blood streaming from him and staining his white robes, he turned his horse, fleeing for his life.

By then, the excubitores had rallied, once more forming a solid circle around me. Cavalrymen from the military districts also helped drive the followers of the false prophet away from my person. For a brief, heady moment, I thought we might yet win the battle.

But that was not to be, the Arabs having split us in two. Each half of the army defended itself as best it could. Both halves, I daresay, would have gone down to destruction had the deniers of Christ exerted themselves against us. Instead of doing so, though, a great many of them poured through the gap in our line not to attack us but to plunder our camp, which lay less than a mile behind the battlefield. Their officers must have screamed and cursed and invoked their false prophet scores of times, trying to hold the men to their principal task, but in vain.

Seeing that, I tried once more to rally the Romans, shouting, "Strike a hard blow, men! Don't let them steal not only the victory but also your goods!"

No one rode forward against the Arabs. Myakes stood close by me, though I did not recognize him till he spoke, a blow having smashed his helmet down over one ear and driven the brim against his forehead so that blood poured down his face. He said, "It's no use, Emperor. If we manage to save ourselves, we ought to get down on our knees and thank God for that much. A plague take everything else—we can always get more stuff."

He was, unfortunately, correct, I realized. I have never been one to go any way but forward, but his words forced me to recognize the difference between going forward with some hope, no matter how small, of success and throwing my life away as surely as if I were slitting my own throat and damning myself as a suicide. "We'll fall back," I said, the words bitter as aloes in my mouth.

And fall back we did, still resisting attack from the front and using some soldiers not engaged there to form a line defending against attacks from our left flank. These, thanks to the mercy of God, were less severe than they might have been, the Arabs being more interested in plunder than in further fighting once our defeat was manifest. Assaults against me also eased as more Roman soldiers placed themselves between me and the foe.

Saving our camp, saving our belongings, I saw at a glance, was hopeless. "We'll make for Sebastopolis!" I shouted to the excubitores and the horsemen from the military districts. "Once we get behind the walls of the town, we can defend ourselves from the deniers of Christ. If they go blithely plundering the countryside, we'll sally forth and teach them the lesson they should have had on this field." Beaten though I was, I looked toward eventual triumph. That trait availed me little here, but would serve me well in days to come.

My greatest fear was that this half of the army would simply dissolve around me, the men fleeing this way and that, leaving themselves easy meat for the Arabs. They must have perceived the danger there, though, and realized their best hope for bodily salvation lay in sticking together. Very few deserted our mass. The fate of those who did—they being quickly snapped up by the enemy—helped persuade the rest not to bolt.

After we had retreated past our camp, swinging wide to the south to traverse it at a safe distance, the pressure against us eased. "Let the cursed Arabs have my bedroll and my cot and my tent," Myakes said. "They don't have me. One of these days I'll get those things back again, or others even better."

More than a thousand years before, the poet Arkhilokhos had sung the same song, having thrown away his shield to escape the barbarous Thracians. In the words of the historian Menander Protector, who recorded the deeds of the first Justinian and his successors, "The changing circuit revealed such things before our time, and will reveal them again, and the revelations shall not cease, so long as there be men and battles."

The sun had nearly set by the time we approached Sebastopolis. As we drew near its protecting walls and towers, the men cried out in dismay, for they saw, as did I, another army moving rapidly toward the city from the northeast. I sent out scouts to hold off the enemy while the rest of us gained safety. These men soon came riding back, not in headlong retreat but shouting for joy: the other army did not belong to the followers of the false prophet, but was in fact our own left wing, also falling back on Sebastopolis.

Commanding them was Leontios. I had rather hoped, considering his sorry performance in the battle itself, that the Arabs had made away with him. God, however, was not so kind. And not only had Leontios brought that half of the cavalry from the military districts out of the fight, but also the several thousand Sklavenoi who had neither fallen to the Arabs nor gone over to them. That struck me as wasted effort. Their fellow tribesmen having proved themselves traitors, how likely was I ever to trust these barbarians again with weapons in hand?

Still, for the moment, the Sklavenoi were a more welcome sight than Arabs would have been. In the failing light, it took us some small effort to persuade the garrison within Sebastopolis we were in fact Romans and not deniers of Christ attempting a ruse. I finally had to approach the walls and shout up a warning about what would happen to those garrison soldiers if they did not open the gates and admit us forthwith. Enough of them had heard and seen me to be convinced, which was as well, for I meant every word of my threats. The gates opened. The army on which I had pinned such hopes passed within, beaten but for the moment secure.

MYAKES

Till then, Brother Elpidios, I hadn't known whether Justinian had courage. He'd never needed to show any, if you know what I mean. He had spirit, he had temper—he had temper and to spare—but you can't tell what a man will do when somebody tries to kill him till you see it happen. He turned out to do just fine, thank you. The biggest problem was keeping him away from the Arabs. He wanted to kill every last one of them himself.

The Sklavenoi, Brother? He spent a lot of the retreat to Sebastopolis cursing Neboulos and every one of the barbarians, ranting and fuming about what he should have done to them when we were fighting back in the Sklavinias. He wasn't joking, either. Like he said there, when he said something like that, he meant it. That worried me.

Then he got quiet. That worried me even worse.

JUSTINIAN

Inside the citadel, I stared at Leontios, wishing I could turn him to stone as the monster Medusa had with her victims in pagan myth. "You disobeyed me," I told him in a deadly voice.

"Emperor, I did what I thought best, seeing how things were," he answered. In fact, against him Medusa might have glared in vain, his head already having been formed from solid marble. He went on, "I've been fighting battles for your father and you longer than you've been alive. I know something about them, that I do."

"You disobeyed me!" This time I, shouted it. "You disobeyed me, and we lost the battle on account of it. The blame is yours—yours!" Looking back on it, the last word was probably a scream.

But screaming at Leontios was like screaming at a post. All he did was bow his head slightly, as a traveler in wet weather will do to keep the rain out of his eyes. "Emperor, I didn't do a thing to lose the battle," he said. "Not one thing. If the special army hadn't betrayed us, we might have won."

If your *special army hadn't betrayed us,* was what he meant, but not even Leontios was blockhead enough to say such a thing to me. Snarling, I answered, "If we'd had a decent attack from the left, not the paltry one we got, we would have smashed the Arabs before the cursed Sklavenoi went over to them. They would have stayed loyal if we'd been winning."

Leontios bowed his head a little farther. "Maybe so, Emperor," he said. "It could be so, I suppose."

He could not have said, *Liar,* any louder had he bellowed it at the top of his lungs. I sprang to my feet. Had I still been wearing my sword, I would have cut him down where he sat. How much grief and torment that would have saved me in years to come! But God does not reveal to mere men what lies ahead, and, in any case, I had taken off the sword on coming into Sebastopolis. And so, rather than striking that large, hard head from his shoulders, I hit him in the face with my fist, as hard as I could.

He too leaped, with a roar of pain. Blood dribbled from the corner of his mouth. I hit him again. This time, expecting the blow, he bent his head down so that my fist slammed into his skull. Pain shot up my arm: he was hardheaded indeed. I hit him again and again. He did not strike back. Had he done so, even once, I would have given him over to whatever half-skilled torturers a provincial town like Sebastopolis boasted. All he did was keep his head down and bring up his arms to protect his face to some degree.

At last, having done to him what, thanks in great measure to his wanton disobedience, I had not done to the followers of the false prophet, I told him, "Get out, and be grateful for my mercy."

He stumbled away, leaving a trail of blood drops on the timbers of the second-story floor. I was certain I had blackened one of his eyes. Maybe, come tomorrow, he would explain his bruises by saying he had walked into a door, as beaten wives, I am told, often do. Had he been truly considerate, he would have leaped off the city wall and broken his neck, but that, I supposed accurately, was too much to hope for.

I stood there in my chamber, breathing hard. Beating Leontios had left me excited in another way. Going to the door, I spoke in a low voice to one of the excubitores standing guard outside it. He nodded and, after consulting for a moment with his comrade, hurried away.

After about a quarter of an hour, he returned with a woman, as I had asked him to do. I barred the door. Smiling, the woman began to pull off over her head the long tunic she wore. "No," I said harshly. She paused, her face puzzled. I shoved her down onto the bed, ignoring her squawk of surprise, and took her as if by force, pretending she was my captive though she was there of her own free will. I took her several times through the night, using her almost as roughly as I had Leontios. When morning came, I rewarded her well, as her complaisance deserved. And, I vowed, I would reward Leontios as he deserved, too.

Although they had suborned Neboulos and the large majority of the Sklavenoi, although they had defeated the army I had assembled against them, the Arabs did not try to bypass the fortress of Sebastopolis and penetrate deeper into Romania, nor did they linger long around the town. The force we still had was too large to let them split up into raiding parties, which it might have defeated in detail on sallying forth, and large enough to remain a threat to their entire army. After burning some fields and pasturelands nearby, they withdrew.

Had I worn Prince Mouamet's shoes, I would have been bolder. But then, I had seen Leontios's quality only too well, while the Arab might have remained ignorant of the depths of his fecklessness. At any rate, scouts having confirmed that the deniers of Christ were indeed withdrawing, I counted myself and the Roman Empire lucky, in that they were not gaining so great an advantage from their victory as they might have done.

A couple of days after their withdrawal was confirmed, the Roman army also left Sebastopolis. Instead of triumphantly advancing into the lands the Arabs had stolen from my ancestors, we were trudging back toward Constantinople in defeat. That was hard to bear, all the more so in light of the high expectations with which I had invested the campaign.

The men from the Armeniac military district soon detached themselves from the army, returning to the farms they tended when their services as soldiers were not required. The men from the Anatolic military district and that of the Opsikion continued westward with the excubitores. So did the Sklavenoi, a remnant less than a third the number Neboulos had brought to Sebastopolis.

On our reaching Ankyra, the horsemen from the military district of the Opsikion prepared to take the southbound road, going back to their farms and villages. I put a stop to that, ordering them to accompany the rest of the army as we proceeded west toward the Sea of Marmara. Some of the men from the Anatolic military district also wanted to break away from the army: at Ankyra, we were already close to their homes. Again, I did not let this happen.

A few days later, we reached Dorylaion, another good-sized town—

or, rather, strong fortress—in the Anatolic military district. Another good road leads south from it into the military district of the Opsikion. Once more, the men from that military district tried to leave the army.

I met with some of their officers, saying, "I have one more task these men can perform for me. I do not think they will find it a disagreeable task, even if it does take them farther from their farms than they might have expected."

"If you tell us what it is, Emperor," one of those officers said, "we'll be able to let them know, and then we won't have the grumbling that's been going through the ranks." His colleagues nodded.

But I shook my head. "Keep them together, and tell them just what I've told you—no more, no less. The mystery will bring them along, I think." I smiled, something I had done little since losing the battle east of Sebastopolis. The officers obeyed me, not least because their curiosity was also piqued.

I had the same sort of conversation with the officers from the Anatolic military district. They too got the bulk of their men to remain in the ranks, though a few, their home villages being so close to our line of march, did succeed in slipping away and resuming the farmer's way of life in which they passed the time between campaigns.

I was less concerned at that than I might have been under other circumstances, for we were moving along easily, deep within the bounds of Romania, and I did not expect the onset of any foe. Indeed, all the men we had left except the excubitores had stowed spears and javelins and bows and arrows—all the weapons save those they wore on their belts—in the supply wagons that rattled along with the cavalry from the military districts.

We had passed Malagina, on the way up to Nikaia, when Myakes said, "Emperor, I know you have something on your mind, but I don't know what. If I ask you straight out, will you tell me?"

"No," I said. He gave me a reproachful look, having sometimes succeeded with such looks since my boyhood. I looked back at him, making my own features, insofar as I could, reveal nothing. He looked more reproachful yet, which I took to mean I had succeeded. Smiling, I said again, "No."

"You're a cruel man, Emperor," he said. Still I held my face steady. Sighing, he withdrew from my presence.

As we traveled the road from Nikaia up toward Nikomedeia, we began passing through country wherein the Sklavenoi had been resettled in large numbers. News of what had passed at Sebastopolis having preceded us to that part of Bithynia, our line of march found many Sklavinian women, often with brats at their side or squalling in their arms, come to learn whether their men had turned traitor, had fallen in the fighting, or had returned against the odds.

Sometimes we would see and hear happy meetings and cries of delight, sometimes wails of grief when a woman learned her barbarous husband was not coming home. Only a handful of Sklavinian women felt obliged to slay themselves from grief on learning that their men had perished. Most who discovered their men missing from the shrunken ranks of the special army assumed those men had run off with the followers of the false prophet to Syria, and so did not deem themselves required to commit suicide to join them in death. Some, indeed, wasted no time in taking up with other barbarians.

Because of these women, the journey from Nikaia up toward Ni-komedeia, which should have taken at most two days, needed more than twice that long. The army, and especially the Sklavinian portion of it, took on more of the aspect of a migration than a military force: I was reminded of the bands of Mardaites—men, women, and children—traveling the military road across Anatolia toward their new homes on the frontier against the Bulgars.

"This, this carnival is disgraceful," Leontios complained, pointing to the disorder and to the unmilitary persons among the Sklavenoi.

I fixed him with my coldest stare. "When I desire your opinion, be sure I shall request it. Until such time as I do, be so good as to keep it to yourself."

"But, Emperor, I—" he began. I squeezed my horse with my knees, urging it up into a trot so I did not have to find out what vacuous opinion he was about to put forward. Not even he was so foolish as to try to keep up with me, which, given the depth of Leontios's folly, says how obvious my move to avoid him must have been.

On our reaching Eribolos, which lies on the gulf of Nikomedeia a few miles south of the town of that name, I ordered the entire army, Sklavenoi and cavalry from the military districts alike, to march west along the coast road by the southern shore of the gulf toward Prainetos, reproducing on the way the journey I had made a few years before to see Neboulos's special army as it was being assembled and drilled. The remaining Sklavenoi were glad, the route taking many of them close to the farms and villages they had established since being resettled in Ro-mania. From the cavalry from the military districts I heard nothing but grumbling: they had thought that, in compensation for being prevented from returning to their homes, they would be allowed to go into Constantinople, and now saw themselves diverted from the city as well.

Some of their officers were sufficiently aggrieved at being turned aside from the imperial city to come to me to complain of it. For such presumption, I would at most times have given them my heartiest imitation of the wrath of God. That afternoon, though, I said only, "I still have one task remaining for your horsemen."

One of the officers, quicker than the rest, asked, "For the cavalry alone? What about the Sklavenoi?"

"Oh, the Sklavenoi will also be involved, never fear," I told him. He and several other men tried to question me further, but I looked enigmatic and said nothing.

That evening, we halted at Leukate, where white, chalky cliffs tumble down steep and sheer to the gulf of Nikomedeia. Far below us, small waves slapped the base of the cliffs, a gentle, murmurous sound. At my order, the Sklavenoi camped nearest the cliffs. I broke the horsemen from the military districts into several blocks, posting them in a sort of cup around the remnant of the special army and the drabs and nasty little children accompanying the barbarians.

Myakes came up to me as I was talking to messengers I was about to send to each encampment of the cavalry from the military districts. Being a longtime companion of mine, he exercised the privilege such men have, saying, "Emperor, I've been looking at the dispositions you've made here. Looks to me like you're going to—"

My own disposition was none too quiet. I held up my hand. He, unlike Leontios, knew better than to go on after a clear signal to halt. "What I am going to do, Myakes," I told him, "is have my revenge." I turned back to the messengers. "Tell the men, without being in any way ostentatious, to arm themselves from the supply wagons and then to await my signal."

"Aye, Emperor," they said as one, and hurried away.

"Emperor, have mercy on them," Myakes said, suddenly and urgently: he had indeed divined my intentions. "These are the ones who stayed loyal. They—"

"Are Sklavenoi," I broke in. "Are barbarians. Are likely to turn against us in any future campaign. Are, as the Holy Scriptures say, broken reeds that will pierce the hands of those who lean on them. Are never going to have another chance to betray us Romans. Do you understand me?"

"Yes, Emperor," he said, and looked down at the ground. Once more, years later, he would ask me to have mercy on my enemies. I told him no then, too. I was right both times.

Having waited until I judged the messengers had reached the encampments of the cavalrymen from the military districts and those men were arming themselves, I summoned more messengers and gave them the next order to take to the soldiers. It was the last order I would give them for the night: "At the signal, rush upon the treacherous Sklavenoi and slay them all. Slay them without mercy. But for them"—*and for Leontios*, I thought, but I knew what I was going to do with Leontios, too—"we would have beaten the accursed Arabs. Now we shall take vengeance upon them."

As the first group of messengers had a little while before, these men answered, "Aye, Emperor." But in their voices I heard the same fierce eagerness that filled my own. Feeling vindicated, I looked round for Myakes. He had gone. Because he had served me so long and loyally, I forgave him his lack of enthusiasm this once.

I turned my attention back to the messengers. "The signal shall be two long blasts from the horn here," I told them.

"Aye, Emperor!" they said again, and, at my nod of dismissal, dashed off with gleaming eyes to pass on my commands. Again I waited. Anticipation made my heart pound ever faster, so that I had trouble judging the passage of time. At last I was certain the messengers must surely have reached even the most distant encampments. I nodded again, this time to the trumpeter. He raised his horn to his lips and blew the two notes of the signal. Standing next to him, I was almost deafened. I had wondered if all the men from the military districts would hear the call. My doubts now vanished, along with some small part of my hearing.

Yet the brief silence that followed was not altogether a product of that stunning call's effect on my ears. The Sklavenoi, who had been raucously celebrating their return to the land in which I had resettled them, paused in their no doubt drunken debauch, wondering what the two blasts meant.

They were not left in doubt for long. The noise rising up into the heavens was not like that which I had heard during the battle near Sebastopolis, nor even like that following my soldiers' breaking into the Sklavinian village from which Neboulos had ruled as kinglet. Upon our breaking into that village after penetrating the circle of carts and wagons the Sklavenoi had thrown up around it, the barbarians—warriors, women, even children—could have been in no doubt as to our intention, and comported themselves accordingly. Here . . .

Here, as I had intended, our onslaught took them altogether by surprise. Their first cries, then, were friendly, even welcoming: they believed the men from the military districts rushing upon them sword in hand had come to join in their revels. Only when they began falling to the Roman soldiers did they realize the trap in which they had been placed, and realize also they had no escape.

How their screams and wails rose to the heavens then! And how unavailing those screams and wails were! Even a well-disciplined force of fully armed soldiers, assailed without warning from three sides at once with cliffs on the fourth, would have suffered catastrophic losses. The Sklavenoi, as they had proved again and again, were anything but well disciplined. They were not fully armed, nor could they fully arm themselves, all their weapons past knives and a few swords being stored in the wagons the men from the military districts controlled. And they were not, or many of them were not, soldiers but the sluts and brats who attached themselves to soldiers.

Everything proceeded exactly as I had hoped it might. It was not simply victory, it was not simply slaughter, it was massacre. Listening to the Sklavenoi dying under the swords and javelins of the Roman soldiers who set upon them, listening to the screams of those who leaped off the precipices of Leukate to avoid the Romans' avenging weapons and to those of the Sklavenoi whom the soldiers herded over those precipices, that being an easier and safer way to dispose of them than any other, was as exciting, as gratifying, as the chastisement I had given Leontios in partial requital for his failure at Sebastopolis.

I was certain some of the cavalrymen form the military districts were saving some Sklavinian women to enjoy before killing them, or perhaps even to keep. Being filled with bloodlust and simple fleshly lust myself, I envied them their acquisitions. However much I lusted, though, I despatched no messenger with an order to put aside one of the yellow-haired women for me. One experience with a Sklavinian wench brought to me at sword's point sufficed for a lifetime. I stood in the darkness in front of my tent, blood thundering in my ears, listening to those who had betrayed me, betrayed Romania, dying as they deserved.

By midnight, it was over. With a squadron of excubitores bearing torches, I walked through the Sklavinian encampment. Death and the stench of death were everywhere. Here and there, my guardsmen and I had to walk on twisted bodies, no open ground showing beneath or around them. For all that, though, there were fewer corpses than I had expected. "Did our soldiers let some of the barbarians escape?" I growled, not concerned over a few women but rather over any large number of men. "If they did, they shall be punished."

Then the excubitores led me to the white, chalky cliffs. Some of them leaned over, arms extended, thrusting out their torches as far as they could. I leaned over myself and peered down. The light the torches cast on the scene at the base of the precipices was meager, but enough. Corpses were drifted there like snow after a winter blizzard. I still heard an occasional moan, not all the Sklavenoi forced over the edge having died at once.

In the morning, I would send some soldiers down there to finish their work completely. For the time being, what I had accomplished would do. And I saw every thing that I had made, and, behold, it was very good.

M Y A K E S

How did Justinian dare to take the Holy Scriptures' words about God and use them to speak of himself, Brother Elpidios? Yes, I think it's an outrage, too. If you want to think God punished him for that sin, how can I argue with you, considering the way he ended up?

But he was Emperor of the Romans, remember—God's deputy on earth. And any man who takes pen in hand uses the words of the Bible to help give his own thoughts shape. I think that's what he was doing, nothing worse. I don't think he had blasphemy on his mind.

Something worse? Oh, the massacre. I did try to stop it. You heard what Justinian had to say about that. The Sklavenoi who came back hadn't done anything wrong; they proved as much *by* coming back. But Justinian wouldn't listen to me. There were times—too many times—when Justinian wouldn't listen to anyone but Justinian.

God was listening? Well, I hope so. I'm an old sinner now, and pretty soon I'll see Him face to face. At least I can hope there's something on the other side of the scales to keep those sins from dragging me down to hell. I can hope. Can't I, Brother?

J U S T I N I A N

Having avenged myself against the Sklavenoi, I dismissed the Anatolic troops and those from the Opsikion, allowing them to return to their respective military districts. As they began their journey eastward, many of them thanked me for having allowed them to take part in my vengeance.

"The pleasure was mine," I said, to which they responded with laughter. But what sounded like a witticism was nothing less than simple truth.

Accompanied only by the excubitores and by Leontios, then I went back to Nikomedeia. The guardsmen marched as if expecting combat at any moment, and so perhaps they were, the country through which we were marching still being that upon which I had resettled the Sklavenoi. But the surviving barbarians, instead of attacking us, fled far away, not wishing to invite further chastisement on themselves.

From Nikomedeia to Chalcedon across the Bosporos from Constantinople, the journey along the military road was uneventful. Ferries waited there to take me, the guardsmen, and Leontios back to the God-guarded and imperial city. Although returning sooner and with less glory than I had hoped upon beginning my campaign, I had lost no great stretch of Roman territory despite defeat at the battle by Sebastopolis.

I invited Leontios to accompany me and one company of the excubitores on the ship that would return us to Constantinople. "Thank you, Emperor; that's very kind of you," he said. "I'm glad you're not upset any more, and that you've gotten over being angry at me." He went up onto the deck of the ferry with a broad smile of relief stretched across his face.

The wind blowing from the wrong quarter, oarsmen took us across the narrow neck of water separating Asia from Europe. Before we had gone more than a couple of bowshots from the quays of Chalcedon, I pointed to Leontios and called out to the excubitores near me: "Seize that man and cast him in chains!"

"What?" Leontios bellowed, like a bull at the moment when the knife makes it into a steer. As the excubitores dragged him down, he exclaimed, "Emperor, I thought you'd forgiven me!"

"What do I care what you thought?" I said while the guardsmen were wrapping heavy iron chains around his wrists and ankles and locking them with heavy iron padlocks. "I never forgive those who wrong me. I punish them—as they deserve."

Leontios kept on bellowing, quite unpleasantly. One of the excubitores asked, "Shall we pick him up and fling him into the drink, Emperor? A few bubbles and it'd be all over. With all those chains on him, he'll sink like a rock."

"No," I said, though I should have said yes. "Drowning the wretch is too quick to suit me. I want him to have plenty of time to think about his crimes and his stupidity. We'll take him back to the city, we'll throw him into a prison, and then—we'll forget about him."

"Emperor, your father never would have done such a thing," Leontios said while the excubitores, resenting him no less than the Sklavenoi for the defeat near Sebastopolis, howled laughter to see and hear him discomfited.

He had tried before to use the memory of my father to get me to do what he wanted rather than what I wanted. Having failed then, he merely proved his own foolishness by making the attempt a second time. "You're right," I told him, remembering what had happened to my uncles Herakleios and Tiberius. "My father would have cut off your nose and slit your tongue, or perhaps put out your eyes, before disposing of you for good. You may thank me for my mercy." The excubitores laughed louder yet. Leontios said nothing. I signaled to one of the guardsmen. He seized Leontios by the hair and smashed his face against the planking of the deck. "You may thank me for my mercy," I repeated.

"Thank you for your mercy," Leontios choked out through cut and bleeding lips. His nose also bled. I made up my mind to reward the excubitor for serving me well.

Constantinople neared, perhaps more rapidly than I might have liked. The simplicity of campaigning appealed to me. Now, the Emperor of the Romans is God's deputy on earth. That which is pleasing to the Emperor has the force of law. Basic tenets of Roman law, aye. But practice and law, here as in many instances, were not identical.

For one thing, I was coming home to my mother, who would pester me to marry again, which I did not want to do (an error, I see now, but I failed to see it then), and to show friendliness toward my daughter, which I wanted even less to do. For another, I was imperfectly enamored of the mass of administrative detail through which I would have to wade on returning to the imperial city. And, for a third, on campaign I did not suffer the constant scrutiny I had to endure at the palace.

The closer I got to Constantinople, the better I understood why my grandfather had abandoned it for the barbarous west. True, Lombards and the Arabs were troublesome there, but I grew ever more certain that was not the only reason for his going. If he was not also seeking escape, I should be very surprised.

But, considering the fate that found him in Sicilian Syracuse, he must have learned—although too late—there was no escape from the dangers dogging the imperial dignity. And I . . . I stayed in Constantinople, and my fate found me there.

Stephen the Persian looked grave. Standing beside him, Theodotos looked like a vulture bereft of carrion. Stephen said, "Emperor, the treasury would have greatly benefited had the revenues anticipated from this past summer's campaign been realized. As things are, however—"

"As things are, we're flat," Theodotos broke in, his voice a harsh croak made all the harsher by contrast with Stephen's smooth almost-contralto.

"Very well, we're flat," I said. "How do we recover from being flat?"

Stephen the Persian shrugged. His jowls, flabby like those of so many eunuchs, flopped up and down. "Most desirable would have been either the continuation of tribute from the Arabs or the acquisition of booty of comparable value. Absent those factors . . ." He shrugged again. "I have done such things as I could to increase revenue for both the public treasury and the privy purse, but we still face a significant short-fall."

"You have been diligent; I will say that much," I replied. That was, if anything, an understatement. Since returning to the imperial city, I had found myself bombarded with petitions and complaints about Stephen's methods of collecting that which was owed to the state. Up until that time, I had not imagined the Greek language contained so many synonyms for *extortion*.

Most of these petitions I rejected out of hand: what man ever pays his taxes with a glad heart? Even where there was some doubt in the matter, I supported my sakellarios, for, when the needs of the subject and those of the fisc collide, those of the subject needs must give way. If the fisc fails, the Roman Empire fails, and, if the Roman Empire fails, the subject goes down in ruin.

I recall no cases where there was not at least some doubt, enough to decide in favor of gaining the needed revenue. Even so, it was not enough.

Theodotos said, "Emperor, I know how we can bring in more gold, if you'll but say the word."

I leaned forward. "Tell me. This is what I want to hear."

With a nod to Stephen the Persian, Theodotos said, "Your sakellarios, he's a clever fellow with the numbers, but he's too kindhearted by half." I looked at the ex-monk with new respect. A great many men had accused Stephen of a great many things, but excessive generosity had not, till now, been one of them. Theodotos went on, "Oh, he's willing enough to squeeze the artisans and the merchants and such, but he's hardly touched the nobles and magnates here in the city."

"What have you to say about that?" I asked Stephen.

"There is some truth to it," the eunuch replied. "Squeezing artisans and merchants makes them grumble, but nothing more. Squeeze the nobles and magnates of Constantinople too hard, and they begin to plot against you."

"Let them plot." Theodotos made a quick chopping gesture with his right hand. "Then they end up short their eyes or their noses or their tongues—or their heads. And the property of proved traitors is forfeit to the fisc."

Both finance ministers looked my way. They could propose, but I had to decide. I nodded to Theodotos. "Let it be as you say," I told him. "The nobles and magnates will not plot against me. If it weren't for my family, there would be no Roman Empire for them to inhabit. We would have fallen to the Persians or to the followers of the false prophet many years ago. Or if I am mistaken, and some of those dogs prove base enough to turn toward treachery despite that truth . . . if that be so, we shall use them as you suggest, Theodotos."

He and Stephen the Persian both bowed their heads. I having made the decision, they went forth and put it into effect. They were good at what they did; I would not have set them in their places had they been anything but good at what they did. From that day forth, money came into the fisc in quantities adequate to make up for the tribute the deniers of Christ were no longer paying.

But oh, how the grandees screeched to have to pay their share to the government that not only kept them safe but kept them rich! By the petitions flooding in to me, by the complaints from those nobles bold enough to beard me in person, anyone would have thought the whole of their wealth was being confiscated, not just that part necessary to preserve the whole.

Some of them, as Stephen had warned me, did worse than carp. These vicious fools I detected in good time, having a fair number of spies of all descriptions scattered about the imperial city. Some of them I ordered mutilated, following Theodotos's suggestion. Others I simply cast into prison, along with the insolent guildsmen and with Leontios. Occasionally, to show my mercy, I would release one or two. The rest simply stayed where they were. Fewer people missed them, I am certain, than they imagined would be the case.

They found company in their prison cells, too, for, men being sinful and imperfect creatures, not all found themselves able or willing to obey the canons set down by the assembled bishops of the fifth-sixth synod. Those who persisted in lewd practices or in the demonically inspired customs of the pagan past deserved punishment no less than those who sought to conceal their wealth—and what they deserved, they received. If I could make it so, Constantinople would be a moral city.

I also had in mind that Constantinople should be a safe city: safe for me, I should say. To that end, my spies watched not only those still free and able to make mischief, but also some of the prominent personages in prison. One of these fellows, a converted Jew named George, brought me word of Leontios. "He has two suspicious characters who visit him all the time," the spy reported.

"Assume anyone who wants to visit Leontios is a suspicious character and go on from there," I answered, to which George, who himself looked like a born conspirator, nodded emphatic agreement. I added, "Who are these people, anyway?"

"One is a monk, a certain Paul, from the monastery of Kallistratos," George said, "and the other a former officer, also now a monk, called Gregory the Kappadokian."

"The plain monk I don't much care about," I said. "Even Leontios is entitled to prayers for the benefit of his soul. In fact, considering the state of Leontios's soul, I daresay he needs more prayers than most other people I could name. But tell me more about this Gregory, who was once a soldier. He may still remember his old trade."

"Right now, Emperor, I don't know any more." George looked crafty, an expression that, by the way the lines on his face fell into familiar patterns, he frequently assumed. "But I can find out."

He sent me a written memorandum a few days later. Gregory the Kappadokian turned out to have been a kleisouriarch, an officer in charge of defending a mountain pass against the Arabs, and had served under Leontios in a couple of his campaigns. More reports on him trickled in over the days and weeks that followed. He seemed to have been a good if unspectacular soldier before donning the monastic robe, and to have no intimate ties to Leontios save their common service: he had no relatives married to any of Leontios's, nor did Leontios owe him money. For that matter, he did not owe Leontios money, either.

I considered flinging Gregory into prison, too, by choice into the cell next to Leontios's so they could talk with each other to their hearts' content. In the end, though, I forbore. But for his continued friendship with a former commander, Gregory appeared to be an utterly ordinary fellow. And Leontios, imprisoned as he was, could hardly threaten me. Reasoning so, I let Gregory stay free and keep on visiting him.

I would not be so naive today.

Before the campaigning season ended that year, the Arabs sent several raiding parties into Anatolia. They did this, I gathered, every year no truce was in force between them and us. These raids, though not large, penetrated deeper into our territory than the followers of the false prophet usually managed to do. I did not take long to find out why: Sklavenoi from the special army were guiding the Arabs through the territory that had once nurtured them.

Receiving that news, I rounded on Myakes. "If I had been sorry about slaughtering the Sklavenoi, I wouldn't be any more."

Infuriatingly, he shrugged. "I don't know about that, Emperor," he said. "You took vengeance on them, and now they're taking vengeance on you. How is one any different from the other?"

"How?" I exclaimed. "I'll tell you how! I am Emperor of the Romans. They are a pack of wretched barbarians. Now do you see?"

All he did was shrug again. In his quiet way, he could be, and often insisted on being, a difficult man. Having been accustomed to his stubbornness from boyhood, I tolerated it in a way I would not have from a more recent acquaintance.

Dismissing him, I summoned a scribe. The man poised reed pen over papyrus to take down my words. "This order is to go to all Roman military commanders in the east," I said, and the scribe nodded. I drew a deep breath before continuing, "Let any Sklavinian traitor captured in the company of Arab raiders within Romania be burned alive as fitting punishment for his treachery. Let there be no appeal from or reduction to this sentence. Let the barbarians be filled with fear so that they no longer abet such debased acts of brigandage."

The chancery having prepared sufficient copies of the order, couriers on fast horses sped it to the military district of the Armeniacs and to that of the Anatolics, the two most likely to be concerned with it. Before the end of the campaigning season, I received several most gratifying reports of incinerated Sklavenoi.

I summoned Myakes and read to him a particularly fine one. "Isn't that splendid?" I said. "Reading it, I can almost hear the Sklavinian's shrieks, almost smell the meat roasting on his bones. This Bardanes who would sooner be called Philippikos has the makings of a first-rate officer. I aim to promote him for the excellent service he's given me."

"If I were you, Emperor, before I promoted him I'd check to see if he ever really did cook any Sklavenoi," Myakes answered stolidly. "Anybody can tell a good yarn. There's people out on the streets of the city who make their living doing nothing else but—and I'm not even talking about lawyers."

I snorted. "I think you've been jealous of Bardanes since he spotted that Sklavinian breathing through a reed."

"You're the Emperor. You can think whatever you like," Myakes said. "Me, what I think is, that story sounds too good to be true. And when a story sounds too good to be true, it usually is."

That made me thoughtful. I have already remarked on several occasions that the worst curse of being Emperor is hearing what people want you to hear, not what is true. If Bardanes Philippikos was sending me fancy stories about how many Sklavenoi he had given over to the flames so as to make himself look good, I needed to know as much. And if he had, he would be a long time regaining my confidence, if ever he did.

The Roman Empire has spies among the Arabs. The followers of the false prophet, worse luck, also have spies in Romania. And the Emperor of the Romans has spies of his own, whom he can send forth to examine the deeds not only of foreign foes but also of enemies and potential enemies closer to home. I sent out two of these men, neither knowing of the other, to learn whether Bardanes had done as he claimed.

Their separate reports came back to Constantinople within days of each other a few weeks later, the gist of both being that Bardanes Philippikos had indeed incinerated a goodly number of captured Sklavenoi. On receiving the second report, I shoved them both under Myakes' nose, asking him, "What have you to say about these?"

Not reading with any great fluency, he needed some little while to make sense of the reports. When he had finished them, he handed them back to me with a single offhand comment: "All right, Emperor, he didn't get caught—*this* time."

"Why, Myakes," I said mockingly, "I do believe you're jealous."

To that he made no reply at all, but turned and took his leave with far less ceremony than was suitable on departing the presence of the Emperor of the Romans. Too late, I realized I had wounded him. Perhaps he truly was jealous. Perhaps he was but hurt I could have thought him so. Emperor of the Romans though I was and am, I have never, from that time to this, dared to ask him. Over the next few days (with, I grant, some friendly overtures on my part), his demeanor gradually regained the gruff familiarity I tolerated from no one else.

MYAKES

Jealous, Brother Elpidios? Why on earth would I have been jealous of Philippikos? Because I was a starving peasant when I took up the soldier's life and he had a patrician for a father? I'd known plenty of blue-bloods by then. It's not angels that come out when they sit on the latrine, any more than it is with me.

Is that blasphemy, Brother? I'm sorry; I didn't aim to singe your virgin ears. I just meant that wasn't the reason. Because I was Justinian's friend—or as close to a friend as Justinian let himself have—and Bardanes came sniffing round the Emperor? That, now, that's closer to the mark. I didn't trust him. He was too smooth somehow, if you know what I mean. Justinian couldn't see it. He never could. He paid for it, too, at the end.

Because Bardanes Philippikos was a heretic who tried to overthrow the sixth holy ecumenical synod? I didn't know that then . . . and I wouldn't have worried much about it if I did know.

You didn't hear that last? Well, never mind. Wasn't important anyhow.

J U S T I N I A N

Shortly after learning that the Sklavenoi who had defected from the service they owed the Roman Empire were still tormenting us, I had equally unpleasant news from the opposite frontier: from, indeed, the uttermost west. Pope Sergios, taking the habitual presumption of the bishops of Rome to a new extreme, refused to ratify the canons to which the bishops I had assembled for the fifth-sixth synod had agreed.

I admit I was not entirely without warning the pope of Rome might behave in such arrogant and senseless fashion, several bishops from the west or under papal jurisdiction having predicted his descent into folly. But I also admit I had not credited their warning, being unable to believe any priest of God could not only ignore but reject canons promulgated by a synod through whose deliberations the Holy Spirit had surely worked.

Such presumption was all the more distasteful coming from the bishop of Rome. Without the military power of the exarch of Ravenna, the viceroy of the Roman Empire for Italy, the pope's miserable city would soon have fallen to the Lombards. Not only are the Lombards savage and barbarous even by standards prevailing in the west, they also profess the Arian heresy.

When I took counsel with the ecumenical patriarch Paul to formulate a joint response to Sergios's insolence, I spoke in anger: "We ought to let the Lombards have Rome and eat it up, and the pope with it. That would serve him as he deserves, the ungrateful wretch."

Paul coughed several times, deeply and wrackingly, before replying. The sickness of the lungs that would claim his life in the following year already had its hooks deep in him. When he could speak, he said,

"Emperor, however much such a course might please you now, it would cause a great scandal throughout Christendom, and would do untold harm to the holy church in the west."

"Pope Sergios is doing great harm to the holy Christian church in the west," I retorted. "How dare he refuse to accept these canons after the synod decided they were proper and just?"

Paul sighed. "I regret the pope's stance no less than you, Emperor. The bishops in Rome being first in honor, they often deem themselves first in authority as well. You are not the first Emperor to discover this." He coughed again.

"I know," I said. "My grandfather exiled a pope for his disobedience. If I have to do the same, I tell you I shall not shrink from it."

"May that not come to pass," Paul said. "It would embroil the church in conflicts better left unkindled. Let us try first to bring the pope to reason."

"Very well," I said. "See to it, then." My father having devoted much of the energy of his reign to restoring unity within the church through the sixth holy ecumenical synod, I did not wish to damage his work by causing another schism. That was not the purpose for which I had convened the fifth-sixth synod. The reverse, in fact: I had intended it to clear up the problems the two previous ecumenical synods had ignored. I truly had not believed the pope of Rome might reject what the bishops prescribed.

A few days later, Paul gave me a draft of the letter he purposed sending to Pope Sergios. It was a small masterpiece of its kind, arguing the case so persuasively and brilliantly that I felt certain even the mulish bishop of Rome would be made to see the light. I wrote I have read and I approve on the draft, then returned it to the ecumenical patriarch.

He let me know when the letter left on a ship bound for Italy. It was, by then, quite late in the sailing season. I was not sure the letter would reach the pope before spring, and did not doubt his reply would not arrive in the imperial city till then. I dared hope Sergios would ponder his course through the winter months and, becoming more moderate with contemplation, would announce his acceptance of the canons when good weather once more permitted intercourse between his barbarous ruin of a city and the heartland of the Roman Empire.

One can always hope.

With spring came a resumption of the Arabs' raids on the eastern frontier of the Roman Empire. As had been true in the previous year, some of Neboulos's Sklavenoi served as guides to the deniers of Christ. I sent messengers renewing my order to burn those barbarians who fell into our hands.

Again, I received from Bardanes the son of Nikephoros vivid accounts of the Sklavenoi he had roasted. Again, they seemed too good to be true, so much so that I once more despatched spies to the east to learn whether he was telling me what he had done or what he hoped I wanted to hear. Again, my agents reported back to me that he had in fact given captives from the special army special treatment. In recognition of his zeal, I promoted him to kleisouriarch.

Spring also brought, as foretold, a reply from Pope Sergios. That reply nearly prostrated poor Paul, weak as he already was from his bodily illness. When he brought the letter to me, he had to be carried to the palace in a litter. His face was hardly more than skin and bones, and his hand looked skeletal as he passed the pope's missive to me.

The letter was in Greek, Sergios being familiar with that language because his family sprang from somewhere near Antioch, although he himself, Paul told me, had been born on the island of Sicily where my grandfather lost his life. Since it was in what is now the chief language of the Roman Empire, I had no trouble understanding it. Having read it, I should have preferred it to be in Latin or some other even more barbarous tongue, so I might have remained ignorant of its import.

In it, Sergios lyingly asserted his legates had affixed their signatures to the canons of the fifth-sixth council after being deceived as to the meaning of those canons. Since they had participated in the synod, their mendacity and that of the pope were made manifest. Sergios further claimed that the canons, decided upon after deliberation of the participating bishops and signed by all the patriarchs save him alone and by myself, went outside the usages of the church and were erroneous innovations. He said he would sooner die than consent to them.

"By the Mother of God," I said to Paul, "nothing would please me better than giving this vain and ignorant bishop exactly what he tells me he wants."

Paul tried to reply, and, after suffering a coughing fit that ended with bloody spittle at one corner of his mouth, succeeded: "Emperor, I pray you in the name of the holy church, exercise restraint. The pope is a fool, but he is also heir to Peter, patriarch of the see of Rome."

"The heir to Peter, patriarch of the see of Rome, is a fool," I answered, reversing his words, "and deserves to pay the penalty for his folly."

"Have mercy upon him, Emperor," the ecumenical patriarch begged.

I tugged at my beard, not wanting in the least to have mercy on any man who presumed to defy me. But Paul, plainly, was a dying man, making this request of me with what was almost the last of his strength. "Perhaps I can put him in fear," I said, "and in so doing warn him of his own fate unless he obeys."

"That would be better," Paul said eagerly, grasping at any straw of conciliation I offered.

And so, on the following day, I sent a letter to Zachariah the exarch of Ravenna, ordering him to send soldiers down to Rome, to seize some of Pope Sergios's closest followers, and to ship them to Constantinople for judgment. In due course, Zachariah wrote back to tell me he had obeyed my commands by sending one of his underlings, a certain Sergios unrelated to the pope, down from Ravenna to Rome with enough men to lay hold of backers of the bishop of Rome.

Unlike Pope Sergios, my Sergios obeyed me in every particular. As quickly as could be expected, he sailed back to Constantinople with two of the recalcitrant pope's prominent supporters: John the bishop of Portus (a town on the sea near Rome, and serving it as a harbor) and Boniface, one of the pope's advisers.

"What have you to say for your master?" I demand when they were brought before me, their hands chained behind them like those of any other prisoners.

Boniface stood mute. John, who had more spirit, however misguided he was, said, "Emperor, the apostolic father will never agree to canons he thinks wrong."

"Then he will have a hard life," I said. "If I plucked the two of you out of your backwards western land, I can pluck him as well, and I will if he does not come to his senses."

"It shall be as God wills," John answered.

Their fate was as I willed. I ordered them cast into prison with those who had tried withholding money from the state and those jailed for violating the canons of the fifth-sixth synod. Since Pope Sergios was both withholding obedience from the state and violating the canons of the fifth-sixth synod, I reckoned that fate fitting for his henchmen.

But, like that of Pharaoh in bygone days, the heart of the bishop of Rome remained hardened. Not long after my Sergios conveyed Boniface and John to Constantinople, Pope Sergios sent me another defiant letter, not only rejecting the canons of my synod once more but also demanding the release of those two men.

Paul the ecumenical patriarch wrote Sergios of Rome another letter, warning him of his error and also of my wrath. It did no good. Sergios's presumption continued unabated, and indeed grew worse. I would have written to Zachariah on the instant, ordering him to arrest Sergios and

convey him to Constantinople, had matters more urgent than the ravings
of a backwoods prelate not intervened.

After defeating us at Sebastopolis, the followers of the false prophet might
well have stolen considerable territory from the military district of the
Armeniacs. This, as I have said, they did not do, contenting themselves
with raiding, using the skulking Sklavenoi to show them where the best
booty lay. We Romans dealt with these raids fairly well, and I had hoped
the lost battle would prove to have no severe consequences for the Roman
Empire.

In this, as in the treacherous dealings with Neboulos on the night
after the battle by Sebastopolis had been joined, I underestimated the
depths of the Arabs' iniquity. And so, the following summer I received
the unwelcome news that Sabbatios, an Armenian prince who had been
loyal to us Romans since Leontios's campaign some years before, had
given his principality into the hands of the deniers of Christ.

I spent much of the summer trying to repair the damage Sabbatios's
defection inflicted on the Roman Empire. Unlike Italy, Armenia is vitally
important to Constantinople. From its mines, we draw much of our iron.
Its sturdy soldiers swell the ranks of Roman armies. And, should a foe
control its passes, he gains the best routes for invading Anatolia.

Furthermore, the Armenians, even if not always of perfect orthodoxy, are Christians. Having them come under the yoke of the followers
of the false prophet was bitter to me, and would surely prove bitter to
them. Sabbatios proving unwilling to pay the least attention to my own
entreaties, I prevailed upon Paul the ecumenical patriarch to write to
him, bidding him reconsider his abandonment of allegiance to the Roman
Empire in light of our common faith.

In this ploy I had considerable hope, Sabbatios having over a period
of years established a name for ostentatious piety. But the wretch had, or
pretended to have, taken umbrage at the canons of the fifth-sixth council
condemning certain Armenian usages—this despite the approval Armenian bishops had given those canons.

"What a satanic hypocrite!" I burst out when Paul sadly gave his
letter to me. "He deserves to come under the rule of the followers of the
false prophet: only they come close to matching his deceit."

"Emperor, I shall pray that Sabbatios may return to his senses," the
patriarch replied. Having spoken, he paused to catch his breath, which
he did with increasing difficulty as his illness advanced. Then he went
on, "And I shall pray for you."

"Thank you," I said. "May God hear your prayers."

He held up a hand. The tips of his fingers were not pink, nor even white, but faintly blue. "I shall pray for you, Emperor, for you have stirred up hatred against yourself and against the Roman Empire—"

"How dare you?" I broke in, my temper as usual quick to kindle.

"How dare I?" he answered. "I dare because I am a dying man. What worse can you do to me than my body is already doing? Soon God shall demand an accounting of my many sins face to face. But I say again, you have stirred up hatred against yourself and the Roman Empire in Italy and the west, in Armenia, and even here in the Queen of Cities, where rich and poor alike groan under the unfair taxes your ministers inflict on them."

"Is it my fault dissembling evildoers abound in both west and east?" I said. "As for the whiners and grumblers here in the city, when have you ever heard of any man who thinks the tax collector a benefactor, even if without taxes the Roman Empire would come crashing down in ruin?"

Paul said, "Emperor, I have told you the truth. What you choose to do with it is your affair. God has granted each of us free will, to use for good or ill."

"You are dismissed," I said coldly. Paul left the palace, not returning for some time. This estrangement kept me from using him to try to bring Pope Sergios to his senses—assuming Sergios had senses to which he could be brought, which was by no means obvious.

The very next day, Sisinniakes, the logothete in charge of petitions, plopped down a great stack of them in front of me. "These, Emperor," he said mournfully, "are almost all of them from people protesting their tax assessments. Not just little people, either, mind you: some of them are officials in your own government, and some others are rich, powerful men who like to hear yes when they ask for something."

"They will hear that I am their Emperor, and I am to be obeyed," I snapped, angry at the coincidence of these petitions' coming so close on the heels of my argument with the patriarch.

Sisinniakes cleared his throat. "Emperor, forgive my saying so, but you're the fifth of your house I've seen on the throne. People respect the house, Emperor, on account of all the fine things the rulers of your line have done, but they don't love you."

"I don't love them, either," I shot back. "Why should I? They do everything they can to cheat the fisc in its hour of need, and they dance and worship demons and fornicate without the least thought for their immortal souls. If they were better, they would be easier to rule."

Bowing his head, he said no more. He did not have quite the same security in offending me as did Paul, being neither a churchman nor on the very edge of death. But if I took his head, I would have been depriving the old fool of only a few years of life. It seemed hardly worth the fuss it would cause.

Trying to get some use out of him, I said, "You told me almost all these petitions had to do with taxes. What about the rest?"

He looked up to face me, smiling a sad smile. "Emperor, the rest are from men and women who have gone to prison because they got caught breaking the canons of the fifth-sixth synod, or else from their families begging to get them out."

"They are sinners and seducers and blasphemers," I snarled. "Let them stay there till they rot, every last one of them." I picked up the pile of petitions and thrust them back into Sisinniakes' arms. "As for these, take them and burn them!"

I do not know whether or not he burnt them. I do know I never saw them again. That was what I wanted.

When spring returned to the world, the ecumenical patriarch Paul finally had the grace to depart from it. The synod of bishops of the see of Con-stantinople having sent me the traditional three names from which I could make my choice of Paul's successor, I selected a certain Kallinikos, he having a better reputation for pliability than either of the other two.

On meeting him, I found Kallinikos's demeanor and physiognomy to accord with his reputation. He was a round little man, with no sharp angles on his face or anywhere else about his person. By the way he leaned forward as if hanging on my every word, he gave the impression of being eager to please me.

Nor, in fact, was that impression false. Kallinikos was eager to please me. Kallinikos was eager to please everyone. He had a great many chances, and used every one of them. He was so eager to please, he would have made a better whore than a patriarch, but I did not know that at the time.

"I want you to draft a letter to Sergios, the patriarch of Rome," I told him, "bidding him to come to his senses, to accept the presence of the Holy Spirit at the fifth-sixth synod, and to acknowledge the canons the bishops established at that synod. His own legates, after all, were present there, as were other bishops from the patriarchate over which he has jurisdiction. Remind him of all this in no uncertain terms."

"It shall be just as you say, Emperor," Kallinikos promised, and it *was* just as I said. A couple of days later, he sent me a draft of his letter for my approval. The text was, if anything, even more fiery than I had hoped. I told him to send it to stubborn Sergios forthwith. For the moment, I was the man he was trying to please, and he was doing a splendid job.

Sergios's reply reached this God-guarded and imperial city as quickly as such things can be expected, given the distance between Rome and Constantinople and the difficulties and delays likely to be encountered on the journey. On account of its contents, though, I would have been as glad had it taken longer on the way, it being full of the same pretentious obstinacy the bishop of Rome had already displayed.

"Emperor, I stand ready to threaten this manikin of a Sergios with even harsher strictures than those of my last letter," Kallinikos declared, "strictures up to and including anathema."

"I thank you for that," I said, and meant it: patriarchs of Constantinople have been known to care more for accommodating themselves to the bishop of Rome than to the Emperor of the Romans. "Sergios did not seem to understand when two of his henchmen were fetched to Constantinople. The time for letters has passed, Kallinikos. I aim to fetch the pope here, to let him answer for his own transgressions."

"How right you are!" Kallinikos exclaimed, also sounding as if he meant it. No doubt he did. He was, however, ready to say *How right you are!* to anyone who told him anything of any sort.

Off went the letter. In it I told Zachariah to do with Pope Sergios as my grandfather had told the exarch's predecessor at that time to do with Pope Martin: to arrest him and bring him to the imperial city so I could pass judgment on him. My grandfather had sent Pope Martin to Kherson. To me, that seemed a good enough destination for Sergios.

Just how good it was, I would find out in due course.

MYAKES

B y the time Justinian became Emperor, Brother Elpidios, his family had been ruling the Roman Empire for more than eighty years. Like he says, people loved the house of Herakleios. People had reason to love it. Without the house of Herakleios, there probably wouldn't be a Roman Empire any more.

Justinian, now, by the time he's writing of here, he'd been Emperor about nine years. In those nine years, he'd taken all the goodwill people had for his family and chucked it right into the latrine. It might not have happened that way if some of the things he'd tried had worked out better—if we'd beaten the Arabs at Sebastopolis, for instance. Who but God can say for sure about something like that?

But what really wrecked things for him was that he went on doing whatever he thought he needed to do right then, and never had a clue that people were starting to spit when somebody said his name. Paul the patriarch and Sisinniakes both tried to tell him—you read me what they said. And you heard for yourself—he wouldn't listen.

Remember something else, too, Brother. Justinian was writing here years after what he's talking about. He still doesn't see or doesn't believe what people were telling him back then. He knew what happened to him. As long as he lived, he never figured out why.

JUSTINIAN

Not long after the letter to Zachariah started on the long journey to Ravenna, I was startled to receive a request for an audience from the monk Paul, who had been identified to me as a warm friend of Leontios's. Not only was I surprised, I was intrigued. This Paul must have known I knew of his attachment to a man who, to put it mildly, I did not find pleasing. Under those circumstances, asking for an audience with me took a certain amount of what was either courage or hubris. Trying to learn which, I granted the request.

Paul put me in mind of my Theodotos: he was intensely certain of his purpose. Also like Theodotos, he wasted no time in small talk. Having risen from his prostration, he said, "Emperor, I have come to ask you to free the brave general Leontios."

"Why should I?" I demanded, my tone halfway between anger that he should dare to say such a thing and curiosity as to why he said it.

"First and foremost, from simply Christian charity," he answered. "No man deserves to be caged like a wild beast, and Leontios less than most."

I shook my head. "As a man, I might do this," I said. That left open the possibility I also might *not* do it, which was far more likely. I continued: "As Emperor of the Romans, I cannot. By his bungling, Leontios cost the Roman Empire far too much to let me casually forgive him."

"But, Emperor, in his earlier campaigns he gained great glory and advantage for the Roman Empire," Paul said. "Should you not weigh the one in the pans of the balance against the other?"

"When he won victories, he was promoted. He was rewarded. How else did he become a rich man, and a general to whom I entrusted a great army?" I said. Paul remained silent—what could he reply to that? Leaning forward on the throne, I asked him, "Are you telling me a man who is rewarded for his successes should not be punished for his failures?"

"No, Emperor," he said; had he said anything else, I would have had him thrown out of the throne room. He had spirit, though, continuing, "But does he deserve to be punished so harshly for a misfortune that partly sprang not from any error of his own but from the treachery of the barbarous Sklavenoi?"

As he had been nowhere near the field by Sebastopolis, he must have spent a lot of time listening to Leontios in his cell. I answered, "I have punished the Sklavenoi, or such of them as I have laid hands on, as they deserved. Shall I treat Leontios as I treated them?"

"No, for he was no traitor, only a man brought down by the treachery of others," Paul said, arguing like a lawyer.

"That is not so; he disobeyed my orders, which, had he followed them, might have brought us victory in spite of the Sklavenoi," I told the monk. He looked down at the floor, again not knowing how to respond. I daresay Leontios, doing his utmost to show himself in the best possible light, had never bothered to mention that small detail. Scowling down from the throne at Paul, I said, "Can you still honestly tell me this wretch deserves his freedom?"

To my surprise, he nodded. "As I said before, Emperor, a tiny, stinking cell is no fit home for a man. If you cannot find it in your heart to forgive him, would you be generous enough to commute his sentence from imprisonment to exile?"

That, I must say, was clever, exile being a common punishment for those who have offended their sovereign. After some thought, I answered, "I shall not do that at this time. I do not reject it out of hand, though. Should I change my mind, or should a proper situation arise, I will think on it again."

"You are gracious, Emperor," Paul said. I did not feel particularly gracious; part of the reason I had said what I said was to make him go away without committing myself to anything. He added, "Leontios will be glad to hear he has some hope of seeing the light of day once more."

I started to tell him not to let Leontios get his hopes up, but then held my tongue. For Leontios to be in prison was torment, as Paul rightly said: I had intended it to be such. But for Leontios to be in prison, thinking each day might be the one on which he was set free, disappointed each night when he lay down on his pallet, hope building again the next morning, only to be dashed once more: was that not torment more exquisite? If Paul wanted to inflict it on his friend, he was, as far as I was concerned, welcome and more than welcome to do so.

"I am glad to see you smile so, Emperor," Paul said. "It gives me hope you will soon show my friend the light of your mercy."

"Does it?" I said, and smiled more broadly.

I walked through the gardens around the palace with Kallinikos. It had rained earlier in the day. Drops of water still glistened here and there on leaves and flowers, and all the trees and shrubs and plants glowed with the special green they take on just after a rain.

My mind, however, was not altogether on the garden. I pointed to an old, run-down church dedicated to the Mother of God that stood near the palace. "Hardly anyone goes in there these days," I remarked.

"A pity," the patriarch said, trying as usual to guess my mood and to accommodate himself to it.

This time, he guessed wrong. "What I have in mind," I told him, "is tearing it down and putting up a fountain and some seats there, so I can have a convenient place to receive the nobles when the weather is fine."

"You want to—tear down the church?" he said, frowning. This was not the sort of request he received every day.

But I nodded. "You can rebuild it somewhere else—in the district of Petrion, say. There aren't that many churches near the Golden Horn now. You need not pay for this," I added. "Since I am tearing this one down, I'll pay for the replacement."

That put a different light on things, as I had thought it might. Now Kallinikos almost purred: "Of course, Emperor. It shall be just as you say." I could see from the gleam in his eye that the church he would build in Petrion would be far grander than the one already crumbling to ruins of its own accord here.

"Oh," I said, as if just thinking of it. "One thing more: I want a public prayer from you as the workmen start to tear down this church." I pointed again toward the tumbledown building.

The ecumenical patriarch frowned again. "A—prayer, Emperor? We have many prayers for the construction of a church, but I do not know of any for the demolition of a church." He risked a jest: "I am certain the followers of the false prophet know several."

I looked down my nose at him, being more than a palm's breadth the taller of us two. "I daresay you can devise one," I said coldly.

Kallinikos's coughing fit would have done credit to his predecessor, although Paul, being consumptive, had the better excuse for suffering such a spasm. "Emperor, if you require this prayer of me—"

"Would I have asked you for it if I did not require it?" I demanded. "I am not in the habit of making jokes, particularly in matters of piety."

Kallinikos stopped coughing. He started shaking. That suited me better. "If, as I say, you require this prayer of me, you shall have it."

"I hoped you would say that," I told him, smiling in such a way as to make him shake even more.

We held the ceremony for the demolition of the church a few days later. Splendid in his patriarchal regalia, Kallinikos raised his arms to the heavens and intoned, "Glory to the long-suffering God at all times: now, forever, and through eons upon eons. Amen." God certainly must be long-suffering, for Him to have put up for so long with such a lump of suet on the patriarchal throne.

Having knocked down the church, I duly erected the fountain and the reception area around it. There, on pleasant days, I passed time with aristocrats from the old families, many of whom affected to regard Constantine the Great as an upstart. We drank wine. We ate sweet cakes. Occasionally, when they felt bold, they would complain to me of the tax assessments Stephen the Persian and Theodotos levied on them. Since the occasions were social, I pretended to listen.

What did my forbearance gain me? Only betrayal.

MYAKES

A re you all right, Brother Elpidios? I haven't heard you sputter that way since the first time Justinian talked about having a woman. What's your trouble now? Oh, calling Kallinikos a lump of suet. Brother, I saw Kallinikos a good many times. If you rendered him down for fat, you'd need a big tun to hold it all.

The prayer when they knocked down the church? No, Justinian never figured out the patriarch meant God was long-suffering for putting up with *him*. A good thing for Kallinikos he didn't, too, or we'd have found out *exactly* how much fat he had in him. Justinian would have cooked him over a slow fire.

Yes, Justinian should have paid more attention to what the nobles were telling him. He should have paid more attention to what a lot of people told him. He didn't listen to me, either. You've seen that. You'll see it again, God knows. Justinian was good at a lot of things. Listening wasn't any of them.

J U S T I N I A N

Zachariah did not bring Pope Sergios back to the imperial city under arrest, as I had charged him to do. He went with an army of soldiers from Ravenna and some of the cities south of it down to Rome, intending to arrest Sergios and put him on a ship.

Unfortunately, however, through some mischance word of what the exarch intended to do reached Rome ahead of him. The people of Rome prevailed upon Zachariah's army not to let Sergios be taken out of the city and carried away to Constantinople. Although Zachariah himself was a fine man, steadfast both in his loyalty to me and in his purpose here, the soldiers under his command, being for the most part of the same Italian blood as the city mob of Rome, were persuaded by them, and mutinied against the exarch.

Some few of the soldiers remaining loyal to Zachariah, he used them to seize the pope in his residence. But his force was so small and that outside so large and inflamed that he lost hope of accomplishing the command I had given him. All at once, it was as if the wretched Sergios were holding him and his few faithful followers, rather than the other way round.

In his letter to me retailing these events, Zachariah maintained he yielded to necessity. Years later, I heard he cowered under the pope's bed, with the mutineers baying for his blood. God knows the truth in this matter. I do not. I do know Sergios, perhaps fearing my vengeance if the exarch were slain, did not let the mob work its full and ugly will upon him. Instead, he was merely expelled from Rome after being reviled and beaten.

Had the exarch been murdered by these semibarbarous Italians, I would unquestionably have sent a fleet from the imperial city to burn Rome to the ground and to bring Sergios here for trial as a common murderer. As things were, I by no means abandoned my intention of arresting Sergios and placing on the episcopal throne of Rome another, more tractable, man.

Before I could make arrangements to bring that to pass, however, another concern forced itself upon me: I received from Thessalonike word that Dorotheos, whom I had appointed general of my new military district of Hellas, had without warning lost his life. Having read so far and no farther in the announcement informing me of this, I assumed him to have fallen to some unsubdued Sklavenoi. But I soon discovered such was not the case. Rather, his horse threw him as he was riding into Thessalonike after hunting. His head smashed into the ground. He lay without speaking or moving for three days before breathing his last.

Military districts need generals at their head. This was especially true of one such as Hellas, with barbarians to the north and to the west. Leaving a vacancy there would have invited the Sklavenoi in the area to make trouble, perhaps negating everything my campaign against them had accomplished a few years before.

As one must do in such circumstances, I pondered whom to appoint as Dorotheos's successor. None of the other officers in Thessalonike at that time had particularly impressed me (nor, for that matter, had Dorotheos; his virtue, such as it was, lay in avoiding serious error, not in accomplishing anything great). That meant I would need to choose a general either in Constantinople or from one of the Anatolian military districts. Who, I wondered, would be willing to leave the imperial city or the long-civilized lands of Anatolia for a frontier district like Hellas?

And then I had what struck me as a happy inspiration. Having a pretty good notion of where the monks Paul and Gregory the Kappadokian were to be found, I sent messengers thither, summoning them to the throne room. While waiting for their arrival, I sent other messengers to the Proklianesian harbor in the southern part of the city.

The monk and the former kleisouriarch did not reach the palace until late afternoon, coming in with the stink of prison still clinging to their clothes. Ignoring that, I waited until they had prostrated themselves before me and arisen before saying, "You want Leontios free, not so?"

Their eyes widened. They glanced at each other, though neither of them turned his head. Cautiously, Paul said, "Emperor, that is so." He could scarcely deny it, but, for all he knew, I was about to order their heads taken for persisting in a desire I had no wish to fulfill.

Instead, I said, "Take him, then, and go." I held out an order to them. "This will authorize his release. You may tell the guards they shall answer to me if they fail to obey my command."

Now they were both frankly staring. Gregory took the sheet of papyrus from my hand as if afraid it would burst into flame if he touched it. His lips moving, he read it to assure himself it was what I had said. When he saw it was, he blurted, "What made you change your mind,

Emperor?" The order said nothing about that, concerning itself only with Leontios's release from imprisonment.

"I am naming him general of the military district of Hellas," I answered. "Three dromons wait in the Proklianesian harbor to take him—and you—to Thessalonike. Once you get him from the prison, go to the harbor without delay. If you are in Constantinople when the sun comes up tomorrow, you are dead men. Do you understand?"

"We do," Gregory said with a crispness proclaiming him a former officer.

"We thank you for your mercy, Emperor," Paul added.

"Go," I told the two of them, "and remember what I have said." They hurried out of the throne room. I never expected to see them or Leontios again. What I hoped was that Leontios, trying to accomplish something great and redeem himself from exile (not that I ever expected to allow him to return to the imperial city), would make the intimate acquaintance of a Sklavinian arrow and die a slow, painful, lingering death. I was pleased at my cleverness in sending him away; not only was he likely to perish, but I would get some use from him before he did. Not even Stephen the Persian could have found a more economical solution—so, at any rate, I told myself.

But the dawn of each new day does not necessarily bring that which one expected the afternoon before, nor that for which one had hoped.

M Y A K E S

W hat would I have said, Brother Elpidios, if Justinian had asked me whether I thought he should let Leontios loose? I probably would have told him he had a pretty good idea there. Leontios mured up in jail made people pity him and try and work for him. Leontios gone, though, would have been Leontios forgotten after a couple of weeks.

But Justinian made one mistake, Brother. He gave Paul and Gregory the order releasing Leontios. That was fine. He had the little fleet waiting to take them to Thessalonike. That was fine, too. And he told the two monks, once they had Leontios, to take him down to the harbor and put him on one of those dromons. And even that was fine. *But he didn't send any soldiers down to the harbor with them to make sure they put Leontios on the dromon and then got on themselves.*

Would I have reminded him to do that? How can I say, after more than thirty-five years? I like to think so, but who can be sure of such things? Any which way, I never got the chance. The company I led wasn't at the palace that evening; we were scattered among several buildings. With a squadron from them, I was watching over the Praitorion, on the Mese not far west of the grand palace, to make sure nobody stole either the papyri or the prisoners stashed there.

The duty was about as exciting as watching paint dry: a dead quiet night if ever there was one. To liven it up, some of the boys and I were rolling dice. Yes, I know that's a sin. Yes, I know the fifth-sixth synod had said so not long before. I wasn't planning on living like a monk, not in those days I wasn't.

Where was I? Ah, that's right. Down on one knee in a back room. All of a sudden, somebody started banging on the front door. It was barred, of course. I'd just won three throws in a row, and I didn't feel like getting up while the dice were hot. I pointed to a new excubitor, a little skinny fellow named John—or maybe Theophanes. After all these years, I forget which. Anyway, I told him, "Go see what the devil that is and make it stop."

Off he went. I heard him talking, but I couldn't make out what he was saying—like I told you, we were in a back room. A minute later, he came running back. "It's the Emperor!" he exclaimed.

"What?" I said. "What's the Emperor doing here, this time of night?"

"Says he's got some business needs taking care of," answered John or Theophanes or whatever his name was.

"Business?" I scratched my head. The only business Justinian usually did in the nighttime had to do with serving girls, and he wasn't about to come to the Praitorion to take care of that. The pounding started up again. I stared at John. "Didn't you let him in?"

"Uh—" He was new, all right.

"Mother of God!" I scrambled to my feet. "He's going to be angry enough to eat us all without salt." John—Theophanes—whoever he was—started back toward the door. "Wait," I told him. "I'll take care of it. He isn't so likely to bite my head off."

Bang! Bang! Bang! From the racket out there, I wondered if Justinian had ordered whoever he had with him to break down the doors. "Open up in there, in the name of the Emperor!" someone shouted: not a voice I knew.

"I'm coming, I'm coming!" I shouted back. When I got to the doors, I slid the bar out of the brackets to either side of them and leaned it against the wall. Then I pulled the doors wide. "Come in, Emp—" I began.

A couple of dozen men stood out there. Several of them were holding torches. All of them but a couple of black-robed monks were holding swords. At their head was a tall, wide-faced fellow in a filthy tunic whose tangled beard reached halfway to his waist. After a couple of heartbeats standing there gaping, I recognized Leontios.

I was too startled to draw my own sword right away. That probably saved my life. Instead of running me through, the way they would have if I'd had a blade in my hand, Leontios and the gang of bully boys he'd scraped together just jumped on me and knocked me down. I tried to fight back, but they started pounding my head on the floor. After that, my arms and legs didn't want to do what I told 'em. They trussed me up like a hog they didn't plan on roasting right that minute.

The racket made the rest of the excubitores come running out to see what was going on. One of the monks shouted, "Many years to the Emperor Leontios!"

"Treason!" John (or was it Theophanes?) cried. He did yank out his sword, and rushed at the monk. A couple of guardsmen followed him. Most of them, though, only stood there. They weren't about to die for Justinian. John and his comrades did die, and in a hurry, too. My heart sank, and I hadn't thought it could go any lower.

"Now what, Emperor?" one of Leontios's henchmen asked. Hearing that title used for anybody but Justinian made my blood boil. I tried to break loose, but no luck. Whoever had tied me up, he knew what he was doing.

Leontios didn't answer for himself. One of the monks spoke up for him: "Now we open up the prison cells where the tyrant has hidden away so many good soldiers and noblemen for so long. With them free, we'll have the beginnings of a decent little army of our own—and one that won't be any too fond of Justinian."

They found the keys to the cells on their own, and didn't have to ask me where they were. I lay there with my hands and feet getting numb and thanked God for that. If they'd put the edge of a sword up against my throat—I don't *think* I would have betrayed Justinian, but who can know something like that for sure? And if I didn't, well, I wouldn't be sitting here talking with you now, Brother Elpidios.

Leontios's men were laughing and joking when they went downstairs to set the prisoners free. Leontios and the two monks, along with some of his ruffians, stayed in that front hall. He spoke to one of the monks: "Paul, I know you always told me the stars said I'd be Emperor one day. I never believed it. I couldn't believe it. I thought I'd die in jail and never come out alive. When Justinian let me out, I expected I'd be dying soon in a different way. Why would he make me general of that godforsaken military district if he didn't figure I'd get killed there?"

"What he thought matters no more," the monk—Paul, I guess it was—answered. "Don't hesitate now and you *will* seize power. Listen to Gregory and me, follow our advice, and everything you want will be yours."

First I heard the prisoners coming, then I smelled them, and then I twisted my neck so I could see them. They took the weapons away from the bodies of the excubitores who'd fought for Justinian, and then disarmed the ones who hadn't fought for him and sent them away. What's that, Brother? *So then because thou art lukewarm, and neither hot nor cold, I will spew thee out of my mouth?* Thank you. That fits very well.

Some more men came into the Praitorion then, with swords and spears and clubs enough to fit out the prisoners who didn't have any. The monk who wasn't Paul—yes, Gregory; thank you again—said, "Here's what you'll do: go to all the districts of the city and spread the word that Justinian's gone crazy and aims to massacre everybody who lives inside the walls. People will believe it—people will believe anything about Justinian. Tell everybody to gather at the church of the Holy Wisdom. I'll go to the patriarch and tell him the same thing—except I'll say Justinian aims to start with him. Once we've done all that, Justinian will fall into our hands like a ripe fig."

I was lying there doing my best to be invisible. It didn't work. Somebody jerked a thumb at me and asked, "What about him?" I tried again to get free of the ropes. That didn't work, either.

But Leontios said, "Leave him be. He's Justinian's lapdog. If we fail, my head goes up on the Milestone come what may. But if we kill him and then fail, you'll all die. Not one of you will live. He's not going to hurt us lying there all tied up. When we win, we can figure out what to do with him."

So there I lay. Outside, on the Mese, the racket got louder than I'd ever heard it in the middle of the night. People were running back and forth, riding back and forth, and everybody who was going anywhere was yelling at the top of his lungs. Most of the yells were just yells, but then I heard someone shouting, "Dig up Justinian's bones!"

I felt the same sort of chill I had when most of my excubitores wouldn't fight for Justinian after Leontios and his toughs broke into the Praitorion. You shout "Dig up so-and-so's bones!" and you want the worst thing you can think of to happen to that person, whoever he is. And the more time went by, the more people were screeching, "Dig up Justinian's bones!"

Gregory came back then—it's not far from the Praitorion to the great church. He was grinning like he'd just tripped over a pound of gold in the street. "Kallinikos is with us!" he told Leontios. Everyone in the Praitorion—except me, and I didn't count—started cheering like a madman. Gregory waited till people calmed down a little, then went on, "Of course, Kallinikos is going to be with whoever talks to him last; we have to make sure none of Justinian's people—not that there are many left—gets near him. He's putting on his robes now. As soon as he's done that, he's going to preach in the great church."

More cheers. Leontios said, "I need to be there, then. Let's go." He started to leave, along with all his followers. For a minute there, I thought they were going to leave me all alone. I got my hopes up—maybe I could wiggle loose after all.

No such luck. Paul remembered me and said, "Now what do we do with him?"

"Sling a spear shaft through his arms and legs," Leontios said. "We'll haul him along with us. That way, he won't get into any trouble or any mischief." So that's what they did. Off I went, upside down, carried on their shoulders. Yes, like a pig heading for the roasting pit, Brother. I was thinking that very thing at the time.

The world looks pretty strange upside down, you know that? You never tried it, you say? I'll tell you, I wish I hadn't.

But while they were lugging me east up the Mese toward the church of the Holy Wisdom, I saw a couple of poor bastards in worse shape than I was. Along came this big bunch of laughing, shouting people, with screams coming out of the middle of it. The people thinned out a little when they recognized Leontios, so he could see what they were up to. That meant I got to see, too. They'd caught Stephen the Persian and Theodotos, who'd done so much to get Justinian hated, and tied their legs together, then tied ropes to their feet so they could drag 'em along the street.

"Mercy!" Stephen screamed. Theodotos screamed even louder: "Mercy, in God's name!"

"What are you going to do with them?" Leontios asked.

"Haul 'em down to the Forum of the Bull and burn 'em alive!" somebody told him, and that set the whole wolfpack baying again. By the sound of things, everybody liked the idea except Stephen and Theodotos. They kept bleating for mercy. Me, I was upside down. I was miserable. All the same, I wouldn't have minded seeing them burn, especially since they were the ones who'd landed Justinian in so much of his trouble.

But it wasn't up to me. It was up to Leontios. Everybody looked at him. He looked at the crowd, at all the eyes glittering in the torchlight. He looked at Theodotos and Stephen. He grinned. If they'd had any hope at all, that grin would have killed it. "Aye, burn 'em!" he shouted. Why not? That made the mob like him and hate Justinian, both at the same time. Off went the eunuch and the greedy monk, their heads banging the cobblestones. Their wails faded in the distance. So did the cheers of the mob, but a lot slower.

"On to the great church," Paul said. Leontios nodded, like he'd forgotten and was glad someone was reminding him.

The church and the courtyard around it were packed. "Make way!" Leontios's henchmen shouted. "Make way for the new Emperor!"

That got people to move aside, all right. Some were still yelling, "Dig up Justinian's bones!" More, though, started shouting, "Many years for the Emperor Leontios!" and "*Tu vincas*, Leontios!"—doing things properly, you see, in the middle of a usurpation.

"I think," Leontios said, "I shall rule as Leo."

"With your beard and hair so long, you certainly have the mane of a mighty lion, Emperor," Gregory said—currying favor in the middle of a usurpation.

Torches and lamps and candelabra made the inside of the church of the Holy Wisdom bright as day, though morning twilight was just beginning to stain the eastern sky. Because I was where I was, I didn't see Kallinikos till one of the ruffians who was carrying me almost trod on his toes. The patriarch wasn't up at the ambo where you'd expect him. He stood down by the baptistery instead.

Seeing Leontios, he bowed to him. "Hello, Emperor, and God bless you," he said. Yes, he'd trim his sail to fill with any wind. "I—" I don't know what he said after that, not for a while, because I got dropped on the floor like a sack of garbanzos, and I was too busy hurting to pay him any heed. For good measure, a couple of people kicked me and a couple more stepped on me, I don't think knowing I was there till their feet found out.

I'd landed on my back. I could look up and see Leontios and Kallinikos kiss each other on the cheek, a pair of smiling Judases. Paul came up and said something to the patriarch. Kallinikos's head went up and down, up and down. Whoever said anything to Kallinikos, he'd nod. He'd do it. If you got to him last, he was yours.

People started yelling: "The patriarch will speak! The patriarch will speak!"

It got quiet. Kallinikos filled himself up with air like a frog about to croak. Then he let it out, all at once: "This is the day the Lord has made! Let us give thanks and rejoice!" After that, he couldn't go on for a while, not through all the cheering. When he did, it was with about the drivel you'd expect: "This is the day of change, of freedom, of hope, of justice, of—"

He probably could have gone on for hours, but somebody outshouted him. Now, it's just as rude to interrupt the ecumenical patriarch as it is to interrupt the Emperor. But Kallinikos didn't care, not this time, and neither did anyone else, because what the fellow yelled was, "We have Justinian!"

J U S T I N I A N

I woke to tumult, some time in the late hours of the night. Only the earliest hint of dawn showed in the window. Beside me, the girl I had taken to bed for my pleasure the evening before stirred and mumbled and rolled over; the soft tip of her bare breast brushed against the side of my arm. I sat up. The racket was very loud, louder than it should have been anywhere near the palace at that hour.

My sitting woke the girl. "What is it?" she asked.

"I don't know, Zoe," I answered. "Whatever it is, the excubitores should set it to rights before long." Assuming the guardsmen would do just that, I leaned over and began to caress her. She sighed, I hope with pleasure, and slid closer to me.

Then someone began pounding on the door to my bedchamber. I snarled an oath, wondering who dared presume to disturb the Emperor of the Romans at his sport. "Flee, my son!" my mother cried. "Foes are in the palace!"

Zoe cried out in fear. Her forgotten, I sprang to my feet. To ward against murderers in the night, I always kept a sword by the bed. Even in near darkness, finding it was no more than the work of a moment. I flung an undertunic over my nakedness and unbarred the door.

My mother stared at me in mingled surprise and dismay. "No, son!" she exclaimed. "Out the window"—she pointed—"and make what escape you can." Zoe came up behind me, wearing rather less than I was. My mother ignored her, sure proof of the depth of her alarm. "Flee!" she said again. "You have only moments—the palace is betrayed."

I thrust the sword out ahead of me, as if to run through an enemy. "Did my great-great-grandfather run from danger?" I demanded. "Did my grandfather? Did my father, when his brothers tried to overthrow him? If they want me, they will find me ready to fight. Where are the excubitores?"

My mother groaned. "Most of them stood aside and let the usurper's men into the palace."

"Who is the usurper?" I demanded, wondering upon whom I should have to avenge myself.

Before my mother could answer, I heard someone around a bend in the corridor say, "The Emperor's bedchamber is that way." Several men came running, their sandals pounding against the mosaic tiles of the floor. To this day, I wonder which of my servants thus betrayed me to my foes. I wonder if he serves me yet. If he does, I wonder how long I can make him last, how much I can make him suffer before dying, if ever I learn who he is.

I had no time to concentrate on the voice, though, for several low ruffians came dashing round the corner. They all had swords. "There he is!" one of them cried, pointing at me in the torchlight. Not wanting the fight to endanger my mother or even Zoe, I rushed toward the traitors, intending to cut my way through them and however many had invaded the palace.

They being many and I one, though, my success was less than I had wished. The first man I attacked fell with a groan, clutching at a gash in his side. But the second, being a better swordsman, kept me at play. "Don't kill him!" one of the other brigands shouted. "Leontios wants him alive." Thus I learned who craved to steal my throne.

"I want *me* alive," my opponent panted, parrying a blow that should have laid his face open.

But, as the ancient pagan saying has it, even Herakles could not fight two. That dog kept me too busy to deal with any of the others as they deserved. One of them tackled me and knocked me to the floor. Unable to slash him as I fell, I hit him in the side of the head with the heavy pommel of my sword. He groaned and went limp. Before I could do anything more, another man grabbed my arm and wrenched the sword from my hand.

"Now we've got him!" my assailants roared. I punched and kicked and butted and bit, learning the taste of their blood. No one came to my aid. Despite all I could do, they swarmed over me, binding me hand and foot. After that, they spent some little while beating and kicking me, whether out of general hatred or because of the fight I had put up I cannot say. I bent my head down, hoping to keep them from smashing my teeth or breaking my nose. Looking back, that seems funny.

"What do we do with him now that we've got him?" somebody asked.

"Take him to the great church," answered the man who had fought me sword to sword. "That's were Leontios is at, and that's where the patriarch, God bless him, is at, too." I cannot imagine why I was surprised to discover Kallinikos had joined those betraying me, but I was.

The ruffians hauled me to my feet. A couple of them thrust their arms through between my arms and my ribcage and hustled me along. Dawn was breaking. In the trees and bushes around the great palace, birds began to sing. I remember that quite clearly. Again, I cannot say why. God, Who knows everything, will know that as well.

Men came up to me and reviled me: like any other dogs, they snapped at what they thought weaker than themselves. I cursed them as foully as I knew how, foully enough to make some of them gesture to avert the evil eye. I hope the curses I sent their way bit anyhow.

As we drew near the church of the Holy Wisdom, a swarm of people came out of it. At their head strode Kallinikos and a man I recognized after a moment as Leontios. I cursed him, too, at the top of my lungs. He took no notice, having already assumed what he fondly imagined to be the imperial manner. "Bring him to the hippodrome," he told the men who had me, "to the stadium where the horses run." Even as usurping Emperor, he remained redundant.

To the hippodrome—and, I suppose, to the stadium where the horses run—we went. As we went, I saw that two of Leontios's followers carried between them a man suspended from a pole. He turned his head and saw me, too. I might have guessed faithful Myakes would not stand by without doing his best to keep me from being overthrown. His best, like my own, had not been good enough.

"God bless you, Emperor," he called to me. One of the brigands walking alongside hit him in the face. Forgetting I was also bound, I tried to break free of my captors and come to his aid. That got me nothing but another buffet of my own. My ears rang.

Into the hippodrome we came. They hauled me to the stretch of track near the finish line, between the main grandstand—which was already black with people—and the Kathisma, the Emperor's seat, from which I had so often watched the pounding chariots come down to the line.

"Leontios!" the people shouted. "*Tu vincas*, Leontios! Leontios, Emperor of the Romans! Many years to the Emperor Leontios!" Listening to their fickle faithlessness, I felt like a husband coming home early one day to discover the wife he had trusted sucking on his best friend's prong.

The men who had charge of Myakes dumped him down on the ground. That made the mob bay louder, many of them, no doubt, believing him to be me. Then the cries grew louder still: an executioner, his features hidden by a black hood, came striding up the track toward me.

"Lord Jesus Christ, Son of God, have mercy on me," I murmured, wishing I could make the holy sign of the cross. Turning to Kallinikos, I said, "If you give me unction before he slays me, God might make the pangs you will suffer in hell for betraying me a trifle less agonizing."

Instead of answering, Kallinikos turned to Leontios for permission: sure enough, the dog had a new master. Leontios had also heard my words. He walked up to me, a broad false smile on his face. When he held up both his hands, silence dropped over the hippodrome like a cloak. Into it, he cried, "I, Leo, am now Emperor of the Romans!"

More acclamations rose, those rather discordant, some men hailing him as Leo, others who listened but did not hear persisting in calling him Leontios. How he styled himself mattered not in the least to me. I knew who he was. I knew what he was. So long as I had breath in me, even if it should be but for the next moment, I would not forget.

He held up his hands once more. Silence fell again. He said, "Out of the love and comradeship I feel yet for the Emperor Constantine, I shall not slay his worthless son Justinian, however much he deserves it."

Now the buzz from the crowd was surprised, confused. I felt surprised and confused myself: did he think he could leave me alive without my seeking to avenge myself and regain the throne rightfully mine? I had known he was a fool. I had not known he was such a fool.

But he was. He went on, "Let Justinian's nose be cut off, as Constantine cut off the noses of his brothers Herakleios and Tiberius. And for good measure, let his tongue be slit, too, that you may never more hear him order the ministers you rightly killed today to steal from you your money, your property, your freedom. Then off he goes to Kherson, and you'll never hear of him or from him again at all."

Once more, the cheers from the grandstand redoubled. True, the mob would not have the pleasure of seeing a head leap from a body and bump along the track while blood fountained from the stump of the neck. But they would have their blood, albeit not so much. And, instead of a quick end to their sport, they could enjoy my screams and moans for as long as Leontios chose to indulge them.

Now he beckoned to the executioner, who advanced upon me. Behind the hood, his eyes were thoughtful: the eyes of any good craftsman measuring the task ahead of him. "Emp—uh, Justinian—it will be easier for you if you hold very still and let me do what I have to do here," he said.

"May you die of the plague," I told him. "May your prick drip pus and wither. May your daughter couple with a dog on the Mese. May the demons of hell tear your flesh from your bones with pitchforks and throw it in the fire to burn forever."

I thought I might as well have been cursing a stone. Everything I said rolled off him, leaving him untouched. I suppose he already bore the weight of so many curses from so many men that one more mattered not at all. He turned to my captors. "Hold him tight, if you please. I'm going to do his tongue first." Maybe my words had got through to him after all. It was cold, cold comfort.

I clenched my teeth so hard, one of them broke. That, at the moment, was the least of my concerns. Matter-of-factly, the executioner went through his bag of tools, finally selecting a small, sharp blade, more a scalpel than a knife. I twisted my head back and forth until someone behind me seized me by the hair and prevented it.

The executioner stood before me. I spat in his face. The spittle soaked into the black hood and was gone. I vowed he would not force my jaws open. Some vows are wasted. He grabbed my beard in his left hand and pulled down. All at once, to my helpless horror, I understood why Alexander the Great had required his men to shave their chins. Despite all I could do, my mouth came open.

Fast as a striking serpent, the executioner slashed me with that little knife. At the same moment, though, I was trying once more to jerk my head to the side. I could not move much, but I did shift a little. And so, instead of slitting my tongue from root to tip, he gashed the side of it, also cutting my gum and the inside of my cheek.

I shrieked, both because the pain was bad and to make it seem worse so he would not inspect the wound to see what sort of job he had made of it. My mouth filled with blood, faster than I can write this. I spat in his face again, a great spurt of red. Some went in through the eyehole of the hood and made him rub at himself to restore his vision: a tiny measure of revenge, but I could take no large ones.

If I could not, he remained professional about the whole business between us. Wadding up a cloth, he stuffed it into my mouth. "Press it against the wound, hard as you can," he told me. "It will help slow the bleeding."

In spite of the rag, blood dripped down my chin. More ran down my throat, tasting of rust. But, with the rag in my mouth, I could not curse the executioner again, as I very much wanted to do. That worked to my advantage, he assuming I did not speak because I could not, and that the mutilation had been successfully accomplished.

As if the executioner were likely to forget, Leontios prodded him: "Now the nose. Remember the nose."

"Yes, Emperor," the fellow answered, which made me try to break free of my captors all over again: that anyone could presume to call this bumbling fool Emperor of the Romans infuriated every fiber of my being.

The executioner rummaged through his tools. This time he drew forth a larger blade than he had used before. He tested the edge with his thumb, shook his head, and stropped the knife against the leather sole of his shoe, standing on one leg like a stork to do so. After another test, he was satisfied and walked up to me once more. The early morning sun glittered off the newly touched-up edge.

"You have to hold him still again," he told the men who had charge of me. "Otherwise, the job won't be as fast and neat as it ought to be." He never spoke of mutilation. I suppose that by thinking of what he did as *the job*, he saved himself the trouble of thinking about what sort of job it was.

I think of this now, looking back at the moment across a gap of a decade and a half. Perhaps I should summon one of my executioners, to find out if I am right. I wonder if they would answer me honestly. I wonder if they have even considered the matter. Every trade has its secrets, and every trade has its blind spots, too.

Looking at these latest sentences, I see that I wish to avoid the narration of what came next, as if, by speaking of something else, I could will that bit of time into nonexistence. The executioner set the edge of the knife against my nose, just below the point where bone gives way to cartilage, and sliced down. The end of my nose, with the nostrils, fell into the dirt at my feet, and that is the last I ever saw of it.

Again, my blood streamed after it. The crowd cheered. "*He'll* never be Emperor again!" Leontios shouted, and the cheers got louder. Again, the executioner, efficient in his craft, pressed a bandage to the hole in my face where my nose had been. That might have kept me from bleeding to death, but made it very difficult for me to breathe.

"Why don't you cauterize the cut?" asked the fellow holding my hair. He laughed nastily. "That'll make this bastard hurt even more."

"From what I've seen, cauterized wounds are more likely to fester," the executioner replied: a serious answer to what he judged a serious question. He turned to Leontios. "Unless you want to give him more pain, of course, Emperor."

"Let it go," Leontios said. "He could have killed me, I suppose, and he didn't. Get him on a ship, get him out of the city, get him out of my sight."

One of his henchmen prodded Myakes with his foot. "What about this one? Strike off his head and have done?"

I expected Leontios would say yes to that. But, through a haze of agony, I saw him shake his big, stupid head. "No, he can go to Kherson, too. The excubitores are *my* bodyguards now; they'd grumble if an officer of theirs died for no reason but that he was loyal."

M Y A K E S

Did I think they'd kill me, Brother Elpidios? Let's put it this way: I hoped they wouldn't. If Leontios hadn't killed me back at the Praitorion, back before he knew whether he could steal the throne, I didn't think he'd order it now in cold blood. But was I sure? *Kyrie eleison*, no! He might have figured the crowd hadn't seen enough blood to satisfy it from watching Justinian get mutilated, and decided to spice up the show with my head.

I didn't mind a bit when my bearers picked me up and slung me on their shoulders again. They weren't taking me to be slaughtered. When that's what your choice is, everything else looks good.

And Justinian, he'd need all the help he could get. Up till then, life had been easy for him. Oh, he'd had family die, but who doesn't? Life's a chancy business. But he'd always had plenty to eat, he'd always been healthy, he'd always been handsome, he'd always had people hop when he told them to hop. Now he didn't have any of that. I wondered if not having it would break him. Emperor to mutilated exile was a long, long step, and here he was with no choice but to make it all at once. Could he? I was glad I was alive to find out.

J U S T I N I A N

They dragged me and carried Myakes through the streets of the imperial city toward the Golden Horn, where waited the ship that would take me into exile at Kherson. News of the traitor's vile act had spread through every corner of the city. People jeered at me as I went. "Cut-Nose! Cut-Nose!" was the commonest cry. How I wished the ground would have opened beneath the senseless mockers, letting them fall into the flames of hell as they deserved.

I could not answer their jeers with curses, not with a rag stuffed into my mouth and another tied around the back of my head and over what had been my nose. A few of the jackals threw stones and rotten fruit at me. Some of them hit. I scarcely noticed. Next to the wounds I already had, those were small things. If only the mob had had a single neck, that I might have cut off its head with one blow!

The pain was fire, and would not cease. Every cobblestone I saw through a red haze. I think my senses reeled for a time, for we reached the quays faster than should have been possible for a party of brigands and ruffians carrying one man and dragging along another who had been wounded.

"Bring him aboard!" called the captain of the ship that would take me into exile. His Greek was peculiar—peculiar enough that I noticed it in the state I was in at the time. With an effort like that of Herakles when in the pagan myth he briefly held up the world for Atlas, I raised my head. That yellow-haired fellow . . . I had seen him before. After a moment, the name came to me: Apsimaros.

My captors laid me on the deck and cut the ropes that bound me. They did the same for Myakes. The torment of blood coming back to hands and feet helped distract me from my larger anguish. Sailors armed with cudgels and shortswords stood over us, as if we were about to dash back onto the wharf. However little I wanted to leave the imperial city, my flesh was at that moment incapable of further resistance. Whether Myakes could have fought them or not, I do not know. Taking his lead from me, as he had for so long, he did not fight.

Seeing us remain where Leontios's men had left us, most of the sailors soon went back to the business of readying the ship to depart. Three or four remained close by, though: enough to overpower us even had we been at the height of bodily strength. Apsimaros shouted orders in his guttural Greek: "Cast off the lines! Man the sweeps!"

When all satisfied him, Apsimaros shouted again. The sweeps bit into the water. Little by little, the ship moved away from the quay, out of the Golden Horn, and toward the Narrows, the strait separating Europe and Asia and sometimes still known by its ancient name, the Bosporos.

Perhaps the sea breeze in my face helped revive me to some small degree. Though incapable of standing, I made it to my hands and knees and crawled toward the stern of the ship. Several sailors accompanied me on the slow, painful journey. Had I tried to throw myself into the sea, I wonder if they would have stopped me. I suppose they would; the Narrows being such a thin ribbon of water, a miracle might have let me swim to land and survive, and they would not have wanted to take the chance—or to explain their lapse to Leontios.

But I had no thought of throwing myself into the sea: neither to escape, for, whether the sailors did or not, I knew I had no hope of making land, nor to end my life, for the only time I came close to suicide, as a small boy, it was from rage rather than despair.

Nor did I completely give myself over to despair even then. I peered back in the direction from which the ship had come until a swell of land hid Constantinople from my view. I slumped down after that, but one thought still burned in my mind: *I will see the city again. By God and His mother, I will.*

BOOK Γ

JUSTINIAN

I remember little of my arrival at Kherson. No, I shall be honest: I remember nothing of my arrival at Kherson. I had taken a fever in my wounds while sailing across the Black Sea, and recall only scattered patches of the journey. That may be as well, many of the memories I have lost surely being ones filled with torment.

I wonder what the Khersonites made of my sudden appearance on their distant shore. Till that ship reached them, I was, so far as they knew, Emperor of the Romans. In fact, when conscious I still considered myself Emperor of the Romans. The rest of the world, however, had a contrary opinion for the time being, and I was in no position to demonstrate how wrong it was.

MYAKES

Matter of fact, Brother Elpidios, Kherson isn't quite the end of the world, even if it is a long ways off and tucked up against the Khazars and the other barbarians who roam over the steppe with their herds. Sailing into it is even kind of pretty. It sits in a curved bay on the west side of the peninsula that sticks down into the Black Sea. The land rises up, almost like a stairway, toward the hills that keep the worst of the winter away.

When we came into the harbor, though, the whole place stank of fish. A lot of what they live on there is dried and salted fish. You hear people talking about bread, but you don't see it all that often. Sometimes they even grind up the dried fish into a kind of meal and bake it into wafers and sheets. They aren't so bad as they sound, not once you get used to them.

Church bells were ringing when we pulled up to their quays. They'd seen us from a long ways off, and they knew we weren't one of the little fishing boats that dot their waters like pepper on top of a stew. We were a real ship, from a real civilized place, and they were greedy not only for whatever we might have brought 'em but for whatever gossip we had, too.

The *tudun* himself came down to the harbor to look us over. The *tudun* is like the eparch of the city, you might say, Brother. Kherson is a town where Romans live and Romans trade, but it's not exactly a Roman town. The *tudun* is in charge of it for the Khazar khagan. He has more say there than anybody else. The Khazars roam right next to Kherson, like I said, and the Roman Empire is across the sea. That would give the nomads every sort of edge in a fight, so there is no fight.

"Are you from Amastris?" the *tudun* asked us in Greek with a funny accent different than Apsimaros's. You know about Amastris, Brother? That's right—one of the towns in Anatolia right across the Black Sea from Kherson.

"No, we are from Constantinople," Apsimaros answered.

The *tudun's* eyebrows went up. He was a funny-looking fellow, fat as a eunuch, with a flat, swarthy face and scraggly whiskers, dressed all in furs and hides. "What do you bring us from Constantinople?" he asked. "We do not have ship from Constantinople for a long time."

"I bring you greetings from Leontios, er, Leo, Emperor of the Romans," Apsimaros told him. That was plenty to make the *tudun* and everybody else who understood Greek start hopping up and down like their tunics had just caught fire. Apsimaros had style. He waited, patient as you please, till they'd simmered down a little. Then he said, "And I bring you Justinian."

Justinian, right then, was lying on the deck. I had no idea whether he was going to live or not. Apsimaros didn't care. He pointed to Justinian, then to a couple of sailors. They hauled him up between them so the *tudun* and everybody else could see he was missing most of his nose.

Several of the dockworkers and touts and whores and such who had come down to see the ship crossed themselves. The *tudun* didn't. He wasn't a Christian. Some of the Khazars follow pagan gods, some follow Mouamet, and some are even Jews.

Whatever the *tudun* was, he asked Apsimaros, "What are we supposed to do with him?"

"If he dies, bury him," Apsimaros answered. "If he lives, let him live, but don't let him leave. Here he stays, for as long as he lives. Leontios"—he shook his head; he wasn't used to Leontios's new name—"*Leo*, I mean, will send you money to keep him here." I don't know whether that meant money for Justinian's upkeep or a bribe to make sure nobody let him leave. Probably both, I suppose.

"Who will take care of him?" the *tudun* said. "He needs someone to take care of him." By the way Justinian hung in the sailors' arms, limp as asparagus that's been boiled too long, that was plain to anybody with eyes.

Apsimaros pointed my way. "This is Myakes. He was one of Justinian's guard captains, and he went into exile with him instead of giving up his head."

"All right," the *tudun* said. "He is not the first exile here. He is not going to be the last exile here, either. We take him."

"The Emperor Leo"—now Apsimaros spoke carefully—"thanks you, and thanks the khagan of the Khazars, too." He turned to the sailors. "Put out the gangplank. Get him off this ship."

They didn't just obey him—they jumped. They wanted Justinian off that ship. I don't really suppose they could have imagined he'd do anything to them, not in the state he was in, but I don't know what else they could have been thinking, either. Apsimaros might have been convinced Leontios—no, I won't call him Leo—was Emperor now, but it didn't seem to have sunk in for the sailors.

They dragged Justinian up onto the wharf. I followed them. I hadn't made any trouble on the ship—didn't see any future in it—so they didn't give me a rough time, either. They even draped one of Justinian's arms around my neck. I'd figured they would dump him on the planks for me to pick up.

"You come with me," the *tudun* said. He pointed off to the south, toward a low building of the red-brown local stone. "We put Justinian there. It is a place for Christian monks, but it has a *xenodokheion*, a guesthouse, too. We see if he lives." He looked at Justinian. His eyes were narrow already. They got narrower. "Right now, I think he dies."

Right then, I thought Justinian was going to die, too. Fever came off him in waves. The wound where his nose had been was raw and inflamed. I wasn't going to admit what I thought, though. "Take me to the monastery," I said. "It's in God's hands, not mine." Yes, I said that. More pious back then than you thought, eh, Brother Elpidios? Well, I daresay we all have a surprise or two in us. Justinian, he had more than that. You'll see.

JUSTINIAN

My first clear memory of exile is waking from deep sleep and seeing Myakes' face above me. Beyond me, and seeming miles above me, were the roof beams of an unfamiliar building. The straw of the mattress on which I lay was lumpy and scratchy; I had never been in such a disgraceful excuse for a bed in all my life.

With awareness came the return of pain. At first I reckoned that the lingering aftereffect of some dream I had been lucky enough to escape, but it persisted. Memory followed awareness by a few heartbeats. Leontios had done *that* to me in the hippodrome, while the people laughed and cheered. Intending to get a sword and kill him then and there, I tried to stand.

"Easy," Myakes said. "I just got done thanking God that you're alive."

I have never been one to heed advice. Here, however, I had no choice, discovering as I did that my limbs would not support me—would, indeed, barely move at my command. The coarse wool tunic I wore was soaked with sweat, not from the effort of attempting to rise, but as if I had just broken a fever. That, I realized, was exactly what I had just done.

Trying to speak, at first I produced nothing save a harsh croak. My mouth tasted of stale blood. The wounds there had trouble healing on account of the moisture from my saliva. But they were not the disabling wounds Leontios had ordered the executioner to inflict. I tried again, and this time made understandable words: "What is this place?"

"A monastery," Myakes answered, adding after too long a moment's hesitation, "Emperor." I forgave him the hesitation, given my state then. After another pause, he spoke again, modifying what he had said before: "A monastery in Kherson."

More memory returned. I needed a distinct effort to nod my head. "Yes," I said, speech coming easier now, "he said he would do that to me."

My voice sounded wrong in my ears, and not only because it was rusty from disuse or because I moved my tongue as little as I could. The tone, the timbre, was not what it had been. With a gaping hole in the middle of my face, I sounded different from the way I had when I was made like every other man.

Cautiously, I brought my hand up to the empty place where my nose had been. It still pained me, as I have said, but at a level far below the agony it had inflicted. It was a cut. It was healing. "How long have I been here?" I asked.

"Five days, Emperor," faithful Myakes said, this time without the hesitation over the title that was, of course, still rightfully mine. "The *tudun* and the monks thought you would die, but your fever ended last night, and now—"

"Now I want something to eat," I said. My insides were a vast rumbling cave. Looking at my hand and arm, I saw how much flesh I had lost—or rather, how much flesh had temporarily melted away from me. That melting, though, could be reversed. Lost flesh, as I and eunuchs will attest, is lost forever.

"I've been giving you watered wine," Myakes said. Stout fellow, he was probably the only reason I had not gone before the judgment of all-powerful God some days earlier. Now he got to his feet and hurried out of the chamber where I lay. From the other beds nearby, I realized this was not a monastic cell, but the *xenodokheion* attached to the monastery. None of those other beds had anyone in it. In Kherson, guests were few and far between.

I had made it up to one elbow by the time Myakes and a monk came back into the *xenodokheion*. The monk carried an earthenware bowl on a wooden tray. I had already resigned myself to fare far rougher than the tender viands I had enjoyed back at the palace, and was expecting something like barley porridge. That, however, was not what the aroma rising from the bowl suggested. I pointed to it, asking, "What's in there?"

"Fish stew, Justinian," the monk answered. How could I upbraid him for failing to use my proper title when, out of charity, he was feeding me?

"It smells wonderful." With no small effort, I sat up straight. My head swam, but I did not let myself topple over. He handed me the bowl, and a wooden spoon wherewith to eat from it.

The stew was hot and salty and rich. The fish in it was either dried or salted, but I did not care, feeling myself restored with every mouthful I swallowed. The salt stung my wounded mouth, but I had lately known worse hurts than that. I did not look up from the bowl until it was empty.

"Thank you," I said to the monk then. "That may be the most delicious meal I've ever eaten."

"God bless you for your kindness in saying so," he replied, sounding not merely surprised but astonished. At the time, I did not understand. Before long, I did. The first bowl of fish stew I ate was surely made with the ambrosia of the pagan gods for a spice. The fifth bowl—no different from the first—tasted good and sated my hunger. The fiftieth bowl—no different from the first—I ate with resignation rather than relish. By the time I ate the five hundredth bowl and then, I think, the five thousandth—no different from the first—I loathed it with a loathing I had thought reserved for an unloved wife. But, in Kherson, eating all too often meant eating fish stew.

I spent nine years in Kherson. The monk, I found later, had lived his whole life there, and he was not a young man. I daresay he had had a surfeit of fish stew by the time he finished cutting his milk teeth. No wonder he was startled to discover anyone with a good opinion of it.

"Wine?" I asked.

"I shall bring you some," the monk said.

When he returned, it was my turn to be surprised. The wine, sweet, fruity, was an excellent vintage, and not one with which I had previously been familiar. "Where does this come from?" I wondered aloud. "I have never drunk of it in Constantinople."

"We make it here; the hillsides are suited to the grape," the monk answered. "We make it mostly for ourselves. It is not a famous wine, so shipping it far across the sea does not pay."

I drained the wooden cup he had given me, wishing for more. Over the long years that followed, I drank a great deal of the sweet red wine of Kherson. Unlike the stew of salted fish that seemed the characteristic local food, it never bored me. But then, the most the stew brought with it was a bellyache. The wine, if drunk in sufficiency, brought oblivion. To an exile in Kherson, oblivion was sometimes the most precious gift God could grant.

I did not know then I would spend so many years away from the imperial city, for I did not fully understand how isolated from the rest of the civilized world—or perhaps I should simply say, from the civilized world—Kherson was. My thought then was to heal, to raise a force, and to return to Romania to cast down Leontios. In the bright glow of returning awareness, it all seemed very easy.

Intending to ask for another cup of wine, I found myself yawning instead. Was the vintage of Kherson so strong? No, I was weak, and had not realized how weak I was. However much I wanted to remain sitting, I could not. As a man will after waking from a fever, I quickly fell back to sleep.

"He's going to make it," I remember Myakes saying. *Of course I am*, I thought, and thought no more.

When my eyes came open again, it was night. Somewhere not far away, a single lamp burned, so the chamber in the *xenodokheion* was not absolutely dark. I remembered at once where I was. I also realized at once I was stronger. This is not to say I was strong; a boy whose beard had not yet sprouted could easily have laid me low. It is a measure of how near heavenly judgment I had come.

Beside me, someone was snoring. At first, I thought it was a carpenter sawing through a thick log. I had no trouble picking out the rhythm: *push*-pull, *push*-pull, *push*-pull. But the fellow was no carpenter, and had no saw. It was only Myakes. I wondered how little sleep he had got while I lay in feverish delirium. Having served me so well through that, he deserved to recover now.

Next to his pallet lay a stout cudgel. Leontios's men had robbed him of his sword, and he must have had neither chance nor money to get another since arriving at Kherson. But he aimed to protect me as best he could, and a club was better than nothing.

I sat up. It was easy, this time: I *was* stronger. Myakes might have fed me as best he could, but he hadn't fed me much. One real meal counted for more than whatever he'd managed to spoon into me while I lay delirious. And, encouraged by how easily I had succeeded in sitting, I stood.

During the time when I was out of my head with fever, someone seemed to have stolen my legs, replacing them with half-baked dough that wanted nothing so much as to buckle under my weight. I swayed like a ship on a tossing sea. No doubt I should have been wiser to lie down again, but that would have been as much as admitting defeat. Besides, I needed to piss.

Breathing hard, I looked around for a chamber pot. The mere act of breathing felt different after my mutilation, and not only because the wound, while beginning to heal, still festered. Air seemed to strike the interior of my body too soon, so that it felt harsh and raw even when it was not. And, when I exhaled, my breath no longer came down over my mustache and lips, something I had not noticed with the topmost part of my mind until its absence brought it to my attention.

Spying the pot at last—one lamp was not enough to illuminate so large a chamber—I made my way toward it. Myakes and I being the only ones in the *xenodokheion*, the monks could have placed it near us, but had not done so, I suppose for no better reason than that they had not thought of it. They were there to give their guests food and shelter, not convenience.

Standing had been hard. Walking was harder. I thought I would fall over at every step; I have had a far easier time managing while drunk. Stooping down to pick up the chamber pot was also anything but easy. But I managed to ease myself without getting the floor too wet, then returned to bed.

Myakes had not wakened when I rose, but the rustle of straw under my body as I lay back down made him open his eyes. Glancing my way, he saw I too was awake. "You all right, Emperor?" he asked.

"With this for my palace, how could I be anything but delighted?" I answered, startling a grunt of laughter out of him. Then I responded to what he had really meant: "I'm better than I was, at any rate. I walked across the room and back just now." I spoke with some small pride, as if I were Pheidippides still alive after having run from Marathon to tell the Athenians of their victory over Xerxes.

"Eat and sleep and rest—that's what you've got to do for a while," Myakes said. "Once you have your strength back, you'll—" He broke off. My likely future must have looked bleak to him.

Not to me. "I'll go back to the imperial city and reclaim my throne," I declared. "How long can Leontios last as Emperor? He's a joke, and not a funny one."

In the dim, dim lamplight, I could not see Myakes' expression well. He must have known that. Even so, he looked away from me, perhaps to give himself a moment in which to gather his thoughts. When at last he spoke, his voice was sadder and more gentle than I had ever heard it: "Emperor, Leontios didn't cut your nose off just for the sake of hurting you, you know."

I slammed into the full meaning of that like a man running headlong into a wall. Myakes was right, of course. Leontios had not mutilated me only to imitate my father's mutilation of my uncles; he had done it for the same reason my father had mutilated them: to disqualify me from ever seeking to regain the imperial dignity.

Because the Emperor of the Romans and the Roman Empire are so intimately connected to each other, it stands to reason that a mutilation to one implies a mutilation to the other. For as long as the Empire has existed, a physically imperfect man has been reckoned unfit to rule. That is why Emperors commonly have eunuchs as their chamberlains—they know the servants in such intimate daily contact with them will not seek to take their place on the throne.

Of itself, my hand went to the part of me no longer part of me. My fingers jerked away from the crusted scabs they found.

Myakes had been watching me. "Now do you understand, Emperor?"

I understood. I understood all too well. I understood why he had hesitated before giving me my title, that first time he spoke upon my regaining my wits. I understood that, to him, it was now but a title of courtesy, a title of pity, not the title of respect it should have been.

That was what it meant to him. Not to me. Clenching my fists, I said, "By God and Jesus Christ His Son, I *will* take back the throne, Myakes. I don't care if I don't have this"—and now I made my hand linger where the fleshy part of my nose had been—"and I don't care about anything else. It—shall—be—mine—again."

"Yes, Emperor," Myakes said, but more as if humoring me than as if believing me. "How will you do it, though? And if, uh, when you do, how can you make people accept you?"

"How will I do it? I don't know yet," I answered. "Once I do, how can I make people accept me? That's easy, Myakes: I'll kill the ones who don't. Once I kill enough, the rest will get the idea, don't you think?"

"Yes, Emperor," he said again.

A couple of days later, having heard I was recovering from my wounds, the *tudun* of Kherson came to pay me a call. The Khazars have had their affairs intermingled with ours since the days of my great-great-grandfather, who persuaded them to join him in attacking the Persians. They also join us in opposing the followers of the false prophet, and have embarrassed the Arabs more than once.

To my way of thinking, they have no right to lord it over Kherson, which properly is, as it has always been, Roman. But the sword and the bow make their own law, and so Ibouzeros Gliabanos, khagan of the Khazars, is also overlord of Kherson.

The *tudun*, his governor here, was barbarously ugly and spoke a vile Greek, but I quickly discovered him to be no fool. "You are to me a problem, Justinian," he said, studying me with a curiosity that, I judged, had nothing to do with my mutilation. Unlike most, he was able to see past it to the man I remained.

"I do not wish to be a problem to you," I answered. However much I despised the necessity, I had to speak him soft, for he held the power here.

"Do you want to be Emperor again?" he asked.

"I am Emperor still," I said simply.

"Then you are to me a problem." He pointed a finger at me. "I do not want a problem with the new Emperor in Constantinople. He send his ships here, we have fighting, we have trouble, the khagan blame me." His nervous expression said more clearly than his words that such blame was liable to be lethal. My respect for Ibouzeros Gliabanos rose; a sovereign who could inspire such fear in his subjects was not to be despised.

"Leontios will do nothing," I said. "That is what Leontios does best: nothing."

The *tudun*'s smile stretched across his wide face but did not reach his narrow eyes. "You say this? He cast you down, and you say this?"

"He did not move to cast me down. His friends moved him." I picked up a bowl and set it down a couple of feet away to show what I meant.

"Maybe they move him to fight, too," the *tudun* said.

Myakes let out a snort, showing he shared my opinion of Leontios. The *tudun*'s gaze swung toward him. But the barbarian shook his head. "You say this. I do not know it is true. I do not want to find out." He pointed my way again. "Justinian, if you live in Kherson, you live quiet. You understand—live quiet?"

"I understand," I told him, and I spoke the truth. But understanding and agreement are not the same.

The *tudun*'s narrow, dark little eyes glinted. He was not the least capable of men, nor the least suspicious. "You live quiet," he repeated. "You make trouble, we know who does." He touched his nose to show what he meant. "We not let you make trouble. We give you back to Roman Emperor." This time, he patted the back of his neck to show what would happen to me were I returned to Constantinople.

"I understand," I said again, though still knowing in my heart that I was the rightful Emperor of the Romans. A nomisma does not cease to be made of gold even if dropped into a latrine.

Those narrow eyes glinted again as the *tudun* studied me. I discovered for the first time the advantage of my mutilation: not only did it draw the gaze to it in horrified fascination, it also made my expression harder to read by changing the contours of my face. "You be good," the *tudun* said severely, as if to a naughty child. He strode out of the monastery, satisfied he had done his duty.

"You're going to have to be careful, Emperor," Myakes murmured. "You're going to have to be patient."

I knew those words, but had never thought they would apply to me. "God is teaching me humility," I said. Myakes nodded eagerly. He wanted me to stay quiet, too. That meant he could stay quiet along with me. He got his wish, though at the time I had not intended that he do so.

A couple of weeks passed before I was well enough to leave the *xeno-dokheion*. I thought I had most of my strength back, though by looking at my body I could see how much flesh I still needed to restore. But what sufficed for walking around in the monastery, I soon discovered, was less than adequate for the greater journeys required beyond its doors. Quickly growing winded, I had to rely on the strength of Myakes, who accompanied me, as much as on my own.

This was so despite Kherson's minuscule size. A healthy man could have walked from one end of the place to the other in half an hour. Even I would not have needed much longer, that first time. To one used to the marvels of the imperial city, being forced to live in Kherson was like having to drink water—and water of poor quality, at that—after wine.

The life of the town, such as it was, clustered close to the harbor. Though ships from the Roman Empire were few and far between, the little fishing boats kept sailing out onto the Black Sea to bring back the catch on which the life of Kherson depended. Many others depended on the boats for their livelihood: carpenters, netmakers, sailmakers, brothel-keepers, taverners.

Over everything hung the odor of fish. I discovered in Kherson that, whichever part of the nose is responsible for the sense of smell, it lies deep within the organ, not at the tip, which had been taken from me. I had no trouble whatever discerning the stinks of fish drying in the sun, fish pickling in salty brine, fish frying, and fish rotting. As time passed, I grew accustomed to those stinks, hardly noticing them. In the early days of my exile, though, they made their presence insistently felt.

A washerwoman emptied a barrel of water out onto the roadway in front of her shop. Soaking rapidly into the dirt—Kherson boasted no paved streets—the water soon vanished, leaving behind only a patch of mud to entrap unwary passersby, and perhaps to enhance the washer-woman's trade.

Seeing that brief puddle, though, gave me an idea. "She'll have more water in there, won't she?" I asked Myakes.

"I expect so, Emperor," he answered. After a brief hesitation, he asked, "Are you thirsty? There will be wineshops for that."

I was not thirsty. I had no doubt he knew I was not thirsty. He was trying to protect me from myself, always a losing battle. I went into the washerwoman's shop. She looked up from the tunics she was wringing out. Her mouth twisted. Then, of a sudden, her faced cleared, or nearly cleared. "You're him, aren't you?" she asked in strangely accented Greek. "Justinian, I mean."

"Yes, I am Justinian." Till that moment, I had never had to humble myself before anyone but my father, and found the experience both strange and unpleasant. Nevertheless, I persisted. Pointing to a wooden hogshead, I asked, "Is there water in that barrel?"

"There is water," she agreed. Then she went on as Myakes had: "Are you thirsty? I will get you a cup."

"No, I am not thirsty," I said. "I want to see myself. May I look?"

She hesitated. Her lip curled again, which should have told me everything I needed to know. But I had been polite. Though she looked troubled, she nodded to me. Nodding my thanks in return, I went over to the hogshead and peered down into it.

In the grand palace in Constantinople, I had a mirror of polished silver as tall as I was, in which I could examine my magnificence when decked out in the imperial regalia. A handsome man had always stared back at me from that gleaming surface. My regalia now consisted of a dirty wool tunic. I had been disfigured. The water in that miserable old barrel seemed an appropriate instrument in which to view myself.

It was dim inside the shop, and dimmer within the hogshead. For a moment, I thought I would see nothing. Then, my eyes having adapted to the gloom, I wished nothing was what I had continued to see.

Everyone knows the seeming of a man new-recovered from illness that all but took his life: the sunken eyes, the skin stretched tight across cheekbones, the expression that says—and says truthfully—he has won a battle against a foe as deadly as any who roars on the battlefield, sword and bow to hand. All that I expected; all that I found. In my imagination, I had subtracted from my appearance most of my nose—or, at least, I had thought I had done so.

I have many times been reminded imagination and reality are not identical, but never more forcibly than on that quiet morning in that humid little shop. In my imagination, the wound was neat and precise, with pink flesh appearing under where my nose had been. In fact, my face took on the aspect of a skull, with a large, dark opening in the center. The presence of my eyes above it could not overcome the horrific, skeletal impression I created even on myself.

Sickened, I turned away from the hogshead, for the first time understanding in my belly why ancient custom forbids the imperial throne to a mutilated man. Who, I wondered, could bring himself to obey the commands of an Emperor whom good fortune had so conspicuously abandoned? What disasters would the reign of such a one bring down onto the Roman Empire?

Turning toward Myakes, I saw he had long ago grasped what I was realizing only now. "You see, Emperor?" he said, meaning the word in its most literal sense.

"Yes, I see," I answered, and, for a moment, despair threatened to overwhelm me. "I see," I repeated heavily, and, after thanking the washerwoman for what she imagined to be her kindness, I spoke again to Myakes, in listless tones: "Let's go."

"Aye, Emperor," he said, compliant as always.

And by that unquestioning compliance he saved me. I strode out of the washerwoman's shop into the warm, bright sunshine. Myakes followed without hesitation. He need not have followed. He need not have accompanied me to Kherson at all, or nursed me when fever from my wounds nearly took my life. Better for him had he stayed behind in Constantinople.

But he had followed and cared for me. He followed still. If he followed me, mutilated as I was, others would follow as well. The logic was as inexorable as any the pedagogue whose name I have long since forgotten tried to inculcate in me, as inexorable as the logic demonstrating the hypostatic union of the two natures of our Lord Jesus Christ, the Son of God.

"I *will* be Emperor again," I murmured, and then, "I *shall* be Emperor again," which partook of more of the flavor of inevitability building in my mind.

Myakes said nothing. I daresay he thought I was mad. But if he thought me mad, why did he still call me Emperor? Humoring a madman, perhaps? Perhaps. But why would he have gone on serving a madman? As exile, I had no claim on him; he could have done better for himself had he abandoned me. To the bottom of my soul, I believe something in him still sensed the power of the imperial dignity clinging to me even in Kherson, as the scent of perfume clings to a woman long after she sets aside the jar from which it has come.

I did not traverse Kherson end to end, not that first day. The smell of fish frying in hot oil wafting out of a tavern near the washerwoman's shop made my stomach growl like a bear. I pointed to the tavern, saying, "Let's get some of that. It will be better than the salt fish they'll give us back at the monastery." I had already had plenty of that.

Myakes looked down at the ground. "How do you propose paying for it, Emperor? At the monastery, they don't ask for money—or they haven't yet, anyhow. If we stay there much longer and Leontios doesn't send any, they will, I expect."

Was I more astonished than I should have been? Maybe I was, but in all my life I had never once had to pay for food, and the idea that I might need to do so now had never entered my mind. Almost as much as the glimpse of my appearance, it brought home to me the brute reality that, in the eyes of the world, I was Emperor of the Romans no more. Well, the world was and is an ignorant place, and I have had occasion to teach it more than one lesson.

Nor had I ever had to worry about money for myself before: for the Roman Empire, yes, but not for myself. I had had everything. I now had nothing. Realizing to the fullest how far I had fallen was dizzying. I found myself swaying on my feet. This, I judge, was also due in no small measure to my remaining bodily weakness. Having recovered from that in part, I had imagined it completely overcome, and now discovered I was in error.

"Let's head back," Myakes said, seeing both my discomfiture and my weakness. And, indeed, he took my arm and bore some of my weight when I faltered. The salty stew was waiting for us when we arrived. I ate of it, then crawled under my blanket and slept like a little child after a hard day's play.

When I woke, I was stronger.

One day not long after that, Myakes said to me, "I expect you'll be all right here for a spell, Emperor. I'm going up into the town."

"What are you going to do there?" I asked.

"Look for work on the docks," he answered. "We'll both be better off if we have a bit of cash jingling in our pouches." He slapped the one he wore on the belt round his tunic. Nothing jingled there, it being empty.

"But—" I began. I can name no rational reason for the pained embarrassment I felt. Myakes had been serving me since I was hardly higher than his knee. He had risked his life more than once on my behalf. Why his proposing to labor so that I might have money so affected me, I cannot say. That it did, I cannot deny.

Myakes, however, would hear none of my inchoate protest. "Got to be done," he said cheerfully. "I've been a farmer and I've been a soldier. After those, dockwalloper won't be so much of a much."

He poured down the wine the monks had given us with our morning porridge—salt-fish porridge, of course—and went out, whistling a dirty song whose tune our pious hosts fortunately did not recognize. That left me with nothing whatever to do and with no one with whom to talk, the monks being occupied after breakfast with their own concerns.

I went into the monastery chapel to pray. A couple of monks there gave me approving looks. After noticing that, I ignored them, wondering how I should address the God Whom I had served all the years of my life, Who had rewarded me with rank and comfort and pleasure beyond those of which most mortal men can dream . . . and Who had then cast me down.

Quoting the Psalmist, I said, " 'The judgments of the Lord are true and righteous altogether.' " Though easy to say, that was hard to accept. The Lord had judged my family harshly: my brother, my father, my wife all struck down young, and now my own fall from wealth and splendor. God had let Satan inflict boundless suffering on Job, whose faith had not wavered.

In the end, God rewarded Job for his steadfastness. That thought helped me shape the rest of the prayer I sent up to the heavens: "Test me as You will, Lord; I am Your instrument. And if it should happen that You grant me return to the Queen of Cities, I shall glorify Your name unceasingly. But if it be Your will that I remain here throughout my span of days . . . I shall glorify Your name unceasingly in that case as well." I crossed myself.

I stayed in the chapel a long time. Next to the church of the Holy Wisdom, it was a hovel, but a house of God is a house of God, no matter how humble. I did not need to think about what to do there; I already knew. And so I remained, while the sun wheeled across the sky.

As evening approached, Myakes returned. He stank of sweat but had money in his pouch. "I won't have any trouble keeping us in coins," he told me. "It was like they'd never seen anybody who wanted to do some work and wasn't going through the motions—or maybe I'm just used to moving faster than these people on account of all the years I've lived in the city."

"All right," I said, still obscurely troubled that he should have to labor with the sweat of his brow for our welfare. But what was the alternative? That I labor myself? For one thing, I had not yet fully recovered my strength after the fever that followed my mutilation. For another, should an Emperor of the Romans have become a common roustabout? I saw that as even less fitting than living off Myakes' stalwart efforts.

Every morning after that, he went off to the docks. Almost every evening, he came back with a full day's wages, sometimes in Roman folles and miliaresia, sometimes in silver minted by the followers of the false prophet, sometimes in coins I had never seen before, coins from out of the barbarous west of the world or the all but unknown east. Kherson was not a great trading center if only the number of merchants who called there was taken into account, but it did draw folk from every corner of the earth.

Myakes was generous in sharing with me what he earned. Though I continued to spend a good deal of time in the chapel, I was also able to make forays into the town and, if the impulse struck me, to buy for myself a cup of wine or some fried fish drenched in vinegar. I had, in fact, the illusion of freedom—freedom, that is, so long as I did not try to leave, or even think of leaving, Kherson.

It was not enough.

MYAKES

Do you know, Brother Elpidios, I wouldn't have minded so much if Justinian had decided to live out his days on the far side of the Black Sea. I'd be there yet, I expect, probably not working so hard now. I'd be an old man there, same as I am here, but I'd have my eyes, and that wouldn't be so bad. Like as not, I'd be sitting in a wineshop, or maybe out in front if the weather's fine like it usually is up there, and I'd watch the pretty girls go by. Every now and then, somebody'd ask me to tell a story of Constantinople, and folks would go *ooh* and *ahh*, and they'd buy me more wine. Doesn't sound so bad, does it?

Justinian might still be there, too—you never can tell. He'd be ugly, no doubt about it, but Kherson's not a big place. People would be used to him by now. Once you've seen somebody every day for years, what he looks like doesn't matter so much. He'd just be old Justinian, who used to be Emperor. And the stories *he* could tell—I'd have listened to those myself.

But that's not how things happened. They could have, easy enough, but they didn't. And so Justinian's twenty years dead, and I'm here, an old blind monk. You can't tell beforehand, Brother Elpidios. Only God knows beforehand, and He never, never, lets on.

JUSTINIAN

While I stayed there in Kherson, days began to blur together in a fashion I had never known before. With nothing to distinguish one from another, they slipped past me without my fully realizing they had gone. I was taken by surprise when the first winter storm roared over the mountains north of the town. Surely only a month—six weeks at the most—had passed since the warm summer day when Leontios and his pack of traitors stole my throne from me. But no, looking at the position of the sun in the sky and the stars at night convinced me that storm was no freak, but came at its proper time.

Not many storms came roaring over the mountains. Although lying the breadth of the Black Sea north of Constantinople, Kherson has winters generally milder than those of the imperial city, this being due to the shielding effect of the high ground. Snow was more frequently an amusement for the children than a drudgery for their elders. And, in fact, Myakes and I had a fine time, or more than one, pelting each other with snowballs and then retreating into the comfortable warmth of the *xenodokheion*.

But, though I continued to live in the guesthouse attached to the monastery, I was no monk, lacking as I did the temperament for the solitary life. One day I borrowed some silver from Myakes—or rather, I asked it of him and he gave it to me—and went walking up into Kherson.

I knew the sort of place I was looking for, and expected to find such a place close by the harbor. Sure enough, when I came to a large two-story building with a muscular fellow lounging outside, a sword on his hip and a club in his hand, I suspected my search was done. Nodding to him, I said, "Are the girls pretty?" and pointed inside.

"Aye, they are," he answered—would a whorehouse bouncer deny it, thereby turning away trade? He looked at me in a thoughtful way. "I'm not so sure they'll think you're pretty, though."

I made the miliaresia jingle in my pouch. "They'll think these are pretty."

He surprised me then, saying, "Maybe, maybe not. This is a town full of sailors. Business is good enough, the girls can afford to be choosy."

He was not offensive about my mutilation, treating it as a simple business problem. That left me untroubled; indeed, it pleased me more than his simply ignoring it would have done. Responding in a like vein, I said, "May I try my luck?"

He studied me again. "You're not going to raise a fuss if they turn you down?"

"By the Mother of God, I swear it," I said, whereupon he started to laugh, as did I a moment later. An ordinary enough oath, yes, but not when offered outside a brothel. Not only did he wave me forward, he opened the door so I could enter.

I had never been inside such a place before. As prince and then as

Emperor of the Romans, I had had women brought to me, and no need to go forth to seek them. Thus I looked around with some curiosity. It was as I might have expected: several women, some comely, some not, sat on chairs or lolled on couches, waiting for trade. They wore thin, clinging tunics cut very short; none of them bothered with drawers. Each and every one looked bored. The hall smelled of cheap scent and old sweat.

A plump fellow, evidently the master of the place, came up to me, looking very important. "What do you want here?" he demanded.

That question I had not expected. Others, perhaps, but not that one. I stared at him, then answered, "I've come to buy some paint."

The whores realized I was jesting before their pimp did. At their laughter, he pasted a broad, insincere smile across his broad, insincere face. "I don't know, friend," he said—when a man like that calls you *friend* stand with your back to a wall and keep one hand on your belt pouch and the other on your knife. He went on, "You're not the prettiest fellow who ever came in here, you know."

I daresay he was not the prettiest fellow who had ever come in there, either, but if I angered him, I would not get what I had come to pay for. And so, as I had for the bouncer outside, I showed I had money to spend. "The silver looks the same any which way."

He ran his tongue over broad, fleshy lips. Even so, he spread his hand. "If I order one of the girls to serve you, I'll make all of them angry— you see how it is? If one of them will go to you by herself, fine. Otherwise . . ." He let that hang.

I turned to the women, not pleading—if I had not pleaded for Leontios, I would not plead before a pack of prostitutes—but showing myself to them and waiting to learn what they would do. What they did was nothing. Not one made any move to join me. I jingled the pouch again. "Twice the money," I said, but, one by one, they shook their heads.

"You see how it is," the brothel keeper said again.

"I see," I said, less angry than I had thought I would be. Like the muscular lout outside, they were matter-of-fact, not scornful. That gave me an idea: "What if I come back after dark, and we go to a dark room?"

"For twice the usual?" one of the girls asked. Yes, it was business.

"A deal," I said at once. She was thin and rather plain, but not outright ugly. And, if she would not be able to see me in the night, I would not be able to see her, either. There in the blackness, I could imagine her as I pleased.

When I went outside after completing the bargain, the ruffian out

there said, "No luck, eh?" Seeing me doing as I had sworn, he was inclined to be sympathetic rather than harsh.

"They told me to come back after dark," I answered.

"Ah," he said understandingly. "I'll see you then, I guess." As I
started to go, he added a question: "Is it true what they say, that you used
to be Emperor of the Romans?"

"No," I replied. I saw that I had disappointed him, but I had not
finished: "It's not true I used to be Emperor of the Romans. I *am* the
Emperor of the Romans."

"All right, chum," he said, in the tones of one humoring a man
mad but not dangerously so—as guardsman for a brothel, he must have
come across a good many of that sort. Even in his amusement, though,
he remained civil.

I had enough money to pay the double rate, but not much more. Instead of going into a tavern, then, or an eatery, to while away the time till
sunset, I walked down to the wharves, strode out on one to the very end,
and peered south over the waters of the Black Sea toward the Constantinople I could not see. No ships from the Roman Empire were tied up
there, only the little local fishing boats. No ship from the Empire had come
in since the one bringing me, unless while I lay in my delirium. I felt very
much alone, very much a mote adrift. If a whorehouse bouncer would not
believe me the Emperor of the Romans, why should I? How could I?

"Because I *am*," I said. A seagull standing near me flapped up into
the air with a startled squawk.

The sun plunged into the sea. I waited until almost all the twilight
had drained from the sky before making my way back toward the brothel,
not wanting to be turned away because I was too visible. On account of
that, I arrived at the place later than I expected, having lost my way more
than once in the gathering gloom.

"Should have brought a torch with you," the guard remarked when
at last I found the proper lane. I shrugged and nodded, yielding the
point—why not? As he had before, he opened the door for me.

My greatest worry was that the one who had said she would go
upstairs with me was already upstairs with someone else. She would eventually have come down again, yes, but imagining her all my own would
have come harder. But there she sat. When she saw me, she got to her
feet. She put out her hand, palm upturned. I crossed it with silver. Having
made sure I had paid her enough, she nodded.

She took me up to a room big enough for a bed and not much more.
She closed the door behind us, and I barred it. Going to the little window,

she pulled the shutters across it and tied them so they would not open. It might have been something less than perfectly black in there, but it lacked little of that perfection.

In the darkness, something rustled: her tunic sliding off over her head. I quickly pulled off my own tunic, then took a step backward toward the bed. It proved to be but half a step away; rather than sitting down, I almost fell onto it, saving myself only by jerking back at the last moment.

Fresh pressure on the mattress said the woman had got down beside me. I groped for her. My hand closed on firm, rounded flesh. I caught her in my arms. She felt like a woman against my skin. She smelled like a woman. I did not need to see her to rise tall and proud.

As I began to caress her, she said, "Don't try kissing me. It would remind me of—" *Of your being noseless.* She might as well have shouted it.

It did not kill my ardor. Nothing would have killed my ardor that night, not after so long without. "All right," I answered, my voice mild as wine three-quarters water. I had not intended kissing her anyhow; who could say where her lips had been and what they had done before touching mine? My own lips and teeth closed on the tip of her breast as my hand went between her legs.

"What do you want from me?" she asked. "You're paying, after all."

Rough games had pleased me now and then in days gone by. Instead of making as if to take her by force, though, I answered, "Treat me like a lover, not a customer." What I wanted, most of all, was to feel as if my mutilation did not cut me off—indeed!—from the rest of mankind. The blackened room in which we lay gave that the lie, but what we were doing helped me not think about its being a lie.

She let out a tiny sigh, as if I could have asked nothing more onerous of her. But then, in the darkness, she played the part well enough. She nibbled my earlobes and kissed my neck and licked my nipples, every now and then teasingly stroking my manhood as she did. Then she took me in her mouth. She was not particularly skilled, but I was not particularly demanding, not then.

"Shall I finish this way?" she asked when I began to gasp.

"No," I said, and so she straddled me, as Irene the Sklavinian serving girl had done all those years before for my first time. But I put my arms around her and rolled us over so I rode her. Not much later, I spurted my seed deep into her. When she began to pull away, I held her to me, for I was still hard. I had not gone twice, one time right after the other without dislodging myself, for a few years, but that night, after such long abstinence, I had no trouble.

She let me have her again. If she took pleasure from it herself, she gave no sign I could discern. When I rolled off her after the second round, she said, "You should pay twice again." But she meant that either as a joke or as a ploy to see if she could get the extra silver from me.

Having faced down angry nobles in the imperial city, I had no trouble with a Kherson whore. "I paid enough," I answered firmly. "I don't think I kept you up here long enough to lose much other trade."

Had she threatened to scream for the bouncer, I do not know what I should have done, he being both larger and, more to the point, much better armed than I. But all she did was sigh and begin to grope around on the floor for the tunic she had doffed. A tiny victory for me, perhaps, but the first I had won since being treacherously ousted from my throne, and so one to cherish.

Finding my way back to the *xenodokheion* in the darkness was another victory, one that at the time seemed as large. On leaving the brothel, I paid a couple of coppers for a torch—nothing came free there— to light my way southward, but the cursed thing went out before I was halfway there, leaving me alone in a darkness almost as stygian as that inside the chamber where I had coupled with the whore.

I stumbled on—literally, seeing (or rather, not seeing) how full of stones and mud-filled potholes the streets were—by God and by guess and by occasional glimpses of stars overhead through rents in the clouds scudding past. So long as I kept going south I told myself, I would eventually come upon the monastery to which the guesthouse was attached.

Such assurances are often less than reassuring even by light of day. In the chilly blackness of night, I might as well have been a little boy murmuring charms against the monsters that dwell only in his imagination and so can follow him even under the blankets of his bed. I was looking around for monsters, I must say, but, as much by luck as by design, found the monastery instead.

When I walked in through the door of the *xenodokheion* I found Myakes, wearing a sword I had not known he possessed and about to come out after me. "Where were you?" he cried out on seeing me, his tone quite different from that by which a subordinate customarily addresses his superior.

One of the monks was hovering in the chamber: "Never mind," I replied in dull embarrassment, not wanting to wreck the reputation for piety I had built up since arriving at the monastery.

Myakes, though not always what one would call quick-witted, was in certain matters no fool. "Oh," he said, realizing where I must have been, and then, a moment later, "Oh" again when he figured out the likely reason I had had to wait so long before faring homeward. "Hope it was worth it." God bless him, he sounded almost as matter-of-fact as the bouncer had been.

"I think so," I said. The monk looked from one of us to the other in confusion, unable to follow our elliptical conversation. *Just as well,* I thought.

M Y A K E S

Easy, Brother Elpidios, easy. We don't ask guests at our *xenodokheion* here to be saints, now do we? Of course we don't. Every man's a sinner, right? The only perfect man was the Son of God.

Yes, Justinian went out and fornicated with prostitutes. Why are you asking me when he admits it himself? Yes, I know he was the man who fought so hard for the canons of the fifth-sixth synod that condemned brothels and those who kept them. No, that didn't stop him. Pretty plain it didn't stop him, wouldn't you say?

A hypocrite? Justinian? Less so than most men I've known. But he *was* a man, and even then well on the sunny side of thirty. Once his wounds healed up, his body drove him, same as it does any man that age. Yes, he fell into sin every now and again. You get rid of every man who's fallen into sin that way every now and again, all of a sudden the world starts looking like a pretty empty place.

Me, Brother? What did *I* do when we were up there in Kherson? Oh, this and that. I was working a lot of the time, remember. Was I working *all* the time? Now, what ever would you mean by that, Brother Elpidios?

J U S T I N I A N

I did not pander to my lusts. Every so often, though, when they grew unbearable, I would ask money of faithful Myakes and go off after sunset to slake them. Some of the other women at the brothel gradually came to accept me, so I did not have to rely entirely on the complaisance or availability of that one.

As I have already said, days and weeks and months in exile began to flow into one another, with little to distinguish any particular day from any other. Only the unusual was worthy of note, and little enough of that happened. A few times a year, a ship from Constantinople or one of the Anatolian cities of Romania, Sinope or Amastris mostly, would tie up in the harbor. Then we would have a brief orgy of catching up on news from the wider world, much of it old news by the time it reached us.

Avid to find out how the Roman Empire was faring, I pestered captains and sailors alike for word of what Leontios was doing. For the first year the usurper's fundament defiled the throne, the answer was, as best I could tell, that he did nothing whatsoever. This in no way surprised me, being in perfect accord with the character Leontios had previously exhibited.

"Everything is peaceful," the seafaring men would say, perhaps hoping to wound my spirits by showing that the Empire was doing well without me.

If that was their intent, it failed. In calm weather, a ship's captain may fall asleep whenever he pleases with nothing evil befalling his vessel. But if he is asleep when a storm blows up, the ship will go to the bottom before he can wake and try to make amends for his carelessness. So I judged it would be with Leontios, and my judgment was vindicated.

That, however, as yet lay ahead, for news from the Roman Empire trickled in slowly. News from all over the world trickled into Kherson . . . slowly. It lay on a trade route that stretched east all the way to the land of Serinda, whence we Romans learned the secret of manufacturing silk during the reign of the Emperor for whom I was named, and west to the island of Britannia and even to another island beyond Britannia, of which geographers may speak but of which I was previously ignorant.

Most merchants travel back and forth across a single section of the trade route, but some, pulled by greed or the desire for adventure, wander far from their homes. In taverns in Kherson, I met men from India—the eastern India, the one Alexander conquered, not the one also known as Ethiopia—and Persia, from Germany (the source of so many barbarous tribes that have harmed us Romans) and from this distant island I mentioned, which is called, I think, Ibernia.

"No, I've never been to Constantinople my own self," a traveler told me in a hideous mixture of Greek and Latin enlivened by a barbarously musical accent, "but I know a man who has. A priest, he was, out of some little town in Gaul—"

"Arculf!" I exclaimed. The odds were against it, I knew, but he was the sole priest from a little town in Gaul I had met in the imperial city.

And may I be condemned to the eternal fires of hell if the merchant did not nod. "Aye, that's the man," he said. "A good and holy soul he is, too."

"Yes," I said, agreeing with him completely. "How did he come to distant Ibernia?"

I needed some time to puzzle out the answer to that. Arculf, it seemed, had in fact not gone to Ibernia but to Iona, a small island off the western coast of Britannia. There the trader's uncle, a certain Adamnan, was abbot of a monastery. Arculf, being shipwrecked there, related his tales of travel in Romania to this Adamnan, who took them down in Latin. And so, knowledge of the civilized world does reach, distantly and in dreamlike wise, even those far-off places.

What happened to Arculf after his ship foundered at this island of Iona, the trader with whom I was drinking did not know. Learning even so little of my old acquaintance, though, brightened that day and several after it, and also gave me my own tavern tale to spin out in later times.

"Not a bad story, for a man without a nose," another merchant judged a few weeks later, and bought me a cup of wine.

"I am Emperor of the Romans," I declared, having already had a good deal of wine that day.

"Not a bad story, for an Emperor without a nose," he said, and the laugh he got gave him the last word.

As I have intimated, no great stretch of time passed before Leontios began demonstrating on the throne the qualities on account of which he had so singularly failed to endear himself to me. A ship crossing the sea from Sinope brought word that raids into Romania led by the Sklavenoi, which had diminished thanks to the vigorous efforts I undertook to combat them, were once more increasing in both frequency and ferocity.

Not long afterwards, news came that the prince of Lazika, whose name, if memory serves, was Sergios, brought his district, which lies on the southeastern shore of the Black Sea east of Trebizond, under the dominion of the deniers of Christ, as Sabbatios the Armenian had with his a few years before.

Both these tidbits reached Kherson months after they happened. Myakes heard the first of them on the wharves, I the second in a tavern. When I brought it back to him at the xenodokheion, he looked thoughtful and said, "The generals in the military districts aren't going to be very happy with Leontios."

I snorted. "Who would be happy with Leontios? No one with his wits about him, that's certain." Then, unbidden, a horrid thought struck me. "By the Virgin Mother of God, Myakes, suppose one of those generals overthrows Leontios and takes the throne while I rot here, across the sea from everything that matters?"

"Don't really know what you can do about that, Emperor," Myakes said. He twisted awkwardly, trying to scratch the small of his back. "Something bit me."

Something had bitten me, too: fear. Back in Romania, as Myakes had said, the generals were undoubtedly seething at Leontios's ineptitude. And, if one of them took it into his mind to do more than seethe, he had the resources with which to topple the sluggard: men and weapons and gold.

And what had I? A pallet in a *xenodokheion* in a half-barbarous town owing first allegiance to the Khazar nomads, and one former guardsman who had constituted himself my servant still. And somehow, incredibly, more than two years had passed since Leontios shipped me into exile. Save for being hale in body once more, I was no closer to returning to what was rightfully mine than I had been when Apsimaros poured my fever-wracked carcass onto the Kherson quay.

"Suppose someone who actually knows how to rule seizes the throne," I said, clutching at Myakes' arm. "Leontios is an easy target, but I can think of half a dozen men who would be very devils to put down."

"So can I," he answered, scratching still. He did not sound greatly concerned. He was always calmer by nature than I, and he had also come to be contented with the life he was living. And yet how can I say that, having spent so long content to live like a beast satisfying animal lusts but no others? Nor, though I did not yet know it, was my exile anywhere near complete.

My trouble was simplicity itself: how was I to go about establishing an army that could retake Constantinople in a town lacking enough men to form a proper regiment, and in a town, moreover, where, being who I was and what I was, I could not hide, and where the *tudun* was determined I should do no such thing? Easy enough to discover the difficulty. Discovering a solution to it was years away.

I had, by then, made a couple of tavern friends I felt I could trust: a half-Khazar named Barisbakourios and his brother Salibas, who sometimes went (and whom I preferred to call) by the more properly Greek name, Stephen. Drunk and sober, they proclaimed they would be glad to help me regain my throne. With faithful Myakes, they made me an army of three. With an army of three, I stayed in Kherson.

News continued to trickle into the town, however distantly removed from the time when it had actually occurred. One of the relatively rare ships from Constantinople itself brought word that the Arabs had seized Carthage. I drank myself senseless when I heard that. One of the reasons my grandfather, Constans, had sailed to Italy and Sicily and his eventual murder in the barbarous west was to protect Carthage from the followers of the false prophet. And now, Constans having given his life to defend it, Leontios fecklessly threw it away.

"Leontios will have to do something about that, Emperor," Myakes said when, the next day, I took word back to the *xenodokheion*.

"Will he?" I had a headache like death, which inclined me even more than I would have been otherwise toward doubting any possible link between Leontios on the one hand and doing something on the other.

"Aye, he will," Myakes answered through a mouthful of salt-fish stew. He was eating in a hurry, as he intended to go up to the harbor to look for work. But he spared me a couple of more sentences, saying, "Losing Carthage is like losing Thessalonike or Ankyra would be. He can't ignore it."

"Who says he can't?" I returned. Ignoring inconvenient difficulties was one of the few things Leontios had proved he did well.

Here, however, Myakes proved correct. Leontios set out a fleet, I learned eventually, and, to my astonishment, succeeded in driving the Arabs from Carthage. Returning in larger numbers, however, they then defeated us Romans. The commander of the Roman expedition, a certain John, sailed back to the Empire for reinforcements, not having enough men with him to stand up to the larger army the deniers of Christ had moved against him.

On his reaching Crete, though, his junior officers revealed a plan of their own: to sail east rather than returning to the west. They struck for Constantinople, having proclaimed one of their own number Emperor of the Romans.

"He has a funny name, a foreign kind of name," the sailor who was telling me the story said, "so people are calling him Tiberius instead of, of . . ." His memory failed until I bought him another cup of wine. "Of Apsimaros, that's it."

"Apsimaros?" I had been drinking wine myself; at that name, I swallowed wrong, coughed, and sprayed little drops of red over the tabletop in front of me. "They couldn't have dug up a bigger nobody if they tried for a year."

Strictly speaking, I suppose that is not true. Phokas, whom my great-great-grandfather overthrew to the salvation of the Roman Empire, had been but a commander of a hundred before a mutiny raised him to imperial rank—in his case, I shall not say imperial dignity. Apsimaros was of higher standing than that.

After dabbing at himself, my informant said, "That's the name, all right. Once you hear it, how can you forget it?" Except, of course, as a means of gaining more wine. "He's in Sykai now, they say, across the Golden Horn from Constantinople, and trying to figure out how to break in."

I bought him still more wine in the hope that he could tell me something else, but he, wine or no, had run dry, leaving me disappointed. To become Emperor, a rebel must seize the Queen of Cities. My great-great-grandfather had managed it against Phokas, for no one defended the vicious tyrant. Leontios had managed against me, seizing the city from the inside out, so to speak. Apsimaros, though, was attempting what I would also have to do when my day came: breaking into Constantinople against opposition. The followers of the false prophet had not managed that. Could anyone?

The next ship up from Constantinople brought the announcement of the accession of Tiberius, Emperor of the Romans, who, it was reluctantly admitted, had once borne the barbarous appellation of Apsimaros. That was all the official word given forth. Myakes got more out of the sailors, who, remembering what they reckoned my former rank, were reluctant—were afraid—to speak to me.

"He bribed Leontios's soldiers up at Blakhernai, that's what he did," Myakes reported. "They opened the gates for his men, and in he came. Did some pretty good plundering, the soldiers he had with him." His sigh said he wished he'd been there himself. But then he brightened. "Ah, that's the other thing: Apsimaros caught Leontios." He beamed from ear to ear.

I shrugged. "Since he's calling himself—miscalling himself—Emperor now, I suppose he would have. Leontios must be shorter by a head." It was my turn to sigh. "Too bad. I wanted to kill him myself."

"He's not dead, Emperor." Myakes beamed wider than ever. "Apsimaros the asp bit him, sure enough, but not to death. He packed him off to the monastery of Delmatos, but first—do you know what he did first?"

"Sooner or later, you'll tell me. Why not now?"

Myakes took no notice of my irritability, and, in fact, cured it with half a dozen words: "Emperor, he cut off his nose."

My hand went of itself to the scarred wound I bore. "He did what?" I said, and then held up my hand. "No, don't say it again. I heard you.

Truly God is a just judge. That comes closer than anything I could have imagined to tempting me to forgive Apsimaros for stealing the throne that belongs to me. I don't forgive—I'll never forgive—but I am tempted."

"He's ruling under the name Tiberius," Myakes reminded me.

That made me shrug again. "He's sitting on my throne. No reason he shouldn't steal a name that belongs to my family, too."

As a matter of fact, though, now that I think on it, my clan had also borrowed the name Tiberius, taking it from the Emperor who ruled just before Maurice and who was, in the days of my great-great-grandfather, a man of good reputation. How and why that Tiberius came to bear his name, I cannot say, he being the first Roman Emperor to carry it since the one in whose reign our Lord was crucified.

"His brother, I hear, is named Herakleios," Myakes said. "Whether that's his real name or one he's put on, I couldn't tell you."

I vaguely remembered that Apsimaros had had a brother who was an officer of some sort. For the life of me, I could not remember what that brother's name had been; in no way had he distinguished himself. Apsimaros would undoubtedly promote him to high rank anyhow: if a man could not rely on his own brother, he could rely on no one. Remembering how little my father had been able to rely on his brothers, I felt relying on no one the better choice.

Then I looked over at Myakes. Had I not relied on him, had I not had him upon whom to rely, I would surely have died not long after my exile began. But comparing Myakes to my ambitious uncles was comparing figs and fingers. Myakes was in no position to supplant me, no matter what he did. Apsimaros would always have to keep one eye on his Herakleios, just as my father had had to watch his brothers Herakleios and Tiberius, just as I would have had to watch my brother Herakleios had he lived.

I said, "I pray to God, Myakes, that Leontios has no one to look after him as you looked after me when I needed you most."

He grunted; I'd succeeded in embarrassing him. "Emperor, I've been taking care of you about as long as I've been a man," he answered after a pause for thought. "I've been doing it so long, I'd hardly know how to do anything else."

He seemed to feel about it the same way I felt about the throne: the one was his destiny as the other was mine. But he was luckier than I, for his calling, unlike mine, had suffered no interruption.

·   ·   ·

Time went on. I never abandoned the hope and intention of regaining my throne, but I had no luck building any sort of force to help me do it. My only new recruit besides the aforementioned brothers, Barisbakourios and Stephen (or, as I have said, Salibas, he answering impartially to both), was a gigantic fisherman named Paul, who was as strong as any other two men I have ever seen. Unfortunately, what God had given him in bulk, he took away in wit, with the result that the fisherman was often called—though seldom to his face—Moropaulos, Foolish Paul.

Carthage remained in Arab hands. Apsimaros, having been part of the fleet that failed to reclaim it, must have regarded it as a lost cause. In the east, though, he beat back an attack by the followers of the false prophet, and that frontier, being the gateway to Anatolia and to the imperial city itself, is more vital for the Roman Empire.

By the news that slowly dribbled into Kherson, Apsimaros displayed more energy on the throne than had Leontios. That this is less than the highest of praise, I freely admit; a dead man would have found it difficult to display less energy than had Leontios.

In the year following his successful defense of Roman territory, Apsimaros sent into exile Bardanes, sometimes called Philippikos, consigning him to the island of Kephallenia. Reckoning this upon my fingers, I find that it must have been in the fourth year of Apsimaros's usurpation, which was the seventh year of my exile. The more I think on it, the more incredible it seems, and yet I am convinced it is accurate.

"What did Bardanes do?" I asked the traveling jeweler who gave me the news.

"Story is that he dreamt he had an eagle shading his head, and was stupid enough to say so in front of somebody who took word to the Emperor," the fellow answered.

"That *was* stupid," I agreed. From time out of mind, the eagle has been the symbol of Roman power and, by extension, of the imperial dignity. No wonder Apsimaros exiled him; he had as much as claimed he would be Emperor one day.

In the next year, the Arabs under Azar attacked Kilikia. Apsimaros's brother drove them back to their own lands with heavy losses. The Armenians also rebelled against the Arabs whom Sabbatios had installed as their overlords. Apsimaros sent men to help them, but the deniers of Christ proved stronger there, driving out the Romans, regaining the territory that had rebelled, and burning alive a good many of the Armenian grandees who had risen up against them.

I know I heard this story in detail far more circumstantial than I recount here, but count myself lucky to remember any of it at all. Sitting not far from the sailor who was spinning it was a small, thin, brown man with wavy black hair and features of almost feminine delicacy. During my time in exile, I had learned that such men came from distant India.

They did not often come from distant India, however; in those seven years, I had seen no more than half a dozen. Thus I looked at this fellow with some considerable interest. Perhaps men from India also come to the imperial city from time to time. If they do, however; they do not come to the grand palace; before my forced journey to Kherson, I had seen never a one.

The man from India also stared at me. I had grown resigned to that from children and strangers, the general run of Khersonites having by then accustomed themselves to my appearance. But the Indian's stare was different from those of many seeing me for the first time: curious, not horrified.

After a bit of staring, that curiosity got the better of him. Picking up his cup of wine, he came over to me as I stood in front of the bar, whereupon, pointing a brown finger at the center of my face, he asked, "Why do you look like that?" His Greek was not very good, and flavored by a singsong accent unlike any I had heard before. He certainly did not know enough of the language to be polite.

"Why do I look like this?" I repeated, to be sure I understood him. He nodded. He being a barbarian, I thought him also a fool, and gave back the sort of answer I should have offered to a Roman twit who put such a question to me: "I lost my nose somewhere, and don't know where to find it."

That got a laugh from the drinkers who heard me. The little man from India, though, nodded again, as if what I had said made perfect sense. "If you want," he said, "I build you new one."

"Oh, splendid," I said. "Will you make it of clay, so that I can paste it onto my face?" I won another laugh with that sally. I laughed myself, bitterly. One winter, the second or perhaps the third I was in Kherson, I had taken a knife and carved a nose out of wood, taking pains to let no one, not even Myakes, know what I was about. Rather than pasting it to my face, I had attached it by means of a cord tied round my head. When it was done, I carried it off to a rain puddle (again making sure no one saw me), donned it, and examined my reflection. My opinion of the result may be inferred from the fact that I never wore it again.

Once more, however; the man from India, rather than giving up or growing angry—as I was certainly beginning to do—replied as if to a serious question: "Oh, no, very much no. I make from flesh of you."

He wore a tunic not much different from mine. Instead of a belt, though, he had a rope around his middle, with a flat wooden box dangling from it in place of the usual leather pouch. From the box he drew a knife that reminded me of the one the executioner in Constantinople had used to try to slit my tongue.

Had I been back at the grand palace, anyone daring to produce a weapon in my presence would have met a quick end at the hands of the excubitores, or perhaps a slow end at the hands of the executioners. His intention in so doing would have mattered not at all; the act would have sufficed and more than sufficed.

But I was in a smoky tavern in Kherson. My hand went to the knife I wore on my own belt, but I did not so much as pull it from its sheath, waiting instead to learn what he would do or say. "Make from flesh of you," he repeated, and, with the knife as pointer, sketched a flap of skin on his forehead, saying, "Do cutting here, you see—you understand cutting?" He knew how limited his Greek vocabulary was.

"I understand," I told him. "You are speaking of surgery."

"Surgery," he agreed happily. "Is word I am wanting, oh very yes. Do cutting here, I say, and it go down over . . ." He pointed to the hole where my nose had been. "Make more cutting." He ran his thumb along the bottom of his own nose. "Sew together, wait for heal, you have again nose. They no do this here?"

"They do not do this here, no." Even in my own ears, my voice sounded far away. To have a nose again . . . I had dreamt of having a nose again, but knew too well how dreams vanish on waking. My hand moved to the scars—smooth now, and painless, from the passage of years—around my mutilation. "Would it be as good a nose as the one I once had?"

Without a moment's hesitation, he shook his head. "No. You still be ugly. You not be very, very ugly no more, oh very yes you not." No, he did not have enough Greek for politeness. As when he took out the knife, though, I remained unoffended. His attitude bespoke a certain basic truthfulness.

I found more questions: "How is it you know how to perform this surgery? Have you done it before?"

"Do it three times, me." He held up three fingers, in case I had not followed him. "How I know how? My brother—is right word, brother?— he do this times many. He . . . *baidyas.*" This, it turned out, was, as best I can set it down in Greek characters, the Indian word for physician, the small brown man being unable to remember its Greek equivalent, if indeed he ever knew it before I said *iatros.* "I do you?" he asked.

As he had not before, I did not hesitate now. "Yes, you do me," I said. At that time, in that place, what had I to lose? He could not very well have made me uglier than I already was. And if I had not died of fever when my nose and tongue were cut, I doubted I should perish of it from what, as I could see, would be a lesser infliction of the knife.

Then he revealed he was indeed a trader. I had shown myself too eager. The glow that came into his eyes had nothing to do with the lamps and torches illuminating the tavern. "What you give me to do this?" he asked.

"What do you want?" I asked, suddenly cautious. As Emperor, I had dickered with the Arabs over tribute, but, till I came to Kherson, that was my only experience with the fine art of haggling. Exile had broadened my knowledge of an art for which an Emperor had but limited use; even so, I knew I was less acquainted with it than a man who had made his living by it from childhood would have been. I tried to distract him by asking an unrelated question: "What's your name?"

"Auriabedas," he answered; that, again, is as close as I can come to rendering it into Greek letters. He was not distracted. "Is gold good in this part of world," he said, a tribute to the quality of our Roman nomismata I could have done without at that moment. He held up a hand, showing thumb and all fingers. "You give five—this many—of gold."

"Five?" I clapped a hand to my forehead. "I am not a rich man." A humiliating thing for the Emperor of the Romans to have to say, but true. "I can give you two." I did not know how much money Myakes had, nor what he could spare.

Auriabedas's fine features assumed a look of tragedy that might have suited him for one of Euripides' dramas. "Is not enough, oh my no," he said. "You not pay five, you stay very very ugly, oh my yes."

"Three, then," I said. "I tell you, I am not made out of gold."

"Five," Auriabedas repeated. He had not much Greek, but, being a canny merchant, had made certain he knew the numbers in our language. "You no want pay, I no want cut." He looked at me. "You no want pay, maybe I say ten soon."

We were two nomismata apart. With a nose, even one that left me uglier than I should have been had my own encountered a club, I could deny I was physically imperfect and hence debarred from the Roman throne. Without a nose, I had no prayer of raising enough support to return to Constantinople; years of bitter exile had proved as much to me. Was I to throw away my chance to regain the throne in a quarrel over a couple of nomismata?

"Five," I said, hoping Myakes had five nomismata to his name.

Auriabedas beamed at me. "I fix you," he said. "You be ugly, but you not have to fuck in dark like I bet now." He cocked his head to one side, seeing if that shot went home—as indeed it did. Not since arriving at Kherson had I taken a woman in broad daylight.

"Come to the monastery tomorrow," I told him. "I will pay you." If Myakes had not the money, I knew whom to rob.

Myakes proved to have the money. He put it in my hands. The only question he asked was, "This fellow's not a mountebank?"

"I don't think so," I said. "If he were, he would boast more about how wonderful he was and how he'd never had any trouble with this surgery and how everyone to whom he's ever set a knife has come out of it handsome as a pagan god. A man who tells me straight out I'll still be ugly after he cuts strikes me as an honest man."

Having weighed that, Myakes nodded. "Maybe you're right, Emperor. Sounds like you've got a decent chance, anyways."

One thing more he did not—would not—say. To let him know I understood it without his words, I said it for him, as it had occurred to me the night before: "Besides, being as I am, what do I have to lose?" His jaw worked. He glanced down at the floor of the *xenodokheion*. But when his eyes returned to mine, he nodded once more. If I was to be Emperor again, I had to have a nose.

I had not told Auriabedas at what hour to come to the monastery. From sunrise on, I paced back and forth, nervous as a cat trying to watch three mouseholes at the same time. I was beginning to wonder if he would come when, a little past noon, he did. "You go outside," he said, pointing. "Need very much see what I do."

Out we went, Myakes walking a pace or two behind us, sizing up the man from India. When he did not say anything or try to dissuade me from my course, I concluded he had decided, as I had, that the fellow at least thought he knew what he was doing.

Auriabedas sat me down on a large stone. The wind was blowing off the sea, so the stink of fish was missing from the air. By then, I noticed its absence more than its presence. Auriabedas gave me a small jar. "Drink," he said, undoing the stopper. "Wine and poppy. I cut, you hurt not so much."

I drank. The stuff had a muzzy taste to it. After a while, the world began to look dimmer than it had, an effect the poppy has on the eyes. I yawned. I felt sleepy, detached, almost floating away from myself.

From his little wooden case, Auriabedas drew the knife he had shown me in the tavern; needle and thread; some linen rags for bandages;

a couple of hollow wooden tubes, each one thicker than my little finger; and, absurdly, a pen-and-ink set. He leaned forward, touching me with surprising delicacy to measure the exact size of the wound he aimed to repair. Then, inking his pen, he drew on my forehead the shape of skin he intended to cut out and fold over the hole in the center of my face.

"It looks like you're drawing a leaf," Myakes told him, he being able to see the shape I was trying to discern from sense of touch alone.

"Leaf, oh yes," Auriabedas said. "For center of nose bottom and for sides. You understand?" He touched the wings of flesh around his nostrils to show what he meant. Then he looked at Myakes, seeming troubled as he did so. "I cut. I hurt. I make pain. You are understanding this, oh yes? I need mans to hold. Not one man. Two mans, three mans, maybeso more mans. Not have here."

I held up a hand. Once moved, it seemed to stay in place of its own accord. "Auriabedas, by God and the Virgin Mother of God I swear I shall not move as you cut me. Do what needs to be done. I shall endure it."

The troubled look did not leave his face. "You say this now. What you do once I start cut, that very very different. I tell you. You hear me?"

"I hear you," I answered. "I shall not move, I tell you. Do you hear me?" I folded my arms across my chest and tilted my head up so he would have the best possible light by which to work. "Begin."

He began.

MYAKES

Brother Elpidios, if somebody told me about it and I wasn't there to see it with my own eyes, I'd call him a liar to his face. You know about poppy juice, don't you? Ah, I thought as much. What it does is, it makes bad horrible pain seem like plain horrible pain. That's all it does. I had some after they put my eyes out. I guess I know.

Well, Justinian, he just sat there like he was a marble statue. Except to breathe, he never twitched, not even once. He didn't scream, he didn't yell, he didn't even hiss. He never once tried knocking Auriabedas's hand away. No, I take it back. Justinian wasn't *just* like a marble statue. Marble doesn't bleed.

If you could stand it, it was fascinating to watch. Me, I'd seen enough battlefields so it didn't bother me too bad. The little brown man made the first cuts right above the top of Justinian's mustache. When

Justinian didn't flinch, he sort of muttered to himself and kept on making little cuts till that whole stretch was raw meat.

Once he was happy he'd chopped Justinian up enough there, he started cutting away at the leaf he'd drawn on his forehead. He cut it from the bottom up, I suppose so the blood wouldn't drip on the line in a place where he hadn't cut yet. Once he'd cut a section, he had to slide the knife under it to free it from the flesh underneath, not that you've got a lot of flesh between the skin of your forehead and the bone there.

After a while, he had the whole leaf free. He gave it a half-twist at the bottom, so it would still be skin side out when he put it over the hole where Justinian's nose used to be. I'd wondered how he was going to manage that. He knew what he was doing, all right. Justinian hadn't made a mistake there.

He sewed the leaf to the raw meat at the very base of what would be the new nose. Justinian didn't wiggle for that, either. "Blood in both," Auriabedas said. "Blood join blood, oh yes, all good." Justinian does a fine job of writing down the funny way he talked. I can hear it in my head, even if I haven't much thought of it over the years between then and now.

I'd wondered what his little wooden tubes were for. He put them into Justinian's nose—or what was going to be his nose—to give shape to his nostrils. Then he did some more sewing and finished bandaging Justinian's face. By then, with all the rags there and more rags around where he'd sliced that leaf-shaped flap out of Justinian's forehead, the little brown fellow had wrapped him up good.

When Auriabedas was all done, he turned to me. He was all smiles. "Now he have nose," he said in his bad Greek. "Hope it good nose. Think it good nose, oh yes. Him brave man. Never see more braver, oh very no. How you say?—deserve good nose."

"Thank you," Justinian said.

J U S T I N I A N

It hurt. Mother of God, how it hurt! When the executioner slashed my tongue and cut off my nose, the pain was also very bad. But those two cuts were inflicted quickly, and, once they had been made, my body could turn immediately to the business of healing. Here, Auriabedas not only cut once but kept on cutting and digging and prodding and poking and then at last sewing. I was glad for the wine with poppy juice, but do not think it did much against my suffering. Any man not dead would have suffered as a result of what the small brown trader did to me.

Two things helped sustain me while he cut. First, I had given him my oath I would neither pull away nor try to stop him while he worked. If a man will not tell God the truth, to whom will he tell it? And second, when the executioner had cut me, it was with the express purpose of keeping me from ever regaining the imperial throne. Every time Auriabedas's knife sliced into my flesh, every time he drove needle and thread through me, he brought me that much closer to reclaiming what was rightfully mine. For that, I would have endured the pangs of hell, much less surgery.

I do not know how long it all took. When at last it was over, Auriabedas gave me more of the drugged wine to drink. Again, it did not take away my pain, though for a little while it made that pain seem almost as if it were happening to someone else, not to me.

While the little man from India was wiping his knife and needle on a scrap of cloth and returning them to the small box he wore in place of a belt pouch, Myakes asked me, "Can you get up, Emperor?"

"I think so," I answered, and then proceeded to prove myself right. As I had after I was mutilated, I tasted rusty blood in my mouth: less this time than before, though. The bandages barely let me see. I turned back toward the monastery and toward the *xenodokheion* where I had spent— no, not spent: squandered—so much time. "Help me back," I told my faithful companion. "Now we'll see how bad the fever gets." If I spent a stretch out of my head and raving . . . *so much the better*, I thought.

I should be hard-pressed to deny that Auriabedas earned his five nomismata. Rather than cutting me and leaving my recovery to the will of God, he came back to the monastery at first daily and then every other day until my healing was well advanced, changing my bandages and putting ointment on the wounds he had inflicted. The pain the first two or three times he changed the bandages—especially the first, as a result of all the blood that had dried on them—was almost as bad as during the surgery.

But the wounds healed more cleanly than I had expected. Perhaps the ointment he favored, a mixture of boiled butter and honey, had some special virtue to it. I have since tried to interest Roman physicians in this blend, but, if Galen or Oribasios failed to speak of a medicament in glowing terms, they refuse to admit it could be of any value. Nor is a mere imperial command enough to change their opinion.

Myakes would always stay close by while Auriabedas did what he had to do with me. After the little brown man peeled off the latest set of bandages, I would ask, "How do I look today?" The first few times I put the question, Myakes pretended he did not hear it, which I took for something less than a good sign.

But after a week or ten days, when scabs had formed over the raw wounds in my forehead and at the base of my nose, he began to look thoughtful rather than carefully blank. "You know, Emperor" he said one day, "it might not be so bad."

A few days after that triumph, I reached two more milestones. Auriabedas approached me with a small knife. "I need to cut stitches, take out them," he said. "Flesh grow good to flesh, oh yes, not need stitches no more, oh no." I submitted to his ministrations. The feel of the thread sliding out through my flesh as he drew it forth with a pair of tongs was strange and repellent, but soon over.

Having accomplished that, Auriabedas bade me splash warm water on the lower part of my face, over and over again, to loosen the dried blood gluing his little wooden tubes to my flesh. Then he used the tongs to pull the tubes free. More blood, this fresh, not dry, followed. Since he took it as a matter of course, I did as well. And, as I expected from his manner, the flow soon stopped.

He tapped at the thin layer of flesh above the former position of one of the tubes. When it held its shape under his prodding, he looked pleased. "You have nose good as I can make," he said proudly.

"I am glad to hear it," I answered. How good a nose it truly was, I did not yet know, but for Myakes' increasingly hopeful comments. I had not yet found (indeed, I had not yet sought) a mirror or still water in which I could view myself, reasoning it would be wisest to wait until I was more nearly healed before doing so. But I reckoned the day when Auriabedas, having taken the bandages from my forehead, did not replace them with new ones as a sign that my healing had advanced far enough.

A monastery was not the ideal place in which to seek a mirror, the monks being by the very nature of the lives they had chosen for themselves opposed to the notion of adornment and ornamentation of the body. I knew a place, however, where that notion was embraced rather than opposed. And so, from the *xenodokheion* I took myself off to the brothel where I had been in the habit of easing my lusts when those grew too strong to be ignored.

The guard standing outside was not the same fellow who had been there when I began patronizing the establishment, nor his immediate successor, either. Yet he had been there long enough to recognize me, which, for a moment, he failed to do as I came round the corner. "You've—you've changed," he managed when I walked up to him.

"I hope so," I answered. He held the door open for me as I went inside, as that first guard had so many years before. From that day to this one, I had not shown my mutilated face there in daylight.

The women lounging within exclaimed in surprise, first at seeing me there with the sun in the sky and then on account of my changed aspect. "What did you do?" they asked, over and over again.

I explained what I had done. Some of them nodded. Some of them made disgusted noises. "May I see myself, please?" I asked. "I came here for the loan of a mirror." That was, in fact, the only reason for which I had come, not having had the crust to borrow—no, to take—more money from Myakes so soon after paying Auriabedas.

Several of the whores had small mirrors, which they used to darken their eyelids and paint their cheeks and lips with red. I looked now in one, now in another. The great scab on my forehead remained, looking as if I had fallen from a horse onto my face. I tried to imagine it gone, replaced by a smooth, pale scar. But I studied it less closely than my nose. As Auriabedas had said, that was still ugly, a far cry from the proud prominence I had once borne. It looked as if someone had smashed it with a rock and done a particularly fine job of flattening it. But it looked like a nose, if a damaged one, not a great gaping hole in the center of my face.

And then, to my astonishment, one of the women took me upstairs to celebrate my improvement in the most enjoyable way possible. "I can't give you anything," I told her—before, not afterwards, to avoid any possible misunderstandings.

She shrugged, which, as she had just got out of her shift, I found inspiring. "Not many men coming in today," she said. "Don't worry about it." And so I did not worry about it. Go to any business long enough, prove yourself a good customer, and you will get favors to which someone walking in off the street for the first time could not hope to aspire.

Afterwards, I strode through the streets of Kherson, looking at the town with new eyes, letting the townsfolk see me with my new face. Not all of them recognized me, which I found almost as satisfying as the girl had been. I went down to the harbor. Myakes, who was rolling barrels of—what else?—salt fish onto a ship, waved to me. I waved back.

One of the laborers with whom he was working walked by and casually slapped him on the shoulder. I envied him, and envy him to this day, that easy contact among equals. It is something I have never known.

As prince and then Emperor, I was set above the rest of the world. After Leontios mutilated me and exiled me to Kherson, the rest of the world, by contrast, was set above me. Having seen life from above and below, I own to preferring the former. Of life at the same level as everyone else, I am ignorant.

Coming down close to the sea, I stared south across it. How many times I did that in my years of exile, I could not begin to say. For a long while there, though, that sea sundering me from Constantinople had seemed wide as the unending ocean that flows on forever past the last land of the known world. Now, all at once, I felt the imperial city to be barely below the horizon, so that, if I went up into a high place, I might see the great dome of the church of the Holy Wisdom revealed in all its splendor and ingenuity.

This was not so, of course, but the feeling had a reality of its own. I had never left off saying I was Emperor of the Romans, not through all the weary, empty years in Kherson. Now, all at once, I felt like the Emperor again, as if robbed of my throne only yesterday, not years before.

"I *will* go back!" I said, fiercely enough to startle a tern walking near me, perhaps in the hope I would throw it a scrap of fish. "It *shall* be mine again!" The tern mewed and flew away. And I, I started back to the *xenodokheion*.

I had not gone far before I met the *tudun*, coming back to his residence after having been away on some business or other. Escorting him were a double handful of his fellow Khazars, swarthy, stocky men in furs and leather. Some of them glanced at me, then looked away: I was not extraordinary enough to be worth staring at. What a triumph!

The *tudun*'s eyes started to slide away from me, too, but then they snapped back. "You Justinian," he said, almost accusingly.

"Yes, I am Justinian," I agreed. My voice was proud.

"What happen to your nose?" he asked. "Not gone no more." He frowned. "No, wait. I hear you have someone cut on it."

"That's right." Rumor was ahead of me, then. I wondered if Auriabedas had been drinking his way through my five nomismata, boasting of his surgical prowess in every dockside tavern. If he got more business from that, I hope he did as well by the rest of his patients as he did by me.

The *tudun* was not stupid, and knew a surprising amount about Roman ways. "You have nose again, you able to be Emperor again. Romans not laugh at you now, you want to be Emperor again." He stared at me, as if daring me to deny it.

I did not deny it: not quite. "I had not thought so far ahead," I told him, even if I would not have said the same thing while taking a holy oath before God. "I had a chance to not be ugly—not to be so ugly—any more, and I took it."

He frowned. "You come here, you promise you don't try and become Emperor again. You say you live here quiet, not cause nobody no trouble."

"I have not done anything differently since I got this new nose of sorts," I answered. Then I held up one finger. "No, I take that back. I've bedded a woman without the room's being so black, she could not see my face."

He snorted. A couple of his bodyguards understood enough Greek to translate that into their own language—which may be even uglier than that of the Sklavenoi—for their companions. The barbarians laughed. One of them pointed to my face and then down to my crotch. He said something else that engendered more laughter. *Didn't cut that off*, was my guess as to its meaning.

"Woman I don't care nothing about," the *tudun* said, snapping his fingers to emphasize the point. "Trouble—I care about. Not want none between Romans and Khazars. I tell you this long time gone—you remember?"

"I remember." I had tried to stir up trouble for the wicked usurpers—first Leontios, then Apsimaros—from the moment I arrived at Kherson. Because of my mutilation, I had failed. Now, like Lazarus, my hopes were reborn.

The *tudun* pointed at me. "You raise trouble, any kind, even smallest bit"—he held his hands close together to show how small a small bit could be—"I tell Emperor Tiberius, see if he still want you to stay here."

That brought me up short. I had not known Apsimaros well (I refused to call him Tiberius, even to myself) before my throne was stolen from me, and word of his deeds that reached Kherson was bound to be sketchy and inaccurate, but he, unlike Leontios, seemed to be no sluggard, and to have a fitting concern for maintaining his place, usurped though that was: why else would he have sent Bardanes Philippikos into exile on the strength of a dream?

"You hear me?" the *tudun* asked. "You understand me?"

"Oh, yes," I assured him. "I hear you and I understand you very well indeed." I understood I would have to be careful as I planned my return to Constantinople. I had understood from the beginning that I would be returning to Constantinople.

Still looking at me in the most dubious fashion, the *tudun* went on his way. I, for my part, returned to the monastery. A monk, not a man I knew, waited in the *xenodokheion*. "Emperor, I greet you!" he exclaimed, and prostrated himself before me on the guest-house floor.

No one, not Myakes, not Barisbakourios, not his brother, had prostrated himself before me in Kherson. Because of that, and because I was just arrived from seeing the *tudun* and listening to his warning to me not to act the part of the Emperor, I stared down at this fellow in some suspicion, wondering if he might not be a stalking horse, intended to goad me into publicly claiming the imperial dignity and thereby giving the *tudun* an excuse to move against me.

"Get up," I told him, and then had an inspiration. "In lands attached to a monastery, all men are equal before God."

He rose, his face wreathed in smiles. "Emperor, how glad I am to see that your reputation for piety is nothing less than the truth."

If he was a traitor, he was an enthusiastic traitor. "Who are you?" I demanded. I did not reach for the knife I wore, but my hand knew with the body's knowledge where it was.

"My name is Cyrus, Emperor," he said, smiling more broadly yet: if a traitor, genial as well as enthusiastic. "I have sailed from Amastris to Kherson for, among other reasons, the pleasure and honor of making your acquaintance."

"And why is that?" I was determined to play my own game at my own speed. If this Cyrus proved the *tudun*'s agent, he would get nothing from me.

He looked around, although the two of us were alone in the large hall. Dramatically lowering his voice, he answered, "Because I have seen in the stars that you are destined to rule the Roman Empire once more."

Again, I did not know how to take that. A man in the *tudun*'s pay would say the same thing, seeking to entice me. And, even if Cyrus was sincere, I still did not know how to respond to his words. That one can foresee the future in the stars violates the proved fact of God's omnipotence, and for that reason is condemned by the holy church. But Cyrus was far from the only churchman to have dabbled in such waters; Leontios's puppetmaster, Paul, also claimed to have seen in the heavens his patron's rise.

Cyrus suddenly seized my hands in his. "Emperor, have faith in me," he said. "When I sailed from Amastris, I had no idea how what I had seen might come to pass, you having suffered such cruel injuries at the hands of your foes. And here I meet you and find you"—he cast about for a word, and found one—"restored. Is it a miracle?"

Gently, I touched my new nose. Flat, aye. Ugly, aye. A nose? Unquestionably. How to explain to a monk I had received it thanks to the arts of a little brown man who scoffed at the notion of Christ's being the

Son of God, or even of there being but one God? I did not explain. If Cyrus wanted to reckon it a miracle, I would let him.

"When do you intend to go back to Amastris?" I asked.

"Go back?" He shook his head in puzzlement. "Emperor, I do not intend to go back. I aim to make myself a place here, and to aid you in recovering your throne in every way I can. Once that is done, I shall return to Romania, but not until then."

If he spoke the truth, he easily passed the test I had set him. Over the next few days, I learned from longshoremen that he had indeed disembarked from a ship from Amastris. "He was an abbot there, I hear," one of them said, which explained how Cyrus had got permission from his superior to abandon his monastery for another, or rather that he had needed no one's permission. Oh, he might have asked his bishop, but then again, he might not have, too, abbots being largely autonomous within the ecclesiastical hierarchy.

In Kherson, he lived as a monk among other monks. If taking orders when he had once given them troubled him, he showed no sign. He spoke more openly about my return to Constantinople than I did. Sometimes he did so within the hearing of Khazar soldiers. I saw how they glared. If he was an agent of the *tudun*'s, either they did not know it or they made a better show of hypocrisy than I suspected to lie within the abilities of such barbarians. I was convinced.

And so, little by little, was Myakes, who initially had distrusted Cyrus even more than I had. "He's the straight goods, Emperor," he said one day when we were drinking wine in a tavern. "I wouldn't have believed it, but he is. Nice to have a man of God who's on our side seven days a week."

"Yes," I said, drawing the word out into a hiss. Kallinikos had been perfectly happy to work with me—and to bless Leontios in my place . . . and to bless Apsimaros in Leontios's place. If I regained the throne, no doubt he would bless me again . . . for a while.

Barisbakourios and Stephen—I more often thought of him that way than as Salibas, Stephen being the good Greek name it was—walked into the tavern. They hurried over to the table where Myakes and I sat. "That monk of yours, Emperor, he's something!" Barisbakourios exclaimed. "You listen to him, the devils of hell already have Apsimaros on their forks, and they're toasting him over the fire." His eyes glowed. He was ready for anything, was Barisbakourios, the best of the handful who had rallied to my side in Kherson.

"People *were* listening to Cyrus, too, and nodding at everything he said," Stephen added. Had his brother gone against me, I think he would have, too. Though lacking the spark of Barisbakourios, he was brave and—because his brother was—loyal. Not all can lead, and without followers a leader is no more than a voice that crieth in the wilderness.

"Were any Khazars there?" I asked.

"No, no Khazars, but a couple of the rich merchants' bodyguards were hanging around the edge of the crowd," Barisbakourios answered. "The longer they listened, the unhappier they got. They're afraid of Apsimaros, the fools."

What they were afraid of was the wrath of the Roman Empire, which, even when the Empire was headed by a usurper so little Roman that he had to change his name to have one fit for putting on his nomismata, was nothing to be despised. I also took the bodyguards' unhappiness to mean that their masters would be unhappy when Cyrus's words were reported to them, and very possibly that the *tudun* would be unhappy, too. If he was, odds were that Cyrus truly did support me.

My other choice in looking at Cyrus was to reckon that he sought to incite me to actions by which the Khazars or the rich merchants (whom I had not previously considered) could justify taking my head. The more I pondered that, the less likely it seemed. The merchants' reach did not extend to Amastris, whence Cyrus had indubitably come. And, if the Khazars intended taking my head, they could do it. They needed no justification: to the contrary. If they did do it, they had no need to fear the wrath of the Roman Empire: again, to the contrary. Apsimaros would shower them with presents on learning they had killed me.

Which, by ineluctable logic, meant Cyrus was unlikely to be an agent, and likely in fact to have seen in the stars that I would indeed return in triumph to Constantinople. Which, in turn, meant—or probably meant—I could trust him. One thing an Emperor soon learns is that men he can truly trust are few and far between.

Writing out the pathway my reasoning followed takes longer than the reasoning itself did to pass through my mind. After taking only a couple of breaths, I raised my mug of wine in salute. "To Cyrus!" I said.

"To Cyrus!" Myakes, Barisbakourios, and Stephen drank with me.

Even with Cyrus vigorously espousing my cause, it advanced more slowly than I would have liked. Having spent so long in Kherson, I felt every added day like another heavy stone dropped onto my back. The first white hairs appeared in my beard while I spent time doing nothing in exile.

Not all the time passed to no good purpose. The scabs crusting my forehead finally fell away, and the raw pink scar under them began to weather on being exposed to sun and air. A year having passed after the

Indian cut me, the scar was no longer pink but a shade only a little paler than the rest of my skin. When I visited that brothel, none of the whores there hesitated to join with me during the day, and they no longer charged me twice the going rate. I was no longer so conspicuous as I had been.

This was true of my physical appearance. In other ways, though, Cyrus's vigorous advocacy of me and my cause was making me more conspicuous than I had been. I was walking into Kherson early one morning when a couple of Khazars on ponies came trotting down toward the monastery where I had stayed so long. Recognizing me, they reined in. One of them said, "You come with us. The *tudun* is to see you now."

I ended up walking into town between their horses. In all the time I had spent at Kherson, the *tudun* had never before honored me by inviting me into his residence: to do that would have been to acknowledge I was worthy of honor. Nor was he in truth honoring me now; it was more that I had become a nuisance to him.

The building to which I was conveyed, while made from the local stone, had the spare lines that said it dated from the early days of the Roman Empire, perhaps from the first couple of hundred years after our Lord walked the earth as a man. I wondered if the governors the Emperors of those times had sent to this distant outpost of Roman soil reckoned their tenure here as much an exile as I did mine.

The Khazars who had led me to the residence turned me over to the guards standing in front; the half-bored, half-alert demeanor of the latter put me in mind of the fellows who had stood outside my favorite brothel down through the years. Their boredom fell away, though, on their taking charge of me.

Rather than doors, the *tudun*'s residence had a carpet hanging over the entranceway, no doubt to imitate the tents to which the governor was more accustomed than he was to permanent housing. Inside, as I soon discovered, this imitation of the nomadic life continued. More carpets lay all over the floors, making my feet feel as if they were stepping on thick grass. Instead of the chairs and couches the Roman governors had used, cushions whose covers were as fantastically embroidered as the rugs did duty for furnishings. The lamps stank of butter.

In lieu of a throne or other high seat, the *tudun* lolled atop a mound of cushions. I looked around, finding none provided for me. Having contemplated remaining upright so I could look down on him, I decided it were wiser to sit, he having a position I acknowledged and I possessing none to which he admitted.

"You have friends making noises over you," he said ominously, "friends making noises about Emperor. Merchants not like."

He said nothing about the khagan of the Khazars, which I found interesting, but, if he was to govern the town, he had to pay attention to its prominent folk as well as to his distant master. I answered his first comment: "I am not responsible for what my friends say. They think I was treated unjustly." I thought the same, but again decided wisdom lay in keeping silent on that. Looking up at him, I went on, "Have any of your spies ever reported that *I* claimed I would go back to the imperial city and regain the crown?"

He did not bother denying he had set spies on me. "They not say that, no." I breathed an invisible sigh of relief, for I *had* said it, but, evidently, only among men who genuinely backed my cause. His words also confirmed Cyrus's loyalty to me. Still, he held the power here, and I had trouble bearing up under his gaze. After a pause, he said, "But your friends, they say what you want, yes?"

Yes indeed. "I cannot control what my friends say," I repeated. "Some say one thing, some say another, as is true of all men. But is it just to condemn me for words I cannot control? Would you want anyone to do that to you?"

Those narrow eyes glinted. He jabbed a thumb at his chest. "I never want to be Emperor of Romans at Constantinople. Never."

"Ah, but suppose your friends started saying you wanted to be khagan of the Khazars?" I shot back. "It would not be true. Would you want Ibouzeros Gliabanos to judge you from their loose talk?"

"I never want to be khagan, either," he said, but that was not the point, and he was clever enough to realize it. From atop that mound of cushions, he stared down at me. At last, grudgingly, he said, "Maybe." He spoke to the guards in the language of the Khazars, which has always put me in mind of the noises an egg makes frying in a pan. Without a word to me, the guards gestured out toward the curtain. They did not follow on my departing. The *tudun* having finished with me, I was no longer of any interest to them.

I reported my conversation with the Khazar governor to my comrades. Myakes, ever the most cautious of us, said, "We have to go easy for a while. If we get the Khazars *and* the merchants angry at us, we lose everything, and fast."

"That's so, but there's such a thing as being too careful, too," Barisbakourios returned. He was ready to sail for Constantinople that day or any day, so long as the ship held him and me—and perhaps his brother as well, though I suspect he would have done without Stephen at a pinch.

Cyrus said, "The truth of your right to rule, Emperor, is no less than the truth of the Lord. And, like the truth of the Lord, it must be proclaimed to those who know it not."

"Sometimes the truth of the Lord is proclaimed loudly, sometimes quietly," I said. "As the Holy Scriptures say, to every thing there is a season. Now is our season for quiet ripening. When the harvest is ripe, we shall reap it."

Cyrus and Barisbakourios protested but, recognizing me as Emperor of the Romans, recognized also that they were bound to obey me. And so, for the next few months, they were less vehement about putting forward my claim, regardless of how proper they knew it was. The *tudun* did not summon me again during that time, proving he was to some degree lulled.

But what I had asked of my followers, however necessary it seemed, went against their grain and mine. Little by little, almost without knowing it, Cyrus and Barisbakourios once more began to speak of my returning to Constantinople and to the throne waiting there. Had the *tudun* sought to silence them when they first began this, I should have eased their eagerness again. But he did not, and so I did not.

And so when, one day, Cyrus stood half preaching to, half haranguing, a crowd of lazy loafers who, like lazy loafers everywhere, took their entertainment where they could find it, he cried out, "In the eyes of God, this Apsimaros and Leontios before him were and are base usurpers, surely doomed to damnation and eternal torment at the clawed hands of Satan and his demons. Here before me stands the rightful Emperor of the Romans. Is it not so, Emperor Justinian?"

I turned to the crowd and, as if seized by something more than myself, shouted in a great voice, "Yes, it is so, every word! I was and am and will be Emperor of the Romans, and will return to Constantinople to wear the crown once more!" How the loafers cheered!

MYAKES

How I wish he would've kept his mouth shut, Brother Elpidios! Yes, that means I was happy enough in Kherson. I had a place to sleep, I had work that wasn't too easy and wasn't too hard, either. I had plenty to eat. I had plenty to drink. If I wanted anything more, I had places where I could go. I didn't go to the same place Justinian used, but Kherson had plenty of them. Never known a town full of sailors that didn't.

But that's not what I'm talking about, not this time. I wish Justinian would have kept his mouth shut because opening it drew notice to him that he didn't want. We'd been making plans, the lot of us. We knew what we wanted to do. We just weren't quite ready to do it yet—and doing it with people keeping an eye on us was ten times tougher than if we'd been able to go about our business with nobody the wiser.

Justinian, though, he was never one for doing things by halves. What's that you say, Brother? You've seen as much? I hope you have, what with spending so much time reading his book to me. Holding back after the *tudun* warned him—it ate at him. He couldn't stand it, no matter how plain the need was.

Afterwards, he felt better. He was all happy and smiling and lazy, like he'd just had a woman after doing without for a long time. What? You don't know what I'm talking about? Oh, that's right, so you don't, poor fellow. Well, you're a holy man, Brother Elpidios, and God loves you. That's . . . very fine.

But you lay a woman, you can get in trouble, too. It's not all fun. She can give you a drippy pipe. You can put a baby in her. Even if you don't put a baby in her, her brothers and her father are liable to find out you've spread her legs, and then come after you with clubs, or maybe knives.

Say you've been bragging. That helps 'em find out. And when Justinian shouted out that he was the rightful Emperor and he aimed to get his crown back, if you wouldn't call that bragging, Brother Elipidios, what would you call it?

J U S T I N I A N

I waited to see what the *tudun* would do after I proclaimed my intention of regaining that which I had inherited from my ancestors. What the *tudun* did, rather to my surprise, was nothing. Perhaps he was weaker than I had thought or than he had presented himself as being, or perhaps the khagan of the Khazars had sent him orders to moderate his treatment of me. I set Barisbakourios to investigate which of those was so.

But the *tudun* was not the only power in Kherson, which, like any frontier town, was rife with alliances running in more than one direction. The older families there looked more strongly toward Constantinople than toward the Khazars. They may also have remembered that Apsimaros, before usurping the throne, had been an officer of the fleet, and so more inclined to use it than Leontios would have been—not that Leontios was ever much inclined to do anything.

I was spooning up the inevitable, inescapable salt-fish porridge in the *xenodokheion* one morning when Stephen burst in, all sweaty and disheveled. "Emperor!" he said. "They'll be coming for you, Emperor!"

"Who will be coming for me?" I demanded, though I already had a fair idea. Myakes was eating beside me. He had been grumbling over my announcing I intended to retake the throne, and I did not care to give him the chance to look at me as if to say *I told you so*, even if he was too well trained in subordination to speak the words aloud.

"The whole lot of the bastards," Stephen said, which, if imperfectly responsive, had more flavor than that porridge of mine. He went on, "They'll kill you if they catch you, or else send you back to Apsimaros."

The prominent folk in Kherson could muster more force than I could hope to withstand. And, if by some chance they chose to give me over to Apsimaros rather than slaying me themselves, he would no doubt make up for their neglect in that matter.

Myakes put down his spoon, brought the bowl from which he was eating to his lips, and gulped down what remained. "Might as well fill my belly," he remarked. "Lord knows when I'll get the chance again." That being full of homely good sense, I imitated his example.

Stephen, meanwhile, was shifting from foot to foot, as if he intended running to the latrine at any moment. "Come on!" he exclaimed, the instant I put down my bowl. "My brother has horses waiting."

I had hardly been on a horse since my exile. Kherson was not a city of such great extent as to make riding needful, shank's mare sufficing for all journeys thereabouts. But we could not stay in Kherson, not now. I sprang to my feet and followed Stephen out of the *xenodokheion* where I had lived for almost nine years. After that day, I never saw the place again.

I should not even have looked back at it had Cyrus not chanced to come out of the monastery as I was trotting away and to call after me, "Where are you going, Emperor?"

Stephen had not told me what Barisbakourios had in mind doing with the horses he had collected. But an answer came to my mind as readily as a sword might come to my hand: "We're going up toward the country of the Khazars." If the *tudun* had kept silent after my assertion of my rights, perhaps his master was indeed more inclined to friendliness toward me than he had been in the past. He could hardly have been less inclined to friendliness toward me than the local leaders of Kherson, not if they aimed to murder me or betray me to the usurper.

"I'm with you, Emperor," Cyrus said, and came running after Stephen and Myakes and me.

Had I been offered while ruling in Constantinople such a horse as one of the beasts Barisbakourios had waiting, I have no doubt I should have ordered a whipping for the wretch rash enough to insult me so. Any horse, however, was better than none, and these beasts qualified, if barely, as *any horse*. I mounted the least disreputable of them, and we rode by side streets toward the north gate of Kherson.

The guards there were Khazars, which probably saved my life. Had they been Khersonites, I daresay they would have refused to allow me and my companions to leave the town. As it was, they shrugged and stood aside. Out of Kherson we rode, heading north.

My first intention had been to ride straight for the court of the khagan of the Khazars, out there on the immense plain from which the peninsula containing Kherson depends like the little ball of flesh hanging at the back of a man's throat. Having just escaped one danger, though, I wondered whether I ought to thrust myself at once into another, for I would be utterly at the khagan's mercy if I arrived at his barbaric court without any sort of invitation on his part.

When I spoke my doubts aloud, the others agreed with them. "Here, I know what let's do," Barisbakourios said. "Let's hole up in Doros. The people in Doros, they don't care what anyone else thinks or does."

Before coming to Kherson, I had never heard of Doros. By then, however, I had been in exile for a quarter of my life. "The town up by the neck of the peninsula?" I said, and then nodded. "Yes, that's a good idea. We'll do it."

Like Kherson, Doros is formally under the control of the Khazars. In Kherson, that formal control has a basis in reality, the khagan making a profit from the port. The folk of Doros formerly derived their income from tolls on trade going into and out of the peninsula. The khagans of the Khazars have for some years been strong enough to forbid them that. Such income as they have these days, as best I can tell, they derive from taking in one another's washing. Having impoverished them, the Khazars no longer bother taking an interest in their affairs.

They are a comely people, the folk of Doros: tall and straight and some of them fairer of hair and of skin than I. That much I had known, from meeting in taverns their traders who came down to Kherson. What I had not known was how nervous being around many of them would make me: those of them who spoke Greek did so with an accent almost identical to that of Apsimaros.

On reflection, that was not surprising. He was of German blood of some sort, and the folk of Doros, it turns out, are Goths. The Emperor for whom I was named, the first Justinian, conquered the Ostrogoths a century and a half ago. We Romans have had few dealings with the Visigoths of the western Iberia, also called Spain, since they ousted us from it while my great-great-grandfather was distracted with more urgent wars against the Persians and Avars and Arabs. (It is said, though—whispered, actually—that he had more intimate dealings with them than those of war, siring a bastard on a woman of their people: a truth the women of my family no doubt wish the men would forget.)

M Y A K E S

See, Brother Elpidios? I already told you about that, long time gone. I know what's what, I do.

J U S T I N I A N

In ancient days, the Goths ruled much of the plain over which the Khazars now roam. The folk of Doros are a remnant of those who did not accompany the rest on their journey to the richer lands of the Roman Empire. They have improved over their ancestors in that they are now orthodox Christians rather than cleaving to the vile and abominable heresy of the Arians.

Barisbakourios had brought money enough to secure us lodgings in a tavern dirtier, smellier, and far more expensive than the *xenodokheion* where I had stayed so long. How galling it was that I, who had formerly commanded the resources of the Roman Empire, should again have been reduced to living off the generosity of my followers. Barisbakourios now being general of the military district of the Opsikion, though, I can truthfully say I have requited generosity with generosity, as I have also requited treason with vengeance.

More of Barisbakourios's money and, I think, some of Myakes' as well, went into persuading Totilas, the leader of the Goths of Doros, not to yield me up to the Khersonites if they asked that of him. The risk there, of course, was that they might pay him more to surrender me, but our bribe did at least raise the stake in the game.

Totilas said, "I do not want trouble from Kherson. I do not want trouble from the Romans. I do not want trouble from the Khazars. I do not want trouble of any kind. I want to stay here undisturbed."

Like a turnip in the ground, I thought. Totilas's nose resembled a turnip, being large and purple and bulbous. *Well, not all of us are turnips. Some deserve the imperial eagle as emblem.* But I had to speak him fair, lest he use his petty power to harm me. "Noble Totilas, I want no trouble, either, but I take it as trouble when evil men band together to kill me or send me in chains to another man who would surely do that. All I want is the chance to live in freedom." *And to take back what is mine.* "God willing, I shall not be in your city long."

God willing, indeed. Acting on the belief that the khagan of the Khazars was at the moment not unfavorably inclined toward me, the first thing I had done after having arrived at Doros was to send Stephen— otherwise known as Salibas—to Ibouzeros Gliabanos, entreating him to accept me at his court. Being of half-Khazar blood, Stephen could speak to the khagan in his own tongue.

If Stephen brought back word that Ibouzeros Gliabanos would accept me, I purposed leaving Doros at once and repairing to his capital on the plain. If, on the other hand, Stephen brought word of a refusal . . . I did not know what I should do then. The best plan I had was to board ship, sail back to Constantinople, and try to raise a revolution. Against Leontios, such a plan might well have succeeded. But Apsimaros had shown himself more alert than the usurper he had usurped.

Totilas scratched that great root of a nose; I do believe I preferred my own, as Auriabedas had repaired it, to the one with which nature had endowed him. "If you do not stay long, maybe there will be no trouble." Avoiding trouble appeared to be his alpha and omega in life. *A turnip indeed*, I thought.

Sure enough, the Khersonite leaders did send a delegation to Doros seeking me. Sure enough, they did offer Totilas a bribe to yield me up to them. But, being most of them tight-fisted merchants, they offered only a tiny bit more than I had paid. I told him, "If you try to take me, I will make as much trouble as I can. I will not go quietly. In fact, I will set fires in my room and all over that building. With any kind of wind, they will cause you all sorts of trouble." Having heard him speak, I bore down on the word as if I were a magician casting a spell.

And so I might have been. He turned so pale even that nose became for a moment the color of ordinary flesh. "Don't do that!" he exclaimed. "Christ have mercy, don't do that." Any leader in any town would have had good cause to fear incendiarism. Put that next to Totilas's fear of trouble, and the game was mine. "I'll send those Khersonites away with a flea in their ear, see if I don't."

He did. They left Doros grumbling. By all appearances, they were unused to having Totilas stand up for the independence of his town. Actually, he was not standing up but being propped up, but the Khersonites did not know that. I breathed easier when they rode away.

Bread in Doros was as rare as it had been down in Kherson. As at the latter place, salt fish formed the bulk of the diet. The Goths of Doros had their own way of preparing it, though, mixing it with cabbage half-pickled in sharp vinegar. I cannot decide to this day whether that was better or worse than the fish stews of Kherson. It was, however, different from them, which at first gave the mixture an appeal the stew had long since lost. Before long, though, fish and sour cabbage also began to pall.

Kherson made better wine than Doros. That did not keep me from drinking a good deal of the wine of Doros while waiting for Stephen to return. Like my great-great-grandfather before me, I became infatuated with a big, yellow-haired Gothic woman, a servant at the tavern. Though not thinking of herself as a prostitute, she proved more mercenary than the whores at the brothel I had patronized in Kherson. Since I had little to give her, she gave me little. All things considered, that may well have been for the best, even if I would not have said so at the time.

I fretted and fumed as the days went by and Stephen remained out on the plain. "I want him here," I told Myakes. "I don't care if he tells me Ibouzeros Gliabanos won't even spit on me. I just want to *know*, curse it. Not knowing is what drives you mad."

"Not me," Myakes said. "Sooner or later, it'll happen. You can't do anything about it till then, so what's the point of getting in an uproar?"

To Myakes, who was not in the habit of looking ahead, the future seemed small and distant, unworthy of special heed. I had done nothing but look ahead since the day I came out of my delirium at the *xenodokheion* in Kherson: Constantinople and the throne beckoned me. The khagan's response either eased my way toward what I saw or cast a great shadow across it. I burned to know which.

Burn as I would, God revealed things in the time He desired, not the time I desired. His will be done, but it nearly led to disaster for me. After leaving me severely alone once I threatened to do my best to burn down his small, ugly, fish-stinking town, Totilas summoned me to his house: Doros was too insignificant to boast any more significant residence for its leader than a hovel somewhat larger than most of the hovels around it.

"Uh, the Khersonites have been here again," he said, nervously cracking his knuckles. "This time, they say they'll give me twice as much as the last time they were here."

This was a thinly veiled—indeed, an unveiled—invitation for me to match their offer. I would have, if I could. I knew how much money my followers had: not enough. I sighed. "What a pity," I said, adding, "This was such a nice little town."

The last sentence was a great whacking lie, but Totilas, as I had hoped he would, caught the past tense contained therein. "What do you mean, *was?*" he said, his nose going a couple of shades darker.

"What I said," I answered. "You don't think I haven't made myself ready for a day like this, do you? My friends and I have been here for weeks now, and made more friends in Doros. About every other building here has a little jug or barrel of oil hidden away in it. Try to seize me, try to do anything to harm me, and my friends—and you don't know who all of them are, I promise you—will go running through the town, tipping over those jars and throwing torches into them."

I have only rarely heard lies so big that did not come from the mouth of a follower of the false prophet. I had recruited one, count him, one follower in Doros, a certain Theophilos, who, while more clever than Foolish Paul, was not much more clever. Nor had my henchmen secreted fuel for incendiaries throughout the town.

But things like the vengeance I had taken on the Sklavenoi and my surviving a mutilation that might well have killed me had given me a reputation for single-minded determination and ferocity. Regardless of whether I had actually done what I claimed, Totilas knew all too well it was the sort of thing I *might* do. Did he have the nerve to call my bluff?

One glance at him proved he did not. His ruddy face went a dirty yellow. His dusky nose went pink. "You are a devil," he exclaimed. "You would not." But he thought I would. Thinking that, he was meat for the roasting.

"Leave me alone, and I shall leave you alone," I said. "Seek to betray me to my enemies and you become my enemy." That was true. If I helped him exaggerate in his mind my capacity to harm my enemies . . . good.

I rose and went back to my lodgings. None of the Goths of Doros tried to stop me. For the next several days, though, men searched frantically through the town. Every container of oil they found was no doubt added to my account. For good measure, I sent Barisbakourios out to buy more fish oil. For some reason, no one in Doros would sell him any.

Totilas, now, was not the man to start precipitate action. In fact, had I not had the misfortune of knowing Leontios, I might have reckoned Totilas the most lethargic man charged with administering any sort of public affairs I had ever met. Nonetheless, he would conclude, sooner or later, that I was running a bluff. When he did, his likeliest action—averse to taking action as he was—would be to sell me to the Khersonites. Did he find the will, he could do it. I knew that better than he.

"Where is Stephen?" The question had been important before. Now, all at once, it was vital, and on our lips all the time, the only variation being Barisbakourios's occasional, "Where is Salibas?"

I was beginning to fear he had suffered misfortune either on the way to the court of Ibouzeros Gliabanos at distant Atil or, perhaps more likely, on the way back from that court: if Ibouzeros Gliabanos was not so well disposed to me as I had hoped, he might well deem it expedient to expunge from the landscape my envoy to him.

My landlord grew visibly more distressed at my presence under his leaky roof; if his distress did not grow voluble as well as visible, this was no doubt because my followers and I made sure to display ourselves, well armed, before him at frequent intervals.

But other armed men began displaying themselves, too, around the tavern where we were staying. For the time being, they fought shy of doing anything more than displaying themselves, that being certain to have caused the trouble Totilas dreaded. But these matters could not be indefinitely delayed.

Three or four days after beginning to muster his force, Totilas approached the tavern where I was for all practical purposes besieged. I expected this would be a demand for my surrender, his coming in person showing more spirit than I had looked for from him.

Myakes said, "He hasn't got a sword in his hand, Emperor, nor one on his belt, either."

He was right. Totilas advanced with both his hands held out before him so I could see they were empty, and carried not only no sword but no knife, either. "Parley!" he called loudly. "I want to parley with Justinian."

"Come ahead," I answered, not showing myself at a window lest he have a concealed archer awaiting the chance to puncture me.

Cyrus opened the door to admit the leader of Doros. Once inside, Totilas said, "Justinian, my men and I are holding a certain Salibas who also goes by the name of Stephen. He's one of your followers, not so?"

"Yes, he's mine," I said, as steadily as I could. Barisbakourios looked as if an arrow from a hidden archer had just pierced him. If Totilas had seized Stephen, he was indeed showing more initiative than the amount with which I had credited him.

Totilas licked his lips. "He says—he says he is coming back from seeing the khagan of the Khazars."

"That's true," I told him, and so it was.

"He also says . . ." Totilas licked his lips. "He also says the khagan of the Khazars, who is my overlord, wants you to go to his court as fast as you can. Will you go?" He sounded pathetically eager, bringing his next words out all in a rush: "Will you please go? That way, I can tell the Khersonites the truth when I say you are not here any more, and they will go away and leave me in peace, and there will be, thank God, no trouble in Kherson. So, will you go?"

How strange, to hear him begging me to do that which I most wanted to do in all the world! Theophilos let out a whoop half the town must have heard—not that that is anything remarkable, considering what a miserable little town Doros is. Barisbakourios no longer looked wounded. By that time, however, I had learned better than to take anything this side of God's holy truths on faith. I said, "Let Stephen come here. If I hear this from his lips, I will go."

"Thank you, Justinian! God bless you, Justinian!" To my surprise, Totilas embraced me before lumbering out of the tavern. He shouted to his men something in which I heard Stephen's name, but I followed no more than that, the rest being in the Gothic tongue.

But he soon proved to have been telling the truth, for Stephen came running in with us. After embracing his brother, he turned to me and spoke in great excitement: "Emperor, Ibouzeros Gliabanos wants you with him. He can't wait to have you there. He says you're the perfect counterweight to Apsimaros."

"Does he?" To Stephen, that was good news unalloyed. To me, it meant the Khazar intended using me as a piece on a game board. I laughed. I intended using him the same way. "I think Ibouzeros Gliabanos and I shall get on very well indeed," I said. "Let's go find out whether I'm right."

Of the journey to the khagan's court I shall say little, little having occurred worthy of mention. I shall note, however, that, while riding up the narrow isthmus of land joining the peninsula on which Kherson lies to the plains north of it, I was able to see the Black Sea on my left and and the Maiotic Bay on my right, which strikes me as interesting enough to record here.

Those plains themselves are also noteworthy: endless undulating grass, as far as the eye can reach in any direction. In Europe, in Anatolia, land has limits and variety: forests and mountains and meadows and cultivated fields. Not there. The plains are vast past any possible imagining, and reach far beyond the relatively small stretch of them I traveled. I did not know whether to be awed or afraid of such un-bounded immensity.

Every now and then, as we traveled east toward Atil, the town in which the khagan kept his court, we would pass a band of Khazars. When I first saw such a band, I marveled that the nomads had not overrun the entire world, for it overspread an enormous area with herds of cattle, sheep, and horses; with men riding round those herds and from one of them to another, and with the felt tents in which dwelt those riders and their women and children.

But there were, as I discovered, surprisingly few of those tents in each band of Khazars, and each band required an enormous stretch of territory on which to pasture the animals by which it lived. Constantly dealing with the herd trains the nomads for martial struggle in a way a farmer's life cannot match: they are ever in the saddle, and accustomed since childhood to riding through gaps in the herds and cutting out groups from among them, tactics they also apply in war. In war, though, their forces, while fierce, are also small, which allows their neighbors to survive.

Barisbakourios and Stephen speaking their language, we were able to ask for food and shelter in the Khazars' tents. The food was of the simplest sort, meat both roasted and sun-dried, curds, and little flat wheat-cakes in place of bread, a proper bake oven being too heavy to transport on their constant travels.

For drink, they made a liquor not from grapes as we do or even from barley like the barbarous Sklavenoi, but from the milk of their own mares. To a man used to wine, the stuff is thin and sour, but it has the same virtue as does wine. And when, having drunk to excess in the evening, one wakes the next morning, it makes one regret such overindulgence even more vigorously than does wine.

The Khazars sleep, and expect their guests to sleep, wrapped in furs and carpets on the ground. This gave me no difficulty whatever. As we were leaving a band one morning, an old man—notable because so few of the nomads live to be old—said something to Barisbakourios, who turned to me: "He is surprised, because most travelers he has seen like sleeping softer."

"Tell him that after nine years of a thin pallet on the stone floor of the monastery xenodokheion, I am sleeping softer," I answered with a laugh. Barisbakourios translated that for the old man. He laughed, too, displaying teeth worn down almost to his gums from years of gnawing at leathery strips of dried meat.

As I have said, each Khazar band took up a wide area of the plain. But the spaces between bands were wider yet. Most of the time while we were journeying to Atil, we might have been the only men on the face of the earth. We hunted partridges and pheasants. Myakes proved to be as good with the bow as anyone else in our band, which made him swagger above due measure.

M Y A K E S

I did nothing of the sort, Brother Elpidios, and I haven't the slightest idea why Justinian says I did. Just because I managed to put one right into the eye of a partridge two days running, I suppose. Nobody else came close to that, not in all the time we were on the road—not that there was any road, mind you. How could anyone blame me if I let people know about it?

The sin of pride, Brother? Oh, no, not me. What do you mean, why not? Because . . . That is, because . . . What does Justinian say next? Maybe it won't be about me.

J U S T I N I A N

From Doros to Atil is a journey of upwards of a month, even for men riding steadily, as my companions and I did. In all that time, the landscape changed little. We could have ridden east for another month from Atil, and it would have changed little. Having departed Doros, we could have ridden west rather than east, and the landscape would have changed little. We could also have ridden north; again, it would have changed little. If I harp on the vastness of the plains north of the Black Sea, it is indeed because of the strong impression that vastness left on me.

At last coming to Atil, now, that was a change. The town the Khazars have made for their capital lies close by the northern shore of the Caspian or Hyrcanian Sea, a body of water known to us Romans more in legend than in fact, though, in the Persian wars after the death of the Justinian for whom I am named, one Roman general did reach it by way of the Caucasus, built a small fleet, and ravaged Persian commerce on it.

A great river, the Volga, flows south into the Caspian Sea. Nearing the sea, its stream breaks up into a number of channels, as the Egyptian Nile does in what is called the Delta on account of its shape. Atil straddles one of these channels, the district to the west being larger than that to the east, though less populous. The khagan's residence is in the western part of the town.

Calling Atil a town, now that I think on it, stretches the meaning of the word. In many ways, it more closely resembles the encampments of the Khazar bands in which I had sometimes passed a night on the journey from Doros. Only a few of the dwellings are of timber or of mud brick; far more of the inhabitants dwell in tents like those of their nomadic fellows. These tents, however, do not wander over the plains, the natives making their living for the most part by agriculture. They sow crops for miles around in the rich soil of the Volga Delta, and bring in a good harvest.

But enough of that. On our reaching Atil, Stephen brought us to the khagan's palace, if a building made of clay and sticks may be dignified by such an appellation. Servants in coats and tunics of fine wool took charge of us and led us to Ibouzeros Gliabanos, khagan of the Khazars.

Rather than a throne, the khagan used as his high seat a gilded cart ornamented with a cloth-of-gold canopy, another remembrance, I suppose, of the nomadic life most of the Khazars lead. The khagan's servitors spoke to Barisbakourios, who translated their words into Greek: "We are to prostrate ourselves before the lord of this land."

He and the rest of my companions went to their bellies without hesitation. I remained upright. Ibouzeros Gliabanos spoke. Barisbakourios and Stephen, who understood him, rose; the others soon followed their example. He spoke again, and again Barisbakourios served as interpreter: "He asks why you did not go down."

"He is the khagan of the Khazars. I am the Emperor of the Romans," I answered. I daresay Ibouzeros Gliabanos took that to mean I assumed we were equal in rank. If he did, I did not correct him. In fact, though, I reckoned myself his superior. The only equals Emperors of the Romans have ever acknowledged are the Persian kings and their successor to power on our eastern frontier, the Arabs' miscalled commanders of the faithful. German kings? Barbarous khagans? They have more pretensions than true quality.

Ibouzeros Gliabanos spoke again. Barisbakourios looked relieved. "He says you are a man of spirit. He says you would not have come to him if you were not a man of spirit."

"Tell him I thank him for inviting me to his court," I replied, studying the khagan as I did so. He was younger than I had expected, being not far from my own age. He had a broad, rather swarthy face, black hair, and a thin, straggling black beard. His nose was low and flattish, not much more impressive than the one Auriabedas had restored to me. His eyes, narrow and dark, seemed clever.

He said, "You have endured much to claim the rule still." Henceforth I shall omit mention of Barisbakourios's translations, which sometimes slowed our speech together to a crawl.

"It is mine," I said simply.

He nodded. "You speak as one who rules should speak. And yet . . ." His voice trailed away. He looked sly. I understood him well enough. I was not the only man to claim the title, and the other sat in Constantinople while I stood here in Atil.

"It is mine," I repeated. "In times gone by, the khagan of the Khazars aided the Emperor of the Romans, Herakleios, who was my great-greatgrandfather, against the Persians. We Romans and you Khazars have fought together against the Arabs. We are allies by interest and allies by blood. In fact, is it not so that my great-great-grandfather once sent a portrait of his daughter to the man who was then khagan, offering a marriage alliance?" My opinion at the time was that this spoke more of Herakleios's desperation than anything else, but I hoped Ibouzeros Gliabanos would not see it the same way.

Ibouzeros Gliabanos turned to a man who stood at the right side of his cart and spoke to him in a low voice. Although Barisbakourios leaned forward as far as he could without falling over, he was unable to make out what the khagan said or the counselor's reply. Ibouzeros Gliabanos then spoke directly to me: "This marriage alliance was never made."

"But it was offered, which shows how close your people and mine have been." I hid my disappointment. What a boon for my hopes it would have been had the khagan proved my distant cousin! He spoke again to the man beside him, who hurried away.

Presently, the fellow returned with a square of gilded wood inset with precious stones and pearls. In the center of the square was the portrait of a young woman in imperial regalia; as an icon of the Virgin is labeled MOTHER OF GOD, so her image was entitled EUDOKIA DAUGHTER OF HERAKLEIOS.

"From the treasury," Ibouzeros Gliabanos said, while I stared at the image of my great-great-aunt, whom I had never known. She was not Herakleios's daughter by my great-great-grandmother, but rather by Martina, through the incestuous connection he formed with her in his later years. I should have disapproved of her for that, but here, so far from home, she did not seem such a distant relation after all. The khagan looked from me to her image and back again. "I thought I remembered we had this old picture."

"It proves what I told you," I said boldly.

"Yes," he said. He and his counselor spoke again. The counselor left once more, returning this time with one of the handful of old men I had seen among the Khazars. The khagan asked him what he knew of the picture. He answered in a quavering voice only a little above a whisper, so I had to wait until Ibouzeros Gliabanos spoke directly to me once more: "He says the reason there was no marriage is that the khagan of those days was murdered before the maiden arrived."

"We know of such things in my family, too," I said, remembering my grandfather's death in the Sicilian bathhouse.

"For the sake of the past then, and for the sake of friendship in the future, I declare you are my guest here, and I will do for you what I can," the khagan said. Though a barbarian, he had proved himself a polite man. That did not keep me from grasping the intent behind his speech. When he said *for the sake of friendship in the future*, what he meant was *for the sake of the debt you will owe me*.

I bowed in return, accepting that. If he did give me the aid I needed to regain my throne, I would indeed owe him a great debt, and would be honor-bound to repay it. And if he did not . . . in that case, how would I see Constantinople again?

Ibouzeros Gliabanos put me up in a tent near the palace. This was no insult, most folk in Atil, as I have said, inhabiting such dwelling places. I was fed well, if curiously, on rice and fish. Rice is a grain grown in the moist soil of the delta thereabouts, and eaten in porridges and stews and casseroles, as it lends itself to being baked in loaves even less well than oats.

I thought I would despair at having to eat fish again, but the smoked, tender flesh of the sturgeon bore little resemblance to the dried fish I had for so long endured at Kherson. The Khazars also preserve the eggs of the sturgeon in salt, a delicacy for which I was slower to acquire a taste, but one of which I eventually grew quite fond.

The khagan having granted me freedom to travel in the city, I crossed the Volga to the eastern half, where the larger half of the population and most of the merchants dwelt. The Khazars sell slaves, honey, wax, furs, and isinglass, all but the last of which are imported into their country from the even more barbarous lands to the north. In exchange, they buy cloth and finished clothing, as well as wine and fine sword blades, though their own smiths produce the ordinary sort.

Ibouzeros Gliabanos was himself a pagan, though among his advisers he numbered pagans of his own erroneous creed, followers of the false prophet, a handful of Christians, and some Jews as well. He was permitted, and he made full use of, a company of twenty-five wives and more than twice that number of concubines. Though not providing entertainment on such a lavish scale to his guests, he did see to it we lacked no companionship we desired.

We got on well, he and I. He invited me to dine with him at the palace more than once. At one of these affairs, he said, "I envy you the spirit that lets you go on seeking what was taken from you. If that happened to me, I hope I would do the same."

"I think you would," I told him, not altogether insincerely.

"I hope so," he repeated, frowning into his wine cup. "I wish I could do all I want to help you. The other Emperor of the Romans . . ." His voice trailed away.

"Is a usurper," I said.

He nodded. "Yes. But he is also strong and rich. The Roman Empire obeys him."

"If I took the throne from him, the Roman Empire would again obey *me*." I spoke with confidence, and why not? If the Roman Empire had bowed to the wishes of Leontios, it would obey anyone set over it.

The khagan drank more wine, then ran his tongue over his lips. "Once you were in Constantinople, far from Atil, you would forget your friendship for the Khazars. I would have no hold on you but gratitude, and gratitude is worth its weight in gold." Yes, he was a ruler of men.

"I will give you any oath you like," I promised. "I would not risk my soul by promising falsely. You must believe that."

"Why must I?" he said, a question that, while imperfectly polite, was very much to the point. He plucked one of the long hairs from his unkempt beard. "I need a way to bind you to me."

"You do not trust my oath?" I did my best to sound injured and offended. In Ibouzeros Gliabanos's place, I should have placed no faith in oaths, either, but I would have let myself be given over to his torturers before admitting as much. I drank more wine myself. The khagan, disdaining the fermented mare's milk of his people, imported fine vintages from Kherson, the Caucasus, and Romania.

He studied me, then found another question, one I had not expected: "Have you a wife back in Constantinople, Justinian?"

"I am a widower," I answered. Poor Eudokia was by then sixteen or seventeen years dead: almost half my life. I had not forgotten her—I shall never forget her, of course—but I did not think of her every day, either.

"I know you Christians are allowed only one at a time, poor fellows," Ibouzeros Gliabanos said, "but even the rules of your religion let you marry again if that wife dies, is it not so?"

"Certainly it is so. Why do you ask?"

"I think," the khagan said slowly, "I think I may have a way to bind you to me as you should be bound. One of my younger sisters, you see, has not yet been pledged in marriage to any man. . . ."

My mouth fell open. I stared at him. He smiled back, looking pleased at his own cleverness. And, indeed, from his point of view, the ploy was nothing less than brilliant. Were I to become his brother-in-law, I would be far less likely to go against his interests, for in so doing I should be harming my own kin.

Well and good. I took another pull at my wine while mulling over the other side of the nomisma. Could I, I asked myself, stomach being wed to a barbarian princess? I had come to the Khazars because they were strong, not because they were civilized. I had not expected Ibouzeros Gliabanos (he being, as I say, a barbarian) to come up with a scheme an Emperor of the Romans might have admired. I *did* admire it, and should have admired it even more had it not put me in such a predicament.

I said, "I will not—I cannot—marry any woman who is not of my faith. This is not only because I am a Christian myself, but also because the Romans would never accept an Emperor with a pagan wife." The khagan had to know that was true. I hoped it would suffice to release me from the trap he had set.

"We have Christians and Christian priests here in Atil," he said placidly, "and you brought one with you, even if we did not. She will become a Christian: I see it is needful. Her name, you should know, is Tzitzak."

"Tzitzak," I echoed. I looked down into my wine cup. It still had wine in it. I drained it, filled it, and drained it again. The chamber in which Ibouzeros Gliabanos, Barisbakourios, and I sat began to spin. "Tzitzak," I repeated. It sounded like the noise a small, hungry finch might make. I looked over at the khagan, who sat waiting courteously to see what I would do. Despite that courtesy, I knew he would not aid me if I said him nay. I tried to bow while sitting cross-legged, and almost fell forward onto my face. Having no choice and knowing it, I said, "I am honored to have you for my brother-in-law."

His face lit up. I think he, knowing something of Roman pride, had expected me to reject the offer even if that meant I should never see Constantinople again. That I did not gave him some clue as to the depth of my desire to regain what was and is rightfully mine, thought to this day I do not think he grasps it in fullness. He put both hands to his mouth and shouted for a slave: "More wine!"

Those words of the Khazar tongue I learned quite well that night: he and I both used them again and again over the next several hours. At the end of that time, the khagan slumped over sideways and began to snore. He and I had had nothing intelligible to say to each other for some little while, Barisbakourios having passed out before either of us.

I got to my feet, surprised to discover I could do so. Weaving down the halls from one wall to another like a ship making a series of tacks against the wind, I made my stumbling way out of the palace and to my tent. Barbarians though they were, the Khazars, as a result of their living in nomadic fashion, had great skill with tents, and the one with which they had furnished me was nearly as luxurious, in their fashion, as the pavilions in which I dwelt while on campaign at the head of the armies of the Roman Empire.

Instead of excubitores, two Khazar guards stood before the entranceway. They nodded to me; I was their charge if not their sovereign. After considerable fumbling, I succeeded in lifting the flap and going inside. There was an excubitor in there: he was snoring, as a matter of fact. I shook him.

Myakes' first move was to grab for the sword lying beside him. "Congratulate me!" I said, causing him to arrest the motion.

"Why is that?" he asked sourly. "For falling into a wine jar?" He was always testy on being suddenly awakened.

"No, for pledging my troth," I answered.

"Emperor, you're very drunk," he said, which, God knows, was true. "Tell me about this in the morning, if you remember any of it then. My bet is, you won't." He pulled a sheepskin up over his head, trying to go back to sleep.

I shook him again. He said something not becoming to my imperial dignity, something pungent enough I wish I *could* have remembered it come morning. I said, "I *am* going to be wed. Her name is—" I hiccuped, not, actually, a bad approximation of Tzitzak.

It might not have been a bad approximation, but it was not good enough, either. "Her name is *what?*" Myakes said from under the sheepskin.

"Tzitzak," I said carefully, managing to get it right this time.

Getting it right did me little good: "Sleep it off, Emperor," Myakes urged, and rolled over onto his side.

"She is the sister of Ibouzeros Gliabanos, khagan of the Khazars," I said, taking some little while to do so: being as drunk as I was, I spoke at about half one's usual speed to make sure Myakes understood me.

He did. He sat up again, letting the sheepskin fall where it would. "You're going to marry the khagan's sister, Emperor?" he repeated. I nodded, and wished I had not, the motion already being enough to make my head ache. Myakes whistled softly; he could see the implications in that. "And once you do, he'll help you?"

"So he says," I replied. "If he will not help his brother-in-law, whom will he help?" Myakes might have answered me. I do not know. The next thing I remember, it was morning.

MYAKES

I don't think I've ever seen anyone so drunk as Justinian was that night, Brother Elpidios. Believe me, that's saying something, too. You make your life as a soldier, you'll run into a lot of people who can pour down the wine. Justinian, though, I'm just amazed he woke up the next morning to remember anything. How did he get from the palace to that tent? Divine providence, you ask me.

And do you know, Brother, from that day to this I've never figured out whether Justinian got that drunk because he was glad he'd finally get the help he'd wanted for so long or because he was disgusted that he'd have to marry a Khazar to finally get the help he'd wanted for so long.

Matter of fact, I was hoping he'd tell me, but he doesn't, not really, does he? Maybe he didn't know himself. Maybe it was both at once. Here in the monastery, life is simple. It's not like that out past the walls.

JUSTINIAN

When I did wake, I wished I would die. I had not spewed up any of the wine I drank the night before, which meant it all remained inside to finish the job of poisoning me. I staggered out of the tent in search of cool, fresh air. In finding it, though, I also found the sun. It sank spears of agony into my head through my eyes.

A new set of Khazar guards stood outside the tent. They had no trouble figuring out what was wrong with me and, I being merely a visitor and not their Emperor, they made scant effort to hide their mirth.

Most of the guards Ibouzeros Gliabanos gave me understood some

Greek. This was for his benefit, not mine, but I used it then. "Cabbage," I croaked piteously. "Can you get me a raw cabbage and pure cold water?"

They found me a cabbage. The water came from the nearby river. It was not very cold and tasted of mud, but it had to do, there being no other. I methodically devoured the entire cabbage, washing it down with long draughts of the water. After a while, my headache and the remaining symptoms of imminent bodily dissolution receded.

Presently, Barisbakourios came out of the khagan's palace and toward the tents where my companions and I were quartered. He looked the way I felt, though rather worse. Seeing me, he said, "Emperor, do I rightly remember that—?"

"You do indeed," I answered. "How is the khagan?"

"Wretched," he answered succinctly. I smiled in much the same way as I had done on learning of Leontios's mutilation: misery does indeed love company.

One of the guards was a decent soul. Without being asked, he fetched the same cure for Barisbakourios as he had for me. While Barisbakourios was imitating a rabbit in a farmer's garden, Cyrus emerged from his tent, rubbing his eyes. I daresay our chatter had awakened him. At the sight of him, that part of my hangover the cabbage had not cured did disappear. "Just the man I was looking for!" I exclaimed, which was true, even if I had not known it until he came before my eyes. Ibouzeros Gliabanos had said there were Christian priests in Atil, but here was my own loyal follower. "I shall want you first to save a soul by converting a pagan to Christianity and then to yoke the two of us together in marriage."

Cyrus might not have drunk too much wine the night before, but he had not been awake long, and his wits still moved slowly. "You want me to—what?" he said, and dug a finger in his ear, as if certain he could not have heard rightly.

I explained. Then I explained again, for Stephen and Theophilos came out of their tens and also had to be brought up to date. Myakes kept on sleeping. But then, of course, he had already heard the news.

Cyrus's eyes glowed. "Emperor, this is the best news I have heard for you since . . ." His voice trailed away. In the long years of my exile, bits of good news had been few and far between.

I found one, though: "This is the best news I have had since I got my nose back." I touched the member I had named. That put into my mind the thought of another member. "Going through with this will be more enjoyable than that was, too."

Everyone laughed except Cyrus, who permitted himself a smile.

Then he said, "Emperor, I shall go the the palace now, to see what arrangements need be made to bring the young woman to our true and holy orthodox faith. I promise I shall be most diligent in instructing her, too, that the marriage may be celebrated as quickly as possible."

"That is good," I told him. "After you meet her, will you do one other thing for me?" He nodded, plainly anxious to please. Being anxious myself, I blurted out my question: "Will you tell me if she's pretty?"

Until such time as Tzitzak was baptized into the holy and saving Christian faith, I could not wed her, nor, by the customs of the Khazars (which are in this regard even more stringent than our own), even set eyes on her. I waited with such patience as I could muster: more, perhaps, than I had possessed before my exile, but no great amount nonetheless. Having concluded the bargain with Ibouzeros Gliabanos, I wanted it sealed.

As he had vowed, Cyrus did teach Tzitzak our beliefs at the best pace he could manage, finding her a willing pupil. The wife of a Roman merchant in Atil served as his interpreter, as chaperone, and also as another witness to the truths inherent in our creed.

"She is ready to be baptized, and to take a proper Christian name in place of the heathen appellation with which she was born," Cyrus said after what seemed forever but was in fact a matter of about three weeks. "Have you any suggestions, Emperor, for what that name might be? Zoe, perhaps, symbolizing the new life she is beginning? Or Anastasia, to honor your mother?"

This question having been in my mind since not long after Ibouzeros Gliabanos proposed the marriage alliance, I had an answer ready: "Neither of those, Cyrus. No, if it please her, let her be called Theodora."

" 'The gift of God,' " Cyrus said, and nodded in agreement. "That is indeed a fitting name for a convert to the holy and orthodox faith, and—" He broke off, his eyes widening, and began again in a new tone of voice: "And she will bear the name of the first Justinian's consort."

"Just so. If I am named for the great Emperor, let her name recall that of his great Empress. You are a learned man, Cyrus; speak to her somewhat of the first Justinian's Theodora, that she may gain some understanding of the fame and honor accompanying the name."

"I shall do as you say, Emperor," Cyrus assured me. He looked sly. "And when news of this wedding, and of the name of the bride, reaches the Roman Empire, I have no doubt that it will create considerable . . . excitement there."

"It had better," I said. "I intend that it should." I wanted Apsimaros to feel himself assailed by great names from out of the Roman past, and thus to feel himself all the more a parvenu, all the more illegitimate, all the more a usurper. Any means I could find to fill him with uncertainty and fear, I would use.

Tzitzak accepted the name Theodora without hesitation, and henceforth I shall refer to her by that name. Her baptism, at a small church used by Christian merchants in the Khazar capital, was by Cyrus's account and that of Ibouzeros Gliabanos a splendid affair (though not so splendid, unfortunately, as to tempt the khagan himself toward Christianity). The Khazar custom I have mentioned precluded my presence.

That accomplished, no impediment remained to our marriage. By the standards of Constantinople, it was celebrated with almost indecent haste. I, however, cared little for the standards of Constantinople, having been away from the imperial city for most of a decade. What I cared about was the chance to return to Constantinople. The marriage seeming necessary for that, I allowed no further delays.

Next to the church of the Holy Wisdom, even next to the churches of Kherson, that in which I was wed was a hovel. I think it was a furrier's warehouse before acquiring its present purpose. The crowns of marriage that went on my head and Theodora's were made of tin, the marriage belt I slipped round her waist (publicly here, again yielding to Khazar usages) of brass.

And yet, somehow, none of that mattered. With Cyrus officiating and the priest whose church it was assisting, the ceremony struck me as even more solemn and splendid than it had when I had wed Eudokia all those years before. I had been but a youth then. Now, half a lifetime later, I brought more of myself to the wedding, so to speak. That may have had something to do with it.

Here, too, I had caused a new soul to accept our saving Christian faith. That mattered very much to me. I also strongly felt the importance of renewing the alliance with the Khazars that had helped save the Roman Empire in the days of my great-great-grandfather and would now, God willing, help save it from the clutches of the usurper.

At last came the moment when, Theodora and I having given each other our vows, I could part her veil and see for myself what sort of bargain I had made with her brother the khagan.

Cyrus had told me I would find her acceptable. Taking another man's word in such matters, though, and especially the word of a celibate, is in itself a sort of act of faith, and not one I could easily or casually make. And so I examined her with no small curiosity and, at first, with something approaching dread.

By the standards of Constantinople, she was not a beauty. She had something of her brother's aspect: her face was flat and round, with high cheekbones, a rather low nose, and dark, narrow eyes set almost at a slant. But, having been in Atil for some time by then, I realized that, by the standards of Khazaria, she was, as Cyrus had assured me, an attractive woman. Her eyes, though narrow, were bright and clear, and she had a fine pointed chin (if Ibouzeros Gliabanos had the same, his beard concealed it).

She was also studying me, as no doubt she had been throughout the ceremony. She had not seen me until then, either, and must have heard of my mutilation and its repair. I wondered what she thought.

She surprised me by speaking in Greek obviously memorized and now parroted: "I shall try to be a good wife for you, Justinian Emperor of the Romans."

I wished I had learned more of the language she spoke. I had picked up a few words since arriving at her brother's court, but for the most part had relied upon Barisbakourios and Stephen to interpret for me: what point to the Emperor of the Romans' acquiring a barbarous tongue? Since the bargain with her brother, I had seen a point, and tried to gain more knowledge of the Khazar speech. "Good," I said now. "I too. For you. Thank you."

It was not a whole sentence, as hers was, but she understood and nodded and smiled, perhaps in some relief. Women of high blood know they are tokens in a game their menfolk play, passing from one house to another as suits the needs of the moment. This marriage, unusually, had been required of me no less than of her. We would both have to make the best of it.

The feast following the ceremony was lavish, in the nomad style: roast mutton and beef, a great plenty of fermented mare's milk and wine both, and a honeycomb which, by their ritual, Theodora and I shared in the hope that our union would be sweet.

Presently I took my bride to the tent appointed for the first night. My companions shouted the usual bawdy advice in Greek. The Khazars were also shouting. I had come to understand a couple of those words, too, from the women Ibouzeros Gliabanos had furnished me before yoking me to his sister. As best I could tell, they were saying the same sorts of things as Myakes and Theophilos and the rest.

A couple of lamps burning butter lighted the inside of the tent, which was piled thick with carpets. In the center, though, lay a square of white cloth about a cubit on a side. All nations except the utterly depraved cherish the proof of a bride's maidenhead.

Pointing to the lamps, I mimed blowing them out and asked, "Yes?

No?" in her language. With my scarred forehead and flat, repaired nose, I knew I was no longer handsome. The whores at Kherson had let me couple with them in the light after Auriabedas cut on me, but Theodora might well have had taste more refined than theirs.

But she said, "No," in Greek and then something in the Khazar tongue I did not understand. She tried to turn that into Greek, but could not; her face twisted in frustration. Then she started to laugh. So did I. We would, I was sure, face the struggle often in times to come.

There are, though, ways of gaining understanding that require no words. I set my hand on her shoulder. She came to me. I held her. She felt like a woman in my arms. Her eyes closed when she kissed me. I thought—I made myself think—nothing of that, it being common among women.

Running over her body, my hands were pleased with what they found. And, when I took from her the long coat and tunic she wore, my eyes discovered my hands had not been mistaken. She was slim, with small breasts and nipples surprisingly dark for those of a woman who had not borne a child. I would have been more surprised—and more suspicious of her virginity—had the Khazar girls with whom I had amused myself not been similarly made. Like them, too, she had only a small, thin tuft of dark hair at the joining of her legs.

Having undressed her, I undressed myself as well. I was ready for her. Her narrow eyes widened to see how ready for her I was. I waved for her to lie down on the square of white cloth. Still nervously watching me, she did so. I knelt beside her, caressing her bare body as I had done while it was clothed.

Patience came easier than it had on my first wedding night, not least because I did not burn so hot as I had in my youth. I took my time, trying to excite Theodora or at least to make her less afraid both of me and of what we were about to do. After a while, clumsily and in unpracticed fashion, her hands began to imitate what mine were doing.

My mouth eventually went where my hand had gone. She sighed. Women encountering that caress for the first time, I have found, are astonished at how sweet it can be. I thought at first to give her full pleasure that way before taking her maidenhead, but then had a different notion. Bringing her nearly to the brink, I kept her there for some little time before entering her.

She was well and truly ready; I slid in with ease until the membrane stopped me. I thrust hard then. Beneath me, her face twisted in pain, but not for long: breaking through, I fleshed myself to the root. As I drew back and then thrust home once more, her face twisted again, this time in a way with which I had long been intimately familiar. She gasped and quivered; her inner muscles squeezed me.

Her eyes, which had been closed, opened. She looked up at me. I was intent on my own pleasure then, having given her hers, but not so intent that I failed to worry whether the sight of my face would curdle her joy. Perhaps my rhythm faltered. She smiled at me, and I stopped worrying.

Having completed the act, I got up off her and looked at the square of cloth. Sure enough, she had been a virgin; she had not bled much, but enough to confirm that. She burrowed under furs while I put my tunic back on and went out into the night to display the proof of what we had done.

Loud, drunken cheers greeted me. "How many rounds tonight?" Barisbakourios whooped, ready to translate my answer for the nomads without Greek.

"The Khazar language doesn't have numbers so big," I boasted. He translated that. The khagan and the other Khazars standing there laughed loud and long. That kind of bragging on that kind of night amused them rather than insulting them, as it might have done under different circumstances at another time.

I went back into the tent, as I had gone back into the palace bedchamber with Eudokia. Then I had gone several rounds before bothering to come outside and display the bloody trophy of conquest. Now, while confident of a second round, I was anything but for the third and beyond. Thus time robs us of our powers, my brash words to the men waiting outside the tent notwithstanding.

When I returned to her and let the tent flap fall behind me, Theodora flipped off the furs under which she had hidden. I took her willingness to show herself to me naked as a good sign; she might easily have retained a larger portion of virginal modesty—or, indeed, she might have been repelled by what we had just done and wanted no part of it thereafter, or as little part of it as she could manage.

That proving not to be the case, I wasted no time in divesting myself of the tunic once more. I caressed her with hands and mouth, as I had done before. Proving slower to rise than I had then (ah, the years!), I taught her what a woman could do with her mouth. That was a time when I wished we had more words in common, although, after some initial hesitation, she grasped the principle with pleasing—very pleasing—speed.

When I went into her, I stroked her tender little button with my finger while thrusting in and out. After a very short time, she gave a mewling cry so loud, I feared the torn edges of her maidenhead pained her. It was not pain, though, but pleasure. I spent myself a moment later, groaning half with delight, half with exhaustion.

We lay side by side afterwards. Her skin was slick with sweat, as was mine. I fell asleep for a while. When I woke, the lamps were guttering. Theodora's motion had disturbed me. She was pouring wine into two cups. I think she would have wakened me once it was poured, had I not stirred sooner. Seeing my eyes open, she smiled and handed me one of the cups.

We managed a third round then, with her proving she had not forgotten the lesson I had given her not long before. I managed thanks to that, coupling with her in the laziest fashion possible, her on her side and me taking her from behind. I gasped, sighed, pulled out of her, and fell back to sleep. She may have tried to waken me again that night. If she did, she failed.

We have done well together, Theodora and I, from our wedding night onward. She took to lovemaking as if, having gone so many years without (for I do not think she was far from thirty when we married), she intended making up the lost time as quickly as she could. With that at bedrock, we found we got on well in other ways, too.

Out of need, we soon learned to speak to each other. She picked up Greek fast, and I learned such Khazar words as I could. I still found the nomads' speech ugly, but now I also found it useful, which made a great difference.

"Now I will give you everything I can," Ibouzeros Gliabanos promised when I spoke to him a couple of weeks after having wed his sister.

"Good," I said. "Now tell me exactly what that will be."

Hearing that, he grew evasive. Had I been khagan of the Khazars, I should have grown evasive then, too. Had he led an army down toward Constantinople, he would have had to fight his way through the country of the Bulgars and then through Roman territory before reaching the imperial city. Alternatively, he might have gone through the Caucasus and into Anatolia, but that would have weakened the Roman Empire against the followers of the false prophet and still would have left him on the wrong side of the Bosporos to take Constantinople, as the Persians were during the reign of my great-great-grandfather.

I should have thought this through more thoroughly before bearding him to make good on his promise. I should, for that matter, have thought it through more thoroughly before fleeing to his court in the first place.

But what choice had I? I could not stay in Kherson, nor in Doros, either. Ibouzeros Gliabanos, at least, was not actively persecuting me.

On seeing that he had no intention of furnishing me with an army, I said, "Give me gold, then. With gold, I can get warriors." How good the warriors would prove was another question. I had given Neboulos and the Sklavenoi gold, but so had the accursed Arabs. But with gold, there were things I could do. Without it, my opportunities would be far more limited.

So much of the wealth of the Khazar khaganate depending on trade, Ibouzeros Gliabanos was an able bargainer. But I had learned a fair amount in my time of exile, and I was desperate, where he was not. I pressed him hard, finally persuading him to part with perhaps more gold than he had intended.

"Bah!" he said, and made a sour face. "Now that you have extorted this money from me, I ought to send you far away, so you do not come to think you can make a habit of it."

If he was angry at me, I did not want to stay close by him, lest he choose to vent that wrath. I doubted causing his sister unhappiness would stay him. And, if he was going to give me gold, I should have liked to be closer to Constantinople than was Atil. Atil, so far as I could tell, was close to nowhere worth reaching. Still, returning me to Doros or Kherson would have been a death sentence: a polite death sentence, but a death sentence nevertheless.

He might have been thinking along with me, for in musing tones he said, "Suppose I send you to Phanagoria. What do you think of that?"

"Phanagoria?" I pursed my lips while thinking. The town is situated next to the peninsula on which Kherson lies, just to the east of the narrow strait joining the Black Sea and the Maiotic Bay. It has some commerce with Constantinople, although less than Kherson enjoys. From it, though, I should likely have been in a good position to observe events at the Queen of Cities. I could hardly have been in a worse position for observing those events than from Atil. And no one in Phanagoria, so far as I knew, had any particular interest in killing me. I nodded to Ibouzeros Gliabanos. "Let it be as you say."

"Good, good," the khagan said expansively. "I shall give you the gold, as I said I would"—he forgot for the moment the difficulty with which he had just been persuaded to say he would—"and you will live like a king."

"No," I told him. He frowned. I explained: "I will live like an Emperor."

He liked that, laughing out loud. "You have the spirit of an Emperor," he said. "I have seen this, and seen it clearly. And Phanagoria is more like a Roman town for you. You will like living there, and my sister will see what living like a Roman is like."

"Yes, I want to show her that," I answered, though Phanagoria would be only a small, debased copy of true Roman life. Then, he having mentioned Theodora, I gave him news I might otherwise have held back for a day or two or let her pass on: "She is with child."

"Good, good," he said again. "This is why you marry."

"Your nephew will be Emperor of the Romans," I said, and watched his narrow eyes gleam as he contemplated the possibilities inherent in that. I contemplated those possibilities, too: having the vicegerent of God on earth be of their blood might bring the Khazars to Christianity whole-sale, which would solidify their alliance with the Roman Empire against the deniers of Christ.

"For this news," Ibouzeros Gliabanos said, "I shall give you more gold." The news must have pleased him as greatly as appeared to be the case, for he kept his promise.

Again we traveled over the vast sea of grass. When the wind blew over it, it rippled and changed color, much as the waves did on the veritable sea. Our journey here was slower, though. Travel by land is always slower, save for couriers and others in a driving hurry, who constantly change mounts to speed themselves along.

Theodora rode on horseback, astride like a man. This would have startled me even had she not been carrying a child, but she took it as a matter of course. In a mixture of her tongue and mine, she said, "The baby is tiny yet. This does not hurt it. Khazars ride horses. I am a Khazar. I ride a horse." She had no need of my old pedagogue to teach her the elements of logic.

What was I do to? Beat her, make her stop riding, and slow us all down? I saw no sense in that. She kept riding a horse. Now that I think on it, whenever she has set her mind on doing a particular thing, she has in the end done it. Perhaps that is one of the reasons we get on so well.

Phanagoria, when we finally reached it, proved a town similar to Kherson, though smaller. It boasted several churches, better than half its populace being Romans. As with Kherson, though, it had a Khazar *tudun* or governor, a certain Balgitzin, who also ruled another nearby town but dwelt in Phanagoria. He dressed in Roman fashion, in a linen tunic, and spoke better Greek than his counterpart farther west.

"I am honored to have the Emperor of the Romans here as a guest in my city," he said when I presented myself to him on my arrival. "And you have wed the daughter of my splendid khagan. Will wonders never cease?" He bowed to Theodora, who had not followed everything he said. Seeing that, he spoke rapidly in the Khazar tongue.

"Yes, we are man and wife," she answered in Greek.

"I will give you a fine house, with many rooms," Balgitzin promised. He was full of promises, Balgitzin was. He was wasted as a *tudun*; he would have been a great success as a Constantinopolitan courtier. A man who made so many promises, though, was liable to have trouble keeping them all.

This first one, though, he kept. A minor noble of the imperial city would not have been ashamed of the house in which he installed us—not, at least, after the aforesaid noble had the house cleaned from top to bottom. Rats and mice and cockroaches and ants never stopped plaguing us as long as we lived there. Having lived much harder in Kherson, I made the best of things here.

Theodora, for her part, was enchanted. As I have previously mentioned, most of the dwellings in Atil are tents. Living within real walls and under a true roof made her feel as if she were inhabiting a palace. "Constantinople must be like this," she said one evening after we made love.

I fear I laughed at her. She got angry. I tried to explain what a small, mean, dingy town Phanagoria was when set alongside the Queen of Cities. She did not believe me. Having now seen one town, she imagined herself an expert on such things, and would not believe any city could exceed Phanagoria. Try as I would, I could not persuade her. She was stubborn in such matters, too.

Balgitzin fawned on us. We had gold from Ibouzeros Gliabanos. Theodora liked salted mackerel. To her, it was new and exotic and tasty. I paid for beef and mutton. I had had enough of salt fish and dried fish for a lifetime.

All my comrades but Myakes went back to Kherson, resuming the lives they had interrupted on my behalf and passing my regards on to Moropaulos and my other followers there who had not left. Once they were gone, I settled down to make myself as comfortable as possible in Phanagoria and to await any good news that might come from the Roman Empire.

Waiting came hard. Curiously, all the years I had passed in Kherson, up until the time when Auriabedas gave me back a nose of sorts, seemed to go by fast as a blink. However much I tried to keep my hopes burning, they had faded then. Now, with hope burning bright once more, each passing day seemed a wasted opportunity. I began spending time by the edge of the Black Sea once more, staring south and west across the water toward the imperial city as if my will could lift me and return me to my proper home.

Stephen, having returned to Kherson, sent me word that all my backers in the town where I had originally been exiled were also alert for any reports coming from Constantinople, and that they, like me, had their hopes aroused. *Emperor, they cheered loud and long when I told them of your marriage to the daughter of the Khazar khagan,* he wrote.

I cheered that marriage myself. After so much sorrow, I was now happy above the mean. When Ibouzeros Gliabanos proposed the marriage to me, I had wondered if I could stand being joined to his sister. Now I wondered how I had lived so long without her.

Her body suited me, her temper suited me, and the converse also held true. We had, in short, fallen wildly in love with each other, something far more likely to spring from the union of a taverner's daughter and the young fellow who sells her father olive oil than a mating between Emperor and princess arranged not with any thought for the feelings of the parties most intimately involved but only to secure an alliance. Call it luck or the will of God: either will do. Whatever the reason, I reveled in something I had not known since my brief marriage to Eudokia, and something which struck me as superior to that.

Spending time with Theodora helped me keep my wits about me as day followed day in Phanagoria. I consoled myself for each day that passed without useful word from Romania either in her arms or simply in her company. Too soon, too soon, the peaceful rhythms of those few brief weeks passed away, never to return.

I was having bread and wine with Theodora one quiet, sunny midday when Myakes broke in on us. No matter how long he and I had been together, I looked up at him with some considerable annoyance; no man cares to be interrupted while in the company of his wife, nor is it proper for even a husband's closest companions to gaze on her overmuch.

Before I could reprove him, though, he said, "Emperor, I was down at the harbor, and Moropaulos just now sailed in from Kherson." We called him Foolish Paul among ourselves, too, the name fitting like a boot. Myakes went on, "I've got him waiting out in the hallway, Emperor. He's carrying important news, news you need to hear."

My annoyance melted like snow in spring. "Bring him in, then," I said. I turned to Theodora. She made no move to absent herself, as a properly modest Roman wife would have done. Being the khagan's sister, she was accustomed to taking part in such affairs. After a moment's hesitation, I decided not to order her away.

In came Moropaulos, twisting slightly to get his great shoulders through the doorway. After bowing to me and then, shyly, to Theodora, he said, "Emperor, that Apsimaros, he just sent a man to the khagan of the Khazars on account of you. Fellow came up to Kherson and then took horse, bound for Atil."

"*Did* he?" I turned to Myakes. "You were right. I do have to hear this." Back to Moropaulos: "What does Apsimaros's man have to say to the khagan, pray?"

"Emperor, he says Apsimaros will send him many presents if he sends you to Constantinople alive. If the khagan doesn't fancy that, Apsimaros says, your head will do."

MYAKES

If it had been Leontios still on the throne down in Constantinople, Brother Elpidios, he would have sat on his backside till Justinian came to him. That was the way he was. Apsimaros stayed quiet too long for his own good, too, but he did finally get moving. I never had anything in particular against him. Up till then, he hadn't done anything to Justinian except hold onto the throne he'd taken from Leontios. He hadn't ruled too badly, either.

I thanked God we had people back there in Kherson. They let Justinian know what Apsimaros was up to, and he knew it before Ibouzeros Gliabanos did, too. Me, I couldn't imagine the khagan of the Khazars turning against the man he'd just married to his own sister.

Justinian, he'd always had more imagination than me.

JUSTINIAN

Turning to Theodora, I asked, "How likely is your brother to betray me?"

"I do not know," she answered. Had she indignantly denied the possibility, I should have been certain her primary loyalty lay with him, not me. As things were, she went on, "If Apsimaros gives him enough, I think he will take it, though."

I wanted to kiss her for that answer, but would not because of the presence of Myakes and Moropaulos. "I think you are right," I said. "I think your brother would sooner align himself with someone calling himself Emperor who is in Constantinople than with a true Emperor in exile."

"That means trouble," Myakes said. "If the khagan tries to seize you or kill you, what do we do?"

"If that happens, we cannot stay any longer in lands the Khazars rule," I said, to which both Myakes and Theodora nodded. I looked toward Moropaulos. "God bless you for bringing this news. Tell my followers in Kherson to be ready for whatever may happen, and you be ready there to bring me word if Apsimaros sends more envoys to the khagan, or the other way round."

"I'll do it, Emperor," he promised. Dipping his head, he hurried out of the chamber. Though as thorough a supporter as anyone could wish, he was always shy in my presence.

"If we have to leave, where do we go?" Myakes asked. "Straight for Constantinople?"

My heart cried *yes*. Myakes' tone, though, suggested he did not think that a good idea. And the more my head examined the idea my heart loved, the more I was—reluctantly—inclined to agree with him. "If we show up outside the imperial city with no more force than a handful of men in a fishing boat, Apsimaros will crush us like a man smashing a cockroach under his heel," I said, hating what logic and reason told me.

Myakes let out a loud sigh of relief. "I think that's just right, Emperor. I don't know how to tell you how thankful I am you think the same way."

"You need men with you, to strike a blow against this Apsimaros," Theodora said—statement, not question—having followed our Greek. Her frown, which I had seldom seen, was amazingly like her brother's. After spending some little while in thought, she said, "Maybe, my husband, the Bulgars. They are not friends to the Romans, and they are not friends to the Khazars, either."

As I had started to say yes to Myakes' notion of sailing straight for the imperial city, so I started to say *no* to Theodora. Having fought against the Bulgars, I was not inclined to think of them as allies. But those wars, now, were more than a decade behind me. Asparukh, their khagan, had died while I was in Kherson. Of his son and successor, a certain Tervel, I knew little.

Glancing over to Myakes, I saw he liked the idea. The more I thought on it, the more I liked it, too—if it proved necessary. "*Theou thelontos*, we are worrying over nothing," I said. "If Ibouzeros Gliabanos shows proper loyalty to his family, I am perfectly safe here."

"Yes, God willing," Theodora said, making the sign of the cross; her acceptance of the true and holy orthodox Christian faith had sprung from deep conviction, not merely the desire to keep from hindering her brother's scheme. "Is it so in Romania, that all family is always loyal to all family?"

"No, it is not so," I said, remembering my father and my Uncle Herakleios and my Uncle Tiberius—and, before that, the struggle between my grandfather's backers and those supporting the descendants of my great-great-grandfather's second wife.

"It is not so among the Khazars, either," Theodora said.

"I didn't think it was," I answered. "We shall hope everything turns out for the best. And if everything does not turn out for the best—which God prevent—if that happens, we shall also be ready there."

Days flowed past, one after another. Having made the journey myself, I knew that Apsimaros's envoy, whoever he was, would be some time traveling across the plains to Atil. If he persuaded Ibouzeros Gliabanos to treachery, word that treachery had been ordained would have to make its way back to Phanagoria before any move against me could take place.

In the meanwhile, Theodora's belly began to bulge with the child she carried. She quickly reached the point of surfeit with salt fish and dried fish, a development surprising me not at all. Thanks to the money I had of her brother the khagan, we had no trouble affording better. The cook Balgitzin gave us also went out every so often and bought fresh fish from the men bringing them off the boats.

Theodora stared in some considerable dismay the first time he brought in a squid as long as his forearm. "You *eat* that?" she asked me incredulously. "It is not a proper fish. I do not like the way it stares at me, and I *do not* like all its—" She wiggled her fingers back and forth, lacking the proper word.

"Tentacles." I did my best to be helpful.

"Whatever they are." She made as if to push the squid away. But when, instead of seeing it whole, she ate slices of it fried in butter (a flavor I tolerated better than she did that of olive oil, to which she took years to become accustomed), she praised its delicate taste and grumbled only a little at its chewy texture. The cook bought more squid after that, and she ate them with good appetite. She did not, however, care to look at them before they were cooked. Nor does she even now, here on the day on which I set down these words.

Every time I saw Balgitzin after Moropaulos came to Phanagoria, I wondered whether the Khazar had yet received orders to make away with me. This was at first foolish, for I knew more about Apsimaros's effort against me than he did—unless, of course, the *tudun* at Kherson had sent him word at the same time as the fisherman came to me. I doubted that,

Balgitzin remaining for some time cordial to me and not striking me as a man schooled in the art of dissembling.

And then one evening, having drunk myself cheerful if not sozzled at Phanagoria's finest tavern (a dubious commendation in such a limited field) along with Myakes, I discovered a squad of armed men—Khazars— outside the doorway to the house in which I and mine were living. They had not been there when the two of us left the place.

Myakes set a hand on my arm to hold me back, the Khazars having four or five presumably sober men to each of us. I shook him off and went straight up to them. "Any of you speak Greek?" I asked. When a couple of them nodded, I found the next logical question: "What's going on?"

They might have answered that question by drawing their swords, in which case I should not be scribbling now. One of the men who had shown he understood Greek answered, "Balgitzin say, you have Romans wanting to kill you. Is true?" It was my turn to nod; I could hardly deny it. The Khazar continued, "We are guards to you—for you—to be sure no Romans kill you."

"Oh," I said, and then, "Thank you very much." I could not object if Balgitzin set guards on me using such a pretext. For that matter, it might not have been a pretext: if Ibouzeros Gliabanos had rejected Apsimaros's request for my person or some significant fraction thereof, he would have reason to think the usurper might resort to more direct means of disposing of me. But if the khagan had decided to go along with the usurper, he gained a plausible excuse for placing warriors near me.

Which was it? I did not know. I could not know. I could only wait. I hated waiting. I had waited a decade for the slim chance I now had. How I hungered to slay them all! But they were many, and I had only faithful Myakes at my side. Suppose we did slay them? Balgitzin could summon soldiers without number. I could not.

I walked past them into the house. Myakes followed. The Khazars bowed to each of us in turn. I barred the door. That only made me feel more trapped, not more safe.

However much I desired to do so, the guards gave me no excuse to complain of their conduct to Balgitzin. When I stayed in the house to which the *tudun* of Phanagoria had assigned me, they remained outside. When I went out, one or two of them came along with me. I even found myself having trouble disliking them. They were but warriors, doing as they were ordered and doing it well.

No murderers with Apsimaros's gold in their belt pouches sprang out from behind a wall to try to slay me. Was that because the guards intimidated them or because they were not there? Again, how could I know?

A couple of weeks after Balgitzin gave me my armed guard, he invited Theodora and me to a feast at his residence that evening. "I thank you," I said. "What is the occasion?"

"A noble has come from the khagan's court at Atil to Phanagoria," he answered. "Of course you remember Papatzun."

"Of course," I lied. Back at Atil, one barbarian had seemed much like another. Those who did not speak Greek—which meant the large majority—might as well not have existed, as far as I was concerned.

But, as I had expected, my wife had no difficulty placing this Papatzun on my bringing her word of his arrival. She looked serious, saying, "This is a man my brother trusts."

"He has not come to Phanagoria now by chance, then?" I said.

"By chance?" Theodora frowned until she understood what I was driving at. "Oh. No. If anyone brings word from my brother to do this or not to do that, Papatzun is likely to be the one. I will learn from him what I can."

"Good." I kissed her, but then warned, "Don't let him know we suspect."

Amusement glinted in her dark, narrow eyes. "Do not fear about this. I will not ask him. I will not ask his friends, if any have come with him. I will ask his slaves. I know a couple of them well. They will tell me the truth."

I kissed her again. "I will not give you any more advice. You don't need it."

"You are my husband." She hesitated long enough to draw in a deep breath before going on, "You are my love. If I can help you, I will do it."

All I knew at that moment was gratitude. I may be reckoned unmanly for not disdaining a woman's help, but, considering how easily Theodora could have chosen the side of her brother and her tribe rather than mine, I knew how lucky I was in her. "You are my Empress, my Augusta, now," I said. "Soon you shall be my Empress in the Queen of Cities."

"God willing," she said once more, making the holy sign of the cross.

"As for the banquet," I said, "we shall see what we shall see."

On meeting Papatzun again, I discovered I did remember him after all: remember his face, at any rate, for we had not had much to say to each other, being largely without a common language. He was not very young, not very old, not very fat, not very thin, not very tall, not very short . . . not very interesting. In Constantinople, I judged, he would have been a secretary in charge of some medium-sized bureau, a man doing a fairly large job well enough to avoid censure but not so well as to get himself promoted out of it.

In Constantinople, such quiet, competent men are common enough. No doubt being harder to come by in Khazaria, they must also have seemed more valuable than is the case within the boundaries of the Roman Empire. This rarity, I judge, accounted for the trust Ibouzeros Gliabanos reposed in Papatzun.

Khazar notions of banqueting require the celebrants to gorge themselves until they cannot move and drink until they cannot see. Having had my fill of fish, I ate beef and mutton. Perhaps having had his fill of beef and mutton, Papatzun ate mackerel, quite different from the sturgeon of Atil. He agreed with me in preferring wine to the drink his countrymen make from their mares' milk.

Despite Balgitzin's services as interpreter, Papatzun and I had little to say to each other. He was polite enough to me; I could no more fault his behavior than that of the guards with whom Balgitzin had saddled me. Every so often, I would glance over at him from the corner of my eye. Once or twice, I saw, or thought I saw, him glancing over at me in the same way. When that happened, each of us quickly looked away from the other.

Theodora, by contrast, enjoyed herself immensely. The banquet giving her the chance to speak her own language unmixed with Greek, she took full advantage of it, chatting animatedly with Balgitzin's wife (whose name I learned but have long since forgotten), taking part in the conversation of the men more freely than would have been reckoned proper at a Roman feast, and, by all appearances, enjoying her conversations with Balgitzin's and Papatzun's slaves as well.

Balgitzin swilled till he began to snore. Papatzun let out a sniff of contempt. I had been to enough Khazar banquets to have learned that the one who passes out first is often an object of contempt, being reckoned weak if not effeminate. In slow, bad Greek, with long pauses for thought between words, Papatzun said, "No—hold—wine."

"No, indeed," I answered. I was by then quite drunk, but not so drunk as to let down my guard. "You, now, you drink like a man." He smiled vaguely, understanding enough of the Greek to know I had not insulted him. I did my best to put the words into the Khazar tongue.

"I am a man," he said in his native language. "You are a man." I wondered if he would run through the conjugation of the verb *to be*, but he just studied me for a while, now making no pretense of doing anything else. After a couple of minutes of this intense scrutiny, he lifted his goblet in what was half salute, half challenge. I lifted mine as well. We drank at the same time, and drank deep.

Presently, Papatzun slumped over like a tree under the woodsman's ax. Having won the drinking bout, I looked around for Theodora. She was not there; she must have gone off with Balgitzin's wife. One of the Khazar's slaves came up to me when, vaguely surprised that I could, I got to my feet. "Take me to my wife," I said when he asked what I required.

Instead, he brought Theodora to me. She looked down at Balgitzin and Papatzun, both of whom sprawled snoring on the rugs. But for those snores, they might as well have been dead men. They would lie there unmoving till sunrise or longer. After that, for some hours they would wish for death rather than imitating it. Having lain as they lay, I knew this well.

Not even the stark shadows of lamplight fully defined the expression on Theodora's face, which, being flatter and smoother than those of Roman blood, had fewer sharp angles to build shadows. Her eyes went from the snoring Khazars to me. "Can you walk home?" she asked.

"I can do anything," I said grandly, which in truth meant I could do very little. Theodora smiled. She knew what kind of talk got poured out of the neck of a wine jar. I do remember that we got home, and I am too large for her to have carried me all that way, so logic compels me to believe I walked. Logic aside, though, I have no proof of this.

Thinking on it, I suppose the guards Balgitzin had given me (or had set on me—I still did not know how to construe their presence) could have done the hauling. But Theodora would have chaffed me about that had it happened, so I still believe I did set one foot in front of the other all the way from Balgitzin's residence to my own.

Once there, I remember asking her, "What did you learn of Papatzun's slaves?"

She seemed impressed at my recalling Papatzun had slaves, let alone that they might know something important. But all she would say was, "I will tell you in the morning." I tried to argue with her. She lay down, as if for sleep. I lay down beside her to go on with the argument, and the wine overwhelmed me, as she must have known it would. Devious, was Theodora.

I have had thicker heads than the one with which I woke up the next day—a few. Headache or no, though, I remembered what Theodora had said before I passed out. We still lay side by side. Shaking her, I asked the same question I had put the night before: "What did you learn of Papatzun's slaves?"

She woke smoothly, as was her usual habit, nor, for that matter, had she drunk herself into crapulence. "You *do* recall." She sounded surprised. "If I thought you would, I would have told you last night. Papatzun has"—her face went cold and sad—"has brought Balgitzin orders to kill you whenever he gets the command from, from—"

"From your brother," I finished for her.

"Yes," she said, and looked away from me. I heard tears in her voice as she went on, "I knew he could do this. I did not think he *would* do this."

Not all the blood pounding in my head sprang from the hangover, not now. Part of that painful drumroll was fury. "Your brother can give orders, but he is in Atil, far away," I said. "His commands will take time to be obeyed. I am right here. I intend to be ready to move tonight."

She did not, at first, fully grasp what I was saying, being caught up in the choices she had made. "He is my brother," she whispered—probably to herself, for she used the Khazar tongue, "but you are my husband. You *are* my husband."

I took her in my arms. "And very glad of it, too," I said. Had it not been for her, no doubt Ibouzeros Gliabanos, Papatzun, and Balgitzin should have succeeded in making away with me. But that was not what I meant, or was, at most, a tiny part of it. I have never heard the act of love praised as a cure for too much wine, but it served me admirably.

Much improved, and knowing now what lay before me, I summoned Myakes. He and Theodora and I spent much of the morning making plans, finding holes in them, and making new ones. At last we had a scheme that satisfied everyone—except Theodora.

"You will leave me behind," she said bitterly.

I nodded. "I will. If I win after tonight, as God is my witness and my judge I will send for you. And if I lose, you will be able to go home safely to your brother. He will treat you well regardless of what happens here. You are blood of his blood, as I am not, and your child will carry my blood as well, which may prove useful to him one day. That, though, is only if I lose." I kissed her, right there in front of Myakes, and, I daresay, scandalized him. "I intend to win."

The feast I laid on that night rivaled the one Balgitzin had given the night before. The food, in my judgment, was better, being cooked in the Roman fashion rather than that of the Khazars. Papatzun might not have found it better, but he found no fault with it, either, not by how much he ate. He drank as heroically as he had the night before, too.

Through Theodora, who was interpreting between us, he said, "You drank me down last night, Justinian, but tonight you are not even in the race. Do you Romans save it up for one night and then give over? A true man is ready to drink every night!" He drained his cup and held it out for more.

I rose as if to fill it myself, carrying the wine jar as I went round behind him. But instead of pouring at once, I set the jar down on the table. Papatzun looked back over his shoulder at me, drunken puzzlement on his face.

Setting down the jar let me free the braided leather cord I was using as a belt for my tunic. His turning his head at just that moment gave me the perfect chance to whip that cord around his thick neck. I tightened it with all the strength I had in me.

Papatzun tried to cry out. He could not—I gave him no air. He tried to reach around himself to seize me and throw me aside, but could not do that, either. His feet thumped on the floor. They grew still surprisingly fast. His face went from the red of drunkenness to a purplish black I had not seen since the Sklavinian woman hanged herself in my pavilion.

Not until the stench of loosening bowels proved him dead did I relax my grip. Then, letting him topple over, I turned to Myakes and Theodora, belting the leather cord back around my waist as I did so. My grin might have been the one on my face after having a woman. "One traitor dealt with," I said. "Now for the other."

Before I could go out the door, Theodora embraced me, saying, "God with you."

"God with us all," I said, not knowing whether I would ever see her again.

When Myakes and I burst outside, the guards Balgitzin set over me, who had been drinking wine and shooting dice by torchlight, sprang to their feet. "What is wrong?" asked the one who spoke the best Greek.

I jerked a thumb back at the house. "Papatzun has been taken ill in there," I said, that bearing at least some nodding relation to the truth. I followed it with a thoroughgoing lie: "He's asking for Balgitzin—says it's life or death."

In the excitement of the moment, none of the guards asked any questions past that. They did what they usually did: told off a couple from their number to accompany me wherever I was going. One of them carried a torch, adding its light to that from the one Myakes carried.

We hurried through the streets of Phanagoria to Balgitzin's residence, where, arriving, we pounded on the door. One of Balgitzin's servitors answering, we told him the same tale we had given the guards.

Balgitzin came out a few minutes later. "What's wrong with Papatzun?" he asked as we started back to the house he had assigned me.

"His belly pains him," I answered. "He has been vomiting, and fears he might die. He says he needs to tell you something. I do not know what it is."

He sent me a hooded glance, wondering, no doubt, if the message pertained to me. Then we pressed on. As far as he knew, I was ignorant of the orders concerning me Papatzun had brought from Ibouzeros Gliabanos. I hid a smile, not that the torchlight was likely to betray it in any case. Soon enough, I would show him what I knew.

We passed the black mouth of an alley opening out onto the street along which we traveled. I stopped and recoiled. "What's that?" I exclaimed, pointing down the alley. "Something—someone—moved in there."

Balgitzin turned toward the alley. The Khazar guard held his torch higher, the better to see down the narrow, stinking lane. Out came Myakes' sword, as if to defend us from footpads.

While Balgitzin stood distracted, I undid my braided belt and whipped it around his neck without giving him the chance to cry out. Strangling is the best way to kill a man when one must be silent doing it. Balgitzin got out no more than one startled, almost inaudible grunt.

Myakes, being without a strangling cord, did the best he could with his blade. Using point rather than edge, he thrust deep into the guard's throat, blood thereby drowning whatever outcry the man might have made. The Khazar dropped the torch and tried to draw his own sword, but toppled into unconsciousness and death with a hand still on the hilt.

I choked the life out of Balgitzin. When his bowels voided their contents as Papatzun's had done, I let his corpse lie in the street along with the rest of the offal there.

Ever practical, Myakes slit his purse and the guard's. "Heh," he said, his whisper loud in the quiet night. "Even a little gold here. And they may think—for a few minutes they may think—somebody else killed these two and kidnapped us. The more time we can buy to get away, the better off we're going to be."

"No arguments," I said. We hurried off toward the eastern gate of Phanagoria—the direction opposite that in which we would have been expected to flee, our friends dwelling in Kherson to the west—and I put my head down to make my features harder to recognize, reeling along as if drunk.

"Here, what's this?" a guard called on our approach.

"Got to get my cousin here back to Tomin," Myakes answered, sounding drunk himself. "Tavern there weren't good enough for him, no, sir—had to come taste the big city, the damn fool. Well, he's still got to go out fishing tomorrow morning, yes he does, no matter how much he had tonight." His chuckle was full of malicious pleasure at my fate.

He sounded absolutely convincing. I almost believed him myself, and I knew better. The guards laughed and stood aside, letting us pass out into the night.

As a town, Phanagoria had little to recommend it, although I lived as well there as anyone was capable of living. Tomin, now . . . if anyone who had to live in Tomin slew himself to escape, I doubt God would reckon his suicide a sin deserving damnation. It lay—and, worse luck, lies yet—about three miles east of Phanagoria: a miserable little place without a wall, without a church, and without a hostel, as I discovered on arriving. The couple of taverns the place did have were taverns only, not places where travelers might put up for the night. The publicans apparently never dreamt anyone might *want* to put up at Tomin for the night, an attitude for which I confess a certain amount of sympathetic understanding.

Tomin exists for one reason and one reason only: a tiny indentation in the seacoast offering ships a little shelter. "We have gold," Myakes said, as if reminding himself, when we lay down against the wall of a building to get out of a chilly breeze and try to rest before dawn. "We can hire a fishing boat to take us to Kherson."

"To somewhere near Kherson, anyway," I said. "I'm too easily recognized to go into the city, I fear, with Apsimaros and the rich men there wanting my head. But you're right, Myakes, we need to gather my followers now."

"And after we do that, Emperor?" he asked, shifting around to try to get more comfortable—or at least less uncomfortable.

"After that?" I sighed. "After that, the Bulgars. Theodora was right: with Ibouzeros Gliabanos turned against me, I have no better choice." As I tried to sleep, I also tried not to think about how bad a choice the Bulgars were likely to be.

I do not remember dozing off, but I must have, for Myakes woke me at dawn by pounding on a tavern door. When the irate proprietor opened up, a show of coins salved his wrath and got us bread and wine, which we ate and drank picking our way through Tomin's muddy alleys to the seaside.

"Look!" I pointed. A real merchant ship was beached there, dwarfing the little fishing boats to either side of it. Some considerable trade exists among the cities and towns along the northern coast of the Black Sea. The only surprise was that this ship had put in at Tomin rather than the nearby Phanagoria. Caught by darkness, perhaps. "We can get out of here faster with him than with any fisherman."

"If he's westbound, aye," Myakes answered. "Probably will be, or we'd have seen him in port yesterday."

"Only one way to find out," I answered, and strode down toward the merchantman.

Her captain, a rough-hewn fellow named Peter, dickered a fare to Symbolon, the nearest port to Kherson, asking no questions once we had paid. I had been prepared to introduce myself as John and Myakes as Myron, but he proved interested only in money, not in names.

We sailed shortly thereafter, having had little intercourse with the folk of Tomin: when the Khazars came after us, as I am certain they must have done on discovering both Balgitzin and Papatzun slain, they might well have concluded Myakes and I had vanished into thin air. Whatever they concluded, they did not catch up to us before we had quitted that part of the world for good.

The one bad stretch I had on the three-day voyage to Symbolon came very early, when Peter put into the port of Phanagoria to unload wine and load smoked fish. Myakes and I spent all our time at the stern of the ship, staring out to sea. But the Khazars did not send men aboard to search for us. On our sailing out of that harbor, Myakes and I finished emptying the jar of wine he had bought in Tomin.

Apsimaros had captained the last ship upon which I had traveled, the one taking me from Constantinople into exile in Kherson. No doubt mercifully, I recall next to nothing of that voyage. I could here set forth the journey to Symbolon in exacting detail, but to what purpose? Only storms make travel by sea anything but dull. We had none, not on that journey. I thanked God, not yet aware of His plan for me.

Myakes and I left the merchantman at Symbolon, a town larger than Tomin but smaller than Phanagoria lying a few miles south of Kherson. There I took a room above a tavern (the folk at Symbolon at least entertaining the possibility of someone's wishing to do such a thing), and Myakes and I divided the money we had with us.

I told him, "Go into Kherson. If we're heading for the land of the Bulgars, we'll need Moropaulos's boat again. Anyone else who wants to come is welcome." I laughed. "One thing sure: I'll know who my true friends are."

"Some of them, Emperor, anyhow," Myakes said. "I've seen that boat Foolish Paul sails. It won't hold many, and that's the truth."

I waved that away. Some who said they backed me would find more excuses than Moropaulos's boat being small to avoid accompanying me on what they reckoned a forlorn hope. "Go on," I told Myakes. "I'll see you back here tonight or tomorrow morning, I expect."

"Aye, Emperor," Myakes said, and slipped away. I had no doubt he would slip into Kherson as readily. He had spent as long in exile there as had I, but I would have drawn notice even had I not been mutilated, and he, I think, would have remained inconspicuous even with a cut nose. Regardless of the setting in which he found himself, he had a knack for making himself at home without drawing undue attention.

Waiting came hard, as it always does for me. I went down into the tavern. I drank a good deal of wine. I ate salt-fish stew. Although having the money to pay for better, I forbore. Symbolon not being Kherson, I had some chance of going unrecognized there, and meant to foster that chance as much as I could. So far as I could tell, no one paid me any particular attention. I was ugly but not hideous, and thereby ideally suited for going unnoticed.

Evening came with no sign of Myakes. After another bowl of that stew—the last, praise God, I ever tasted!—I went up to the room I had bought for the night. Though taking no woman up there with me, I did not sleep alone. I crushed all the bugs I could, but, like the Spartans at Thermopylae, was defeated at last by superior numbers. Eventually, later than I would have liked, sleep found me.

I woke before dawn, whether from nerves or bedbugs I cannot say. Going downstairs, I discovered myself the only one awake in the place, and so, less than happy with the world, returned to my room once more until I heard someone moving about below. I went down again, and breakfasted on wine and an egg cooked with cheese, that being the only choice besides fish porridge.

Sometime during the second hour of the morning, Myakes strode into the tavern. I did not rise from my stool: I sprang from it. Had he waited any longer before arriving, I daresay I should have smashed the top of my head from leaping straight up into the ceiling.

His smile was impudent, he having known the state in which I would be. "Boat's at the wharf, Emperor," he said. "Let's go."

I left the tavern without a backward glance. When we were about halfway down to the harbor—a short journey, Symbolon hardly being any sort of metropolis—I asked, "How many companions have I?"

His face clouded. "Me and Moropaulos. Barisbakourios and Stephen. Theophilos. I thought he'd be up in Doros, but he was staying with Stephen. That's it."

"Not even Cyrus?" I said in dismay.

"Not his fault, Emperor," Myakes said. "I couldn't get word to him in the monastery—he got himself in trouble there for gallivanting off the last time without so much as a by-your-leave. Didn't want to wait around, spend any more time in Kherson than I had to."

"All right," I said. "Good enough. As for the others who would not come—a plague on them." More than a few had cheered me in Kherson when I declared I would take back the imperial throne. Cheering was easy. When it came to anything more than cheering, where were they? As if invisible. "I'll have my vengeance on them, too, by God and His Son. But first the Romans." I hurried down toward the fishing boat, Myakes half-trotting beside me.

Foolish Paul waved from the boat. I waved back, though my first sight of the vessel that would, I hoped, carry me to the land of the Bulgars made me wonder how it had sailed from Kherson to Symbolon, let alone from Kherson to Phanagoria bringing me news of Apsimaros's move against me.

I also cast aside some of my dismay at the failure of more Khersonites to rally to my standard. Moropaulos's boat was crowded with him and Theophilos, Stephen and Barisbakourios in it. Adding Myakes and me would make it very crowded. It did not look as if it had much room for provisions aboard, either. I shrugged. Other supplies failing, we could, I supposed, catch fish.

Moropaulos waved again. "Come on, Emperor," he called. "The sooner we leave, the sooner we get there." A broad, foolish grin spread over his broad, foolish face.

Two or three of the dockside loungers any harbor in the civilized world attracts turned curious eyes my way. I wished Moropaulos had not chosen that exact moment to address me by my imperial title. If searchers from Kherson or Phanagoria came to Symbolon, they would have no trouble learning I had been there. I consoled myself with the thought that they were unlikely to be able to find out whither I was bound.

Stooping on the edge of the pier, I scrambled down into Moropaulos's boat. The fisherman steadied first me and then Myakes. After undoing the lines holding the boat to the pier, Moropaulos and Theophilos plied a couple of long oars to get us out into open water. Once we were there, Foolish Paul, who struck me as being far less foolish now that I encountered him in his proper element, raised the sail, turned it to the best angle to take advantage of what wind we had, and sent us heading northwards.

When we sailed past the lighthouse with which Kherson feebly imitates fabled Alexandria, I shook my fist at the town. "May I never see you again!" I called across the water, a wish that has come true. "And may I punish you as you have tried to punish me!" I am still fulfilling that wish even as I write these words.

Above Kherson, the coast of the peninsula on which it lies curves up to the north and west. We stayed in sight of land at all times. As I had guessed, between tacks Moropaulos let his nets down into the water. The catch was small, but enough to keep us fed, each of us taking turns roasting his fish above a tiny brazier. A bucket of seawater always stood close by, lest a sudden great wave overturn the brazier and spill burning coals onto the deck.

Being small and lighter than the dromons in which I had previously traveled, the fishing boat had a motion on the water different from theirs. I felt every movement of the sea, and proved myself a man able to take such motions as they came. Poor Stephen, being less fortunate in that regard, ate little and spent a lot of time hanging over the leeward rail.

We traveled past the headland marking the westernmost extension of the peninsula on which Kherson lies, past the mouth of the Danapris, and then past that of the Danastris. Most nights, we simply beached the fishing boat, keeping watch alongside it till dawn. A couple of times, we put up in little trading towns by the edge of the sea. They were to Doros as Doros is to Constantinople; having said so much, I shall draw a veil of merciful silence over any further description of them.

From the mouth of the Danapris to that of the Danube, where the Bulgars live, is not a long voyage, and seemed all the shorter in comparison to the distance we had already come. Up to that time, the weather had been good. Oh, the winds for the most part blew from the northwest, requiring a good many tedious tacks if we were to beat our way westward, but they were not violent, and the sea, Stephen's opinion to the contrary notwithstanding, remained gentle.

All that changed two days after our sailing past the mouth of the Danapris. Clouds filled the sky, clouds so black and thick and roiling, I at first took them for the smoke of a great fire somewhere. The wind freshened and began to howl. The light chop in which the fishing boat bobbed turned into waves that first buffeted the boat and then began to toss it about the sea.

The storm blew up almost as fast as I can record its coming. Less than half an hour after I spied the clouds on the western horizon, rain started drenching us. The day went black as midnight. Every so often, a lightning bolt split the sky overhead, giving us all momentary, purple-tinged glimpses of the heaving sea. The roar of the thunder put me in mind of God's voice summoning us to judgment.

"Can you steer for shore?" I screamed to Moropaulos.

He shook his head. "No," he shouted back. "I don't even know which way the shore is, not for sure. Sea's doing the steering now, not me—sea and the wind." He brailed up the sail. "I *think* the wind's still out of the west. Don't want to get blown too far away from land."

I shook my fist at the heavens, as I had at Kherson. Leontios had not been able to keep me down, not for good. The rich traders in Kherson had not been able to make away with me. When Apsimaros tried to move against me, he could not do so without my learning of it. When Ibouzeros Gliabanos sought to betray me, I learned of that, too, and struck first. Having escaped so much, having achieved so much, was I now to perish at God's hands?

"No!" I shouted, loud as I could, and shook my fist again.

The storm grew ever worse, despite my defiance. The fishing boat spun like a top, waves smiting it from every direction. The lightning showed those waves tall as hills, tall as mountains. Soon one would surely strike us wrong and capsize us, and then everything would be over.

After we went sliding down from yet another wavecrest deep into the trough behind, someone clutched the soaked sleeve of my tunic: Myakes. He had been fearless for so long, but now a flash of lightning showed the terror on his face. "We're going to die, Emperor!"

"No," I said, thinking him right. But then, the boat wallowing out of the trough, my spirits rose with it. I raised a defiant shout: "No!"

A wave broke over the bow, drenching both of us and almost sweeping me over the side. "We're going to die," Myakes insisted, spitting out saltwater. "I beg, you, Emperor, on my knees I beg you"—and he did fall to his knees—"promise God that if He spares you here, you'll have mercy on your enemies."

"What? Mercy?" I shook my fist at the heavens for a third time. "If I have mercy on even one of them, may God drown me now!"

And the storm stopped.

MYAKES

A miracle, Brother Elpidios? I don't know if it was a miracle, or if we'd come out the other side of the squall line or whatever it is sailors call those sudden storms that blow up out of nowhere, or what. I do know it happened just the way he writes it, though. He's right. I was frightened to death. You can fight a man. How do you go about fighting the sea? One minute I was certain sure we were sunk and drowned and food for the mackerel and the squid and the tunny that had been feeding us for so long up in Kherson. The next—

The next minute, Brother Elpidios, the clouds were flying away to the east, and the rain went from sheets to spatters and then stopped, and all at once when we were in the trough of a wave the crest of the next one wasn't higher than the top of our mast, and the sun came out, and—

It sounds like a miracle to you? If you think I'm going to argue very hard, you can bloody well think again.

J U S T I N I A N

From that moment forward, I knew I should prevail, God having by sparing me given an indubitable sign He approved of my purposes. All of us, working with buckets and cups and a small bronze cooking pot, bailed as much of the sea as we could from the fishing boat. By the time the long, weary task was done, we stood ankle deep in water. Having been knee deep before, we reckoned that great progress.

By God's providence, the rigging had survived the storm. Like our tunics, it flapped wetly. But the sail filled with the gentle breezes following the storm, and let us sail slowly toward the west, the direction in which the sun was now setting. We were out of sight of land, and spent a chilly night on the sea. Making sail again the next morning, though, we spied the shore no later than the third hour.

On our sailing closer to that shore, we discovered we had reached one of the several mouths of a considerable river. "Does the Danube break up before it flows into the sea, the way the Volga does?" Barisbakourios asked, the simple word *delta* evidently being unfamiliar to him.

He, his brother, Theophilos, and Foolish Paul all looked toward Myakes and me. None of them had been in his part of the world before. We being Romans and this having been Roman territory before the Bulgars raped it away from my father, they expected us to know the answer.

And Myakes, who had accompanied my father on his ill-fated campaign against the Bulgars, did know. "Aye, that's the Danube, all right," he said. "All we have to do now is sail up it a ways and wait for the Bulgars to notice us." He shook his head. "No, that's not all. We have to hope they feel like talking with us instead of killing us for the fun of it."

"A point," I admitted. I had been so full of thought for what the Bulgars might do for me, I had not asked what I might do for the Bulgars. After a moment's doubt, though, I straightened in the battered fishing boat. "I do not—I will not—believe God, having spared me from the storm, will let me perish at the hands of the barbarians."

"Here's hoping you're right." Myakes was seldom inclined to take on faith the goodwill of potential foes.

With Moropaulos skillfully using the steering oar and turning the sail so as best to catch the wind, we made our way up one of the channels of the Danube, waiting to be noticed. I began to wonder whether any Bulgars lived in that part of the land until I saw a large herd of cattle grazing in the distance. Where there were animals, there their masters would also be found.

And, before long, one of the Bulgars riding with the cattle spied the boat on the river and came riding up to the riverbank for a better look at us. Barisbakourios and Stephen called to him in the language of the Khazars, and he shouted back to them, but neither side could understand the other.

My turn, then. "Do you speak Greek?" I called across the water. Some Bulgars did, I knew, having acquired the tongue either from the luckless Romans who had inhabited the land they now ruled or from traders coming up out of the Roman Empire.

The good fortune that had smiled on me since the storm abated continued. "Greek? Yes, I speak little Greek," the horseman answered. "Who you? What you want here?" He leaned forward on his horse like a hound seeking a scent. Every line of his body seemed to shout, *Are you fair game? Can I slay you?*

"I am Justinian, Emperor of the Romans, the son of Constantine, Emperor of the Romans," I answered, and had the satisfaction on watching his jaw drop and him go slack with astonishment on the ugly little pony he rode. I continued, "I have come to see your khagan, Tervel. Will you take me and my friends to him?"

For all I knew, the barbarian might have thought I still sat on the throne in Constantinople. True, I had been cast down ten years before, but who can say how swiftly, if at all, news reaches a Bulgar herder? Maybe he thought I had come to take supper with my fellow sovereign, and would then return to the Queen of Cities.

On the other hand, maybe he merely thought me a liar. But if I lied, I lied on a scale greater than he had ever imagined. "You stay," he said. "Not go. I bring you another man. He talk toward you." Riding away, he booted the pony up into a gallop, getting a better turn of speed from the animal than I had expected.

"Shall we beach the boat, Emperor?" Moropaulos asked.

"Yes, do," I said. "We've come to see the khagan. If the Bulgars fall on us before we can do that . . ." I did not go on. But if the Bulgars chose to fall on us before I could see the khagan, I had no place else to go in any case. Tervel was, and how well I knew it, my last hope.

The fishing boat glided up onto the muddy bank of the Danube. We all got out of it as fast as we could. Solid ground, however muddy, beneath my feet for the first time since escaping the storm felt monstrous fine. I walked up from the mud to the grass beyond and lay at full length upon it.

Myakes came over and sat down beside me. "If I ever go to sea, Emperor, I mean to say, if I'm ever that stupid—"

"What? You won't even cross from Constantinople to Asia?" I teased.

"Maybe I'll go that far," he said. "Maybe. And maybe I won't, too." Plucking a blade of grass, he set it between his teeth, as if to say he was at one with the ground from which it sprang.

We rested for perhaps two hours before that first Bulgar returned not with one but with several of his fellows. One of them wore gold hoops in his ears and a gold armlet on his left wrist: a chief of sorts, unless I missed my guess. He did not dismount, staring down at me from horseback. In better Greek than his countryman had used, he said, "I hear Justinian had the nose of him cut off when they threw him out of Constantinople."

"I did," I answered, and touched first my repaired nose and then the scar on my forehead above it. "You see how the surgeon covered the hole with skin, so now I have a nose again, even if it is not such a good nose as I owned before."

Having studied me, he answered, "Why do you want to see the khagan?"

"I shall discuss that with the khagan," I answered haughtily. "Or is he in the habit of talking over his business with everyone he chances to meet?"

As nothing else had done, that show of arrogance went far toward convincing him I was what I said I was. Like the first Bulgar who had found me, he said, "You have to wait here a little while." He shouted orders in his own tongue to his men, a couple of whom rode away. Returning to Greek, he told me, "They will bring horses for you and your friends to ride."

While we waited, I introduced my companions to him and learned he was called Omurtag. He paid me the compliment of not asking again what I wanted of Tervel. But for the Bulgar who had found us, none of his followers spoke Greek. Seeing that, I realized how fortunate I had been on the initial encounter.

The Bulgars he had sent forth returned to the riverbank more quickly than had been the case after the first meeting. Moropaulos was the only one of us not an experienced horseman. He also fretted over his boat, saying, "What shall I do without it?"

"If I win," I said, "I'll make you rich enough to buy twenty boats, a hundred boats. If I lose, you'll die in battle or Apsimaros will cut off your head. You won't need this boat either way, will you?"

"But this is *my* boat," Moropaulos said, showing how he'd got his name. After a while, we cajoled him into leaving it behind. He awkwardly scrambled up into the saddle of the horse the Bulgars identified as the calmest of those they had bought. *Calmest* proved less than identical to *calm*, but Foolish Paul managed to keep from being pitched off onto his head.

We rode south and west from where we had come to solid ground. The countryside resembled the plain across which I had traveled to reach the court of Ibouzeros Gliabanos, but was not so limitless; to the south, silhouetted against the sky, I could see the mountains separating the land the Bulgars had stolen from us from that still under Roman rule.

Omurtag being a man of authority in his own right, he commandeered the services of a band of Bulgars we encountered as evening drew near. Thus we had plenty to eat, plenty to drink even if it was fermented mare's milk, and tents in which to sleep. The accommodations were similar to those we had had of the Khazars, one band of nomads apparently living as much like another as peasants near Thessalonike live like peasants near Nikomedeia.

We rode out again at first light the next morning and, after riding all day, came to Tervel that evening. Atil, where Ibouzeros Gliabanos dwelt, had come more than halfway toward transforming itself from a nomadic encampment to what might one day become a considerable city. The camp at which Tervel ruled had barely begun the same process. The Bulgars had built a wooden fence around a good stretch of territory surrounding Tervel's tent and those of his followers, but the khagan and his men still made their living from the herds that fence enclosed.

A rider went ahead to announce my arrival to Tervel. The fellow came back with permission for me to go on and meet the khagan. Omurtag, knowing which was Tervel's tent, led me to it. A couple of slaves—Romans, by their looks and by the Greek they spoke with each other—tended to the party's horses. Perhaps having learned who I was, they stared and stared at me.

I wonder whether Tervel's curiosity would impel him to come out and greet me, but he waited for me to go to him, he being after all sovereign in this place. The interior of his tent glowed with lamps of glass and silver—Roman plunder—till it was almost bright as day, though the lamps burned butter rather than oil as they would have done in Romania. More plunder—golden bowls, silver wine pitchers—gleamed in the lamplight.

Tervel, sitting there cross-legged on the carpet, wore plunder, too: a woman's jeweled earring in each ear and a necklace of nomismata. Since he had succeeded his father not long before, I expected him to be hardly more than a youth, as had been true for me. But he was a man of close to my own age, a battle scar seaming his right cheek, his face almost as lined and weathered as that of any other nomad.

My followers prostrated themselves before him; I bowed, as I had to Ibouzeros Gliabanos. When I straightened, he was studying me through narrow eyes like those of the Khazar khagan. "I think you really may be Justinian," he said in Greek as fluent as mine. "I guessed some mountebank was coming to fool me, but you have not only the wound—fixed some sort of way, I see—but also the look of the man I remember seeing."

"Have we met?" I asked. "Were you on an embassy to Constantinople? I hope you will not be angry if I say I do not remember you there."

"We have met." His smile showed excellent teeth. He somehow contrived to make them look very sharp. "It was not in Constantinople. I have never been inside Constantinople. But you have come here before. I saw you then. I fought your men, to try to keep them and you from getting back inside the Roman Empire. We failed"—he shrugged—"but not by much."

"No, not by much," I admitted. "That was half a lifetime ago for me." Much of my reign had been half a lifetime ago for me. "You would have been young to fight then."

"My first battle," he agreed. "You Romans should never have got away. We should have trapped you and killed every one of you."

I should be stretching a point if I said I liked Tervel from the outset. But I could tell at once that he and I, agreeing or not, would always be able to understand each other. We thought alike: half-measures satisfied neither of us.

I said, "When my father came here with his army, he should have destroyed every one of you Bulgars. Then my campaign would not have been needed."

"When your father came, and all the ships vomited out their soldiers, we thought he was the most fearsome man in the world," Tervel answered, smiling that unpleasant smile once more. "Then we found the soldiers only knew how to run away from us. They fought better with you leading them, I must say."

"Why—thank you," I said in some—more than some—surprise. Up till that moment, whenever people compared me to my father, they always found me the lesser. So much had I come to take that for granted, the possibility it might not be so smote me with the force of Paul's revelation on the road to Damascus.

Tervel either did not notice my confusion or controlled himself so well, he revealed nothing of his thoughts. He said, "And now you come to me without an army at your back, Justinian. Tell me why this is. Did I not hear you married the daughter of the Khazar khagan? Is he not your friend?"

"I married his sister," I said. He inclined his head, accepting the correction. I went on, "I think he would be my friend, if he did not think being Apsimaros's friend counted for more."

"Ah," Tervel said. "He can afford to be Apsimaros's friend. The Khazars have no borders with the Roman Empire. We Bulgars do. We have never been friends with the Emperors of the Romans: not with Constantine, not with Justinian"—one eyebrow lifted ironically—"not with Leontios, not with this Apsimaros, either." He folded his arms across his chest, waiting to see what I would say next.

"That will change, if an Emperor of the Romans owes his return to his throne to the khagan of the Bulgars." I was careful to use the indicative, not the subjunctive, Tervel having shown he grasped subtle shades of meaning.

"Taking Constantinople would not be easy." He used the subjunctive. "My countrymen who have seen the city do nothing but talk about how strong its walls are."

"Apsimaros got into the city," I returned. "I too shall find a way."

"Maybe," he said. "Maybe." He stretched, lithe as a wildcat. "I need not decide this at once. Drink and eat with me, and tell me of how you came here from Kherson. Unless I am wrong, this will be worth hearing."

Clapping his hands together, he shouted for slaves. Like the others I saw in the country of the Bulgars, they were Romans, poor souls. They brought us roast mutton and wine, the khagan preferring it to his people's native strong drink.

Tervel had me speak in some detail on the repair of my nose, the Bulgars being more ignorant of surgery of any sort than we Romans. "Do you think you could teach my people to cut so?" he asked when I was through.

"I doubt it," I answered. "I paid as little attention as I could to what Auriabedas was doing to me. Myakes here watched. He'd have a better notion of how the operation was done than I do."

"Not good enough to teach it to anybody else," Myakes said quickly. "What I was trying to do was not to puke."

"Too bad," Tervel said. "Noses get lopped often enough, it would be worth knowing what this foreigner with the name I cannot say did. But go on, Justinian."

I told of traveling to the court of Ibouzeros Gliabanos, and of my marriage to Theodora, with which he had shown himself somewhat familiar. Then I spoke of my journey to Phanagoria, of the khagan's betrayal, and of how I had dealt with Papatzun and Balgitzin. Tervel and the other Bulgars who understood Greek clapped their hands at that.

I also told them of how God had chosen to spare me out on the sea as I was sailing to their land, finishing, "And so you see, O Khagan, I am truly destined to enter the Queen of Cities and avenge myself on all who wronged me."

"So you say," Tervel replied, voice betraying nothing. He was no more a Christian than Ibouzeros Gliabanos—less, in fact, for the khagan of the Khazars tolerated all faiths, including the true one, in the lands he ruled, while the Bulgars saw Christianity as connected with Roman rule, and so suspect.

"With your help or without it, I am going on to Constantinople," I said.

"I believe you," Tervel said. "You are a man who keeps promises—I see that. If you go without my help, though, I do not think you will have a glad time of it."

Although thinking him likely to be right, I would sooner have had my new nose cut off than admit as much. "I would like your help," I said, "but I will go on without it." This ignored what had to be as evident to Tervel as it was to me: that, should he order, I would go nowhere but into whatever grave the Bulgars gave me.

He also ignored the fact, perhaps deeming its mention impolite, perhaps finding it too obvious to need mention. As Ibouzeros Gliabanos had before him, he said, "If you win, you will be inside Constantinople, and you are liable to forget whatever help you had getting there. How do we seal this bargain so I will get the reward I'd deserve?"

"I cannot marry your sister," I said, "nor even your daughter." In theory, I suppose, I might have done that, Emperors tending to make their own law on such matters, but I had no wish to put aside Theodora.

On the contrary. And then, as I seldom did, I remembered Epiphaneia. "I cannot marry your daughter," I repeated, "but I can give you mine."

I had not seen her, of course, since my treacherous overthrow and exile. Before that time, I had seen her as little as I could, and would have seen her less than that had my mother not continually tried to make me act as a father toward her. That I did not wish to do, and would not do. All I could think of, whenever I set eyes on her, was that she had caused the death of her mother Eudokia, whom I had loved.

A decade's separation and near forgetfulness, I discovered, had not caused this feeling to ease, any more than that same decade had slaked my desire for vengeance against Leontios and Apsimaros. Nor did my marriage to Theodora, happy though it was, ease the pain of having lost Eudokia. Thus I felt not the slightest hesitation in offering the barbarous Bulgar the child of my flesh. In its way, that too was an act of vengeance.

"Tell me of this daughter," Tervel said, his voice so elaborately casual, I knew he was interested.

Having given him her name, I went on, "She would be seventeen now, I think. Now"—I help up a hand—"I have heard nothing of her since I was overthrown. It may be she has wed in that time: she would have been a small girl then, you know. It may even be she is no longer among the living, though God forbid it." I said that, I own, more for fear of losing the bargain than from concern for her safety. "But if she lives, and if she is not wed or has not accepted the monastic life, I swear by my God, the one true God, to yoke the two of you together in marriage."

"That is not a small promise," Tervel said slowly. He spoke in his own language, to enlighten those of his noble company—boyars, the Bulgars call them—who spoke no Greek. I could not understand their startled exclamations, but I could not mistake them, either.

Myakes leaned toward me, whispering, "Emperor, the Augusta your mother will—"

"Obey," I broke in. "My mother is not here, Myakes, nor are you she. Remember it." He bowed his head in acquiescence.

"That is not a small promise," Tervel repeated, fortunately having missed Myakes' comment and my equally soft-voiced reply. The khagan went on, "But it is a promise full of conditions. Maybe these are conditions you cannot speak to now, because you do not know enough. And maybe, too, you know more than you say. What will you do, Justinian, if you find your daughter is dead or cannot marry me?"

For a moment there, I hated him. But it was my own weakness I was hating, hating cruel necessity that caused me to come before him, as

I had come before Ibouzeros Gliabanos, as a beggar. A beggar I was, though, and so I would remain until Constantinople was mine once more. If I could not make Tervel sweet, that time might never come. And so I said, "Khagan, if for any reason you cannot marry my daughter, I will name you Caesar."

Beside me, Myakes stiffened. Tervel's eyes went so wide, they were almost round. "You would do this?" he said.

"I would," I replied. "I will."

"But, Emperor"—Myakes was whispering again—"Caesar is—"

"I know what the title of Caesar is," I said aloud, both to him and to Tervel. "It is the highest title in the Roman Empire, save that of Emperor alone. The only difference between the Emperor's crown and the Caesar's is that a cross surmounts the Emperor's."

"Good," Tervel said. "I do not want a cross on my crown. I am not a Christian. I do not wish to become a Christian."

I wished he had not said that. The Roman Empire had not had a pagan Caesar since before the days of Constantine the Great. The Roman Empire, so far as I knew, had never had a Caesar who was at the same time a barbarian. None of that mattered longer than a moment. If Tervel did not aid me, I should be in no position to grant titles to anyone. And, relatively speaking, titles are cheap.

"I must think on this." After widening, Tervel's eyes narrowed. "Does it mean that, if you die, I become Emperor of the Romans?" His smile said this was not intended to be taken altogether seriously, but the hungry expression that followed said he wished it were.

Shaking my head, I replied, "I will not lie to you," by which I meant I saw no profit in lying. "For one thing, my wife is with child. For another, if you are not a Christian, you will never be Emperor of the Romans."

"You speak freely," he observed.

"I could tell you any number of pretty lies," I said. "They might make you help me now, but they would make you hate me later."

"You tempt me, Justinian," Tervel said. "I will not tell you yes now, and I will not tell you no, either. I will think on this, as I said I would, and I will give you my answer when I decide. Until then, you are my guest."

"You are kind beyond my deserts," I replied. That was probably a lie, but a lie I was obligated to tell. Tervel gave not a hint of what he would do with me if he decided not to give me the soldiers I had asked of him. I did not inquire. If he would not aid me, I cared little as to what happened next.

He set me up in a tent surprisingly similar to the one in which I had dwelt by the palace of Ibouzeros Gliabanos. Slaves—Romans—tended to my needs. After the first couple of nights, I took a good-looking woman named Maria into my bed. I loved Theodora no less, but she was far away, the slave woman close by. Maria was resigned rather than eager, but one seldom finds more in a slave.

A week after my first coming before him, Tervel summoned me to his tent once more. I went with outward impassivity as complete as I could muster, but with my heart pounding and my stomach knotted within me. How strange, how grim, that my fate should depend on the whim of a barbarian chieftain who was a lifelong enemy of the Roman Empire.

I bowed before him, as I had bowed before Ibouzeros Gliabanos: he was master here, not I. More often than not, I scorned the nomads for their lack of anything approaching proper ceremonial. This once, I welcomed their barbaric abruptness, for with it I learned more quickly what I wanted to—what I had to—know.

Without preamble, Tervel said, "I will give you soldiers. We will go down to Constantinople together, you and I, and see if we can set you back on the throne you lost."

My heart pounded harder than ever, but now from joy rather than concern. "If I reach Constantinople with an army at my back, I *shall* rule again."

"May it be so." Tervel sounded polite, but not altogether sincere. A moment later, he explained why: "If you win, everything will be as you said. Either I will have your daughter or I will be Caesar. And if you lose, my armies will still have their chance to plunder the Roman lands between here and Constantinople."

"That is true," I said. "But if I win, as I expect to do, your armies will have to come back here without plundering their way home. We will be allies then, and allies do not ravage each other's lands." And then, unable to contain my eagerness another instant, I burst out, "When shall we move against the Queen of Cities?" Nomads, I knew, were always ready to ride out at a moment's notice.

But Tervel said, "In ten days, or perhaps half a month. I have sent messengers to my cousins to the south and west, asking them if their men will ride with us."

"You cannot simply order them to ride?" I said in some surprise.

"If you Romans invaded us, we would all stand together," he answered. "But I cannot tell them to take their men to war outside their grazing grounds. I hope they will join us, though."

"I will reward them if they do," I said. Bowing again, I added, "But not so richly as I will reward you."

"Good enough," Tervel said. "May it be so." Again, though, he sounded less concerned than he might have. As Ibouzeros Gliabanos had before him, he purposed using me for his own ends. His lands marching with those of the Roman Empire, he could use my cause as a plausible excuse for what would in fact be an invasion. I regretted the evils the Empire would suffer as a result, but saw no alternative. I had come too far to go back. Forward was the only way left.

When we marched, we marched without Tervel's cousins. Though my war against them after I had subdued the Sklavenoi lay many years in the past, the Bulgars inhabiting the lands near the former Sklavinias still remembered me with something less than fondness. "We do not trust the Emperor with the cut-off nose," one of them told Tervel. "If you are wise, you will not trust him, either."

Under other circumstances, I should have been flattered at the Bulgars' still fearing me after so long. As things were, I mourned the support I would not have. Tervel did not fret about trusting me. He had no need to fret. I was in his power. If I displeased him or alarmed him, he would put me to death, and that would be that.

The Bulgars who did ride with us, I am sure, had their minds more on loot and rape and murder than on restoring me to the throne of the Roman Empire. Any soldiers are more apt to dwell on the pleasures of their trade than on the purposes for which their rulers employ them.

As we rode south toward the mountains, the landscape took on a familiar look—or so I thought, at any rate, although I had seen a great many landscapes since. Not wanting to put the question to Tervel, I asked Myakes, "Are we not heading toward the pass we used to get back into Romania when we were campaigning against the Bulgars?"

"I think we are," he answered. "I'll tell you something else, too— I'm bloody glad we've got the Bulgars with us this time, not trying to keep us here."

"So am I," I told him. Instead of showing proper march discipline, the Bulgars straggled out across the land, as if they were the flocks they tended. If one of them spied a rabbit in the grass, he would ride off and try to kill it, eventually either rejoining his comrades or not, as he thought best. But the more I associated with the nomads, the more I came to respect them as warriors. Their horses seemed tireless, and subsisted on what they pulled from the ground as they traveled. The men were no less hardy, going on long after Romans or Arabs would have had to halt.

Having noted this same endurance among the Khazars, I was pleased to have it at my disposal.

No. I overstate that. The Bulgars were not at my disposal. They were at Tervel's disposal. When we traversed the pass in the Haimos Mountains and entered Roman territory, he sent them out broadcast to plunder the countryside. He had made no promises to keep them from doing so before I had regained my throne. If I had to guess, I would say he did not expect me to regain it. I did not discuss this with him. The event would prove him right or wrong.

Roman frontier guards at the southern end of the pass rode forward to resist what they mistakenly took to be one of the many small Bulgar raiding parties that had so troubled the land in the quarter-century since the barbarians, as divine punishment for our sins, succeeded in establishing themselves south of the Danube. Now, though, I intended using the Bulgars as divine punishment for Apsimaros's sin of usurpation, and for that of Leontios as well, if he still lived.

On discovering we were a veritable army rather than a band of bandits, the Romans rode away far faster than they had ridden forward. Whooping, the Bulgars rode after them, slaying a few and bringing a few back for questioning. Most of them were Mardaites and other easterners whom I had resettled to hold this frontier. I was somewhat irked to see them so incontinently flee, but did not blame them overmuch, they being so outnumbered.

"Justinian! It is you!" one of them exclaimed in Greek with a guttural Syrian accent years on this chilly frontier had been unable to efface. "We heard they cut off your nose, not that they just smashed it. I saw you in Sebasteia when you arranged to move us here. Have you come to take back the throne?"

"I have," I declared, whereupon the Mardaite burst into cheers.

One of his companions, however, was imprudent enough to shout out, "Tiberius Apsimaros, Emperor of the Romans!" Two Bulgars were holding the man. I glanced at a third nearby, who was not at that moment tending to any prisoners. The Bulgar drew a knife. I nodded. He plunged it into the frontier guard's belly, again and again. The Bulgars holding him let him fall, writhing and shrieking, to the weeds and dirt.

With his screams as background, the rest of the Mardaites wasted no time in acclaiming me. Some, no doubt, were satanically dissembling, but I let them all go, to spread word of my coming and, I hoped and expected, to bring more Roman soldiers over to my side along with the Bulgars.

A few of the barbarians grumbled at watching the prisoners leave their hands still intact and breathing, but I said, "You have just entered the land of the Romans. Do you think you will have no chances for sport later?"

Tervel shouted something in his own language. The Bulgars calmed themselves. Shifting to Greek, Tervel told me, "You did right. You are right. The Romans you let go will do us more good alive than they would give us amusement."

"That was also my thought," I replied, and then, pointing southward, continued, "And now, shall we ride on?" Tervel dipped his head in agreement and waved to his host. We followed the frontier guards into Romania.

The main road running south and west from the pass toward Adrianople and away from the Queen of Cities, we abandoned it, traveling south along the seacoast toward Constantinople instead. Watching gentle waves slap against the shore, I found myself thinking of anything but the gentle waves I had survived out on that same sea.

As we came down toward Mesembria, the most northerly of the Roman coastal cities, we discovered that most of the villages in our path had been abandoned. Myakes snorted, saying, "Those frontier guards you let go, Emperor, they spread the news, all right—the news the Bulgars were coming. Nobody cared whether you were with 'em or not. People heard that, they ran."

"I fear you're right," I answered. "No help for it now."

A little later, Tervel rode up to me. "Shall we lay siege to Mesembria?" he asked.

I shook my head. "No. Taking it gets us no closer to seizing the imperial city, and besieging it wastes time we do not have."

"This is sense," he agreed after a moment's thought. "If you fail, we will capture this town on the way north." In his mouth, *if you fail* sounded like *when you fail*. As with most men, he did what he did primarily for his own purposes, not out of any special charity of soul.

That evening, we encamped only a couple of miles outside Mesembria. Some of the Bulgars rode out to pillage the suburbs beyond the wall. And, to my surprise, one of the locals rode into our camp. He did not come alone, either. but at the head of a flock of some five hundred sheep chivvied along by a couple of herdsmen who looked as if they wished they were somewhere, anywhere, else.

The man on horseback—a young fellow, probably born about the time I succeeded my father—dismounted and prostrated himself before me. In a loud voice, he said, "Emperor Justinian, I bring your army these sheep, and with them I bring myself." His Greek had some of the same Syrian flavor as that of the frontier guards the Bulgars had captured.

"Rise," I told him, and he did, with the fluid grace of a well-trained warrior. "I accept the sheep, and I accept you as well," I said. "Tell me your name, so that I may know whom I thank."

"Emperor," he said, "my name is Leo."

M Y A K E S

Yes, Brother Elpidios, *that* Leo, the one who's Emperor now. Up till then, nobody outside of Mesembria had ever heard of him, nor many folk inside Mesembria, either. But he found himself a way to get noticed, that he did. When everybody else was running away from Justinian, he ran toward him.

What? What would he have done if Justinian had lost? Probably gone back to Mesembria and tried like the devil to pretend he never had anything to do with him. He likely would have got away with it, too. Leo was the sort of fellow who could tell you the sun rose in the west, and you'd believe him.

Yes, you're right, Brother. It's *just* the same way as Leo has moved against the holy icons, as a matter of fact. When he took the throne, he swore he wouldn't fool around with the faith, didn't he? Of course he did. Every Emperor does. But then a few years later he started going on about whether it was proper to make images at all, and—what was it? last year? year before last?—didn't he toss the patriarch out on his ear and put in his own man?

What? Leo's chum Anastasios isn't limber enough to lick his own privates like a dog, so he licks Leo's instead? I'm going to have to watch out for you, Brother Elpidios. Every once in a while, you can still surprise me. Yes, of course I accept your apology. It's the Christian thing to do, after all. If you want me to set you a penance, why don't you read to me for longer than you'd planned?

J U S T I N I A N

Well, Leo, when I tell you I am pleased to meet you, I want you to know I'm not saying it just for politeness' sake," I answered. "You are the first Roman who has not only shown me my proper respect but also helped me toward getting my throne back. On account of that, I name you my spatharios here and now."

He bowed low. His black eyes glowed in his narrow, swarthy face. "Emperor, you are generous to me," he said.

"You've earned it," I told him. Spatharios is a handy title. The spatharios of a petty noble who brags of his authority makes everyone around him laugh. An Emperor's spatharios, on the other hand, may be a person of considerable importance. Or he may not: he may be a man with no more power than the petty noble's spatharius, but one whom the Emperor, for whatever reason, has chosen to honor with the title.

I had no idea which sort of spatharios Leo would make. If he proved useful to me, I would give him power commensurate with his rank. If not, no harm done.

"Tell me of yourself," I said. "If you say you were born in these parts, I'll be surprised."

Smiling, he shook his head. "I cannot, Emperor. I spring from Germanikeia, on the edge of Syria. I was a little boy when my parents brought me here. That would have been at your order, wouldn't it?"

"So it would," I agreed. "And now you've given me another reason to be glad for that order." He bowed once more, pleased at the compliment. And I—I was pleased at the mutton. I shall not deny also being pleased at Leo, who, though young, seemed both clever and energetic.

I presented him to Tervel, as much to see how he would react as to honor him. His eyes widened, and he said, "Khagan, I tried to kill you once. I shot an arrow at you when you came down raiding into Romania, but I missed."

"When Justinian came up raiding into the land of the Bulgars, I tried to kill him," Tervel returned. "He tried to kill me, too. I failed. He failed. You failed. Now we are together."

"And now we shall not fail," I said. Tervel and Leo both nodded. "Once we get down to Constantinople," I added, "the soldiers will abandon Apsimaros the usurper, returning their allegiance to me. My family, after all, has ruled the Empire for almost a hundred years. What has this Apsimaros done, to make him worth keeping? Nothing, I tell you. Nothing! Nothing!" My voice rose to a shout.

Tervel and Leo nodded again.

From Mesembria down to the imperial city, the army I and Tervel led had but little fighting to do. The Bulgars who spoke Greek—perhaps one of them in four—would smile broadly at me on that journey, saying, "They fear us. See how they fear us."

"Indeed they do," I would answer, not wanting to discourage them. But, while some of it may well have been fear on the part of my foes, more, I think, was strategy. Constantinople had been attacked before, but no foreign enemy had ever taken it in battle. My great-great-grandfather, however, had put paid to a vile usurper. I expected to do no less.

Fewer Roman soldiers than I should have liked abandoned Apsi-maros to come over to me. Many of those resuming the cause of their rightful master did so at the urging either of Myakes, whose acquaintance with some of their officers went back to the days before my throne was stolen from me, or of Leo, who demonstrated for the first time but not the last a gift for persuasive speech remarkable in one of his years.

Apsimaros's men did not try to hold us at the Long Wall. I thought briefly of Philaretos, my former father-in-law, who had commanded the garrison along the wall, and wondered if he still lived. We reached Constantinople on the seventh day after passing Mesembria. The last glimpse of the city I had had was from the deck of the dromon taking me, freshly mutilated and half blind with pain, off into exile. Apsimaros, I remembered, had captained that dromon: one more requital needed.

"Coming home, Emperor," Myakes said, pointing to the walls looming up over the southeastern horizon.

"Coming home," I agreed. "I've been away too long."

We rode closer. As the true height and length of Constantinople's fortifications became clear to Tervel, he brought his horse close to mine. "I have seen Roman cities," he said. "Men I have sent to the city here have told me of it, as I said when you first came before me. I always had trouble believing them. Now I see with my own eyes they were telling less than the truth, not more."

We encamped outside the northern part of the city wall, the tents of the Bulgars and those Romans who had joined us extending from Blakhernai hard by the Golden Horn south and west as far as the Kharisian Gate, about a quarter of the distance down toward the Sea of Marmara. Near that gate, the aqueduct of Valens enters the imperial city. It has, unfortunately, been useless to Constantinople since the days of my great-great-grandfather, when the Avars, during their siege of the city, destroyed almost a mile of it. No Emperor since had enjoyed the leisure or the resources to make the necessary repairs.

Soldiers on both the outer and inner walls stared out toward us, watching our every move. Mounting one of the ponies on which I had ridden down from the land the Bulgars had stolen from us Romans, I approached the walls so I could speak to the warriors manning them, being certain that, once they were certain it was indeed I who came before them, they would renounce Apsimaros the illegitimate and acclaim me once more.

Myakes rode with me, offering his usual pragmatic advice: "Don't draw within bowshot of the walls, Emperor. If Apsimaros hasn't put a price on your head, I'm a big green sheep."

"We already know he has put a price on my head," I said. "He was willing enough to pay it to my brother-in-law, that's certain. And as for the confidence you show in me, I do thank you very much." Myakes blew air out through his lips, a snorting sound likelier to come from a horse than a man.

Tervel rode along, too, a few paces behind me. Though wishing he had stayed in our camp, I could hardly tell him so, he having served as my benefactor since I arrived in his country seeking aid. But I did not want him to see me fail, and feared his presence would make me more likely to do so.

With no help for it, I rode on, ignoring him as best I could. Also ignoring Myakes, I drew close to the walls, close enough to let the soldiers see me, to let the veterans among them recognize me, and to remind them of where their loyalty should lie. They stirred, up on the walls, waiting for me to speak. They could have pincushioned me with arrows, but no one shot. I took that for a good sign. Tervel, prudently, had stopped at the distance Myakes had suggested for me. Myakes himself, whatever he thought of my boldness, remained at my side.

"I am Justinian, Emperor of the Romans!" I shouted to the soldiers. "Justinian son of Constantine son of Constans son of Herakleios Constantine son of Herakleios, of the house that saved the Roman Empire from the fire-worshiping Persians and the followers of the false prophet both. I have returned to reclaim the throne rightfully mine."

For a moment, only silence followed my words. I quietly sat my horse, awaiting the great roar of approbation and delight that would lead to opened gates and to my sweeping back to power. From the top of the outer wall, a soldier cried, "Hey, Justinian, aren't you missing a nose for this kind of duty?"

The wretch, the scoffing Thersites, could not have been above thirty yards from me. He and his comrades could see perfectly well that I bore a nose which, if perhaps less lovely than the magnificent appendage with which God had graced me, was nonetheless adequate for all legitimate purposes, including the purpose of establishing my own legitimacy as ruler.

But, caring nothing for whether he lied or spoke the truth, he continued to cast scorn on my physiognomy. And, emboldened by his licentious freedom of speech, others showered me with differing sorts of insults. "How do you like riding the barbarian mare you bought?" one of them shouted. I shook my fist at him, that surely being a reference to Theodora rather than to the gelding on which I was then mounted.

"You come down here with an army of Bulgars and you call yourself Emperor of the Romans?" another soldier said. "If you love them so well, why don't you go off and be Emperor of the Bulgars?"

More abuse and insults rained down from the walls. At last, a couple of soldiers shot arrows that stood thrilling in the dirt not far from my horse's forefeet. I rode away, believing they would next shoot at me intending to hit, not to miss.

Tervel's face remained impassive on my coming up to him. "They did not hail you as you hoped," he said, a statement of the obvious I could have done without.

"They mocked your men as much as they mocked me," I said. Tervel said nothing, and his face continued to reveal nothing. Myakes suffered one of his unfortunate, unbecoming, and untimely coughing fits. Despite that, my own words gave me an idea. "Let the Romans come forward," I told Tervel. "Let them and me go up and down the whole length of the wall, showing the garrison that Romans do support me and persuading the soldiers to abandon the usurper and return to me."

"We will do this," Tervel said, with no hesitation I could discern. "It is the best hope you have." How good a hope it was, he did not express an opinion. Nor did he say what he might do if it failed.

The next morning, small bands of Romans rode up and down the length of the wall, haranguing the soldiers inside the city and urging them to come over to my cause. Accompanied by Myakes and, at his usual discreet interval, by Tervel, I myself traveled down past the Kharisian Gate, the southern limit of the Bulgars' encampment.

I spoke as I had on first approaching the city walls. Now Myakes added his voice to mine. Among others, the formidable Leo was speaking on my behalf elsewhere along the walls. If I could not persuade the soldiers myself, I reckoned the two of them most likely to do it for me.

What sort of promises Apsimaros was making inside the imperial city, I cannot say with certainty. Whatever they were, they and the familiarity of having been ruled for seven years by the usurper kept the soldiers on the walls from going over to me. I judged them to feel a certain amount of sympathy for my cause, as none of them, no matter how close I approached, tried to slay me with an arrow or a stone flung from a

catapult. But none of them made any move to admit me into Constantinople, either, nor did I note any signs of strife among them implying
one faction wished to do so but was prevented by another.

Having shouted myself hoarse to no visible effect, I returned dejected to the encampment the Bulgars had established. Shortly thereafter,
Leo also rode into camp. "What news?" I called to him. This was foolishness on my part, for any news he had worth giving would have been
sent to me on the instant. Knowing as much now, however, did nothing
to help me then.

Leo shook his head. "I'm sorry, Emperor," he said. "They seem very
stupid and stubborn."

"Justinian, how are we going to get into the city?" Tervel said. "By
my sword, everything I had heard of these walls is only a piece of the
truth. I would be mad to throw my army at them."

"I did not ask you to do that," I answered. I had not asked because
I did not think he would do it, and I did not think an attack would
succeed if he did do it. I had not adequately considered the walls from
outside until then. When I was a child, the Arabs had assailed the Queen
of Cities with siege engines of the sort the Bulgars lacked, and to no
avail. They had also challenged us Romans on the sea, where the Bulgars
had no ships whatever.

Tervel had that same thought in a different context, saying, "We
cannot make this city starve, either, not when boats bring in food in spite
of everything we are able to do on land." In truth, we could not do that
much on land, either, lacking as we did the manpower to extend a tight
siege line along the whole length of the wall. I had counted on the
soldiers' renouncing Apsimaros at my return. To find that hope mistaken
was a bitter blow.

"Can't hardly quit now," Myakes declared. "We've come too far for
that."

"Yes," Tervel said, but I liked neither his tone of voice nor the look
on his face. He could quit our venture without a qualm, return to the
lands north of the Haimos Mountains, and, by means of booty and slaves
taken, reckon the raid a success. He could take me with him, to use as
pretext whenever he cared to attack Romania again. Only gaining the
city now would keep me from that fate, but how to gain it?

"We'll try again tomorrow," I said, with luck sounding more confident than I felt.

I went to different parts of the wall that next day, traveling past the
Golden Gate down toward the Sea of Marmara in my effort to persuade
the soldiery within the Queen of Cities to abandon the usurper and return

to their rightful and proper affiliation. I had no more success, however, than I had enjoyed, or rather not enjoyed, on previous days. Some soldiers continued to revile me on the grounds that I was noseless, despite the refutation of that argument being there before their eyes. More cursed me for having come with a host of Bulgars at my back.

To that charge, I found myself hard-pressed to respond. Perhaps I should have been received more favorably had I come straight down to Constantinople in Moropaulos's fishing boat. At the time I began the journey, I had thought it more likely I would be seized and beheaded.

That still struck me as having been highly likely. In any case, I had no choice. The die, as Julius Caesar said, was cast. I harangued the soldiers on the walls from first light of dawn till dusk deepened into night. They would not open the gates for me. More dejected than I had ever been in all my life, even in the black days shortly after my mutilation, I rode back toward Tervel's encampment, back past the Golden Gate, back past the Kharisian Gate, back past the ruins of the aqueduct of Valens.

My supporters seemed as downhearted as I was. The men from Kherson had marveled no less than Tervel at seeing Constantinople. Now, though, its splendor took on a sinister meaning for them. "How are you going to get in there, Emperor, if they won't open up?" Barisbakourios asked gloomily.

"Whatever you do, Emperor, it's going to take something special," Leo agreed. He had again been unable to persuade the garrison to renounce the usurper.

Tervel stood listening quietly to our conversation. Eventually, the khagan of the Bulgars would suggest withdrawing to the lands he ruled, the lands north of the mountains. I saw no choice ahead but to go with him, to pursue my dream even as it receded before me, to become the glove inside which rested his hand. Part of me would die every day, but the breathing husk that remained would be enough for him and to spare.

Moropaulos, in his earnest, dull way, ticked off points on his fingers: "We can't go over the walls—we're not hawks. We can't go under the walls—we're not moles." He knew nothing of mining, but the Bulgars knew nothing of mining, either, which made him correct. He went on, "We can't go through the walls—we're not woodpeckers." He laughed, but only for a moment. Then his heavy face curdled to sadness. "That doesn't leave anything."

The rest of my followers looked similarly dejected. So did Tervel, although art might have substituted for emotion on his features. For one moment, downheartedness threatened to overwhelm me, too. Then, ever so slowly, I straightened, where before I had slumped. "We are not hawks," I said in a voice that made my comrades turn toward me and pay my words close heed. "We are not moles. But perhaps, by God and His Mother, we can be woodpeckers."

"Only person a wood pecker'd do any good is a eunuch," Myakes said.

I glared at him so fiercely that he subsided, mumbling apologies. Pointing south toward the aqueduct of Valens, I said, "The channel there does not bring water into the imperial city these days, nor has it for eighty years or so. But it still goes into Constantinople. God willing, so shall we."

"What if they have guards in there, Emperor?" Stephen exclaimed.

"Then we'll fight them," I replied. *Then they'll kill us*, I thought. "But I never remember guards being posted in the aqueduct. Do you, Myakes?"

Where a moment before he had been good for nothing but making crude jokes, now he sounded surprisingly thoughtful. "No, Emperor, I don't, not ever. Nobody thinks about the aqueduct, not these days."

I was thinking about it, thinking about the prospect of making my way through several hundred yards of pitch-black pipe. I wondered how big around the pipe was. Would I be able to stand upright in it, or would I have to crawl all that way? If I did have to crawl, finding guards there was less likely. But who could guess what might have denned there in the many years since water had stopped flowing?

"Who's with me?" I asked, deliberately not thinking of any of these things.

Faithful Myakes spoke first, I think, but he beat out my followers from Kherson—and also Leo—by only a fragment of a heartbeat. None of the other Romans who had joined me since I came down with the Bulgars said a word. Neither did Tervel. I tried to make out his expression in the fading light, tried and failed. Was he discomfited at seeing what he had reckoned certain failure suddenly sparked with another chance at success?

If he was, he was not so discomfited as to keep me from making the effort. On the other hand, he did not offer any aid, either. He simply stood aside and let me and my backers do as we would—washed his hands of us, so to speak, as Pilate had done with our Lord. All the risks were ours, and all the planning was ours, too.

Not, I must say, that much planning was involved. We had to get up into the opening, go through the pipe, and get down into the city. It would be simple—or it would be impossible.

"Torches," Stephen said, "so we can see what—"

"No." I cut him off. Pointing toward the aqueduct once more, I continued, "We have no way to tell whether bricks have fallen out or mortar come loose, or whether the pipe itself has cracked. If the usurper's soldiers see light in the aqueduct, whether everything has been dark and quiet since my great-great-grandfather's day, they'll be waiting for us inside the city, and that will be the end of everything."

"All that way in the dark?" Theophilos shuddered.

Though dreading that myself, I told him, "Stay here, then." My voice, I daresay, had a lash to it. Having seen what might be a way into the city, I was wild to try it.

"A pry bar," Myakes exclaimed. "No telling what we'll have to move."

"I know where to get one," Leo said. That, I confess, made me raise my eyebrows. This was only the third day on which he had been in the neighborhood of the imperial city. But he hurried away with every sign of confidence. My new spatharios was proving a man of no small resourcefulness.

"Rope, too," Myakes called after him. He waved to show he had heard. To me, Myakes said, "Rope'll give us a way down where we might not have one otherwise."

Leo came back a few minutes later with a coil of rope around one arm and a stout iron crowbar about a cubit long in his other hand. "Excellent," I said, and then turned to Tervel. "Have we a ladder tall enough to let us climb up into the water channel of that aqueduct?"

"I don't know," he answered. When he seemed inclined to say no more, I folded my arms across my chest, making it plain I should not be satisfied without his giving me a more responsive reply. Grudgingly, he went on, "I will see. If we do not, we can make one by lashing two or three shorter ones together."

"Good enough," I said. "Now, I have one more favor to ask of you."

"What is it?" He did not sound happy. What he sounded like was a man who felt what he had thought to be a puppet jerking his arm.

"When we go up into the pipe, I want your men to attack the wall," I told him. "I want them to make an enormous din, so any noise from us goes unnoticed." When he simply stood there, saying neither yes nor no, I added, "By this time tomorrow, you will be revealed either as my son-in-law or as a Caesar of the Roman Empire."

His face did not show what he thought. It seldom did. Up in the country he ruled, he had seemed hopeful about my prospects, but that hope must have faded when few Romans came over to me, and faded again when the garrison of the imperial city held it closed against me.

Maybe hope revived in him. Maybe he simply thought he would be rid of me. "I shall do it," he said.

The ladders the Bulgars had were *not* long enough. When they lashed two of them together, the resulting contraption still had a bend in the middle on being forced more or less upright, as a man's leg has a bend at the knee. My followers examined it with doubts that, had they been applied to religion, would have amounted to wicked atheism.

Although having those same doubts myself, I suppressed them. "It will serve," I insisted. "It does not have to hold us long—only long enough to get us up into the aqueduct."

I wanted to wait until midnight to enter the aqueduct, but was persuaded to begin earlier, around the start of the fourth hour of the night, because I had no way of knowing how long the journey through the channel would take. I hoped to drop down into Constantinople while it was still dark, so as to be able to pick for myself the way in which I would first confront the soldiers and people of the city.

Several grunting Bulgars carried the spliced ladder to the base of the ruined aqueduct and raised it high. I wonder if they should have joined three, not two, together, it being barely long enough for its required purpose. Changing matters at that point, though, would have taken time I did not wish to spend.

I started up the ladder. It did flex at that joint, as a man's knee might have done. I climbed as fast as I could. If it broke under my weight and sent me tumbling to the ground, drama would turn to unseemly farce in the blink of an eye.

It held. Gasping, I got to the top. I reached into the opening of the channel, which was something less than a yard wide: a tiny thing, seemingly, to have supplied the imperial city with so much water. My fingers closed over sticks and twigs. I threw the bird's nest away and scrambled up into the pipe.

It was too narrow for me to turn around in it. "I'm in!" I shouted, almost as if I had entered a woman. I had to hope they would hear me down below.

The ladder scraped against the broken end of the aqueduct: someone else was on it. I scuttled farther down the pipe, to give whoever it was room to climb in. "Don't put more than one man on this cursed thing at a time." It was Myakes' voice. I might have known he would let no one come between me and him. Cursing, he made it into the pipe in the same ungainly way I had used. "You there, Emperor?"

"I'm here." His bulky body cut off what little light had come from the opening of the channel. "We'll both move down now."

That came none too soon, for someone else was already climbing toward us: Barisbakourios, followed by Stephen, then Leo, then Moropaulos, with Theophilos last of all. By the time Theophilos joined us, I was some distance down the pipe, moving ahead in utter darkness.

Some men, I have heard, suffer a deadly fear of being enclosed in a small space. Had any such sufferer been among us, he would without a doubt have gone screaming mad. Not only were we literally in a space of small compass, again and again banging our heads or barking our backs when we rose up more than the pipe would permit, but it seemed even smaller than it was because of the utter lightlessness there. It would have been easy to imagine the pipe closing in on us until it squeezed us as an Aesculapian snake squeezes a rat. Fortunately, none of us was afflicted by this sort of morbid imagining.

M Y A K E S

Brother Elpidios, I tell you the truth, I never came so close to pissing myself as I did in that damned pipe. I was blinder then than I am now. I can tell the difference between light and dark to this day. I can't *see* anything, mind you, but I can tell the difference. There wasn't any difference to tell, not inside that pipe there wasn't. It was all black, nothing else but.

I would have had the screaming hobgoblins in there, I think, if it hadn't been for Justinian. What? No, he didn't pat me on the shoulder and keep me brave, or anything like that. Yes, I'll tell you what I mean, if you let me, Brother. What I mean is, if I'd gone to pieces in there, I figured he'd tell somebody to cut my throat or knock me over the head, and then everybody behind me would have crawled over my body and gone on.

Let me put it like this: frightened as I was, part of me knew it wasn't a *real* fear, if you know what I mean. I was doing it to myself. I could feel I was doing it to myself. I couldn't stop doing it, but I could slow me down a little.

And I knew being afraid of Justinian *was* a real fear. Can't think of one any realer, not offhand. Stand between him and getting into the city then and you'd end up with footprints up your front and down your back—and a knee in the balls for good measure.

Was I more afraid of Justinian than my own imagination? Brother Elpidios, you'd best believe I was. You would have been, too.

W e were not the only living things in the aqueduct pipeway. I have spoken of the nest my hand found when I climbed off the ladder. A couple of bats flapped past me, too, squeaking indignantly at having their seclusion disturbed. Hitting out at them, I succeeded only in barking my knuckles.

Skitterings told me mice or rats had climbed the masonry of the wrecked aqueduct to make their homes in the pipe. None of them ran toward me; they all fled away, sensing that I and the men with me were larger and more dangerous than they.

I crawled headfirst through spiderwebs beyond number, wondering what their patient weavers found to eat in this dark, wretched hole. More than one spider dropped down onto me and crawled away. At first I swatted at them, but, finding crushing their soft, hairy bodies more re-volting than letting them run on me, I soon desisted. Soft cries of disgust from my followers said not all the eight-legged creatures were descending on me.

How far had I come? In the Stygian darkness, I had no sure way to judge. Something like panic ran through me. Was it a spear-cast? A bow-shot? A mile? Had we reached the wall? Had we passed it? I stopped. Myakes promptly ran into me, each of the others colliding in turn with the man in front of him.

"Wait," I said. "Quiet." Echoing weirdly up the tube through which we crawled came the sounds of battle. Tervel, then, had kept his pledge to me. But so attenuated were the sounds, I could not use them to judge how far or how long we had traveled. On asking my companions, I dis-covered that their opinions varied so widely as to be of little value.

The argument threatened to engulf us as thoroughly as darkness had done. "Wait," I said again. "Let us assume we've come about a bowshot, say, two hundred fifty cubits." That was in the middle range of the guesses they had put forth. "From now on, I will keep track of how many times my right leg advances. For each of those times, I will add one cubit. It will not be a perfect reckoning, but better than the nothing we have now."

No one argued with me. I was in the lead. I had a plan, where the rest had none. And I was the Emperor. Muttering under my breath to keep the count straight, I moved on once more. They followed.

If my beginning guess was right, we should have been approaching the outer wall. Setting my ear against the rough side of the pipe, I tried to find out whether I could hear the Romans who were resisting the Bulgars' onslaught. All I could make out was my own blood pounding. Sighing, I went on.

At the count of, I believe, three hundred seventeen, my hand came up against an obstruction. A moment later, my head ran into it, too. "Hold up," I said to Myakes and the rest behind me. I felt of the obstruction. It was an iron grate, rough and scaly with rust under my fingers. At some time after the Avars had worked their destruction, then, Roman engineers had done their best to make sure no one could do as I was doing. By the feel of the iron, though, it had been a long time ago, and forgotten since. Explaining what I had found, I ordered, "Pass the pry bar up to me."

Leo, who was still carrying it, handed it to Stephen, from whom it went to Barisbakourios, Myakes, and me. The artisans who had installed the grating had cut holes into the channel, in which they inserted the ends of the bars of the grill. Working as they had been doing under cramped, difficult circumstances, they had not made the fit perfect, as they otherwise might have done. That carelessness, and perhaps the feeling that they were taking needless precautions, caused them to leave space into which I could set the pointed beak of the pry bar.

Using it was not easy, even after having set it in place. If I could have stood on my knees, I would have been in excellent position to exert full leverage. The pipe was too low and narrow to permit that, however. I had to lie at full length, as both my arms, which otherwise would have supported me, were engaged in prying.

With a sharp snapping sound, a piece of the grate flew off. It hit me in the back, and then hit Myakes in the head. We both cursed, there in the cramped blackness. I tugged at the grate. It still refusing to come free, I used the pry bar once more. When the next chunk of rusted iron broke away, it hit me in the head; I felt blood trickling through my scalp.

I tugged again. The grate shifted under my hands, but remained in place. I had to break off two more pieces of iron before I could wrestle it out of its position. Even then, it being essentially as wide as the channel in which it was set, I could not simply put it to one side. I and my followers had to scramble over or under it to advance. Moropaulos, the bulkiest of us, had a dreadful time. I feared he might prove a cork in the bottle for Theophilos, but at last he made it past the grate.

Then I had to remember the count of cubits. In my exertions, I had for the moment lost the exact number, but I did not admit that to Myakes and the rest of them. On we went, one obstacle overcome. Forty-seven

cubits, or rather, forty-seven advances of my right leg, later, I ran headlong into another grate. I hissed in pain, it having struck close by the
place where the chunk from the first grate had hit me.

This new grate was as scabrous with rust as the first had been. Since
I now carried the pry bar, I went straight to work. I needed to break the
grate at only three places before becoming able to shift it. Once we had
all struggled past, I said, "If my reckoning is true, we've passed beyond
the inner wall and are now inside the city."

Theophilos started to raise a cheer. Myakes hissed, "Shut up, curse
you, or we're all *dead* inside the city."

We crawled on. Having come so far, I began to wonder how I would
be able to leave the aqueduct. Dropping down into a cistern half full of
water from other sources, although it might clean us of the filth through
which we had been traveling, struck me as being less than ideal.

But God, Who had heard my pledge and saved me from the storm,
provided for me once more. Looking ahead, I spied on the inside of the
pipe a short strip of light in what had been darkness absolute and im-
penetrable. Hurrying to it, as best I could hurry in that cramped place, I
discovered a door had been set into the roof of the channel, no doubt
for the convenience of workmen who might have to enter to clear ob-
structions. Like everything else pertaining to the aqueduct, the door had
not been cared for since my great-great-grandfather's day. Its timbers had
shrunk and split, allowing a little moonlight to pierce the darkness. I
wondered if we had crawled past other doors in better repair, but then
decided I did not wish to know.

Crawling past this door, I rolled over onto my back, using my legs
to push up against the boards. Had it been latched, I would have attacked
it with the pry bar. But it swung back easily. I stood upright, savoring
that position, and looked around to get my bearings. Considering how far
we had come in the blackness, my reckoning proved quite good. We were
about a bowshot inside the inner wall, and considerably less than that
distance from a large cistern. As well I had found the doorway, I thought.

"Anyone trying to find out what that noise was?" Myakes hissed
from inside the pipe.

"I can't see anyone," I answered. "Pass me the rope. I'll make it fast
to one of the hinges here, and we can all climb down."

"No. I have a better idea," Myakes said. "Moropaulos is a big, strong
fellow. Let him hold the rope while the rest of us go down. Then he can
tie it to a hinge and climb down himself. That way, we only have to trust
the old iron once, not seven times."

His plan indeed being better than mine, we adopted it forthwith.

The rest of us crawled up onto the top of the aqueduct. Moropaulos stood in the doorway, the better to brace himself. I had intended to be first man down, but Myakes again took the lead from me. I do not know to this day whether he was testing Foolish Paul's strength or making sure no opposition waited below.

Whichever it was, he soon called, "All's well, Emperor. Your city's here waiting for you."

I went down hand over hand, having first wrapped the rope around my leg and over the top of my instep to give myself some additional purchase should a hand slip. A minute later, I stood in an unpaved alleyway in Constantinople, a stone's throw north of the Mese. "I've returned," I whispered, as if saying it was what made it true.

Leo descended next, then Stephen, Barisbakourios, and Theophilos. Foolish Paul's feet were a man's height above the ground when the iron hinge to which he'd tied the rope tore free of the cement and bricks under his weight. He landed with a thud and a shout, the rope streaming down after him. He scraped one knee—through all our knees were already raw from a longer crawl than ever we had done as infants—but, praise God, was otherwise unhurt.

I looked at all my companions in the moonlight. The pale radiance sufficed to show how filthy and tattered they were, which doubtless meant I was filthy and tattered as well. Seven men to overthrow the greatest city in the civilized world! One of the pagan dramatists of Athens wrote a play about seven men against a city, but I recall neither the playwright nor the city the seven men opposed.

"We'll go to the Mese," I said. "We'll find a fountain on a street corner and clean ourselves as best we can. Then we'll go to the grand palace. We'll get inside any way we can, and then we'll slay Apsimaros." With my rival dead, I reasoned, no one would oppose my reassuming the throne rightfully mine.

No one moved. I barked at my followers. Barisbakourios said, "Emperor, this is your city. We don't know which way to go." He kept looking around, even here down on the ground. "I don't think I believed all your stories of the imperial city, the ones you'd tell back in Kherson. But you meant them, didn't you?"

"Of course I did," I answered, setting out for the chief boulevard of the city. Myakes strode along beside me, Constantinople also being familiar to him. The others, even Leo, followed slowly, cautiously, as if on the verge of being overwhelmed by the size and magnificence of the city through which they walked.

They exclaimed in wonder at the length and width and paving of the Mese, and at so many people being on the street at an hour well past midnight. We were a large enough group to deter robbers, and also large enough for others to think us robbers and depart in haste. Grimy as we were, a couple of whores came up to us. They hissed curses at me when I sent them away; we lacked the time for even the most pleasant distractions.

While we were splashing water on our faces at a fountain, a squadron of horse came riding along the Mese toward the walls, their harness jingling. When the light from the torches they carried fell on us, their leader called, "Here, you men! Who are you?"

Had I listened to reason, I should have either fled or lied. If reason spoke to me, I heard nothing. At last back in my beloved city, I drew myself up proudly and said, "I am Justinian, Emperor of the Romans, the son of Constantine son of Constans son of Herakleios Constantine son of Herakleios. Who, sir, are *you?*"

The officer's chin dropped to his chest. So did Myakes'. Leo, I remember, clapped his hands together, once, twice, admiring my audacity. Had the officer and his soldiers been perfectly loyal to the usurper, they could have cut me down where I stood. The fellow's mouth worked. When he spoke, though, he gave no order to attack, instead whispering, "Holy Virgin Mother of God."

"I have returned to take back my throne," I said, and drew my sword. "Will you stand by me, or will you fight?"

Smashing a lump of quicksilver with a hammer could have created no greater scattering than did my words. A couple of the riders wheeled their mounts and galloped back toward the palace, crying, "Justinian is in the city! The Emperor is in the city!" They might have thought they were warning Apsimaros, but, by those cries, their hearts knew who their true sovereign was.

Others galloped away down side streets. Few of those said anything at all. My guess was that they aimed to sit out whatever turmoil sprang into being as a result of my sudden and unexpected arrival, then obey the orders of whoever finally seized control of the throne. Still others, that astonished officer among them, rode forward on the route the whole squadron had been taking. They too shouted my name, and some of them, intending to do so or not, also shouted that I was Emperor.

And eight or ten men did not ride off in any direction. Bowing in the saddle to me, one of them exclaimed, "Command us, Emperor!"

Over the long years of exile in Kherson, Myakes had rehearsed for me many times how Leontios and his henchmen had seized control of the imperial city the night I was overthrown. Now I could imitate the blow that had toppled me. "Ride through the streets of the city," I told the horsemen. "Shout my name. Raise a great commotion. Let everyone know I have returned and I am in the city. Tell anyone who wants to help to do as you are doing and rouse the people."

"Emperor, we will!" they declared as one man, and they rode off in all directions, shouting my name at the top of their lungs.

"What now, Emperor?" Myakes asked.

"First the palace," I answered. "Once we lay hold of the usurper, the game is ours. Then we seize Kallinikos." Hungry anticipation filled my voice.

We trotted along the Mese toward the palace, which lies close by the sea. As we moved, confusion spread all around us. People spilled into the street, many of them still in their nightshirts. More and more of them began shouting my name, some in disbelief, others in delight. We ran on.

Had the soldiers on the wall united against me, I still could have been thwarted. But some of them favored me while others did not, the result being that no one did anything. They did, I will say, maintain their watch against my Bulgar allies, that being a matter of most elementary prudence.

My comrades, all save Myakes, to whom the splendid buildings and plazas and monuments adorning the Queen of Cities were familiar, exclaimed again and again at them. They exclaimed at the column of Markianos, at the church of St. Polyeuktos on the other side of the street, at the Praitorion, at the round Forum of Constantine, at the church of St. Euphemia and the bulk of the hippodrome beyond it. I exclaimed at the hippodrome, too—in hatred, having last seen it when my blood spilled into the dirt there.

They were just beginning to exclaim at the Milion at the end of the Mese, and at the church of the Holy Wisdom not far past, when I, refusing to be distracted, led them south off the Mese toward the palace. "Gawk later," I said harshly.

Torches and bonfires blazed all around the palace, a low, rambling building. People streamed in and out, some soldiers, some not. I had never seen, never dreamed of such activity late at night; the palace might have been an anthill stirred by a stick. Before long, thanks to the abundant light, someone spied me and my followers and loosed a nervous challenge: "Who comes?"

"Justinian, Emperor of the Romans!" I shouted back. Audacity and only audacity had brought me so far. Never again would I put my faith in anything else.

Myakes plucked at my torn sleeve. "Emperor, they outnumber us a hundred to one. If they—"

"Shut up," I snapped, for everyone who had heard my voice was staring my way. I brandished my sword, as if to say I would cut down the first man who dared defy my right to rule.

Still sounding very nervous indeed, the fellow who had challenged me said, "The Emperor, uh, Tiberius, uh, Apsimaros, uh, the usurper, hearing you had somehow sneaked into, uh, come into the imperial, he, uh, well, he took flight is what he did. Half an hour ago—can't be more. So, uh, the palace is yours. Welcome, uh, welcome home, Justinian, Emperor of the Romans!"

"*Tu vincas*, Justinian!" people shouted, as if I were being acclaimed for the first time.

I waved the sword again. Silence fell; I might have slashed at speech. "I am not *becoming* Emperor of the Romans," I said. "I *am* Emperor of the Romans. I *have been* Emperor of the Romans. All this is mine by right." For ten long, lonely, dreadful years I had said that, in Kherson, in Doros, in Atil, in Phanagoria, in the land of the Bulgars. How many had believed me? I had half a dozen men at my back here, no more. But I had been right all along.

BOOK Δ´

JUSTINIAN

As word spread from the palace that Apsimaros had run away, both those who had thought to stay loyal to him and the cursed lukewarm saw I looked like winning and came over to me. By sunrise, fighting had ceased.

By sunrise, also, I had ordered a house-to-house search for the fugitive usurper. Alas, it did not catch him in its net. A naval officer before presuming to advance his station, he escaped the city in a small boat. I offered a large reward to anyone who would bring him to me alive. "Or if not," I said, "his head will do." I laughed. How I laughed!

My mother wept to see me, even though, by the time she did, I had changed from the filthy tunic in which I entered Constantinople into a robe suited for the Emperor of the Romans. We embraced as if we had never exchanged harsh words. "My son," she said, and then, proving herself of my house in spirit if not in blood, "you are avenged."

"Not yet," I answered. "Not fully. Not till Apsimaros stands before me, loaded with chains. But he will." I smacked one fist into the other palm. "And Leontios and Kallinikos are already in the hollow of my hand." I smiled, anticipating.

"Your face," she said sadly. "Your poor face."

"It could be worse," I told her. "Leontios is uglier than I am these days, by all I hear. And he'll be uglier yet when I'm through with him." I changed the subject: "Tell me—my daughter Epiphaneia, is she well?"

My mother's face glowed as if a lamp shone through it. "She is indeed. Do you know, I think this may be the first time you have ever asked after her."

"Is she wed?" I persisted, wondering which half of my bargain I would have to keep with Tervel.

"No," my mother replied. "Neither of the usurpers would permit her betrothal. They feared any man who married her would plot against them because of who she was. And, of course, she was still very young while Leontios disgraced the throne. In fact, she—"

"Good." I interrupted her. "If she is unwed, I can marry her off to Tervel the Bulgar, to repay him for the men who helped put me back on the throne." Without those men, I never would have been able to approach the city and enter the pipe that brought me into it. Tervel might not have been confident of my triumph, but had helped make it possible—and his army remained encamped just beyond the wall. Keeping our bargain seemed the better part of wisdom.

"You would give the child of your flesh to minister to the lusts of a barbarian?" my mother whispered, turning pale. "It cannot be."

"If she is still unmarried, it shall be," I said. "It's either that or let Tervel tear up the countryside—and break my oath to him, too."

"It cannot be," my mother repeated, more firmly this time. "As she judged herself unlikely to be allowed to wed a man, she became a bride of Christ year before last, and dwells in the nunnery dedicated to the Mother of God near the Forum of Arkadios."

"In that case, you're right—it cannot be," I agreed. "I'll have to name the Bulgar Caesar instead." She began to gabble at that, too, so I left her. Not even the Emperor's mother may scold him against his will, a telling proof of the power inherent in the imperial dignity.

On leaving her, I intended to go and speak with Tervel, but Leo and some city folk I did not know hailed Kallinikos before me. "Emperor!" cried the patriarch, prostrating himself before me when his captives released him so he could do so. "Congratulations on your glorious return to the imperial city!"

I stared at him. He was, I saw to my astonishment, so base of soul as to be absolutely sincere. He had abandoned me to consecrate Leontios, abandoned Leontios to crown Apsimaros, and now stood ready, or rather sprawled ready, to abandon Apsimaros for me once more. He had the perfect temperament for a whore. A patriarch, however, needed judging by different standards.

"Wretch!" I shouted, and kicked him in the face—not hard, not even hard enough to break his nose. "You are the spineless slug who announced Leontios's accession with the opening words of the Easter service, as if he were Christ come again. And now you think you can serve me once more? You have never been so wrong in all your life, and that says a great deal."

"Mercy!" he wailed, as he should have done from the beginning—not that it would have helped him, not that anything would have helped him.

"When I was coming down to Constantinople, I swore a great oath to have mercy on none of my enemies," I replied. He shrank in on himself, like a loaf of bread falling when the oven door opens at the wrong time. Then, thoughtfully, I asked, "Has the pope in Rome yet accepted the canons of my fifth-sixth synod?"

Blood dripped down his cheek where I had kicked him. Though he still groveled on his belly before me, his face showed sudden hope. "No, Emperor, the wicked, stubborn fellow has not. He still thunders defiance at the synod inspired by the Holy Spirit. Only spare me, and I shall send anathemas against him that—"

"Be silent," I told him, and he was silent. After some little while passed in thought, I snapped my fingers and smiled. "I have it! The very thing!"

"Excommunication?" Kallinikos asked. "A drastic step, Emperor, but, should you require it, I—"

"Be silent," I said again, and then spoke to Leo: "Take him to the executioners. Let him be blinded with red-hot irons, and then let him be exiled to Rome. Thus I not only punish his betrayal but also warn the pope, whatever his name is these days. . . ." Kallinikos did not answer, past bleating like a ram as it is made into a wether. No one else knew. Shrugging, I went on, "Whoever the pope is, he needs to remember I have my eye on him." I pointed to Kallinikos. "Take this offal away."

Away he went, still bleating. I never saw him again. He never saw anything again. Leo was laughing as he led him thither. "You'll need a new patriarch now," Myakes remarked.

"I know," I answered. "I have the man, too: one who was loyal to me at cost to himself, not disloyal at gain for himself."

Myakes looked sly. "I know what you're going to do: you're going to name Cyrus."

"That's just what I'm going to do," I said. "He was loyal to me. How can I be anything but loyal to him? He's earned the patriarchal throne. He'll be glad to get out of Kherson, too—what man wouldn't? But first things first." I started out of the palace, on the mission I had begun when the matter of Kallinikos interrupted me. "I have to see Tervel."

Looking down from the wall at the khagan of the Bulgars, I saw him and his army in a light different from that in which I had viewed him when we marched on Constantinople together. All the gates of the imperial city remained barred against the Bulgars, as against any other barbarians.

From a couple of steps beyond the ditch in front of the wall, Tervel waved to me. "You are on your throne again! Well done!" The words were fulsome enough. The tone . . . the tone was that a man uses when a friend has some unexpected piece of good fortune fall into his lap: he is glad for his friend, no doubt, but cannot help wondering why the good fortune did not come to him instead.

"I am on my throne again," I agreed, wishing I could repudiate every promise I had made. But, with Apsimaros uncaptured, with his brother Herakleios an important commander in Anatolia, I could not afford to affront the Bulgars. "Now I can give you what I swore would be yours."

Now he hesitated before speaking. He had not thought I should be in a position where I had to make good on my promises. In such a position, I think I startled him by doing so. Carefully, he said, "You will give me your daughter to wed?"

"No, I cannot do that," I said. "I learn that she is a nun, and does not wish to come forth from her convent. But I told you that, if the marriage could not be, I would make you Caesar, and that I will do, and gladly. Come into the city in a week's time, and I will grant you the robe and crown of your office, and rich gifts besides."

"My men, who have come so far for you, would like to see the city before then," he said.

"They may," I said, and he brightened, doubtless hoping I would be foolish enough to allow his whole army into Constantinople at once, thereby giving him the chance to seize it. Quickly, I laid that hope to rest: "They may enter in parties of a hundred, and two hundred may be in the city at any one time. I will stock taverns where they may drink their fill for free, but if they rob or rape or kill, I will punish them as if they were Romans. Agreed?"

"Agreed," he answered. I was not lavish, but neither was I so niggardly as to rouse wrath—and now I held the Queen of Cities.

To show him I would abide by my pledge, I ordered the Kharisian

Gate opened at once, that he might send his first contingent of Bulgars into the city. The nomads stared in astonishment at Constantinople, they being even less prepared for its magnificence than my followers from Kherson. Seeing their wonder, I smiled and turned to Myakes, who had accompanied me out to the wall. "I wonder what Theodora will have to say about the imperial city here, thinking she knows all about cities because she has seen Phanagoria."

"That will be something, all right, Emperor," Myakes agreed. He was watching the Bulgars coming into Constantinople. When he saw Roman soldiers accompanying most of them as guides—and, though it remained unsaid, to keep them out of mischief—he relaxed. In thoughtful tones, he asked, "Have you talked to the lady your mother about marrying the Khazar?"

"Not yet," I answered. Then, thoughtful myself, I went on, "I think, for the time being, I shall dwell in the palace at Blakhernai, here in the northwestern part of the city. It will put me close to the encampment of my allies, the Bulgars."

"Uh-huh," Myakes said: a peculiar noise, difficult to transcribe in Greek letters. I took it to mean he was of the opinion I chose that course not because it left me close to the Bulgars but because it left me far from my mother. Such speculation I refused to dignify with a reply.

When I went to the palace in the Blakhernai district, I found only a handful of servants and slaves there, both Leontios and Apsimaros having been in the habit of residing in the grand palace. But many of the servitors there were men and women and eunuchs I had known before my exile. One of the eunuchs explained why that was so: "If we were thought to be loyal to you, Emperor, but the usurpers could not prove treason against us, they sent us away from their presence, to a place where nothing was ever likely to happen."

"They did the same to me," I exclaimed, and the chamberlain bowed low. My exile had been harsher than his, but not even Auriabedas could have repaired his mutilation.

I discussed with the eunuchs at the Blakhernai palace my plan for raising Tervel to the rank of Caesar. The one who had explained why I found so many familiar faces there, a certain Theophylaktos, said, "Where shall we get the proper regalia, Emperor? No one in your house has ever named Caesars, only junior Emperors. We have no proper crowns, we have no proper robes. . . ." Besides such concerns, that Tervel was a barbarous Bulgar faded into insignificance for him.

"Take one of my uncles' crowns and cut off the cross atop it," I said. "Tervel knows that's the difference between an Emperor's crown and a

Caesar's, because I told him as much. Since we've had no Caesars for so long, no one in the imperial city will know any more than that."

"True," Theophylaktos said, sounding surprised at having the matter so abruptly settled. Then he looked worried once more. "But what of the robe this Tervel is supposed to wear? The moths will surely have had their way with—"

"So what?" I said. "We'll put him in an imperial robe. No one will know if that's not perfectly proper, either. And no one will care. We'll say it's a Caesar's robe, Tervel will be wearing a Caesar's crown, and we're proclaiming him Caesar. That should settle things."

"Most irregular," the eunuch muttered. But he bowed and composed himself to obey. My entire return to Constantinople had been most irregular, but he did not mention that. Since I was now undisputed master of the imperial city, anything I ordered became regular because I ordered it.

As I had commanded, so it was done. Tervel and his guards quietly came into the city two days before that on which I would fulfill my promise to him. During those two days, he rode through as much of the city as he could, so that I saw little of him. "I never believed my envoys," he said, as he had before. "Now I see they said less than they might have done."

Criers had also gone through the city, ordering the people to appear before the palace of Blakhernai at the start of the fourth hour of the day, to see me create the new Caesar. As my father had crowned me, so I intended to crown Tervel myself. Since I was setting the crown on his head in my capacity as Emperor, the patriarch's presence was superfluous and dispensable. As well, too, for Kallinikos, having tried and failed to reaccommodate himself to me after acquiescing in my overthrow and mutilation, had already sailed off, blinded, into exile at Rome. I felt sure the ship bearing him would reach its destination safe: with him aboard, it would sail before any breeze.

Palace servitors threw coins into the crowd around the rostrum the artisans had hastily erected in front of the Blakhernai palace. Already, the engraver Cyril had provided coins bearing my image and the number twenty, signifying the twentieth year of my reign. By my reckoning, I had never been rightfully removed, and I intended making my reckoning that of the whole Empire.

"*Tu vincas*, Justinian!" the people shouted as I strode forward to take my place on the platform.

They had acclaimed Leontios and Apsimaros as fervently as they now acclaimed me. How I longed to turn soldiers, Romans and Bulgars together, loose on them, to show them playing the prostitute had its price. Regretfully, I set aside the notion, having made other plans for the day.

"I *have* conquered," I said. "The wretch who stole my throne lies in prison, while the pirate who robbed him of it in turn has shown his cowardice by fleeing the imperial city. The house of Herakleios is restored, as God ordained."

They cheered, loud and long. They dared do nothing less. Some of them, no doubt, were examining their memories and their consciences, wondering if I could learn they had cheered my overthrow ten years before. They had been fools to cheer then, but were not so foolish if they wondered thus. I intended trying to learn exactly that. When vengeance is God-ordained, it must be thorough.

"I have conquered," I repeated, and then made my voice go hard: "No thanks to you, no thanks to any Romans, that I have. My one true ally was Tervel son of Asparukh, khagan of the Bulgars. Upon him, then, I confer the rewards you Romans might otherwise have claimed. Attend me, Tervel!"

Clad in a plain white tunic, the khagan joined me on the platform. He stared out in wonder at the multitude there to witness his aggrandizement. In a soft voice, he said, "I have never seen so many people gathered together in one place in all my life. How do you feed them all?"

"We manage," I answered, and raised my voice once more: "People of Constantinople, I now raise Tervel the Bulgar to the rank of Caesar, in recognition of his services to me." Theophylaktos the eunuch draped an imperial robe, glittering with pearls and gems and golden threads, around the Bulgar's shoulders.

Tervel grunted in surprise. "This thing is as heavy as armor." He looked down at himself. "Prettier than armor, I will say." He smiled.

With my own hands, I set on his head the crossless crown of the Caesar. "Behold Justinian Emperor of the Romans and Tervel Caesar!" I shouted to the gaping mob. "We are friends and allies, joined against thieves and robbers."

With one accord, the people prostrated themselves before the two of us, men, women, and children alike, so that we saw only their backs and the napes of their necks. A headsman would have had an easy time of it, striding through the crowds lopping heads as a farmer with a scythe cuts down wheat. Most of them, I daresay, deserved nothing better.

"Arise!" Tervel shouted in a great voice, his first—and last—command as Caesar. The people hastened to obey. Some of them shouted the acclamations traditional upon the accession of a Caesar, wishing him many years and good fortune. Those acclamations sounded thin, though,

and not only because of going so long unused as to be half-forgotten:
some Constantinopolitans, I thought, did not care to lavish such praise
on a barbarian.

I had no great delight in doing as I did, but, having begun it, did it
as thoroughly as I could. "When Tervel Caesar returns to his own country," I told the people, "we shall honor him with many presents: gold and
scarlet-dyed skins and pepper." Such are the presents that have pleased
barbarians for hundreds of years. Tervel proved no exception to the ancient rule, puffing out his chest and looking pleased.

The people cheered, which made him even prouder than he had
been. I hid a smile. He thought they were cheering his rank and my
munificence. Knowing the city mob as I do, I knew also that what delighted them most was the announcement that he would be leaving Constantinople for his homeland.

That announcement delighted me less than it did the mob. Tervel's
having a country of his own, a country carved out of Roman territory,
remained galling a quarter of a century after the Bulgars, humiliating my
father, established themselves south of the Danube. To every thing there
is a season, and a time to every purpose under the heaven, says the Book
of Ecclesiastes. For now, Tervel remained my friend and ally. Later . . .
later would be a different season.

A few days later, the khagan rode north, his saddlebags nicely heavy
with gold, bulging with skins, and packed with pepper. The latter he
reckoned as much a marvel as anything else he found in Constantinople.
"It *bites* the tongue!" he exclaimed, on my serving him a kid roasted with
peppercorns. The sharp flavor made him drink immoderately, a benefit
he also appreciated.

I having kept my promise, he kept his as well, and restrained the
Bulgars from plundering as they rode north. And why not? He had made
more profit dealing with me than he could have got by stealing from me.
That he kept his pledge by withdrawing peacefully also helped me secure
my hold on the heart of the Roman Empire, no small matter with Apsimaros still at large. Rumor said he had sailed up toward Thrace, but
rumor was not enough. I wanted the usurper.

But Apsimaros was not the only illegal ruler about whom I concerned myself. One of my first actions on returning to the imperial city was to order
Leontios's guards *not* to tell him I had reclaimed that which was mine. Tervel having departed, I went in full imperial regalia to the monastery of Delmatos and commanded the usurped usurper brought before me.

"Down on your belly before the Emperor of the Romans!" my ex-cubitores shouted, and Leontios prostrated himself in his filthy tunic. The prison stench came off him in waves.

"Rise," I said.

Clumsily, he got to his feet. Not only was he covered with dirt, but his shaggy, unkempt hair and beard, which had had only a light frosting of gray ten years before, were now snow but lightly dusted with soot. In the center of his broad face was a broad hole. The executioner had done a more thorough job on him than on me, which disheartened me not in the least.

Imprisonment having done nothing to quicken his wits, he stared at me some little while before saying, "You're not Apsimaros," and fol-lowing that a moment later with, "You're someone else." Finding he re-mained not only fatuous but also redundant made me laugh out loud. A frown turned his features even uglier than they had been before. "I know your voice, don't I?"

"I should think you would, Leontios," I replied. "Or shall I call you Leo, the Lion?" I shook my head. "No. No one else did."

His eyes went wide, but not so wide as the hole where his nose had been. "Justinian!" he exclaimed, and made the sign of the cross, as if he had seen a ghost. "But it isn't—you can't—you aren't—you've got—"

I affirmed every one of his incoherent denials: "It is I. I can rule. I am Emperor. I've got a nose." I smiled at him. "You look remarkably hideous without one."

"*Kyrie eleison*," Leontios gasped, turning pale beneath his grime. "*Christe eleison.*"

"God and Christ may have mercy on you," I said, "but I shall have none, and, since that is at God's command, my own guess is that the demons in hell will torment you through all eternity: what you deserve, for raising your hand against the Emperor of the Romans."

"I spared your life," he said. "I did not kill you."

"You did not think you needed to kill me," I told him. "The lesson I draw from that is not to make such mistakes myself. Having lost your nose, you shall lose your head as well." I gestured to the guards. "Take him back to his cell. Now, instead of every day being the same as the one before and the one after it"—a condition I knew all too well from my weary years in Kherson—"he has something to look forward to."

The guards laughed. Myakes laughed. I laughed. Leontios, the hu-morless wretch, failed to see the joke.

· · ·

A few weeks after my return to the imperial city, a messenger still stinking of horse sweat dashed into the Blakhernai palace, shouting, "Emperor! Emperor! We have Apsimaros!"

Although normally reckoning highly important the dignity of my office, on that glad occasion I took no notice of it whatever, letting loose a whoop of delight that made the tax official with whom I was talking jump in alarm. "Is he alive or dead?" I demanded. "Where was he taken?"

"Up in Apollonias, on the coast of Thrace," the messenger answered—rumor, for once, had spoken truly. "He's alive—in chains and on the way down to the imperial city. What happened was, he paid for lodging up there with a nomisma that had his own face on it. The tavern keeper recognized him and gave the word to the city garrison—"

"Which had already declared for me," I interrupted happily.

"Which had already declared for you," the messenger agreed. "Apsimaros was taken by surprise—he never got his sword out of the scabbard."

"A pound of gold for the news," I said, whereupon the messenger let out a whoop even louder than mine. He started dancing where he stood.

The bureaucrat said, "Emperor, this news should also end any difficulties you have with Herakleios, Apsimaros's brother."

"By the Virgin, that's true," I exclaimed. Apsimaros, it turned out, had summoned Herakleios from the military district of the Anatolics on receiving word that the Bulgars and I were advancing on Constantinople, intending to use his brother to command an army against me. But, by the time Herakleios got the news and the force he brought with him sailed from southeastern Anatolia, the imperial city lay in my hands. Unable to land in the vicinity, he had come ashore at Abdera, about halfway between Constantinople and Thessalonike. I had feared he and the usurper would be able to unite against me, but that would not happen now.

I had given Barisbakourios a small army of my own, drawn from the city garrison, to maneuver against him and keep him from advancing toward the Black Sea coast, the direction in which I believed (accurately, as it fell out) Apsimaros had fled. When I shouted for couriers, they came in exclaiming, having heard the news the messenger from the north had brought. I told them, "Send word at once to Barisbakourios. Let him make it known to the soldiers following Herakleios that the false emperor they supported is now in my hands. We shall see how long they go on following the fallen usurper's brother."

The couriers rode out within the hour. I also sent riders to the military districts in Anatolia with the same news, so that any generals thinking of rising in support of Apsimaros would be persuaded to think again. I bade those latter riders learn which officers in the military districts were most favorably inclined toward the usurper and, so long as they were able to do so without touching off rebellion, arrest the traitors and send them back to Constantinople for punishment.

Apsimaros came into the city a few days later. Apollonias lying by the sea, I had thought the men of the garrison would put him on board ship so he might get to Constantinople faster, but the commander of the cavalry company explained why they had not: "The son of a whore used to be a ship captain, Emperor. Who can say whether some of the sailors used to serve with him? They might have helped him get loose. My boys—I know them, Emperor, and I picked the best ones."

"Good enough," I said on his explaining himself. "Better than good enough, in fact." I turned to Apsimaros. "Have you got anything to say before I give you what you deserve for stealing my throne?"

"I did not steal your throne," he answered in his peculiar Gothic accent. "I took it from Leontios, who did not know what to do with it. When it was mine, I did well with it." Accent or not, he had some courage and more in the way of brains than Leontios could ever have aspired to.

"It was not yours, any more than it was Leontios's," I said. "And while you were on it, you tried to get rid of me."

"I wish I would have done it, too," he replied. "I should have flung you overboard when I was taking you to Kherson. Worse luck, I did not see the need." He shook his head. The chains with which he was adorned clanked mournfully at the motion.

"Take him to the monastery of Delmatos," I told his captors. "Have them put him in the cell next to Leontios's. I am sure the two of them will have some interesting things to say to each other." I laughed at the thought.

Apsimaros said, "They cast you down because you were a cruel, hard man. You have not changed, except to grow worse. I may not live to see it, but they will cast you down again."

"No, they won't," I answered. "No one will. Everyone who is or might be or might become my foe will die before getting the chance to strike." He started to speak again. I hit him in the face, and he fell silent. To the soldiers, I said, "Take him away." I am Emperor of the Romans. The last word is mine.

When he was gone, Myakes said, "He's not like Leontios, that one. I'm glad he panicked when he heard you were in the city. If he hadn't, he'd have given us a tough fight. You ought to take his head now, and have done."

"Soon," I said. "Not yet. I'll take his head and Leontios's at the same time. I want to do a proper job of it, one that the people who see it will remember for a long time—and that will warn everyone who dreams of rebelling."

"All right," he said. "Maybe you'll have this Herakleios in hand by then, too."

"That would be very good," I agreed. "And I am certain to have a good many other officers. Putting all in all, I can make a show the people will enjoy—and so will I."

"You've waited a long time, Emperor," he said.

"By God, I have," I burst out. "But I will make up for that, too. Everyone who crossed me before I was exiled, everyone who backed either of the usurpers—those people will pay. How they will pay! If I have mercy on even one of them . . . you saw the will of God there, Myakes."

"Yes, I saw it," he said. "You've kept your promise, that's sure enough."

Not being certain of his tone, a matter in which he had more license than most in the Empire, I asked, "Are you arguing against anything I've done?"

"Oh, no, Emperor," he said emphatically. "After the storm, after you got into the city, how could I argue with anything you've done?" A moment later, he added, more than half to himself, "What good would it do, anyhow?"

"None whatever," I told him and he nodded, having already known that.

MYAKES

Brother Elpidios, when we rode south with Tervel's Bulgars, I figured it was the forlornest forlorn hope you ever did see. When we went into the aqueduct, I figured Apsimaros's soldiers would be waiting inside the city to slaughter us. When Apsimaros ran away—when Apsimaros ran away, Brother, I figured God really was on Justinian's side.

That's one reason I quit arguing with him. The other was that Jus tinian decided God was on his side, too. Now, Justinian had never been much for listening to anybody else. He even knew that was so. But once he got his crown back . . . once he got his crown back, what he said went.

And if you didn't like it, you went, too—off to the headsman, like as not.

And if you didn't go to the herdsman, you went some other way. Justinian had had a lot of time to think of interesting ways to get rid of people. Turned out he hadn't wasted it, either, not a moment's worth.

Yes, I kept quiet. No, it wasn't brave. But you don't have the vaguest notion what Justinian was like in those days, Brother. You would have kept your mouth shut, too, believe you me you would.

J U S T I N I A N

Herakleios lasted three weeks to the day after his brother Apsimaros came into my hands. What I had hoped would happen came to pass: on learning of the usurper's capture, his brother's supporters melted away until he was left with a band any self-respecting bandit chief could have bested. And one of his few remaining followers promptly proceeded to betray him to Barisbakourios.

"How are you going to reward him, Emperor?" Myakes asked. "With thirty pieces of silver?" He laughed, to show it was a joke.

It did not strike me funny. "Betraying a usurper's brother is hardly the same as yielding up the Son of God," I replied. "I'll give this fellow two pounds of gold." That made Herakleios more expensive than our Lord had been, but Judas, of course, did not—could not—get full value for Him.

Barisbakourios brought Herakleios into the imperial city a few days later. I rewarded my old comrade from Kherson more substantially than the soldier who had given him Herakleios: it was then that I named him general of the military district of the Opsikion, a post that, along with being one of the most important commands in the Roman Empire, paid its holder thirty pounds of gold a year. At the same time, I sent Theophilos, who, to my surprise, had served Barisbakourios well as his lieutenant general, to head the Karbisianoi, the Aegean fleet, a post paying five pounds of gold a year. The Aegean then being quiet, my assumption was that he could do no great harm in the position, and might do well.

As I had been with Leontios and Apsimaros, I was eager to speak with Herakleios, who had been the last man in arms against me. Barisbakourios led him before me; though not so decked in chains as Apsimaros had been on reaching Constantinople, Herakleios wore manacles that clanked when he went down in an awkward prostration. "You know what I will do with you, of course," I said as he got to his feet once more.

"You'll kill me some kind of way," he answered. "I don't doubt that for a minute." He had a guttural accent like his brother's and resembled him in bodily appearance, too, being tall and slim and lighter in complexion than most Romans.

In a couple of sentences, he also proved he had a good understanding of the way the world works. "You're right," I said. "You deserve nothing less."

He had courage. His shrug made the manacles clank again. "I hope you have the courtesy to make it quick," he said. "I wasn't the one who overthrew you. All I did was try to keep my own brother on the throne. I lost, and now I'm in your hands."

It was not begging. It was nothing like begging. He might have been reminding me of an appointment I had next week. Never before, never since, have I seen a man discuss his fate so dispassionately. His calm words swung me toward agreement where tears and histrionics would have earned him an ending opposite that which he craved. "Fair enough," I told him. "You'll not suffer."

"For which I thank you," he said, and then, still dispassionately, continued, "I never would have guessed you'd pull this off."

"God was on my side," I told him, to which he had no answer. I asked him a question about which I had been wondering since my days up in Kherson: "Is your name truly Herakleios, or did you change it when your brother changed his?"

"Herakleios is the name my mother gave me," he replied. "Had we both changed at the same time, he would have become Herakleios and I Tiberius. I was named for your—great-grandfather, is it?"

"Great-great," I said.

"Your great-great-grandfather, then, the famous Herakleios who saved the Roman Empire. My brother wanted to do the same thing." He raised an eyebrow; as I have noted, he kept his sangfroid in the face of death remarkably well. "You will admit, the Empire needed saving after three years of Leontios."

I shrugged. "Your brother became my enemy the instant he had the crown set on his own head instead of recalling me after he cast down Leontios."

"How could he?" Herakleios sounded honestly curious. "Your nose was lopped. I see you have had it repaired—you must have found a very clever surgeon—but I do not think you had done that back in the days when my brother first became Emperor of the Romans."

In that he was of course correct. But he was also my prisoner, under sentence of death, and I, not his brother, Emperor of the Romans. Nothing required that I answer him. Rather than doing so, I gestured to Barisbakourios, who in his turn gestured to the men under his command. They led Herakleios away to await his fate. To his credit, he did not tax me about the inconsistency he had exposed.

News spread rapidly of my return to Constantinople and my reassumption of the imperial power stolen from me ten years before. In Thrace, the pursuit first of Apsimaros and then of Herakleios brought word of my arrival to every town and village. In Anatolia, the officers I sent out to take over for any suspected of retaining their loyalty to the previous usurper let the soldiers and peasants know I was firmly in command in the imperial city.

I also sent messengers announcing my return to Oualid in Damascus, the new miscalled commander of the faithful having succeeded the accursed Abimelekh only a few months before I regained the throne. Merchant ships took the news to Alexandria, to the Phoenician cities—and to Kherson and Phanagoria.

Not long before autumn storms made travel on the Black Sea too unsafe to contemplate with equanimity (although, as I knew from horrifying experience, deadly storms could arise on that sea at any time), a merchant vessel from Phanagoria came down to Constantinople. Its captain, a certain Makarios, sought an immediate audience with me. On my servitors' learning he bore a message from Theodora, his request was granted at once.

After prostrating himself before me, he said, "Rejoice, Emperor, for your wife has borne you a son, and both were well, the latest report I had before sailing."

By then, I had grown accustomed to rewarding men who brought me good news. "Half a pound of gold for Makarios here!" I called out. The sea captain bowed himself almost double. A eunuch scribbled a note on a waxed tablet, thereby insuring the command would be remembered. "Has the boy been baptized?" I asked Makarios.

"Yes, Emperor, he has." Regardless of whether he had just become a richer man, Makarios suddenly looked apprehensive. He coughed a couple of times, nerving himself to continue. At last, he did: "Emperor, he was baptized as Tiberius."

The throne room grew very quiet. Courtiers and excubitores stared at me, wondering how I would respond to that. Well they might have; though Tiberius was a name my family used, it was also that which

Apsimaros had ruled. Putting those two facts together, I thought I understood how and why the name had been bestowed. "Tell me," I said to Makarios, "did Ibouzeros Gliabanos have a hand in naming the baby?"

"Why—yes, Emperor." He sounded astonished. "How could you know that?"

"Because my dearly beloved brother-in-law the khagan of the Khazars was, is, and always will be a trimmer. He could not have known I had beaten the usurper when the boy was born, could he?" I asked. Makarios shook his head. I went on, "Had I lost, the name would have pleased Apsimaros, since he stole it himself. And it . . . suits me well enough." I wondered if my uncle Tiberius still lived. I had not bothered to find out about him and his brother Herakleios. Come to think of it, I have not bothered to find out about the two of them to this day.

Makarios said, "Emperor, I am to tell you that your wife misses you and longs to come to Constantinople and lay your son in your arms."

"I miss her, too," I answered truthfully. "Her confinement being safely past, I shall send a fleet to Phanagoria—or to Kherson, if she'd rather; let the rich men there sweat to see the Augusta pass through on the way to the imperial city, after they tried to murder me—to bring her back to me. They can sail tomorrow, or I will know the reason why."

"Emperor, I beg your pardon, but you'd do better to wait," Makarios said. "I count myself lucky to have got here without bad weather. It's late in the year, it truly is."

"If I command the fleet to sail—" I began.

Makarios dared interrupt me: "Only God commands the weather, Emperor." Courtiers gasped. Since I had already executed a good many who opposed me, they thought the sea captain likely to be next. And killing him would have saved the fisc half a pound of gold.

But I refrained. The only thing I said was, "I hope that Cyrus has heard of my successful return, so he can come to Constantinople from Kherson this season."

"I don't know the man, Emperor; I'm sorry," Makarios said. "But the ship that brought the news to Phanagoria had touched at Kherson first, so I expect he knows about it, whoever he is."

"No one of any particular importance," I said. "He's only the man I've picked as the new patriarch of Constantinople."

"If he's no one in particular, who knows whether—" Makarios abruptly fell silent, hearing all of what I'd said, not the first part alone. I dismissed him and then dismissed him from my thoughts; that I can dredge his name from my memory as I write these words surprises me.

Cyrus, as chance would have it, arrived in Constantinople a few days later with a harrowing tale of tempest survived on the sea. Since I had my own story of that sort, the two of us traded them. That done, I summoned him to supper, at which time he said, "Emperor, you honor me beyond my deserts by raising me to the patriarchal throne."

"Nonsense," I told him. "You left a safe and comfortable post in Amastris to cross the sea and come to my aid because you saw—however you saw—I would be Emperor again. You having had faith in me, I now have faith in you. Loyalty I reward with loyalty, just as I reward treason with death."

He bowed his head. "May I give you the service you deserve."

"I expect you will," I answered, and he has, no doubt about it. He having arrived in Constantinople, the local synod, as was its duty under canon law, presented me with his name and those of two nonentities as candidates for the patriarchate, knowing in advance what my choice among them would be. Despite modesty, he has, I must say, made a splendid ecumenical patriarch.

And, as I told him at that supper, I was also proceeding with vengeance against those who had overthrown me ten years before and against those who espoused the cause of the usurper Apsimaros rather than my own. I made no secret of the vengeance I was taking; I have never made a secret of the vengeance I still continue to take. At my order, artisans erected several gibbets atop the inner wall to the city, so that I might edify the people by causing them to contemplate the fate of those stupid enough to have opposed me.

First to be hanged on the gibbets was Apsimaros's brother Herakleios. As I had promised him, his end was quick and easy. While he dangled there, I caused Apsimaros to be brought out of his cell under heavy guard to view the corpse. For the usurper's end I had something more elaborate in mind. Meanwhile, however, to keep the people in a contemplative mood, I executed various of the other officers who had been imperfectly loyal to me.

As Makarios had known it would, the season of autumn storms soon arrived; I was glad Cyrus had managed to come into the imperial city before travel became so dangerous only a desperate man would think about it. As ecumenical patriarch, he celebrated the glorious festival of our Lord's birth in the church of the Holy Wisdom.

A week or so before Lent began, I chose to put an end at last to Leontios and Apsimaros, thereby giving the city mob of Constantinople, in a rowdy mood in any case before the onset of the solemn season, something out of the ordinary to talk about and celebrate. To assure a large crowd in the hippodrome, I decreed a day of chariot racing. This sport, which I am given to understand was a commonplace up to the reign of the Emperor whose namesake I am, is reserved for special occasions these days, partly because the partisans of the rival teams are still given to riot and all manner of unseemly behavior to show their support and partly because the races are ruinously expensive and not even the imperial fisc can afford to offer them frequently.

Along with the horse races, I also announced a triumphal procession through the imperial city, from the Golden Gate to the hippodrome. People crowded under the colonnades on either side of the Mese to watch.

First came a company of excubitores, gorgeous in gilded parade armor with bright-dyed cloaks streaming after them. Behind them walked civilian servitors carrying sacks of silver miliaresia, from which they threw coins into the crowd, the occasion, while auspicious, not calling for gold.

After the men with the money glumly tramped Leontios and Apsimaros, each in the filthy tunic he had worn while imprisoned in the monastery of Delmatos, each with his hands manacled in front of him. So the people could tell which wicked usurper was which, a secretary with a large sign bearing each man's name followed him. And, for the benefit of the many who could not read, the secretaries called out the names of Leontios and Apsimaros in loud voices, as well as their crimes: "These vile worms dared rebel against the vicegerent of God on earth, Justinian, Emperor of the Romans!"

"*Tu vincas*, Justinian!" the people shouted, for I rode in a chariot drawn by white horses directly behind the overthrown usurpers. I waved to the right and then to the left, acknowledging the appropriateness of the old salute on this day, as on the day when I first reentered the Queen of Cities.

At my side marched faithful Myakes, who, of all my guardsmen, did by far the most in trying to prevent my ouster and who served me so long and well in my exile. Not for anything on earth would I have deprived him of the opportunity to share in avenging the outrages Leontios and Apsimaros had inflicted upon us.

MYAKES

Truth to tell, Brother Elpidios, by then I just wanted it over with. I would have been every bit as happy if Justinian had taken Leontios's head, and Apsimaros's, too, and then gone on with the rest of his business. Leontios had had his nose sliced, after all, and he'd been locked up for seven years. And I've already said I didn't have anything special against Apsimaros.

But nobody was going to change Justinian's mind. He'd wanted a show, and he was going to have himself a show. It was as simple as that. Who'd tell him anything different? He was Emperor of the Romans. Anybody who didn't like it would end up hanging on the wall, same as Apsimaros's brother Herakleios and his chums.

And the people had themselves a good time, same as they do at any parade—same as they did when Leontios stole the throne out from under Justinian, come to that. They cheered Justinian and threw things at Leontios and Apsimaros. If you didn't know better, you had to figure they'd stay on Justinian's side forever. If, I say. If.

J U S T I N I A N

Behind me came the stalwart friends I'd made in exile: Cyrus first among them, in his patriarchal regalia; Barisbakourios and his brother Stephen; Foolish Paul, without whose fishing boat we never would have reached the land of the Bulgars; and Theophilos from Doros, who kept improving. With them walked the spatharios Leo, who had served me so well on my return journey to the imperial city.

Another company of excubitores brought up the rear. Like that heading the procession, this company wore fancy parade armor. But the men had everyday weapons at hand, lest some ready-for-aught conspirators attempt a rescue of either usurper—although, in truth, why anyone would have wanted to rescue Leontios passes my comprehension.

Eggs and fruit and the occasional stone flew at Leontios and Apsimaros both. Without being so ordered, the driver of my chariot increased the distance between them and us so we should not be similarly pelted by accident or by malice under cover of accident. The stratagem succeeded, though I had a surfeit of the gagging stench or rotten eggs by the time we reached the hippodrome. But I was not dripping with them, as the two usurpers were.

A great cheer rose from the crowd in the hippodrome on our entering through the gate the chariots normally use. The races having been completed, the excubitores led the way around the churned-up dirt of the track toward the stands opposite the Kathisma: to the spot, in other words, where Leontios had had me mutilated a bit more than a decade before.

Now Leontios and his fellow usurper Apsimaros stumbled after the guards, the shackles they wore clanking with each step they took. On their nearing the grandstand, a chorus posted on the second level of the imperial Kathisma burst into the thirteenth verse of Psalm 91: "Thou hast attacked an asp and a basilisk, and hast trampled down a lion and a dragon!"

I turned my head to speak to Cyrus: "Surely the Lord wrote that verse for me, and surely He inspired you to recall it."

"Emperor, it is my duty and pleasure to serve you," the patriarch replied, modestly casting down his eyes.

No one will deny the city mob is foolish, fickle, and ever demanding new amusements. But neither will anyone deny that the people of Constantinople are the cleverest, best-educated folk in all the civilized world. Understanding at once the verse's multifarious aptness, they burst into a deafening storm of applause. The lion of course signified Leontios, the asp Apsimaros. Some of the more sophisticated no doubt also took in the double meaning of the basilisk, which at the same time implied both reptilian horror and a petty king, a true king or Emperor being not just *basiliskos* but *basileus*.

"This is the day the Lord hath made!" Cyrus cried, as Kallinikos had when I was being deposed. Then the people had cheered to see me cast down; now they applauded as I was raised high. Were I to be overthrown again, they might cheer once more, but that shall not come to pass, anyone who might dare such an outrage no longer being among the living.

When I say I was raised high on that day, I speak not only metaphorically but also literally. Myakes stepped forward and pushed Leontios and Apsimaros down before me. They bent their backs almost as if in prostration; Leontios, I saw with no small amusement, got horse dung in his bushy beard. And I, I sprang atop them, setting one red imperial boot on Leontios's back, the other on Apsimaros's, symbolizing in terms the veriest clod might understand my domination over them. The chorus sang out the prophetic verse once more, and the crowd acclaimed me and derided those who had defiled my throne with their presence on it.

"Mercy!" Leontios squealed beneath me. "I did not slay you. Have mercy!" Apsimaros, more manly or merely without hope, kept silent.

I ground my booted foot into Leontios's back. He groaned, but made no move to try to throw me off: excubitores stood round him with swords and spears and bows, ready to punish such insolence with bitter torment. The leeches in the stands, baying laughter at the usurpers' humiliation, would have laughed even louder to see blood flow. However little Leontios knew, he knew that much, having listened to their cheers while my blood spilled for the mob's delight.

Still standing atop the two toppled tyrants, I shouted to the crowd, as loud as I could: "Let them be taken to the Kynegion, there to have the sword sever their heads from their bodies!"

Most of the people cheered, jeering the usurpers and applauding the fate I had decreed for them. Leontios's shoulders began to heave under me, not because he was trying to throw me off but because he was shamelessly weeping. Up in the grandstand, I heard catcalls among the cheers, these surely coming from the more bloodthirsty, those who would sooner have had the executions carried out before their avid eyes.

That privilege, however, I reserved for myself. To placate the masses, I shouted out another announcement: "We shall have a second round of races here in the hippodrome tomorrow!" Universal rapture greeted that proclamation.

My springing down from the backs of Leontios and Apsimaros signaled to the mob the end of the day's festivities. I tasted the tone of their voices as they streamed out of the hippodrome. Despite not having watched the usurpers' heads leap from their bodies, they seemed well enough pleased with what they had witnessed.

Excubitores stirred Leontios and Apsimaros to their feet, and the two of them rose. Apsimaros was pale, his lips pressed against each other until they almost disappeared, but he did his best to show a brave front. Leontios, by contrast, presented a disgusting spectacle, and would have done so even without the horse dung in his beard. Not only did his tears of terror cut pale lines down his filthy cheeks, but greenish snot flowed out of the hole in his face where his nose had been and trickled through his mustache.

"The sooner the world is rid of you, the more pleasant a place it will be," I told him: an aesthetic judgment as well as a moral one. Incapable of coherent speech, he blubbered at me. "To the Kynegion," I told the guardsmen.

They had to drag Leontios to the amphitheater by the sea northeast of the church of the Holy Wisdom, his legs refusing to carry him. Apsimaros walked. I rode in the chariot behind them.

Was the masked executioner waiting there the man who had mutilated me? No one had—no one to this day has—admitted knowing which executioner that had been. I remain . . . most interested in learning, but at the time passed lightly over the question, other matters being more immediately urgent.

In the center of the Kynegion stood a chopping block, like that for poultry but larger. The stains on it were old and dried and dark, I having been in the habit of hanging rather than beheading the officers who had supported the cause of the two usurpers. Some fresh stains would go on it now.

The executioner had a sword on his hip, a weapon larger and thicker-bladed than a cavalryman's sword: one made for chopping. Bowing to me, he asked, "Which of them first, Emperor?"

Having been weighing that very question in my mind as I traveled from the hippodrome, I replied without hesitation: "Let it be Apsimaros. That way, Leontios can see what lies ahead for him."

Leontios moaned. Apsimaros nodded to me. "If I had won, you would have ended here," he said. He walked to the block, knelt, and laid his head upon it. "Strike hard," he told the executioner. The fellow looked my way. I nodded. Apsimaros was doing his best to die well. I would allow it.

Up went the sword. Leontios's eyes followed it with horrified fascination, though it would not bite his neck . . . yet. Down it fell. Anyone who has been in battle, or for that matter anyone who has watched and listened to a butcher cutting up a carcass with a cleaver, will know the sound it made on striking home.

Apsimaros's head sprang from his body. A fountain of blood, brightest red in the winter sun, gushed from the stump of his neck, drenching the head, the dried grass on the floor of the Kynegion, and the chopping block. His legs kicked wildly; but for the manacles, his arms would have flailed, too. He pissed and shit himself, the stench plain even through the overwhelming iron smell of blood.

Leontios slumped forward in a faint. I walked over and kicked Apsimaros's head to one side; my boots already being crimson, contact with the blood-soaked relic would not mar them. To one of the excubitores, I said, "Wash this off so people can see who it is—was—and take it to the Milion for display."

"Aye, Emperor," he said, while his comrades dragged the rest of Apsimaros's corpse out of the way.

No doubt wanting to be helpful, the executioner told the guardsman, "I have baskets here. You can use one to carry that."

"Ah, good," the soldier said. "Thanks."

Other soldiers hauled Leontios over to the chopping block and positioned him so the executioner could do his work. But, before the man could raise that heavy sword, I said, "Wait. I want him to know what is happening to him, just as he knew when he tormented me."

Obediently, the executioner waited. Leontios remaining limp, one of the excubitores stooped and pinched his earlobe between the nails of thumb and forefinger. This produced the desired effect; Leontios writhed and twisted and opened his eyes. On doing so, he discovered his head lay on the block. He let out a hoarse scream—"No!"—and tried to twist away.

"Seize him!" I cried, and several excubitores did exactly that. Even after they forced him back to the proper posture, though, he kept shouting and twisting his head from side to side: exactly as I had done when the executioner serving him had tried to slit my tongue. As the soldiers had done then with me, so now one of them seized Leontios by the hair and held his head still. The wretch tried to bite, his teeth clicking together. It did him no good.

Even so, the executioner did not make a clean job of the kill, as he had with Apsimaros. He had to strike twice, the first blow merely spraying blood in all directions and turning Leontios's screams to half-drowned gurgles. At the second, though, the death the usurper so richly deserved was visited upon him at last.

"I do beg your pardon, Emperor," the executioner said as Leontios's blood poured out over the ground. "I should have done better there." He sounded professionally embarrassed, as a builder might after erecting a house with a leaky roof.

"Never mind," I told him. "He earned what you gave him. Had you taken his head with a carpenter's saw, I should not have said a word against you."

"A carpenter's saw?" the fellow exclaimed. By the way he recoiled from me, he found the idea more nearly appalling than appealing. Executioners are, from my dealings with them, a conservative lot, very much set in their ways.

Leontios's body kept twitching a good deal longer than Apsimaros's had done, whether because the executioner had required two strokes rather than one or simply because he was too stupid to realize he was dead I could not say. Helpful still, the executioner gave the excubitores another one of those baskets in which to carry Leontios's head, then went off to wash the blood from his blade and examine the edge for nicks to be honed away before his next tour of duty.

I watched as the excubitores set the heads of Leontios and Apsimaros on pikes in front of the Milion. Placards proclaimed their crimes to the crowd. Turning to Myakes, I said, "Amazing how far two heads go to make up for ten long years of misery."

"So it is, Emperor," he said. "Now that you've avenged—"

"Avenged?" I broke in. "Not yet!"

"But . . ." Myakes hesitated, as well he might have, before going on. "You've dealt with the patriarch, there's Leontios and Apsimaros, you've already taken care of Apsimaros's brother, there are all those dead officers—"

I interrupted again: "Plenty more where they came from, by God and His Son, and I aim to root out every one of them, too. I've hardly started sweeping the bureaucracy clean of traitors, and you know what I owe the Khersonites. I'll give it to them, too; see if I don't. I am not yet avenged, Myakes. I have barely begun."

"Can't you let this be enough, what you've already done?" he said.

"While one who opposed me remains alive, it is not enough," I replied. "Treason is a wart on the face of the Roman Empire, and I will cut it off."

Hearing the iron in my voice, he bowed his head. "Yes, Emperor," he said quietly.

MYAKES

I did try, Brother Elpidios. I thought, when he came back to power, he would get rid of the two usurpers and the most important people who had backed them, and then he'd get on with the business of being Emperor again.

It didn't happen. I wish it had. But he'd been thinking about revenge, eating revenge, drinking revenge, breathing revenge, dreaming revenge, all the time he'd been in exile. Once he got the chance to take it, he took and took and . . .

This wasn't the only time I tried to get him to slow down, to think about what he was doing, to see if maybe he'd had enough. You just saw how much good it did me. As time went on, I tried less and less often. What, Brother? The sin of despairing? Well, maybe it was. The sin of not being listened to, that's certain.

JUSTINIAN

With winter wearing on toward spring, the logothete in charge of petitions approached me with a rolled-up parchment. This was no longer the elderly—indeed, the ancient—Sisinniakes, who had died during my years in exile, but a certain Philotheos, the successor appointed by one of the usurpers. Thus far, having nothing more against him than that fact, I had permitted him to remain in office.

After prostrating himself and gaining my permission to rise, he handed me the parchment, saying, "Emperor, this petition for return from exile comes to you from an island in the Ionian Sea, Kephallenia by name. The petitioner is a certain Bardanes, son of the patrician Nikephoros, who, he writes, is also sometimes known as Philippikos." Seeing me stir, Philotheos said, "Am I to gather that this man is known to you, Emperor?"

"I first met him almost twenty years ago," I answered.

"Ah. I see." The logothete coughed delicately. "Are you aware of the crime for which he was sent into exile on this distant, inhospitable island?"

"Yes, word of that reached me in the distant, inhospitable land to which I was sent into exile," I said, which served to take Philotheos's toploftiness down a peg. "He dreamt of an eagle, and Apsimaros heard about it."

"This is correct." Philotheos licked his lips in anticipation of what would follow. "Do I assume, therefore, that, should you deign to recall him, you shall to so to requite him as you did those two whose heads remain on display at the Milion?" His tone said he had confidence in the assumption.

So much confidence had he, indeed, that his jaw dropped on my saying, "No." I went on, "I gave the usurpers what they deserved: they were my foes. Bardanes Philippikos always served me well. Not only do I intend recalling him, but I shall restore him to the rank formerly his. Prepare for my signature the necessary orders for his release and convey them to the governor of Kephallenia, whoever he may be." The island and its affairs, such as they were, had before that moment not drawn my notice since my return to Constantinople.

Looking flabbergasted, Philotheos went off to do as I had ordered of him. From behind me, I heard another cough. I turned to find Myakes' face set in disapproving lines, as it often was at that time. "Emperor, Bardanes has done well enough on Kephallenia all these years," he said. "Why don't you leave him there for the rest of his days?"

"Now that the whole Roman Empire recognizes me as Emperor once more, I can repay all my debts," I answered: "the ones I owe to those who wronged me, and the ones I owe to those who served me well. When we were campaigning in Thrace, Bardanes might well have saved my life from that Sklavinian hidden in the river."

Myakes snorted. "The only thing that poor barbarian wanted was for the lot of us to go away so he could run without anybody seeing him. He was about as dangerous as a weanling calf."

"You were jealous then of the favor I showed him," I said. "Are you still, after so many years?"

"Call it whatever you please." He stubbornly stuck out his chin. "I say that anybody who dreams of becoming Emperor isn't safe to have around. Let him stay on his island and imagine he's Emperor of that."

"I told Philotheos what to do," I said. "He is doing it. When Bardanes returns, I may use him. He was a good commander. Deny it if you can."

"I don't like it." As was often true, Myakes did not know when to yield.

"I did not ask whether you liked it. I explained my reasons for doing it, which is more than you deserve. I have made my will clear, and my will shall be done. Do you understand that, Myakes?"

He bowed his head at last. How could he do otherwise? I was—I am—the Emperor.

MYAKES

He would have done better to listen to me, Brother Elpidios, then and some other times, too. Or maybe in the end it wouldn't have mattered, anyway. No way of telling that, not really. If you change one thing, most of the others stay the same. You never can know, not for certain.

But, considering how things ended up, I wish Bardanes had stayed on Kephallenia.

JUSTINIAN

All winter long, I had been making plans for Theodora's entrance into Constantinople—and for that of little Tiberius, too. I wanted to see my wife's face as I paraded her down the Mese. From Atil and from Phanagoria, she imagined she knew what the imperial city was like. I smiled whenever I thought of that: she was like a man who, having seen two copper folleis, fancied he could tell his neighbors about a gold nomisma.

I also wanted to remind her how much I valued her, and to show I cared for her still, despite my having returned to the heart of the civilized world. Accordingly, as soon as spring approached, I sent Theophylaktos the eunuch to Phanagoria with a good-sized fleet to take my wife from Ibouzeros Gliabanos and bring her back to the imperial city.

No one said a word to me about the earliness of the season. When I commanded the fleet to sail, sail it did. Having been away from The-odora for most of a year, I was impatient to have her by my side once more, and even more impatient to set eyes on the son I had never seen. I knew, too, that the fleet would have some considerable layover in Phan-agoria while Theodora came thither from whatever part of Khazaria to which she had removed herself—Atil, most likely—on my departure from Phanagoria for the land of the Bulgars.

Not to stretch the tale unduly, the fleet turned out to have sailed too early in the season for its own safety. A storm blew up on the Black Sea the day before the fleet would have made port at Phanagoria. Theo-phylaktos survived, but several ships went down and more than three hundred sailors drowned.

This news I gained from Makarios, the merchant captain who the fall before had brought me news of Theodora's confinement and the birth of Tiberius. He had got to Phanagoria ahead of my fleet, escaping the storm, and set out after the survivors limped into that town. After re-counting the unfortunate tale, he added, "The *tudun* of Phanagoria also told me to give you a message from Ibouzeros Gliabanos."

"Did he?" I said, amused. "Go ahead." I expect it to be a warning against killing any more officials the Khazar khagan had sent out to gov-ern the cities he ruled.

But Makarios said, "He told me to tell you two or three ships would have been plenty to bring your wife back here to Constantinople. He says you didn't need to throw so many men away doing that. Did you think you were taking her by force?" He held up a hasty hand, as well he might have. "These are his words, Emperor, not mine. All I'm doing is delivering them."

"I understand that," I said. "I am not angry at you. But the Khazars will pay for their insolence. All the cities up there will pay for what they did to me. If I were you, Captain Makarios, I'd trade along the southern coast of the Black Sea, not the northern one. Once I am through with those towns, they will have little to trade."

"Thanks for the warning, Emperor," he said, but I could tell by the way he said it that he did not believe I intended my words to be taken literally. He having brought me good news, I hope his business has not suffered in the subsequent years of my reign.

•   •   •

Two months and more passed by before Theophylaktos and the ships of his fleet still floating returned to the imperial city. I bore the delay with such patience as I could, knowing from my own experience how long news and people took to travel across the tremendous breadth of the steppe.

At last, though, a messenger brought word that the fleet was pulling into the Golden Horn, whose harbors were closest to the palace at Blakhernai where I still dwelt. Hurrying up to the roof of the palace, I saw the ships with my own eyes. On one of them would be my wife and son, although they were not so near as to let me make them out. I called orders to the servants and departed.

The fleet was just tying up at the docks when I rode up on a bay gelding: a much handsomer piece of horseflesh than the Bulgar pony aboard which I had come down to Constantinople, even if lacking in both intelligence and endurance by comparison. As I hurried down the pier toward Theodora and Tiberius, I prayed they had had a smoother voyage on the Black Sea than my last one.

"Justinian!" A familiar voice made me spot one waving hand among many. I waved back to my wife, who held up my son for me to see.

I stared and stared at the child of my flesh, he who will succeed me when that flesh is subjected to the common fate of all mankind. He was plump and reddish and, like his mother, had a full head of dark brown hair. After noting these characteristics of his, I noted one of my own: intense surprise that I could view a child of mine without being filled with anger and hatred, the only emotions suffusing me whenever I set eyes on my daughter Epiphaneia.

Sailors having extended the gangplank from the ship to the wharf, Theodora left the vessel and entered the imperial city. "Justinian, here is your son," she said in Greek that showed she had been practicing with merchants or priests during her sojourn in Khazaria, and she handed Tiberius to me.

My hands were unpracticed at holding babies. Tiberius cared not at all. Seeing me smile at him, he smiled back, enormously. I laughed, and so did he, a baby's squeal of joy unadulterated. Whatever his elders might have thought, he cared no more about my nose's being less that it might have than he did about the unpracticed fingers out of whose grip he tried to squirm. His sublime indifference to my features would of itself have sufficed to endear him to me.

Then, continuing to hold him in the crook of one arm, I turned and used the other to wave out to Constantinople, imitating my wife's diction as I did so: "Theodora, here is your city." I could not resist adding, "Is it not almost as grand as Phanagoria?"

Taking a wifely privilege, Theodora stuck out her tongue at me. "You told me stories about Constantinople," she said. "I thought you were as big a liar as a bard who sings songs to my brother the khagan. Now I see you did not tell the truth because you did not say enough."

"Tervel the Bulgar told me the same thing," I answered. "His ambassadors would come back from the Queen of Cities and say what they saw, and he would not believe them. When he saw for himself, he too knew they had been keeping much to themselves."

"I want to see all of this city," Theodora said. "If it is mine, I need to know it."

"Soon you will see the most splendid pearl in the necklace, when I crown you Augusta and Tiberius Emperor in the church of the Holy Wisdom," I said, pointing southeast to show her where in the city the great church lay. Because of its height, the exterior of the huge dome was visible from most of Constantinople, though no one, viewing only the exterior, could gain the smallest inkling of the magnificence housed within.

After we had stood talking for a little while—and after Theophylaktos had got down on his hands and knees, not to prostrate himself before me but to kiss the tarred, gull-dung–smeared timbers of the harbor belonging to his native city in thanksgiving for having come home safe at last—a commotion at the foot of the pier made me look in that direction. Approaching amidst a considerable retinue was a litter carried by bearers with eagles embroidered on the chests of their silk tunics. The walls and even the handles of the chair were gilded; silk worked with golden threads curtained the windows.

Theodora's eyes, already wide, grew wider. "Who rides in this— thing?" she asked. Her Greek, though much improved, had no words for what she was seeing.

One of the attendants opened the door to the litter. The woman who descended wore robes very much like mine. "Come with me," I said to Theodora. "I'll introduce you to my mother." Word of my wife's arrival must have reached the grand palace almost as soon as it got to me.

My wife inferred a good deal from my tone. Quietly, she asked, "You and your mother do not like each other?"

"Not always," I answered, as quietly. "God willing, you and Tiberius will make a difference." That, after refusing my mother's urging to remarry, I had wed a barbarian princess had made a difference, and not a good one. But a grandson would set no small weight in the other pan of the scale. Raising my voice, I said, "Mother, I present to you my wife, Theodora, who shall be Augusta, and my son Tiberius, who continues our line. My wife, I present to you my mother, the Augusta Anastasia."

Politely, Theodora inclined her head. "I greet you, mother of my husband," she said. The words were Greek, but I got the idea she was translating them from Khazar ceremonial.

"Welcome to Constantinople," my mother said, and then, more warmly, "Welcome home." She held out her arms. "Let me see your son."

She knew how to hold an infant, having gained experience with me, with my brother Herakleios, and, now that I think on it, with Epiphaneia as well. She smiled down at Tiberius, and he up at her: he would smile at anyone who smiled his way. He made the sort of noises infants make when they are happy. And then, his grandmother still holding him, he pissed himself.

I thought she would be annoyed. She started to laugh. "These things happen," she said, and turned a thoughtful eye my way. "They happened with you." To Theodora, she added, "He is a handsome boy."

"Thank you," my wife said. She turned and called in the Khazar language, waving as she did so. A slave woman who had accompanied her on the ship from Phanagoria came hurrying up. Theodora took Tiberius from my mother and handed him to the woman. She spoke some more as well. Not having used the barbarous jargon of the nomads who dwell north of the Black Sea since my own departure from Phanagoria, I understood not a word she said, but context made her desire plain: that Tiberius's deplorable state be corrected. This duly came to pass.

My mother said, "I know Justinian will have you live with him at the palace he has chosen for his own, Theodora, but you must bring your grandson to me often, so I can see him and play with him."

"I will do this," Theodora replied. If she saw anything unusual in the separate households my mother and I maintained, she kept quiet about it. I do not believe she did, it being the custom among the Khazars for the khagan to live apart from even his closest family.

Theodora having ridden across the steppe with me from Atil to Phanagoria, I felt certain she would prefer a horse to a litter for the far shorter journey from the harbor to the Blakhernai palace. A litter waited nonetheless, to convey Tiberius (and, incidentally, the slave who had charge of him) to the palace.

My mother's eyes grew wide when she saw Theodora swing up into the saddle, riding astride like a man. Somewhat to my surprise, she said nothing; she had made up her mind to be polite to my wife, even if more for Tiberius's sake than on account of Theodora's own multifarious virtues.

I rode back to Blakhernai alongside Theodora: a little ahead of her, in fact, not only because I was Emperor but also because I knew the way. She exclaimed at everything, as any newcomer to this God-guarded and imperial city will do. But, for her, *everything* was more all-encompassing than it might have been for, say, a Roman from an Anatolian town. "Stones in the roadway!" she murmured at one point, the very idea of paving being exotic to her.

"Yes," I said happily, as if I had invented cobblestones myself.

She kept craning her neck. "All the buildings are so high," she said; we were riding between rows of three- and four-story apartment houses, nothing at all out of the ordinary for Constantinople. People on the balconies overhanging the street peered down at us. Some of them waved. None presumed to empty chamber pots on our heads, which has happened before in the history of the city. "So high," she repeated. "Why don't they fall down?"

From time to time, in earthquakes, they do fall down. I forbore to mention that, saying instead, "Our builders know what they're about."

She accepted it: how could she do otherwise, this being her first journey through Constantinople? When we got to the palace wherein I had dwelt since returning to the imperial city—and where I dwell yet—servants and slaves and eunuchs came out and prostrated themselves before us. Though the Khazars have a somewhat different ritual, she grasped what that meant. "These are all yours?" she asked in no small astonishment.

That I understood; her brother the khagan, though living in great luxury, had but a fraction of my retainers. "These are some of what is mine," I answered proudly—and truthfully. "They are also some of what is yours."

Theophylaktos, ever so delighted to be back in the imperial city, took charge of Theodora then, conveying her to the chamber off the hall of Okeanos that had been readied against her arrival. I saw no more of her until we dined together as the sun was setting. By then, serving woman had plucked her eyebrows, powdered and rouged her cheeks, painted her lips, and curled her hair. She would never look like a woman born in the Roman Empire, but she looked more like one than I had ever seen her. "You are lovely," I told her.

"Am I?" She shrugged. "In Khazaria, we decorate horses like this, not women."

From that day forth, though, she voiced no further complaints against Roman fashion. And she praised the food highly. Full of roast goat soused with fat myself, I said, "These are the dishes they imagined they could make in Phanagoria. Now you taste them as they should be." A servant poured me more wine. "The vintages are better, too."

"Yes," she said emphatically, having also been sampling those vintages.

Presently, Theophylaktos escorted her to my bedchamber, then departed to let us celebrate a mystery in which he had no hope of sharing. Two or three of the serving women would no doubt be downcast at Theodora's return, for the attentions I had given them in her absence would cease, except, perhaps, for occasional amusements.

"My wife," I said, barring the door.

"My husband," she answered. A proper Roman wife would have cast her eyes down to the floor in modesty. Theodora boldly met my gaze. I had not the heart to reprove her, not when she had proved herself loyal to me at her brother's expense. For treachery, the sword; for its reverse, rewards.

All at once curious, I asked, "What did Ibouzeros Gliabanos say when you came back to him and Papatzun didn't?"

Her smile was exactly that which I should have used had I been in her place. "He said many, many, very many very bad things. But all the time he said them, the way he said them was—" Running out of Greek, she used a word in the Khazar language, expecting me to know what it meant.

And, for a wonder, it was a word I chanced to recall. "Admiring?" I said, giving it to her in the tongue of the Roman Empire.

"Admiring, yes, thank you," she said. "Like he hated and had pride for you at the same time."

That probably went a long way toward accounting for the khagan's mocking message after my fleet met shipwreck. Having thrown in his lot with Apsimaros, he must have hoped I would fail in overthrowing the usurper, but, on my success (and, indeed, on my successful escape from his trap before that), he could not help but show a certain reluctant respect.

Theodora looked from the barred door to the bed in front of which I stood. Pointedly, she said, "Did you call me here to talk about my brother?"

I burst out laughing, half scandalized, half delighted. As I knew, Theodora had been a maiden the night we wed. But, on being properly introduced thereto, she had come to take no small delight in that which passes between man and woman. Once I left Phanagoria, she would have done without. Of my own amusements in that regard during the time we were apart, I said nothing, nor did she inquire, knowing the man's prerogative in such affairs.

But we were apart no longer. After putting out all the lamps in the bedchamber save one alone, I divested her of the robe she wore. Even by the light of that single lamp, I saw how childbirth had changed her body. Her breasts were larger and softer than I remembered, her hips thicker, the skin on her belly looser and marked with fine pale tracings it had not held before the child she'd carried stretched it. As far as fleshly perfection went, the serving maids with whom I had been dallying in Theodora's absence were without doubt her superiors.

None of them, however, had saved me in time of need. None of them had stood apart from their brothers to save me. None of them had given me a son to be Emperor after me. And so, while they were pleasant and diverting, Theodora was my wife.

After I made myself naked, she had no cause to complain of the salute I gave her, wordless though it was. When we embraced, standing there by the bed, my lance stood between us, but only for a moment. "So warm," she said, moving it to rub against her belly.

Before long, we lay down together. Each of us knew what pleased the other; I had nothing in which to instruct her, as I had needed to do when bedding a new serving girl. Once kisses and caresses had excited us both, she rolled onto her back, her legs open, inviting me to complete the conquest of her secret place.

That I wasted no time in doing. Theodora's breath sighed out as I thrust myself deep into her. Her thighs gripped my flanks, I rode her until she gasped and called out my name and what I have always taken to be a string of Khazar endearments, though I have never asked her the meaning of the words.

I had not yet spent myself within her, as I had usually done at her moment of delight when we enjoyed the marital couch before my enforced departure from Phanagoria. Enormous in the dim lamplight, her eyes looked past me, through me, rather than at me. Realizing my lance retained its temper, she murmured, "Go on. Oh, go on"—again, immodest, but in its way immensely flattering.

On I went. Again she tensed beneath me. Again she quivered. Again she called my name. And, this time, I sent my seed deep into her womb a moment later.

"You are a big man, a great man," she said admiringly. "You go on and on, you make me crazy for you." She mimed clambering atop me and taking me by force.

I laughed with her, a laugh not far from exhaustion. The truth of things—a truth I kept from her—was that I kept on and on because I took less pleasure from each single stroke than I had before Tiberius passed out through the way on which I was now going in. The sheath into which I thrust my sword now fitting more loosely than had been the case, I had to work harder to reach my full pleasure. Her giving me less satisfaction was, precisely and in inverse proportion, as those learned in arithmetic are wont to say, the occasion for my giving her more.

Having thus labored long and hard, I fell asleep, awakening sometime later from a vivid erotic dream of the sort commonly sent by Satan to tempt us Christians away from the paths of virtue. This particular erotic dream, however, was sent not by Satan but by Theodora, who had amused herself by finding a way to revive my manhood while I lay snoring. Once I was not only revived but awake, she impaled herself on me and, moving slowly and languorously, brought both of us another round of joy. Though unsure whether I could complete my half of that wordless bargain, in the end I managed it.

We both slept then, waking only with the sunrise. The bedclothes bore stains from my seed dribbling out of her in the night: not the stains of maidenhead overwhelmed, as on the first night, but those of a deeper, longer-lasting intimacy. "I am glad you're with me again," I said, and, despite her body's being somewhat less enjoyable than before, I spoke the truth.

My having chosen to dwell at the palace in the Blakhernai district rather than the grand palace furnished the opportunity for a parade through most of the imperial city when the time came to crown Theodora Augusta and Tiberius junior Emperor. This met with the raucous approval of the Constantinopolitan city mob, more of whom were able to gape at the procession that would have been the case had we gone only the short distance from the grand palace up to the church of the Holy Wisdom.

It also met with Theodora's approval, for it allowed her to see the many monuments and churches and splendid buildings lying along the Mese. We did not solicit Tiberius's opinion, as he was still far too small for it to matter in any way. From somewhere—God only knows where—Theophylaktos produced an imperial robe of a size appropriate for a baby. When dressed therein, Tiberius looked absurdly majestic—and, I must say, majestically absurd.

Ceremonial required Theodora to hold Tiberius up for the people of Constantinople to see and to admire throughout the entire procession.

This proved one disadvantage of making the aforesaid procession longer; not far past the column of Markianos, she whispered to me, "My arms will fall off."

"Keep going anyhow," I whispered back; departing from tradition was dangerous. When she looked mutinous, I added, "Besides, they all love him." Her face softened, for that was obviously true. Women cooed and men smiled at the spectacle of a plump, good-natured baby—which Tiberius was—decked out in a miniature version of his father's magnificent robes.

"So sweet!" a woman exclaimed, and heads close by her bobbed up and down in agreement.

"You see?" I said to Theodora.

"I see," she replied, but, never being one to shy from speaking her mind, she added, "I wish you carried him a while." Then, proving how much better her Greek had become, she made a pun, saying, "I carried him nine months already."

"My turn will come inside the great church," I said. She subsided, recognizing that against necessity one struggled in vain. Ceremonial and necessity, when mentioned in matters pertaining to the Emperor of the Romans, might as well be one and the same.

We passed through the Forum of Constantine, paraded by the church of St. Euphemia near the hippodrome, and came up to the Milion, which marks the end of the Mese. The heads of Leontios and Apsimaros were still on display in front of it, both somewhat the worse for wear but distinguishable one from the other on account of Leontios's mutilation.

Deliberately, Theodora turned her back on the last remains of the two usurpers. "Revenge," she said, "is good."

"Truly God was wise when He sent me to your brother's court," I told her, receiving in return a proud smile.

Not far past the Milion stands the church of the Holy Wisdom. "It is the biggest building I have ever seen," Theodora said, peering up and up and up at the massive structure of golden sandstone. From the outside, the massiveness of the church is its most noteworthy feature. Like an egg, it hides its riches within a plain shell.

When we went into the narthex, the outer chamber before the worship area itself, Theodora exclaimed at the mosaics. "Yes, they are fine," I agreed, "but you will find work that comes close to them at the Blakhernai palace, and work to match them in the grand palace. However . . ."

We went on, into the naos itself. Cyrus the ecumenical patriarch waited for us beside the golden altar table. And he waited longer than strict ceremonial would have dictated, too, for Theodora, having decided to stare up into the great dome, stood transfixed, apparently unable to go forward.

Following her gaze, I also looked up into the dome. Having come to the great church many times, I normally took even such a marvel for granted: so familiarity enslaves us all. Now, though, I saw as it were with new eyes, viewing it, thanks to Theodora, as if for the first time once more. The sunbeams streaming through the many windows ringing the base of the dome, light striking off the golden tesserae in the dome itself, shifting if I moved my head by so much as a digit's breadth . . .

"It floats in the sky," Theodora whispered. "Nothing holds it up but the light. It is not part of the building."

None of that, of course, was literally true. And yet every word of it seemed true. Having once begun to stare up into the dome myself, I needed a distinct effort of will to look away. I touched Theodora on the arm, which called her back to herself. Together, we approached the altar. Now Theodora could see and appreciate the marble and precious metal that had been lavished on the great church. Before, the overmastering splendor of the dome commanding her attention, no lesser marvel had been able to show itself to her.

Cyrus prayed, beseeching God's mercy and lovingkindness for me, for my family, and for the Roman Empire. When I became Emperor of the Romans, George, then ecumenical patriarch, had set the crown on my head, but it is the Emperor who crowns both the junior Emperor and the Augusta. The assembled grandees having added their acclamations to those of Cyrus, the patriarch handed me the first of the crowns I was to bestow.

"Behold the Emperor Tiberius!" I cried, and set the crown on my son's head. I kept hold of the crown as well, it being made for a fully grown man. On feeling something brush against his hair, Tiberius whipped his little head around, trying to find out what it was. When he saw the crown, he grabbed for it; his hands were beginning to obey his will. Once he had seized it, he tried to bring it down to his mouth so he could chew on it, as he did with everything that came within his reach.

"Many years to the Emperor Tiberius!" the nobles and bureaucrats of Constantinople cried. The acclamation was more casual than on many such occasions, many of the grandees being diverted by the junior—very junior—Emperor's antics. From the women's gallery came more laughter and sighs of amusement: the noblewomen shared affection for a baby with their humble cousins on the street.

Tu vincas was not a shout that went up at the coronation of any junior Emperor, conquest being the prerogative of the ruling Emperor. I could not even leave the crown on Tiberius, as I should have done had he been older. Once I had satisfied the symbolic requirement of placing it on his head, I took it away again. Tiberius reached for it, and howled when he could not get it.

More laughter rose and echoed from the dome. Theodora rocked Tiberius in her arms till he calmed. Having waited for that moment, I took the second crown from the hands of the ecumenical patriarch. The Augusta is more often crowned in the Augustaion, the enclosed open space south of the church of the Holy Wisdom, but I performed the ceremony inside the great church, combining it with the coronation of my son. Theophylaktos had grumbled a little at the proposal, but not much. And, being Emperor, I had my way.

At my gesture, Theodora slightly inclined her head. I set the crown on it, saying, "Behold the Augusta Theodora!" Tiberius, meanwhile, beheld the crown on his mother's head, let out a squeal of delight, and tried to get it, imperially certain it had been placed there for his amusement alone.

Over the echo of that squeal, more acclamations rang out. Most were in Latin, the ceremony for crowning the Augusta having changed less over the years than that for the Emperor. Indeed, it was my great-great-grandfather who changed the official title of the ruler of the Roman Empire from Augustus to the simple word Emperor.

"Thank you," Theodora said when the acclamations had faded. "God bless you." I nodded, well pleased, having wanted her to use those words to remind the grandees she was of Christian faith even if of Khazar blood.

I took the first crown from Cyrus once more and, accompanied by my wife (who still carried our son in her arms) and the ecumenical patriarch, went out through the narthex to the entranceway to the church of the Holy Wisdom. The crowd out there—people lacking the importance to be admitted to the great church to witness the coronation ceremony with their own eyes—burst into cheers to see Theodora adorned with the Augusta's crown. They cheered even louder when, as I had done inside the church, I set the junior Emperor's crown on Tiberius's small head.

Servants flung coins into the crowd from sacks they carried for the occasion: gold and silver both here. Rather than watching the city mob struggle over the largesse thus distributed, I went back into the great church. Again, the nobles and high functionaries shouted out fulsome acclamations for the newly crowned Tiberius and Theodora.

They had, no doubt, acclaimed Apsimaros a year before. They had, no doubt, acclaimed Leontios as fulsomely ten years before. They would, no doubt, acclaim some other vile, worthless usurper as fulsomely should he chance to overthrow me.

I did not aim to give the whores the chance.

My mother beamed at me, saying, "I am very glad to see you using the grand palace once more. I know your memories of those who dwelt here before you came back are unpl—"

With a sharp chopping gesture of my right hand, I cut her off. "This palace has a larger dining hall than the one at Blakhernai."

"Reason enough," my mother said. "I am also pleased to see you reconciling yourself with some of the people who remained busy in the imperial city after you were forced to leave. That way lies security." I made no answer. She was in any case not seeking one, as she swung all her attention to Tiberius. "How is the littlest Emperor?" She punctuated that by tickling him under the chin. By way of reply, the littlest Emperor squeaked with delight.

One of the spatharioi I had appointed since returning to the city, a certain Helias, came up to me and said, "Emperor, everything is ready."

"Good," I told him.

He was about to go when a cook came running out of the kitchen, crying, "Who is this black devil who wants to work with us?" He made the sign of the cross. "I have never seen such an ugly man in my life!"

"Oh, that's my cook," Helias answered. "I call him John, because I can't pronounce his real name. He's an Indian or an Ethiopian: something like that. He *is* ugly, but he can really cook. He's put a belly on me since I bought him six months ago, I'll tell you that. When I heard the Emperor had a banquet in mind, I brought him along to help."

"Let me see him," I said, curious to learn whether he would resemble Auriabedas.

The cook trotted off, returning in a little while with a fellow who in fact did not much look like the little man who had restored my nose. This man was tall and muscular, with skin black rather than brown and hair growing in tight little curls. His features were hard and coarse, his nose, though seeming undamaged, even flatter than mine.

After clumsily prostrating himself, he spoke in bad Greek: "Emperor, you eat my food, you like my food."

"All right, John," I said, and, diverted by his strange appearance, gave him a nomisma, which he took with a loud, shrill whoop of delight. I turned to the cook who had brought him into my presence. "He may be ugly, but he seems to have no harm in him. Let him cook, so long as he does not bother the rest of you."

Bowing, the cook led John back into the kitchens. That proved well timed, for the invited guests began arriving shortly thereafter. One by one, they prostrated themselves, bowed to my mother and to my wife, and let eunuchs take them to the places assigned them at the tables. Having been seated, they began drinking wine and talking shop with one another, as men of similar trades will do when cast together.

None of them paid any special attention to the magnificence of the hall in which they were enjoying themselves. It was, for these function-aries of intermediate to high rank, a familiar setting. All of them had frequently come to the grand palace while Apsimaros and, before him, Leontios, had set their fundaments on the throne. Some of them I re-membered from the days before my exile; a few I remembered from as far back as the days of my father's reign.

I greeted them with the nineteenth verse of the twelfth chapter of the book of Luke: " 'Soul, thou hast much goods laid up for many years; take thine ease, eat, drink, and be merry.' "

My mother, whose piety, always deep, had strengthened further in the years of my exile, looked sharply at me. I returned my blandest stare, and she subsided. The bureaucrats and courtiers I had assembled—they must have numbered about sixty altogether—lifted their cups in saluta-tion. "May you also be merry, Emperor," one of them called, whereupon the rest gave forth with loud agreement.

Food began coming out of the kitchen then: oysters and spinach, octopus and leeks, prawns in cheese with garlic. I had no idea what share in all this John the black man from India (or wherever his homeland lay) had had, but the dishes were uniformly excellent. My guests might have taken the dining hall for granted, but good food they appreciated, and were loud in its praises.

After the prawns came roast boar in garum, the piquancy of the fish sauce complementing the meat's fatty richness. Again, the courtiers lauded the viands to the skies. Pork is a poor man's meat, but the wild boar is of different substance from the humble, garbage-eating pig, and these connoisseurs recognized and appreciated the difference.

They sighed over geese stuffed with figs and plums and served on a bed of cabbage, and moaned almost as they might have done over a beautiful woman when the servants carried from the kitchen lambs glis-tening with the fat in which they had been baked. Crushed mint leaves were sprinkled over the carcasses, which still smoked from their time in the oven. To add flavor to the meat, the cooks had also inserted peppercorns and tiny quills of cinnamon into the flesh. Biting down on one of them prompted a man to reach for his wine goblet.

As my guests had toasted me before, so now I pledged them. Lifting my cup, I waited until I had their attention before saying, "To the memory of the days that have gone before."

They drank—how could they not drink, when the Emperor of the Romans proposed the toast? But they did not understand; I could see as much in their faces. My mother also looked puzzled. I caught Theodora's eye. She smiled at me. I smiled back.

We all paused a while for another cup of wine before the servants brought in dessert. My mother, who had been dandling Tiberius at every moment in which she was not actually eating, now discovered he had fallen asleep in her lap. "Will you excuse me?" she asked. At my nod, she rose, holding her grandson in her arms. To the guests, she said, "I have my sweet here." They nodded, some, no doubt, having grandchildren of their own.

Theodora leaned over toward me. "This will make it easier," she said.

"It will," I agreed. "Less explaining to do."

In came the cake, full of dates and cherries and sweetened with honey. In, also, came Myakes, resplendent in the gear of a captain of excubitores. Knowing him to be my crony, the courtiers accepted his presence as nothing out of the ordinary, for which I was glad.

"Is something wrong?" I asked.

He shook his big head. His beard shone in the torchlight; I was surprised to notice how gray he was getting. We were none of us so young as we had been. "Not a thing, Emperor," he said. "Helias sent me to ask you when we'd be starting." He looked a trifle sour at that. But I knew what he could do, and so had assigned the chief role here to the spatharios, to see what he would make of it.

"I don't think it will be very long," I answered in a low voice. A few of my guests leaned forward to try to hear what I was saying to Myakes, but only a few, most being less obvious in their inquisitiveness. I went on, "They'll want to be departing soon, as they expect to rise with the sun tomorrow. I won't delay them. Is the nomisma ready?"

"Oh, aye, Emperor," he said in a hollow voice. "Helias's little joke."

He did not approve. I did, saying, "I like it." He shrugged, bowed, and departed.

About half an hour later, taking advantage of a lull in the conversation, I rose, thus formally ending the banquet. The functionaries, familiar with such ceremonial dicta from the time during which Leontios and Apsimaros sat on the throne, rose as one man and, with fulsome praises, thanked me for the boon of my company. Along with Theodora, I departed by the doorway leading toward my bedchamber. The guests left through the other door, the hallway outside of which took them straight to the entrance.

But that was not the only passage in the grand palace leading to the entrance. Theodora and I doubled back through the maze, she following close behind me, trusting me to know the way. And so I did, despite a long absence and visits only rare after my return. Even before stepping out of the door, I heard voices raised in complaint and argument.

Through the complaints, Helias kept saying, "This is all at the express order of the Emperor."

"Well, where is he, so that we may protest to him?" one of the functionaries demanded, his voice full of indignation.

"Here I am," I said, showing myself. Armed and armored excubitores surrounded my erstwhile guests on three sides and, now that I had appeared, moved to cut them off from access to the grand palace as well.

"What is the meaning of this?" that same loud functionary asked, loudly.

"The meaning is simple," I replied. "The lot of you prostituted yourselves with the usurpers. For your whoredom you shall pay. 'Thou fool, this night thy soul shall be required of thee.'" Where before I had quoted the nineteenth verse of the twelfth chapter of Luke, now I used the verse following, the twentieth. Pointing to the big-mouthed wretch, I said, "Go up to Helias."

As if in a daze, he obeyed. My spatharios tossed a nomisma in the air, caught it, and looked to see whether it showed my image or that of the Son of God. "Emperor, it is the Emperor," he told me.

"That is the power of the sword," I replied. Fitting action to word, Helias drew his own sword, which came free from the scabbard with a rasp of metal. Without a word of warning, he drove it deep into the bureaucrat's belly, twisting his wrist to insure the stroke was mortal. The bureaucrat fell with a shriek, futilely clutching at his torn flesh.

The other functionaries shrieked, too, in horror and anticipation rather than anguish, though their anguish would come soon enough. I pointed to one of them, whom I chose at random. "You. Go to Helias." When he balked, I added, "Whatever happens to you afterwards, it will be worse if you disobey me now."

Trembling, the fellow approached my spatharios. Helias tossed the coin again. He looked at it, then toward me. "Emperor, it is the face of our Lord."

"These days," I said, "we no longer use the cross, out of reverence for Him Who was crucified on it. The gibbet serves instead. Truss up this son of a whore and hang him, once you've found out how many of his traitor friends go with him."

Two excubitores seized the functionary. Thoughtfully, Helias had made sure he brought plenty of rope. Even more thoughtfully, he had brought gags with which to silence the cries of the men bound and awaiting execution. That, however, lessened the racket only a little, for my guests, realizing they were all fated for one death or the other, howled like dogs crushed under wagon wheels. They surged against the excubitores, only to be driven back by bared blades.

One by one, with me picking some and Theodora the rest, the functionaries and bureaucrats, weep and bawl and blubber and foul their clothes as they might, were compelled to go before Helias for the toss of the coin. As I recall, rather more than half of them were put to the sword, the rest bound and gagged and then hauled off to the gibbets to meet the fate fortune had decreed. The last few died (or were gagged) cursing me. Die they did, though.

When the last one had been cut down, I spoke to the excubitores: "Take this carrion and throw it into the cemetery of Pelagios with the suicides, for these vile beasts brought their deaths upon themselves." Turning to Theodora, I added, "Tomorrow morning, the servants will have to wash down the walk with buckets of water, lest this blood draw flies."

"Good," she said. "Yes. We will do that."

We went back into the palace. We saw no servants as we hurried toward the bedchamber in which, I suppose, I had been conceived—the night's work had put fear in the hearts of everyone who heard it, as I had hoped it would. Once in the bedchamber, we coupled like ferrets, both of us heated red by the spectacle we had watched. Theodora bit my shoulder, hard enough to draw blood. "Have to get a bucket of water poured on that, too," I said. We laughed, loud and long.

MYAKES

Look, Brother Elpidios, if Justinian felt like getting rid of people who had done something to him, I didn't have a word to say against that. Besides, people who had done things to him had done things to me, too.

But he's right. I wasn't happy about this. It wasn't that I was jealous of Helias. Really, it wasn't. It's just that I didn't see much point to slaughtering the men Justinian felt like killing that night. The only thing they'd done was, they'd kept working while Leontios and Apsimaros were Emperor. If they hadn't kept working—them and people like them—the Empire would have started falling apart. Why did he blame them for that?

And if he was going to kill them, he shouldn't have made a game out of it. I was a soldier for a long time, Brother; killing is a serious business, or it should be. Doing it that way makes it cheap. Degrades it, you say? Yes. thanks. That's a word I wouldn't have come up with on my own.

Justinian said he wanted the people afraid of him. And they were, all right. But when a ruler is strong and they know he'll land on them if they get out of line, that's one kind of fear. If they're afraid of him on account of they don't know *what* the devil he's liable to do next, that's fear, too, but it's a different kind. Justinian either didn't care about the difference or couldn't tell there was one.

He'd sworn he wouldn't spare one of his enemies. The way he acted, he was making sure he'd have plenty of 'em.

JUSTINIAN

When morning came, my mother raised a fuss, as I had known she would. "They were traitors to our house, and so deserved whatever fate I chose to give them," I told her. She would have kept on complaining, but I turned my back on her and walked out of the grand palace.

Outside, servants were still busy cleaning up the mess. Had I had it to do over, I would have had the excubitores slay the functionaries farther from the palace: something to remember in case I decided to play the same game again instead of inventing a new one.

Having called for a horse, I rode west from the palace to the city wall to view the gibbets that had gone up there the night before to accommodate those of my guests to whom chance had given that death. A couple of gibbets stood empty, as more than half the functionaries had been put to the sword. I was sure I could find deserving men for those empty gibbets, and vowed to myself they would not stay empty long.

Only a few crows and gulls attended the corpses, the meat not yet being ripe. Down below the inner wall, people stared up at the bodies on display, but not with such avid curiosity as they had immediately after my return to the capital: to the Constantinopolitan urban sophisticates, mere executions had lost some of their power to entertain, if not to edify.

I also surveyed the dead courtiers with something less than the pleasure I had expected. Turning to one of the guards, I said, "The trouble with these wretches is, they didn't die well. Once they knew that would be their fate, they should have accepted it. Herakleios—the usurper's brother—was worth all of them and more besides."

"Yes, Emperor," the guard answered. What else could he possibly have said? If he disagreed with me, he might have gone up on one of those empty gibbets himself.

Having viewed all of last night's guests, today's executed traitors, I rode back to the Blakhernai palace, to which, by that time, Theodora and Tiberius had also returned. "You go, and your mother shouts and shouts at me," Theodora said. "I tell her I think they should die, too, and she shouts louder."

"My mother *will* speak her mind," I said. "Anyone would think I was related to her." For a moment, Theodora looked puzzled at that. Then understanding spread over her face and she laughed.

In truth, I was not paying full attention to her words or my own. Ever since my mentioning Herakleios up on the wall, he had been in my mind. As general of the military district of the Anatolics, he might well have been able to give me a harder fight than he did. Most of west-central and southwestern Anatolia fell into that military district. Had he stayed there and resisted with his full power, he would have been harder to overcome than he was, caught with a scratch force in Thrace after I had seized Constantinople.

Summoning Myakes, Leo, and Helias, I put my sudden insight to them: "God did not speak from a burning bush to ordain that the military district of the Anatolics should be as it is. Any general there has to think of becoming a usurper, if for no other reason than that he commands such a large army."

"He needs a large army," Helias said, "to help fight the Arabs."

"Not *that* large," I answered, "and the soldiers would still be there, only under two commanders rather than one."

"Ah." Leo's eyes lit. "You want to divide the military district, not pension off soldiers. Yes, that is good, I think, or at least not bad."

"If you do it that way, who would the new general be?" Myakes asked.

"Barisbakourios writes that a tourmarch of the military district of the Opsikion, a certain Christopher from Philippopolis in Thrace, has done good work and deserves a reward," I said. "Do any of you know this man?"

Myakes and Helias both shook their heads. Leo, however, spoke up at once, saying, "Yes, he is a good fighter. He gave the Bulgars fits a few years ago, when he was still in Thrace." That Leo should have known Christopher surprised me not at all. By then, I had come to suspect that, if I asked him about some petty Frankish noble in a land no Roman has seen for a hundred years, he would have furnished accurate particulars without batting an eye.

"What will you call the new military district, Emperor?" Myakes asked.

"Not the military district of the Philippopolitans, I hope," Helias said. "No one could hope to say it." He had stumbled over it himself. We all laughed.

Leo said, "How about the military district of the Thrakesians, after Christopher of Thrace?"

Having savored that, I dipped my head in assent, like pagan Zeus in the *Iliad*. "Let it be so," I said, and so it was. Christopher, receiving his new appointment, worked diligently to separate the men and town under his command from those remaining in the military district of the Anatolics. He did this, of course, to enhance his own position, but it served my purposes, too, placing two potential rivals in an area that had formerly known but a single powerful—too powerful, sometimes—leader.

When I invited a couple of dozen bureaucrats of middling station to a feast at the Blakhernai palace, only eight of them came to the Anastasiakos dining hall. The rest were suddenly taken ill with such an astonishing variety of diseases that anyone would have thought a whole wave of plagues had suddenly descended on Constantinople—which God prevent from ever actually taking place.

With so few guests attending, we all gorged ourselves, the cooks having prepared far more than our small party could consume. I thought we could have done better still, but some of the bureaucrats seemed slightly off their feed, for no reason I could fathom.

"Here," I told them after the servants cleared away what was left. "I had planned to give each of my friends five nomismata, but, since so many of your colleagues were taken ill, each of you gets three purses, not one, and fifteen nomismata in all." I passed out the presents with my own hands.

"God bless you, Emperor," they gasped out almost in unison, and, on my giving them leave to go, all but fled the palace.

Turning to Theodora, I remarked, "Anyone would think they expected to find soldiers waiting for them out there."

"I do not know why," she answered in her slow, deliberate Greek. "This is not the grand palace." We both found that very funny.

Our guests having departed, I summoned Myakes. Before the feast, I had taken pains to learn the dwelling places of all the functionaries I would invite. At my order, Theophylaktos brought me this list, a pen, and a jar of ink. I lined through the names of the men who had joined me at supper. That done, I gave the list to Myakes, saying, "Gather your men together and arrest everyone whose name you see here. I want all of them back at this palace before the sun comes up tomorrow morning."

"Yes, Emperor," Myakes said. "I'll see to it." He had never had my fire, and some of what he had had was gone out of him. But he would obey, even if he persisted in asking questions like, "What will you do with them?"

"Wipe their noses," I snarled. "Get you gone." He bowed and departed.

MYAKES

Yes, of course I knew what he'd do with them, Brother Elpidios, or I had a pretty good idea, anyhow. No, I didn't want to see him do it, especially not so soon after the last massacre. But he gave the orders. If I didn't do what he said, I figured I'd be next up on a gibbet. All he could think about, near enough, was paying back everybody he thought had ever wronged him.

I took a look at the list, divided it into four parts, and sent out four troops of excubitores. I led one of them. I can do my own dirty work, I can. First door we knocked on, the fellow we came for opened it himself. "You don't *look* sick," says I to him. He tried to slam the door, but I stuck a foot in it and my boys went in and grabbed him. His wife and brats were wailing behind us when he left.

The other three were just as easy, and none of them looked sick, either. Back we went to Blakhernai. Getting all four of them hadn't taken two hours. "Have mercy on us!" they kept saying, over and over. "In the name of Christ, have mercy!"

But that wasn't for me to say. It was up to Justinian. I didn't think any of those sixteen poor bastards would get away with his neck. Turned out I was wrong, though.

All the bureaucrats who had refused my invitation to dine having been assembled, I inspected them. One, a thin, pale fellow with shadows under his eyes, coughed wetly, rackingly. Thick yellowish mucus kept streaming from his nose, which he wiped on the sleeve of his tunic.

"You are . . . John son of Eusebios, the customs inspector, not so?" I said.

"Yes, Emperor." He coughed again. "I am sorry I could not"—still more coughs—"join you tonight, but may I ask why your men hauled me from my bed?"

"No, you may not," I told him. He bowed his head, whereupon snot dripped down onto his sandals. "Go home and go about your business." I turned to Myakes. "Give him an escort, so no footpad falls on him in the night." To Theophylaktos, I added, "See that John is sent fifteen nomismata in the morning."

"Yes, Emperor." The eunuch bowed. John, afflicted or not, suddenly walked with longer, straighter strides as the excubitores led him out of the palace.

My giving him presents eased the minds of the other guests brought so late to the dining hall. John having departed, however, I said to those bureaucrats, "One of your number truly was ill. What have the rest of you to say for yourselves? When the Emperor of the Romans summons you to a feast, should you not make every effort to attend him?"

They all began talking at once, some trying to justify claiming illness while hale, others still trying to claim illness despite healthy appearance. In the course of a day's work, the Emperor of the Romans normally hears a good many lies. In the course of a few minutes, I heard as many lies as I normally do in a day's work.

"Enough!" I said at last, whereupon the bureaucrats mercifully fell silent. "The plain and simple truth is, you did not come because you were afraid of what I might do to you."

"After what happened at your last feast, Emperor," one of them blurted, "can you blame us?"

"Of course I can blame you," I answered. He cringed. They all cringed. "The men I had killed after my last feast were every one of them traitors," I went on. "Are *you* traitors? Do you think I think you are traitors? Do you think you are traitors? Is that why you stayed away from me?"

I listened to denials as empty and pointless and useless as their pretenses at sickness had been. Had I believed them, the only course left open to me would have been to promote every one of the rascals making them, or perhaps to order Cyrus the patriarch to declare them numbered among the saints.

But I did not believe them. Their evident good health and their equally evident fear of me convicted them all. "Liars!" I shouted, cutting through their babble. "By your own actions shall you be judged. If you do not trust me, how can I be expected to trust you? You are all sacked, every last one of you."

This they bore up under with equanimity. I heard one of them mutter to another, "Better to lose my position than my neck." Doing their deceitful best to appear dejected, they turned and made for the door of the dining hall where they had not eaten.

"Stop!" I said sharply. "I did not give you leave to go. When I say you are sacked . . ." Now I stopped. They would find out soon enough. Meanwhile, at my order, the excubitores bound their wrists behind them. "Is everything in full readiness?" I asked Myakes.

"Oh, yes, Emperor," he answered, rare in that he was loyal and obedient even when not altogether happy with my purposes. "What with that John who really was sick, we even have one left over."

"Fine. Let's get on with it, then," I said. At swords' point, the excubitores made the functionaries leave the palace of Blakhernai. We marched them to a dromon moored on the Golden Horn not far from the palace: not far from the pier at which Theodora had reached the imperial city, either.

Torches blazed by and on the galley, which carried a full crew of oarsmen and sailors. Two piles of coarse canvas, smaller than the sail, stood on deck. So did stacked stones, as if for a catapult. One by one, the miscreants I had seized stumbled up the gangplank onto the dromon. The captain was a young fellow named Stephen, whom I had recently raised to the dignity of patrician. He prostrated himself on the deck as soon as I came aboard.

"Rise," I said impatiently. "I want this done."

"Shouldn't be too hard, Emperor." He looked at the prisoners, nodding on approval on seeing them already in bonds. "No, shouldn't be too hard. They aren't going anyplace." His smile gleamed in the torchlight.

At his orders, the sailors cast off the lines mooring the dromon to the wharf. The rowers backed oars, then turned and took us out of the Golden Horn, past the lighthouses marking the channel, and into the middle of the Sea of Marmara. Lamps and torches and candles made Constantinople glow and twinkle far more brightly than the star-strewn sky overhead.

"What are you going to do to us, Emperor?" asked one of the bureaucrats who had not cared to enjoy my hospitality. "Are you exiling us to Anatolia?"

"You'll know soon enough," I answered, "you before all the others." That did little to reassure him, but reassuring him was not my object. To Stephen, I said, "Have we gone far enough yet?"

"Should be fine, Emperor," he answered. "We're about halfway between the city and the other shore." He pointed east toward Chalcedon, whose lights were far fewer and of smaller extent than those of the imperial city.

"Well, then," I said, and nodded toward a couple of the excubitores who had boarded the dromon with us. "Deal with the curious one first."

Going over to the piled canvas, they picked up one of the sacks there and threw it over the bureaucrat's head. Before he let out more than one startled squawk, they knocked him down, tying the mouth of the bag securely shut with a length of rope. The other end of the rope they tied to one of the stones. Ignoring the frantic kicks from within the sack, they pushed it and the stone into the Sea. It sank very quickly.

"No, Emperor!" the other disloyal bureaucrats shouted. "Not us, Emperor!" "We didn't do anything!" "We're innocent!" "Have mercy!"

At my nod, the excubitores popped the second one into a sack, tied the sack to a stone, and shoved sack and stone and all into the water. The outcries from within cut off as abruptly as if the fellow had been decapitated.

Bawling like steers, the rest of the bureaucrats tried to break away from the guardsmen who hemmed them in. One succeeded and, being chased by two excubitores, leaped into the Sea of Marmara of his own accord. I wondered if he could swim with his hands tied behind his back. By his floundering, I doubt he could have swum had they been untied. He spluttered a couple of unintelligible curses or pleas before his head sank beneath the surface and did not rise again.

Methodically, the excubitores threw sacks over the other bureaucrats and flung them into the sea. "There goes the last of them," Myakes said when it was done. He rubbed at his calf; one of the men being sacked had managed to kick him. "What now?"

"A good night's work," I answered. "Now we go back to the palace, of course, unless you know of someone else who needs killing so badly, it won't keep till morning."

He shook his head. "That's not what I meant, Emperor. What now? What comes next? You'll have people afraid to come to your feasts and even more afraid not to. Is that what you want?"

"Of course that's what I want," I answered; Myakes was not usually so dim. "People who fear me will be too afraid to plot against me. They'll obey instead."

"Unless you make them so afraid, they think striking at you is a better bet than waiting to see what you do next," Myakes said.

"If I kill enough of them—*once* I kill enough of them—the rest will be too cowed to let a thought like that enter their minds," I said. Myakes looked as if he wanted to argue further; I cut him off by saying to Stephen, "Take us back to the harbor. We're through here."

"Yes, Emperor," he said, and gave the oarsmen their orders.

On my return to the Blakhernai palace, Theodora asked, "All good?"

"All good," I answered. "We have a couple of sacks left over, as a matter of fact." I explained about the bureaucrat who leaped into the sea before the excubitores could give him his new, all-encircling cloak, and wondered whether God would condemn him as a suicide. That done, I finished, "If you have anyone in mind for a leftover, let me know, and I'll tend to it."

"I think about it," she answered seriously.

Having made it clear to the people—and, most of all, to the people possessed of authority—in Constantinople that I aimed to rule as King Stork rather than King Log, I was afforded few opportunities over the next couple of years to exhibit storklike behavior, as no one dared risk my displeasure in any way. Life was good.

This is not to say the executioners spent those two years drowsing in the sun and letting their swords rust. Traitors kept emerging, some being denounced to me while others I ferreted out on my own. A few heads were usually on display at the Milion. But I saw no further need for such salutary and sanguinary lessons as I had administered after my banquets.

Matters touching on the neighbors of the Roman Empire also remained largely quiet during that time. The Bulgars came south over the border into Romania a couple of times, but the raids were no more than nuisances. I wondered if they were Tervel's way of gaining some of the booty my successful return to the throne had cost him. Whenever I sent complaints, the raids stopped . . . for a while.

In the east, Oualid proved a less aggressive ruler of the deniers of Christ than Abimelekh had been before him. He did despoil the churches of Damascus of their wealth, and also, in his arrogance, supplanted Greek in his chancery with the Arabs' own barbarous and guttural tongue. The previous miscalled commander of the faithful had attempted the same measure, only to abandon it on discovering how ill-suited to the task Arabic was. Oualid, with barbarous presumption, has persisted and persists even as I write.

Here in the imperial city, Tiberius learned to walk and to talk. He soon proved as strong-willed as any member of my house, shouting "No!" whenever he found himself checked in any way. When shouting failed, he screamed or threw things or tried to bite. Albeit the despair of the servants, he made me quite proud.

The popes of Rome still refused to subscribe to the canons of the fifth-sixth synod. But when Sisinnios, an ancient monk from Syria, died a mere twenty days after being selected bishop of Rome, his successor, Constantine, another Syrian, proved more reasonable in these matters than several of his predecessors had been.

And Constantine and I discovered a common interest not long after he became bishop of Rome. The bishop of Ravenna having joined the majority, Constantine ordained a certain Felix as his successor.

It had long been the custom for each new bishop of Ravenna to give the pope a written pledge of obedience on assuming office. This Felix refused to do, claiming that, Ravenna being the capital of Roman Italy and Rome, as he put it, merely a backwater, he would do as he saw fit, not as Constantine saw fit for him to do. In this assertion he had the strong backing of Stephen, the exarch of Ravenna, the Roman viceroy in Italy.

Just as Felix presumed upon his dependent relationship with the bishop of Rome, so Stephen presumed on his dependent relationship with me. The exarchate of Ravenna by its nature gave the holder of the officer considerable autonomy, but Stephen, far more than other exarchs before him, forgot he was merely the viceroy of the vicegerent of God on earth. Had Felix's rebellion against Constantine succeeded, the next rebellion would have been against me.

Still, I might have been inclined to sit idly by and let Constantine fight his own battles had not Leo said, "Emperor, if you can rid him of this turbulent priest, won't he be more reasonable about your synod?"

"A reasonable pope?" Almost, I was moved to laughter. But Constantine had not made himself nearly so hateful to me as some earlier bishops of Rome—and I had already discovered Leo's talent for underhanded dealings of all sorts. "Well, we shall see."

Ravenna, lying as it does in the middle of a swampy bog, is as nearly impregnable by land as makes no difference. If I was going to bring

Stephen and Felix under my control, it would have to be by sea. The nearest Roman ships were in Sicily, under the command of the patrician Theodore, and to him I wrote of my requirements.

He followed my orders perfectly, or better than perfectly. Sailing up to Ravenna with a fleet of dromons, he invited Stephen, Felix, and other local dignitaries to a feast outside the walls. All unsuspecting, they came, whereupon he seized them, got them back to his ship without a man of his being hurt, and brought them to Constantinople.

On their reaching the imperial city, I had them brought to the throne room in the grand palace, which, being far more magnificent than any chamber at the Blakhernai palace, was far more suitable for occasions of solemn grandeur such as this. Theodore, a big, bluff man with a bushy black beard, led in the captives, who were weighted down with chains that clanked at each step they took.

Felix and the other villains threw themselves down on their faces before me, grizzling out cries for mercy. I descended from the gold and emerald-encrusted throne, the pearl *prependoulia* that dangled from my crown brushing against my cheeks. I kicked Felix in the ribs as he crouched in the posture of prostration. "Mercy?" I shouted, standing over him. "I have no mercy on any of my enemies, and anyone who rebels against the authority of the Roman Empire is an enemy of mine. Look at Leontios. Look at Apsimaros. Look at them and think how easy their ends were next to those you shall have. You knew better, and flouted my will regardless. Death for you—death for you all!"

My courtiers clapped their hands at the sentence. The miscreants from Ravenna groaned and trembled. Theodore, sounding interested, even eager, asked, "What sort of death, Emperor?"

"I'll leave my executioners to please themselves," I replied. "With fire and knives and weights and water, they can make each death different, and every death take a long time. Tomorrow is time enough, though. For tonight, let them—let everyone—think on the fate awaiting them. Take them away!"

Away they went, moaning. Away I went, well pleased with the day's ceremony. They, no doubt, lay on the filthy straw of their cells, their heads full of nightmares over what was to come. I lay on soft linen—and I also dreamt of what lay ahead for them.

In my dream, I saw Bishop Felix as an old man, which he surely would not become did I slay him, his beard being as black as Theodore's. He stumbled toward me, hands outstretched, groping for me, calling my name, begging for continued existence. He touched me—and I awoke.

Theodora's small hand rested on my arm. But I lay some time awake, pondering the message of the dream, and reluctantly concluded I had no choice but to let Felix live, lest I go against God's will by destroying the possibility of his older self. *Very well,* I said to myself. *He shall live. But he shall not go unpunished.* I slept soundly the rest of the night.

When morning came, I made the arrangements necessary for my changed plans, then had Felix brought to the Blakhernai palace. The excubitores pushed him down on his face in front of me. "I have decided to spare your life," I said without preamble.

"God bless you, Emperor," he said. "I pray that—"

I cut him off. "Instead of executing you, I shall have you blinded and exiled to the regions of Pontos." Having listened to Cyrus, I knew how dreary a place it was. Without his sight, Felix would find it drearier still.

He coughed and spluttered. I might have let him keep his life, but nothing that made it worth living. "Please, Emperor . . ." he managed at last.

"Take him to the kitchens," I told the excubitores. "The executioner will be waiting for us." The guardsmen hauled Felix to his feet and herded him down the passageway. I followed, curious to witness the process the executioner had described for me earlier in the day.

In the kitchen, the cooks were curious, too, crowding around the executioner until he had to shoo them back to give himself room to work. Among the cooks was Helias's black slave John, who looked like a shadow of the men of normal hue.

"All ready, Emperor," the executioner said on seeing me come in behind the prisoner.

"Then go ahead," I said.

He had the excubitores stand Felix next to a high table where the cooks did their mixing and kneading. While the traitorous bishop of Ravenna dolefully waited, the executioner picked up a long wooden peel and thrust it into the oven in which my daily bread was baked. Instead of drawing forth a loaf, however, he took out a silver bowl that had been heated almost red-hot. Handling the peel as skillfully as any baker, he set the bowl in front of Felix, who tried to recoil from its heat but was prevented by the guards.

The executioner poured a jar of hot vinegar into the bowl. A great cloud of noxious vapor rose from it. Into this vapor the executioner had the excubitores bend Felix's head. He himself, with the skill he had learned as part of his trade, forced the recalcitrant bishop to open his eyelids, so that the surface of his eyeballs was exposed to the caustic fumes. Felix howled like a wolf and did his best to twist away. He could not.

After what the executioner judged sufficient time, he let Felix lift his head from the fumes of the boiling vinegar. Felix's whole face was red, as if scorched. His eyes looked as if the executioner had scraped their surface with a file, or perhaps as if they had been rubbed with sand, as a mason will sand down marble to make it smooth. But they were not smooth: on the contrary. I could tell at a glance Felix would not see again.

"Well done," I told the executioner. "Just as I desired." Felix would have been weeping, I think, but no tears flowed from his eyes, which were horribly swollen along with being blistered and abraded. To the excubitores, I said, "Take him to the harbor and put him aboard the ship waiting there to take him to Amastris." Which place, from what Cyrus had said, was as close to living death as made no difference. "He shall never trouble Ravenna again." And off into exile Felix went.

MYAKES

And, a few years later, Brother Elpidios, back from exile Felix came. Once Justinian was cast down, he got his bishopric back, even if he was blind. And do you know what, Brother? He spent a few days at this very monastery before he sailed on toward Ravenna.

I'd only been blind a couple of months myself then. We spent a deal of time talking, he and I did. He told me some useful things, because he'd had longer to get used to it. He'd found, same as I was finding, being in a monastery helps. You go to the same places every day, do the same things. And you don't usually have to fret about where this or that is, because you don't own this and you don't own that, either.

No, I don't know what sort of bishop he made once he got to Ravenna again. I never heard a word about it. Ravenna's a long way from here. For all I know, he might still be bishop. But I'll tell you, Brother, if I've found anything in all these years, it's that I don't know much.

JUSTINIAN

Not long after I blinded Felix and executed the rest of the rebels from Ravenna, Helias came up to me and said, "Emperor, may I talk with you for a little while?"

"What is it?" I asked. By his manner, I judged it was a matter of some importance—and of some delicacy, too.

"Emperor," he said, taking a deep breath, "I don't quite know how to tell you this, but I fear Leo is plotting to steal your throne from you."

If he had thought to gain my attention, he had succeeded. "Do you?" I said. "Why do you think that?"

"It only stands to reason," he answered. "He's too clever for his own good by half, and he's always going around snooping into other people's affairs. I don't like the way he watches me out of the corner of his eye, either."

"All that is as may be," I answered, "but I must tell you that I am glad Leo is diligent in my behalf. I want those who serve me to give me good service. If I have only fools to do my bidding, I shall be in great danger."

"But a clever man will serve himself while claiming to serve you," Helias said.

"You have given me no evidence whatever that Leo is plotting against me, though," I told him. "I cannot condemn him for doing his work too well. If you have any evidence, I will hear it. Until then, do not trouble me with this charge."

Helias bowed and went away. A few days later, a patrician who was called Mauros on account of his extremely black beard came to me with a similar accusation, and with a similar lack of evidence as well. On questioning Mauros, it became clear that he had not plotted his charges along with Helias, but had made them independently.

That two men should devise identical indictments of Leo, neither knowing what the other was doing, made me more concerned about the young spatharios from near Mesembria than either accusation would have on its own. Accordingly, I summoned Myakes and asked him what he thought about Leo.

I had not told him why I sought his opinion. After his usual pause for thought, he replied, "Emperor, if you're asking me whether I like Leo, the answer is no, not very much. But if you're asking me whether he's good at what he does, why, you'd have to be blinder than Felix to say no."

"Yes, I know he's good at his job," I said. "Is his job the only one with which he's concerned?" Seeing that Myakes did not follow, I spelled it out, alpha-beta-gamma: "Does he want mine?"

"Ah, that's what you want to know," he said, enlightenment quickening his features. He thought some more before going on, "If he does, Emperor, I haven't seen it. If I had, I'd tell you in a heartbeat—you know that. If I had, I'd have told you already—you know that, too."

Since he was correct, I thanked him and sent him on his way. No more than two weeks afterwards, the patrician Stephen warned me Leo aspired to my place. Again, I questioned him. Again, he had no solid proof. His claim was unconnected to those of Helias and Mauros, as best I could determine. I dismissed him as I had dismissed them.

His words, however, combined with those of Helias and Mauros, sent me to watching Leo more closely than I had before. In nothing that I saw, in nothing that my privy agents discovered, was the slightest hint of disloyalty. What those agents did discover, however, was an enormous gift for dissembling. Thus, while married, Leo maintained no fewer than three concubines in different quarters of the imperial city, each of them convinced he cherished her alone, as was his wife.

A man capable of such deception was also capable of hatching and nursing plots against me, plots difficult of detection. That he had not done so (or that I had not detected him doing so) proved little. I began to cast about for ways I could be certain his undoubted abilities were used for my benefit rather than to my detriment.

Thanks to the workings of divine providence, such an opportunity was not long in coming. Beyond the northeastern reaches of Roman Anatolia lie the mountains and valleys of the Caucasus. Some of the peoples of this region favor Rome, some incline toward the Arabs' miscalled commander of the faithful, while most back whichever side has given them more presents most recently.

Among the most consistently pro-Roman tribes in the Caucasus is that of the Alans. The followers of the false prophet, however, had recently extended their influence over the Alans' neighbors, the Abasgians. Fearing they would be next, the Alans sent an envoy to me, seeking aid against their neighbors, who now had Arab soldiers alongside them.

"I know the very man to lead your resistance against the deniers of Christ," I exclaimed. "I shall give you my own spatharios, Leo, who by his nature is well suited both to war and to complex bargaining." I spoke with vehemence enough to impress the Alan greatly, nor was I telling him anything less than the truth. "With him I shall send the sum of five thousand nomismata, that he may hire soldiers or make bargains"—a euphemism for *pay bribes*—"as he sees fit."

"God bless you, Emperor!" the Alan exclaimed. "You have given me and my prince more than we dared expect."

"Leo shall sail for Phasis, the Black Sea port onto which your country opens, no later than next week. I am confident he will do great things for you."

If Leo suspected he was being banished, he gave no sign of it. "I'll tie their tails in knots, Emperor," he said. "Send me after them. I haven't been on that side of the world since I was a little boy, and never up in those mountains." He smiled. "I hear the women in the Caucasus are pretty, too."

"Business before pleasure," I said sternly.

"Oh, of course," he answered, as if surprised I could have thought anything else. "But if pleasure comes along, I won't send it packing." Given his philanderings here in the imperial city, I believed him.

He sailed for Phasis a few days later, along with the Alan envoy and the gold. In due course, he reached the town on the eastern shore of the Black Sea and wrote to me that he was going into the interior of the country there, leaving the money behind so that it would remain safe until such time as he decided exactly how it might best be disbursed.

Having heard that much from him, I put him out of my mind. The Caucasus being so remote, his success, if he found some, would be gratifying but not vital, while his failure would not send an Arab host storming toward Constantinople, as had happened in the days of my youth. I wondered if he would prove as ingenious as he appeared.

And then, a few weeks later, Helias brought before me a little old wrinkled man who stank of leather. "Emperor, this is Theodoulos, the bootmaker who fashions the imperial footgear. Tell the Emperor what you've told me, Theodoulos."

"Yes, yes," Theodoulos said—thickly, for he had only a few teeth. "This Leo, this spatharios"—a word on account of which he sprayed me with spittle—"he came into my shop, and he asked me, he did, he asked me . . ."

"What did he ask you?" I demanded.

"Yes, yes, that's right. He did ask me," Theodoulos said. "He asked me, he did, all right—"

"The dye," Helias prompted.

"No, no, not ready to die yet," Theodoulos said, though at that moment he was closer to dying than he knew. But then, somewhere in the darkness of his wits, a lamp was lighted. "Oh, the *dye*. Yes, yes. Leo, he asked me, he did, what dye it was I used to get just that shade of, shade of, shade of, of red on the imperial boots."

"*Did* he?" I said. "He had no business asking you that." That shade of red is reserved for the Emperor alone. Had Leo not been interested in becoming Emperor, it would not have concerned him.

"Emperor, you should recall him and strike off his disloyal head," Helias said.

"I should like to recall him and strike off his head," I answered, "but, if I should, do you think him more likely to come back to the imperial city or go over to the Abasgians?" Helias's face told me what he thought. Thinking the same thing myself, I went on in meditative tones: "A man with his gift for intrigue could severely trouble the Roman Empire."

"That is so, Emperor," Helias admitted, "but will you let him go free and show others closer to home a man can prosper through treason?"

"He shall not prosper," I said, and then again, in an altogether different, almost startled, tone of voice, "He *shall* not prosper."

"What will you do?" Helias asked me.

"That is *my* affair," I answered, not wanting him to get a glimpse of the way my mind worked: though dispraising Leo's disloyalty, he might have some of his own. To Theodoulos, I said, "Half a pound of gold to you for what you have told me of Leo."

"God bless you, Emperor," the bootmaker exclaimed, and prostrated himself again.

Dismissing him and Helias, I called for a secretary. The man having arrived, I dictated a letter. When I had finished, I said, "I shall want a fair copy of that before noon, so that I can sign it. It must be on a dromon bound for Phasis this afternoon."

"Yes, Emperor," the scribe replied. "Of course, Emperor." He knew perfectly well what would happen to him did he fail. But, being employed to write, write he did, and I affixed my signature in the scarlet ink reserved for the holder of the imperial dignity. A courier on a fast horse took the letter to the harbor and stayed there until with his own eyes he had seen the dromon depart.

It returned to this God-guarded city within three days of the time I had reckoned to be the fastest possible. Its captain, a weatherbeaten veteran named Agapetos, hastened to the Blakhernai palace as soon as it tied up at one of the quays along the Golden Horn. On being told he had come, I summoned him directly into my presence and even forgave him the time-wasting ritual of prostration. "Tell me at once whether you have accomplished the task I set you," I said.

"Emperor, I have," Agapetos answered. "The gold the spatharios Leo left behind in Phasis was still there. Obedient to your command, I took charge of it and have returned it to Constantinople. Even as we speak, it is being carried back to the imperial treasury."

"Splendid," I said, and then again, "Splendid. Pharaoh of Egypt set the Israelites to making bricks without straw, and an ambassador without money is as useless as a brick that has no straw. The native tribes of the Caucasus will surely complete Leo's ruination."

"Yes, Emperor." Agapetos did not ask why I wanted Leo ruined. That was not his affair, and he knew it. He made the perfect sort of servant for me: he did exactly as he was told, he did it well, and he never, ever, asked why.

I always kept close track of the ships coming to this God-guarded and imperial city from Kherson, Phanagoria, and the other towns on the northern coast of the Black Sea. I had scores still unsettled with the folk of those regions; the more I learned of their doings, the better I could prepare my own when that time came.

Not long after I gave Leo his comeuppance, a ship captain out of Phanagoria sought me out, coming to the palace at Blakhernai. When the eunuch Theophylaktos learned what message he bore, he passed him on to me. "Say on," I told the captain after he had prostrated himself.

"Thank you, Emperor," he answered. "As I said to your steward here, along with my usual wax and tallow and hides, I have a message from the khagan of the Khazars for you."

"Do you?" I murmured. "Ibouzeros Gliabanos has not had much to say to me since I returned to Constantinople. I thought he owned a sense of shame. Maybe I was wrong. Well, what does he say?"

"Emperor," the captain said uncomfortably, "he asks your leave to come to Constantinople himself, to visit his sister and you."

Had I been drinking wine, I daresay I should have choked. As it was, I coughed a couple of times before saying, "He does, does he? He dares?"

"Aye," the unhappy emissary answered. "He told me to tell you he didn't kill you when you were in his capital, and he thought you'd do him the same favor. He's camped on the steppe near Phanagoria, waiting for your word. If I tell him you grant him leave, he'll sail with me, my next trip into the city."

For one of the rare times in my life, I was not instantly certain what to do. Tell Ibouzeros Gliabanos to stay far away? Tell him to come and then slay him? Had he not been my wife's brother, I should have done that, but he was. Tell him to come and let him escape? I had gone safe out of Atil, regardless of what happened later. But letting anyone escape my vengeance had become bitter as wormwood, bitter as myrrh, to me.

Instead of giving the fellow his answer on the spot, I spoke to Theophylaktos: "Put him up for the night here in the palace. In the morning, I shall tell him what I have decided."

"It shall be as you say, Emperor." If my indecision startled Theophylaktos, I never knew. He prided himself on his imperturbability, the only time I saw it breached being when he returned to the imperial city after the ill-fated journey to get Theodora back from her brother.

As he went off with the ship captain, I went back to talk the news over with Theodora, whom I found spinning flax into thread with three or four of her serving women. Having dismissed them, I told her of Ibouzeros Gliabanos's desire to visit Constantinople.

"My brother to come here?" she said, her narrow eyes widening. "He puts his head in the mouth of the wolf." Her Greek had grown much more fluent in the time since her arrival in Constantinople, but she still flavored it, as she does to this day, with turns of phrase calling to mind the steppe whence she sprang.

This one struck me as particularly apt. "Yes, he does," I replied with a certain amount of anticipation. "How shall we requite him for trying to have me killed in Phanagoria?"

Theodora looked troubled. "He let you live before," she said. "He wed me to you. When you killed his men and fled to the Bulgars, he cared for me and for Tiberius. He has treated you badly, but also well. And," she added, "he is my brother."

I sighed. "For your sake, then, you want me to let him come and to treat him well? I love you, but God will turn away from me if I do not avenge myself on all my enemies."

"If my brother were truly your enemy, you would be dead now, and I would be back at Atil." Theodora looked a challenge at me, as if daring me to deny her words. Seeing I could not, she went on, "And the saddlebags—no, you would say the scales—are even on both sides. He has done you well and harm both. It is a balance. God will forgive you."

What she was also saying was that she would not forgive me if, having invited Ibouzeros Gliabanos to the imperial city, I then turned on him. I sighed again, having feared that would be her response. "Very well. He may come. I will remember the good he has done me, especially since you are the biggest part of that good."

"Thank you!" she exclaimed, and, casting her arms around my

neck, kissed me until I could hardly breathe. Shortly thereafter, we adjourned to the bedchamber, where she threw herself on me and rode me as a jockey rides a racehorse. Such immodest and unfeminine aggression was on occasion extremely enjoyable and even complimentary, she having learned from me everything she knew of love between men and women.

Having been thus persuaded both intellectually and lectually, I summoned the ship captain when morning came and told him Ibouzeros Gliabanos was welcome to visit the imperial city. "And I swear by God and His Son that no harm will come to the khagan of the Khazars through any action on my part or on the part of my servants," I added.

"I shall tell him you have taken this oath, Emperor," the seaman said. "He did not insist on it as a condition for coming, but wanted to learn whether you would offer it of your own free will."

Had I not already known Ibouzeros Gliabanos was a canny, cautious man, his behavior in this regard would have instructed me. He did not demand the oath, which would have implied he failed to trust me. He did not even mention it, which proved the best way to extract it from me. Though a pagan and a barbarian, the khagan of the Khazars was no fool.

The ship bearing the khagan and his retinue sailed into Constantinople a bit more than a month later. I greeted him at the Golden Horn, as I had his sister on her arrival, and, as I had done with her, brought a troop of excubitores both to protect myself and for the sake of pomp. Having made the acquaintance of the khagan in Khazaria, Myakes was the logical choice to head the troop.

Ibouzeros Gliabanos strode up the quay toward the excubitores, Theodora, and me. A little man I correctly assumed to be an interpreter walked a pace behind him and to his left. The rest of the Khazars followed. All of them, the khagan included, kept looking this way and that, as if having trouble believing what they saw.

Having bowed to me and embraced his sister, Ibouzeros Gliabanos spoke in his own language, the interpreter rendering his words into Greek for me: "I thought I knew what a city was, but I see I was wrong."

Theodora clapped her hands together. "I said the same thing when I came here," she exclaimed—in Greek.

The interpreter having performed his office, the khagan spoke with a hint of sadness perceptible even though I did not grasp his words until they were translated: "You have become a Roman, my sister."

"I have," Theodora said in Greek, and then went on in the Khazars' tongue. She translated for me: "I told my brother he gave me to a Roman as a wife, and that I have become of my husband's people, as a wife should."

"I knew that already," Ibouzeros Gliabanos answered, and Theodora nodded proudly. Had she not warned me against her brother's myrmidons, I should not have survived to return to this God-guarded city. The khagan then spoke to me, saying, "Now I understand why you wanted so much to come back."

"For the sake of the city, do you mean?" I asked, and he nodded—I shall henceforth omit mention of the interpreter, a man scarcely memorable. I said, "Yes, I am glad to live here again, but I came back because it is *mine*."

"You are a king," he said, and it was my turn to nod. Turning to the excubitores, he recognized Myakes. "A king who is a good king will have good subjects. Is it well with you, Myakes, who traveled with your king when only you thought he was one?"

"It is very well with me, Ibouzeros Gliabanos," Myakes answered, with a bow for the khagan.

"Do I guess rightly that you had somewhat to do with the passing of Balgitzin and Papatzun?" Ibouzeros Gliabanos asked.

Myakes shrugged, his gilded scalemail jingling slightly at the motion. "They obeyed their rulers. I obeyed mine." Had I known he could give answers as diplomatic as that, I might have sent him to Damascus to dicker with the miscalled commander of the faithful.

Ibouzeros Gliabanos dipped his head, also appreciating the reply. To me, he said, "While I waited to hear if you would receive me, I had word of another of your servants. Because he knew you and some of your followers had spent time with me, the prince of the Abasgians sent to me, asking if I knew a Roman spatharios named Leo. But he was not with you then."

"No, he wasn't," I agreed. "What did the Abasgian say of him?"

To my surprise, the Khazar grinned at me. "He said you did not have anyone else in the whole Empire who was as big a liar as this Leo."

"Did he, by God?" I said. "Well, he wasn't far wrong."

"He said this Leo was still leading the Alans in war against his people, even though he had no money to pay the Alans, as he'd been claiming. The prince said he'd captured this Leo—"

"Good!" I exclaimed.

This seemed to disconcert Ibouzeros Gliabanos, but he went on, "But the Alans rescued him and they're still fighting the Abasgians. The prince's messenger was confused, which means the prince was likely confused, too."

"I'm rather confused myself," I told the khagan, and then, in a low voice, I said to Theodora, "It is as well that I sent Leo to the edge of the world. Were he closer to the imperial city, he would be too dangerous to trust. In the Caucasus, at least, I have some use from him."

"Yes," she said. "His eyes look every which way at the same time."

Ibouzeros Gliabanos said, "You must show me this city, Justinian. I have heard so much of it. Now I see I did not hear enough."

"Tervel the Bulgar said the same thing," I answered. "So did your sister. So does everyone who has heard of the marvels of Constantinople without having seen them."

"Ah, Tervel the Bulgar," the khagan of the Khazars said. "We do not always get on well with the Bulgars, either those to our north or those to our west. How do you like Tervel as a neighbor?"

"Without him, I'd not be here talking with you today," I said, "but that does not mean he has not been difficult sometimes." Bulgar raiders had begun harassing Thrace in larger numbers lately. The embassy I sent to Tervel to complain of that had, for the first time, returned without obtaining satisfaction of any sort.

"Maybe we could both fight him at the same time," Ibouzeros Gliabanos said, "and squeeze him between us like a seed between thumb and forefinger."

"Maybe," I said unenthusiastically. Having the Khazars on the northern border of the Roman Empire struck me as being no more desirable than having the Bulgars there. My preference would have been for all the steppe nomads to vanish off the face of the earth and, in so doing, to take the Arabs with them.

I installed Ibouzeros Gliabanos and his retinue in the Blakhernai palace. Aside from scandalizing the servants with demands for fermented mare's milk and molesting one of the maids, they behaved well enough. The khagan spent much of his time talking with his sister and making the acquaintance of his nephew. Having had any number of children by his retinue of wives, he knew well how to ingratiate himself with Tiberius.

Not caring to be in his company more than necessity demanded, I dedicated to others the task of showing him around the imperial city. I did have hopes that encountering Cyrus, whom he had met in Atil, in the splendid surroundings of the great church might cause him to be persuaded as to the truths of our holy and orthodox Christian faith, as his sister had been. In this, however, I was disappointed. I consoled myself by remembering how richly he deserved to burn in hell for eternity for having tried to slay me. God's justice surely would not be denied in the world to come.

If Ibouzeros Gliabanos intended any moves in concert with the Roman Empire, as I believe he did, he also was disappointed. I tolerated him on account of past favors and his relationship to my wife, but I would never, ever, trust him.

He realized this after a time, saying, "I could give you all the herds and all the gold I have, and you would not send me a single soldier in exchange."

"That is true," I replied. "Tell me, though, whom you would rather have for a neighbor: a man who will do nothing against his will even in exchange for gold, or a man who will do anything at all, so long as he is paid for it."

Despite their swarthy cast, his cheeks flushed red. Having taken Apsimaros's gold in payment for the blood of his own brother-in-law, myself, he recognized the point of the gibe.

Perhaps that was what made him decide to take ship once more a few days later. But the sailing season was drawing to an end, and I can understand his desire not to be away from his barbarous people through the winter season. Were one of them to prove as devious and disloyal as he was himself, he might have found himself in a predicament with which experience had made me entirely too familiar.

Then again, too, he might have wondered whether, if I had him in Constantinople the whole winter long, I would yield to temptation and arrange for his sudden, untimely passing from this life to that of eternity. I confess I was wondering the same thing myself. Had he not been Theodora's brother . . .

But he was, and so I had to let him go, however much I regretted it. Not even the Emperor of the Romans realizes every dream in full.

Before boarding the ship that would take him across the Black Sea, he embraced his sister and said to me, "I thank you for letting me live."

Since he chose not to dissemble hypocritically, I followed the same course, answering, "Thank your sister, not me."

"I have already thanked her. I thank you as well." All his retinue had gone aboard the ship by then. He hurried after the rest of the Khazars, as if worried yet that I might change my mind.

With Theodora beside me, I could not. But, as I watched his ship sail toward the Bosporos, I regretted not having had the foresight to post a couple of dromons at the strait's outlet to the Black Sea so they might incinerate the vessel, him in it, with liquid fire. A storm at sea would almost surely have been blamed for his demise. The sailors who did the deed would not have blabbed, knowing as they must how I requited those betraying me.

For my wife's sake, I let him go: such are the follies of uxoriousness. He is khagan of the Khazars even yet. Once I settle with Kherson and the other cities thereabouts, that will be time enough to deal with him.

The Bulgars' raids having grown intolerable, I resolved to punish them as they deserved despite their being ruled by a man whom I had myself created a Caesar of the Romans. Assembling the cavalry forces from the military districts of Anatolia, I ordered them to cross into Thrace so they could teach Tervel that his exalted rank did not bring with it the privilege of preying on the Roman provinces adjacent to the lands he ruled, lands themselves Roman by right. This was in the twenty-fourth year of my reign, the fourth since my return from unjust exile.

When I returned to the imperial city, I—

M Y A K E S

Wait a minute, Brother Elpidios. Where's the rest of it? What do you mean, what do I mean, the rest of it? The part where Justinian talks about the campaign against the Bulgars, that's what. Didn't you skip a leaf or two or three in the codex there?

What? You didn't? That's all he says? Well, I will be—no, that's something I've finally learned it's better not to say in a monastery. But it's hard to believe, all the same. Up till now, he's pretty much told the whole story, even if he and I don't always remember things the same way. There's a lot missing here, though, one devil of a lot.

What do you mean, why didn't he tell it? How should I know? I'm not Justinian. I can think of a couple of reasons off the top of my head, though, that might have something to do with it. For one thing, this part would have been written right near the end of his reign. Revenge was all he had in his mind, or pretty close to all, anyhow. He didn't get much revenge against the Bulgars.

And that ties in with the other reason I can think of. Justinian botched this campaign every way you can think of. He was never a man who was easy to embarrass, but when he looked back on things here, if he wasn't embarrassed, he bloody well should have been.

Was I there, Brother Elpidios? Oh yes, that I was. I saw the whole mess, right up close. I was lucky to get away with my own neck. So was Justinian.

All right, I'll tell you about it, since Justinian didn't, and since most of the people who were there are bound to be dead by now. So Justinian didn't let out a peep, eh? Isn't that something? I can hardly believe it, and that's a fact.

Like he says, the cavalry from the military districts crossed over from Anatolia into Thrace. They rode up the Black Sea coast. Justinian sailed up to Ankhialos, just south of Mesembria, to meet them there. He brought the excubitores along, which was how I got lucky enough to come.

Ankhialos, of course, means "next door to the sea." If the place weren't next door to the sea, there'd be no reason for it to exist. Now that I think about it, there isn't much reason for it to exist anyhow. Why anybody would bother having it and Mesembria both is beyond me. Yes, I know nobody asked my advice. Justinian sure didn't, for true.

Anyway, there we were, waiting for the cavalry from the military districts to come up and join us so we could attack the Bulgars. You can see the Haimos Mountains, the border between Thrace and the Bulgars' country, from Ankhialos, and you can see Ankhialos from the mountains, too, because they dip south close to the coast. The Bulgars were watching us, though we didn't know it yet.

Ankhialos wasn't what you'd call ready to have an army show up on its doorstep. God in heaven, Brother Elpidios, we excubitores drank the taverns out of wine in three days all by our lonesome. Justinian had to detach a couple of dromons to go on up to Mesembria and bring back more before his guards started fighting each other instead of the Bulgars.

One by one, the regiments of cavalry from the military districts trickled up the road to Ankhialos. Justinian wanted to wait till he had everybody there before he hit the Bulgars a lick. "Concentration, My-akes," he said to me, till I got sick of hearing it. "One strong blow is better than half a dozen puny ones."

"That's so, Emperor. No doubt about it," I finally told him. "If we wait around too long, though, the barbarians are going to know we're up to something, and have a pretty good idea of what. We've got a lot of soldiers here already. If we take 'em by surprise—"

"Concentration," he said again, and I shut up. Trying to tell Justinian anything he didn't want to hear wasn't easy and wasn't particularly safe even before he got his nose slit. Afterwards—well, I could get away with a lot with him, because I'd been through so much with him. But I didn't want to push it, if you know what I mean. Concentration he wanted, and concentration he got.

But it wasn't very concentrated concentration. What do I mean? It's like this: there's a fair-sized plain west of Ankhialos. That's where the troops from the military districts made their camps. But they camped the same way they'd come up from Constantinople: by regiments, one here, one there, one over yonder. Yes, somebody should have been in overall charge and made them all join together and turn into a proper army. But the only somebody who could have done that was Justinian, and he didn't bother.

The other thing he didn't do was keep enough sentries out around the camps. "You worry too much," is what he said to me when I complained about that. "The Bulgars will be shaking in their shoes when they find out I've brought a proper Roman army against them. They won't fight. They'll run away."

"That's what your father said, almost thirty years ago," I answered. "Look what it got him."

For some reason or other, that made him angry, and he dismissed me. Once he had an idea in his head, you couldn't knock it out with a hammer. I thought about asking him why he'd thought the Bulgars could fight Romans when he'd come south with Tervel, but figured they couldn't when he was coming north against Tervel. I didn't bother. It wouldn't have done any good.

Like I said, Ankhialos wasn't as ready as it should've been to supply that "proper Roman army" Justinian was so proud of. The granaries emptied out as fast as they would have if locusts had got into them, and some of the cavalry regiments hadn't even got there yet. Some of the people in the town complained to Justinian that he was eating them out of house and home.

What? How much good did that do? How much do you think, Brother Elpidios? He only killed one of them, I will say that for him.

Where was I? Oh, yes, that's right—we were starting to run out of grain. We were running low on fodder for the horses, too, now that I think about it. And so what happened was, the army started wandering over that plain west of Ankhialos, trying to keep themselves and their animals fed. They might have been a flock of sheep, the way they ate everything down to the ground.

What? Oh. Yes, Brother, one of the farmers complained to the Emperor. He hung him on a gibbet. After that, the farmers did what farmers always do when soldiers come robbing: they ran for the hills and took whatever animals they could with 'em.

I wished Leo was there, instead of off in the Caucasus. Christ, I even wished Helias was there, instead of back in Constantinople minding the store for Justinian. The Emperor had made it very clear he wouldn't pay any attention to me. Both of them were sneaky enough, they might have found some way to get him to listen.

But they weren't there. Justinian didn't listen to anybody. He'd go from one scattered camp to the next. He said he was inspecting the regiments. Maybe he even thought that's what he was doing. It looked like wasting time to me, and I was starting to think we didn't have much time left to waste.

I was right, too. Much good it did me.

The day I'm thinking about, Justinian was visiting the camp of the soldiers from the military district of the Opsikion. He'd gone to them before. He trusted them further than he did a lot of the other troops there, I suppose because Barisbakourios was their commander. He wasn't with the army either, though, which was a cursed shame, because he was one more Justinian might have heeded.

Barisbakourios had sent his lieutenant general to Thrace instead— a weedy little fellow named Theodotos. He wasn't worth much, as far as I was concerned. Some of the men in his regiment had been trained to do acrobatics on horseback. He had them showing off for Justinian when some sort of commotion started in the camps north of his.

"What's going on?" Justinian asked. It was, at least, the right question.

Theodotos didn't even try to find out. "Probably nothing, Emperor," he said indifferently, and then, to his pet acrobats, "Keep on, boys." He turned to Justinian again. "You'll like this next bit, I promise you."

But we never got to see the next bit. A couple of horsemen who weren't acrobats came pelting down toward the camp of the men from the military district of the Opsikion. They were screaming something. It didn't take us long to find out what, either. "The Bulgars!" they shouted. "The Bulgars are attacking! All's lost! Run for your lives!"

Brother Elpidios, you never saw people disappear so fast in all your born days as those cursed acrobats. One moment they were there, the next they were nothing but little dots on the southern horizon—and getting littler faster than you'd believe.

If Theodotos had been worth a follis, he would have rallied his men and sent them off to drive the Bulgars back. If he'd been worth half a follis, he would have rallied them and used them to protect the Emperor. What he did do was squeak "We're ruined!" and then jump on his own horse and gallop off almost as fast as those acrobats.

Well, that did it. That did it and then some, as a matter of fact. "Hold, men!" Justinian shouted, but the soldiers from the military district of the Opsikion weren't about to hold. They'd seen their friends run away, they'd seen their commander run away, and the only thing they wanted to do was run away, too. And that's what they did. They figured Justinian couldn't stop the lot of them, and they were right.

And they weren't the only ones. Everywhere I looked, I saw Romans running or riding south, fast as they could go. Tents in some of those other encampments were going up in flames. Justinian, I suppose, had been right about concentration after all. One strong blow had turned out better than half a dozen weak ones. Only trouble was, the Bulgars gave instead of getting.

A few of the troops from the Anatolian military district did put up a fight. The battle was lost before it got started, though. The Bulgars just ignored the Romans who were fighting back—weren't very many of 'em, Lord knows—and went after the ones who were running. They killed some of those, and plundered what the rest left behind. When a man's decided he's going to run, he'll throw away anything he's got so he can run faster. All the Bulgars had to do was follow along and pick up the flotsam and jetsam, you might call it.

Near as I could see, Justinian was going to stay there cursing the Roman soldiers up, down, and sideways till the Bulgars noticed him and scooped him up. I wondered what Tervel would do with him if they carried him north of the mountains. I wondered, but I didn't really want to find out, because I figured whatever Tervel would do to Justinian, he'd probably do to me, too.

And so, when Justinian showed no signs of going anywhere on his own, I said, "Emperor, we'd better get back to Ankhialos. Once we're inside the walls, the Bulgars won't be able to do anything to us."

"That's true," he said, as if it hadn't occurred to him—and it hadn't, either. So off we went, heading east and a little north over the plain toward the town. I wasn't the only one who'd had that same idea. The Romans who weren't fighting and weren't running south as fast as they could were making for Ankhialos.

Pretty soon, we made up a good-sized band. The horsemen pulled me and the rest of the excubitores up behind them, so we rode double. That let everybody move faster, which made all of us happier, let me tell you. The sooner we got some nice tall stonework between the Bulgars and us, the better we'd like it.

I was riding near Justinian a couple of furlongs from Ankhialos when his horse quit on him. Poor beast must have hurt itself, lamed itself some kind of way, because it just wouldn't go on no matter how he swore at it and no matter how he booted it.

"Another traitor!" he shouted, and leaped down out of the saddle. His sword was already in his hand. If the Bulgars had come at him, he'd've fought hard—nothing wrong with his courage. If you haven't seen that by now, Brother, you're blinder than I am.

But he would not stand being crossed, not for a moment, not even by a horse. Slash, slash, and he cut both the animal's hamstrings. Beast screamed like a woman as its back legs went out from under it. "If I can't have you, the Bulgars will get no joy of you," Justinian said, as if it *was* a woman. He scrambled up onto somebody else's horse and rode pillion the rest of the way to Ankhialos.

The Bulgars, thank God, didn't try storming the town. If they'd tried, they might have done it. The soldiers who were in there, I don't think they would have put up much of a fight. When you got down to it, though, it didn't matter much. Tervel had done what he'd set out to do. We weren't going to invade the Bulgars' country, not after he'd stomped the cavalrymen from the military districts we weren't.

More Romans got into Ankhialos after the band that had formed around Ankhialos. They'd had to do real fighting to reach the city. Some of them brought in trophies: a few heads, bows and arrows, a couple of the boiled-leather shirts the Bulgars wear instead of chainmail.

Justinian ordered the excubitores to confiscate all those prizes. "What for, Emperor?" I asked.

"We'll display them on the walls of Ankhialos, to impress the Bulgars with our might," he answered. With anyone else, I would have laughed. It made a pretty fair joke, after what Tervel had just done to us. But he wasn't joking. I could see that. He wanted trophies up there, just as if we'd won the battle. Maybe he thought we did. I tell you, Brother, I didn't have the nerve to ask.

We stayed in Ankhialos till the third day after the fiasco. Then the Roman troops in the city boarded the ships moored in the harbor and sailed back to Constantinople. We never tried fighting the Bulgars again, not as long as Justinian lived. That's the story he didn't want to tell there. I guess now you can see why. I wouldn't have been very proud of it either.

Now that I've yattered away for a while, Brother Elpidios, your voice should be all fresh and rested. What *did* Justinian like well enough to admit in writing he'd done it?

I received from Cyrus the ecumenical patriarch word I had long been awaiting, namely, that he and Constantine the bishop of Rome had at least the beginnings of an understanding concerning Constantine's acknowledgment and acceptance of the canons of the fifth-sixth synod I had summoned before being sent into exile.

"Excellent," I told Cyrus. "About time we see some sense from a Roman pope."

"Yes, Emperor," he said, nodding. "I think your treatment of Felix made Constantine see cooperating with the Roman Empire is a wiser course than opposing its might."

"A good thing for him he has seen it," I answered. "If I weren't busy elsewhere, I'd use him as I used Felix. Or rather, I'd use him as I would have used Felix if I hadn't had that dream that told me to spare his useless life."

"A dream may be the voice of God, Emperor," Cyrus said. "You were wise not to risk divine anger."

"I thought the same," I said. Why God thought the rebellious bishop of Ravenna deserved to remain among the living was beyond me, but no mortal man could oppose His desire and hope to prevail. Shifting my thoughts from what I had been unable to prevent to what I might be able to accomplish in times to come, I asked Cyrus, "How close, precisely, has Pope Constantine come to accepting the canons of the fifth-sixth synod?"

"He does still have reservations on a few of them, Emperor, but expresses those much more temperately than have previous bishops of Rome," the patriarch replied. "He may, if God be kind, accept those canons almost in their entirety."

Almost complete acceptance was indeed more than any previous bishop of Rome had shown himself ready to grant, but struck me as inadequate nonetheless, being a partial rejection of canons inspired by the Holy Spirit. "To which of them does he still object?" I asked.

"In particular, the thirteenth and the thirty-sixth," Cyrus said. "To refresh your memory, Emperor, these are—"

"I know what they are," I snapped. "The thirteenth requires a married man ordained a deacon or priest to keep on cohabiting with his wife rather than putting her aside, as is the ignorant practice throughout the patriarchate of Rome. The other states that your rights as patriarch of Constantinople are the same as those of the arrogant bishops of Rome, their primacy to be due solely to seniority. How can the popes object to that, it having been stated in the acts of the first ecumenical synod of Constantinople and in those of the ecumenical synod of Chalcedon?"

"Do not ask me to fathom the western mind," Cyrus said, "for I cannot. But with the principle already enshrined in the acts of the ecumenical synods, as you say—and your learning is marvelous, marvelous—perhaps we need not insist on its formal acknowledgment here."

"Perhaps," I said grudgingly. "What of the thirteenth canon, then?"

"The thirteenth canon does allow clergy in barbarous lands to retain their previous practices where those are not clearly forbidden," Cyrus said. "That offer, if not grounds for agreement, is at least grounds for negotiation."

"Very well," I said. "Go ahead and negotiate with Cyrus, since he seems willing to talk. Yield as little as you can, and accept nothing before submitting it to me for approval."

Cyrus bowed. "It shall be exactly as you say, Emperor, in every particular."

I was surprised that he needed to reassure me on the point. Did it prove other than exactly as I said in every particular, Cyrus's tenure as patriarch of Constantinople would come to an abrupt end. I had raised him to the patriarchal dignity because of his loyalty to me; should that loyalty falter, Kallinikos's fate would also fit him.

While he and Constantine sent letters back and forth, a desultory war with the Arabs broke out in southeasternmost Anatolia. The deniers of Christ, after some months' fighting and after Roman forces fell into confusion because of quarrels among their generals, succeeded in breaking into Tyana, north of the Kilikian Gates. They were unable to go farther, though it gave them a base from which they might later try to effect deeper penetration into Romania.

Under other circumstances, the fall of Tyana would have filled me with fury. But I paid little heed to it, nor has it much concerned me since. For one thing, the negotiations with Rome at last seemed likely to bear fruit, and gaining the pope's acceptance of the canons of the fifth-sixth synod counted for more with me than losing a dusty Anatolian fortress.

"The only remaining sticking point," Cyrus reported to me after exchanging a couple of letters with Constantine, "is the thirty-sixth canon, the one proclaiming Constantinople's authority equal to that of Rome, and Rome's primacy that of honor and seniority alone."

"Are you truly certain this point is adequately covered in the canons of the first ecumenical synod at Constantinople and that held at Chalcedon?" I said.

"I believe so, yes," Cyrus replied.

"You do not feel the dignity of your see impaired if the bishop of Rome rejects this one canon?"

"Emperor, I do not," the patriarch said.

"I have seen since naming you that you are zealous in protecting Constantinople's ecclesiastical rights and privileges," I said, whereupon Cyrus inclined his head in modest acknowledgment of the praise. "If this does not trouble you, I shall accept it."

"That is splendid news, Emperor," Cyrus exclaimed. "I confess, I had looked for you to be more refractory. I shall write to Bishop Constantine at once; I'm certain he will be as delighted as I am."

"Go ahead and write," I said indulgently. "Let us have this matter settled, it having hung over us for almost twenty years."

Under other circumstances, Constantine's preposterous obstinacy would have filled me with fury. As things were, however, it, like the faraway trouble in Anatolia, mattered little to me. I was engaged in the work that would be—that *will* be, by God and His Son!—the capstone of my revenge against all those who wronged me during the time in which I was denied my God-given right of sitting on the throne and ruling the Roman Empire.

Arrogant, cowardly little manikins that they were and are, the rich men who rule in Kherson—ruling, by their way of thinking, being defined as playing Roman influence off against the power of the khagan of the Khazars, as centered in the Khazar *tudun* in the city—had presumed to try to take me into custody and deliver me up to Apsimaros, that the usurper might deprive me of my head.

And not only shall I avenge myself upon them. I intend to remove Kherson from the map, to wipe it off the face of the world as a man wipes shit from the cleft of his buttocks, to leave no single stone, no brick, standing upon another. Nine mortal years I passed in that wretched, fish-stinking town. Only in the monastery where I dwelt and in the brothel where I took occasional comfort did I find the slightest trace of human kindness for a soul in anguish. Those I would let stand. The rest? Let fire take it!

Furthermore, the Khersonites are the only ones who remember seeing me with my mutilation. I also intended, and yet intend, to remove all memory of that from mankind. That an Emperor of the Romans should have suffered the humiliation of being allowed to couple with a whore only in darkness absolute, and then for double the going rate, shall be as forgotten as the ultimate fate of the ten lost tribes of Israel.

When I fall upon Kherson, I purpose doing so in force so over-whelming, the Khersonites shall be able neither to resist nor to summon the Khazars to their rescue. Ibouzeros Gliabanos, having survived his visit to Constantinople, might be tempted to thwart me there. That I will not allow.

Reasoning thus, I began gathering dromons and merchantmen to carry troops and horses not only at the imperial city but also at Kyzikos and Nikomedeia. To command the expeditionary forces, I chose my spatharios Helias, Stephen the sailor who had aided me with the bureaucrats reluctant to join my feast, and black-bearded Mauros, reckoning them well suited to my purpose.

"Helias," I said to the spatharios, "you shall govern the new Kherson when the expedition has succeeded in destroying the old. We will settle it by means of merchants and artisans transplanted from elsewhere in the Empire."

"Yes, Emperor," he said, making a show of submissiveness. "Just as you say, Emperor." He coughed a couple of times, then went on, "You are aware, of course, of the grumbling among the property owners of the city at the taxes they have had to pay for your force."

"Theirs is to obey," I growled. "Mine is to decide what the Empire requires. If they grumble, their heads will decorate the Milion, which has looked rather bare of late. Keep your ear to the ground, and bring me the names of those who complain. Have your friends do likewise. We shall nip this in the bud."

"Of course, Emperor." Bowing deeply, Helias departed.

Myakes, who had stood silent by the throne while Helias and I conversed, spoke up after the spatharios left. "That's trouble, Emperor."

"What, Helias?" I said. "I think he's safe enough."

Myakes' shoulders went up and down in a shrug. "You know I don't much like him, so I won't waste your time with what I think there. But remember when Stephen the Persian and Theodotos were squeezing Constantinople so tight fifteen years ago? That got you hated, and it helped Leontios send you into exile."

"I'm ready for trouble this time, Myakes," I said. "Let it come. I'll make a bigger slaughter here in Constantinople than I intend to make in Kherson." Thinking about it was plenty to make my member rise in anticipation.

"Emperor, isn't it better not to have trouble than to smash it when it comes?" Myakes asked.

"I need the great fleet to send against Kherson," I replied. "If building it causes no trouble, well and good. But I shall build it, whether it causes trouble or not." I folded my arms across my chest. "I have spoken." Having spoken, I expected no further comments from Myakes, and in that I was not disappointed. He has never failed me through disobedience.

M Y A K E S

You see how it was, Brother Elpidios? Every so often, I would try to get him to listen. Christ on His cross, even Helias tried to get him to listen. He wouldn't do it. We might as well have been talking to the city wall. Justinian was going to do what Justinian was going to do, and if the world didn't like it, he figured, that was the world's hard luck.

Yes, he bent a little for Pope Constantine. Less than you'd think, though, and he'd seen dickering in the church always had a bit of give-and-take to it. Anything outside the church, it was all take and no give. And even with Constantine, Justinian wasn't the one who did most of the bending. You'll see, I expect.

J U S T I N I A N

Cyrus came to me in a state of high excitement, waving a sheet of parchment. "Emperor, not only has the bishop of Rome agreed to all canons of your fifth-sixth synod save only the thirty-sixth, but he has requested your leave to come to the imperial city so that he might personally show forth his affection for you."

"Has he?" I said. "Well, he is welcome here, since he accommodated himself to me more than I to him. You may write and tell him I shall be pleased to receive him when he comes."

"I shall send the letter this very day," Cyrus said. "But, Emperor"—he assumed an expression of concern—"what if you are away from the imperial city when the holy bishop of Rome arrives? You have been traveling a good deal of late, and—"

"And I aim to go right on traveling," I broke in. "Preparations for the expedition against Kherson go better when they are under my eye. If I'm away when he comes, either I'll return or he can come to me. But I will not keep myself locked up in Constantinople to wait on any man—most especially not for a backwoods bishop with a pretentious title. Is that plain?"

Cyrus's eyebrows climbed on his hearing my true opinion of the pope's view of his own importance. "It is most plain, Emperor," he answered after a moment. "But who can receive the bishop of Rome in your absence?"

"As I say, I won't be absent long at any one time. Surely you can keep Constantine happy for a little while." I laughed. "And even if I am in Nikomedeia or Kyzikos, a Roman Emperor will be residing in Constantinople."

"The Emperor Tiberius?" By his face, Cyrus could not decide whether to be dismayed or delighted.

"He's five years old now," I said. "I don't expect him to rule yet— I don't expect him to rule for many years—but he can serve as my substitute in ceremony."

"I suppose that's so, Emperor." Cyrus looked like a man casting about for objections but unable to find any. He left the grand palace to compose his reply to Pope Constantine and extend my invitation to the Queen of Cities.

That afternoon, I asked my son, "How would you like to welcome the pope of Rome if he happens to come here while I'm out of the city?"

"I don't know," he answered. "Can I cut off his head if he doesn't do as I tell him?"

I folded the boy into an embrace. "By Christ and all the saints, you are truly my son!" I ruffled his hair, which was almost as dark as Theodora's. "I'm proud of you."

"Can I?" Tiberius asked eagerly.

"I'm afraid not," I said. "He's supposed to be making a friendly visit, so people would be upset if he went back to Rome without his head."

"All right," he said, his voice grudging. Then he brightened. "Can I put his eyes out, the way you did with the bad patriarch and the bishop who was a dirty rebel?"

"I don't think we'll have to do that, son," I said. "If he were being disagreeable, then we would have to think about it. It would make all the churches in the west very upset with us."

"So what?" Tiberius said.

"They were upset with us before, when I was a boy, and my father went to a lot of trouble to make friends with them again," I said. "I don't want to make them angry now unless I have no other choice." I rumpled his hair again. "But I do like the way you think."

"You won't let me *do* anything, though," he complained.

He sounded very much like my uncles, Herakleios and my son's semi-namesake Tiberius. How they chafed as junior Emperors under my father, and how, once they grew to manhood, they tried to supplant him. Casting a speculative eye on my Tiberius, I wondered whether, in ten years' time, he would be tempted to seize the reins of power before having any right to do so. If he did, he would regret it as much as my uncles had done after their bid for the throne failed. Kin could prove more deadly than common traitors, being liable to retain one's trust too long by virtue of their blood ties.

M Y A K E S

As things worked out, Brother Elpidios, Justinian wasn't in Constantinople when Pope Constantine got close to the city. The Emperor had gone down to Kyzikos, to see how the fleet there was doing, when messengers got to Constantinople saying Constantine would be there any day.

What, Brother? Me? I was in Constantinople. No, I didn't go to Kyzikos with Justinian. He took along Helias and Stephen and the other officers who'd be heading for Kherson as soon as everything was right. He knew I didn't much care for his plans, and so he just left me out of them. We'd been together for thirty-five years and more, him and me, and now it was like I wasn't there any more. It hurt, I'll tell you.

Cyrus the patriarch forgot Justinian wasn't there. He came to the Blakhernai palace himself instead of sending over a flunky, the way he would have done if he knew he couldn't talk to the Emperor himself.

"You planned all of this out ahead of time," I reminded him when he started having kittens right there in front of me. "Justinian hasn't fallen off the edge of the world. He's in Kyzikos or Nikaia or maybe even Nikomedeia by now. He'll either come back here or see Constantine in one of those places. Tiberius can welcome the pope to Constantinople."

Tiberius reminded Justinian of himself as a boy, eh? He reminded me of Justinian, too. Back when Justinian was little, I'd wondered how he'd ever manage to live to grow up without somebody hitting him over the head with a rock first. I wondered the same thing about Tiberius. But Justinian doted on him. Blood calls to blood, they say, and like to like. That was one place where I wasn't ever going to tell the Emperor what I thought, believe you me I wasn't.

Once Cyrus calmed down and stopped running around like a chicken with a fox on its tail, he did pretty well. We had a few days to get ready. For a wonder, Theophilos, who wasn't what you'd call bright, sent word ahead that the bishop of Rome had got to him instead of letting Constantine come on to Constantinople without any warning. Those were the kinds of surprises you didn't want to have.

When Constantine finally got there, he landed at the seventh milestone outside the imperial city. That let Cyrus spread himself, as the saying goes. Out he went, dressed in his fanciest robe. Out went Tiberius, in one of Justinian's old robes and a crown that must have belonged to one of his great-uncles once upon a time. What he looked like was a pretty little ferret in a doll's robe. Out went Theodora, who never quite figured out how vicious her son was.

Out went the nobles, the new ones Justinian had made and the handful of old ones still left alive. And out streamed the people, in swarms and droves. The idea of a pope in the imperial city was a spectacle that ranked right up there with the hippodrome. The last time a pope had come to Constantinople was during the reign of Constans, Justinian's grandfather. The last time a pope had come to Constantinople without being in chains . . . I don't know how long ago that was. A bloody long time, I'll tell you.

Anyway, up came the dromon, and beached itself within spitting distance of the seventh milestone. What? Yes, I was there, guarding Tiberius's nasty little neck. We all went out to meet Constantine—Tiberius, Theodora, and Cyrus ahead of everybody else—everybody but the excubitores, that is.

Constantine was out of Syria, and spoke Greek as his native language. He wasn't just a barbarian from the west, in other words—he understood showmanship. He waited till the people who counted were close enough to see what he was doing before he let the captain let down the gangplank. He must have been saving the robe he had on for just that moment, too. It outshone Cyrus's the way a bonfire outshines a lantern.

Despite turning green as an unripe fig when he saw that gorgeous robe, Cyrus kept his wits on what needed doing. He coughed a couple of times, till Tiberius remembered his line: "In the name of my father, I, the Emperor Tiberius, welcome your holiness to the imperial city."

"Poor servant of the servants of Christ that I am, young Emperor, I thank you for your gracious welcome," Constantine answered in gutturally accented Syrian Greek. He looked east, toward the walls and big buildings of Constantinople on the horizon. "I look forward to seeing your great capital, and to meeting your father, the grand and glorious Emperor of the Romans."

He laid it on with a trowel, Pope Constantine did. Well, he hadn't

come all that way to tell Justinian what a wicked fellow he was. If he'd
been stupid enough to try that, they'd have chosen a new bishop of Rome
right afterwards, because the one they had wouldn't have been worth
anything to 'em any more.

But that's just chatter, Brother Elpidios. We had some fine horses
from the imperial stable waiting for Constantine and the other churchmen he'd brought. They were all tricked out fancy, with gilded saddles
and bridles and with saddlecloths of imperial crimson. Along with his
gaudy robe, Constantine was wearing a camel-hair cap that reminded me
of nothing so much as a woven cowflop, but he was the pope, so who
was going to tell him he couldn't?

Cyrus the patriarch rode alongside him as they paraded back toward
Constantinople. They were thick as thieves, talking about God and Christ
and how to deal with recalcitrant bishops and all sorts of other holy
things. I heard bits and pieces of it, because I was marching along by
Tiberius's litter, which wasn't far away. If I'd known then what I know
now, I'd have understood a whole lot more of it.

We went into Constantinople through the Golden Gate. Constantine had been staring at what he could see of the city over the top of the
wall—and at the wall, too, come to that. When he finally got inside, he
stopped his horse, took a long look around, and said, "I wouldn't have
believed it, no matter how many things I've heard."

Everybody who sees Constantinople for the first time says something
like that.

Constantine went on, "Rome is a skeleton of what it used to be.
Here at last I see a great city in the flesh."

Just like an Anatolian peasant boy who's come to join the army—
like me, say, getting close to forty years before then—he kept ohing at
this and ahing at that as we rode down the Mese toward the house of
Placidia near the church of the Holy Wisdom, where he'd stay till Justinian got word he was there.

He wasn't a bad fellow—Constantine, I mean. Put three or four
cups of wine in him and he got friendly, same as anybody else. Put a little
more in him and he wanted to wrestle. He'd been a pretty fine wrestler
in his younger days, especially, I guess, if you listened to him tell it. Only
trouble was, he hadn't seen his younger days any time lately.

What's that, Brother? A bishop wrestling? Well, he did. And do you
know what he'd say? He'd say that if it was good enough for Jacob, it was
good enough for him. I couldn't figure out any way to argue against that,
and I'll bet you won't, either.

Anyhow, Constantine and the rest of the churchmen from Rome

had a fine old time in Constantinople. They'd visit a new church or two every day, and at night—ask me no questions and I'll tell you no lies, Brother Elpidios.

Some of them were downright disappointed when Cyrus's messengers finally tracked down Justinian. Sure enough, he was in Nikaia, on his way from Kyzikos down to Nikomedeia. He sent the messenger who'd caught up with him back to Constantinople with a letter telling Pope Constantine to meet him in Nikomedeia.

Off went the pope. Off went the bishops and priests who'd come along with him. They were getting what they'd come all the way from Rome for, and do you know what? Most of 'em really did look as if they could have waited another couple of weeks to have it.

JUSTINIAN

My expeditionary forces against Kherson being nearly ready to sail, the arrival of Pope Constantine in the imperial city proved more nearly a nuisance, an interruption to that important business, than anything else. But, having granted him leave to come, I could hardly refuse to treat with him once his journey was completed.

Nikomedeia made a good enough place for the two of us to meet. Although damaged by Arab and Persian invaders, it has been repaired and refortified, its hilltop stronghold being especially difficult to capture. And the harbor there, though not large, is well sheltered from the elements.

Constantine, however, chose to travel by land. We met not far outside the wall. He dismounted from the post-horse lent him, approached me, and prostrated himself as any other Roman subject would have done. "Emperor, I thank you for calling me to the Queen of Cities," he said in a Greek rather harsh.

He being no ordinary Roman subject, I waited until he had risen and then prostrated myself before him in turn. "Holy Bishop of Rome, I thank you for coming here and restoring perfect peace in the church," I replied, rising myself.

We beamed at each other. I would have treated Felix of Ravenna harshly in any case, and was glad to see myself reaping such a large profit thereby. Constantine said, "Even this small city of Nikomedeia bustles with such activity as is rarely seen in Italy and the other western regions."

You are in a civilized land now, I thought, but did not say as much out loud. What I did say was, "I am glad Romania pleases the bishop of Rome"—a subtler reminder of the same thing.

Constantine said, "I, for my part, am glad we have been able to agree on the canons of the holy synod you summoned twenty years ago, and that you recognize the need for abandoning the thirty-sixth, which is odious in the eyes of the episcopal successors of Saint Peter."

Few of the bishops under the jurisdiction of the patriarchate of Constantinople would have dared be so free-spoken with me. Indeed, Constantine took his prerogatives as seriously as I took mine. "I have been persuaded that canons from two previous ecumenical synods cover the same ground, yes," I replied, yielding his immediate point but not the larger issue.

The immediate point sufficed. "Let us rejoice in our peace and unity," Constantine said. "If I celebrate the divine liturgy here, Emperor, will you take of the Lord's body and blood from my hands?"

"I should be honored," I replied; I should have been slighted had he made no such suggestion. "The church of the Holy Wisdom is the finest in Nikomedeia."

Constantine's face lit up. "I have seen the church of the Holy Wisdom in Constantinople. If this one is anywhere near so fine—"

"Hardly," I said, laughing. "No church I have ever seen comes close to the great church in the Queen of Cities."

"God forbid that I should disagree," Constantine exclaimed, "lest I be revealed in His eyes as a liar."

"The church of the Holy Wisdom here is no mean hovel," I assured him, "and of course the presence of the pope of Rome ornaments any church." We smiled at each other, both of us intent on wringing maximum advantage from our meeting. I went on, "Nikomedeia's other accommodations should also suit you, even if they prove less splendid than those you enjoyed in Constantinople."

"I am sure I shall be contented here," he said. "I have had only comfortable lodgings and courteous dealings with Roman officials. Your governor Theophilos was particularly generous of his substance and his time."

"I am glad to hear he gave you the honor you deserve," I said. Theophilos, though not the brightest man God ever made, had shaped better as the commander of the Karabisianoi than I looked for on naming him to the post. Though relying on his advisers, he did not hesitate to overrule them when he judged them mistaken. More than that, one could hardly ask from any man.

I quartered the bishop of Rome and his followers in a wing of the hilltop stronghold in which I was also residing. He grew quite merry over wine. I said, "At the divine liturgy tomorrow, I want you to pray for the success of the fleet I am going to send against Kherson to avenge myself upon the rich merchants there."

" 'Vengeance is mine, saith the Lord,' " he said, and then giggled. "Not mine, mine, but mine, the Lord's, you understand." Like a lot of men with a deal of wine in them, he was more precise than he needed to be.

" 'An eye for an eye, and a tooth for a tooth.' The Lord says that, also," I reminded him.

"He doesn't say anything about a nose for a nose." The pope giggled again. I let him live, he being obviously drunk and I having in any case long since avenged myself upon Leontios, who wounded my nose. Constantine held up his hands, as if to make scales. "One passage here, one passage there. Which with more weight?" He shrugged. "Emperor, I did not come here to quarrel with you. I shall pray for your fleet."

"Good," I said. "For that, you and the church can keep all your privileges in Italy." He was effusively grateful, but giving him what he already had cost me nothing, whereas extracting more from him would have required troops and poisoned the ecclesiastical peace we were confirming here.

As the evening wore on, Constantine not only challenged one of my guardsmen to wrestle, he broke the fellow's collarbone. He was most contrite, and prayed over the excubitor afterwards, but poor Paul's arm is not all it should be even on the day I set down these words.

The bishop of Rome was somewhat the worse for wear the next morning, but did nonetheless celebrate the liturgy as we had arranged. Nor did he use the excuse of the previous night's drunkenness to evade the promise he had made there. Before everyone in Nikomedeia's church of the Holy Wisdom, he asked God's favor for my "expedition to punish the wicked Khersonites for their numerous sins."

When I came up to take the miraculous bread and wine from him, I said, "Pray also that I may be forgiven my sins."

"I shall, Emperor," he answered, "in the same breath I use to pray for the forgiveness of my own."

He stayed in Nikomedeia another few days, then set out for the distant and backwards west once more. Word recently came to me that he was stricken ill on his journey; I do not know whether he has reached Rome safely. If not, I shall have the nuisance of beginning afresh with a new pope once the matter of Kherson is settled.

•   •   •

Mauros, Stephen, and Helias were all sailing with that portion of the naval expedition departing from Constantinople, giving me the opportunity of reminding them one last time of their orders: "When you get to Kherson, put everyone you can catch there and in the cities nearby to the sword. Spare no one. They had scant mercy on me; I have none on them. Is it understood?"

"Yes, Emperor," they chorused. "As you command, so shall we do."

"Good, good," I said. "I have waited six years for this moment. You will understand that I want it done perfectly, just as I say it must be."

"Yes, Emperor," they repeated.

"Very well," I said. When they started to leave my presence, I held up a hand. "Wait. One thing more." They looked most earnest and attentive. I continued, "I have given Bardanes Philippikos leave to sail with you as an officer in charge of a troop of soldiers. Watch him closely. If he performs his duty well, I want to know of it. If he performs poorly or shows any sign of disloyalty, I want to know that, too."

"Yes, Emperor," they said yet again, knowing they held Bardanes' life in the hollow of their hands. Although I had permitted the exile to return from Kephallenia after I ousted Apsimaros, I had heeded Myakes to the extent of not entrusting him with any position great or small, merely suffering him to live in Constantinople as a private citizen. He having begged me to let him prove himself—*I would die for you, Emperor*, he wrote in his petition—I granted him this small boon. If he lied, he would indeed die for me.

At the harbor the next day, when the fleet was to sail for Kherson, Bardanes came up and prostrated himself before me. "Emperor, by God and His Son, I swear to you, you shall not regret this choice," he said.

"Words are free," I said. "Words are easy. Show me what you do, Bardanes. Deeds mark a man. Show me what you do, not what you say. Helias and the others proved themselves that way."

His handsome, swarthy face assumed an injured expression. "Did I not prove myself, Emperor, when I saved you from the Sklavinian hiding in the stream?"

"A lifetime ago," I told him, adding, "Before you began to dream of eagles." Swarthy though he was, he flushed. "Perhaps that was but happenstance. Perhaps it was but foolishness," I went on, thinking as I had always thought that ever mentioning it was certainly foolishness. "But, because of it, you shall have to earn your way into my esteem once more."

"Emperor, I will!" he cried, so fervently that he was either sincere or one of the worst actors ever born.

And so he accompanies the fleet, its commanders having been warned to take careful notice of everything he does. If he is indeed as devoted to me as he proclaims, he will make a useful servant, being a man both clever and daring. The only one who I am certain surpasses him in those regards is Leo, and Leo lingers yet in the Caucasus. If he were here, I think I would see how clever he was without a head.

Strange. When I took up this writing, recording what I recall of my deeds and my life, I was chronicling the distant past. Now at last, having spent more than a year and a half on the task, I have reached the present day. Having said everything I have to say, I can but set these words aside and await further occurrences.

And yet, having taken up the pen, I find myself loath to put it down. Writing has grown to be a habit as regular as a goblet of wine with my meals, and as pleasurable. Flipping through these leaves, I see I have been very frank—perhaps too frank. I suppose, to keep my pen busy, I could go through this volume and excise those portions not fully redounding to my credit. That, too, would be writing of a sort. But what point to it? No one's eyes but mine shall ever see these words, I am certain of that. Theodora and Myakes are the only ones who know the nature of this exercise. In the great scheme of things, Myakes is of no consequence, however agreeable he has been to me over the years. And my wife, I am certain, will let nothing damaging to me ever see the light of day.

Let the words stand, then. Let them stand. Now I wait, and shall write more as the stream of time brings fresh events to my view.

I was tempted to record the news from Kilikia, which is very much of a piece with that of the previous year. But the fortresses we Romans lost are of such small consequence that I need not waste ink setting down their names. In any case, I will set all that aright in next year's campaigning season, or at the latest two years hence. Kherson and the surrounding towns come first.

What does prompt me to take up the pen is the first word from the fleet that had crossed the Black Sea. The word is good. In high excitement, the messenger from the dromon newly tied up at the Golden Horn told me, "Emperor, Kherson is ours. The folk there weren't expecting us, and they didn't even try to fight back."

"Splendid," I told him. "What went on before you sailed back here?"

He began telling off points on his fingers. "We have the Khazars' *tudun* there, and a fellow named Zoïlos—"

"I remember Zoïlos," I said. "A rascal if ever there was one."

"Yes, Emperor," he said. "We also have forty other prominent men from Kherson, all of them in bonds the whole way across the Black Sea."

"Good enough, good enough," I told him. "The executioners have been pining for want of fresh meat, and now they have it. Well, go on."

"When Mauros and Stephen and Helias got Kherson in their grasp, Emperor, they took seven other rich men and roasted them on spits over a bonfire," the messenger reported. "I saw that with my own eyes. They screamed for a long time, and the smell of cooking meat made you hungry till you remembered what it was. And they—"

I held up a hand. "Wait." I tried to decide whether I wanted the executioners to imitate what my men in Kherson had done. The savor of roasting meat would be very fine, but giving such specific orders was liable to cramp the executioners' style, depriving them of the opportunity to exercise their ingenuity. Realizing I did not have to settle such affairs on the instant, I waved for the fellow to continue.

He said, "Emperor, then they took twenty more men, tied their hands behind them and put them on a ship out past the harbor. They cast boulders onto the ship till it sank and drowned the prisoners."

"That sounds like a lot of trouble for a small result," I said critically. "They could have tied each man to a boulder and pushed him off a gangplank to accomplish the same thing. If they'd set the boat on fire, now—but they were using fire for the other torture, weren't they?" I sighed. "Well, we can't have everything. I suppose they thought it made a good spectacle."

"I wouldn't know anything about that," the messenger said.

"All right. Let it go, let it go," I said, inclined to be generous. "In the general massacre, it wouldn't have mattered much, anyhow. Men, women, children—" Something changed in the messenger's face, although I doubt he was even aware of it. Sharply, I demanded, "What's wrong?"

"Nothing," he said, but then, seeing deception useless, he changed his tune: "Emperor, not all the children are dead. The soldiers and sailors saved some, because they were so young, you understand, to sell into slavery, and—"

"They did *what?*" I said, and the messenger turned pale. "They did *what?* They disobeyed my direct order? They ignored the will of the Emperor of the Romans? Have they gone mad?"

Miserably, the man said, "I don't think so, Emperor. It's just that— killing children is hard, even for soldiers with orders. If they were slaves—"

"Fools!" I shouted. "Blunderers!" I bellowed. "Idiots!" I screamed. "Is it so hard for them to do as they are told? No more, no less? Is it so hard?" I hit the messenger in the face. He staggered back, clutching at his mouth with both hands. "Answer me!" I roared.

I had split his lower lip; blood dribbled down his chin and into his beard. "For-for-forgive them, Emperor," he stuttered. "They meant no harm."

"So *you* say," I sneered. "I shall hear it from the lips of the men I sent to Kherson to do a simple job." After shouting for a scribe, I dictated an order to him: "Mauros, Stephen, and Helias are commanded to return to this God-guarded and imperial city with the fleet entrusted to them in order that they might attempt to explain to their sovereign the gross dereliction of duty of which they are guilty."

"I shall make a fair copy of that, Emperor, and—" the scribe began.

"Never mind." I snatched the papyrus from his hands, scrawled my signature below the order, and thrust it at the messenger. "Take this back to your ship. Take it across the Black Sea. Deliver it to the officers there. It requires immediate obedience."

Even then, the scapegrace tried to argue with me: "Emperor, it's late in the sailing season. If a storm comes up on the sea—"

"It will drown a lot of whoresons who deserve nothing better," I said. "Now get out of my sight, while you still have a head on your shoulders." He fled. So did the scribe.

Dear God, how am I to carry out my vow of vengeance for Thee if the men through whom I must do my work thwart me at every turn?

"The fleet from Kherson is returning, Emperor." The messenger spoke the words, then withdrew from my presence as quick as boiled asparagus. I terrify everyone these days: my power is very great.

Riding out to the harbor to meet the incoming dromons, I saw but a remnant of the great expeditionary force I had sent forth. I went out to the very end of a pier and shouted a question at the closest ship: "Where is the rest of the fleet?"

"Sunk or scattered, Emperor." The answer came faint and thin over the sea. "We fought through a storm, and we must have lost thousands."

I threw back my head and laughed till the tears came. "Just what you deserved," I said. "See how God punished your disobedience to me? If you'd done as you were told, you will still be safe and comfortable in Kherson."

What was left of the expedition against Kherson limped into port. I confess to exulting on seeing the poor, mean state they made: a visible exemplification of what fate reserves for those who heed not the commands of the Emperor of the Romans.

From one of the battered dromons came Mauros. Seeing me waiting for him on the pier, he fell to his knees and then to his belly. With his face still pressed to the tarred planks, he said, "Forgive us, Emperor—I beg you! We did not fully grasp the depth of your wrath against the Khersonites."

Instead of giving him leave to rise, I kicked him in the ribs, as I had with the rebellious bishop, Flavius. "Lackwit!" I shouted, and kicked him again. "Cretin!" Another kick. "Jackass!" Another. "All you had to do was do as you were told. I wanted everyone in Kherson dead, every building wrecked. Now I'll have to send out another expedition to do a proper job of smashing things up."

He did not move as I kicked him; had he moved, I should have ordered him put to the sword on the spot. "Mercy, Emperor!" he gasped on my falling silent. "Mercy, I beg of you."

"That depends on whether you deserve it," I answered. "Where are Helias and Stephen? Did they drown? Are they here?"

"Neither one," he said. "They're still back in Kherson. When your order to return reached us, they didn't dare come back to the Queen of Cities to face you. I dared, and here I am."

For that, I let him get to his feet. "What of Bardanes?" I asked him.

"He is staying in Kherson, too," Mauros replied, adding, "and he was the one who kept us from killing the children there, as you commanded."

"A rebel, in other words," I said, and Mauros nodded. "And Helias and Stephen are either rebels, too, or will be rebels in short order." Mauros nodded again, as if to say he himself was the soul of virtue. That I discounted, though his presence in Constantinople spoke better of him than the others' ominous absence. "The next force I send will bring them all back in chains for my judgment."

"Emperor, you should know you've frightened all the towns in those regions," Mauros said. "The next fleet you send may find nowhere to land, and the men may have to fight their way ashore if by some chance it does gain an anchorage. The Khazars can send soldiers to those parts faster and easier than we can."

"And I let Ibouzeros Gliabanos live!" I cried, striking my forehead with the heel of my hand in bitter repentance for that folly.

"No doubt you thought it was best at the time," Mauros said, giving me what sympathy he could.

I would not hear him. Every curse I had hurled at the army he and

Helias and Stephen commanded, I now rained down on my own head. Slowly and with no small struggle, I returned to myself. "If those traitors refuse to do my will," I ground out, "I shall have to force them to obedience, as I aimed to force Kherson and the other cities up in the north to obedience."

"What shall I do?" Mauros asked.

"You?" I withered him with a glare. "You'll stay here in the city, that's what, and better than you deserve." He bowed his head. Seeing the nape of his neck, I nearly ordered his head stricken from his shoulders on the instant. He had, however, returned to Constantinople in the face of my known displeasure, this bespeaking a certain basic loyalty to my cause. On account of it, I let him live, and am still wondering whether I made the proper choice.

"Punishment," I said.

The men whom I had summoned to the Blakhernai palace nodded solemnly. So much military talent having been invested in the previous expedition against Kherson, I was reduced to leaders I should not otherwise have chosen. Christopher, the officer whom I had recently sent to command the new military district of the Thrakesians, chanced to be in the imperial city. He at least was certain to know his business. With John, the city prefect, and George the Syrian, my minister of public finance, I fear that their undoubted loyalty counted for more than their military talent.

George had a guttural accent that put me in mind of Pope Constantine's. "How are we to bring back Helias and Stephen and Bardanes?" he asked.

"However seems best once you've crossed the Black Sea," I answered. "I can't give you a large army—I don't have a large army to give you—but the rebels will not have any great force behind them, either."

"What about the Khazars, Emperor?" Christopher asked. A sensible soldier, he studied the ground before advancing over it.

The question was sour as vinegar in my ears, and burned my wounded spirit as vinegar burns wounded flesh. "I will give you the *tudun* to restore to his place," I said. "And I will even give you that whoreson Zoïlos, to sweeten up the Khersonites and help detach them from the rebels."

"I hope that works," John said. "By God, I hope that works. What sort of shape are the two of them in, Emperor?"

"No one has been carving pieces off them, if that's what you mean,"

I told the city prefect. By the way he nodded, that was exactly what he had meant.

"You are merciful, Emperor," George the Syrian exclaimed.

"I am *not*," I said indignantly; given my vow on Foolish Paul's fishing boat out on the Black Sea was an insult, implying as it did that I was failing to fulfill my promise to God. I went on, "It's only that the executioners and I have been talking about how to make them last longest and hurt most, and haven't got round to working on them yet."

"Whatever the wherefores, they're here, they're whole, and we'll use them," Christopher said. I was glad to have found him within the Queen of Cities; he showed a quick pragmatism that looked like being very useful.

"If you see Ibouzeros Gliabanos, or treat with an envoy of his," I added, "explain that I do not wish to harm him. I could have harmed him here, had I had that in my mind. My aim is to punish Kherson and the other towns in that part of the world for what they did to me when I was exiled to those regions."

"I hope he hears us," said John, who was something less than filled with optimism as to his prospects for success.

"He will hear you," I said. "He will hear you because you speak for me, for Justinian, Emperor of the Romans. He knows my might."

When John, George, and Christopher sailed for Kherson a few days later, I went out to the harbor to watch them depart. The men were quieter than I should have liked. "They aren't happy about sailing at this season of the year, Emperor," one of the ship captains said. "They know how easily it can storm."

"They can risk the ocean's storm—or they can risk mine," I said. He bowed his head and went aboard his vessel.

Among those glum soldiers and sailors, one fellow stood out: a tall, gangly man with, I believe, the longest neck I have ever seen. "Smash them all," he said, over and over. "Smash them all." Drawing his sword, he slashed at the air.

"Who is that?" I asked, pointing his way.

"He is one of Mauros's spatharioi," George the Syrian answered. "His name is John, like the city prefect's; they call him Strouthos."

"John the Ostrich, eh? I like that." *Strouthos* can mean either *ostrich* or *sparrow*; since there are many more sparrows than ostriches, that is the more common use of the word. Here, though, the other plainly applied.

George said, "He would make a good hound. He always does as he is told. Now he has been told to kill, which he enjoys."

"Good." I beckoned to the gangly man. "You! John! Come here."

He looked up in some surprise, having been locked in his own private reverie of death and devastation. When he recognized me, his eyes—pale eyes, unusual among us Romans—went wide. He walked over to where I stood and gave me the clumsiest prostration I have ever received in all my years on the throne.

"Rise," I said, and rise he did. I am not short, but he towered over me. "I hear you're quite a killer," I told him.

His face lit up, as if a beautiful woman had said, *I hear you're quite a lover.* "Emperor, I do my best," he said.

"I hope your best will be very fine indeed," I said. "Kherson has a whole host of men in it who want killing. When your officers point you at those men, I want you to dispose of them without even the slightest thought of mercy. They deserve none. They are my enemies, and the enemies of the Roman Empire."

"They'll tell me what to do," John the Ostrich said, working it out in his mind ahead of time so he would know what to do when the moment came. Had he had to think at the moment of truth, likely he would have failed. "They'll tell me what to do, and I, I'll *do* it." He did not slash the air again with his sword; the bodyguard standing behind me wordlessly made it plain to even the dullest individual—from which John was not far removed—that doing so would prove fatally unwise.

Although he thought slowly, he had come up with the right answer here. "Obey your officers; they will obey me; all will be well."

John's head bobbed up and down on that long neck like a dandelion puffball in the breeze. "I'll do that, Emperor," he said. "I hope they give me plenty to kill." He prostrated himself again, then went back to his dromon.

"You see, Emperor?" George the Syrian said. "A hired murderer, nothing more, nothing less."

"So less as he is *my* hired murderer, I don't care," I answered. "Use him with care, lest he turn in your hand."

"Yes," George said heavily. "Too many tools have turned in our hands, there on the far shore of the Black Sea."

"That's why you're going out," I told him: "to turn them back the right way once more." He nodded and boarded ship himself. Seeing him go made me wish he cut a more properly martial figure; in the gilded mail-shirt that showed he was a commander, he looked more like a jumped-up tax collector decked out in armor than a warrior. He *was* a jumped-up tax collector, of course, but why did he have to look like one?

•   •   •

Betrayed! The Son of God had only one Judas to contend with. Lord, Lord, dear Lord I have worshiped all my life, why inflict them on by the scores? Are my sins so great?

I do not care. It does not matter. They may betray me, but they cannot beat me. Stinking fly-specked turds, they should know that already. If they are too stupid to remember my past, I shall remind them. Oh yes, I shall. I shall flay them and break their bones and slice their flesh and burn their privates with torches and red-hot iron. Then I will roll their bodies in vinegar and brine and draw out their guts a finger's breadth at a time. Last of all, only when they are at the point of death, I shall put out their eyes, that they may have seen what comes of disobedience.

Has Bardanes a wife and children here? Has Helias?

MYAKES

Ever since Justinian came back from Kherson, Brother Elpidios, I'd wondered now and whether he was drinking from a full jar of wine, if you know what I'm saying. I wondered more when he aimed everything he had at Kherson and the other towns on the far side of the Black Sea. Aye, some of the folks up there had done him wrong, but not *that* wrong. The one who'd done him real dirt was the khagan of the Khazars, but he let *him* live. Go figure.

When he got the news of what had gone wrong for the second fleet he sent up to Kherson, I really do think he went crazy for a while. What you were just reading there, it sounds like he went crazy, doesn't it?

It happened like this. I was—

What's that, Brother? Why did I keep on serving him if I thought he'd gone mad? No, it wasn't on account of I thought he'd take my head if I quit. I did think that, as a matter of fact, but it wasn't why I stayed. Why, then? You don't understand? I'll tell you why, Brother Elpidios. I guess the easiest way to put it is, I'd been serving him so long, it never even occurred to me I could do anything else. I'd been at his side thirty-five years by then, or maybe a bit more than that. Most marriages don't last so long. Somebody ups and dies, husband or wife.

And besides, every now and then he'd listen to me, a little bit, anyway, and what he'd do wouldn't be as horrible as what he might have done. And so I kept telling myself I was doing some good. And I was. *Some* good. Looking back, I've got to say it wasn't enough.

Does that answer your question? Good. Where was I, then? Oh, yes.

I was heading up the throne-room guards when a messenger came running in. Poor bastard looked scared to death. I found out why a minute later, too—he was the one who had to break the news from across the sea to Justinian.

I've never seen a man who looked so much like he wanted to stay down there forever once he prostrated himself. Justinian had to tell him three different times he could get up before he finally went and did it. "Emperor," he said once he couldn't keep quiet any more, "it's all gone wrong up in Kherson."

"What do you mean, it's gone wrong?" Justinian's voice didn't have any feeling in it anywhere. His eyes, though—his eyes were measuring that messenger for a coffin. I've never seen anything like it in all my born days, and I never will now—that's certain sure.

"It's gone wrong," the messenger repeated, and then, the poor sod, he had to tell how. "We landed outside Kherson," he said, "and Helias and Bardanes and the Khersonites and the Khazars said they wanted a parley. So George and John and Christopher went into the city with the *tudun* and Zoïlos—they were going to give them back anyway, you know—and—"

Justinian clapped a hand to his forehead. "Don't tell me they were such imbeciles as to go alone?" he said, like a man in pain.

"Emperor, they were," the messenger said miserably, "and the Khersonites slammed the gates shut on them, and there wasn't anything any of us could do about it, on account of we were outside and they were inside. And they didn't come out and they didn't come out, and then the gates opened up again all of a sudden, and our people didn't come out, but . . . well, they did, because the Khazars had George's head on a pike and John's on another one, and we weren't ready to fight them, not really, so they must have captured a couple-three hundred of us, and then—"

"What of Christopher?" Justinian broke in.

"I don't know, Emperor," the fellow answered.

I didn't know then, either. Years later, cooped up here in the monastery, I found out. The Khersonites and the Khazars in Kherson sent the *tudun* and Zoïlos and all the prisoners off to Ibouzeros Gliabanos. Along the way, the *tudun* died. They slaughtered Christopher and all the captured soldiers—I heard three hundred, but I don't know if that's right or not—to give him slaves in the next world. They aren't Christians, the Khazars, not even close.

"Emperor," the messenger said after a little while, "that's not the worst of it."

"God and His Son, what could be worse?" Justinian said, still in that toneless voice, like he couldn't take in what he was hearing. But he took it in, all right. He wasn't giving anything back, that's what it was, nothing at all.

The messenger licked his lips. I remember that. I was thinking, *This is what he really, really doesn't want to tell.* But he didn't have any choice, not any more he didn't, and so he blurted it out in a rush: "Emperor, they've declared Bardanes Emperor up there."

After that, nobody said anything for—oh, I don't know how long. If anybody breathed during however long it was, it must have been by accident. Theophylaktos the eunuch's eyes got big as hen's eggs. If he were here, he'd probably tell you mine were the same size.

Or maybe not, on account of maybe all he was doing was watching Justinian. That was most of what I was doing, too, but every now and then my eyes would move away for a heartbeat or two. Believe me, Brother Elpidios, that was most of what everybody in the Blakhernai throne room was doing.

Justinian couldn't very well watch himself. He watched the messenger instead, till the poor son of a whore must have thought his head would be the next one on a speak in front of the Milion. And then, in a quiet, even voice, Justinian said, "By the time I am through with them, Bardanes and Helias will wish they were Leontios and Apsimaros."

I think that was the most frightening thing I ever heard in my life, Brother Elpidios.

And then, just like he wrote it, Justinian asked, "Does Helias have a wife in the city? Does Bardanes?"

He didn't need long to find out.

JUSTINIAN

Ha! Helias did have a wife in the city, a woman named Zoe. He had a couple of brats, too. I sent soldiers to fetch them all to the Blakhernai palace. I sent a man to bring Cyrus the ecumenical patriarch here, too, to pronounce her divorce from her husband. Conspiracy against the Emperor has been a legal ground for dissolving a marriage from very ancient days.

And then I had another happy thought and made another summons. I thought it was particularly fitting.

One of the traitor's children proved to be a nursing babe, the other a toddler. Zoe held them both in her arms while I told her the crime of which her husband was guilty. She hung her head. False tears streamed from her eyes.

Cyrus droned out the formula of divorcement, along with all the whys and wherefores that made it binding straightaway. Now Zoe wept in earnest, at being sundered from the man who had betrayed me. The patriarch had done his job. He left.

"Now," I said to Zoe, "you are in law free of the man who was your husband."

"Your will be done, Emperor," she whispered.

"Oh, my will shall be done in this matter," I said, "in every way." I pointed to the children she still held. "They are of the traitor's blood. His line shall not continue."

Zoe began to scream. She turned, as if to run. Excubitores blocked her path. More excubitores advanced on her, seized her, and took the infants from her. Her shrieks grew loud. They echoed sweetly from the roof of the the throne room. They redoubled yet again when a man dressed all in black and wearing a black hood strode into the chamber.

Zoe saw him going over toward the guardsmen who held her children. She screamed, "No, Emperor, not them! Kill me instead! Not them!"

"They are of the seed of the traitor and rebel," I said. "You are not. Now that you are divorced from him, you need have no more concern for him and his."

"My babies!" Zoe cried. The excubitores held her fast when she tried to break free and run to them.

I nodded to the executioner. He did his job smoothly and with great dispatch—he cut the throat of the older child and then, a moment later, of the baby as well. They did not suffer. They died almost before they knew they were hurt. Their blood poured down onto the tesserae of the throne-room floor. Not nearly so much blood as a full-grown man holds, I noted. The servants would have no trouble cleaning up the mess.

Zoe's wails went on and on. "Hear me!" I said sharply. For a moment, she quietened. I went on, "Now that you have no children and are also bereft of your husband, you stand in need of consolation. Surely the love of another man will make up for your small losses here today."

"No!" she screamed, and much abuse of which I took no notice.

I clapped my hands together, once, twice, three times. Into the throne room came John, Helias's Ethiopian cook. "Behold," I said, "your new husband."

John leered at Zoe. I had not thought she could shriek louder than she already had done, but I was wrong. A weedy little priest named Basil tiptoed in after John. He was another of those useful people who did as they were told.

Now, as he had been instructed, he read the marriage service before John and Zoe. John's responses were eager nods. Zoe's were screams or noes. I told Basil, "The woman is distraught. She does not know what she is saying. You are to interpret those as affirmatives."

"Yes, Emperor," he said dutifully. The crowns of marriage—cheap copper ones; no point wasting better on the likes of them—were set upon their heads, and Basil pronounced them man and wife.

I nodded to John. "Consummate your marriage." His Greek was not up to that. I simplified the matter: "Now you take her." Those words he had no trouble understanding. I had earlier urged him to seal their union in the throne room itself. Even though he was only a black barbarian, he did not want to do that. I had set aside a chamber nearby instead. To this he now led—dragged—his bride, while I led the party of well-wishers shouting bawdy advice as they went.

The door slammed shut. Presently, after some small commotion within, Zoe began to scream on a note different from the one she had used up until that time. The excubitores and courtiers standing in the hall with me took this as a sign the marriage union had been accomplished, and so did I. We burst into cheers.

After a while, the door opened and John came forth. Zoe was no virgin. I had not given him a square of linen with which to prove he could show he had taken her maidenhead. But his smugly satisfied expression proved all that needed proving: this despite a couple of claw-marks on one cheek.

Behind him, I saw Zoe, loosely wrapped in the tunic he must have torn off her. She sat on the edge of the bed. Her feet dangled down toward the floor. Her face was buried in her hands. Racking sobs shook her body.

"What kind of bridegroom thinks one round is enough?" I demanded of John. "Remember, she is yours. Go back and do your duty to her properly."

He was a young man, so he needed little urging. He looked thoughtful for a moment. Maybe he wondered whether he was ready to rise again so soon. Then he grinned—he was ready. His teeth, as always, seemed especially white because they were seen against his dark skin. He closed the door. The well-wishers and I waited until Zoe started to scream again. Then we applauded to drown out her racket.

After I encouraged John to show his paces, he proved a man of formidable stamina. No doubt he had suffered long deprivation in such matters because he had been a slave. Perhaps, too, he was excited because he got to swive the woman who had ordered him about.

However that was, I decided not to wait around outside the bed-chamber until his first night—or rather, his first day—was done. Let him have his good time. I had other things to do. And for now, Helias was punished as well as he could be until he himself fell into my hands.

Now to accomplish that—and to deal with Bardanes the usurper.

"Get up, Mauros," I said roughly.

He rose from his prostration. He was a frightened man. I could see white all around the irises of his eyes. "You summoned me, Emperor," he said. "I am here to serve you." His voice did not waver. I give him so much.

"And serve me you shall," I said. "You came back when the others stayed in Kherson to betray me. I thank you for that. Now you shall be the instrument through which I chastise them."

"Tell me what you require, Emperor, and I shall give it to you. You need have no doubt of that." Again, Mauros sounded sure of himself.

I was also sure of myself. "I shall give you another fleet, Mauros," I told him. His eyes kindled. I give few men the chance to redeem them-selves. He knew it full well. "Along with the fleet, I shall give you cat-apults and rams and every sort of siege engine we have stored here in our armories and arsenals."

"You will want me to take Kherson, then," he said.

"Not only that. I want you to raze the walls to the foundations. It will never close itself up against me again."

"I am here to serve you," Mauros repeated.

I held up my hand. "I was not finished," I told him. He hung his head in sorrow because he interrupted me. I gave him time to reflect on his many sins. He may have sinned against God. He had surely sinned against me. I went on, "I intend for you to slay every man, woman, and child inside the walls."

"I understand, Emperor," he said.

"You had better." I know I sounded angry. I *was* angry. Mauros cringed. That pleased me. "If you and Stephen and Helias had done what I ordered you to do in the first place, we would not have trouble now. The Khersonites would be dead. They deserve death. Helias would be my governor in that part of the world. Any number of unfortunate things would not have happened. They would have had no need to happen."

Mauros licked his lips. He knew how I had punished Helias through his children and through Zoe. "You will have no cause to be disappointed in me, Emperor," he said.

"I expect to be pleased with you, Mauros, not disappointed," I replied. "In fact, I can think of only one thing that would disappoint me."

He licked his lips once more. With great care, he said, "Since I do not wish to disappoint you in any way, Emperor, please tell me what that one thing is, so I may be certain to avoid it."

"Failure," I said.

"Emperor?" His face went blank. Artfully blank? I do not think so. I think he simply did not understand.

"Failure." I said it again. "Carry out your orders as I have given them to you and all will be well. Do anything but carry out my orders, fail in any particular, and by God and His Son, Mauros, I swear you will end up envying Helias before I am through with you. I will slaughter every kinsman of yours, no matter how distant. I will kill every friend you have. I will kill every shopkeeper you ever met. Every one of them will have a long, hard time dying. You will watch them with the one eye I leave you after the executioners do their first work. Then, maybe, if you are lucky, you will—eventually—die, too."

He quivered. "Emperor, I have already told you I will do everything in my power to see your will is done in Kherson. But, but—"

"I shall accept no excuses here, Mauros," I broke in. "None. Do you hear me? Succeed, and I will reward you richly. Fail, and you pay the price of failure. Sometimes the world is a very simple place."

"But, Emperor, God is greater than I am," he said. "God is even greater than you, Emperor. It is possible, by His will, that I fail through no fault of my own. What if the Khazars come back to Kherson? How can I fight them and the Khersonites at the same time?"

"I did not summon you here to listen to excuses," I snapped. "If you do not command this expedition, you shall be judged to have have failed in advance. Everything of which I spoke just now will fall due. Shall I have the excubitores lay hold of you, so I can begin on your relatives?"

"Have mercy, Emperor!" he wailed. "I shall do as you bid me."

"Good. As I said, it is very simple. Avenge the Roman Empire—avenge me, the Emperor of the Romans—on Kherson and the Khersonites. It should not be difficult in any way. The town is small and half barbarous. Only if you fail me have you any need to fear. And you shall not fail me, shall you, Mauros?"

"Emperor, I dare not," he said. I nodded in approval. At last, he understood everything he needed to understand.

•   •   •

Mauros's fleet is now sailing for Kherson. I wish it had left a few days sooner. Loading the necessary siege gear onto the transports did take time. If I had only wanted to execute Mauros, I did not need to send him on an expedition bound to fail to give myself an excuse. I could have taken his head and had done. I care nothing for Mauros, one way or the other. I want Kherson in ruins and its people dead. They deserve to be dead.

With the fleet sail a number of light, swift vessels. Through them, I shall learn everything that happens in the northern region. "The season is late, Emperor," Myakes said when he heard me order them along. "We've already had storms. You're liable not to see some of those little fellows again."

"I don't care," I answered. "Some will get through. They will tell me what I need to know. The rest can sink, and their sailors drown." I glared at him. "Are you a traitor, too? Do you want to keep me in the shadows of ignorance? I know there are traitors everywhere, Myakes, but I had not suspected *you*."

"If you think I am a traitor, you know you can take my head," Myakes said stolidly. "I won't run away."

I let him live. Perhaps it is a mistake. So many have betrayed me lately, why not Myakes as well? But I would, I think, sooner suspect Theodora, her brother after all being the altogether unreliable Ibouzeros Gliabanos, whose eyes I should have burned from his head when he dared show his altogether despised countenance here in the Queen of Cities, whose skin I should have flayed from his shrieking, bleeding carcass in digit-wide strips, whose life I should have taken from him as he purposed taking mine from me.

Well, if I should change my mind and decide the captain of excubitores needs death, he was right to remind me I can give it to him at any time. I shall sleep on it and see what I decide in the morning.

MYAKES

So he *was* thinking of getting rid of me, was he, Brother Elpidios? It makes me sad, I won't say it doesn't. But if I told you it surprises me, I'd be lying. There at the end, nobody and nothing was safe from him. His mind must have been slipping—do you notice how his writing is different all of a sudden? These last few sections, the only time he wrote fancy was when he was thinking of how he wanted to torture his brother-in-law before he killed him.

Remember, a lot of people had betrayed him by then. Of course, one of the reasons they betrayed him was that they hadn't done or hadn't been able to do what he'd ordered. They figured he'd kill them if they came home after that, so why not rebel instead? If they won, they'd live, and if they didn't, he couldn't kill 'em any deader than he would have otherwise.

And once the first people started betraying him, he thought everybody would. That just made things worse. He didn't pick what you'd call smart ways to stop it, either, did he? That business with Mauros, now. Any which way, it was going to make Mauros hate him. If Mauros takes Kherson and slaughters everybody in it, he still comes back hating Justinian. And if he doesn't take it . . . He'd come back once after things went wrong, and look at the thanks he got for it. Would you call twice tempting fate? Would Mauros? How much could Justinian expect any man to bear?

He'd borne a lot himself. It made him expect a lot, too.

J U S T I N I A N

God and His Son Jesus Christ be praised, the accursed usurper and traitors and rebels in Kherson shall soon receive some of the punishment they deserve; even though death in battle is a quicker end than they deserve, I trust the Lord Almighty to make their eternal fate correspondingly more painful as recompense for His mercy in this transient world.

Yesterday, one of the courier ships I attached to Mauros's force returned to the imperial city with word that he had overthrown the Kentenaresion Gate of Kherson by means of a ram. And today I have the report from another that the Gate of Syagros is also down. Soon, I expect, the fleet will return with word of a town extinguished and with the persons of Bardanes and Helias, upon which I shall wreak my vengeance.

And now Theophylaktos comes with word that yet another courier is arrived in the imperial city. Strange to think how Kherson must now be days destroyed, even if word of its overfall reaches me only at this instance. I can, I think, afford to be generous to the messenger bringing me the news. And all the complaints I had over my treatment of Mauros are now shown up as the vaporous maunderings they were from the beginning. Put the fear of God and the Emperor in him and he performed well enough.

•   •   •

Treason! Treachery! Deceit! Cheating! Lies! Trickery! Cowardice! That pox-ridden pile on the arse of humanity, Ibouzeros Gliabanos, has sent an army to Kherson to keep my men from punishing the place as it deserves. How are my soldiers to oppose Kherson and the barbarous Khazars at the same time?

I should have killed him. I should have castrated him. I should have slit his tongue. I should have slit his nose. I should have blinded him. Come to the Queen of Cities again, Ibouzeros Gliabanos. Come. I shall coax you with honeyed words once the rebellion is put down. Come. You will like it so well, you will never want to leave. You will never leave— not in one piece.

M Y A K E S

After that, Brother Elpidios, the couriers stopped coming for a while. Justinian didn't know exactly what was going on, up there by Kherson. I don't think he ever did know, not really. I know I didn't, not then. I've pieced it together, bit by bit, from things I've heard over the years here in the monastery.

The Khazars hadn't sent enough men to be sure of licking Mauros. Like Justinian says, he didn't have enough to fight them and the Khersonites both. They all called a kind of a truce to try and sort things out.

While the truce was on, Bardanes got out of Kherson and ran off to Ibouzeros Gliabanos. Somewhere around then, Mauros and his soldiers figured out that they weren't going to be able to take Kherson, not with the Khazars' troops so close. Mauros knew what would happen to him if he went back to Constantinople without taking the place. Justinian had been very clear about that, hadn't he, Brother? Not quite so clever as he thought he was, eh? So Mauros declared for Bardanes.

I suppose it would have been about this time that Helias heard what Justinian had done to his children, and to Zoe, too.

Ibouzeros Gliabanos made Mauros's men swear an oath that they wouldn't hurt Bardanes no matter what. He also made them pay him a nomisma a man, for the privilege of not having to fight his soldiers. Once they'd done that, he gave them Bardanes, though after that everybody called him Philippikos.

Like I told you, Brother Elpidios, nobody in Constantinople knew all the whys and wherefores. All we knew was that Mauros wasn't sending back any more reports about how well things were going. He wasn't sending back any reports at all.

What is Mauros doing? Why does he stay silent? Why do I not hear from him? What plots is he hatching? If he dare not speak to me of what he purposes, does he think me a blind man, unable to see these things for myself? I know what he has in his mind. I know what he must have in his mind. He can have only one thing in his mind.

Treason.

Were he loyal, I should have heard of him long since. Since I have not heard, he cannot be loyal. What is he doing, up there in Kherson? He must have taken Bardanes' cock up his arse, to choose the stinking rebel over me. Let them come. Let them all come. We shall see how happy they are once they try to take the Queen of Cities from me. Bardanes and Helias shall have no stinking Khazars to bail them out then.

No one takes *me* by surprise. Like hundred-eyed Argos in the pagan myth, I see everything. Nothing escapes me. But I cannot see Kherson so well as I should like, not from Constantinople I cannot. I must watch the rebels as close as I can. Too much can happen in Kherson before word of it reaches the imperial city. I must be nearer, to get news sooner.

Where, then? Where? Amastris? No—closer than Constantinople, but not close enough. What of Sinope? Aye, Sinope! Nowhere closer to Kherson, not on this side of the Black Sea. I have men from the military district of the Thrakesians here in the capital, a couple of regiments. Have to pick up more troops along the way. The men of the military district of the Opsikion. Barisbakourios and his men. If they are not loyal, no one is.

And Tervel is with me. He lent me some soldiers to send to Kilikia to fight the Arabs. I will use them to fight the usurper instead.

Look at this. Look at these words. Hardly Greek at all. Where are the balanced clauses? The participles? The genitive absolutes? How my old pedagogue would scorn this style. What was his name? I still do not remember. As for the Greek, I do not care. After Bardanes is dead, and Helias, and Mauros, I will make it worth reading. Now it sets down my thoughts as I have them. It is enough.

On to Sinope! No time to lose!

Fight with Theodora in the tent here. Once too often, she says, "You should not have left Constantinople."

"I have to see," I tell her. "I must know what Bardanes is doing, the instant he does it. I cannot wait. I dare not wait."

"You should have stayed," she says again. "Here, marching through the countryside, you are a turtle out of its shell."

"A turtle that stays in its shell is a turtle that can't see," I say. "I must know what they are doing. I must, I tell you."

Stupid bitch, she cannot see what is in front of her. "You stick your head out of your shell, you see them chop it off," she says. "You stay in where you belong, they never get you. They never have a chance to get you."

I cannot go back. I must not go back. Why does she keep trying to put second thoughts in my head? Does she plot against me, too? "Shut up!" I scream. "Shut up! Shut up!"

"No!" She shouts, too. "You need to listen to me, Justinian! You are making a mistake. You should have stayed back in—"

I hit her then. The back of my hand. Hard across her face. Her eyes—big, big. Red on her cheek. Her mouth bleeds. A little. Not much. Only a little. I am the man. I am the Emperor. I have the right.

She is a barbarian. She does not understand. Tries to hit me. I am too fast. Too strong. Grab her arm. Throw her down on the folding bed. Stand over her. Breathing hard. Hard. Yes, hard. Jump down on-to her.

"No!" she screams again.

I am the man. I am the Emperor. I have the right. No is not for me. She fights. I am too strong. Take her. Take that! Argue with *me*? Wonderful! Best since that yellow-haired Sklavinian toy. No rape since then. Long time. Too long. Should not have waited.

She claws my face when I pull out. The Sklavinian baggage hanged herself. This one may stick a knife in me. Ha! Let her try. I set drawers to rights. She starts to cry.

First Kill Bardanes. Kill Helias. Kill Mauros. Kill the Khersonites, the Phanagorians, the Goths in Doros. Kill them all. Then Theodora will be happy.

Amastris. Dreadful hole. No wonder Cyrus left. Makes Kherson look like a city. Christ, what a thing to say! But true, true. Marched by now. Halfway to Sinope. More than halfway. Faster. Must push faster.

MYAKES

Whew! Rest a bit, why don't you, Brother Elpidios? That's hard stuff to take. I knew he was coming apart at the seams while we were marching to Sinope, yes. I think everybody who had anything to do with him knew he was coming apart at the seams. But listening to him, you wouldn't have thought it was as bad as that—not even close. He'd always wanted to pay back the Khersonites, and there's never been an Emperor who was happy about rebels rising up against him. Nobody thought it was anything more than that.

And maybe, if things had worked out different, it wouldn't have been. You may as well go on, Brother. Why not? Can't be much of that left.

JUSTINIAN

Sinope. At last. God be praised. I stand at the end of the land. I spit out into the sea. Almost I can hit Kherson, Phanagoria. Almost. I look across. Nothing but water. The towns? Just below the horizon. So it seems. Ships go back and forth. All the time. Boats, even. One must be in port. Maybe more than one.

Theodora speaks with me again. I let her. Now she knows not to quarrel with the vicegerent of God on earth. She will be better for it. God would not have led me here but to destroy my foes. I will destroy them all. No mercy.

I look to the harbor. There must be a ship in port.

A ship from Kherson! Found!

Sailed for Constantinople. They sailed for Constantinople. While I was marching here. Curse them to hell. Satan fill their bones with molten lead. Demons stab them with red-hot pitchforks. Fiends rip their flesh to pieces. Days ahead of me. Curse them to hell.

Theodora says not a word.

MYAKES

M̲e, Brother Elpidios, I think Theodora was dead right. Justinian should have stayed in Constantinople and made the rebels come to him. Taking the imperial city is always the hard part in a civil war. As long as you hold the center, you hold the Empire. If you leave it, you're liable to be in trouble.

But going to Sinope wasn't the worst idea in the whole world, either. Sinope is closer to Kherson than Constantinople is. Sinope is also closer to Constantinople than Kherson is. If Justinian had heard Bardanes and his pals were getting ready to move against the capital, he had time to get back.

Or he would have had time. Bardanes left for Constantinople while we were still heading toward Sinope, and stole a march on us that way. He got a bigger start toward the imperial city than Justinian thought he could.

Oh, yes, I was there when he got the news. The fellow who brought it just thought he had an interesting bit of gossip. He didn't know—he couldn't have known—Justinian was in Sinope. He turned as many different colors as a mullet being boiled when he got hailed before the Emperor.

He told him the news. He didn't have any choice about that. We all looked at Justinian, waiting to see what he would do. Have you ever heard a lion roar, Brother? You have? Ah, good. You know how, when you hear it, your belly knows you should be afraid before your head does? The noise Justinian made was like that. My hand went halfway to the hilt of my sword before I realized it was just a noise and couldn't hurt me.

"We have to go back," Justinian said, and he was right about that. "We have to beat the cursed, stinking rebels back to the imperial city."

He was right about that, too, if he wanted to go on being Emperor. But Bardanes had a good start on us.

JUSTINIAN

B̲ack to the city. On the road, back to the Queen of Cities. Rain, turning the road to mud. Christ, why rain *now*? Has God turned His face from me? Is it because I spared Ibouzeros Gliabanos when I had vowed to kill all who wronged me? What else can it be? I made the vow. I broke it. Now I am punished. Lord, have mercy. Christ, have mercy.

Rain, turning the road to mud. Christ.

We crawl. We limp. With the rain turning the road to mud, we lurch on. The horses tire. They slow. We crawl.

Where are Bardanes and Helias and Mauros? Out on the sea, out on the sea. God, let this storm that slows me drown them. Do not forsake me, sinner that I am. Blow up a new storm to sink the rebels and Ibouzeros Gliabanos dies at my hands. I know not how, not yet, but it shall be. I will make my word good.

In the tent, the third night out from Sinope, Theodora says, "Once you have killed the rebels, do not go out of Constantinople again."

For her sake, I let her brother live. But that is done. I say, "No." We nod at each other, wary as a Roman soldier and an Arab. She puts a hand on my shoulder. She forgives. *She* forgives. Lord, have mercy on me.

Christ, have mercy on me. Rain, turning the road to mud.

Amastris again, dull and dead as before. The horses half dead, too. Not enough fresh ones. Rain every day since we left Sinope. Where is Bardanes? Did this storm roar through the Black Sea? Did it take the rebels' dromons down to ruin? God, let it be so. God, make it be so.

The soldiers slog on. They say not a word. They know the need. But they are as tired as their horses. Sometimes they cannot ride, or the horses sink. They march. They sink. Three drown in the mud.

Past Amastris. Where is Bardanes? Every horseman I see fighting his way east, going about his business, puts me in fear. Will the rider hail us? Will he say we are too late? Will he say we have lost the race? Is the rebel at Constantinople? May it not come to pass! Heaven forbid!

Damatrys. Ten miles from Chalcedon. Under the shadow of St. Auxentios's hill. Beacon fire on top of the hill, part of the chain of beacon fires that warns when the Arabs invade. Are there beacon fires for rebels? Would to God there were, to burn them up in.

Another horseman on the road. He sees us. Some of the riders had gone into the fields. They feared my soldiers. This one rides up. "Emperor!" he calls. "Justinian!" My regalia is the color of mud. Everything is the color of mud. He needs a little while to spot me. When he does, he says, "Emperor, Philippikos is in the city."

"Did anyone fight to hold him out?" I ask.

"Emperor, not a soul," he answers.

My hand goes to my ruined nose. Now I know a worse hurt. I look round at my army. The word hits the men like an arrow in the guts. To come so far. To labor so hard. To fall so short. I see their minds. *Now we are not the Emperor's soldiers*, they think. *Now we are rebels and bandits*.

"In Kherson, I was Emperor of the Romans with one subject," I shout. Faithful Myakes steps up and waves. Good after all I did not kill him.

"Two subjects, soon," Barisbakourios says. He remembers I gave him his rank.

"I am still Emperor now," I say. "I got Constantinople back once. I will get it back again."

Four men cheer. Five. Six. Worse than none. Like a dying ghost of what a cheer ought to be. Hope drips out like blood from a cut vein.

The rider still sits his horse. "Emperor. There is more."

Morning. Barisbakourios is—

M Y A K E S

Poor sod, he couldn't bear to write it, eh, Brother Elpidios? God help me if I blame him. If you want to know the story, though, you'd better know the whole story. The first thing Helias did when he got into Constantinople and found out what Justinian had done to his wife and children was, he went after Justinian. Well, Justinian wasn't there, and neither was Theodora.

So the next thing Helias did was, he went after Tiberius. Tiberius wasn't with us—he'd stayed back in the city with his grandmother. Anastasia knew what was liable to happen to him, too. She'd taken him to the church of the Mother of God next to the Blakhernai palace. The way that fellow coming out from Constantinople told it, she was sitting in front of the church when Mauros and John Strouthos got there.

Tiberius was inside. He was holding onto the altar with one hand and to a piece of the holy and life-giving wood from the True Cross with the other, and he had amulets draped round his neck. Outside, Anastasia was begging Mauros and John the Ostrich to let the little monster live. She said he was too young to hurt anybody. She was right, too, but if he'd had time . . .

Anyway, it didn't work. Helias had told John to get rid of Tiberius, and John wasn't about to change his mind once he got told to kill somebody. And Mauros hated Justinian almost as much as Helias did—you've seen why. He said, "Helias's children were too little to hurt anybody, too."

John the Ostrich didn't waste time arguing with Anastasia. He went into the church, broke Tiberius's grip on the altar, took the holy wood away from him and tossed it down on the altartop, and then put Tiberius's amulets around his own neck. I don't know why he bothered. They hadn't done Tiberius any good. He brought out the brat. Then he and Mauros took him over to a little porch close by, stripped off his robe, stretched him out like a sheep at slaughtering time, and cut his throat.

When the horseman told all this to Justinian, he just sat there on top of his own horse for the longest time. Then he said, "I will kill them all." He brought it out flat, the way I'd heard him do before, the way that would make you feel like somebody stuffed a handful of snow down the back of your tunic. Not this time, though. The words were there, but not the fury that made them frightening. Something had broken inside of Justinian. I don't know how to put it any better than that. For as long as I'd known him, he'd always been the one to grab fate by the balls and squeeze till things happened the way he wanted them to happen. Not any more. Not after that. He wasn't doing the moving. He was being moved instead.

I don't think I was the only one who felt that, or who felt something like it. I don't know how many men we had when we made camp that night, there under St. Auxentios's hill. I do know one thing, though: the next morning, we had a lot fewer.

Justinian was going to talk about that, wasn't he? Why don't you pick up from where you stopped when I started running my mouth?

J U S T I N I A N

Barisbakourios is gone. To think—I called him loyal. Many men from the military district of the Opsikion with him. And some of the Thrakesians. And some of the Bulgars, too. The ship sinks. The rats dive into the sea. Fools. No safe harbor near. Can the ship float? Does it matter?

I am forty-two. I think I am forty-two. My father did not live so long. Nor my grandfather. Nor my great-grandfather. I am old. I burn hard. I burn fast. Now I burn out.

Theodora beside me. She does not weep. She cuts her cheeks. Blood flows, not tears. Nomads mourn so. She forgets she is a Christian. God forgets I am a Christian.

Scouts must go forward. Rebels between us and Chalcedon?

Followers of the usurper? Must know. Can we get to Chalcedon? Get to boats? Get to Constantinople? Must try. Mine.

Scouts back. Enemy soldiers not far west. I call the men together. I order the attack. The men stare. They mutter. They do not form by companies. Not by troops. They do not attack. I should kill them. How?

They do not seize me. They do not give me to Bardanes, to Helias, to Mauros. They stay with me. They will not attack. Maybe they will defend. Maybe they will defend and win and then attack. Maybe maybe maybe may—

Morning again. More men gone. Not so many. When I come out of my tent, Myakes orders a cheer. The men shout. The ones who are here. Not the others. A better cheer than the last one. A good cheer? A better cheer.

Maybe they will defend. The usurper's men do not attack. Maybe they fear me. They should fear me. If I can go forward, I will beat them. I order the men forward. They will not go.

More of the usurper's men about. Fewer of mine. Again, fewer of mine. They forsake me. God forsakes me. Five generations, all in ruins. The sixth generation, cut down in ruins. God forsakes me. I do not forsake God. I pray. Let me go on, I pray. Let me slay my enemies, I pray. I have enemies left alive. It is not right. How can I die with enemies left alive?

Avenge me, God. If it be Thy will that I die without slaying Ibouz-eros Gliabanos, avenge me. I read once of a bishop who was a heretic, who suffered what the physicians called an abdominal obstruction and died vomiting shit out of his own mouth. If I must die, give the Khazar this death, I pray Thee.

Bardanes' men spying on the camp. Trying to see what I have left. My men shoot arrows at them. They ride away. A cheer, almost, that sounds like a cheer. My men can fight. They have fought. *Will* they fight? For me? How to make them?

Dead. Barisbakourios dead. The best of the ones from Kherson. Dead. Loyal. Loyal as could be, till these last days. Dead. Hunted down. Killed. Dead.

Do the rebels lie? No. They shout at our camp. They know. I have heard lies. I have told lies. I know lies. They tell the truth. A staff I hoped to lean on. First fled—now dead.

•　　•　　•

My men melt now like snow in spring. They trickle away. They dribble away. They stream away. Myakes comes to me. "Emperor," he says, "run away. Hide somewhere. Hole yourself up. Bardanes is nothing much. He won't find you."

"I never run away," I said. "I never did. I never will."

"What about when the Bulgars hit us outside Ankhialos?" he says.

"Not the same," I answer. "I never run away from the Queen of Cities."

He bows his head. "Never a dull moment around you," he says at last.

"Go on." I clap him on the back. "Save yourself. Go on. No one will look for you."

"I wouldn't know what to do without you," he says. "Maybe, some kind of way, we'll beat the bastards yet."

Someone stays loyal. A small miracle. One more miracle, God?

M Y A K E S

He's probably right, Brother Elpidios—I could have gotten away. It never would have occurred to me on my own. I turned him down without even thinking about it, same as I would have if he'd told me to worship Mouamet. I might still have my eyes if I'd run, but I don't suppose I'd be a holy monk now. What? It all worked out for the best, you say? I—oh, never mind.

The only time he had any juice in him was when he talked about revenge. That was what fed him, the last part of his life. He never quite figured out it could feed other people, too, though. He got his. He made other people want to get theirs. When they wanted to pay him back, he wondered why. But he didn't lay down at the end. He fought on. I give him that much.

J U S T I N I A N

I wake to more desertions in the morning. Around the third hour of the day, with the sun halfway up the sky, a rider comes. "Truce!" he shouts. "Truce! Hear me out!"

I hope the bandits have fallen to fighting among themselves. If they have, I can play them off, this one against that. "Go ahead," I tell him. "Say your say."

"My commander is Helias, chief general to the Emperor Philippi-kos," he says. "By God and His Son, he swears that none of the soldiers who leave Justinian's army will be harmed in any way because they fought for him till now. He's lost; Philippikos has won. Anyone with eyes in his head can see that. Anyone who wants to keep eyes in his head had better see that. Day after tomorrow, Philippikos overruns this camp. Anyone who's still fighting for Justinian is going to pay."

"Helias leads that army?" I called to the horseman.

"Aye." He peered in at me. "You bloodthirsty madman, you'll pay, sure enough, when he catches up with you."

"Me?" I cried in a great voice. "That vile, murdering son of a whore you call your master, let him come. Let him come with an army of ten thousand against me alone. He wantonly murdered my son, and thinks to escape unscathed? Christ, let him come! Let him not wait so long! Let him come tomorrow. No—let him come today!" I drew my sword and brandished it. "Let him come this minute, and I will cleave his filthy head from his shoulders."

"He'll come when it suits him, not when it suits you," the messenger answered: a whipworthy rogue if ever there was one. "It's not like you're the Emperor any more. He doesn't have to do what you say."

"Kill him!" I shouted to my men. "Kill him for the disgusting, de-based liar that he is."

A couple of arrows flew out toward Helias's toady. Coward that he was, he fled away from the camp, back to the savage brute's other diseased arse-lickers. I shouted in triumph to see him run, but even then my own men were slipping out of camp.

Morning again. I have three hundred left. At Thermopylai, the Spartans won glory forever against the Persians with no more.

But the Spartan three hundred would not flee, would not run, would not give up, would not abandon, would not think of themselves ahead of the cause. My men . . . ?

Evening. Maybe a hundred remain. They eat well. Why not? We have food for an army dozens of times this size.

These are the last words I shall set down in this book. After I write them, I shall send for Myakes. Perhaps he will escape. Perhaps my words will live, even if it be God's will that I do not. Ah, Ibouzeros Gliabanos, I should have slain you and kept my vow. See what loving your sister brought me?

I am Justinian, Emperor of the Romans, the son of Constantine, Emperor of the Romans, the son of Constans, Emperor of the Romans, the son of Herakleios Constantine, Emperor of the Romans, the son of Herakleios, Emperor of the Romans. Romania is *mine*.

MYAKES

You know, Brother Elpidios, when one of Justinian's slaves—maybe the last one who hadn't run away by then—brought word that he wanted to see me, I wondered if he was going to take my head—just to make sure he'd done it, you might say. That was about the only time when I really thought about running off. In the end, though, I didn't. I'd been doing what Justinian told me for too long by then to break the habit, I expect.

"Tomorrow we fight," he said when I walked into his tent. "Tomorrow Helias dies. He killed my son, sure as if he'd cut his throat with his own hands."

Justinian says we had a hundred men left? I don't think so, but all right. Helias had thousands—I know that. He could squash us like a man squashing a bug and never set eyes on Justinian himself. What's that, Brother? Had Justinian forgotten he'd killed Helias's children, or did he think it didn't matter because they deserved what they got and Tiberius didn't? Truth to tell, I don't know. It amounts to about the same thing either way, wouldn't you say?

He handed me the codex—the very one you've got there—and he said, "After I win tomorrow, give this back to me."

"All right, Emperor," I told him. I understood what he meant, even if he couldn't come right out and say it.

"Fight hard, Myakes," he said, and clapped me on the back like we were talking in a tavern. "Always fight hard." He knew all about that. Nobody can say anything different there. I nodded my head and went away. The book? I stowed it in my own knapsack.

By the next morning, we didn't have a hundred men left. I don't think we had fifty. To this day, Brother Elpidios, I don't know why we had any. A few people will stick to any cause, I suppose. What? Do I mean me? Who else would I be talking about?

We put on our armor and we waited: me, a couple of other stubborn excubitores, a few men from the military district of the Opsikion, a handful of crazy Bulgars, and Justinian. He trotted his horse back and forth in front of us as if we were fifty thousand. He looked splendid in his gilded chainmail. If only he'd had a real army to lead.

About halfway through the morning, up came Helias. *He* had a real army. I don't know how big it was—big enough and then some, I'll tell you that. But now he was as wild for revenge as Justinian ever had been. When he saw Justinian there in front of him at last, he forgot about all the soldiers he was leading. "Murderer!" he screamed, and set spurs to his horse, and charged.

"Murderer!" Justinian screamed back at him, and he charged, too.

We all yelled ourselves hoarse, Justinian's little band. If he cut down Helias, who could say what that army would do? His own force had shrunk in a hurry. Who was to say it couldn't grow again in hurry, too?

Over on the other side of the line, all those however many thousand men Helias had with him went quiet as the tomb. They were thinking the same thing we were, sure as the devil, only our up was their down. If Justinian nailed Helias, everything was up for grabs again.

If. If, if, if. We were thinking with our hearts, the forlorn little guard Justinian had. Like he said himself, he was past forty by then, and he hadn't done anything you'd call fighting from horseback since before he got exiled. He'd exercised, yes, but it's not the same thing. Helias was, I don't know, fifteen years younger, something like that, and he really knew what he was doing.

We didn't need long to see that. The first pass they made at each other, Helias knocked Justinian's sword out of his hand. The next time around, Justinian went after him with a dagger. No quit in Justinian— never any quit in Justinian. He didn't try and run away. If he didn't have any weapons left, he'd fight barehanded and hope for a break.

He didn't get one. Helias hit him a whack with the flat of his blade that left him swaying in the saddle like he didn't know the difference between stew and Easter. When Helias saw he couldn't fight any more, he got an arm around his neck and dragged him out of the saddle. Then he jumped down himself, and drew his dagger.

Justinian tried to kick him. It didn't work. Helias knelt down beside him. Justinian started to yell something. It might have been, "Em—!" Maybe not, too. We'll never know now. Whatever it was, Justinian never finished, on account of Helias got to work with that knife.

A minute later, he stood up. He was holding Justinian's head by the hair. I think it tried to bite him. No, Brother Elpidios, not really—a joke. If Justinian could have, he would have, but he was done. It was over. At last, it was over.

Helias's men let out all the cheers they'd been holding back while they waited to see whether he'd live. They rolled forward over us. It wasn't a battle. It wasn't anything like a battle. Only a couple of us fought.

No, not me, Brother. I ran back to my tent and grabbed the knapsack with the codex in it. Then I tried to run. Why did I do that? If you'd asked me then, Brother Elpidios, I couldn't have told you. I just did it. Now, after all these years, the way it looks to me is, I'd been doing what Justinian wanted for so long that a little thing like him being dead wasn't going to change the way I acted.

I don't think it ended up hurting me. So I got caught a hundred cubits away from my tent instead of two hundred. So what? I wasn't going to get away. Nobody who stayed with Justinian till the end got away, I don't think.

Theodora? Now, that's a good question. I have to tell you, I don't know what happened to her. From that day till this, I've never heard. Maybe she's in a convent. Maybe they sent her back to her brother. Maybe they killed her, and kept quiet about it afterwards. Helias might have. Maybe she's somebody's concubine, or somebody's wife. Make up your own story. I can't help you there.

Me? Thanks to the fancy armor I was wearing, the lugs who had hold of me figured out who I was. They dragged me off to Helias. He already had Justinian's head mounted on a spear. "Ah, Myakes," he said. "So it comes to this."

"It comes to this, sure enough," I answered.

"What am I supposed to do with you?" he said.

"What are you asking me for?" I said to him. "If it had come down the other way, I'd've tried to see that you died faster than Justinian would have wanted, anyhow."

"Yes, I believe you would have," Helias said. "You never stopped Justinian from being vicious, but sometimes you stopped him from being *as* vicious. Does that make you better for doing something or worse for not doing more? Hard to say, isn't it?"

I looked over toward Justinian's head. His eyes were still open, but they were just dull glass. A fly was walking on one of them. I said, "He raised you up, too, Helias, and you bit his hand."

"He would have taken my head if I hadn't," he said. "You love him too well, Myakes—I don't want you running around loose. But I don't quite have the stomach to kill you, not when you did do *something*, anyhow, to make his evils less. I'll throw you in a monastery, and take your eyes to make sure you don't come out."

"If that's what you've got in mind, I'd sooner you did kill me," I told him.

He didn't listen. He didn't have to listen, not to the likes of me. He gave the orders, and his bully boys dragged me off to take care of 'em. It wasn't what you'd call a fancy job. They didn't bother with silver bowls and boiling vinegar, the way the executioner had with Felix. They hauled me over to a fire and heated up a couple of skewers, the kind you'd use to roast meat. Then one of them got a thick leather gauntlet from some-where, grabbed a skewer, and burned out my left eye with it. He did that one first because it was on his right side, I guess.

What do you mean, what did I do? I did just what you'd think. I screamed and did my damnedest to get away, only I couldn't. Did it hurt? You bet your balls it hurt! It hurt worse than anything else that's ever happened to me. Then the fellow with the leather glove got the other red-hot skewer out of the fire. The very last thing I ever saw, Brother Elpidios, through the tears that were streaming down my face, was that glowing iron, coming right at me.

I heard the fellow who'd blinded me throw down the gauntlet. "Off to a monastery with him," he said, "and better than he deserves, too."

"Ahh, Myakes wasn't so bad," one of the others said, like I was dead instead of just wishing I was. "Here's his knapsack. Let him take it along." He must have opened it then, I suppose to see if anything in there was worth stealing. He saw the codex. "What's he doing with a book?"

The one who'd stuck skewers in my eyes—ugly bastard; I remember that, oh yes I do—he laughed like a jackal. "Who cares? He can keep it—it'll give him something to read." He thought that was the funniest thing in the world, and so did all his stinking chums.

But that's how Justinian's book got here, Brother Elpidios, in case you ever wondered. That's how you finally got to read it, even if I never have.

What can I say? The book is done. My story's done, because I haven't had any story to speak of since I came here. It's been the same thing over and over and over, and it'll keep on being the same thing till they wrap me in a shroud and lay me in the grave. I suppose, for a man with no eyes, it's better that way. No story, no, but no surprises, either.

And Justinian's done. Maybe it's better that way, too. I don't know. Justinian, he was nothing *but* surprises. For better and for worse, you never knew what he'd do next. Whatever it was, he went at it hard as he could. If he'd been better at choosing . . . ahhh, if he'd been better at choosing, he wouldn't have been Justinian.

And now that you've read the whole book and you've heard every-thing I've got to say about it, I suppose *we're* done, too, eh, Brother Elpidios? Brother? Are you there, Brother?

E L P I D I O S

I, Elpidios, the sinful monk, set down these words on the last leaf of the codex in which the Emperor Justinian recorded the deeds of his life, reckoning up and arranging what occurred in each period thereof without confusion, so that the reader might at once understand what events, whether warlike or ecclesiastical or of any other sort, occurred at any time during the Emperor's life on earth.

Not ignorant of my own lack of knowledge and paucity of expression, I hesitate now in the task I had previously set myself, of adding the events recounted in this life to the chronicle of the history of the world I have been contemplating. I hesitate also because of the multitude and variety of sins Justinian showed forth during his lifetime, sins of which any reader might better be left unaware.

For, as I think, in most circumstances one enjoys no small aid in reading of the deeds of those long ago. If I should write such a book and anyone was to find therein anything useful, he ought to give the appropriate thanks to God and pray for the Lord's aid to my lack of knowledge and sinfulness. Though I may be guilty in this regard of ignorance and of the laziness of a groveling mind, I think I shall set aside this life of Justinian, on the grounds that separating sin from virtue in the said life is beyond my poor talents. Let this codex go on a shelf in the monastic library, in the hope that, some day, a man with greater talent than mine may find for it a fitting use.

If I do come to write my chronicle, I shall craft it from sources more malleable and more in accordance with my own judgment and understanding. The Lord will surely forgive my errors, for working according to one's ability is pleasing to God. Amen.

HISTORICAL NOTE

Justinian II was born in 669 (or perhaps 668). He became Roman (as he styled himself) or Byzantine (as we would be more likely to call him) Emperor on the death of his father, Constantine IV, in 685, was ousted from the throne by Leontios in 695, regained it by overcoming Tiberius III Apsimaros in 705, and was again overthrown—and this time killed—by the forces of Bardanes Philippikos in 711.

Along with Justinian, the following people appearing in *Justinian* are actual historical personages: Abimelekh (Abd al-Malik, caliph, 685–705), Agathon (pope, 678–681), Anastasia, Apsimaros (Tiberius III—Emperor, 698–705), Arculf, Asparukh, Balgitzin, Bardanes Philippikos (Emperor, 711–713), Barisbakourios, Basil (bishop of Gortyna), Benedict II (pope, 684–685), Boniface, Christopher, Constantine (pope, 708–715), Constantine IV (Emperor, 668–685), Cyrus (patriarch, 705–712[?]), Daniel, Epiphaneia (name fictional), Eudokia, Felix, Florus, George, George I (patriarch, 679–686), George the Syrian, Gregory the Kappadokian, Helias, Herakleios (Apsimaros's brother), Herakleios (Constantine IV's son), Herakleios (Constantine IV's brother), Ibouzeros Gliabanos, John (admiral), John (archbishop of Cyprus), John (bishop of Portus), John (eparch of the city), John Pitzigaudis, John Strouthos, John the cook (name fictional), John V (patriarch, 669–675), Kallinikos, Kallinikos I (patriarch, 694–705), Kyprianos, Kyriakos, Leo II (pope, 682–683), Leo (Leo III, Emperor, 717–741), Leo (mint functionary), Leontios (Emperor, 695–698), Makarios, Mauias (Muawiyah I—caliph, 661–680), Mauros, Moropaulos, Mouamet (Muhammad—Abimelekh's brother), Myakes, Neboulos, Nikephoros the patrician, Oualid (Walid I—caliph, 705–715), Papatzun, Patrikios Klausus, Paul (the monk), Paul III (patriarch, 688–694), Paul the magistrianos, Petronas, Polykhronios, Sabbatios, Sergios (officer), Sergios I (pope, 687–701), Sergios of Damascus, Sisinnios (pope, 708), Stephen the exarch, Stephen the patrician, Stephen the Persian, Stephen/Salibas, Tervel, Theodore I (patriarch, 677–679), Theodore of Koloneia, Theodore the patrician, Theodotos, Theophilos, Theophylaktos, Tiberius (Constantine IV's brother), Tiberius (Justinian II's son), Tzitzak/Theodora, Zachariah, Zoe (Helias's wife: name fictional), Zoïlos.

In addition, the following persons mentioned in the novel but dead before the time in which it is set are historical: Athalaric, Constans II (Emperor, 641–668), Constantine I (Emperor, 306–337), Eudokia (Herakleios's daughter), Herakleios (Emperor, 610–641), Herakleios Constantine (Emperor, 641), Heraklonas (Emperor, 641), Honorius I (pope, 625–638), John (bishop of Thessalonike), Justinian I (Emperor, 527–565), Kosmas, Leontios, Martin I (pope, 649–655), Martina, Maurice (Emperor, 582–602), Maximus the Confessor, Menander Protector, Mouamet (Muhammad), Paul II (patriarch, 641–654), Peter (patriarch, 655–666), Phokas (Emperor, 602–610), Pyrrhos I (patriarch, 638–641, 655), Septimius Severus (Emperor, 193–211), Sergios (patriarch, 610–638). All others, including Brother Elpidios, are fictitious.

The two most important sources for the reign of Justinian II are the chronicles of Nikephoros and Theophanes. I have read both in the Greek. Both use some older common source; each also offers information the other lacks. Justinian's modern biographer, Constance Head, downplays some of the more horrific episodes in the Emperor's second reign, episodes recorded only in the chronicle of Theophanes. I must respectfully disagree with her interpretation. The kinds of things Theophanes has Justinian doing strike me as consistent with his actions and personality as described in the Liber Pontificalis and in the Syriac chronicle of Dionysius of Tel-Mahre, to which Head did not have access (although she did use the later Syriac chronicle of Bar-Hebraeus, who draws on Dionysius's work).

I have for the most part stuck very close to the historical record of Justinian's career, which is quite sufficiently amazing without embellishment. I altered the actual events of the sixth ecumenical synod in a couple of ways, first by having Makarios of Antioch present when his fellow monothelite Polykhronios tried to raise the dead (Makarios had actually been condemned and removed from office by then), and second by having Bishop Arculf of Gaul take part in the synod. Arculf was in fact in Constantinople at the time, but as a pilgrim on the way home from Jerusalem. His native town here is fictitious, and his meeting with Justinian II is conjecture on my part. I should note here that theology was so vital to the world of the late seventh and early eighth centuries, and so intimately intertwined with politics, that a novel of this sort, which appears to place undue stress on it, in fact severely understates its importance.

Most details of Justinian's private life are also conjectures. It is, however, worth pointing out that Theodora did act in her new husband's interest and against that of her brother on very short acquaintance with Justinian, which may perhaps speak well for him in that regard.

I have followed Richard Delbrück's conjecture that Justinian had his mutilated nose surgically repaired while in exile (in fact, I dare take the liberty of saying here that I made a similar conjecture myself before learning of Delbrück's, which has—some—iconographic evidence to support it). Auriabedas is fictitious, but Indian surgeons at the time were in fact the world's leaders in what we would call plastic surgery, and could and did perform operations such as the one I describe Justinian submitting to. Details of the procedure are from Guido Majno, *The Healing Hand: Man and Wound in the Ancient World* (Cambridge, Massachusetts, 1975).

The only place Myakes appears in history is in the melodramatic scene during the storm on the Black Sea. His relationship to Justinian and his ultimate fate are novelistic inventions.